A WHISPER
TO THE LIVING
and
PARADISE LANE

Ruth Hamilton

A WHISPER TO THE LIVING and PARADISE LANE
A CORGI BOOK : 0 552 14958 6

This WH Smith edition first published 2001
Copyright © Ruth Hamilton 2001

1 3 5 7 9 10 8 6 4 2

including

A WHISPER TO THE LIVING
Originally published in Great Britain by Corgi Books,
a division of Transworld Publishers
Copyright © Ruth Hamilton 1989
Set in 11/12pt Plantin by
Phoenix Typesetting, Ilkley, West Yorkshire.

PARADISE LANE
Originally published in Great Britain by Bantam Press,
a division of Transworld Publishers
Copyright © Ruth Hamilton 1996
Corgi edition published 1996
Set in Plantin by
County Typesetters, Margate, Kent.

Corgi Books are published by Transworld Publishers,
61-63 Uxbridge Road, London W5 5SA,
a division of The Random House Group Ltd,
in Australia by Random House Australia (Pty) Ltd,
20 Alfred Street, Milsons Point, Sydney, NSW 2061, Australia,
in New Zealand by Random House New Zealand Ltd,
18 Poland Road, Glenfield, Auckland 10, New Zealand
and in South Africa by Random House (Pty) Ltd,
Endulini, 5a Jubilee Road, Parktown 2193, South Africa

WHSmith plc, Greenbridge Road,
Swindon SN3 3LD.

www.whsmith.co.uk

Printed and bound in Great Britain by
Cox & Wyman Ltd, Reading, Berkshire.

A WHISPER
TO THE LIVING

Ruth Hamilton

in loving memory of my parents.

*Also for Allison Williams, a true friend
who is sadly missed.*

Acknowledgements

Many thanks to: My two sons who tolerate me while I write; Diane Pearson for her patience and encouragement; Lyn Andrews who made me carry on through thick and thin; Dr Sonia Goldrein for her help, support and advice; the *Bolton Evening News* and the *Liverpool Echo* for factual guidance; the people of Bolton and Liverpool, my two home towns; friends and colleagues in Kirkby, especially those at Millbridge, Millbrook, Northfield and Springfield Schools.

This is a work of fiction. However, Bolton is a real place and although I have altered names of some streets and roads, these actual locations do exist. Any resemblance to persons living or dead is coincidental. I had a tale to tell and I set it in one of the places I know and love best.

'The fall of a leaf is a whisper to the living.'

English proverb

Contents

Part One: The Fall of a Leaf . . .

1	Beginnings	13
2	Neighbours	25
3	My Immortal Soul	32
4	Changes	41
5	Moving on	52
6	Encounters	68
7	Communion	77
8	The Killing	94
9	On the Run	114
10	New Pastures	122
11	Losing Faith	136
12	Fighting Back	145
13	The Worst of Times	174
14	The Best of Times	186

Part Two: . . . is a Whisper to the Living

1	Martin and Simon	215
2	Edna and Simon	245
3	With Premeditation	253
4	Tensions	269
5	Disruptions	277

6	Laughter and Worry	288
7	The Rape	300
8	Repercussions	315
9	Confrontations	333
10	Dénouements	348
11	Dolly's Lot	361
12	Departures	369

Part Three: Anne   391

Author's Note   415

Part One

The Fall of a Leaf ...

I

Beginnings

On 28 January 1940, I was born dead.

My mother, Nancy Byrne, after suffering for forty-eight hours on a horsehair sofa under the stairs, placed me as gently as she could on the peg rug in front of a cold range, then collapsed on to the stone floor beside me.

Fortunately for both of us, the widow from next door had, with the help of her two sons, managed to clear a way through the nine-foot drifts of snow, thus enabling Dr Clarke to put in a somewhat tardy appearance. This had been one of the worst winters in living memory and Bolton had ground to a virtual halt.

My mother, small-boned, fragile – no more than five feet tall, had produced an oxygen-starved infant whose head, swollen and blackened from long imprisonment in the birth canal, seemed larger than its body. Mrs Hyatt from next door, before busying herself with paper, kindling and coal, hastily bundled the motionless girl-child into a blanket which she then stuffed into a cardboard box.

Tom and Freddie Hyatt, her strapping fourteen-year-old twins, were dispatched upstairs, from whence, with much cursing and clattering, they fetched my mother's bed. The infant remained ignored in its box, the doctor's main concern being for the state of Nancy Byrne's health, for the lower part of her body had lost all feeling.

It was therefore a very shocked Tom Hyatt who heard my first mewlings, who stared down into my makeshift coffin, his mouth agape, Adam's apple bobbing wildly as he tried to attract the doctor's attention.

I was snatched from the box and carried through to the scullery, where Dr Clarke cleared the obstructive matter from my throat, permitting me to express my anger at the incompetence with which I was surrounded.

I believe that my character was formed almost completely in those first few moments of life. My fear of small spaces, my attitude to authority, my tendency not to trust or depend, all these were born with that furious ear-splitting scream.

I was given to my mother, who smiled wanly and said, 'Eeh, she looks about six months old already.' To which Dr Clarke replied, 'Well, she must weigh at least eleven pounds – you're very lucky, both of you.'

My mother did not feel lucky. Firstly, she was in no two minds that my father had set his heart on a boy. Secondly, this infant did not look at all normal – in fact, it was ugly to the point of revulsion. And lastly, most importantly, would she, Nancy Byrne, ever walk again? From the waist down she had no sensation at all; it was as if she had been cut off at the middle.

I was a bitter disappointment to her. Had I been pretty, or even manageable, then I might have been forgiven for being female. But there I was, bald and blue-black about the face, screaming incessantly, a hideous reminder of the uselessness of her lower limbs.

She handed me to Mrs Hyatt. 'Here, you take her home, love. I can't cope with her while I'm this road. Give her a bottle or something.'

So I spent the first two or three weeks of my life at number 22, while, in the kitchen of number 20, my mother drank Mrs Hyatt's beef tea and concentrated on her toes.

Her two short white legs lay stiff and still on top of the army greatcoat that served as quilt for the bed and she stared at them for days on end with never a word for the nurse who came in daily or for Mrs Hyatt who fed her, washed her, emptied her bedpans.

Now that the thaw had set in, visitors began to arrive, aunts bearing black-market fruit and cigarettes, uncles with bottles of stout and words of encouragement. They visited me too, declared me to be a fine lass, but still my mother would have none of me.

By the middle of February, Nancy Byrne's self-hypnosis began to pay off. She moved first her toes, then her feet, after which happy event she set about the business of learning to walk again. This proved a painful process, because her spine had been damaged during confinement, but her determination was so great that she was fully mobile by the time I was two and a half weeks old.

She collected me from next door, carried me home in a hand-knitted shawl and, with her usual deliberation, began to know and love me. As she explained to me in later years, 'You see, lass, you can only do one thing at a time. The road as I looked at it, I had to get me legs back. If I'd have never got me legs back, I'd have given you away. Better a foster Mam with legs than a real Mam stuck in a bed or on a chair for the rest of her life. And I didn't want to be looking at you and blaming you for me legs, 'cos it weren't your fault. But human nature, aye, mine included, being what it is, I would have blamed you in a way. Anyroad, all's well that ends well as they say.'

My father, far from being disappointed, was delighted with his daughter. As a regular soldier fighting, as he put it, 'for King, country and a pair of bloody boots as 'll fit', he was home infrequently, but he lavished me with love, attention and such gifts as could be obtained during those war-torn years.

And it was a terrible war, both inside and outside our house. While German planes droned their nightly song overhead, my mother, who would go nowhere near the air-raid shelter in the back yard, would sit in the darkened kitchen clinging to me under the table, a rolled-up *Bolton Evening News* clutched tightly in her hand. When the all-clear sounded, she would creep out furtively, turn up the gas mantle and begin her own war on the cockroaches, battering them to pulp with the paper and crunching them into the flags with the wooden soles of her clogs.

Thus, having learned early on to count cockroach corpses, I was quite numerate by the time I began to attend nursery class at the age of three. Also, once my mother had recovered from her disappointment at my not being a boy, she determined to make the best of things and began the task of teaching me to read and write at a very early age. I was, as a result, precocious and very advanced in comparison to my classmates at All Saints nursery.

The mills were still turning out cotton in spite of

the war and my mother returned to her work as a doffer and spinner just after my third birthday, abandoning me to the tender mercies of the Sisters of the Cross and Passion, who had little patience with a waif as maladjusted as I seemed to be. I had been baptised by Father Sheahan in Mrs Hyatt's scullery a few days after my birth, and was therefore designated Catholic, although my mother no longer practised her religion.

Until I was three, my world had been very small. It contained me, my mother, a father who visited occasionally, our immediate neighbours, an aunt or uncle who would drop by from time to time and the parish priest whom I hated with an unreasoning venom known only to small children. I disliked his long black cloak, which terrified me, especially when the wind shaped it into something unspeakable and nightmarish. I loathed his silly biretta which sat on his large head like, as my mother put it, a pea on a drum. Most particularly, I objected to his big red hands reaching down, patting me on the head, or, worse still, lifting my chin so that I had to look into his grey, lifeless face. The face shaped itself into a smile sometimes, a smile that never reached the eyes.

When my world was made larger, I noticed the same unamused eyes in the faces of the nuns and although I didn't recognize it yet, my quarrel with Catholicism had begun.

Miss Best was not a nun. She wore proper clothes and her legs showed. Also her eyes smiled, but not all the time. They were not smiling now. 'Annie Byrne, get into your cot. Now – this minute!'

'No.' I stamped my new red clog onto the polished floorboards. It was daft, going to bed every afternoon. I had never been to bed in the afternoon before. Bed was for night, not for daytimes. The cots were set out in rigid rows, canvas structures on folding metal frames, each with a pink or blue blanket. Under every pink or blue blanket lay a child, round eyes popping as they stared at me, the sole dissenter.

'Come on now, Annie, take off your clogs.' For answer I kicked out at her, narrowly missing a lisle-stockinged leg.

At that moment the door was thrown open and there stood Sister Agatha, headmistress, despot, monarch of all she surveyed. From her right hand there dangled a short leather whip which she was tapping gently against her thigh through the thick folds of her voluminous habit.

'What have we here?' Her Irish voice held none of the pleasant lilt common to most of my own immigrant uncles.

Miss Best all but curtseyed. 'Oh . . . Sister . . . it's just that little Annie doesn't like to lie down in the afternoon.'

After a bone-chilling silence, the nun spoke, her voice cracking with anger. 'Doesn't like? Doesn't like, is it? Well, we'll just have to see about that now, won't we? Get into that cot now, this instant, you bold girl.' I said nothing, but some devil in me made me drag my eyes from the whip, forced me to stare up at her, straight into those icy eyes.

'Did you hear what I said? You're not deaf as well as stupid, are you? Did you hear me, girl?'

'Yes.'

'Yes, what?'

Miss Best put a hand on my shoulder. 'Yes, Sister. You must say yes, Sister.'

'Yes, Sister,' I muttered through clenched teeth.

Sister Agatha drew Miss Best aside. Although my heart was pounding in my ears, I caught snatches of their whispered conversation.

'. . . very advanced, Sister . . . more like a six year old . . . doesn't need the sleep . . .'

'They must conform, Miss Best . . . grow up delinquent . . . mother lapsed . . . child too big for her boots. . .'

It looked to me as if Miss Best was getting into trouble and it was all my fault. Quietly, I slipped off my clogs and lay flat on the cot, pulling the blanket high over my head. The two women stopped talking. I knew they were staring at me, for I could feel the chill of the nun's eyes as they swept over my body.

This was my first remembered encounter with compromise. Many more were to follow, but this became, for me, a point of reference. For a long time afterwards, whenever I had to relinquish my principles in order to keep the peace, I would say I was 'doing my Best', for Miss Best was the one who taught me to make room for people, to consider others as well as myself.

Fortunately, I knew nothing of what lay in store for me. I would be 'doing my Best' for many years to come.

We war babies grew up quickly. Each day, we set off for school, gas masks swinging from our shoulders, stopping off at Connie's corner for a ha'porth of cocoa and sugar, scurrying into the playground to stand in regimented rows beneath the eagle eye of Sister Agatha, then lining up once more for our daily dose of cod liver oil and orange juice.

I became outwardly docile, realizing quickly that

I must have no opinion, voice no objection, because if I did, I would invoke the wrath of my elders and invite the alienation of my peers. Nevertheless, I established myself as pack leader, organizing play-times, inventing games of dragons, of princes and princesses in which I always played the chief role.

Just after my fourth birthday, I was moved into the infants' class because of my ability to read and write. I was heartbroken, not so much because I had been placed with a nun, for Sister Immaculata was near-human, the exception that proved the rule, but because I had to leave behind my beloved Miss Best. However, I settled quickly into the new routine, enjoying the challenge of learning, soaking up like a sponge everything that was on offer.

The sirens often sounded as we left our school. They were part of our lives and we never hurried when they began their raucous wailing. Even at three and four years of age we were responsible for ourselves, negotiating main roads, scurrying across trolley and tram tracks, making our own way home through mazes of terraced streets and cobbled entries.

I never went straight home, but stayed with Mrs Hyatt till my mother came back from the mill. But one afternoon, as I passed my own house on my way to Mrs Hyatt's, I noticed that our front door was open. I heard voices and muffled crying coming from within, so I sat on the step and listened. It had been my experience thus far that anything worth hearing would never be spoken in front of me.

So it happened that I learned of my father's death as I sat on a cold doorstep with nobody to comfort me. It was a chilly September afternoon in 1944. I stared up our sloping street towards Derby Road, remembering the times I'd watched my father running down faster and faster towards me, how, when he had reached me, he would pick me up high in the air, tossing me about, making me squeal and giggle. I recalled the smell of him, tobacco and beer, sometimes whisky.

I had always snatched the Glengarry from his head, cramming it down onto my own yellow curls as he sang 'A Gordon for Me'. He would never come again. Never. My Daddy was dead. My Daddy who always took me to the lions in the middle of Town, under the big clock.

No, he couldn't be dead, not my Daddy. He'd be there with the lions. It was a mistake. Grown-ups were always making mistakes.

As fast as my legs would carry me, I was up and away to the top of Ensign Street, down Derby Road towards the town. The sirens were screaming again, but I never heeded them, so intent was I on reaching my goal. Blindly I ran past the deserted market place and through Moor Lane, stopping only to catch my breath as I reached the Civic Buildings.

The Crescent was empty of people; no vehicle moved and though dusk had begun its descent, not a single lamp was lit as I climbed the Town Hall steps towards the lions. I sat, shivering on the stone slabs waiting for my father. Opposite, I could see the memorial to those who had lost their lives in the previous war, the war during which my parents had been born.

Somewhere, bombs were falling, but I was used to that; I had never lived in a world at peace. When the bombers had finished vomiting their contents onto Manchester, a thin, cold drizzle began to fall, wetting me through to the skin within minutes. A warden found me there sometime during that night, but I was not grateful to him, for even in my weakened state I fought to maintain my vigil.

'I'm waiting for my Dad,' I insisted.

'Nay, lass. Tha can't stop 'ere. Jerry'll be back, more than likely.' He picked me up and I hit him full in the face with a clenched fist. 'I'm stopping. I'm waiting for my Dad. They said he's dead, but he's not . . . he's not. He always comes to the lions. Please let me stay, Mister . . .' But the man was already carrying me down the steps to a waiting policeman who shone a dimmed torch into our faces.

'I reckon she's bloodied tha nose, then, 'Arry.'

'Aye, she 'as that. But she's in a fair state, wet through an' all. Tha'll 'ave to tek 'er 'ome.'

'Where dost live, lass?' the policeman asked.

'I'm not telling you.'

'Oh, well then.' The policeman removed his helmet and scratched his head. 'Well, in that case, we'll 'ave to tek thee to t' Cottage 'Omes.'

The Cottage Homes? That was for children that nobody wanted, that had no mams and dads. Still, if I hadn't got a dad, I might as well go and live at the Cottage Homes. But then, if I did, I might never see my Mam again. And I did have a Dad. I did.

'Number 20, Ensign Street,' I muttered.

'And what's yer name?'

'Annie Byrne.'

'How old are you?'

'Four and a half and a bit.'

'By. Tha's a clever lass for four and a half and a bit. What are you doing stuck out 'ere with old 'Arry an' a couple o' pot lions?'

'I've told you once. I'm waiting for my Dad.'

'Right. Well where's yer dad comin' from?'

I thought hard before answering, 'Italy, I think.' The two men looked at one another over my head before Harry handed me to the policeman, whispering as he did so, 'They've told 'er 'e's dead.'

I stiffened in the policeman's arms. 'They haven't told me nothing. They never tell me nothing. But I heard them saying it.'

There was a lot of rain by this time and the policeman's muslin-draped torch gave little light, so I wasn't sure that I saw tears running down his face. He raised his head, craning his neck towards the sky. 'Sod you,' he shouted and his voice was high and strange. 'Sod you bloody bastards.'

Normally, I would have been fascinated by such interesting language, but by this time I was too tired, wet and worried to wonder anew about the anomalies of grown-ups and their rules, one law for them and another for me.

When we finally reached home, my mother was in a state of total hysteria, laughing and crying at the same time, clutching at my hands, slapping me for my naughtiness, then hugging me in her relief. I was shocked to the core when Mrs Hyatt got up from her chair, crossed the room with her waddling gait and hit my mother very hard across the face. I could not understand this at all.

But I was given little time to wonder, for they stripped me off and wrapped me in a warm blanket, then we sat, my mother and I, the policeman and Mrs Hyatt in the four chairs that surrounded the kitchen table.

My mother, after drawing several shuddering breaths, said, 'Annie, your Dad's not coming home any more.' The gaslight flickered and I stared at the spluttering mantle, trying to fix my attention on something – anything other than what was being said to me.

The policeman took my hand in his. 'Tha'rt a big, fine lass, Annie. Yer dad 'as died for 'is country. When yer older, you'll be proud of 'im.'

'Who killed him?' I asked, of nobody in particular.

'Why, the Nazis, luv – the Germans,' answered the bobby.

'The ones that dropped the bomb on Emmanuel Street and killed Rosie Turner?'

'Aye, lass.'

'The ones that dropped the bombs tonight?'

'That's it, Annie, they're the ones.'

A terrible anger rose in me, heaving in my throat like vomit. I fought for breath, pushing away the hands that reached for me. Something in my chest swelled and swelled until I felt I would burst. I had to do something bad, something really bad to let the anger out. Jumping up from the table so quickly that my chair fell away, I flew to the window and threw back the blackout.

Staring up into the rain-filled night sky, I screamed at the top of my voice, 'Sod you bloody bastards.' And my mother, who would normally have berated me for such gross misconduct, pulled me into her arms, pressing her tear-soaked face against mine.

'That's right, lass,' she sobbed. 'You tell 'em.'

2

Neighbours

Apart from the war ending, two things of note happened during the sixth year of my life. Firstly, old Mr Higson from the end house, number 30, died on the outside lavatory. We children received this news with a mixture of sadness and revulsion, the former because he had been kind to us and the latter because we didn't think anyone should die with his trousers down.

The second event, which was not completely unconnected with the first, was that my mother started courting.

Mr Higson's youngest son, Eddie, who had been a prisoner of war for several years, was allowed out of the Infirmary to attend the funeral. Thin almost to the point of emaciation, he went with his older brothers to thank the neighbours for their kind thoughts and floral tributes. His appearance appalled and fascinated me. A cadaverous head was not improved by flesh of a yellowish shade which seemed to be stretched like parchment over forehead and chin, only to darken in great shrivelled hollows where cheeks should have been. His eyes were sunken too, small navy-blue dots set well back in circular craters of bone. The nose was prominent, wide-nostrilled and with a gristly bump near the top, while his lips were thin almost to the point of total absence, giving the mouth the appearance of a slit in the fold of some ageing newspaper. This whole death's head was crowned by an incongruously vigorous mop of crinkly dark hair, all flattened and shiny with grease.

Eddie Higson had never been married. My mother immediately pitied him for his poor condition and took to visiting him at the hospital to which he had had to return immediately after the burial of his father.

During these visits, for which my mother prettied herself up with powder and rouge, I was left with Mrs Hyatt who voiced her disapproval of the affair regularly – not to me, but to her two sons. Freddie, the elder by ten minutes or so, made little response to his mother's mutterings, while Tom, who always seemed to feel a degree of responsibility towards me, would whisper, 'Hush, Mam. Not in front of the lass.'

I was fond of Tom. He always brought me sticks of barley sugar on a Friday when he got his wages and sometimes, when I was daydreaming, I imagined that Tom might be my uncle. Not my Dad, nobody could replace my Dad, but Tom was the best uncle anybody might wish for.

I sat in Mrs Hyatt's rocker by the fire, sucking my stick of barley sugar. Mrs Hyatt took a rice pudding from the range oven and banged it down onto the table between the two men.

''E's got sly eyes. I never did like 'im. When yer dad were alive, 'e never liked 'im neither.'

'Listen, Ma,' drawled Freddie. 'Me Dad never liked nobody, specially when he got near the end. People with cancer isn't noted for their sense of humour.'

Mrs Hyatt clipped Freddie round the ear with the oven cloth. 'Bit of respect when you talk about yer dad. And it were nowt to do wi' cancer. It were to do with . . . well . . . with other things.' She cast a furtive glance in my direction, then mouthed a few silent words at Freddie and Tom.

'That was all just talk, Mam. Nothing was ever proved,' said Tom. 'And mind what you say. Little pigs have big ears.'

I reacted not at all, pretending to concentrate on the sticky sweet as I stared into the fire. Tom went on, his voice almost a whisper, 'Nancy Byrne has her own life to lead now. You can't go telling her who she must go out with and who she mustn't. And she knows nothing about . . . all that, I'm sure she doesn't. What's more, that tongue of yours will get you into trouble one of these days, mark my words. What you're saying about Ed . . . about you-know-who is nothing short of slander. Aye, you'll choke on that tongue, you will.'

Mrs Hyatt bristled visibly, her back straightening, her head moving slightly from side to side as she spoke. 'Slander, you say? Slander? Why do you think he joined up so bloody quick, eh? 'E's no flaming 'ero, I can tell you. And who's to speak up now? Aye, answer me that one – if you can. With 'alf Emmanuel Street flattened and them as was involved cold in their graves? Oh aye, it's all forgotten now, isn't it? But I've not forgot, the dirty evil bast . . .'

'Be quiet, Mother.' Tom stood and raised his hand. 'Hush your noise. Give the man the benefit of the doubt.'

'And what about 'er?' Mrs Hyatt jerked a thumb in my direction.

'I'll watch out for her,' answered Tom.

'Aye, well. You'd best grow eyes in t' back of your 'ead, then.' With this final remark, Mrs Hyatt grabbed her coat from its peg and, picking up a tall white jug from the dresser, announced her intention to go to the outdoor licence for a drop of stout.

A few minutes after her departure, Freddie went out to the air-raid shelter – which he now used as a pigeon house – to tend his prize birds, leaving Tom and me as sole occupants of the kitchen.

I gazed into the fire once more, wondering yet again if I could trust my instincts and place my faith in Tom. Most grown-ups got mad if you asked questions. Those who didn't get mad treated you as if you were soft in the head or something. But Tom never got mad with me. Would he now? There was only one way to find out. Without turning my head, I asked, 'Is he a bad man, Tom?' The clock ticked noisily.

'I don't know, Annie.' This was promising. Adults were usually so positive, so sure of their ground – an admission of indecision could be a step in the right direction.

'What did he do?' I asked carefully.

He came slowly round the table, then squatted down on his haunches in front of me. 'Annie, love – I can't answer your questions. But I will say this to you. If anything ever worries you – anything at all – you come straight to me. Right?'

'Right.'

'You know I was there when you were born. If it hadn't been for me . . . well, never mind all that now. You're almost a little sister to me, Annie. If anything ever happens to you . . . if anybody . . . well, you just come straight to your Uncle Tom.'

'I will.'

'No matter what?'

'No matter what, Tom.'

Footsteps in the narrow lobby made him rise to his feet. My mother, flushed and smiling, burst into the room, her eyes sparkling as she cried, 'He's coming home Friday, Tom. Ooh, I can't believe it. He's near ten stone again – he was only seven and a half when he got back. I'm that excited – we must have a party. And guess what, Annie?'

I stared at my radiant mother as she threw her handbag down onto the table and ripped off a white cotton glove to reveal a narrow gold band with a small shining stone set into its centre. 'Your Mam's engaged – you're going to have a new Dad, Eddie's going to be your Dad. Isn't that great news?'

I looked from Tom to my mother, then back to Tom.

'Well? Have you nothing to say, Annie?' she cried.

My hands were shaking as I rose to my feet and I gripped the fireguard tightly as I positioned myself next to Tom, leaving the table as a barrier between us and her.

'He will not be my Dad,' I heard myself say. My mother, seeming to deflate visibly, sank down onto one of the ladder-backed kitchen chairs.

'No, I know he won't be your real Dad, but he'll be your new Dad.'

'NO. NO. HE WON'T.' I stamped my foot on the hearthrug. 'You are choosing him, Mam. I'm not. If I wanted a new Dad, then I'd choose my own. And I don't want one, anyway. Especially him. He's ugly and . . . and . . .' I groped for words, then Mrs Hyatt's statement, after echoing in my head for a split second, fell out of my mouth. 'He's got sly eyes,' I announced.

The silence that followed was nearly deafening. My mother looked almost pleadingly at Tom, but he turned his back to reach a pipe from the rack to the side of the range.

'What can I do with her, Tom?' For answer, he shrugged his shoulders.

'She can't run my life for me. I'm too young to be . . . well, you know, to be without a husband. I need to settle down again and I know he's right for me. And I might not get another chance, being as I've got An . . . being as I'm not on me own.'

Tom stuffed tobacco into the bowl of his pipe before turning to face her. 'It's a bit soon for the lass, Nancy. Billy's not that long gone, maybe the child needs to serve out her mourning.' The implication that Nancy herself was not mourning did not miss its mark.

'You can't mourn forever, Tom,' she said quietly. 'And kids gets over things quicker than what we do. She'll get used to him.'

Tom stared at my mother for some time before answering, 'If you say so.' Whereupon he turned to light a spill at the fire.

'You don't like him, do you, Tom?'

'I've no feelings either way, Nancy. You know him better than I do, though I daresay there's folks round here as have known him longer. Anyway, what should you care about the opinions of a lad not yet twenty?' He applied the spill to his pipe, puffed for several seconds then swung round to face her once more.

My mother turned her gaze on me. 'You coming home then, Annie?'

I kicked at the rug with the toe of my clog.

Tom nudged me gently. 'Get on home then, lass.'

I made up my mind there and then that should my mother become Mrs Eddie Higson, then I would move in with Tom, Freddie and Mrs Hyatt. It seemed a simple enough solution. If my mother loved Mr Higson more than she loved me, then I would go and live among people who really cared for me.

It had not yet occurred to me that I would not be allowed to put this plan into action. But, having found Tom, the one adult in whom I could place a measure of trust, I went home if not happy then at least comforted, believing I had discovered some if not all of the answers.

3

My Immortal Soul

Like many ugly babies, I had developed into an acceptably attractive child. Although I outstripped my peers by a good couple of inches in height, a fact that often made me a target for Sister Agatha's wrath (since I was the most visible victim in my class), I was blessed with an abundance of soft yellow curls and wide-spaced green eyes. Other assets included two sets of fine strong limbs that made me an adequate competitor in games involving either sex and a respected adversary when it came to combat of any kind.

Of course, like most females, I was not satisfied with my appearance. My mouth was too big for my face, my nose silly, small and freckled, my knees were lumpy, making the long calves appear thin, while my elbows always protruded at odd angles from the few skimpy dresses I owned.

Nevertheless, I was reasonably at peace with myself, having established my leadership at school, having learned to live with, if not to like, the various compromises required by the adults who dominated my life.

My mother was fond of me; of that I was fairly sure. During the long years of war we had shared a bed, shared our hiding place under the solid squareness of the kitchen table, we had divided equally between us our odd meals of dried egg and blackened potato. We had also pooled our fears, my mother often turning to me with her worries, making me far older than my years.

Our dependence was mutual; often I played the role of comforter when she returned from long fruit-less hours of queuing for food or when, in the dark hours, she would turn to me in her loneliness, her tears wetting my pillow as well as her own. For her part, she nursed me through those black days after my father's death, never once leaving my side until I had wrung myself dry of grief. 'We must stick together now, Annie,' she would say. 'You're all I've got and I'm all you've got.'

I began to plan our future, seeing it mapped out before me with all the clear simplicity of a five-year-old mind. 'I'll never leave you, Mam. When I'm fifteen, I shall be a hairdresser and we'll get a shop. You won't have to work in the mill any more and I shall keep your hair pretty for you.' And she would smile her sweet sad smile, looking all the while into the flickering flames of our ill-fed fire, wondering, probably, about her own future.

She was only twenty-seven when my father died, a beautiful, tiny woman with Titian curls, grey-green eyes and the sort of walk that made men turn and stare when she passed by. I knew that my mother was pretty, but I never thought of her as young or marriageable. We had had a Daddy, my Daddy. Never in my wildest imaginings did I think that she might want, or need, to replace him.

So when she turned to Eddie Higson, she turned away from me, threw away all my carefully thought out plans, dismissed me almost, from her thoughts, from her heart and from her life. She stopped loving me, stopped caring about me. And no amount of cajoling or bribery on her part or on his could alter my very set opinion.

I became louder, more boisterous at school, seeking trouble, accepting my punishments almost gladly, because I was no longer lovable and deserved to be punished. My teachers, alarmed at this change in me, sent for my mother.

'She has gone wild, Mrs Byrne. We have all tried.' Sister Agatha raised her eyes ceilingward, her hands rattling the large rosary that hung from her waist, because she held no whip at this moment. She never held the whip when a parent visited. 'We in the convent have offered umpteen decades to implore our Blessed Lady to intervene.' She turned her steely gaze on me. 'But nothing at all seems to be setting this . . . this poor child back on to the right path.'

My mother squirmed in her chair, putting me in mind of Willy Walford from the Cottage Homes, an orphan boy who came for his lessons with his head shaved against the nits. He was a squirmer, was Willy Walford. And here was my mother carrying on the same way, the only difference being that she was bigger and had a full head of hair.

I knew I was getting angry. My mother might not love me any more, but I didn't want old Sister Nasty Knickers (as we called her on the sly) making my own Mam squirm like somebody from the orphanage. I fixed my gaze on the statue of the Immaculate Conception with the blue-glassed night light burning at its feet.

'Have you anything to say for yourself, Annie Byrne?'

I shifted my eyes towards the black-robed figure

which, silhouetted against the window, looked like a grim monster from hell.

'No,' I replied, my voice clear and high.

'No, what?'

'No, Sister.'

The nun came round the desk and stood in front of me and my mother and although this left but a few inches of space between her and us, I determinedly held my ground, though my mother did scrape her chair back a fraction, which made me even more angry and impatient.

'Did you or did you not write those . . . foul words on Sister Immaculata's blackboard?' There was a long silence.

'Answer the Sister, Annie.' I felt very annoyed with my mother. Although her accent was never strong and her speech was virtually free of the usual Bolton colloquialisms, here she was, trying to talk dead posh just because we were in old Nasty Knickers' office. My mother was afraid of Sister Agatha! Well, so was I, but I wasn't going to let it show.

'Yes. I wrote them.'

Sister Agatha's lip curled into a snarl. 'Then I suggest you learn to spell, girl. The undergarment you mentioned in your scribblings begins with a K. And my name, young lady, is Sister Agatha.'

My mother's face was bright crimson by this time. No doubt she had already been informed that I had inscribed on the blackboard 'Sister nasty nickers is a wicked old wich.' It had only been for a dare anyway. Peter Bates had promised me his biggest, silverest bolly-bearing if I'd do it. And I'd done it, while Peter Bates had not, as yet, fulfilled his side of the bargain. I would deal with him later. Even if he did have irons on the soles of his clogs, while I had only rubbers on mine, I'd deal with him. I knew where to kick the boys to make it hurt.

'Come on now, girl. Do your catechism,' Sister Agatha was now saying. 'Show your Mammy that we've taught you something, at least. Who made you?'

'God made me.'

'Why did God make you?'

'God made me to know Him, love Him and serve Him in this world and to be happy with Him forever in the next.' I paused for breath.

'And have you any idea at all of what that means, Annie Byrne? It means that you are to be a good girl for the sake of your immortal soul.'

My immortal soul was something I had not yet managed to come to grips with. Sister Immaculata had drawn an immortal soul on the blackboard only last week. It was like a balloon. When it was full of grace, it was round and coloured in with bright pink chalk. When it was empty, it sagged and had no colour at all. Except, of course, for the black spots of sin covering it like an attack of measles. And there again, you only got the measles if the sins were venial. Should your misdemeanours be mortal, then the soul would surely be black right through to the core – black, deflated and totally without shine.

Of the location of my immortal soul I was unsure. Perhaps it was in my chest where I got the bad feelings when I was angry; perhaps that swelling, choking sensation I got was my immortal soul erupting and letting all the grace drain away. But I wasn't sure. Sometimes I knew that my soul was in my belly where I often suffered pain after a bout of naughtiness. The whole thing was a terrible worry and I tried not to dwell on it too frequently.

'And you will be making your First Confession soon, Annie Byrne. After which you will receive the most Blessed Sacrament of all, the Body and Blood of Jesus Christ.'

I felt sick. I had no notion of cannibalism and therefore no opinion on the subject, but this did not sound quite right to me. I looked pleadingly towards my mother, who was no help at all. She just sat there staring at her shoes, her face grim and still crimson.

Sister Agatha tutted her annoyance then, warming to her subject, went on in a shrill tone, 'My goodness, child, have you not a grateful bone in your body? Jesus Christ suffered for you, died for you . . .'

I didn't hear the rest, because here was something I could latch on to, something I appreciated and understood. Jesus Christ was a hero. He had died for me. Well, my Dad had done the same; he was a hero too, he had died for me, for all of us, in fact. Why, he'd even died for old Nasty Knickers, though I felt sure she didn't deserve it. My Dad had died so that the Nazis would stop bombing the mills and our houses. They were hopeless shots, Nazis. Four or five times they'd had a go at Trinity Street Station and missed. And they didn't just miss a bit, they missed by miles.

'Are you listening to me, Annie Byrne? Would you look at that now, Mrs Byrne. She's away daydreaming while we're here, the both of us, concerned with the survival of her immortal soul.'

My mother nudged me none too gently with her elbow. 'Whatever are you thinking about, Annie?'

'Nazis,' I replied, looking straight at Sister Agatha. Perhaps my original half-formed idea had been to elaborate, to tell Sister Agatha that I now understood the theory of martyrdom, that I was beginning to appreciate the fact of Jesus's sacrifice. But something held me back and that single word, dropped into the room from the mouth of a five-year-old, seemed to have almost as devastating an effect as another bomb on Emmanuel Street. Sister Agatha nearly sat down on the edge of her desk as she groped for support, her right fist clenched tightly over her left breast, while my mother's chin dropped, her gaping mouth allowing her a vacant and rather idiotic appearance.

'Did . . . you . . . hear . . . that, Mrs Byrne?' gasped Sister Agatha. 'This child is wicked . . . wicked, I tell you!'

I waited for my mother to speak, hopefully in my defence, but no answer came, though her tongue moved in her mouth as if she were trying to shape her thoughts.

Sister Agatha began to pace back and forth across the room, throwing her arms wide then crossing them over her chest, looking for all the world like an ugly black crow trying to get off the ground. 'She called me a Nazi . . . a Nazi – you heard her, Mrs Byrne.'

She marched towards me, her claw-like hand pointing towards my face, the extended index finger stopping about an inch from the end of my nose. I looked straight at her, didn't flinch, made no move away from her and I could see plainly that my bold-ness was not appreciated.

'You will go, Annie Byrne, into the corridor. There you will say a decade of the Holy Rosary before the Sacred Heart. You will not stand, you will kneel and you will have no cushion for your knees.'

Knowing I had done something bad, but having no real concept of what my sin had been, I toyed with the idea of standing my ground. Had my mother not been there, had I not been a witness to her lack of sympathy for me, I probably would have chosen to remain and take a whipping. But knowing that my mother would neither support nor defend me, I took one last look at her mortified expression before creeping out into the corridor to stare at the effigy in the corner.

It was a statue of a long-haired man in a red cloak, patience and suffering etched deeply into its face. One hand lay across its chest where a heart dripping vivid red blood sat on a plain white undergarment. This was the Christ who had died for me. This was the Christ whose Body and Blood I would have to receive. I still felt sick.

I touched an icy bare foot, tracing the toenails with the end of my finger. Well, this was definitely not body and blood. I scraped away a bit of the flesh-coloured paint to reveal chalky white plaster underneath. Then, kneeling on the cold marble floor, I took the beads from my pocket and began to count my way through the Our Fathers, the Hail Marys and the Glory Bes. My knees hurt. On the end of my rosary, another Christ figure dangled, this time crucified and made of base metal and I swung this item about a bit to relieve the monotony.

I knew I didn't believe in what I was doing, in what I was saying. None of it made any sense. I shut my eyes tight and fought to believe, reaching down inside myself, trying to locate my immortal soul, hoping that it would inflate and fill with grace as I prayed. Nothing happened. I shuffled about the floor, trying to ease the agony in my knees.

When I opened my eyes and gazed once more at the dripping heart, my stomach heaved and I vomited noisily onto the clean black and white floor before sliding down into unconsciousness. They found me there eventually, cleaned me up, put me into a nursery cot and gave me sips of water and a cool cloth for my head.

From that day on, Sister Agatha ignored me almost completely. She never seemed to look directly at me again, avoiding me whenever possible, delegating my punishments to beings lesser than herself. Occasionally, I caught her looking at me sideways, but as soon as I met her eye she would turn away quickly, leaving in the space between us an atmosphere I did not yet recognize as shame.

My contempt for her grew then lessened as other, more pressing, events pushed her from my mind. She was, after all, a person of no importance.

4

Changes

'See what Eddie's got for you, Annie. Come on, hurry up.'

I pretended not to hear, whipping my newly chalked top into further frenzy until it skidded to a halt among the cobbles at the pavement's edge. Sheila Davies, my best friend for the moment, straightened from her task of marking out a hopscotch on the flagstones. 'Yer Mam's shouting, Annie.'

I picked up my top and sauntered over to Sheila.

'Why don't you go and see what she wants?' she asked. 'I think you're right daft not playing with all them things he's bought you.'

She was right, I supposed. There I was with a veritable treasure trove – a scooter, a skipping rope set in varnished wooden handles with ball-bearings for smooth turning, a dolls' house with curtains and smart furniture, all ignored out in the air-raid shelter. I couldn't explain, not even to Sheila, why I wouldn't play with the things. In truth, I found it difficult – indeed impossible – to explain to myself why I couldn't, or wouldn't take advantage of Eddie Higson's generosity.

'Get in here now, Annie!' The tone of my mother's

voice precluded the possibility of any further attempts to ignore her.

On entering our kitchen, I found Eddie Higson sitting, as usual, in the big rocker, my father's rocker. This was placed to the left of the range and sideways on to the window, a position chosen by my father because the light enabled him to read his *Bolton Evening News* until dusk forced us to use the gas.

I resented Eddie's presence in my Dad's chair, resented his presence in our house, the way he would put his feet up on the fireguard while my mother fetched him pint pots of thick, stewed tea and wedges of window pie. I had always loved window pie; it had been my favourite, made specially for me and only for me. Now I refused it, just as I refused to share anything with this man who had invaded my house, stolen my mother and spoiled my life.

But this time, it was not going to be easy, for Eddie Higson held in his lap a beautiful ball of blue-grey fur, a tiny scrap of feline life that mewed and clawed gently at the man's fingers.

'It's a little cat, Annie,' he announced, his small deepset eyes narrowed in anticipation. Did he think I was daft or something? I'd seen cats before. My heart went out to the little creature. I longed to pick it up, stroke it and love it, make it my very own. It would love me in return, I knew it would.

'It's a Persian,' said my mother. 'Eddie's paid a bob or two for that, I can tell you.'

I knew what was expected of me. I knew what I wanted to do – I wanted to do the very thing that was required of me, to take the kitten, express my gratitude and forge a link that both he and my mother were waiting for – depending on, almost.

I wandered to the dresser and picked up my copy

of *Robinson Crusoe*, the one my father had bought for me during his last leave.

'Well?' enquired my mother. 'Aren't you going to thank Eddie for getting you such a pretty little cat? Smokey, he's called.'

I flicked through the pages of my brightly illustrated children's version, then snapped the book shut loudly. 'I don't want a cat,' I said, carefully avoiding looking at Smokey whom I wanted in that moment more than I'd ever wanted anything before in my life.

'Bloody hell,' cursed Higson. 'There's no pleasing some folk. What does she want, then?' he enquired of my mother who simply raised her arms in a gesture of despair.

'What do you want, then?' he asked of me.

I placed my book back on the dresser. 'Nothing,' I replied.

'She bloody hates me, Nancy,' he shouted, furious now. He hurled the kitten to the floor and I steeled myself not to flinch as its little body hit the peg rug. My breathing quickened and became shallow as that familiar feeling of anger and confusion rose in me, overwhelming me almost, filling my chest to bursting point. I had always known instinctively that this was a cruel and vicious man, but now the living (or dying) evidence lay at our feet, mewling piteously before the fire. I also knew that had I accepted the cat, his fate would have eventually been similar, for Higson would have used the animal to get at me sooner or later. I was full of hatred for Higson, full of contempt for my mother, who was stupid, so stupid not to see through this terrible man.

She ran now and picked up the kitten, cradling it in her arms as she screamed at me. 'Now look what you've done, Annie. Poor little thing.' Obviously, she was blind as well as stupid. I took a slow and deliberate breath. 'I didn't do it, Mam. He did.' I pointed an accusing finger at Eddie Higson. 'He is a bad man,' I announced. 'And I don't want him in my house.'

Higson crossed the room in two strides and hit me full across the face with the flat of his hand. This was the first time he had hit me, but I knew, with an unwavering certainty, that it would not be the last, that should my mother marry this man, then I would suffer for a long time to come.

'Don't touch her,' screamed my mother. 'Don't you ever hit her, Eddie.'

Although my face smarted from the blow, I stood my ground as he glowered before me. 'Don't hit me again,' I said quietly, simply repeating my mother's words and staring full into his small, deep-sunken eyes.

I never found out what happened to the little cat, but I wept bitter tears for him in the privacy of the air-raid shelter. When my tears were dried, I took the scooter and the skipping rope down the back street and flung them onto the Emmanuel Street bombsite. The dolls' house followed suit, but it looked incongruous sitting among the dust and rubble of ruined homes, so I picked up a half-brick and destroyed it as efficiently as the German bombers had wiped out the real houses that once stood there.

At the end of my destructiveness, I felt exhausted but victorious. One battle at a time. If I won enough skirmishes, I would surely win the war.

The real war broke out, of course, after the wedding. Considering our impoverished state (since Eddie

44

Higson was still unfit for work) and taking into account the post-war shortages, it was a lavish affair. The reception was to be held in my grandfather's house, which was a large one, in the centre of a high terrace on Vista Street at the top of Daubhill. The street was aptly named, because from my grandfather's house you could see for miles across the moors surrounding Bolton. We had even had a grand view of Manchester as it burned after one massive raid, three or four sets of cousins pressed against the upstairs windows marvelling at the orange brightness of the night sky.

The wedding took place at All Saints in August 1946. The church was filled to bursting with aunts, uncles, cousins and friends of my mother from the mill. Higson seemed to have no friends. His two brothers and their wives and offspring were in evidence, but apart from them, he had few supporters.

My mother had decided against bridesmaids, knowing full well that I would be, at best, an unwilling participant and that my absence from such an entourage would attract comment and cause embarrassment.

In fact, I did not really attend the service, escaping early on to a small side pew next to a confessional box, where I busied myself studying a spider that was carefully constructing a web across a corner of the door. This was Saturday. By Wednesday night the web would be in ruins when the first sinner would cross the confessional threshold at seven o'clock.

I wore a silly pink satin frock with smocking on the bodice and a wide sash that kept coming loose and trailing on the floor. On my feet I had black patent ankle-strap shoes which had cost, so I had been informed, an arm, a leg and a cartload of coupons.

My mother was dressed in powder blue crepe and wore a hat with a small open-weave veil. She looked pretty, but rather like a fragile china doll with her painted rose-bud lips and pink-rouged cheeks.

Higson looked clean, at least, though rather uncomfortable in his greenish-grey suit with the wilting carnation hanging from a button hole. But then, I thought, no self-respecting flower would survive long in such unsavoury company. His hair, usually crinkly and springy, was plastered flat to his head with a liberal application of grease. There were some improvements – even I had to admit that, because he didn't really look like something off a pirate's flag now. The face was rounder and fuller, the skin a more acceptable colour. But nothing would ever improve that nose, nasty black bristles poking out of the nostrils, the whole thing hooked like the beak of some flesh-eating bird. He was, in my opinion, a very ugly man.

I would not smile for the photographs. My mother, gritting her teeth and trying to hang on to her patience on this happy day, rubbed at my scuffed shoes with her wisp of a handkerchief and told me to smile, for goodness sake. There was nothing to smile about, so I carried on frowning and dragging my toes in the dust.

As most of my relations, including my mother's father, were Irish, a small ceilidh band had been engaged and my grandfather's large front room had been emptied for the dancing.

I had just one interesting cousin called Eileen. Her father, Paddy Foley, had deserted Eileen and her mother two years previously, so I had, of late, come

46

to identify with the fatherless girl. Her mother, Nellie, was my mother's sister, though they did not look alike. Nellie was tall, thin as a reed and dark-haired, with the pale skin so often found in those of Irish descent. My mother, prettier by far than Nellie, had a softer, gentler look about her.

Eileen herself was plain to the point of ugliness, with straight mousy hair and strange eyes that darted about constantly as if she were frantically searching for something.

We took ourselves off to the top of the house, right up to the attic, away from all the fiddling, shouting and stamping of feet. We sat side by side on an old army trunk, our heels dangling and bumping gently against its side. She stared at me with all the wisdom of a ten-year-old, those odd, quick eyes seeming to pierce through my skull right to the very centre of my thoughts.

'You don't like 'im, do you?' She put an arm around my shoulders. Unaccustomed, of late, to such empathy, I allowed a few tears of self-pity to run down my face and she dried them, none too gently, with the rough-ribbed cuff of her grey cardigan.

'Me Mam says as 'ow you'll get used to 'im, like,' she went on. 'You'll be better off than what we are at any road – once he can get work. At our 'ouse we've seen nowt but bread and drip for a week now. See.' She opened a brown paper bag. 'I've fetched loads of butties up and a bottle of stout – we can 'ave our own party.'

'No!' I made up my mind quickly as an idea flashed across my brain with all the sudden brilliance of a streak of fork-lightning. 'Save my half, Eileen. I'm running away.'

Expressing no surprise, as Eileen had ceased to

feel surprise at a very early age, she merely asked, with great calm, 'Where to, like?'

I thought about this for some seconds. 'Well, I'd go next door, but they'd only find me straight off and drag me back. I think I'll go to . . . to . . . Blackpool. That's it, I'll go to Blackpool.'

She stared down at her white blancoed canvas shoes. 'Where will you live?' she asked. This was getting a bit complicated for me.

'I'll find somewhere. I can sleep on the pier or in a tram shelter. And . . .' I began to warm to my subject. 'And I'll get food off people on the sands – bits of picnics and that.'

Eileen shook her head wisely. 'They'll only bring you back. They always do – I've been fetched back four times now – mind, I never got as far as Blackpool, but it makes no difference. They'll always get you in the end, Annie. Then you'll get a right good 'iding off yer Mam. Nay. You'll have to go 'ome with them and make the best of it.'

She was right, of course. They did always get you in the end. I sighed deeply, trying to imagine what life was going to hold in store for me. I had already been banished from my mother's bed, was already forced to sleep cold and alone in the small front bedroom.

And I'd have to eat with him, sit with him in the kitchen every evening. There was no privacy in the house, no bathroom. If you wanted a wash, you used the tin dish in the slopstone. If you wanted a warm wash, then you heated water on the range or on one of the two gas rings in the scullery. Weekly baths took place in front of the kitchen fire in the metal tub from the back yard. Which was all very well when there was just me and my mother. But now, with a stranger in the house, how would we manage?

I sobbed my unhappiness into my fingers, squeezing the tears in my palms until they ran right up to the elbows. It was the unfairness of it all that frustrated me. Grown-ups could do exactly as they pleased. We just had to fit in, were forced to fit in. We had to wait until we, in turn, became adults before we could have any choice at all in things that really mattered.

'Don't take on, Annie,' whispered Eileen. 'Don't let them know 'ow you feel. Just carry on going t' school and do your booklearnin'. I've 'eard as 'ow you're clever at school. They can't take that away from you now, can they? You'll likely get a scholarship when you're eleven – oh aye, you'll pass for t' grammar alright. Then you can be what you want, do what you want.'

'What can I be, Eileen?' I gripped her hand tightly.

'Ooh, anythin'. Well, nearly anythin'.'

I thought about this for a few minutes, my sobs beginning to subside.

'Could I be a teacher, Eileen?'

'I reckon as 'ow you could, yes.'

'Then I could tell people what to do instead of them telling me. Only I'd be a nice teacher like Miss Best with legs. I could never be a nun. I don't like nuns.'

Eileen, a not too frequent attender at St Gregory's, which was also under the tender auspices of the Passionists, agreed with me wholeheartedly. She sat, tugging at her hair, twisting it about her fingers. Perhaps she thought if she twisted it for long enough it would go curly.

'I'm goin' to work in a shop,' she announced. 'A food shop. If they don't pay me proper I can always pinch enough to eat.' She grabbed a sandwich from the bag and swallowed it in two bites. For a moment or two I forgot my own troubles and thought about poor Eileen.

Auntie Nellie worked full time in the mill, yet there was never enough to eat, seldom any coal for the fire. Most of the time, Eileen did not go to school, simply because she had little to wear. For days on end, her mother would lock her in, telling her that the house was being watched and should Eileen ever open the door, let alone step outside, then she, Auntie Nellie, would surely be informed by her spies.

This poor ten-year-old child was, therefore, left without food to eat, without fire to warm her, while her mother, who did not always come home as soon as the working day had ended, spent her wages in the Swan or the Black Bull, returning only once her purse was empty and her belly full of ale. Surely my life, even with Eddie Higson in it, could not be as terrible as Eileen's?

'Do you get frightened when you're shut in?' I asked.

She nodded quickly.

'Shall I come sometimes and put a bit of bread or maybe an Eccles cake through the letterbox?'

Now she was shaking her head vehemently. 'No. They'll only find out. Whatever you do, they always find out.'

'But it's not fair,' I cried. 'You should go to school like me and you shouldn't be locked in on your own all day with no dinner.'

She put a finger to her lips. 'Shush. Nobody knows, 'cepting you. If me Grandad ever found out, he'd flay me Mam, you know he would. Then me

Mam would go for me – aye, she would that – and where would that get me, eh?'

'But it's not fair!' I shouted again.

She looked at me wisely, shaking her head as if exasperated at me for expecting it to be fair.

We sat together for a long time until the room grew chill, two girl children separated by four years, connected by the strangeness of our lives, she with the crazy mother, I with the horrible so-called stepfather. Yet we drew strength from each other as we sat there waiting, waiting for our day to come. It would be a long wait, we knew that. It would reach beyond this room, this house, this day and into dimensions as yet uncharted. But our strength, joint and separate, lay in our youthfulness, in our unspoken hope that we would be survivors.

Thus began my journey into my mother's second marriage, my pathway into a hell I could never have imagined. So fierce was the heat in my particular hell that when, some three years after this wedding day, I learned that Eileen and her mother had perished in their gas-filled scullery, I felt not only pity and grief, but something approaching envy too.

Eileen had not survived. I was condemned to live.

5

Moving On

Our house in Ensign Street was a slum. Although my mother did her best, scrubbing floors, blackleading the grate two or three times a week, making sure her doorstep and the two or three square feet of flags outside the front door were donkeystoned daily, she was fighting a losing battle.

We were constantly overrun by vermin; in the night the kitchen and scullery floors would become blanketed in silverfish and cockroaches, while mice and even rats put in regular appearances around the meat safe and under the slopstone.

It was a poorly built two up two downer, with a sloping scullery attached at the back and a brick air-raid shelter in the yard. The roof leaked with monotonous frequency and the bedroom walls were decorated with a variety of moulds, some wet and green, some white and furry.

Facilities were, to say the least, primitive. At the bottom of the back yard was a tippler toilet consisting merely of a wide earthenware pipe which protruded from the flagged floor, the seat being a crude circle of badly splintered wood with a hole in the middle. There was no flushing mechanism. A suspended bucket in the pipe simply emptied itself into the open drain below once the contents became heavy enough to make it tilt.

Next to the lavatory was a midden, a low wall over which debris and decaying food were thrown. Two or three times a month, the cart would rumble up the back street and men with rags wrapped around their mouths and noses would shovel the putrid contents of middens onto the open lorry, thereby disturbing the rats' nests, causing the creatures to panic and move once more towards our homes in search of food.

Yet there was a predictability about life in Ensign Street, a monotony that made us feel secure in spite of our unclean environment.

Because most of the women worked on weekdays, washing was done on Saturdays. Each household had its own posstub and posser and the pounding of wood on metal, the swish of garments in water, the scrubbing of sheet against washboard, these sounds were our dawn chorus at the beginning of each weekend. Should it rain, then these activities must take place in the sculleries and tempers were always frayed on inclement Saturdays, for no-one, not even the most hardened of heathens, would dare face the contempt of her neighbours by washing on a Sunday, however bright the weather.

Once the clothes had been rinsed and forced through the rollers of the wringer, they were hung across the back street to dry, row upon row, three or four lines to every house and woe betide any child found playing round the backs on washdays. Inside the kitchens were pulley lines where the wash was hung to air once brought in or, in the event of rain, clothes would be transferred straight from mangle to pulley, thus forcing the residents to live in a steam-filled atmosphere for the whole day.

The rentman came on Saturdays too, when he knew that the women would all be about their washing and could not, therefore, hide from him. He had a small moustache like Hitler and a large black book to write in, but he was a pleasant enough man and always gave me a mint imperial or an Uncle Joe's mintball.

On Tuesday evenings, the clubman arrived, collecting our pennies for the Providence cheques with which we bought most of our clothing. He had bright red hair, a tooth missing at the front and he did bird imitations. At least, he used to, though once Eddie Higson moved in with us the Provvy man never stopped again, but just took his money and left quickly. I was pleased in a way. It made me realize that I was not the only one who disliked Higson.

Wednesday night was insurance night. Like most poor people, we set aside a few coppers each week so that we would not be buried as paupers.

Lamp Eel came on Friday evenings, the sad carthorse dragging its load up the back street while his master, who always wore a trilby hat with a flower stuck to the brim, called in a high voice, 'Lamp eel, lamp eel, come on Missus, bring out your dead . . . lamp eel. . .', and we would rush out of our houses to inspect whatever was on offer this week. Lamp Eel, whose original function had been to deliver oil for lamps, sold just about everything from donkeystone to sets of china, though where he got the stuff during the shortages nobody seemed to know. His cart was wonderful to behold and to hear, for it shone like a million jewels and jingled magnif-icently as pans and bottles clattered together whenever his cartwheel hit a rut between cobbles.

So although my mother had married a man I despised, I took comfort from the familiarity of my surroundings, drew solace from the continuing routine, reassuring myself that nothing had really changed, that life was still, more or less, the same. I knew every flagstone, every crack, every cobble that paved my walk to and from school. I was even allowed to the shops now and had made friends with the keepers, enjoying a chat in the fruit store or the Co-op, pretending to be grown-up as I commented on the price of a gas mantle, the cost of a tape of Aspros or a packet of Fennings Cooling Powders. The Co-op was my favourite place, because I loved the smells, loved to watch the staff as they deftly shovelled up potatoes or scooped precious sugar into blue bags. I would breathe in the odour of ground coffee, the scent of hanging bacon, the perfume of the earth that clung in wet lumps to potatoes and carrots. If there was a heaven and if there were smells in heaven, I knew it would be just like the Co-op.

But for recreation, the bombsite was my favourite place, because again I could play shops, resting an old door on two piles of bricks for a counter, grinding up brick dust to 'sell' as sugar, using small stones for fruit and sweets. I had never seen a field except from a distance, had never needed a field, for I had, right on my doorstep, a real adventure playground. Of course, the bombsite was forbidden territory, a fact that made it all the more attractive to us and we never minded the trouble we got into for playing there.

Tom Hyatt remained my dearest friend. He was twenty now and a very great age this seemed to me. He had become a qualified tradesman, a painter and decorator and he brought me sweets every Friday when he got his wages. As soon as Lamp Eel had been and gone, I would rush next door to visit and collect my bounty, sitting in the big rocker with dolly mixtures and halfpenny spanishes while Tom told tales of the great houses beyond the moors where he was working. During the first few months of my mother's marriage, Tom often asked, 'Are you alright?' and I would nod, not wanting to worry him.

There were some beatings, just a few, but my mother and Eddie Higson ignored me for the most part. I was left more and more to my own devices and although this neglect did not make me exactly happy, at least I was free to do much as I pleased.

So when I discovered that we were moving, that Eddie Higson had found a job of sorts, that we would be leaving the street and Tom and the bombsite – and yes, even my school suddenly became attractive when I thought of moving to another – I felt as if my world had been completely shattered.

Higson was out. I faced my mother across the kitchen table where she was rolling out pastry, arms covered to the elbows in flour. This time, I was fully determined to dig in my heels and get my own way. They couldn't do this to me. Hadn't they done enough already?

'You and him can go if you want, but I'm going nowhere. I'm stopping here and that's that.'

She wrapped the pastry round the rolling pin and transferred it to a blue-rimmed enamel dish.

'Ah, so you're stopping, are you? And who'll pay your rent and do your dinner? What about your washing and who'll drag you out of bed every morning for school, eh?'

'I don't know and I don't care.'

'Well then, I suggest you start knowing and caring pretty damn quick. We are moving up Long Moor and that's flat. Now stop being so daft and pass me that pan of mince off the range.'

I banged the large iron pan hard onto the table, causing utensils to rattle and fly about. My mother pushed a lock of hair from her face, leaving a smudge of flour on the end of her nose and I studied this as she spoke.

'Eeh, it's a lovely house, Annie. Wait till you see it, just you wait. It's got a back-boiler and a bath-room – well, a sort of bathroom, just like a big cupboard off the front bedroom. And we're getting the electric in – proper lights and a cooker.' She paused in her labours to look at me. 'Listen, Annie. Your Grandad has give us the deposit – some money, like, to put down. Now that's a secret and you mustn't tell nobody, even your cousin Eileen, for Grandad can't do it for everybody and we don't want to cause no fights. Can't you see what this means, love? We're to have a mort-gage, a proper mort-gage instead of a rent book. It'll be our house, not the landlord's. Won't you try to see I'm doing what's best?'

It was hopeless. I'd have been as well off talking to the wall, yet still I went on. 'But it's not what I want, is it? Nobody ever asks me about anything in this house. I just get told what to do – not asked – told. And if I don't do it then I'm in trouble.' I stopped for a second to draw breath. 'You went and married him and I have to live with him. I can't choose, I never get the chance to choose. Now you say I've got to leave my own house, my Dad's house, and go piking off to live where you want to live. Well, it's not fair. I don't want to live up Long

Moor with electric and a bathroom.'

'Do you want to stop here with rats and cock-roaches, then? Is that what you want, to stop in a filthy slum the rest of your life?' She was waving the rolling pin in the air now. 'Now you listen to me, our Annie. Six sisters I've got and every last one of them married to some no-good lump of an Irishman, every one of them up to their eyes in muck and kids they can't feed. Well, I never married an Irishman, because apart from your Grandad they are the scum of the earth. Your Dad was a fine man, a Gordon Highlander and he would have looked after us if he'd lived, oh aye, your Dad would have done right by us.'

She must have seen my lip quiver, because she continued in a quieter tone, 'But he didn't live, Annie. Get that into your head, will you? And now he's dead, Eddie has took us on, both of us, and he'll do his best now he's on the mend. Oh, Annie . . .' She came round the table and took my hand in hers. 'All I've ever wanted is me own front door, me own bit of garden with a few daffs and marigolds. It's got a bit of garden at the front, you know. And there's fields nearby where you can play and the tram stops right outside the door to take you to school.'

I wrenched my hand away. 'You go then. You go and catch the tram, because I'm stopping here. I shall move in with Mrs Hyatt and Tom and Freddie. Tom'll look after me.'

My mother sighed deeply before saying 'Tom won't be there, love.' My fists clenched into tight balls as I asked, 'What do you mean?'

'Tom's off to America soon, lass. He's away to seek his fortune and I can't say that I'm surprised . . . Annie . . . where are you going . . .?'

But I was already off and down the lobby, into the

street and hammering on Mrs Hyatt's door. A startled Mrs Hyatt peered through the window, then I had to wait, hopping from foot to foot until she finally let me in.

'Is Tom there?' I gasped.

'Aye, he's just sat down for his tea. I . . .'

I flew past her and into the kitchen. Tom paused with a forkful of food in his hand as he saw me standing breathless in the doorway.

'Whatever's the matter with you, Annie? You look like you've seen a ghost . . .'

I swallowed hard. 'Is it true?'

'Is what true?'

'That you're going to America?'

'By the hell.' His fork dropped with a clatter and he pushed his chair back from the table. Looking past me, he spoke to his mother. 'See? I told Nancy not to tell her. I told her I wanted to do it in me own time and in me own way.' He looked straight at me now. 'Yes, it is true, Annie. I'm going, sooner or later.'

'Why? Why, Tom?' My voice was full of pleading as I choked back the tears. How many more people would I lose? Did I have to lose everyone I loved?

'I'm going for a better life, Annie. There's more chances over there, I'll get a good job, better training . . . oh heck, how do I explain all this to a child?'

Mrs Hyatt came to stand beside me, her aproned bulk filling the small space between dresser and table. She placed a fat, heavy arm around my shoulder, but looked at Tom as she said, 'Nay, Tom. This is no child. This one were never a child, God love 'er.' Then to me she said, 'I'll still be 'ere, you know. And Freddie. We'll look out for you – you've only to bang on the wall.'

'But Tom said he'd always be here, Mrs Hyatt,' I sobbed. 'He said he'd always look after me . . . and he tells lies, just like all grown-ups.'

It seemed to me that this was the last straw, the final betrayal. My Dad gone, my Mam's affections and attentions directed elsewhere, now Tom was going . . . I would be alone. Utterly, completely, totally alone, no adult on my side, nobody to turn to for comfort or love. Even Tom, my Tom, whom I had begun to trust, was deserting me.

'Is it far to America?' I gulped between tears. 'Can I get there on the tram or a trolley-bus?' But I knew the answer before it came and confirmation arrived in the form of a choking sound from Mrs Hyatt, who turned away quickly towards the dresser. But she was not laughing at me. There was no laughter in those sagging shoulders.

'No, Annie,' said Tom. 'It takes a good few days on a ship to get there.'

I ran to him, flinging my arms about his neck and he drew me gently into his lap. 'Take me with you, Tom. I'll be a good girl, I promise. Just take me with you – please.'

Mrs Hyatt, who was weeping openly now, her wide back shaking with sobs, said, 'You're not the only one as'll miss 'im, Annie. Nay, 'e'll be very sadly missed, will our Tom.' Then she went through to the scullery, clattering the pots and pans to drown the sound of her sobbing.

'You'd want your Mam, Annie,' said Tom gently. 'You know you can't leave your Mam. She'll be needing you one of these days when you're a bigger girl.'

'She doesn't need me, Tom. She's got him.'

'But you love your Mam, don't you?'

What a daft question this was. Even the best of adults seemed to ask daft questions. Of course I loved my Mam. But did she love me? If she had loved me, would she have needed that dreadful Eddie Higson, would she have married a man like that? And would we be moving up Long Moor if she loved me?

'Yes, I love my Mam, Tom,' I answered, almost wearily.

'And if you ever need anybody to help you, or just somebody to turn to, Freddie and my Ma will be here to see to you.'

Obviously, Tom didn't know anything about the proposed move. Briefly, I wondered whether or not I'd get into trouble for telling the Hyatts our business, for Mrs Hyatt was, in my mother's book at least, a busybody and a gossip. But I couldn't keep it to myself, so, throwing caution to the winds, I blurted out, 'We're moving, Tom. Up Long Moor. They're making me go with them. But if you'd stop here instead of going to America, then I could get back and see you and . . .'

Mrs Hyatt bustled into the kitchen, drying first her eyes, then her hands on a corner of the capacious apron. 'Long Moor, you say? When?'

'I don't know, Mrs Hyatt. Soon, I think.'

'Well!' She lowered her bulk into a chair. 'Well, I'll go to the foot of our stairs! What have I always said, Tom? What have I always said? Ideas above 'er station, that one. By! Next news, she'll be 'avin' tea parties wi' bone-china cups and lace doyleys. I'd not be at all surprised if she stopped talkin' to the likes of us.'

'Shut up, Mam. Before you go too far again.'

But Mrs Hyatt was not going to shut up, not for

anyone. She was on her high horse and she'd probably stop there till she fell off, or got kicked off – and Tom was too gentle a man to go hard on his mother.

'Buying a house then, is it, Annie?' she asked, her tone sweetening.

'Yes. My Mam says we are to have a mort-gage.' Instead of a rent book, my mother had said. Perhaps it was bigger than a rent book, or a different colour. Though it sounded more like an exotic fruit to me.

'Well, we'll just have to see 'ow your Mam goes about paying her mort-gage while she's married to that soft bugger. Oh, 'e doesn't fool me, Tom. Like I said before, 'e's no bleeding 'ero, comin' back snivelling from a prison camp after sittin' it out for four bloody years. I'll bet 'e built no escape tunnels. Only reason 'e joined up was over that lass . . .'

'Watch what you're saying, Mam.'

'Anyroad, Nancy'll have to work all the hours God sends for 'er fancy ideas. 'Cos there's no road as 'e'll pay for much. And shortage o' money's not the only thing she'll be worrying about . . .'

'Nancy knows nothing about all that, Mam. And neither do you if the truth were but told.'

'Don't talk to me about truth, Tom Hyatt. Are you going to eat this or not?' When Tom made no reply, she snatched his plate from the table, then, jabbing the air with Tom's fork as if to emphasize every word, she said, 'The truth is dead, Tom, dead and can't speak up for itself. And 'e seems to me to be the right type to . . .' she faltered, placing the fork on the plate. 'Alright, Tom. 'Ave it your own way. Maybe I am wrong, maybe I've said too much in front of this one.' She gestured towards me. 'But I do know this – something about you-know-who is not quite right. And I can't 'elp 'aving me say. Speak as I find, I do.'

She wobbled into the scullery and we heard her, as she scraped Tom's dinner into the slops bucket, muttering not quite to herself 'there's no smoke without fire' and 'a wrong un if ever I saw one'.

Tom took my chin in his fingers and gently turned my face towards his. 'Look, lass. I'm sorry if it looks like I'm letting you down, but I'll be back some day with all kinds of tales to tell you – and presents for you too. Oh yes, I'll bring back some fine presents for my little Annie. You're a sensible girl, got a good head on them shoulders. Now listen to me. Just you stick up for yourself, do what you think's right and do your best at school. I shall write to you every week from Philadelphia – for that's the name of the town I'll be bound for – and you can write to me. How does that sound? You'll have a pen pal in America.'

I knew I was beaten. I had no way of preventing Tom from going to America, no way of changing my mother's mind about moving to the other end of the town.

When I got down from Tom's knee and crossed the room towards the door, I was aware that I was letting him go there and then, for he had already left me, was making plans for a new start away from me. He didn't love me, couldn't love me. Perhaps I really was not lovable, perhaps nobody would ever love me enough to stay with me.

Within the space of two years I had lost the three people who had been most important to me. With my father, I had had no choice, but with my mother and Tom, I felt I had made a conscious decision to let go.

But that decision was just an invention of mind, a pride-saving piece of my imagination. Because, in truth, I had had no choice in any of these matters.

*   *   *

I was forced to admit to myself, however grudgingly, that Long Moor Lane was a great improvement on Ensign Street. Although the rooms at the back of the house had flagged floors, there was a proper kitchen instead of a scullery. This large, single-storeyed square was attached to the rear living room and its unplastered brick walls were painted in a light shiny green colour.

My mother was proud of her new kitchen, especially after she had replaced the low slopstone with a proper porcelain sink and had purchased a kitchenette, a tall cupboard, green to match the walls and with many compartments and drawers fitted into it. She also bought a real cooker which she tended with loving care, forever polishing and cleaning its various surfaces, while in truth she still depended greatly on the living-room range, though she would never have admitted her distrust in the new-fangled gadgetry with which she was filling our home.

For many months she would not switch on the new electric lights unless she had a cloth in her hand to protect herself against the unknown. For a while, she even wore wellington boots for such occasions, having heard or read somewhere that rubber soles 'stopped it going through you'. She adhered rigidly to the use of her flat irons until Eddie Higson proved, by plugging in the new iron to the ceiling light fixture and surviving, that she might try an easier way of pressing the clothes.

Our living-room range was another novelty, being constructed of a beige ceramic material that required no leading and having a raised area of tiles set on to the floor in front of it. In the recesses to each side of the chimney were floor-to-ceiling cupboards in which we stored crockery and such linens as we owned, thus making redundant the large mirrored dresser that had always dominated our Ensign Street kitchen.

There was no lobby in this house, just a small square vestibule leading straight into the front room, which had a wooden floor, a source of great pride in my mother's book. This room also had cupboards in the recesses, but while the living-room cupboards were panelled in wood and strictly utilitarian, these were ornate by comparison, their upper portions being glazed and leaded. Into these compartments went my mother's few treasures, bits of cut glass, framed photographs, a plaster saint or two and a set of white demi-tasse coffee cups, a wedding present for which she had never found a use. A square of moss-green secondhand carpet was acquired and my mother spent many hours varnishing and polishing the surrounding floorboards.

But outside, there was still the midden and the tippler lavatory and no amount of fancy cupboards and instant lighting could compensate, in my mother's mind, for these two festering sores. So when Eddie Higson's window round became reality, when he had finally purchased bucket, leathers and goodwill, my mother began to save with a grim determination known only to the victims of true deprivation. We were forced to eat strange meals, soups thick with lentils and barley, meat and potato pies with the emphasis strictly on the potato, scones without raisins, jam butties without margarine. The closest Eddie Higson and I ever got to camaraderie was then, as we stared blankly at one another across a table that held these odd offerings.

I had never had many clothes, but now I began to

look shabby and down-at-heel, was forced to curl up my toes so that weekday clogs and Sunday best would last a few months longer. She stopped smoking too, which meant that her temper became less than even and I learned to keep my distance at certain times, like after meals when she most craved a Woodbine. Eddie Higson took to rolling his own, using bits of paper and a strange machine like a miniature mangle, often including the contents of discarded dog-ends he had picked up in the street, occasionally treating himself to an ounce of fresh tobacco.

To give him his due, he worked hard during those first few months at Long Moor Lane and, after reading several borrowed tomes on the subject of plumbing, he undertook, with the help of his brother, the installation of our new bathroom.

He divided the back bedroom into two equal parts, put in new windows, then fixed a bath, a wash-basin and a flushing toilet into one of the two new rooms, leaving the other half as a small third bedroom. The cupboard which had incorporated the old bath became a walk-in wardrobe where my mother, who must have felt like the Queen Bee (being the first on the block to have a proper bath-room) hung her sparse trousseau.

The second bedroom, up another flight of stairs, was an attic room with a three-sided sloping window set into the roof. This was my room, my very own domain with an interesting view up and down the road and plenty of space for my bed and the newly acquired tallboy and dressing table.

The houses across the way were smart corporation dwellings, their occupants mere tenants, so my mother, a home owner, was on no more than

66

nodding terms with them. Although she still worked in the mill, still came home with her hair full of fluff and the soles of her shoes encrusted with tiny steel rings, she declared herself to be up-and-coming now and announced that she would, in future, be voting Tory.

My attic window enabled me to see over the rooftops to the moors that surround Bolton like a huge green dish. My mother had told me that Bolton was so named because it sat in a dip between moors and that it had therefore been named, originally, Bowl Town.

Now that we lived on one of the moors, albeit on a main road, the air was cleaner, clearer and fresher than in the centre of town where the trapped dampness was so valuable to millowners whose spinning factories depended on a wet atmosphere.

As a town-dweller, I did not, as yet, find myself attracted to the greenness beyond the roofs. Like any seven-year-old, I required playmates, the company of my peers, so I came down from my tower to explore my new surroundings, venturing a little further each day into the unknown.

It was time to establish my territory.

6

Encounters

My first encounter with other children came, of course, when I began to attend St Stephen's school. This was five tram stops up the road towards Harwood, though most of the trams were buses now and not so much fun, so I often saved my penny fare by walking the distance to and from school.

Standards at All Saints must have been high, because within a week I was in and out of first-year juniors and put to work with the eight-year-olds.

I loved the school right from the start. All the teachers had legs; no more flapping habits and rattling rosaries to disturb my peace of mind.

There was a priest though, because the school was attached to a church – in fact, the church itself was an infants' classroom, the altar and the first few pews being partitioned off during school days, while the rest of the benches were piled around the walls, ready to be brought out for Sundays and Holy Days of Obligation.

The priest was Father Cavanagh. He was fat and bald and wore a long black cloak with a clasp of metal chains at the throat. I didn't like him, but then I had never expected that I would. Priests, like nuns, were odd, legless animals from whom I expected neither kindness nor sympathy. This one, like most of them, asked a lot of questions. His voice was high and silly, the Irish brogue so thick that until I got used to him, he would have to repeat himself several times before I understood him. But he was, at least, a patient man and he spoke to me slowly, mouthing his words as if addressing an idiot or a deaf-mute.

'You'll be making your First Communion then soon, Annie?'

'Yes, Father.'

'And your family will be along to the Mass for to see you take the Blessed Sacrament?'

'I don't know, Father.'

He patted my head. Priests always did that and I hated it, it made me feel like a dog at its master's feet. He turned to my teacher, Miss O'Gara. 'They never come to the church, you know. I'll have to be paying them a visit, I'm thinking.' He looked back at me. 'You know, Annie, once you've made your Communion, you'll have to come to the Mass every Sunday or 'twill be a mortal sin?'

I nodded. This was familiar territory; we were back to the immortal soul business again.

'And you must come regularly to Confession to prepare yourself for the Blessed Sacrament.'

'Yes, Father.' He patted my head once more.

'Is your Mammy a Catholic then, Annie?'

'I think so, Father.'

'And your Daddy?'

'I haven't got one, he was killed in Italy when I was four.'

The priest took a step away from me, a puzzled expression appearing on his wide face. 'Ah well, 'tis sorry I am to be hearing that, child. But tell me now, is there not a man living at your house just now?'

'Yes, Father. Eddie Higson.'

Father Cavanagh glanced quickly at Miss O'Gara. 'Is he your stepdaddy then, Annie?' he enquired of me.

'No. He is not my stepdaddy, Father.'

Father Cavanagh removed his biretta and passed a fat hand over his bald pate. Miss O'Gara stepped forward and whispered something into the priest's ear.

I heard his sigh of relief before he spoke. 'Ah. So they are married. Well thanks be to God for that at any rate. Now, Annie. If your Mammy has married Mr . . . Mr Higson, then he is now your stepfather both in the eyes of the law and by the rules of your faith. Are you understanding me?'

This I would not pretend to accept. It was bad enough having him pat me on the head all the time and listening to his stupid questions, but this was going too far.

'No. He is not my stepfather,' I said quietly. 'My Daddy was my father and I don't want a stepfather.'

Father Cavanagh tutted his dismay, then shaking a finger at me he said, 'You know your Commandments, do you not?'

'Yes Father.'

'And is not the fourth "honour thy father and thy mother"?'

'Yes, Father.'

'Then surely you must honour Mr Higson, for he is looking after you as a father would, caring for you, is he not? It will be a mortal sin for you not to honour your stepfather, Annie.'

My stomach turned over. Whatever I did, wherever I went, there were adults tying me in knots, confusing me to the point of madness. And the worst offenders were these priests and nuns with their laws about this and that, telling me what I must think, what I must believe, how I must act – even who I must be.

But I kept cool, nodding my assent. My lips had formed no lie, but that nod, with its mute falsehood, laid yet another stain on my immortal soul which was by now, I felt sure, so pitted with black holes that it might have been used to drain cabbage.

I took my place next to Josie Cullen who was eight and nearly as tall as I was. We did not sit together by choice, but simply because we were both on the same page of the sum book and sum books were always one between two. Yet in spite of the fact that our proximity to each other had been forced upon us, we were fast becoming friends.

Josie and I were termed tomboys because neither of us wore ribbons or hairslides, nor did we play sedately like the other girls. We were frequently dispatched to the washroom after playtimes, for we seemed to attract dirt, gathering it about our persons like a pair of magnets collecting filings. The boys liked us, respected us almost, as we were not averse to a bout of rough and tumble and while Josie was conker champion of St Stephen's, I excelled at marbles, cleaning out the boys' stock of glass alleys and bolly-bearings with a frequency that alarmed them and won their admiration.

Josie nudged me. 'Take no notice of 'im. 'E's a soft old sod.'

I gaped at Josie. She had already made her First Confession and Communion. She would have to tell Father Cavanagh in the confessional that she had called him a soft old sod. I voiced my concern in a whisper.

'Don't be so daft,' she hissed back. 'For a kick-off,

I can always disguise me voice. Or I can go down to St Patrick's and tell some other soft sod as I've called this soft sod a soft sod.'

This was terrible. Now I had two immortal souls to worry about – mine and Josie's! 'You can't call a priest a soft s . . . a name like that, Josie. It's a sin. You'll go to hell!'

'Oh shut up, Annie. You're beginning to sound like a bloody soft sod yourself . . .'

Although I was worried by all this, I felt elated somehow. I suddenly knew that it wasn't just me, that I wasn't the only one who entertained bad thoughts about people, important people too, like priests. But I would never have dared to voice my contempt as Josie just had. Whenever I got bad thoughts, whenever my temper rose, I became over-whelmed by guilt, weighed down by the knowledge that I was heading for certain damnation. But if Josie felt any guilt, she never showed it.

She chewed now on the end of her pencil. 'What's eight eights?' she asked.

'Sixty-four.'

'How do you do that, Annie?'

'Do what?'

'Sixty-four just like that, without having to go back to one eight is eight.'

'I don't know.'

'You must know.'

'Well I don't.'

'See? I told you you were a soft sod.' Furtively, she passed a sticky square of chocolate across the desk and I pushed it into my mouth before Miss O'Gara could spot it.

'Want another?'

'No. Save it for playtime. Where did you get it, anyway?'

'Paper shop.' She copied down another sum. 'I nicked it. It's dead easy at Warburton's. Anyroad, there's never any toffee coupons at our 'ouse.'

I almost choked. I was eating stolen chocolate. Thou shalt not steal, that was number seven on the list of Commandments. Josie's soul must be as black as hell itself. Mine too, since I was sharing her spoils. Or would the stains be brown? Chocolate was brown . . .

'Annie Byrne. Have you finished those sums?'

'No, Miss.'

'Then get on with your work and stop daydreaming.'

I got on with my work.

Eddie Higson blamed me for a lot of things. Firstly there was the atmosphere in the house, which was not good as I spoke to him seldom, going for days on end without even looking in his direction. Then there was the fact that I would not, even when I did deign to speak to him, call him Dad. When I spoke of him, he always got his full title and this angered him greatly whenever it happened within his hearing. He blamed me for shouting too much, singing too much, being too quiet. He blamed me for the cost of living and most of all for being alive, for being another man's child.

As time went by and it began to appear that my mother would have no more babies, he apportioned this problem to me also, saying loudly and often that I had 'ruined' my mother by being born such a huge great lump. Of this I took little notice,

73

because I was impressed by none of Higson's opinions and was determined to minimize his influence on my life.

But I was afraid of his quick, blind rages, tense in his presence and I took to absenting myself from the house for hours at a stretch, taking refuge in Josie Cullen's chaotic but happy household.

The Cullens lived in a corporation house in Ince Avenue at the back of the library. There were so many Cullens that they were forced to eat in relays, the littlest ones often being sent to sit on the stairs with a bowl on their knees and one spoon between two or three.

Mrs Cullen put me in mind of Mrs Hyatt from Ensign Street, being of similar build and nature. Although her house was already filled to bursting, she always found space, time and a wedge of bread and dripping for me. 'There y' are, lass. Get outside o' that, it'll stick to yer ribs. Now, our Josie, get that wash in to soak. And where's our Allan? ALLAN!' she would scream through the ever-open door, 'Get thisen in 'ere while I mend yer pants.'

Mrs Cullen would then turn to survey her rumbustious troop. 'Right now, Ellen, get down that corner shop and ask fer five o' spuds on tick. Be nice. Smile at the woman for God's sake. Martin, get that knitting needle off our Tony, 'e'll 'ave 'is bloody eye out like a lolly on a stick in a minute. An' get that bloody cat out o' the cupboard, Cathy. Yes, I know she's lookin' where to 'ave 'er kittens – find 'er a box in the front room an' a couple of old *Evening News*es. Now. 'Oo's took the bloody lid off me bloody kettle? Annie love, go an' 'ave a look round t' back garden will yer? An' while yer about it, see if you can catch sight o' me fryin' pan. Only they've been playin' 'ouse again, so you'll likely find a cup or two while yer at it . . .'

I loved every minute I spent in that smelly, untidy house. There was nowhere to sit, scarcely an inch of room to even stand in, but at the centre of it all was Mrs Cullen, her great belly heaving with laughter as often as not, calmly dealing with each crisis as it arose, spreading her love and generosity equally amongst all-comers.

When I would go home, always reluctantly, I could not help comparing my mother with Mrs Cullen. Long hours in the mill were taking their toll and it was plain that my mother was not a happy woman, for her face, once rounded and well-fleshed, was becoming sunken and seemed to be acquiring new and deeper lines with each passing day. Even her Titian hair was losing its vibrance, while her shoulders became rounder, as if they were carrying a great invisible weight.

Higson, on the other hand, appeared to be thriving on good food and fresh air and had regained most, if not all the strength he had lost while in the prison camp. But however many windows he cleaned, however many spools my mother doffed, however many frames she tended, there was never enough money in the house.

Furthermore, now that men had returned from the war and had recovered from wounds of body and mind, they were reclaiming their jobs and my mother was forced to agree, with reluctance, that she would eventually take an evening shift at the mill. This bitter pill was sweetened by the offer of promotion to supervisor in charge of two rooms and as this meant an increase in rate, her money would not be noticeably reduced.

The elevation in her status should have cheered her and improved the atmosphere at home, at least between her and him, but still the long silences continued. I knew that my mother was very unhappy and I understood enough to realize that Eddie Higson was responsible for her state of mind. This was one thing for which I could not blame myself, because I was being as good as I knew how to be, was keeping out of 'his' way as frequently as possible, spending my time at the Cullens' or in my attic room.

But for many months now, I had not heard my mother laugh, had seldom seen her smile. The marriage had been a mistake. Even at my tender age, I could sense this. Yet I derived no satisfaction from having been proved right.

7

Communion

Father Cavanagh persuaded them both to attend my First Communion and they looked so embarrassed and out of place, never having been inside St Stephen's before, that I rather wished the priest had kept his nose out of our business. I wore a long dress of creamy-white satin, a veil with a stiff crown of artificial flowers and new white shoes. In my hands I carried a nosegay of mimosa and gypsy grass, together with a white missal and a rosary that my father had had blessed by Pope Pius XII himself.

The priest placed the bread on my extended tongue while an altar boy held a solid gold plate under my chin in case of crumbs. Should the body of Jesus Christ crumble, then it must crumble only onto precious metal.

I blessed myself, trying to feel solemn and dignified and waited for the wafer to melt, for I had been forbidden to chew. It stuck to the roof of my dry mouth and I hoped that Jesus wouldn't mind too much when I edged it away with my tongue, for this thin consecrated biscuit now embodied Christ, who had died for me.

I felt empty of grace and of breakfast, as we were forbidden to eat or drink before Communion. We new communicants, eight boys and seven girls, went obediently back to our families while Father Cavanagh droned his solemn way through the rest of the Mass.

Then it was over. Now I would have to be very, very good, for every misdemeanour I committed would have to be relayed through the black grille of the confessional and right into Father Cavanagh's ever-inquisitive ear. If sins were left untold and if the Blessed Sacrament was allowed, therefore, to descend into a stomach full of sin, then this would be a sacrilege, for which crime there would be no absolution.

Yet I felt nothing at this, my first communion with Jesus Christ. What I had expected to feel, what I should feel, I didn't know, but I was sure that I should not feel so . . . so ordinary, that Jesus should be filling me with grace and happiness, that I should be inviting Him, welcoming Him into my heart and soul. And when I returned to my pew and saw Eddie Higson sitting next to my mother, my loathing for him hit me with renewed force and I fell to my knees to make yet another act of contrition. 'Lord I am not worthy that Thou shouldst enter under my roof; say but the word and my soul shall be healed. O my God, I am sorry and beg pardon for all my sins . . .'

After the Mass, there was a party in one of the classrooms and we were given a breakfast of sorts, sandwiches, biscuits and orange juice. My mother and Higson stood awkwardly to one side, while the rest of the parents, obviously regular churchgoers, grouped themselves about the room, exclaiming over what a lovely Mass it had been and didn't their Mary look sweet in the white frock and wasn't Jimmy quite the little man in his new suit.

Father Cavanagh, when he entered the room, made a bee-line for my mother. As consecrated shepherd of this particular flock, it was his bounden duty to round up the stray sheep first. The priest beckoned me to follow, which I did with reluctance as the food was disappearing fast and I hadn't had much.

'Well now,' he was saying. ''Tis lovely to see the pair of you here, so it is. And you'll be after setting a good example for little Annie here now, won't you?'

My mother nodded while Eddie Higson stifled a yawn – he was not used to being out of bed so early on a Sunday.

'And will you be attending the Mass in the future then Mr . . . er . . . Higson?'

'Depends on the weather. I sometimes do a few houses on a Sunday if the week's been bad.'

'You work on a Sunday? On God's holy day? Mercy in heaven, isn't that a sin now?'

Higson shrugged. 'Well, you work on a Sunday, don't you? I reckon Sunday's about your busiest day. And if we all did what you're suggesting, they'd have to shut all the hospitals for a start, wouldn't they? So do we just leave people to die being as it's Sunday?'

'Ah well now, that's a different matter altogether, for hospital work is essential and as for my work, well . . .'

Eddie Higson interrupted loudly. 'So's window cleaning if it pays my bills.'

The two men glared at one another for a few seconds, then Father Cavanagh turned to my mother.

'Will yourself be bringing Annie to the Mass then, Mrs . . . er . . . Higson?'

'I'll try, Father.'

'Yes, yes, you do that. And isn't it time you made your Easter Duties? I have not seen you at Communion, Mrs Higson.'

'I'll bear it in mind, Father.'

'Aye, you do that now, and God bless you.'

The priest moved on to speak to the other parents and Eddie Higson grabbed me by the arm and dragged me out of the classroom. My mother followed at a slower pace crying, 'But she's not had her party, Eddie . . .'

'Bugger her party. We're getting out of here.'

Then, at the far end of the corridor, I spotted two familiar figures making their way towards us. With a great cry of joy, I wrenched my arm free and began to run, coronet and veil slipping unheeded to the floor.

'Aw, we missed it, luv.' Mrs Hyatt enfolded me in her large heavy arms then Tom pulled me away from her, lifting me up, swinging me into the air just as my father had used to do.

'You've not gone to America, then,' I said happily.

'Not yet, Annie.'

'But you're still going?'

'Aye, he's still going,' said Mrs Hyatt before moving on to greet my mother.

'Are you alright, Annie?' Tom whispered.

'Yes, I'm alright.'

'Is he . . . good to you?'

I looked over my shoulder at Eddie Higson who was standing a little way apart from my mother and Mrs Hyatt. 'I don't take any notice of him,' I said. 'I just keep out of his road.'

'He doesn't hit you or anything?'

I shrugged. 'Not much. When are you going anyway?'

'Next week.'

This news dropped like a stone into my stomach and I had to swallow deeply before I could say, 'I wish you wouldn't, Tom.'

'Tell you what, Annie. You wait for me and I'll come back and marry you when I've made me fortune. How does that sound?'

'Daft,' I said, but I knew I was blushing.

My mother and Mrs Hyatt joined us now.

'Will you come and have a cup of tea with us then, Florrie – and Tom, of course. And I've a scone or two and a bit of window pie left – come on back with us.'

'Aye, we will that,' answered Mrs Hyatt. 'And I'm sorry we missed your Communion, Annie, but it's a fair stretch from Ensign Street up here – more ways than one, eh, Nancy?'

The walk back down Long Moor Lane was uncomfortable, for neither Tom nor Mrs Hyatt spoke to Eddie Higson after the initial greeting. My mother and he walked in front while I skipped along behind, one hand in Mrs Hyatt's, the other in Tom's.

They were, of course, very impressed with the house – or least, Mrs Hyatt was. Tom had little to say on the subject, but his mother oohed and ahed over every detail, especially when it came to the bathroom and the walk-in wardrobe.

Eddie Higson, after drinking just one cup of tea, went out to collect money from his customers. In truth, I felt, he went to get away from Mrs Hyatt who, apart from casting the odd furtive glance in his direction, had ignored him almost completely.

When there remained just the four of us, Mrs Hyatt, more relaxed now, said to my mother, 'By, tha looks a bit weary, lass.'

'Yes, well, it's tiring at the mill. I'm starting evening shift soon, so it should be a bit easier.'

Mrs Hyatt stirred her second cup of tea slowly. 'And who'll be looking after 'er while yer out?' she asked.

'Oh, Eddie'll see to her.'

'Will 'e now?'

I felt Tom's leg brush past mine as he kicked his mother's shoe under the table. My mother, bristling slightly, spoke up. 'He's quite capable of seeing to the child, Florrie. Fact is, Annie can very near take care of herself.'

'Aye, 'appen she might 'ave to an' all from what I've 'eard.'

In the silence that followed, you might have heard a feather, let alone a pin drop. My mother rose with exaggerated quietness, taking with her the teapot as a signal that the Hyatts were no longer welcome, then she said softly, 'That, Florrie Hyatt, was all talk and you know it. And if you've come all the way from Ensign Street to cause bloody trouble, you can just damn well get back where you belong.'

Tom, leaning an elbow on the table, put a hand to his forehead. 'Cut it out, Ma. I've told you before and I'll say it again – no good can come of this.'

But Mrs Hyatt, her colour heightening, jumped up from the table as fast as her bulk would allow. 'Leopards doesn't change their spots, Nancy Byrne – ooh, I'm forgettin' meself, aren't I? Nancy 'Igson, I mean. What can't speak can't lie an' them as is

82

dead don't get up and talk for theirselves, do they?'
Her face was darkening to a purplish hue.

'They don't need to. You do all the talking for
them. Who the hell do you think you are, anyway,
Florrie Hyatt? Mouthpiece of Bolton? Why don't
you get under the clock in the Town Centre, maybe
they'll give you a loud-hailer.'

''E did things. You know 'e did.'

'I know nothing, Florrie and neither do you.'

Tom looked anxiously at me, then waved an arm
towards the door, asking me, with a raised eyebrow,
to step outside with him, but I shook my head. I was
not going to miss this. For once, I might learn something about Eddie Higson.

Mrs Hyatt continued. 'I know 'e were wild and
evil, that's what I know. 'E were a bad lad and bad
lads becomes bad men.'

My mother slammed the teapot back onto the
table, causing cups and spoons to rattle. 'Do you
want me to get the law on you, Florrie Hyatt? Is that
what you want, a big scandal? Because I will, you
know, I shall get a solicitor. And if Eddie knew what
you were saying . . .'

'Why, what 'ave I said?'

'That he's a bad lot.'

'Prove me wrong, then.'

'Oh no, you prove you're right. I know enough
about the law to know the onus is on you. Innocent
till proved otherwise, Florrie Hyatt. You just
remember that. Whatever happened all those years
ago – if anything ever did happen – was before I ever
lived in Ensign Street and if you hadn't kept your
great mouth flapping it would have died a death by
now. Eddie's a good man. He works hard, he's got
the house nice – what more proof do you want?'

83

Tom looked quickly at me. 'There's a time and a place for this sort of thing. Have neither of you any consideration for this child? And you listen to me, Mam, once and for all. A lot of lads sow wild oats but turn out decent. So shut up, will you?'

This was, by now, totally beyond my comprehension. As far as I could work out (and it wasn't very far) Eddie Higson might have done something bad and then again, he might not. Whatever he might have done had made Mrs Hyatt go a funny colour and Tom said it was something to do with sewing. I had never seen Eddie Higson sewing. It was always my Mam who did the mending and stitching and sewing on of buttons.

Whatever it was all about, Tom and his mother were leaving and I might never see Tom again. As my mother and I stood in the doorway watching them walk away, I felt the tears of self-pity pricking my eyelids. I had not enjoyed my First Communion day one little bit.

Swiftly, I pulled myself away from my mother and ran down the road, the long satin skirt lifted high and bunched carelessly in my two clenched fists.

'You won't forget me, Tom?'

He looked down at me, his own eyes suspiciously wet. 'No, I'll never, ever forget you, Annie.'

'And you'll write to me?'

'That I will. Soon as I get there.'

Mrs Hyatt bent to give me a kiss and whispered in my ear, 'Remember, lass, any bother at all an' tha comes fer me an' Freddie. OK?'

'OK.'

I sighed deeply as they walked away. Grown-ups were such a puzzle to me, telling half a tale, warning you about things you couldn't understand.

But I was to understand only too soon what they had meant, what they had been trying to guard me against. I was eight years old and teetering on the brink of a nightmare that was to last for many years to come, a bad dream from which I would not wake until I had gained considerably in age and experience.

For a while at least, forgiving Tom and Mrs Hyatt would not be easy, for they might have protected me if they had tried harder. But they were, after all, no blood kin to me and I was no responsibility of theirs.

Forgiving my mother would, strangely, be easier, because I would have to care for and protect her from the evil in our midst.

But I would never, as long as I lived, forgive Eddie Higson for what was about to happen to me.

Mrs Cullen was having a clearout.

This was something she did two or three times a year and it was carried out with a precision that fell a long way short of the military. The idea was, as she put it, to 'shift all th' upstairs muck to downstairs an' all t' downstairs muck out ter t' back o' the 'ouse, then kick it about till it disappears'.

We lined up on the stairs like a chain-gang, playing a game of pass the parcel with objects of varying size, shape and incredibility. We handled torn sheets, rag rugs, jerries without handles, half-sets of false teeth, corsets with the whalebone whipping free about our ears, toothless combs, bits of lino and oilcloth and several dozen back copies of the *Bolton Evening News*, some turning yellow with age.

Once this lot was piled into the narrow hallway, there was scarcely room for Mrs Cullen to make her descent past all the children who had gathered on, around and under the mound of debris.

'Now,' she announced, her huge breasts heaving with exertion. 'Tha mun get this lot out the back, then we mun mek a start on t' front room. Allan, put them corsets down. No, yer can't keep 'em. What the 'ell are you plannin' on doin' with 'em anyroad – makin' a rabbit 'utch? No, Josie, you are not 'angin' on to that jerry for growin' daffs in, yer don't know where it's been. Or, more ter t' point, yer do know where it's been. An' Martin – put them false teeth down – hey, not on yer Dad's chair this time! Where's our Josie gone wi' that jerry? Annie – put that bloody kettle on, lass, I'm fair clemmed . . .'

On this particular Thursday night, we had started on the front room, which was the worst room in the house, having been given over to the children as a place to play, leaving only the large kitchen as true living space for this huge family. The front room was so bad that even opening the door to get in required careful planning and Lizzie, being the smallest of those old enough to walk, was pushed through a tiny gap in order to remove the main obstacles from behind the door, thus enabling the rest of us to enter the room.

Once inside, we met a total and glorious chaos. There were large matted tangles of wool and string, three-wheeled skates, wooden crates with pram wheels and lengths of rope attached and what seemed to be about a hundred cardboard boxes in various sizes and states of decay. Although nothing was intact, everybody had a good reason for wanting to keep some of it.

Allan wanted the boxes as he was a compulsive collector and needed 'things to keep things in'. He also had grandiose ideas for the crates on wheels and insisted that he could get the skates mended by an old farrier up Breightmet who had taken to skate-mending now that horses had become fewer and farther between.

But Mrs Cullen was ruthless in her insistence. Everything must go into the back garden where it would join last year's mouldering and rusting heaps of prams and broken furniture.

We had just begun to transfer the last of the rubbish into the hallway, when a sharp rapping at the door made us pause, a sudden and miraculous silence falling over the whole ensemble as we pondered. Would it be rent, water or gas? Had they come to turn us off, turn us out or was it just the bum bailey? The latter would have come as no surprise and little threat, for few bills had been paid and there was nothing worth the bailiff's trouble to carry away, the few sticks of furniture that had survived the seven children being too scarred and battered to be of any value whatsoever.

Mrs Cullen paused, a finger to her pursed lips, then she whispered, 'Tha'd best open t' door, Annie. Say yer not family, at least that's the truth. Tell 'em to come back tomorrer – wi' a pick-axe an' a police escort.' Josie giggled and Mrs Cullen clipped her gently round the ear. 'Shut up, our Josie. It might even be the flamin' priest an' I can do wi'out 'im 'Oly Maryin' all over me back kitchen an' me in t' middle o' me clearout.'

I crept surreptitiously down the hall and opened the door just a crack.

'Can you come back tomorrow?' I whispered through the gap, trying not to giggle as Josie's stifled snorts of laughter reached my ears.

'No, I can't come back tomorrow. Get out here now.'

I must have stiffened visibly because Mrs Cullen came forward, negotiating her way carefully around the pile of rubbish.

''Oo is it, luv?'

I opened the door to reveal Eddie Higson standing on the step, a Woodbine making his lip curl even further into the snarl that usually occupied his face when he looked at me.

'Get yourself home,' he snapped. 'It's way past your bedtime.'

I stood my ground. 'I'm helping Mrs Cullen,' I said, trying to keep my voice steady, trying to keep the fear out of it, trying, most of all, not to lose face in front of Josie – I didn't want her to know how much I feared this man who was supposed to be my stepfather.

Eddie Higson swept a contemptuous eye past me towards Mrs Cullen and her brood, bringing his gaze to rest finally on the vast mound of debris at our feet.

'I reckon Mrs Cullen's got enough helpers of her own. She doesn't need you. Anyroad, happen she should get the council to shift that lot.'

Mrs Cullen drew herself up to her full five foot two, arms clasped beneath the pendulous bosom. 'My 'usband will see to all this when 'e gets in from the ropewalk. You go, Annie luv.'

'Aye,' Eddie Higson said, pulling the cigarette from his mouth and grinding it underfoot on the step. 'Come on. Get yourself out of this midden before you catch something.'

Mrs Cullen's body seemed to swell with anger as she stumbled closer to the door. 'This is no midden, Eddie Higson.'

'Oh aye?' he drawled. 'Well, you could have fooled me, for I've seen less on a corporation tip than what you've got here.'

Mrs Cullen was at the door now and she faced him, her complexion reddening as her anger rose. 'Aye, well, 'appen you spend a lot o' time up at corporation tips. Most people usually manages ter find their own level, their own place, like. I see you've found yours. So get back ter t' tip where you belong. Only don't tek Annie wi' you. She don't belong on no tip.'

'That's why I'm taking her home. Out of this bloody tip. You want to watch yourself, Mrs Cullen. You'll be having the Health round next and getting yourself fumigated.'

'Fumigated? It's your bloody gob wants fumigatin'. We may not 'ave t' poshest bathroom up Long Moor, but at least we 'ave an 'appy 'ome, one as your Annie's glad to run to. Poor little waif can't get away from 'er own 'ouse quick enough, seems ter me.'

Eddie Higson was shouting now as he said, 'You slovenly old bitch, you. She'll not be coming here no more, I'll see to that. And her mother will too when I tell her what a state this place is in. Get here now, you,' he screamed at me.

'No. No, I'm not coming,' I cried, the tears beginning to flow down my face and into my throat, choking me so that I had to fight for breath.

'Get here now or I'm coming in for you.'

Mrs Cullen pushed me behind her then stood in the doorway, her legs spread wide. 'You'll 'ave ter get past me first. An' I'm not lettin' you in my 'ouse wi'out a fight, you bad-mouthed bugger, you. Come on then. Try it. Just you try to get in. Don't forget, my George'll be 'ere in a minute. 'E'll sort you. You'll be climbin' no bloody ladders fer a week or two if 'e gets 'is 'ands round that scrawny little neck o' yours.'

I could hear Mrs Cullen breathing heavily in the silence that followed and I held my own breath, fighting back the sobs.

'Are you coming or not?'

'No,' I managed to gasp.

'I'll beat the bloody living daylights out of you, lady,' he yelled. 'You'll have to come out of that pigsty sooner or later and I'll be waiting.'

Mrs Cullen, after slamming the door in his twisted face, turned to look at us, leaning heavily against the stair rail for a few seconds before speaking to me. 'Now don't tek on, lass. You can double up wi' our girls tonight – till yer Mam gets back off 'er evenin' shift at anyroad. Likely she'll come and collect you once it's all sorted. Don't worry, 'e'll calm down, it'll all be forgot, you'll see.

'Now come on, you lot. Get this muck shifted before your dad gets back an' breaks 'is neck over it. I'm goin' to warm a drop o' milk fer Annie. Lizzie, see if yer can find a clean cup. Martin, get in that meatsafe see if there's a bit o' brandy left. Bring 'er through to the kitchen, Josie. Come on now, come on. . .'

My mother did not come for me at the end of her shift. I spent the night at Josie's house and it was not comfortable, for there was little room in the bed which contained four of us, two at the top, two at the bottom, like sardines in a tin.

Things were not made easier by Lizzie who wet the bed and everyone in it, which I later discovered to be a regular occurrence. For the whole of the next day at school I reeked of drying urine, a smell I recognized now as that which usually surrounded Josie, Lizzie and most of the rest of the family. I was also covered in spots, tiny red bites bequeathed to me by all the other creatures that occupied Josie's bedroom.

When I reached home that afternoon, Eddie Higson had not yet returned from his round. My mother was at the living-room range, her back towards me as I entered the room and she seemed, at first, to have little to say. When she turned to face me, I understood why she was so quiet, because her cheeks were bruised, her lower lip swollen to twice its normal size and one of her eyes was closed and surrounded in purplish black flesh.

She had received my beating. Because of my disobedience, because of my cowardice, my poor little mother had been beaten half to death by a man who must surely be crazed to inflict such wounds on his wife.

I ran to her and she flinched as I flung my arms about her waist. It was obvious that her body, too, was hurt.

Easing herself gently away from me, she pressed me into a chair. 'Annie, love. Things is hard enough without you making this kind of trouble. Why didn't you come home when you were told?'

I hesitated before replying, 'Because he was nasty to Mrs Cullen, Mam. He called her a slovenly old bi . . . well, a bad name. He showed me up in front of my friends.'

'Friends? Friends, love? Can't you smell yourself? They're mucky folk, Annie. You shouldn't be mixing with mucky folk. Oh, I wish I'd come and fetched you home after my shift, but I couldn't – not like this.

You'd be best stopping away from the Cullens in future.'

'I like them,' I said stubbornly, yet immediately torn between wanting to agree with my poor hurt mother and wanting to defend those who had been good to me.

'You should have come home when he first came for you.'

'I don't want to come home with him. I don't like being here with him. Why can't you be here? Why can't you work days like you used to?'

'Because I can't, love. It's as simple as that.'

Flinching visibly, she lowered herself into a squatting position in front of me. 'Now, listen, Annie. You're a big girl. I fell downstairs last night – you understand? I fell down the stairs. Now I've got a letter here from . . . er . . . from Dr Pritchard. I want you to go down to Millhouse mill and give it in to Ernie Bradshaw. Nobody else. If Ernie's not there, you bring this letter back. Can you remember that?'

I nodded and she went on. 'Only I can't go into work looking like this now, can I? I'd likely frighten the mill cat to death – let alone me mates if they saw me like this. So after tea, when the hooter's gone off, you get your coat on and go down Folds Road. You catch the 45 and get off at the stop after the bend. Go up Millhouse Lane till you get to the mill – you can't miss it, it's about the same size as Buckingham Palace. Ask for Ernie Bradshaw, second floor. And remember, that letter's for him and only for him.'

She rose painfully and took a step back. 'While you're there, Annie, have a good look round. And I mean a good look – you see what it's like in there, take it all in. Because except for today, I don't want you ever setting foot inside a mill again.' She reached out her hands in an imploring gesture. 'You've got chances, Annie. Chances I never had. Things are going to change, specially for women, you mark my words. Well, I want you to take them chances.' Her hands closed into tight, gripping fists. 'Take them, use them opportunities. Because I'll never rest in me grave if I know you're a spinner or a doffer.'

'You're . . . you're not going to die, are you, Mam?'

Her face stretched into as much of a smile as the damaged tissue would allow. 'No, lass. I'm not shuffling off just yet, not till you're a doctor or a lawyer or . . .'

'An Indian chief,' I said, finishing off the rhyme.

'You're going to be something great, Annie. I've always known it, right from the start when you brought yourself to life. There's something in you, something I can't put me finger on, so you'd best put your own finger on it, love. Because the choices are there for you; they weren't there for me – it was the mill at fourteen and I've never known any other life. But you will, oh aye, you will.'

She placed my meal on the table in front of me. 'Remember, Annie. I fell downstairs.'

'I'll kill him, Mam,' I said quietly.

As she turned from me, I thought I heard her say, 'You'll have to get in the queue for that.' But I wasn't sure.

8

The Killing

It was an experience I would never forget.

Now that the trams and trolleys were gone, I had finally got used to the new buses, but this time I was going in the wrong direction, down the moor rather than up, travelling back towards Town and, it seemed, backwards through the century too.

The further down the road I got, the untidier the area became until, at the bottom of Folds Road where I alighted from the bus, it seemed that I was back in Ensign Street, for the tiny Victorian terraces ran in deep rows to the left and to the right of me as I walked down Millhouse Lane. Each street seemed so like Ensign Street, so neglected and small and squalid, that I began to appreciate my mother's ambition to move up the moor.

Had I really lived in a house as small as these were? Had I really played in those narrow, cobbled backs with open middens so close and never noticed the smell?

Our own midden up Long Moor Lane was now a coal shed, while the building that had once housed the tippler was used to store tools and Eddie Higson's buckets and leathers. Oh yes, we had come a long way up in the world, but what price were we paying? And would I have to tell in confession that my mother had taken my beating and that I wanted Eddie Higson dead?

I stopped at the mill gates as I pondered, realizing after a few minutes that, yes, I would indeed rather live in Ensign Street without him than up Long Moor with him. Perhaps we could leave him and go back? But no, even after the beating, she would never leave her new bathroom. And, of course, as a Catholic, she could not abandon her husband no matter what he did to her.

I clutched in my hand the envelope that held a sheet of lies, a tissue of total fabrication that would protect Eddie Higson. Shouldn't I tell somebody the truth? Instinctively, I knew that in order to protect my mother, I could never, ever tell anyone about what had happened in the house. Someone had to look after her. It would have to be me. And how many more times would she have to 'fall down-stairs'? Was that the price she would have to pay for her bathroom and electric light? And what would he do to me once she went back on evening shifts? Would he beat me too? Would I need a note to say I'd fallen down the stairs?

It was all too much to worry about, so I snapped out of my trance; if I stood here much longer, I'd be home late and I didn't want to have my mother worrying. And I needed to get back to make sure he didn't beat her again, because if he did, I would surely be there to find a way of hurting or even killing him.

Six flagged steps led up to a side door and I pushed this open to find before me another flight of stone stairs which I climbed until they turned to yet another flight. Up and up I went until I found a huge door with a large white number two painted on to it.

This I had to push hard, for it was very heavy and had a spring to keep it shut.

I stepped through that doorway and into a hell on earth that almost knocked me back out again. The noise was incredible. Row upon row of frames filled the room. The workers, sandwiched between the machines, obviously got as little consideration here as they did at home, where the mill-owning land-lords packed them into hovels, dozens to the acre.

Each spinning-frame was covered in what appeared to be a million moving parts, rattling and clanging, spools filling with cotton, filling so quickly that the women had to run to keep pace with the work.

I watched them for a few moments, fascinated by their deftness as they doffed the full spools and replaced them immediately with empty ones, each time feeding the cotton through a maze of metal rings. Even from the doorway, I could see the sweat pouring from the women's faces, could make out vast damp patches on their clothing as they moved swiftly up and down the frames.

The air was wet and heavy; the temperature in the room must have been hotter than the hottest days I could remember, days when tar melted and pave-ments became too fierce for thin soles, let alone bare feet. This was where my little mother had spent her life since she was but six years older than I was now. I felt my own sweat pricking my eyes as it ran down from my hair; after one minute I was wet to the skin, clothes sticking to my back, palms slick with moisture.

A man came forward and dragged me back out on to the cool landing where the sudden quiet was almost deafening.

'What do you want here then, little lass?'

'I'm looking for Mr Bradshaw, my Mam's boss.'

'That's me.' Bright blue eyes twinkled and he brushed a hand through his light brown hair. 'It isn't every day a bonny lass comes up here and asks for me. I think my luck must be changing. Now, what's it all about?'

'It's about my Mam.'

'Eeh well. You're Nancy's lass aren't you? I can see the resemblance now. I wondered where our Nancy was tonight. Nothing up, I hope?'

I handed him the note and he tore at the envelope swiftly. It was not from the doctor at all – I recognized my own mother's writing.

Ernie Bradshaw leaned against the wall before speaking again. 'Tell her the job's safe. I just hope she is, that's all. And you can tell her . . . well, tell her Ernie sends his best. How is she?'

'She's hurt.'

'I know that. What's your name now – Annie, isn't it?'

I nodded.

'Well, Annie, you tell your Mam as Ernie will be up to see her. Tell her that if . . . if he's in, then she must leave a sign. Now, let me think a minute.' He paced about the landing, all the while stroking his chin and I thought what a nice man he seemed, friendly-looking, easy to talk to.

'I know,' he said suddenly, turning in mid-stride. 'Tell her if he's in she must leave a small stone on the front doorstep. Now, can you remember that?' This man seemed to know and understand my attitude to Eddie Higson, otherwise he would not be confiding in me now. Was he a friend and not just a boss to my mother?

'Yes, I can remember that, Mr Bradshaw.'

'Call me Ernie. Everybody else does. Now, can you keep this secret?'

'Yes, I can, I'm good at secrets.'

'You won't tell your Dad?'

'He's not my Dad. I tell him nothing.'

'Aye, so I've heard.' He grinned at me. 'I'm very . . . fond of your Mam, Annie. If anything ever . . . well, if anybody ever hurt her . . .'

'She fell downstairs, Ernie.'

'Aye.' He waved the note. 'So it says here. And I'm a monkey's uncle.'

So it looked as if my mother had confided in this man, had told him that she was unhappy with Eddie Higson, that all was not well up Long Moor Lane. Well, I wasn't surprised; this was a man you might take to, confide in and trust.

'Give her . . . my love, will you, Annie?' He pressed a half-crown into my hand. 'And that's for you, for being such a bonny lass. Don't forget now. The boss sends his love.'

'Oh thankyou, Ernie, I've never had a whole half-crown before.'

'You deserve it, love. Now get off home and see you look after that Mam of yours. Ta-ra now.'

'Ta-ra, Ernie.'

Once outside, I looked back at the building, craning my neck to see the top of the stack where thick smoke was belching forth into the sky. She had been right. I would never want to set foot in there again. Except for one reason. I'd like to see more of Ernie Bradshaw.

I got the chance to see him again, not just once, but many times. The first few visits he paid us were during the school holidays and the three of us spent long afternoons laughing and joking in the kitchen.

On the third occasion I was sent out to play and to keep an eye out for Eddie Higson in case he got home early; when I came back into the house my mother, whose face was healing nicely, looked flushed and happy and she had changed her dress.

'Where's Ernie?' I asked innocently.

'Oh he's . . . in the bathroom. He won't be a minute.'

'I wish we could swap Eddie Higson for Ernie,' I whispered.

'Keep your thoughts to yourself, Annie . . .'

My mother's affair with Ernie Bradshaw was beautiful. During those summer months she blossomed into her old self again, began laughing and singing 'Burlington Bertie' like she had used to, wore cheap, pretty clothes and make-up, bought some bright clip-on earrings and coloured beads.

She was quiet when Eddie Higson was around though, and so was I, because I knew too much to say or do anything that might puncture the frail bubble that was her happiness.

I learned to knock at the door before entering if there was no stone on the step, learned to watch in the back street for the familiar sight of Higson's ladder as it bobbed its way home on his shoulder, learned to live with my sins by framing my confessions carefully and rehearsing my piece each time before chanting my list of errors through the grille.

Ernie and my mother spent many afternoons together and although I was often excluded, they sometimes took me out to the Jolly Brows and once to Southport on a charabanc. What the neighbours must have thought I never knew; certainly my mother was not aware, in her bliss, of anything beyond the fact that she was infatuated with this man, that she had to be with him at every opportunity. But I knew in my bones that we were living on a knife's edge, that sooner or later Eddie Higson would find out and we would all suffer as a consequence. But it was no use; when I voiced my fears, she simply refused to hear me.

Once she returned to her evening shifts, my mother made arrangements for me to sleep at Rita Entwistle's house, nominally to keep Rita company as she, too, was an only child, but really to keep me away from Eddie Higson. Rita's mother and my mother worked together and although Rita was never a really close friend, she was, at least, clean and generous with her toys.

My friendship with Josie remained close and constant and I visited the Cullens whenever I could, was still happier in their house than I was anywhere else.

I was also receiving regular letters and parcels from Tom in Philadelphia, so my life, apart from the great worry about my mother and Ernie, continued on an even keel for several months.

When my mother began to get fat, I took little notice. Some people were fat, some were thin; nobody bothered much about shapes and sizes in those days. It was Mrs Cullen who inadvertently told me the reason for my mother's increased girth. We were sitting out at the back of the house enjoying a sunny September afternoon. Around us were piles of 'clear-outs' among which the little kids played while we elders – Josie, Allan and I – sat drinking dandelion and burdock with Mrs Cullen.

'What dost want then, a brother or a sister?' Oh no, not again. Surely there were not going to be eight Cullens? I noticed that she was not looking at Josie or at Allan as she spoke.

'Are you talking to me, Mrs Cullen?'

'I am that, lass. Did you think I were askin' our Josie? Don't you think I've done my share then? Nay, I'm 'avin' no more. I'm even thinkin' o' sendin' George off ter Siberia ter mek sure.' Her great belly shook with laughter. 'But it's time you got a little playmate, isn't it? Eeh, I can see yer now, pushin' yer pram round Long Moor. Aye, it's not before time. 'Ow old are you now?'

'Eight and a half,' I answered, hoping I didn't sound too stunned.

'Big gap, that. Still, never mind, eh?' She was staring hard at me now. 'Eeh lass – didn't you know, 'aven't they told you?'

I shook my head.

'Well then, tek no notice o' me, I could be wrong. It's just I've 'ad so many meself I recognize t' symptoms, if yer get me meanin'. She might just be puttin' a bit o' weight on, luv.'

I was trying to organize my thoughts. A brother or sister, a baby in the house, how did I feel about that? I concluded that my feelings were mixed. With a new baby about, Eddie Higson would be pleased and would perhaps take even less notice of me – that would be a good thing. But a baby would take my mother's attention too, leaving her with less time for me. And what about poor Ernie? She wouldn't be able to have a lie down with him in the afternoons any more, not with a baby to feed and change. Perhaps Ernie would go elsewhere now and we would both miss him.

'By the way, Annie,' said Josie. 'We're moving, you know.'

Oh no, not again! Mrs Cullen laughed at the expression on my face.

'We're movin' across the road from you, Annie,' she giggled. 'You'll be able ter stick yer 'ead out o' t' winders an' yell across at us.'

Thank goodness for that, at least. 'We've got a swap for a four bedroomed,' said Allan. 'Though I think the real reason is the council wants to get at this lot and clean it up.'

Mrs Cullen roared with laughter. 'Aye. 'Appen they'll move us every time as t' garden gets full!'

'When are you moving?' I asked, just for something to say, something to take my mind off the possible changes at home.

'Couple o' weeks,' answered Mrs Cullen. 'Now you get off 'ome an' see is yer Mam needin' you. If she's the way I think she is, she'll be needin' all the 'elp she can get. Oh, before you go – come 'ere a minute.' I bent down so that she could whisper in my ear. 'Tell 'er to go careful wi' that Ernie feller. Don't worry, I won't say nothin' ter nobody. I saw 'em together in Town last week an' once before at your door. Tell er . . .' Her voice dropped even lower. 'Tell 'er 'e's wed wi' three kids of 'is own.'

I fled homeward, my face burning with shame. I'd begun to pick things up at school, dirty words about what men and women did together, stories of bad women who would 'go' with anybody, even married men. Although I wasn't yet fully aware of what it all meant, I didn't want my Mam to be a bad woman.

When I opened the front door, all was quiet, yet the air seemed to crackle with an atmosphere, a bad feeling that soaked out of the living room, through the front room and right into the vestibule. I opened this second door quietly and stood rigid, waiting for I knew not what.

'You filthy bitch.' His voice was ominously quiet. 'Trying to pass it off as mine, were you?' I flinched as I heard flesh strike flesh. 'I'm sterile, you dirty piece. Sterile, do you hear me? My chances of fathering a child are about a million to one, they told me that in the hospital.'

He hit her again and I heard her moan of pain before she spoke between gasps. 'But . . . there is a slight . . . chance of you . . . isn't there? And there's been . . . nobody . . . nobody.'

'Tell that to the cat, you stupid bag. How often have you let me at you lately, eh? And do you think I'm blind, with your new frocks and your earrings, walking round like a bloody tart? That is not my kid. Whose is it? I'll beat it out of you, I will, I will . . .'

Now the sounds were different. This time it was not flesh on flesh, but something solid hitting something soft. I didn't know what to do, where to turn. For what seemed like hours I remained riveted to the spot, sweat and tears pouring down my face. He was speaking again as he kicked her.

'I used to say she'd ruined you, didn't I? Well that was just a joke, you see, just a joke. I'm not joking now though, oh no . . .'

Suddenly galvanized, I shot through the house and into the living room. My mother lay at his feet in front of the range as he drove his foot again and again into her belly which she was trying to shield with very bloody arms. So involved was he in his task that he did not notice me as I crept behind him and brought the rolling-pin crashing on to the back of his skull.

He went down like a stone and I raised my hand

to strike again, would have finished him off there and then, but my mother, raising herself slightly said, 'No, Annie. Get the doctor. He's killed my baby.' I noticed then that the rug beneath her was soaked bright red, that her skirt was sodden with blood, that more blood was pouring down between her thighs.

Instinctively, I grabbed some towels from the pulley line and packed them as tightly as I could between her legs, then I flew out of the house, not to the doctor's, but back to Mrs Cullen. She would know what to do. Mrs Cullen always knew what to do. Within minutes, Allan had been despatched for the doctor, Josie put in charge of the household, while Mrs Cullen and I ran, as fast as her bulk would permit, back to our house.

There was no sign of Eddie Higson. Obviously, I had not hit him hard enough, I thought viciously as I looked down at my mother whose lifeblood seemed to be covering the living-room floor.

'Get down to the prefabs, Annie,' said Mrs Cullen. 'They've got them fancy fridges, ask for ice. Go on, 'urry up.'

I picked up a bucket and ran down the backs until I reached the prefabs where I disturbed half a dozen residents with my screaming. They piled the ice into my bucket and, not thinking to thank them, I sped back home. But I was too late, for my mother was already being lifted into the ambulance. Mrs Cullen held me back, because I was all for getting in the vehicle too and I heard myself screaming my mother's name as the driver slammed the door and shot off at great speed.

'Is she dead?' I moaned.

'Nay, lass. She'll be alright in a day or two. Are you stoppin' at Entwistle's tonight?' I shook my head. 'No. Rita's down with the chicken pox. I'll have to stop . . .' Oh no, I couldn't bear it. 'I'll have to stop here.'

'Did 'e beat 'er up, luv?'

'Yes,' I answered flatly. 'But she'll say she fell downstairs.'

Mrs Cullen shook her head. 'That's what they always say. There must be more folk fallin' down t' bloody stairs than there is folk walkin' up 'em. Now listen, Annie. Like as not that bugger's gone off down the pub for the night. 'E'll be terrified o' what 'e's done, you see. With any luck, 'e'll not be back till late. If you get worried about yer Mam, I'll send George down the Infirmary, see 'ow she is. You know where I am. If you need me, just come down. You stop 'ere, see if the doctor brings any news. 'E's a nice feller is Dr Pritchard, go an' see 'im a bit later on. Are you alright now?'

I nodded, unable to speak. Mrs Cullen wobbled away, turning as she reached the edge of the pavement. 'Don't you worry now. Come round later if you like.'

I was frantic after she'd gone, driven almost out of my mind, pacing about the house like a caged animal, couldn't sit down, couldn't stand in one place for two seconds at a time. What should I do? What could I do? Panic flowed over me in waves, a blind, unreasoning feeling that was not really connected with what had happened, because my mind would not, just now, fix on any of it. This was fear in its purest sense, for I could not discover its real source. Yes, my mother was hurt, yes, I feared for her life – somewhere inside me I knew all that. But it was as if I were facing a tiger, a wild beast with an unpredictable nature that might pounce at any time and I ran from this invisible animal, room to room, storey to storey, until dusk fell and I knew that this house could no longer contain me.

The doctor's wife opened the door to my hammerings and looked at me as if I were something the cat had dragged to her doorstep.

'Yes? Can I help you?'

'I want the doctor, Dr Pritchard . . .'

'There is no surgery just now, I'm afraid, but if you'd like to come back in, say, fifteen minutes . . .'

'I want to see him now. It's an . . . an emergency.'

She looked me up and down again as if assessing my worth, her cool eye somehow making me feel better, because I was used to this type, had got used to this type at All Saints. She might have legs, but this one was a real nun if ever I saw one and I could deal with nuns any day of the week – yes, even now. She ushered me through to the waiting room.

Dr Pritchard was a kind and gentle man with a far-seeing eye and a respect for humanity that was unusual in a man of his calling. He treated everyone with equal respect, always bent a willing ear, always had a smile and a jelly-baby for a child, even during rationing.

He joined me on the brown leather waiting bench.

'Hello, Anne. Now, you'll want to know about your Mummy, won't you?'

I nodded and he took my hand in his.

'Well, dear, I have telephoned just now to the hospital and she is in no danger whatsoever. They are managing to replace the blood she has lost and apart from being a little tired and bruised, she is doing fine, just fine.'

This was another thing I loved about this dear man. He always explained things like what made your blood clot when your leg bled and why you should never scratch your chicken pox.

'What about the baby?' I asked quietly.

He paused before replying, 'The baby is gone, I'm afraid, Anne.'

It was then that the tears came and I leaned heavily against this man as I wept, clinging to his tweed jacket as my tears poured down the front of his clean white shirt. He leaned back and pressed a button on the wall. His wife appeared in the doorway after a few seconds and he spoke briskly to her. 'Warm tea, Edna – warm, not hot and with two teaspoons of sugar.' He dried my eyes on his capacious handkerchief and instructed me to blow my nose into the same. She stood in the doorway, an expression of disdain tightening her already bitter features.

'Tea, Edna.' She slammed the door behind her as she disappeared.

'Are you feeling better now, Anne?' He always called me Anne. I liked that.

'A bit, Doctor.'

'Crying's good medicine, you know. Better than all the stuff in the chemist shop. It's like – let me see now. You know how the sky goes black and the air hangs heavy before a summer storm?' I nodded. 'And then after the thunder and the rain there's a lovely clean feel to everything? Well crying can be like that. It clears the brain.'

'Is she hurting, Doctor?'

'No. They have put her to sleep. When she wakes up she will be all mended.'

'But with no baby.'

'That's right, dear. We could not save the baby.'

Oh God, how I hated that Eddie Higson. How would I face him now after all this? How could I live with a murderer? My mother was alive, but he had killed her baby, I knew that. My knowledge of anatomy was limited, but I was sure he had killed my unborn brother or sister.

'What's sterile, Doctor?' He sat bolt upright and stared at me before attempting to answer this one.

'It means . . . well . . . bearing no fruit. Or, in the case of an animal or a person, it means bearing no young ones, no babies.'

She entered then with the tea, thrusting the china cup and saucer into his hands as if she would as soon approach a snake as come near me. After she had left without a word for either of us, Dr Pritchard asked, 'Why were you asking about the word "sterile" Anne?'

Instinctively, I was on my guard. 'Oh, it's something I heard at school. I knew it was to do with . . . well . . . babies and all that, but I wasn't sure what it meant.'

'Ah.' He leaned back once more and studied me as I sipped my tea.

'Tell me, Anne,' he asked after several seconds. 'How did your mother come to be so hurt?'

I stiffened. What should I say? If I told the truth, would Eddie Higson be locked up? And would that be what my mother would want? I decided to go cautiously. 'I wasn't there when it happened, Doctor. I think she fell down the stairs.'

The doctor sighed loudly. 'Yes. That's what she said, too, so I suppose she must have fallen downstairs, mustn't she?'

He looked meaningfully at me and I answered meekly, 'Yes, Doctor.'

He took the cup from my hand and led me through the hallway to the front door. 'Come and see me again, Anne. And don't worry, your Mummy is in very capable hands.'

I felt better now. The panic had left me; something about this warm and gentle man had calmed and soothed me. I had only to get through the next few days and my Mam would be home again.

I let myself into the darkening house and crept into the kitchen to make a bit of toast at the grill. Now I would have to look after myself, but as for him – well, he could go to the devil for his dinner. If the worst came to the worst, I at least had friends, could eat with Josie or Rita. He had nowhere to go and that was what he deserved.

When he staggered in at about eleven o'clock, I was on the sofa in the back living room, still fully dressed and with my mother's coat over me for warmth. Although I had been asleep, I woke the instant he entered the house, pulling the coat over my head, feeling, as an ostrich must, that if my face were invisible then he might not see me at all. I heard him switch on the light, then go through to the kitchen. He was making something to eat; I could hear the kitchenette compartments opening and closing, the sound of bread being cut on the board, the click of the cheese-dish lid.

He sat then at the table, not three feet away from me and I listened to the disgusting noise he always made when he ate.

What would he do to me? I knew he would never let me get away with it; I had hit him over the head with the rolling-pin and he was not one to forgive and forget. Also, I could smell the beer on him; the fumes permeated the room, soaked through my mother's coat and into my nostrils with a sickening intensity. Eddie Higson did not hold his drink well. I shivered as I awaited my fate.

I was suddenly blinded when, in one movement he crossed the small space between us and whipped the coat from me, throwing it across the room and almost into the grate where lay bloodstained towels and the twisted wreck that used to be my mother's best rug.

'Get up,' he growled. 'And where's your mother?'

I looked up into his hideous face. 'She's in the hospital.'

He threw back his head and laughed. 'Aye and that's where you'll be and all if you ever pull a trick like that again.' He pointed to the back of his head.

'She's . . . she's lost her baby, the doctor says.'

'Good. And what else did the doctor say? Does he know how she lost the kid?' He seemed frightened and I made him wait for a few seconds before answering, 'No. She told them she fell downstairs – again.' I did not manage to keep the venom from my tone.

'Get up when I tell you! From now on, you do exactly as I tell you – you hear me?'

I made no reply, but got up and stood by the sofa. He grabbed my arm tightly. 'You do whatever I say. Otherwise, I'll kill the bloody pair of you – you and your filthy mother. Because she'll pay for this, by Christ she will. And so will you. You knew all about it, didn't you? Well so do I now, 'cos a chap in the Star put me right tonight. I know the rat's name, rank and number now and his number's very near up, I can tell you. Ernie bloody Bradshaw, eh? I'll twist his sodding neck round for him; he won't know whether he's coming or bloody going by the time I've done with him.'

'He's bigger than you,' I ventured.

'Is he now?' His tone was sarcastic. 'And I've got brothers, so he can be as big as he likes. Now get up them stairs you and into that bath. You're as black as the ace of spades.'

I fled while the going was good. How was I going to warn Ernie? I would have to get to him tomorrow somehow and tell him that Eddie Higson was after him. What if I couldn't? I had no money for busfares, no money for anything and I wasn't going to ask Higson for money. I would have to walk, yes, that's what I'd do. School was still out, this being the September wakes week, so tomorrow I would go to the hospital to see my mother and, on my way back, I would wait at Millhouse mill for the evening shift to come on, then I could tell Ernie to keep his wits about him in case Eddie Higson carried out his threat.

The water was not very warm as the fire had gone out, so I had no intention of lingering in the bath. I scrubbed myself clean, wondering all the while how my mother was and whether or not I would get to Ernie in time.

Higson pushed open the bathroom door and stood leering at me. There was no lock on this door as Higson had declared himself averse to locks; had not his own father perished while bolted into the backyard tippler?

The look on his face was horrible as he approached me, his eyes glazed, his mouth open in a weird and nasty grin. He bent down, picked up the sponge and began to wash me, the smell of stale beer on his breath making me heave almost.

Then he made me stand, lifting me up by the armpits. Muttering words I could not hear, he soaped my chest then my legs, his hands forcing my thighs to part so that he could touch me in a place I had never imagined to be touchable except by myself when washing or drying. So this was to be my punishment. I stood perfectly still while his fingers probed my body, wishing that he would beat me instead. Anything, anything at all would be better than this.

His voice thick now, he asked, 'Do you love me?'

God, the man must have been drunk. Could anybody love a man who did this? He thrust his other hand into his pocket and began to move it quickly, then, after a few seconds of frantic activity, he sighed and knelt down on the floor at the side of the bath.

But my punishment was still not complete, for now he jumped up and grabbed me so tightly by the hair that I felt some of the roots snap away.

'You tell anybody – anybody about this, I'll kill the both of you – understand?'

I nodded mutely, my head moving just a fraction in his cruel grip.

'I'm going to teach you a thing or two – right?'

Again, I nodded.

'And you'll learn to enjoy our little lessons. Yes, you and I are going to get to know one another really well.'

He released me and I fell down into the water as he left the room, slamming the door behind him.

Fiercely I scrubbed my body in the icy water while red-hot tears of shame coursed down my cheeks. I did not understand what had just happened to me, but I feared it and hated it. And who could I tell? How could I find words to frame this terrible act that had been perpetrated against me? How would I prevent it from happening again?

I did know one thing though. Tomorrow I would run away to someone who would care for me, someone who would understand. Ernie Bradshaw would have to take care of himself. Until my mother got out of hospital, I must disappear, get to the other side of Bolton, as far away from here as I possibly could.

The rest could take care of themselves. I was put into this world to survive and survive I would.

9

On the Run

The next morning, I was up by 5.30, creeping about the house like a burglar in my efforts not to waken him. My body still hurt, partly because I had scrubbed myself so hard with the loofah after the assault, but mostly because of the attack itself which had left me bleeding slightly through the night.

Quietly, I opened the bottom-right-hand drawer of the kitchenette where he kept his money, silver in a spinning-ring tin from the mill, copper in a larger wooden cigar box. I would not ask; I would simply take because by this afternoon I would be beyond his reach and among others who loathed and despised him.

I took a shilling's worth of copper for busfares and then emptied the whole of the silver tin into my schoolbag. From the kitchenette cabinet, I picked up the remaining bread and cheese, then, pausing only to collect my mac with the hood, I left the house by the back door, having decided that I was less likely to be seen from the backs. Even at this early hour there were people about, colliers in particular, who often faced a long ride or even a long walk before their working day could start.

I walked all the way to the centre of Bolton, keeping to the backs except when I reached Crowley

Brow, a large bend in the road that was, in fact, a bridge over a very steep drop where water sometimes ran and I stared down for a few minutes into the dried-up bed before continuing on my way.

Everything around me seemed so normal. How could the world carry on like this, as if nothing had happened? Birds sang, early buses began to run, the sky was lightening in a promising way. And I was the one out of step, the one with the beaten-up mother and the dead brother or sister. I was the one who must live with a monster. Nobody cared. I tried to concentrate on not walking on the cracks. 'Stand on a nick, you'll marry a brick and the ghosties 'll come to your wedding,' chanted my mind as I went along. But it didn't work. Nothing could rid me of this crawling flesh where I could still feel the filth of his hands on me.

When I reached the middle of town, I walked to the cenotaph and paused before the statue of a mother holding a dead or dying son in her arms. In a few weeks, I would be laying my father's cross here, just as I had done every year, a plain white wood cross with a red flower at its centre. At home I had a scroll from the king, to commemorate Sergeant William Byrne, Gordon Highlander, 'who gave his life to save mankind from tyranny. May his sacrifice help to bring the peace and freedom for which he died.' But where was my peace, my freedom? Where was my mother's peace? Had my father died just so that we might be handed to another kind of tyranny – oh, there were no bombs this time, but war was war, however small the scale.

And that other hero, Jesus Christ – where was He now with His forgiveness and His goodness and His 'Suffer little children to come unto me'? Suffer little children was damn right, for I was suffering, suffering beyond all measure. I was eight years old and on the verge of believing that there was no sense in life because life hurt, and that there was less sense in death, especially sacrificial death, which was futile as it solved no problems for those of us who must continue alive.

I stopped for a cup of tea and a piece of toast at an early café on Deansgate. The woman looked at me suspiciously, for it was only seven o'clock. 'You're about early, love.'

'I'm meeting my auntie,' I lied easily, yet amazed at my presence of mind. 'We're getting the train for Blackpool.'

'Ooh, lovely. Wish I was coming with you – here have a bit of marmalade with that . . .'

I ate mechanically, like a machine that must be oiled and fuelled, pushing the food down my tightened throat, scalding my mouth with the hot sweet tea. When I had finished, I sat in the café for a while. It was still a bit soon to call on people, whatever the reason, so I crossed over past St Patrick's and on to the railway bridge by Trinity Street Station. Had I been in a better frame, I would have enjoyed this, because I loved to stand looking down on a train as it pulled in, loved to be enfolded in that cloud of steam and smoke, was a budding train fanatic were the truth known, being in possession of a list of engines longer than most of the boys', though I usually collected my numbers at a smaller station, having been forbidden by my mother to venture too frequently into the centre of Town.

I caught the 39 up Deane Road and walked through as this would kill yet more time and once again I was amazed at the size of the houses, at the proximity of the rows and, most of all, I was shocked by the stench of poverty. But when I reached Ensign Street I found, to my horror, that the houses were mostly empty, windows broken or boarded over. Our own house was not occupied and it was plain that the Hyatts too were gone.

I ran across to number 17 and hammered on the door. Surely by half-past nine there should be somebody about in Wakes Week – only a few colliers and busdrivers and the like worked in Wakes Week. A head appeared at an open upstairs window. 'Annie!'

'Hello, Mrs Maguire. I'm looking for the Hyatts.'

She pushed her head through the gap. 'They got put in James Street, lass. The bombs made these houses unsafe, you see. We'll be going ourselves soon. Do you want to come in?'

'No, thanks. I'll get to James Street.'

She paused fractionally before speaking again. 'She'll not be there, love. They'll be up at All Saints – wait there till I come down then I can talk to you proper . . .'

But I didn't wait. As soon as she closed the window, I ran off towards Derby Road and across to the church, arriving just in time to see Freddie and a lot of other men, all dressed in black, lifting a coffin through the church gates. I stopped in my tracks, thunderstruck. Who was dead? And where was Mrs Hyatt? She'd be inside the church, wouldn't she? I walked forward slowly and spoke to a weeping woman who made little sense at first.

She bowed her head as the coffin passed her and I did the same.

'Salt of the earth, salt of the earth,' said the woman before blowing her nose into her handkerchief.

'It's Mrs Mort, isn't it?' I asked. She looked down

at me. 'Oh, Annie, hello love. Fancy you coming all this way. Mind you, we were all neighbours, weren't we? She'll be missed, will Florrie. Pity Tom's not here, but still, I doubt he's heard yet . . .'

I leaned against the railing for support, toast and tea rising in my gorge and I swallowed hard to stop myself from vomiting. Mrs Hyatt dead? Where would I go now? And why could I feel no real grief for this lovely lady who was dead? 'How . . . I mean, what happened?' I managed.

'Heart attack, love. Out like a light, she went. Are you coming in for the service?' I shook my head. She followed the cortège into the church and I stood in the street, my head buzzing with exhaustion and the strangeness of it all. The one person who might have understood was being buried this very day. I looked up at the sky. Somebody up there, in that heaven of Sister Immaculata's, had it all wrong. Or was I being punished yet again? But now, I must find somewhere else to go, somewhere to stay for a while. My Grandad's? No, he would send or even take me home tonight. I could never tell him that I didn't want to go home and why, because I could not find the words for his ears and even if I could, he would make a fuss and Eddie Higson would kill my mother and me.

Aunts and uncles fell, of course, into the same category. I would have to find somewhere to be alone, absolutely alone until my mother got out of the hospital. And, strangely, my desire to visit her had gone, because my body was dirty now, had been dirtied by Eddie Higson's vile hands and I could not, as yet, countenance the idea of seeing my mother. She was alright. Dr Pritchard had said she was alright. So now, I must play for time, keep away from Higson, think things through.

I bought a bottle of lemon pop, two candles and a box of matches from Connie's Corner, then walked down the Ensign Street backs until I came to our old house. The gate swung open easily and I stepped into the tiny yard, just avoiding the corpse of a large rat that lay to the left of the empty midden.

The air-raid shelter was unbelievably dark, yet I took a strange comfort from the blackness, was glad that I could now concentrate my thoughts without fear of disturbance or distraction. But however long I thought, whichever course my mind took, it was always circular in that it brought me back to the same point. I could not, would never be able to, tell anyone about what Eddie Higson had done to me and to my mother. He was evil, truly evil and if I were to seek help, then he would surely finish off both of us.

And so the air-raid shelter became my home. I carefully rationed out my bread and cheese, anxious to save Eddie Higson's money for a real emergency. But as night closed in, I became chilled to the bone and, huddled in my corner, I decided that I must have a blanket. This would be my goal for tomorrow – to acquire more food and some kind of warm covering for the nights. I slept little, merely dozing in the cramped cold, easing myself from one uncomfortable position to another, all the time tense and on my guard in case he came and found me.

The next day I stole three flannelette sheets from the backs in James Street and a blanket from a line behind Cannon Street. My second night was, therefore, warmer but no more comfortable.

After that, I never went out again. I had run out of food, drink and candles, but an apathy had descended upon me, my head hurt and was burning and I coughed almost incessantly. On about the fourth day, I knew I was dying and I didn't care too much about it, even if my immortal soul was black from stealing. My head was filled with words and pictures all jumbled together and I slipped from time to time into blissful unconsciousness, only to be wakened by the coughing and the rasping noise of my own breathing.

They found me and took me to the Infirmary, though I remembered nothing of my journey there. I had something called pneumonia and had Mrs Maguire not recognized my name in the *Bolton Evening News*, had she not remembered seeing me in the street, had she not instigated the search of the area, I might never have been discovered.

My mother visited me in my ward and, as I got better, I went to see her in the other ward. Eddie Higson never came near, though I understood that he had been the one who had reported me missing. I told my mother nothing. In fact, once my illness was over, I began to wonder if I had imagined Eddie Higson's attack on me, for I had had some strange nightmares in my delirium.

My mother was allowed home before I was and she came to visit me each day, once bringing flowers from Mrs Cullen and Josie, another time a doll from Rita and her parents. The police questioned me, but I gave them no answers. I was dismissed with a telling off for being such a naughty girl and, towards the end of October, I returned home.

He was there when my mother brought me in.

'How are you, Annie?' he asked, pretending to be pleasant.

I stared at him and knew it had been no dream.

Gripping my mother's hand, I said, loudly and clearly, 'You can go to hell.'

My mother's hand clutched mine tightly, but Higson merely chuckled, saying 'I see she's back to normal, then.'

He turned to the sports page and carried on reading. And I knew there and then that whatever he did to me, I could overcome it. There was no way he could hurt me any more than he already had and I intended to emerge victorious. How little I knew!

10

New Pastures

It happened again, of course. I was not always able to sleep at Rita's house and he got to me whenever he could, each time putting me through the same sick ritual, though it varied slightly as the years went by and he began to collect and scrutinize my under-wear, looking for the tell-tale sign of menstruation, waiting, as he put it, for me to ripen.

By the time I was ten years old, I knew about sex, knew what Eddie Higson was planning for me, yet I managed to live with it, taking each day as it came, accepting, as children tend to accept, that things were far from right but that I could do nothing to alter or improve my situation.

My mother withered again; of Ernie Bradshaw I saw and heard no more except I knew that he had left the mill. Whether or not he got his beating, I ceased to care. But now I felt sure that I could never tell my mother about what was happening between Higson and me.

'You tell her, you tell anybody and next time I do you proper, ready or not – understand?' I never answered him, just sat or stood wherever he put me and let it happen, whatever he did, I just let it happen.

When I passed my scholarship, he said I could not

go to St Mary's but, for once, my mother put her foot down and got a grant for my uniform, a nasty set of brown and yellow clothing that was all several sizes too big so that I would get my wear out of it. The hat was a monstrosity, a wide-brimmed brown velour with a yellow band and a badge in the front. Even the knickers were brown and long in the leg while the coat looked like something rejected from army stock.

We stood, my mother and I in front of her big mirror and she oohed and ahed over my appearance, her eyes glistening with pride and unshed tears.

I felt nothing except revulsion as I looked at the sight of myself in the mirror, was aware of little except the soreness of my tiny breasts and the pain between my thighs.

'You must work hard,' my mother was saying now. 'Work hard and get them exams you do at sixteen, then you can stop on and do the others when you're eighteen.'

My eyes met hers in the glass. 'I'd rather go to boarding school,' I said. 'I want to get away from him.'

'You can't, Annie. Anyroad, he never hits you now, does he? I mean, we've had no trouble since . . . well . . . since I lost the baby.'

'Since he murdered your baby.'

'Now, Annie love . . .'

'Don't defend him, don't you dare. He's a murderer and a wicked man.'

'We've all got our faults, Annie. Look at me and how daft I was over that Ernie Bradshaw. I just pushed your Dad too far, that's all . . .'

'HE IS NOT MY DAD. My father is dead and that . . . animal is nobody's father. He is not fit to be a father . . .'

'Alright, Annie. Now get that lot off while I sew the nametapes on. Will I put one on your vest as well?'

'No!' I did not want to take off my vest, could not allow my mother to see the bruises. It was getting so hard, this business of protecting her.

Just then Higson entered the room and I paused in the act of removing the gymslip, allowed it to fall once more around my calves so that I remained fully clothed.

'What's this then?' he snarled. 'Bloody fancy-dress parade?'

'I'm just getting her ready for her new school, Eddie.'

He threw himself onto the bed and lay there staring at the two of us, a wicked smile distorting his face. 'I don't see why she needs all that fancy book-learning,' he said. 'All she'll do is finish up wed and then what good will her education be?'

I turned slowly to face him. I knew I would suffer later, yet still I had to say it. 'My education will keep me out of the mill. It will also make sure I don't finish up married to a window cleaner.'

He raised himself to a sitting position. 'You'll be lucky if anybody marries you.'

'Oh, I'll find somebody, don't you worry. And I'll make sure he's a big man who can fight my battles.'

He blanched and I knew he was worried in case I came out with it all there and then in front of my mother. I decided to keep him worried.

Gathering all my strength, I forced myself to sit at the foot of the bed and, keeping my tone light, I went on, 'You see, there are people in this world I just don't like. You know the sort – they say things and do things that hurt. Well, when I'm old enough to have a boyfriend I'll give him a list and say "get them for me". That'll be good, won't it?'

He jumped up and stormed out of the room without a word.

'Ooh, Annie, you shouldn't upset him like that!'

'Upset him? I wouldn't dream of it, Mam.'

St Mary's was a Catholic Grammar School for girls. It sat on top of a mound between Daubhill and Deane Road and it turned out young ladies of varying abilities, many reaching Oxford or Cambridge, some becoming adequate seamstresses and housekeepers, others going on to be teachers, a few, a very few, entering the Passionist convent after several years' constant indoctrination and brain-washing.

Although this was, for me, a golden opportunity in educational terms, I felt like a little child again, especially on my first day when I travelled on the 39 with girls twice my size, sixth formers who, although they wore the same uniform, carried it with panache, with flair – a tilt of the hat, a tightening of the belt to emphasize a true womanly shape.

There were six hundred girls in the school, most on scholarships, some fee-paying. Once again, I was back with the Passionist nuns, though many of the staff were lay teachers. The atmosphere in the school bordered on the sinister, was holy and serious enough to allow fear into the hardest breast among the ninety-odd new starters. Corridors were dark and occupied by a collection of plaster saints dotted around to remind us of the real reason for our being here. First and foremost, we were to become holy; education was secondary and incidental compared to this prime and vital objective.

The Headmistress was a Mother St Vincent, four feet two of solid dynamite and with a tongue that lashed like a whipcord. There were rules, rules and more rules. Never run in the corridors, say grace before eating even a sweet, speak to a teacher each time you meet one in a corridor (the staff must have been exhausted after a day's answering of a thousand greetings) keep your gym shorts long – to test the length, assume a kneeling position and measure no more than four inches from hem to floor – and so on.

Each morning we lined up before Mother and sang Latin dirges after which we prayed, then listened for at least ten minutes to a lecture on behaviour and deportment before marching to the sound of an ill-played piano to our various and wide-spread destinations.

As a first-year, I was destined for St Gertrude's building, which was separated from the main school by a garden through which we were forbidden to walk, being forced instead to take a circuitous route past the tennis courts. During that year I spent much of my time sneezing because I was, more often than not, drenched through to the skin by that famous Bolton rain as I passed, with monotonous regularity, from building to building. Each time we changed buildings, we changed shoes, 'indoors' for inside and 'outdoors' for out. Uniform inspections were carried out after Mass Register (we had to account for our Sundays too) each Monday and scorn was poured on any poor girl who had lost the brown gloves or whose shoes were of inferior quality.

Nevertheless, I settled to my various tasks, took to French, Latin and English Language and Literature like a duck to water, coped, just about, with maths and hated history right from the start. Sister Olivia, who had a severe speech impediment which caused her to spit as she spoke, was our history teacher. We mocked her with the usual viciousness of youth and those of us who sat on the first four rows talked of bringing in umbrellas (brown, of course) to protect ourselves from Sister's leaky mouth. I felt sorry for her, but this pity of mine did not endear me to her subject which I dismissed as pointless, as everybody was dead and I could not see the virtue in learning lists of battles and treaties that nobody had respected anyway. I knew enough about Chamberlain now to realize that bits of paper promising peace were a waste of ink.

The science facilities were poor, as science was not quite ladylike or pretty and was definitely not holy. But we still managed to create a fair amount of mayhem with a couple of bunsen burners, one or two pipettes and the odd sheep's eye or earthworm.

My chief regret was that Josie Cullen had failed to gain a place and was destined, therefore, for another school – St Anne's, which was a secondary modern and churned out mill-fodder or, at best, waitresses and shopgirls. Josie was clever – I knew that – and I was annoyed with her for not trying. But, in Josie's book, St Mary's girls were a 'right soft lot' and she was determined to be a 'hard case' and earning by the age of fifteen.

For my own part, I began to excel, particularly in English and French, in which subjects I came out top of the class on most occasions. My essays were often read out to the whole school, an honour I learned to accept without blushes. When it came time to produce the school magazine, I wrote almost all the first-year contributions, selling my pieces to the other girls for pocket money.

In my second year, a shocking thing happened, a thing that caused me to pull myself up and assess my situation anew. Sheila Davies, my friend from those hopscotch and skipping-rope days, who had also gained a place at St Mary's, died of kidney failure. The school choir sang her requiem and I sat staring at the small light-wood coffin in All Saints Church, my heart and mind filled with grief and sadness. She had been so alive, so vibrant. Now she was gone, gone for ever. What if this were to happen to me? If I were struck down in this way, then I would not be given the chance to work out how to make sure Eddie Higson got his just deserts in this world.

As the coffin was carried out past us, I made my decision. Surely here, in this holy place, I could get help? Surely a priest, a man of God would come to my aid and rescue me?

But I would not speak to Father Sheahan of this parish, or to Father Cavanagh from my own; better, in this case, the devil I did not know.

After much deliberation, I chose St Patrick's, as it was far enough away from both the churches I knew so well, yet near enough for me to reach for tuppence on the number 45.

I sat in St Patrick's the very next evening, waiting until every sinner had passed through the confessional, making sure that I would be the last. I wanted to know that no believer lingered to listen to what I must say once I got inside the box.

It was a pretty church, stone-built and with beautiful stained-glass pictures in the arched windows. I gazed at the Stations of the Cross, vivid portrayals of Christ's suffering that lined the walls of this and every Catholic church. The scent of incense lingered in the peaceful air. For a few moments, I began to understand why people came here, because the tranquillity was somehow hypnotic and comforting. Then, at last, it was my turn. I genuflected as I left my pew, hesitating for just a second or two before entering the confessional.

I closed the door quietly behind me and knelt on the deliberately uncomfortable plank near the floor, making the Sign of the Cross on my forehead, chest and shoulders before beginning. 'Bless me, Father, for I have sinned. It is three weeks since my last confession.' The priest, a dark shape at the other side of the grille, yawned audibly. I was, after all, the last of a very long queue of penitents. 'Tell me your sins, child.'

'I have taken the name of the Lord in vain twice – I said God when I was angry.'

'Anything else?'

'I laughed at Sister Olivia because she was spitting when she talked and she can't help it.'

'We must not mock the afflicted, child. Go on.'

'I tell lies. I honestly can't remember them, Father, but I do tell fibs. I stole a sixpence from a girl at school, but I put it back in her desk the next day.'

'Good girl. Anything more?'

'I listened to dirty talk at school, but I didn't join in.' I hesitated. I had to do it now. It was now or never . . .

'Go on, my child.'

Seconds passed. I could feel the sweat dripping down my forehead, running along the bridge of my nose and I wiped my face with the sleeve of my blazer. He sounded kind and gentle like Dr Pritchard. Perhaps God was real after all, perhaps He had sent me here so that He might perform one of His miracles. I found myself praying, really praying, begging for God to intercede on my behalf, to show me the way, to show this hidden priest the way . . .

'What is troubling you?' asked the tired, pleasant voice.

'I . . . I do not honour my . . . stepfather and I can't honour him. Ever.'

'Oh, I see. And why is that now?'

I paused, then passed a piece of paper under the grille. 'That is my name and address, Father. I am not of your parish, but I want your help.'

The shadow behind the partition picked up the paper then straightened in its seat.

'In what way can I help you . . . er . . . Anne?'

I cleared my throat before continuing, 'The man who is married to my mother has been . . . well . . . doing things to me for about four years. I want it stopped.'

A brief silence followed. 'What sort of things, Anne?'

'Dirty things.'

'You'll have to be more specific.'

I swallowed hard. 'He touches me where he shouldn't. He says if I tell anyone, then he'll kill me and my mother. He already murdered my mother's baby before it was born. My mother was in hospital because he'd kicked her half to death.'

'What do you want me to do, child?'

I thought about this. 'I want you to make him stop. I don't know how, but you must. Perhaps you could . . . well . . . talk to him, tell him he'll go to hell and all that if he doesn't leave me alone. But you have to come in the evening and during the week, when my mother will not be there.'

I heard the priest shuffling about behind the

grille as he prayed almost under his breath.

'Anne. Are you telling me the truth?'

'Yes!' It had never occurred to me that I might not be believed.

'You said yourself not a minute ago that you tell lies, child.'

'I do not lie in the confessional, Father.'

'And you have heard . . . dirty talk at school?'

'Yes, but that's nothing to do with this.'

'I have to be sure, Anne, for it is another person's sin you are telling me. And I have to admit to you, child, that I am at a loss. I have never had to deal with this kind of thing before. I will pray. We must both pray. Now, make an act of contrition.'

'Oh my God, I am sorry and beg pardon . . .' What the hell was I doing here? What kind of a fool was I? I knew Eddie Higson had a grudging respect for, even a fear of the church in spite of his bold words to Father Cavanagh, but could this man really do anything for me? Still, I had tried. From now on I would have to try everything – everything, that was, except telling my mother directly. Because soon, I would reach the age when Eddie Higson would do the really bad thing to me, the thing he had been promising for so long now. Against that, at least, I must protect myself.

The next assault took place the following evening. This time Higson wanted me to touch him, was on the point of opening his trousers when I managed to escape, naked and screaming, down the stairs and out into the back yard. He stood shaking in the doorway as I screamed my fury into the night sky. 'Come in, Annie. I won't do it again, I promise.'

'I don't believe you!'

'Stop shouting. Come in or they'll have you locked up as a mad woman.'

'Touch me again and I'll scream.'

'Alright then, come in.'

I rushed past him and through the house up to my attic room where I swiftly put on my nightie. All kinds of plans were running through my head. Perhaps I could loosen the rungs on his ladder so that he would fall to his death in the street, whereupon I could go and smash his dead face with the heel of my shoe and wipe him out of my mind forever. Or I could push him under a bus or put poison in his tea – he'd never notice the taste, he always drank it black and stewed. But I didn't know where to get poison, hadn't the strength to loosen his rungs, wasn't big enough, yet, to push the bastard under a bus.

He didn't come near me again that week and I decided that screaming had not been a bad idea.

Father Keegan, from St Patrick's, arrived on the Friday evening. He shut himself in the living room with Higson and I crept down, terrified, to listen at the door.

'Your daughter confessed to me earlier in the week, Mr . . . er . . .'

'Higson. She's my stepdaughter.'

'Ah, yes.' There followed a long pause.

'What did she tell you, then?'

'That, I am not at liberty to divulge, Mr Higson. The confession is a confidential matter between God, Priest and sinner. You, as a Catholic, must surely know that.'

Higson cleared his throat and when he spoke again, his voice was high in pitch. 'Then why are you here?'

'To tell you that your stepdaughter is unhappy in this house, to ask you, beg you to . . . make her life easier.'

'In what way?'

'I think we both know what I'm talking about, Mr Higson.'

I heard the shovel in the scuttle as Higson fed the fire, probably to give himself time to think. He spoke again, his voice more confident now. 'She's a fanciful lass, is our Annie, very – what's the word now – talented, yes that's it. She's forever making up stories and writing them down. She even wins prizes for some of them.' His tone was wheedling now. 'So, you see, sometimes she doesn't know where her imagination's taking her. She does imagine things, you know. Her head's crammed full of nonsense – I put it down to her age; she's at that funny age, you see . . .'

'I'm not too sure of that, Mr Higson. She strikes me as a very level-headed young person. And I feel sure that she would not bring her imagination with her into the confessional.'

Higson coughed again. 'What are you going to do about it, then?'

'There is nothing I can do. My hands are tied by the laws of my faith. I only wish there were something I could do.'

'Then bugger off.'

He couldn't help me, he couldn't! I pressed a fist to my mouth to stop myself from crying out.

Father Keegan was saying now, 'I may be a priest, Mr Higson, but I am also a man. I tell you now that if the child ever comes to me again with her tales or imaginings – whatever you choose to call them – then I will quite simply take it upon myself to beat the living daylights out of you.'

'And break your own sodding commandments?'

'I too have a Father Confessor, Mr Higson. My soul is easily cleansed. Is yours?'

I heard a chair fall back as somebody stood up.

'So you'll give me a hiding? You and whose bloody army?'

'I and God's army, Mr Higson.'

'Try it then. Go on, you soft bugger with your big girl's frock on – try it, I dare you. Come on, man, get your fists up.'

There followed a crack like a pistol shot, a thud as a body hit the floor, then complete silence for several seconds.

I was just about to enter the room when the priest emerged, biretta in hand, tears coursing down his cheeks.

'Tell me to go for the police, Anne. I cannot break my promises as a priest, but you can ask me, outside the confessional, to intervene on your behalf. Please, Anne . . .'

'We can't get help, Father. He would kill me and my mother. I suppose it was stupid of me to expect him to listen to you.'

The priest squatted down in front of me. 'Anne, there must be a way.'

'There is no way, Father. I dare not even tell my mother what is happening.'

'Shall I tell her?'

'No!' I cried vehemently.

He rose and placed a hand on my head and this time I was not like a dog at its master's feet, for I could almost feel the goodness of this man flowing into me as he intoned 'in nomine Patris . . .' over me, his voice broken by sobs.

After he had left, I ran out and sat on the wall. Go for the police? As if I could! For a start, would a bobby believe me, a bit of a kid, while a grown man denied everything? And I couldn't imagine myself walking into the police station and saying all this to a man in uniform.

I knew now that there was absolutely no help for me. Everything I did in the future must come from within myself. What I could do, I didn't know, but I was sure that I must carry on protecting myself and my mother in the only way I knew how, by keeping silent.

When, after several days had elapsed, Higson recovered from the priest's blow to chin and pride, he renewed his assaults on me, threatening now to gag me if I screamed. He did not, for the time being at least, try to make me touch his vile body. But he told me, in no uncertain terms, that should I wander again into the parish of St Patrick, then he would surely cut my throat.

Again, I must bide my time.

II

Losing Faith

School became my place of refuge, somewhere I could do well in the eyes of my peers while not faring too badly in the opinions of my teachers. Although the emphasis was very much on religion, a subject that was taught for at least forty minutes a day, we got the opportunity to explore languages and English literature, in which spheres I rapidly developed strong interest.

Home was another matter altogether. Apart from my usual problem, my mother, always tired from the mill, usually exhausted with worry about finances, was too engrossed in her own daily routine to spend much time with me. But she would occasionally pause on her way out to the evening shift to say, 'Do your homework, Annie. Work hard, I want to see you do well.'

And I was doing well, in spite of, or perhaps even because of my home life. The most difficult thing, at first, was that because I knew I was not, could not be normal, that I was the only person in the world with such a terrible secret to hide, I found myself acting all the time. After a while, the acting came naturally and 'putting on a face' became a pleasure to me. Being cheerful, appearing happy, boisterous and very much a leader made me popular with the other girls and so, after a while, I became two people almost – one for school and one for home.

My acting talent did not go unnoticed and even during my first two years at the school I was involved in several productions, playing minor roles two or three times a year. The Cullens, who had moved into a four-bedroomed house opposite us, came to see me play one of Cromwell's soldiers in *When Did You Last See Your Father?* This was an absolute scream, because they filled the front row and their main aim in life seemed to be to make me laugh. Apart from that, they had all helped me learn my lines, so when it came to 'Ho there, a pike – prick me this dog's hide' all seven of them chanted it with me while Mrs Cullen ran up and down the row, boxing ears. My mother came to see me act whenever she could get the time off or when we did a Saturday matinee. When we performed *Assorted Scenes from Shakespeare*, she wept over my Juliet and so did I because I froze partway and lost my lines. But I really did have some wonderful times at school, which compensated in no small way for the agony I still suffered at home. Rita Entwistle often had other friends to stay now, so between the hours of five and ten I was completely at his mercy. He struck at irregular intervals too, making it difficult for me to plan my homework and I often sat up well into the night studying and writing essays. But I was getting stronger and more aware all the time. I would have my own back, I knew it in my bones.

Though life at school had its pleasant side, it was by no means a bed of roses. One of the bigger show-downs came one Monday morning as Sister St Thomas, our class teacher, was calling out the Mass register.

'Anne Byrne. I see that you have not been attending Mass these last three weeks.'

I rose to my feet. We had been trained to stand when addressed by a teacher. 'That's right, Sister.'

'Why not? Is there some illness in the house, or some other reason why you have not attended?'

'No, Sister.'

'Then why have you not been to church? Missing Mass, as we all know, is a sin of omission and is not venial, but mortal. Why have you suddenly started collecting mortal sins, Anne Byrne?'

I looked around at my classmates whose eyes were fixed on me.

'I . . . do not believe in mortal sin, Sister.'

Sister St Thomas' pen fell to the floor and a girl rushed forward to retrieve it.

'You do not believe? You do not . . . well then, I suppose that if you don't believe in it, then it cannot exist.'

'I did not say that it does not exist, Sister. I simply stated that I do not believe in it.'

The nun raised her eyes to heaven. 'Then you must make an act of faith, Anne. You must make yourself believe.'

'I can't, Sister.' I was speaking the truth, voicing my truth, my thoughts, yet it was as if I were listening to somebody else. But I was weary, too weary for lies, too tired, just then, to carry on acting. For once, I had lowered the barricade and was indulging myself by this foolishness. Was I seeking attention, begging for help, looking for punishment? All my life I had, it seemed, been a rebel. But now, at thirteen, I was becoming restless, moody, unpredictable. Sometimes, I was not in control, not in charge of myself. Here I was, in a classroom full of Catholics, defying a teaching nun, decrying the Faith, attempting, feebly and stupidly, to shake the very foundation on which the school was built.

There was a ripple of movement in the room and Sister St Thomas gripped the edge of her desk as she asked, 'Why not? Why cannot you make yourself believe like the rest of us can?'

'Because it doesn't make any sense,' I answered loudly and clearly. Had I really said that? And why couldn't I hold my silly tongue? Perhaps the unthinkable was actually happening – perhaps I was going out of my mind.

The nun got to her feet. 'Come along with me now. The rest of you will study the notes we made yesterday on the gifts of the Holy Ghost. There will be no talking while I am out of the room.'

I was hauled before Mother St Vincent, whose head barely reached my shoulder, so she sat me down while she paced the room, her tiny hands clasped over her flat chest.

Now, here was a woman to fear. No-one ever defied Mother. Yet I was strangely calm and detached as she delivered a long and vitriolic lecture, a sermon that would normally have made my ears burn and my head bow in shame. My answers to her quickly fired questions came, at first, in monosyllables, then suddenly, inexplicably, I didn't care any more, didn't give two hoots what she did or said. She was just a woman, a very small woman who knew nothing about things that really mattered, who had escaped with others of her kind to the safety of the convent where, untouchable, unhurtable, she could pray and teach a bit of advanced Latin, the odd smattering of Greek. She never scrubbed a floor or donkeystoned a step, seldom deigned to speak to the lower members of her order, those silent shadows who flitted about in large grey aprons, shoulders bowed from carrying heavy buckets, hands cracked by scalding water and carbolic soap. Deliberately, I met her steady gaze as she spoke.

'So what you are saying then is, at the end of the day, that you are not a Catholic.'

'I think I am not a Catholic, Mother.'

'And yet here you are, taking advantage of a Catholic education in an excellent Catholic school.'

'There are other non-Catholics in the school,' I pointed out. 'We have three in our class alone . . .' Was I never going to shut up?

'Those girls attend with special permission because their parents admire our standards. They have not had the same benefits as you, have never been baptized, were never given the opportunity to choose the right path to heaven . . .'

'I believe that there is no right path, Mother.'

'And how old are you, to be so sure of what you believe?'

'Thirteen.'

'And you, at thirteen, know better than the rest of us who were put here to teach you?'

'There are other religions, Mother. I will find the one that is right for me one day.'

She continued to look me straight in the eye without having to stoop, though I was seated while she still stood. 'Do you go to Confession?'

'Not any more, Mother.'

'Then we shall pray for you.'

'Thank you.'

Her lips pressed themselves tightly together before she spoke again. 'Are you being sarcastic, Anne Byrne?'

'No, Mother, there's nothing wrong with praying. It's just that it's not only for Catholics – praying's for everybody.'

We stared at one another for several seconds, our combat silent though continuing. Then her expression changed and I knew that she was no longer angry with me. But I had not won, if indeed victory was my goal, because I could scarcely bear to face the sorrow and pain that showed so plainly in her eyes.

Mother retired to the window where she stared out silently on to St Mary's Road. She sighed deeply several times, her hands clutching now at the massive rosary that hung from her fragile waist. After a few moments of contemplation, she turned to face me once more. 'You are far too clever for your own good, Anne Byrne. That is the only conclusion I can reach.'

'No, Mother,' I said quietly. 'I am not clever enough yet to work out what I do and don't believe in. I have read a lot of books and will read a lot more. I am sure that I will sort it out once I get older.'

She reached out her hands in an imploring gesture. 'But Anne, can't you see what you are doing? Better a Protestant than a lapsed Catholic. Better no chance at all than one thrown back into the face of the Lord.'

I suddenly realized that this was the first time I had ever been granted the privilege of a proper, intelligent conversation with a nun. I was being treated as a human being rather than as a stray lamb and I decided that I respected this woman and that she, in her turn, held a grudging respect for me. This was no tyrant, no despot. Mother St Vincent and I had something in common, something that showed at last. We were both actors, each playing her part, each doing what was necessary in order to survive. How could I fear and loathe someone so vulnerable? How could I despise her for living in a convent when I too sought shelter from my own grim realities?

She stared at me now, her eyes full of questions, her quick glance seeming to assess the answers before they came.

'Somebody, or something, has shaken your Faith, my dear. Could you tell me who or what it was?'

I gave no reply and I could see, from the great intelligence in her face, that she expected no answer to such a question, at least, not from a thirteen-year-old girl. But she had done me the very great honour of asking it.

'My faith may come back, Mother,' I said, wanting to comfort this little woman whose reputation for viciousness had now been completely disproved, in my book at least.

'I understand, Anne, that you missed your Confirmation when the Bishop visited your parish three years ago. Why was that now?'

'I was ill in bed with tonsillitis, Mother. I've had tonsillitis off and on ever since I caught pneumonia about five years ago.'

'Ah yes, yes indeed. I know we've sent extra work home for you when you've been afflicted. That's a terrible disease, is it not? I had it myself for years until they removed the tonsils and the adenoids.'

She approached me now, standing just inches away from me as she asked, 'Will your Faith come back in time for your Confirmation by the Bishop next year?'

'I don't know: I wish I did know.'

'Pray for yourself, Anne. Something about you disturbs me. We will offer a Novena in the convent.

You may go now. God bless you, my dear.'

'And may He bless you also, Mother. Thank you for being so understanding.'

'Well now,' she said, smiling at me and deliberately thickening her brogue, 'isn't me bark worse than me bite?'

'I would say so, Mother – but do I tell the others?'

She threw back her tiny head and laughed. 'Ah no, that would be going too far. When you're my size, you need a card or two up your sleeve.'

My heart went out to her. The words were on the tip of my tongue, just waiting to leap out and please her – 'yes, Mother, I'll get confirmed . . .' but I held them back. It was easy to know other people, easy to work out what they wanted and required of me. But there was one person I didn't know at all, one person whose moods and attitudes altered, it seemed, every time the wind changed. Would I ever get to know Annie Byrne?

All during that night, I thought of Mother and her questions, tossing and turning in my bed, my mind a turmoil of jumbled thought. What had shaken my faith was the faith itself with its frigidity, its cold, clear-cut attitude to mankind. And yet within that faith there were real people, good, generous and intelligent men and women like Father Keegan and our Mother St Vincent. They must be the exception that proved the rule; they must, in spite of their cleverness, be misguided.

It seemed to me that most Catholic leaders could see only good or bad, black or white, everything cut and dried, rules to adhere to, laws that must never be questioned.

Catholicism left no room for moderation, no space

for compromise. It required blind acceptance and stupidity; as far as I could see, it precluded intelligence and I could not understand how it captured people of integrity, people like Mother St Vincent. No matter how hard I might be pushed, persuaded, cajoled, I could not allow a bishop to lay his sanctified hand upon my unbelieving head. God, Whoever He was, created not just pretty flowers, charming animals, pleasant people. He also produced items like Eddie Higson. God made mistakes. And because the Faith commanded me to believe in God's perfection and omnipotence, I could not allow myself to embrace it.

I lay in my bed watching the sun rise over the moors. Another day was dawning. Perhaps this day would hold the answer, the answer to the main question. Who was Annie Byrne?

12

Fighting Back

The learning process had been clearly defined for me; listen to a teacher, take notes, copy down the bibliography, read the books on the list, write more notes, produce the essay. So, although I had no teacher for this unscheduled subject, I set about the task of learning about myself in the same mechanical way, turning the pages of memory, re-creating my own history and writing it down in a carefully coded shorthand that no-one but myself would ever decipher. And at last I understood Sister Olivia's mutterings about the importance of background, about a country without a history being like a man with no memory. My past was suddenly important to me.

Although I did not yet recognize or understand it, I was inventing my own therapy, defeating depression by allowing my anger to pour outwards onto paper, exorcizing frustration through the painting of bold word-pictures. It was like talking to some invisible person and the writing of my short memoirs became an obsession almost.

I recognized early on in my research that people, like ants, lived in colonies, were interdependent and that I, a very small worker, could only know and judge myself by discovering how others saw me.

While assessing their attitudes to me, I found myself in turn judging them and I soon had a large ring-file filled with studies of the various characters who had touched my life thus far.

'What are you up to, Annie?' My mother's voice floated from the bottom of the attic stairs. She seldom came up here; this was my domain and I was therefore responsible for keeping it in order.

'I'm writing, Mother.'

'For school?'

'Yes,' I lied, glancing down at the 'shorthand' notes I was currently compiling on the subject of Edna Pritchard, wife of our doctor, mother to my friend Simon.

'As long as you haven't got your head stuck in one of them daft library books again . . .'

Yes, my bibliography was indeed strange. At first, the historical novels had been an escape for me. They provided easy reading, were repetitive, predictable – history was history no matter how fancy the embroidery, the dead remained dead no matter what. But the books were teaching me things, things I might never have come across in the normal course of my life. Normal. Now there was a word to conjure with, a concept difficult to define. Was there anything 'normal' about my life? And how 'normal' were other people's lives?

Through the borrowed books, I had stumbled, quite by accident at first, on certain clues that might equip me for . . . for what? I faced it squarely before writing the word in my complicated code. Revenge. And because that was what I wanted, because that was where all this self-discovery and soul-searching was leading, I wondered sometimes if I were a good or even a nice person. I would not be confirmed, I could not be a proper Catholic or even a watered-down Christian. I was out of step, out of place . . .

'Just make sure you get that homework finished, that's all.'

'I will. Hasn't Angela arrived yet?'

'No, love. I'll leave the door on the latch so's she can let herself in. Eddie'll be late – he's gone up to his brother's. And don't be stopping up all night talking to Whatsername. I want you coming out top of the class again . . .'

My mother. So vulnerable, so transparent, so easy to write down. Her wants were simple. She needed me to be what she might have become had she not remained stuck in the mill all her working life. She was honest, good, caring, hardworking and very naive. Already she looked up to me because I was 'getting an education'. Yet this did not prevent her from laying down her law whenever she had time and opportunity, for beneath that façade of gentleness there lurked an iron will, a determination so grim that I would never have dared to bring home a book with bad marks in it. About once a month she would scrutinize my homework and although she did not understand some of the contents, she was swift to pounce on anything less than a seven out of ten. 'You're not trying, Annie . . .' She seldom raised her voice when she accused me. It would have been easier if she had shouted, but she would say the words in a sad and quiet voice that cut right through me. All her eggs were in one basket; had my brother or sister been allowed to live, then she might have depended less on me, on my success. But I was her reason for living; on account of me she slaved night after night in that filthy mill. I owed everything to her and was acutely aware of it.

Because of my mother, I was edging my way towards a solution that might protect both of us, was growing up quickly, speeding up the process by learning, observing, absorbing anything and everything that might serve my purpose. Although revenge was what I desired, protection for my mother and for myself was what I needed. She, most particularly, must not be hurt any more.

The books she complained about had taught me much. From them, I had learned about rape, had discovered what incest meant. Not that it would be incest – even if he did ever manage it – but it would be damned near, him being married to my mother. The burning question throughout had been – had I brought all this on myself? Had I pushed Eddie Higson into such a pattern of behaviour by treating him with so much disdain right from the start? But no, an echo from the past, already noted somewhere in the diaries, prompted me to know otherwise. Florrie Hyatt from Ensign Street, dead and buried these five years, spoke out loudly and clearly – ''e joined up on account o' that lass' and 'a bad bugger if ever I saw one'. What did you know, Mrs Hyatt? And how much did Tom know? Should I ask across so many miles of ocean?

Also, was my mother weak for sweeping such warnings under the carpet? Or was she simply afraid to be alone, was she insecure, dependent on marriage? Perhaps for my mother a bad marriage was preferable to none at all. But surely she didn't know, couldn't know what he was doing to me. I was too important to her. If she had known, or suspected, then she would definitely have tackled him and it was the fear of such a confrontation that had prevented me from telling her. Twice he had beaten her, once almost to death . . .

I flicked through the pages as I waited for Angela Marsh, my next piece of research, to arrive. On the first sheet was my Dad – or as much of him as I could remember, six foot four in his socks, a fine strong man with a wickedly loud laugh and a bristly chin. Then Tom, Freddie, Mrs Hyatt, Sheila Davies . . . and Eddie Higson. Even on the page, he made me shiver as I conjured up in my mind's eye the image of his face leering over me while he bent to touch my body. Oh God, how I hated the hooked nose, those mean thin lips, the stink of his breath, that corrugated black hair, the small deep-set blue eyes. I heard myself screaming aloud and this sound brought me back to reality, making me grip the edge of the table. Had anyone heard? Had my mother left for the mill, was Angela in the house yet?

No-one came. I buried my face in my hands for a few seconds, forcing myself to breathe slowly and evenly. Control was the key; sometimes, I seemed less controlled now, at thirteen, than I had been at eight or nine. My body was changing – that was obvious, especially to him and to me. I now measured five feet and five inches in height, wore a size six shoe, had a definite waist and small breasts and a great deal of physical strength. So now he depended on blackmail, approached me more warily and less frequently, because even wits as dim as his could not fail to recognize that I was acquiring the bodily power with which I might, one day, overcome him.

Intellectually, I was streets ahead of him and it was on my intellect that I was depending totally.

But my emotional development was another matter altogether and I feared my feelings, was terrified that one day they might get out of hand, that I might commit murder or, worse still, run to my mother, turn for help to the law, scream out in the street and tell the whole world of Eddie Higson's crime.

I thought, not for the first time, about the police. I'd watched them in the streets many a time, chasing lads for fighting and scrumping apples, or telling folk the time and how to get to Affetside, checking up at night to see if doors were secure. They seemed ordinary somehow, just men dressed up, nothing unusual. How could I find the words for such ordinary men and what would happen anyway? Prison for him, shame for my mother and me. And to achieve even that, it would need to be a good day, a day when I was coping well, when I was fluent and confident with strangers. On a bad day, I might not even be believed . . . No. The police were well out of this; I could not turn to them. Instead, I wrote pages and pages, full accounts, searched my memory for the tiniest of details. This was my sole outlet. Perhaps one day, somewhere in the distant future and after my mother was dead, I would set this tale in another time, dress it up, have it published . . .

'You there, Anne?' I pushed the diaries into a drawer and went to open my bedroom door. Angela Marsh began her ungainly ascent of the attic stairs. Angela, at fourteen, was a fee-paying non-Catholic who had not moved up at the end of last year because she had failed her terminals. She was therefore in a class with younger girls and she treated us, on the whole, with a degree of contempt because she was experienced. Most good Catholic girls of thirteen were not interested in Angela Marsh's experiences. But I was not a good Catholic girl and Angela's knowledge, which she seemed only too willing to impart for a small fee, might prove very useful to me.

She stood in the doorway breathing hard. 'That's a lot of bloody stairs,' she grumbled.

'Never mind – see, I've got lemonade and cakes.'

Her eyes glistened with greed as she sat down on my bed and I handed her a glass and a plate which she accepted without thanks. She was a plump girl with large breasts, dark red hair and white skin. With her mouth full of cake, she spoke. 'Don't forget – you do my French homework for a whole month.'

I nodded mutely. She flicked a few crumbs from her ample bosom. 'Right,' she said. 'So you've got yourself a boyfriend and you want to know all about it?'

'Yes.' I hesitated. 'I don't want to . . . get into any trouble. I know this may sound silly, Angela, but I . . . er . . . want to know how far to go. You seem so clever about these things, but I'm just so ignorant. How far do you go?'

She grinned lewdly. 'Well, I've never done it. You know what I mean?'

I smiled at her encouragingly and she went on, 'I don't let them . . . you know . . . put it in me. I've got periods now – have you?'

'No.'

'Well, you might get away with it then. But I daren't – my mother would kill me if I got pregnant. So I just . . . well . . . let them touch me and sometimes I touch them.'

I had to go warily now. 'How do you stop . . . it . . . happening?'

She shook her head slowly. 'I've had a few near misses, I can tell you. It's not easy because sometimes . . . well . . . girls want to do it too, you know. I mean, it's only natural. But you see, it's a case of not driving them too far, hold them back a bit . . .'

'What do you mean?'

She swept a superior look in my direction 'Christ, you don't know much, do you? And you're supposed to be the clever one?' She giggled and crossed her fat legs, one hand straying to her face to pick at a large ugly spot at the side of her nose. 'Look, for a start I make sure there's other people there – like in the back row at the pictures or behind a house with a light in the window. If he gets me on the floor or up against a wall, I usually . . . well . . . you know . . .'

'No, I don't know, Angela. And if you're not going to tell me, then you'll be doing your own French homework.'

She stared at me for a while and I thought she was going to get up and walk out. Then, because even she, the hard case of the class, could feel embarrassment, she came across the room to where I sat in my chair by the window and, in a whisper, she explained to me how she used her body to please the boys without actually allowing copulation to occur.

'Satisfied?' she asked, her cheeks scarlet as she stepped away from me.

I turned to look out of the window and asked, as casually as I could, 'What would you do if someone tried to force himself on you, tried to make you do it?'

I heard the bed creak as she threw her large frame onto it. 'That's what nearly happened to me a few weeks ago with Steve. He's older than me – nearly nineteen. It's the older ones you've got to watch. And you see, with boys, once they get excited . . . you know . . . swell up, they sometimes don't know what they're doing. I'd let him . . . well . . . unfasten my bra and once he got my blouse off, he just went crazy.' I could hear the pride in her voice. 'It's with me being so big. Anyway, the next thing I knew, he was pulling his trousers down. Christ, I was terrified . . .'

'So what did you do?' I turned to face her. 'What did you do, Angela?'

'I kicked him in the balls!' She began to roll about the bed, her body convulsed with almost hysterical laughter. I waited for a few moments.

'And that stopped it?'

'Stopped it? Stopped it?' she howled. 'I reckon it stopped him for a week or two.' She calmed down gradually. 'Since then, I've stuck to boys my own age, ones that have never done it. Don't go with anybody older, Anne. They're the ones that get you into trouble, they're the ones that force you. Once they've done it, they want to do it again and they're not satisfied with the other stuff. Has your boyfriend ever done it with anyone else?'

'I don't think so.'

'Who is he?'

'You wouldn't know him.'

'Ah – frightened to tell me his name in case I take him off you?'

'No.' There was, of course, no boyfriend. And now I had heard all I needed to know, I was no longer interested in the company of this very boring girl. 'I think you'd better go now, Angela. After all, I've your homework to do as well as my own.'

'Please yourself.' She flounced out of the house with an unattractive pout of her small lips and I watched her as she walked down the road, wide hips jerking from side to side, chest thrust out, sturdy legs mincing along, ankles swaying slightly as she balanced her weight on the cubed heels of her black plastic shoes. Yes, Angela had been quite useful.

After she had disappeared, I came out of the house and went to sit for a while on the library wall. This had always been the unofficial meeting place for us – the Cullens, myself and, when he could escape, Simon Pritchard. Here we had all gathered as children to play 'walk the wall, close your eyes, if you fall, mud in your eyes' and 'salt, pepper, mustard' on the steps. Here we had met to swap comics, to play marbles on the pavement, to exclaim over ladybirds and hairy caterpillars trapped in matchboxes – with air-holes of course.

Simon joined me after a short while, his eyes darting constantly towards the house on the next corner in case his mother should be peeping from a side window. Edna Pritchard was a spy and I had written her down as such. She was a mean, hard-faced woman and I pitied Simon for having to live with such a mother, one who twitched at her lace curtains all the while, one who watched, it seemed, everyone who passed along Long Moor Lane. She didn't like me. Because she didn't like me, the same devil that had prompted me to defy the nuns often came to the fore in her presence, made me go out of my way to greet her in the shops, to open doors with a flourish, to offer assistance with her loaded baskets. I suppose Simon's mother amused me in a way. His father, Dr Pritchard, was a different kettle of fish altogether, lovable, warm, dependable, humorous. So while I pitied Simon for his mother, I could only envy him for having such a fine father, one I might have chosen for myself had I been granted but half a chance.

'What's up, Simon?' I asked, looking into the pale thin face. He ran a hand through his hair. 'Homework. Bloody homework,' he muttered.

'Don't talk to me about it, Simon. At least you're not getting persecuted for not being confirmed. Just be grateful you're at a non-Catholic school. They're all praying for me up there – rows and rows of little nuns in long black frocks – all praying for Annie Byrne's immortal soul. You can't move for praying nuns. I'd rather meet a praying mantis than a praying nun, any day of the week. Come on, cheer up – it can't be as bad as all that.'

He grinned widely, his whole face changing as he began to chuckle. 'You're having me on again, Anne . . .'

'I'm not – honest. Cross me heart, hope to die, cut me throat an' spit in me eye. It's murder. The headmistress is being nice to me. I'm under her wing and I don't fit because she only comes up to my knees. It's a very sinister situation, because Mother is never nice to anybody. Some of the girls are jealous of me because I'm getting preferential brainwashing in her office. On top of that, the parish priest keeps coming to our house, trying to get me to go to confirmation class with all the ten-year-olds. I daren't answer the door. Even my mother's a bit on their side, though she never sets foot in a church. I feel persecuted. Homework's nothing compared to that.'

'Oh heck. What are you going to do about it then?'

I shuffled along the wall and whispered in his ear, 'My mother's confirmation name is Winifrede. Don't tell anyone – it's a closely guarded family secret.'

'Winifrede?' he yelled before guffawing loudly.

'Shush. Can you imagine it? I suppose I could go through with it and choose a glorious name like Gorgonzola or Heliotrope . . .'

'Or Rumpelstiltskin . . .'

'But it has to be a saint's name. And saints are so good and so boring that it's difficult to pick one out. I think St Peter's about the best because he was a terrible sinner. Then there's always poor old doubting Thomas. I could be Thomasina or Petra . . .'

'Or Petrol-ina or even Paraffin-ina . . .' He laughed so much that he fell backwards off the wall and into a rhododendron bush. I dragged him out and back onto the wall, was just beginning to dust him off when his father's battered Morris stopped at the edge of the pavement and Dr Pritchard stepped out to join in.

'What's all this?' he smiled.

'Your son fell off the wall, Doctor. A couple of years ago that would have cost him two marbles or this week's *Beano*. . .'

'Oh Dad . . . Dad . . .' gasped Simon. 'She's thinking of calling herself Gorgonzola or Petunia . . .'

'I never mentioned petunias . . .'

'Ah. Changing your name, then?' Dr Pritchard joined us on the wall.

I tried to sober up a little. 'It's . . . it's for confirmation. I'm meant to get confirmed and choose another name . . .'

'You already have a perfectly good name.'

'I know, Doctor. But I'm supposed to choose a second one, one I'll never use . . .'

'Just as well,' chuckled Simon.

I gave him what I imagined to be a withering glance, then turned back to his father. 'Simon and I were just discussing the possibilities. But I shan't need a name because I'm not getting confirmed. Do you think that's wrong of me, refusing to be confirmed when everybody seems to want me to go through with it?'

'Especially the black widows . . .?'

'Praying mantis, Simon.' I kicked him gently on the shin. 'Am I being terrible, Doctor?'

The tall man folded his arms across his chest. 'Depends on the reason. Are you just being awkward or are you genuinely against confirmation?'

I thought about this for a while. 'I'm not against it. I just don't want it for me, that's all. On the other hand, I might be acting difficult. It's hard to say.'

'Yes . . . yes. I expect you find it easy to understand what you know and impossible to understand what you feel . . .'

'That's it, Doctor! That's it exactly.'

'There, you see? Another perfect diagnosis. What would the neighbourhood do without me? You are suffering from adolescence, my dear. This is a condition from which you will, unfortunately, recover sooner or later. It's the worst of times and the best of times . . .'

'You're stealing from Dickens again, Dad.'

'I know, Simon.' He shook his head in mock weariness. 'It's so difficult to be original all the time – even for someone as brilliant as I am.'

He was so lovely to be with, amusing, comfortable and comforting.

'How's it going with you, Simon?' he was asking now.

Simon's head dropped a little. 'So-so, Dad,' he mumbled.

Dr Pritchard ruffled his son's hair and I, as witness to this affectionate gesture, suddenly felt jealous.

'Another case of acute adolescence, eh?' said the

doctor. 'Maybe I should work on a cure? Yes, it's a funny old age, is thirteen. Neither man nor boy, neither fish nor fowl . . . though some of you can be pretty foul at times.' He looked at his watch. 'Come along then, son. We mustn't keep your mother waiting, must we? And I've a surgery to run.' He paused. 'The good thing about being thirteen is that you can sit on the library wall . . .'

'And the bad thing,' grumbled Simon, 'is that while you're sitting on the wall, you're not doing your homework.' He looked genuinely troubled and I realized, not for the first time, that Simon was having a problem keeping up at school. And I couldn't offer to help, because that would make Simon and Dr Pritchard think I was some kind of big-head, better than the doctor's son, a real clever-clogs. As for Simon's mother – well, she'd made it plain enough that she couldn't stand the sight of me. Anyway if Dr Pritchard was so gifted, why couldn't he help his own son? Furthermore, I'd enough troubles of my own at the moment, hanging around here or at the Cullens' house to keep out of Higson's way, doing my own homework in fits and starts on the bus, in the dinner hour, in the middle of the night or at tea-time before my mother left for the mill. And when I wasn't doing homework, I was working on the other thing, writing my story, doing research, planning a solution, trying to overcome the sudden bursts of nervous energy that often hit me without warning.

'Are you going home now, Anne?' Dr Pritchard was asking.

'I'll sit here for a while.'

He looked at Simon. 'Go and start Genevieve – no choke.' He tossed the keys into Simon's hand. 'I'll let you drive her home.' Home was only fifty yards away. 'But don't move till I'm a passenger.'

Simon ran round the car and jumped into the driver's seat.

Dr Pritchard turned to me. 'Why do you spend so much time sitting here in the evenings, Anne?'

I shrugged my shoulders lightly. 'I don't always sit here. Sometimes I visit the Cullens or other friends.'

'But you're here quite often – I've seen you.'

'I'm not doing any harm. It's a free country isn't it? No curfew?' My hackles were rising again. 'I like to watch the world go by – is there anything wrong with that?' How dare he? At least I didn't hide myself behind lace curtains, at least I was an observer rather than a spy . . .

'No. There's nothing wrong with that, Anne. It's just that you seem . . . very tense?'

I jumped down from the wall. 'I'm alright, Doctor. Are you ordering me to go home?'

He cleared his throat. 'There are some odd characters about, Anne. You're growing up now, becoming quite an attractive young lady. Some men are not trustworthy – not beyond dragging a young girl off into the bushes or into a car.'

'I can stick up for myself, thank you.'

'That's what they all say – until it's too late.'

He was only trying to be kind, only trying to warn and protect me. Yet I was suddenly angry with him for preaching to me about a subject already so dangerously familiar. Briefly, I wondered how he would react were I to tell him right here and now in the street, tell him that my particular nightmare would not leap from a car or from behind a bush, but would and already did pounce on me in my own house.

'Be careful, Anne,' he was saying now.

I boiled over, erupted with all the fury of a long-dormant volcano, words spilling like white-hot lava, pouring out in torrents to engulf the innocent, missing the guilty by miles. 'Stop telling me what to do! All of you keep telling me . . . nuns, priests, now the flaming doctor . . . have none of you anything better to do? Go to church, get confirmed, do your homework, don't sit on walls. How old will I have to be to make the tiniest decision for myself? I'll sit where I bloody well want – they can twitch all the curtains in the lane and I'll sit here! I'll sit here till midnight if I want to – I'll sit here till tomorrow . . .'

His hand was on my arm now and, in spite of my fury, I noticed the hurt in his eyes. Oh, to hell with him! Why shouldn't he feel pain, why did it always have to be me, just me?

'Calm down, Anne – please . . .'

'Why don't you get in that car and look after your own, Doctor? Why don't you take Simon home and give a hand with his homework? I don't see why you should worry your head over me – I'm just Annie Byrne from across the road, on a bloody scholarship, not fit company for Mrs Pritchard's son . . .'

'Who said so?'

'She doesn't need to say it, does she? I can tell from the way she looks at me, as if she wished I'd crawl back under my stone . . .' Tears pricked my lids and I knew that my anger was about to be drowned.

'And I don't like to hear you swearing. It doesn't suit you, Anne.'

Why wouldn't he fight back, give me something to sharpen my teeth on, give me a good reason not to cry? I'd had enough, more than enough of patience, understanding, condescension.

'You swear, Doctor. I've heard you on Sundays when you're fixing the car. But I'm not supposed to because I'm a girl and only thirteen, is that it? What can you expect of somebody so low-born? I'm one of the servant classes, remember that. Twenty years ago, I'd have gone straight from school at fourteen into the mill or into service. Why – I might even have swept your floors for you, Doctor.' This was my mother speaking. These were her words, drummed into me when I didn't come up to scratch at school. 'I can only be what I am. Education will not make a lady of me.' The tears were a hair's-breadth away now and my voice was rising in pitch, beginning to crack.

'You sound very bitter,' he said quietly.

'Perhaps I am.'

'Don't be bitter. Please, don't be bitter, love.'

I must apologize, I must! Not only had this man never done me any harm, he had always been someone to respect, to revere almost. Why take it out on him?

'I'm sorry, Dr Pritchard.'

'It's quite alright dear – I do understand and I'm not just being kind and platitudinous – look it up in the dictionary when you get home, eh? What you're going through is something that can be explained. All girls go through these changes, these moody and difficult times. You're fortunate in a way, because you can express yourself.' He turned to look into his car where Simon sat waiting patiently, then, almost to himself he said, 'And yet the more intelligent ones often suffer more acutely.' He stared at me for a few seconds then took a step towards the pavement's edge. 'Come and have a chat with me sometime soon. Remember Anne – you're not alone.' As the car hopped away with Simon at the wheel, I heard my mind's voice saying, 'Oh yes I am, Dr Pritchard.' If only he knew!

I stayed near the wall for a while, drying my few tears furtively with the cuff of my cardigan. When at last I regained a degree of composure, I began the short walk home. I watched the 45 as it dropped its passengers, noting that Higson was among them. He walked along on the other side, pausing by the pillar box to light a Woodbine.

From the opposite direction a black shape loomed large, its girth seeming to increase as it passed the ironmonger's, the chip shop, the Co-op on the corner. The cloaked figure crossed the small side street, waddled past the shop on our corner and along the block till it reached our house where it came face to face with Eddie Higson. I leaned on a gatepost and watched this encounter between priest and sinner. They had both seen me; there was no escape. After taking a deep breath, I crossed the road and joined them.

'Father Cavanagh wants a word,' snapped Higson.

I walked between the two men, opened the front door and led the way through to the living room. It was customary to offer food and drink to a visiting priest. Father Cavanagh in particular was obviously used to over-indulging in both – the size of his stomach demonstrated his fondness for food, while his nose, which shone like a rampant flame in the centre of his yellowing face, spoke volumes about the state of his liver. The fire was dying. I made no move towards the kitchen for refreshments and we stood, the three of us, in an awkward semi-circle with our backs to the range.

Higson cleared his throat. He'd probably had a pint or two and I could see that he was not in the best of moods. 'What can we do for you then, Father?'

The priest removed his biretta. ''Tis about the confirmation I'm here. Annie should be attending classes on a Thursday to prepare herself.'

'Aye, well – that's nowt to do with me. I reckon I'll go up for a bath.' Higson turned to leave.

'Sure, 'tis indeed your business, Mr Higson, as well as mine and the girl's. Are ye not interested in this child becoming a member of the Faith, the one true Faith?'

Higson turned on his way to the door. 'You'd best talk to her mam about that. Remember, she's not my kid.'

'She's your stepdaughter, Mr Higson . . .' The priest's voice tailed away as he found himself addressing a closing door. He now turned to me. 'You won't come, then?'

'No.'

He eased his large frame into the fireside rocker. 'Why not? Why won't you come to the classes?'

'Because I'm not going to be confirmed.'

His eyes flashed cold anger. 'If you'd been confirmed when you ought to have been – four years ago . . .'

'Then I would have had no choice. As it was, I was ill in bed. And it wouldn't have meant anything if I'd had no choice, would it? Now, I'm old enough to choose and I am choosing.'

'But your Mammy wants you confirmed,' he said, his tone wheedling. 'Honour thy father and thy mother. You're but a child yet, only thirteen years old. How can you expect to be allowed to make choices? Think of your Mammy now . . .'

Blackmail. How used I was to that! But no, I'd had enough and would not allow any more of it.

Higson suddenly re-entered the room and I almost laughed aloud when I noticed the sheepish look on his face. He was afraid, frightened to death that I might tell this black-robed ignoramus what my 'step-father' was doing to me. After all, hadn't I told a priest once before?

'I think you'd better leave, Father,' he said. 'You'll get nowhere with her once she's made her mind up.'

The priest struggled out of the rocker and stood swaying at the edge of the rug. I suddenly realized that he was drunk, that he was probably often drunk, that he depended on whisky to get him through ordeals like this one. A strange mixture of pity and contempt flooded into me as I stared at the large bumbling fool who granted absolution, administered sacraments, represented the gateway to salvation.

'And you allow her to make up her own mind?' he shouted.

'What do you want me to do?' Higson yelled back, his confidence restored. 'Drag her up to the church by the hair and chain her to a pew? If she says she's not coming then she's not coming and that's that.' He folded his arms and stood, feet slightly apart, obviously enjoying every minute of his own Dutch courage.

'You're supporting her then, in this sin, Mr Higson?'

'He's not supporting me, Father. I don't need supporters.' Especially him. I needed him like I needed a broken neck.

I turned to the priest. 'I think it would be best if you left, Father.'

Yes, he had better go. I didn't want two rows in

one evening – my one-sided argument with Dr Pritchard had been enough. I was relatively safe now. My mother would be back in less than an hour, so I didn't need the priest to hang around and preserve me.

"'Tis small wonder she has never honoured her stepfather, Mr Higson. You are not fit to have in your care the soul of a young girl, especially a young Catholic girl. Are you ever to Mass these days? Ever to Confession or Holy Communion?'

For answer, Higson opened the door wide. When the priest made no move, he shouted, 'Get out and don't come back. Just leave her alone, will you? Come on you old drunk before I kick your backside out of here.'

Father Cavanagh pointed a finger, none too steadily in Higson's direction. 'You are excommunicated,' he pronounced.

'Excommunicated?' Higson threw back his head and laughed. 'Listen lad, I quit – bloody years ago, I can tell you. Get back to your whisky bottle and your rosary beads.'

The priest, speechless and purple in the face, stumbled out of the room. Higson followed him, slammed the front door, then came back into the living room. He was shaking. In spite of his brave words, he feared the Church. Like all Catholics, he had been indoctrinated from infancy and even now, he half expected a bolt of lightning.

'Bloody cheek!' he joined me in front of the range, his hands reaching out for the little warmth that came from the dying fire.

'Get that fire seen to and make some tea,' he snapped.

I stared at him levelly, forcing myself to meet the

deep-set and bloodshot gaze. Knowing that I was inviting yet more trouble, I stood my ground. 'Do it yourself,' I said quietly. 'I'm not your servant.'

He pulled me roughly towards him, forcing my body against his and I struggled in vain to free myself. When would I learn to keep my big mouth shut?

'You're asking for it, you are,' he whispered, his spittle wetting my face. 'And you're going to get it. Know what I mean?' Yes, I knew what he meant. And no, there wasn't time for him to start on me just now.

'Are you going to do the fire?'

I nodded.

'And make the tea?'

'Just let me go.' He stank of beer, sweat, tobacco and bad teeth.

He released me so suddenly that I fell back against the range oven, banging my head on the mantel shelf. Whether it was the sharp pain, or simply a culmination of all that had happened that evening, I didn't know, but something in me snapped and I flew at him, my hands clawing at his face then beating against his chest. Someone was screaming, sobbing, cursing and only when his hand came over my mouth did I realize that these sounds had been coming from me. His breathing was laboured now and he had to struggle to hold me still.

'Listen, you little bitch,' he gasped. 'I've told you before and I'll tell you again – you do exactly as I say. If you don't, then I'll get your mother and you, the bloody pair. Understand?'

I tasted salt. Something warm and thick was dripping from my mouth. He howled like a wolf and sprang back, but even then my teeth maintained a

166

bulldog grip on his finger until he brought up the other hand and sent me reeling across the room with a single flat blow. I caught sight of myself in the flower-bordered mirror, saw blood on my face and ran to the kitchen to swill his filth down the sink. My stomach heaved and I vomited noisily into the white porcelain, my hands gripping the edge to stop me sliding to the floor. I must hold on, had to keep sane. This was not the way, could not be the way. I was behaving like an animal, a wild beast – no. Animals did not carry on like this – they had order, a kind of discipline in their lives. What was happening to me? Where was my order, my discipline?

Some time later he came through to the kitchen, the stink of Dettol, with which he had no doubt bathed his hand, mixing with all the other scents that clung to his malodorous person.

'Try that again and I'll kill you,' he announced, his voice dangerously quiet.

Kill me, I wanted to say. *Kill me and you'll hang.* But this was not the time. Today had been a disaster and yet, out of this series of storms a plan was forming, spreading its tiny roots in my brain. Although I was uncertain of the details and felt very unsure of the outcome, the seeds were sown and I knew I would have to be not just cool, but icy cold to carry it out. So I shovelled coal and made the tea while he nursed his damaged finger.

When my mother came in, she commiserated with him about his poor hand, said that people should be sued for leaving nails sticking out of window frames. My, it was a mess and no mistake – if she didn't know different, she'd swear he'd been bitten by a mad dog. As she knelt at his side to apply a bandage, he looked at me over her bent head, a smile of triumph playing over his ugly, weathered features.

My skull ached where it had hit the mantelpiece and I was tired to the bones of all these charades. Yet I summoned up the energy to feel annoyed at the sight of my mother kneeling at his feet, the soles of her shoes crusted with steel rings, her hair dotted with cotton, the back of her work frock still damp from her labour.

'I hope you're well insured,' I said to Higson. 'You can get lockjaw from a rusty nail – there's no cure. It's a horrible death too.'

'Ooh, Annie.' My mother glanced up from her task. 'What an awful thing to say.'

'Well – I'm only being practical. It stands to reason – anybody who climbs ladders for a living should be well insured. It's just common sense, that's all. He might break his neck, mightn't he? I'm off to bed now.'

She got up off the floor wearily. 'Just you wait there, our Annie. Is that alright, Eddie? Not too tight?' He grunted and she turned to lean against the table as she spoke to me. 'All I ask, Annie, is for some peace when I get home from the job. Going on about him getting lockjaw and breaking his neck – it's not very nice, is it? Can't you have a bit of respect?'

'People have to earn respect,' I said, as calmly as I could.

'Have you two been arguing? Have you? Can't I even go to work now without worrying about you giving cheek, Annie? What's got into you these days, eh?'

'Ask him. He's your husband, supposed to be the man of the house . . .'

'Annie!'

'Oh leave me alone, Mother. Just leave me alone!'

I stamped out of the room and slammed the door behind me.

'Let her go, Nancy,' I heard him say. 'Bloody priest's been down again mithering her – she's got a right bee in her bonnet over it.'

'She still won't get confirmed then?'

'Nay. She as good as threw the drunken old bum out of the house.'

'Oh Eddie – she didn't . . .'

'Just let it go, woman. For goodness sake – can't you see she's at a funny age . . .?'

Yes, he'd said that before, hadn't he?

I switched on my light and looked across into the Cullens' front room. Martin was standing in front of the fireplace staring into the mirror. He did that a lot these days. The single bare bulb in the centre of the parlour (as Mrs Cullen called it) shone down on Martin, making his hair a lighter red than it really was. He was a strange lad, the odd one out in that large family. Although he was Josie's twin, the two of them were like chalk and cheese. While Josie continued open and voluble, Martin seemed very reticent at times, as if he, like me, were planning something, a secret he could not share.

I took the diaries from the drawer and added the notes about Angela, who had confirmed what I already suspected. The plan unfolded as I wrote and I scribbled furiously in spite of my aching head. It was dangerous, but wasn't my situation already fraught with danger? This would simply accelerate matters, take me off the knife's edge, put me in charge. If I lost my gamble, then at least I would go down fighting instead of remaining as I was now, a sitting duck for him to take pot shots at whenever he pleased.

To ensure that I would not weaken, I forced myself to go back yet again through these notebooks, reaffirming that I was right, that these things had really happened to me, that none of it was my fault. I must fuel my anger, feed my resolve, make sure that I would not relent at the last moment.

Oh Mam, Mam . . . what would you say if you could read all this now? What did you think of me all those years ago when I told you I hated him, that he made me shiver, that his eyes were sly? Did you care? I bet you thought I was an odd little thing because of all I'd been through, losing my Daddy and all. Then that stray bomb had been enough to frighten any small lass and make her wary . . .

I pushed the book away and stared blindly through the window. Yes, she probably thought I'd been shell-shocked for a long time, because the blast had been deafening, terrifying. We had sat there under the table for hours until a warden, his feet crunching on splintered glass, had dragged us out. We were the lucky ones, we residents of Ensign Street, because half the next road had been blown to kingdom come. For weeks after that, I had searched for Rosie Turner, not believing, not wanting to accept. Then gradually, Rosie had faded, slipped away out of focus, leaving just a vapour-trail of memory. Now that too was gone and I could not even imagine what she had looked like.

Everyone had said that I was an unusual child, 'highly-strung' according to my mother's family, 'precocious' in Sister Agatha's book. My mother probably never expected me to react to Eddie Higson in a normal way, because I had not led a normal life. Few war babies had enjoyed a normal life.

I left the table, switched off my light and went to lie on the bed. Yes, I would do it – I would, I really would! Remember, I told myself. Remember the first beating . . .

We got back to the house on the wedding night. For reasons I could not fully understand, I shut myself in the small front bedroom with a pair of scissors and painstakingly cut to ribbons the awful pink dress I had been forced to wear. He beat me that night and my mother did not succeed in stopping him. So, on the night of my mother's wedding, I received the first of many such beatings, beatings I would never forget, would not allow myself to forget. Because my mother did not approve of his hitting me, he always got me on my own after that first time. I could not fail to notice how his face changed as he hit me, those small piggy eyes glazing over, the mouth wet, wide and panting.

I groaned and turned over, forcing myself to recall line for line what was written. I must face up to the past before I could organize the future.

Christmas 1946. My mother out shopping. Higson bending over me. Faded colours in the peg rug, handmade on winter evenings from strips of clipped-up skirts and coats. A shine on the range, black-leaded earlier that day. Festoons on the ceiling, an orange lantern in the doorway. On the dresser a small Christmas tree with arms like bottle brushes. Smells. Pie, yeasty bread, mince tarts. Cherry Blossom polish on the boot that rolled me over towards the heat. A bitter taste in my mouth, vomit laced with hatred. Sounds. A hiss as an air-pocket exploded from the fire's red depth. Breathing. Panting. Gasping. He was dying. Only a dying man would make such noises. Following him.

Standing in the doorway as he leaned over the slop-stone, his back towards me, legs apart, one hand moving in front of him. A splash, then a groan as he reached over to seek support from the wall . . .

Remember Tom. 'Are you alright, Annie?'

'Yes.' I could never tell Tom about the beatings, could not let him know how naughty I was. Just as I couldn't tell my mother. Why? Why couldn't I say, *Mam, he hits me when you're out. . .?* Because she might side with him, might agree that I deserved my punishments. There was always a reason for the beatings. I'd been playing on the bombsite, giving cheek, answering back . . . always a reason. But what had triggered him? He was alright at first, just ignored me. This question I could never answer.

Don't sleep, not yet, not now. Allow the anger, feel the pain. Where were you, Mam, all those times when I needed you, when it first began in Ensign Street? At the mill? Shopping? Passing the time of day with a neighbour, a friend? Shall I blame you, my mother?

The move to Long Moor. The baths. Soap bubbles, lather on my chest, calloused hands caressing my body. A huge finger, topped by a black-rimmed nail, forcing, pushing, tearing . . . no!

Sweat bathed my head, ran in small rivers down towards the pillow. There is me, just me. But my memory is clear, my anger deep, my body strong. He will never know my fear, my sweat, my tears. No-one to help. No-one to trust. Just me, only me. I am Annie Byrne. Annie Byrne is a thirteen-year-old girl with a secret. Holy Mary, Mother of God, where are you? Sleep is coming. My thoughts are disjointed, I am wandering lonely as a cloud, Mr Wordsworth. Too tired to get up and take off my clothes. Tomorrow, I shall be all creased. Like his face, tramlines on the forehead, white in ugly brown skin. A shallow forehead. No brains. Shallow. A pool of water, a pool of blood. Soon there will be blood. Every month, my blood. Whose blood, Annie? Whose blood? Wake up, that's it, wake up! Whose blood, Annie?

I stumbled out of bed and tore off my clothes, flinging them carelessly on to the chair, groping in the dark for my nightdress. Strange, I thought, how a plan could be finalized in a dream. It was complete. Before my blood came, I would have his. Or die trying. The proverbial worm was about to turn.

The dreams were bad that night. I was hitting out at everybody, screaming at Dr Pritchard and Simon, setting fire to Edna Pritchard's lace curtains, yelling at my mother, calling her a traitor. He eluded me completely. Always there was a long corridor between me and him. He stood far away, yet near enough for me to see the leer, the Woodbine smoke curling from a corner of his lip. I walked, but could not run. They reached out from doorways trying to stop me and although I eliminated them one by one, my mother, the doctor, Father Cavanagh, I still could not reach the right one, the one at the end with the ladder on his shoulder. Obscenities poured from my lips, echoing, bouncing off close walls.

I woke sobbing in the miserly light of dawn, my pillow saturated with tears, the dream shattering into fragments for which I groped desperately, trying to piece them all together before true consciousness would deny me access.

Remember . . .

13

The Worst of Times

There was a gap at the end of the bath, a space between end panel and wall where the wooden maiden sometimes stood with towels airing on its rails. With my eye, I measured the gap, then I climbed, fully clothed, into the empty tub as I ran through this final rehearsal of my piece. The mechanics might prove easy in comparison to the real acting I would have to do, the smiling, the sigh of pretended pleasure, the encouraging flutter of eyelashes.

I was not old enough for this. Female survivors in the books had been mature. Young ones always fell prey to Vikings, Romans, Cromwell's soldiers. Those who escaped were women of experience, twenty, thirty years old. But I had learned from them, hadn't I? Hadn't their small triumphs become mine? The books were fiction, I knew that. Yet writers must get their ideas from somewhere, from some central store of actuality and fact. I must believe, I must be prepared.

It would happen right here on the bath mat, black and yellow with a penguin woven into the middle. That awful big thing would be pushed inside me, would tear me apart on the penguin rug. Afterwards, he would have to kill me, because once it had happened, I would not be able to remain silent. Already I felt half-crazy some of the time, my nerves stretched like tight wires, my whole body tense and waiting. Rape would make me crack, I knew it.

So now, I must become the aggressor, because if I continued to do nothing, then it might not even be rape. Sometimes, in the newspapers, it was not rape because the woman didn't say no. My word against his – he would never risk that, because he knew I had ten words for every one of his. And I wasn't a woman, I was just a girl, he'd go to prison with enough proof. Yes, he would kill me. Then he would sneak out of the house and get what they called an alibi, probably from his brothers. It would be murder by person or persons unknown. I could not allow myself to become a file in the police station, a file never closed.

Joannie Walker. I'd never met her, never known her, but her name was burnt into my brain by my mother and the *Bolton Evening News*. Joannie Walker had disappeared in 1948 when she was seven years old. She was used as an example to all of us, don't talk to strangers, don't get into a car or a lorry. Her body had not been found and the file remained for- ever open. Well, I had never talked to strangers, had never got into a car. I smiled grimly as I climbed out of the bath, my assessment complete. No, Mam. I don't talk to strangers, but it happens all the same in your lovely bathroom with your delightful husband. The thing you don't talk about because it isn't quite nice – it's already happening to your daughter. Dear me, what a terrible world. Isn't fish an awful price these days and shall I put the kettle on?

No! NO! She did love me, she couldn't know, mustn't know . . .

Tonight. It had to be tonight or I might snap completely, lose my nerve and forget all my carefully made preparations. Now, while I was on my guard, I could and would orchestrate the whole thing. What if it didn't work? What if he got me? No . . . better now, while I was keyed up for it. What if I killed him? They'd put me away – not quite in prison, I probably wasn't old enough for that. But they'd put me away, wouldn't they?

Oh stop what-iffing, Annie Byrne! No alternatives. Just you. Just you and him, you or him, one winner, one loser.

It was Thursday. My mother left early on Thursdays to work out her two rooms' timesheets for the foreman. I went down to see her before she left, looking at her as if for the last time.

'What are you staring at, Annie? Is my face dirty or something?'

'No. I was just thinking how pretty you are.'

'Me? Don't talk so soft. Mind you, I was alright in my day, I can tell you.'

'You're still alright. It's just that your face is a bit thinner than it was. How old are you?'

'As if you don't know! Anyroad, never ask a woman her age. She'll usually lie through her teeth even if they're not her own. If she doesn't lie, you still can't trust her, because a woman who'll tell her age can never keep a secret.'

'You're only thirty-six. . .'

'Aye. Going on ninety.'

She tied her mill apron round her waist, a large pocket divided into two sections by a single vertical seam. This was where she kept the spools when doffing, in this pocket she smuggled home empty tubes for firewood. I watched her as she dragged a careless comb through soft Titian waves, kept my eyes on her every movement while she found her bag and purse, changed slippers for work shoes, drew on the dark blue cotton-spotted coat.

'Are you alright, Annie? You're standing there like cheese at fourpence. Is there something you want to tell me?'

I stared at her and knew in that moment that I would never be able to tell her. Even if I ignored Higson's threat to harm her, I could not destroy this little woman because I loved her too much. That it would destroy her I did not doubt. The idea of it, the thought of it, would tear her apart. And I knew her, better than he ever would. I recognized her power, knew her temper and her determination, saw the steel behind the softness, realized that a mighty though untutored brain nested beneath those gentle curls, behind the smoke-grey eyes. Yes, if I were to tell her now, or ever, she would take off the coat, pick up the meat knife and wait. Small she might be, cowardly she was not. The consequences would finish her. It was my battle and I would fight it alone.

'No. I've nothing to tell you. I thought I might go for a walk, freshen my brain up a bit.'

'Good idea. But make sure you . . .'

'I know. Finish my homework.'

'And don't backchat Eddie. You're getting just a bit big for your boots, you are. I don't know.' She shook her head. 'Give them a bit of education and they know it all.'

'Would you marry him again, Mother?'

'What a bloody daft question and me nearly late for the bus! The answer to that is for me to know and for you to wonder about . . .'

'You wouldn't.'

She tapped the side of her nose. 'Keep it out, Annie. There's things you just don't ask about. He could be better, could be worse. And so could you. I'm off. Make sure the kettle's boiled for him.'

After she had left, I felt lonelier than I had ever been in my life. Even the ticking of the mantel clock seemed slow and I found myself wishing that he would hurry up, come home, get this thing started and done with as quickly as possible. I sat still as a stone at the table, hardly daring to breathe as I heard the gate squeak. I listened to the scrape of his ladder as he dragged it up the yard, heard him walking slowly, so unbearably slowly, towards the back door. Sputum rattled in his chest and I felt myself flinch as he spat another of his vile messes on to the flags outside.

His brow was raised in surprise when he found me sitting in the living room. His meal was in the range oven and I got it for him, watching his eyes widen in further astonishment as I set the dish in his place. I usually left him to collect his own meal when my mother was out and I hoped, desperately, that my behaviour was not too uncharacteristic. Still, in for a penny, in for a pound – the old saying flashed across my mind as I hung the cloth on the oven door.

'Stew again?' he asked as he removed the pan lid from the plate.

'Thursday's always stew. Payday tomorrow.' I tried to smile, but my face, numb and stiff, did not quite obey me.

He ate noisily like a pig at a trough, slurping the food, chewing small lumps of meat with his mouth wide open. He was revolting.

The spoon clattered into the dish. 'Talking to me now, are you? What's brought this on?'

'Just trying to be civil. Nothing wrong with that, is there?'

I walked carefully across to the mirror and began to brush my hair. This, according to the books, usually got them going. I gripped the brush tightly so that my hand would not shake and tossed the waist-length hair over my shoulder, stroking it in what I imagined to be a sensuous way.

'Somebody been looking at you, then? Some daft lad got his eye on you? I've told you before – if I find you with anybody . . . who is he?'

'Nobody. Not that I'm aware of anyway.'

'Keep away from the lads. Do you hear me? You do as I say.'

'There are no boys. That's the truth.'

I heard him scrape back his chair. 'Taking an interest in yourself, aren't you? What's all this in aid of?'

I turned and placed the brush on the edge of the table. My voice trembled slightly as I spoke. 'It's dirty – my hair, it needs a wash. I'll just go up and see to it.' Again, I half-managed a tight smile.

'Aye, well. Happen I'll come up and rinse it out for you. It doesn't do to go leaving soap in your hair – you might get nits.' He licked his lips salaciously. 'I'll be up in a minute to give you a hand.'

Halfway up the stairs my right knee suddenly buckled and I saved myself by gripping hard on the cast-iron handrail. I was breathing fast, too fast and my head swam. I managed the last few steps with difficulty, stumbled into the bathroom, turned on the taps and crumbled a violet-scented cube into the water. For a few moments I sat on the rim of the bath, forcing myself to calm down and breathe at a proper rate. After removing my clothes, I took a last look at myself in the glass over the washbasin. Whatever happened in these next minutes, I would never be the same person as I was now. If he didn't come up after all my preparations, my will would crumble. If he raped me, then I would probably not live to look at my own face again. I tried to say farewell to the white shape in the mirror, but I couldn't quite do it. Because if I won . . . oh God, how could I win against a grown man? What the hell had I been thinking of? This was crazy . . . mad . . .

A creak on the stairs, then a heavier footfall. He is coming. Remember the plan, pull yourself together. I am in the bath. My hands are shaking as I reach into the space at the end. The poker is heavy, iron with a solid brass handle. I place the poker in the bath, not quite under my body but out of sight on the side nearest the wall. Bits of ash and coaldust float on the surface. Do something! I reach for a sponge and squeeze violet-scented water over my body. If I survive this day, I shall always hate the smell of violets.

The door is opening. He walks across the room and sits on the edge of the lavatory seat, his eyes glued to my breasts. The end of the poker digs into my calf. But this is better than leaving it in the space, better than hoping for the chance to kneel, reach over and grab it. What if he drags me out of the bath right away? This time, he intends to do it, all of it, because he has received my unspoken message. I soap my body slowly, following the plan's minutest detail.

He is coming towards me now. He kicks off his shoes, tears away trousers, shirt, pants. The muscles on his arms are like great ropes, his chest is broad and covered in ugly black hair. I try to smile, try not to look at that horrible threatening thing that sticks out in front of him, blue-veined and swollen.

'Get up. On your knees,' he says hoarsely. I obey cautiously, anxious not to disturb the poker. Now! I grope for a towel, one eye closed. 'Just a minute.' I try to make the pain sound real. 'I've got soap in my eye.' Behind the large yellow towel, I reach down for the poker. Yes, his eyes are closed as he caresses himself. Thank goodness for this man's predictability! The other hand comes down to touch my hair. Suddenly I am cold, cold and angry. Nothing to lose now. He is guiding my face towards . . . A corner of the towel is in the bath. It is easy, so easy. The fool keeps his eyes closed as I swiftly drop the towel and drive the tip of the poker between his outspread thighs. All my strength goes into this action, one hand on the handle, the other halfway down the blackened metal shaft. There is no need for, no chance of a second blow . . .

I stood at the side of the bath, watching as he began to drown. He had jack-knifed forwards, face down in the water while I scrambled sideways to avoid his falling body. There were bubbles above his head and I stood as if fascinated by the patterns they made as they broke the water's surface. I climbed over his legs which lay crumpled on the penguin mat, reached down and pulled out the plug. No, I would not commit murder. No, I would not ruin my life, have myself marked as a criminal. He was not worth that, not worth anything.

Now I shook, trembled so violently that my teeth, chattering hard and uncontrollably, bit into my tongue several times. Without drying myself, I pulled on my clothes as quickly as numb fingers would allow, then, still shivering, I wrapped a towel around my frozen shoulders. There were fewer bubbles now and his face was still immersed in the last of the water. Steeling myself, I bent over, took two handfuls of wet crinkled hair and heaved him out of the bath on to the floor. Vomit and bathwater spewed from his mouth and over the linoleum. Like a robot I carried on with my task, fetching and carrying, wrapping the contents of his stomach in wads of newspapers, carrying these bundles downstairs and throwing them to a sizzling death in the depths of the fire. I took the long-handled string mop and cleaned the bathroom floor, shifting the dead weight of his inert body so that I might reach all the water and mess. The automaton I had become lifted his clothes from the lavatory seat and, holding them at arms' length, carried them across the landing and dropped them onto the bedside rug. Finally, I fetched the poker and dug it deep into the fire, turning over the blackened newspapers, piling coal on top of the evidence.

I huddled over the fire for a long time, my ears straining for the sound of movement from upstairs. When, after an hour or more, I had heard nothing, I crept back up the stairs and stood in the bathroom doorway. His eyes were open, his mouth twisted in agony. My knees began to shake again, so I grabbed the doorframe to steady myself as I addressed him. 'You'd better get up, hadn't you?'

'Help . . . me,' he groaned.

'No!' Then my voice dropped to a whisper. 'You'll have a bit of explaining to do now, won't you?'

His face was white with shock and his body, usually tanned, seemed to be turning blue with cold.

'Listen, you,' I went on, determinedly fortifying myself with words. 'What you've been doing to me these last few years is not right. I'm thirteen now and

I know what you've been up to right from the start. I've read about creatures like you – you're dirty, dirty filthy scum. Pity the Germans didn't finish you off – they'd have been doing the world a good turn for once. But I'll do it. If this kind of thing carries on, I'll get you.'

He cried out in pain as he tried to move and I took a firmer grip on the jamb to stop myself from falling. 'I swear on my own father's death that you will pay, Eddie Higson. I might even tell my mother what you are, because I'd rather be dead and I'm sure she would too if she realized what she's been living with all these years. Anyway, you're in no position to carry out your threats just now, are you? Take this as a warning, Higson. I could kill you right now and nobody would blame me. But I won't because I can't be bothered. As long as you realize I'm capable of it – understand? Touch me again and I'll kill you. Touch me again and you'll never be able to sleep, because you'll know that one night I'll come after you – with a big sharp knife.'

I closed the door and left him there naked and frozen halfway to death already. I had to negotiate the attic stairs on hands and knees because my body was suddenly disobedient, impossible to manage. Sugar for shock. I crawled into my room and reached up for the bottle of pop on the bedside table, my hand trembling so violently that I could scarcely unscrew the cap. I poured the liquid down my burning throat, my head filled by the sound of the glass bottle as it rattled against my teeth.

The door shook on its hinges when I pushed myself against it, forcing my spine to straighten while I fought to control the involuntary violence of nerve and muscle. The bottle slid from uncertain fingers, contents spilling as it travelled across brown and beige lino towards the long fringe of my bed-cover, a reject from the mill, woven in Bolton sheds out of cotton spun by my mother, or someone like her . . . He was dragging himself across the lower landing. We'd got the quilts two for the price of one. And some towels. Yes, I remembered the towels, four green, two blue . . . Someone moaned in the room beneath mine, moaned then howled like a stricken animal. And some flannelette sheets, pink with the hems not done properly.

Instinct made me crawl, in the end, onto my bed where I immediately lost consciousness. There was no bridge between wakefulness and sleep, no more thinking time, because I simply collapsed into a welcoming darkness, remaining motionless and without dreams until morning.

I woke with a start at about seven o'clock. The house was silent. All the horror of the previous evening flooded into my mind and I staggered across the room to stare at the colourless face in the tallboy mirror. Had I really done all that? I looked round. The floor was stained with orange pop, the bottle lay between door and bed. And yes, something more, a new pain, a grinding discomfort . . .

'Annie? Annie?'

I cleared my throat. 'Yes?'

'You'd best come down, love. There's been a bit of an accident . . .'

I took off my crumpled clothes as quickly as I could, pulled on a nightie and my dressing gown, then went carefully down the two flights of stairs.

My mother was sitting at the table, a cup of tea in her hand. She poured a cup for me and I sat down opposite her. My hand shook as I guided the tea to my parched lips.

'Annie? Annie, love? Whatever's the matter?'

The room swam. 'My . . . my period,' I managed, before falling into her arms as she rushed to my side. She helped me on to the sofa.

'Dear God in heaven,' she muttered. 'What a to-do, eh? He's in hospital – fell off his ladder yesterday, caught himself in an awkward place. And as for you, lass – well, you look like a boiled sheet . . .'

She covered me with the blue work coat and began to rub some life into my hands. 'I had to get the ambulance to him . . . looks like you should have gone and all. Will I get the doctor?'

I shook my head. 'No. But I need a couple of Aspros.'

I watched her as she bustled about making more hot tea for me, filling a hot water bottle, fetching aspirin and yet more tea.

She perched on the edge of the sofa. 'You'll be alright, lass.'

'Yes, I know.'

Then I was sobbing, crying my heart out into that beautiful hair as she rocked me in her arms. She was crying too and her body felt so small, so frail as I hung on to her, my mother, my own lovely tiny mother.

'Oh my poor lass, my little girl,' she whispered between her own sobs. 'It's alright, love. I know all about it, I know . . . I know.'

Oh Mam, Mam. You don't know. God forbid that you ever must.

14

The Best of Times

He was in hospital for weeks. According to my mother, who visited him regularly, his injuries had required surgery and he remained in considerable pain for a long time. Strangely, this knowledge gave me no satisfaction and I began to realize that revenge was not really what I wanted. My prime concern was for my own safety and for my mother's wellbeing and I knew that there was still much to fear if and when his recovery became complete. But I managed, for some of the time, to block my mind of such worries, to postpone them at least, because there was little to be achieved by wearing myself down even further.

The window round was temporarily taken over by a friend of Higson's, a drinking companion from the Star. So although this man took his share, we were not too badly off as there was just the pair of us to feed during this period.

I mended slowly and needed several days off school; my mother put this lethargy down to my age, said that starting periods was worse for some girls than for others and that I was one of the unfortunate few. I was sent to see Dr Pritchard who, after peering into my eyes, declared that I was not anaemic, that I was a disgustingly healthy specimen and if all his patients were like me he'd be out of a job in ten minutes flat.

'Still getting the blind rages?' he asked with a twinkle in his eyes.

'Not so often now. I . . . well . . . cry for nothing and laugh at stupid things – things that aren't really funny . . .'

'Hmm.' He leaned back in his chair. 'Hormones. They're a bugger, you know.'

I lifted my chin in pretended defiance. 'Yes, they're a bugger, Doctor.'

He laughed heartily at this and I noticed once again what a handsome man he was, especially when he laughed and made crinkles at the corners of those gentle blue eyes. He ran a hand through the untamable mid-brown hair and I realized that Simon had inherited the straight thick eyebrows from his father, whose own forehead was usually completely hidden as he never seemed to plaster his hair back with Brylcreem. It was a strong face too with features that were clearly defined, especially the square jaw which had a slight cleft not quite in the centre.

'And what makes you cry?' he asked now.

'Books, mostly – stories about people. And Beethoven on the wireless.' For a reason I could not explain, I felt able to tell this man anything. Well, not quite everything, but I did not mind him knowing me.

'Yes,' he said, 'Beethoven can hurt a lot. He was a great big bear with a sore head, that man. Bad enough having all that music rattling round in your skull without going deaf as well. Sometimes, I think only people who've led a tortured life can write good music – or good books, come to that.' He looked me up and down. 'You need a holiday,' he announced.

'I've never had one.'

'I know that. But you need one all the same.' He pondered for a few seconds. 'How about a quick day trip to Blackpool with Simon and me? Time I had a day off too, come to think of it.'

I stared down at my shoes. Mrs Pritchard wouldn't like it. Mrs Pritchard wouldn't allow it.

As if reading my thoughts, he said casually, 'Just the three of us?'

I found myself grinning at him. 'Can I be cheeky, Doctor?'

'Have you ever been anything else?'

'Well, there's somebody else who needs a day out just as much as I do. Please could we take my mother too? Make it a Saturday or a Sunday – he's still in hospital, so she could go.'

'Hmm. Of course your mother can go with us.' He paused. 'I take that "he" is your stepfather?'

'Yes. But I . . . don't call him my stepfather.'

'You don't like him.' This was a statement rather than a question, but I answered all the same – 'No, I don't.'

He rose and walked to the window. With his back towards me he spoke, almost to himself, 'Not easy living with somebody you don't like. Strange thing, a family. A bit like workmates, I suppose. You just have to get on with the situation whether you're suited or not.'

'You can change your job, Doctor . . .'

He turned round, seemed almost surprised to see me, as if he'd been about to lose himself in deep thought somewhere.

'That's right, Anne. But you can't change your family, can you? Would you if you could?'

'Not my mother.'

'But you'd change him?'

'I'd swap him tomorrow for a . . . a jar of tadpoles. In fact, I'd pay somebody to shift him.'

'Does he beat you?' The ground was becoming dangerous, yet I still answered, 'Not any more.'

He leaned on the window sill, hands thrust into his trouser pockets where I heard coins jingling. He was daft with money, was Dr Pritchard, never kept a wallet, stuffed it into any old pocket, often left a heap of coins out by his car when he'd been messing about with hub caps and wheel nuts. Yet whenever we found this treasure, we always, always gave it back to him. Even when we'd found a whitey one day – a whole five pounds – we'd taken it to him straight away . . .

'What does he do then, Anne, to make you dislike him so?'

I shrugged my shoulders as lightly as I could. 'He eats with his mouth wide open, slurps his tea at a distance of about three feet from the cup, snores like a stuck pig . . . shouts, loses his temper . . .'

'Hits your mother?'

'Once or twice he has, yes.'

'I thought so.' He came back to sit at his desk. 'The important thing is not to let yourself hate him. Hatred makes people bitter and negative, eats away their personality, destroys creativity – hatred is a waste of energy.' He leaned back in his chair and stared at me. 'My advice to you is that you must ignore him as much as possible. He won't go away, but at least you won't notice him so much. And we'll have a lovely day in Blackpool while he's nursing his . . . wounds.' He smiled wryly. 'How did that happen, by the way? I didn't see him – come to think

189

of it, I don't think he's ever been to the surgery – he went straight to casualty in an ambulance, didn't he?'

'Yes.'

After a short pause, he asked again, 'How did it happen?'

I looked as steadily as I could into the calm blue eyes. 'He fell off his ladder.'

'Strange place to get hurt falling off a ladder. Your mother says he must have landed very awkwardly to sustain such a severe injury.'

'Yes. Yes, he must have landed awkwardly.'

I could no longer meet the constant gaze and I began to fiddle about with the buttons of my cardigan as if getting ready to leave. He knew something, I could sense it. The pores on my arms opened and I felt tiny hairs prickling as they stood on end. I was aware of his eyes on me, knew he was probing my soul for the answer to an unspoken question. He was clever, yes. But could he read minds?

'What's troubling you, Anne? What is it really?'

Oh to have someone like him for a father! 'Nothing I can put words to, Doctor. Probably just hormones or whatever you call them.'

'Sure?'

I finally managed to look him in the eye. 'Positive.'

Please God, it was all over now. Surely Higson would not dare, not again. Or would he? And if I did tell this lovely kind man what had happened, what would I achieve? There'd be no home for me because I'd be put somewhere safe, or, if they locked him up, no window-cleaning money for my mother, no way to pay the rates or the mortgage . . .

'Some day you will tell me, Anne.'

I shifted in the chair. 'I'd better be going, Doctor.

The waiting room's pretty full out there . . .'

'I always have time for you, my dear.'

Kindness. These days I could scarcely bear it without tears threatening. And suddenly, I longed to run round the desk and hug him, to have some good, clean contact with a man who might have been my father had the fates been good to me. But I let the moment pass and rose hurriedly to leave.

'Saturday morning, then – nine o'clock sharp,' he said. 'I'll let you know if I have any trouble getting a colleague to stand in for me, but I think it will be alright. We'll pick you up.'

'Thanks, Doctor.'

I sped home to give my mother the news, expecting her to be as delighted as I was at the prospect of a day out.

'You what?' She threw the oven cloth onto the table, her grey eyes wide with surprise and shock. 'What the hell are you up to now, Annie?'

'Nothing. I'm up to nothing. He just said I needed a change for the good of my health and I asked if you could come too. What's wrong with that? What's wrong with a day at Blackpool?'

She lowered herself into a chair, her eyes still glued to my face. 'What's wrong? Well, if you don't know, then I wonder if it's worth my while telling you!' She picked up the cloth and began to fold it this way and that as she chose her words. 'Look, Annie. They're a different class – a different type of folk to us . . .'

'That's true. Dr Pritchard always votes Labour . . .'

'He never does!'

'She votes Tory, of course, so they cancel one another out. Simon says it's funny on voting days. They have this agreement not to go because it's a waste of time with them voting opposite, then they both sneak out and vote. Of course they smile secret smiles afterwards, thinking they've outdone one another . . .'

'Eeh well. You'd think he'd vote Tory, him being educated.'

'That's where you're wrong, Mother. And I thought you were the one who wanted to do away with class. You've always told me that if I got an education I could be anything, mix with anybody. I'm just an early starter, that's all. And I'm starting mixing now and you're coming with me.'

'It's not the same, Annie love. They're born to it.'

'Born to what?'

She bit her bottom lip before whispering, 'Money. They're born to money.'

'Rubbish, Mam! She was, perhaps. But he works hard for his wages, you know that. He's a worker the same as you.'

'Aye. And he's a walking flaming dictionary as well. I wouldn't know what to say to him, Annie, honest I wouldn't.'

'Now who's being daft? There's no need for you to be lost for words – ever. Who goes round all the chippies begging crossword pages out of the wrappings? Who's read all of Jane Austen, most of Charles Dickens and half the blinking *Canterbury Tales*?'

'Mucky book that – what I could understand of it . . .'

'I'll get you a translation – a modern version – for Christmas. If you'll come to Blackpool.'

She got up and began to set the table, reaching plates from the wall-cupboard and cutlery from a drawer in the small sideboard. 'I'll think about it.' She clattered a cup into its saucer.

'No you won't. You're coming.'

'Who says so?'

'I say so! Just for once, let me be the boss, eh?'

'Just for once? You've always been a wayward little devil . . .'

'Yes, but I nearly always do what you say. Nearly . . .'

'Aye. And how near's nearly?'

I decided to try another tack. 'Right then, have it your own way, Mother. Dr Pritchard and Simon will be here at nine o'clock on Saturday. What do I tell them? She can't come, she's got a previous appointment with the Prime Minister, just popped out to number ten for a chat? Or shall I say you're not well, then he'll fly in with his box of tricks and prescribe a day in Blackpool? Of course, I could tell the truth and say you won't go because you're not good enough for them.' I paused and watched a sparkle arriving in the quick grey eyes.

'Honest to God!' she exclaimed. 'What did I do to deserve you, eh? What harm have I done in this world? I've done my best, worked my fingers down to the bone . . .'

'Made sure you got an education,' I mimicked.

'Shut up, you cheeky young minx, you! By God, you'll make one hell of a politician, you will. I reckon you could make the bloody birds fly backwards. Whatever shall I wear?'

'Clothes, Mother.'

'And what about my hair?'

'There's nothing wrong with your hair. Put a scarf on anyway – Blackpool's a windy place . . .'

'See?' she said to the sideboard. 'See? She's got an answer for everything, this one has.' She looked back at me. 'And you know I'm frightened of cars. Especially his. Every week, there's half a dozen men pushing him home.'

'Yes, well – don't make any rude remarks about his car. He's very attached to it.'

'So I've noticed. He operates on it every Sunday just to keep it alive. It should have had the last rites years ago, that thing. I reckon it's held together with faith, hope and plasticine.'

'Mother. Are you a coward?'

'No. But I'm no Amelia Whatsername either.'

'Nobody's asking you to fly the Atlantic – or even the English Channel. All you've got to do is sit in a car, smile, get to Blackpool and enjoy yourself.'

'With the doctor?'

'With the doctor.'

She reached into the range oven and brought out a pie, crusty-gold and steaming through the herring-bone pattern across the top.

'Smells good,' I remarked.

'Oh that's right, butter me up. Go and get the spuds and carrots out of the kitchen. They're drained and in the steamer. And I'm blinking well drained too!' she called as I disappeared.

I smiled to myself as I collected the vegetables, listening while she grumbled – for my benefit, of course. 'Sit in a car and smile all the way to Blackpool? That's if we ever get there in that bone-shaker.' Bang, bang – that would be the salt and pepper arriving on the table. 'I don't even like Blackpool that much.' Bang, bang – sugar bowl and milk jug. 'And I've nothing to wear.' Bang – probably the pie knife.

I re-entered with the vegetable dishes. 'Did you say something, Mother?'

'Yes. I'm talking to the fire-back. I might as well, mightn't I? You'll probably sail through life getting your own road, you. Remember how you flattened Sister Agatha when you weren't the size of two pennorth of chips? Then you went and got round that Mother Thingy at St Mary's and you with no intention of getting confirmed. Now you think you're getting round me as well, don't you? I should tell you where to get off, it would do you some good. Anyroad, how come the doctor invites you out? What about the rest of his patients?'

'Well, he'd need about six buses, wouldn't he?'

'So why choose you?'

I grinned. 'Because I'm special.'

'Aye. Special and damned cheeky.'

'He knows I'm cheeky – he said so today.'

'Not a bad judge then. Oh well, happen I'll go if the rain holds off.'

The rain held off. After greeting our benefactors rather stiffly and properly, my mother clambered into the front passenger seat where she sat bolt upright while Simon and I stifled our giggles in the back. Fortunately, the engine was quite noisy and we were able to hold a whispered conversation in comparative peace.

'Your mother looks terrified.'

'She is.'

'Mine's furious. She's probably taking it out on the furniture, costing us a fortune in Johnson's Lavender . . .'

'Oh. Does she know you're with us – with me and my mother?'

'I didn't mention it and I don't suppose Dad did.

They . . . er . . . don't talk much. She knows we're going to Blackpool, though.'

'Oh dear. Did she want to come?'

He shook his head slowly. 'You must be joking. Blackpool's common – it's where street people go. You'd never catch my mother in Blackpool. She tolerates Southport on the odd occasion, but that's just because the shopping's good.'

'What are you two whispering and giggling about?' called Dr Pritchard as he negotiated a left turn while my mother, white as a ghost, clung to the door and to the edge of her seat.

I struggled with my laughter. 'Oh we're just . . . passing the time of day. Isn't it a lovely car, Mother? Genevieve, she's called.'

'Yes. Lovely,' she muttered between clenched teeth and I dug Simon in the ribs to stop him exploding.

To be fair, Dr Pritchard's driving was sufficiently distinctive to strike fear into the heart of the most seasoned traveller. My mother, who had never been in a car before, was quite shocked when our driver repeatedly gazed round to indicate buildings of architectural merit, when he took his hands from the wheel to illustrate a point, when he seemed to be colour-blind with regard to traffic lights. Even I, who had made several journeys in cars belonging to the parents of classmates, was rather unnerved each time he cursed after one of his many near misses.

'Bloody fools,' he grumbled. 'Weekend drivers, you see. They come out like a rash on Saturdays and Sundays.' He put his head out of the window to yell at a rag and bone man, 'Oi – pull over. I'm a doctor on urgent business.' The poor ragman heaved his pony and cart on to the pavement while we jerked forward, gears grinding and wheels screaming.

At last, my mother could contain herself no longer and I sat back to enjoy what would surely follow.

'Dr Pritchard?'

'Yes, Mrs Higson?'

I gripped Simon's hand tightly; I dared not look at him properly, but from the corner of my eye I could see that he was stuffing a handkerchief into his mouth.

'You drive like a maniac, Doctor. I feel as though we're in the hands of a raving lunatic!'

'What?' We ground to a shuddering halt next to a fence. Everyone bounced forwards and back again with a spine-jarring abruptness. Simon and I, who could contain our mirth no longer, climbed out of the car and pretended to become engrossed in the wild flowers at the roadside. But we stayed very close to Genevieve – we would not miss this for the world.

'Does she realize what she's taking on?' whispered Simon.

'I'll bet five bob on my mother any day of the week.'

We spat on our palms, then shook hands to seal the bargain.

My mother's voice came strident and clear through the car's open windows. 'It's a wonder we're not all dead! Four sets of red traffic lights you went through in Preston.'

'Three. And they were amber.'

'Four, Doctor. I can count, you know.'

'Ah yes. But can you drive?'

'No. I can't do major surgery either, but I like to be damned sure that the bloke with the knife is flaming qualified!'

'I am qualified.'

'Ah yes. As a doctor or as a driver?'

I looked at Simon. 'Fifteen–love to my mother.'

'Mrs Higson, I drive every day of the week . . .'

'Do you now? Pity they did away with the bloke with the red flag then, isn't it? Though I daresay you'd have run him over in five minutes.'

'Now, let's be sensible . . .'

'How many notches on your gun so far, eh? It's a wonder they don't clear the roads when they know you're coming. How did you manage to miss that poor old lady a couple of miles back – error of judgement, was it? I reckon she's gone home now to have her heart attack in peace . . .'

Simon sighed heavily. 'Thirty–love,' he admitted grudgingly. Words poured from my mother's mouth in a seemingly endless stream and I smiled as I remembered how she'd worried about what she would say to the doctor. That she was enjoying this scene was obvious, but I found myself hoping that things would not get out of hand . . .

'Mrs Higson. Would you like to walk the rest of the way?' A nudge in my ribs said thirty–fifteen.

'Walk? Walk? I'd rather flaming well crawl than put my life in your hands for another yard!'

There followed a very brief pause, then both doors opened and my mother and Dr Pritchard spilled simultaneously and untidily out of the car.

'Come on, Annie!' she cried. 'We'll find a bus home.'

'Oh Mother – be reasonable . . .'

'Reasonable? Me? Tell him to be reasonable.' Her face glowed and I caught sight of the beauty she had once been. She turned the full force of her not inconsiderable temper on him now. 'I don't know about Pritchard, this here's Dr Jekyll! Put him behind a steering wheel and he changes into a monster!' While she, my darling Mam, had turned into a human being, feelings on show, little body bristling with energy, her eyes wide with passions that were usually well hidden. Had she ever been like this with Higson? Oh no, never a cross word there, seldom a sign of life in her at home. What a transformation! But here she was with a real man, a normal man, a person who allowed her to express herself, someone who had dragged her into the light where she could be seen as she really was, a powerful and rather splendid woman. I bit my lower lip. She had been like this with my father. Although I remembered little of their relationship, I knew I was catching sight of it now. It was healthy, beautiful, yet disturbing, because I realized now how much she had lost, how much she had failed to regain in her second marriage.

Dr Pritchard walked round the back of the car and came to stand next to Simon and me. 'Anne is not walking,' he pronounced. 'She has had some medical problems of late and I insist that she rides in the car.'

My mother drew herself up to her full height, straightening her spine and raising her chin as she spoke. 'Medical problems? Huh! she will have bloody medical problems once you've wrapped her round a lamp post two or three times. She'll be six months in hospital the road you're driving!'

The tall man took a step towards this very tiny but very angry woman. He looked down at her for several seconds then suddenly, he threw back his head and laughed. Dr Pritchard was endowed with one of those laughs that come straight from the belly, a laugh that could not be ignored or denied. It was more infectious than 'flu in hot weather and soon Simon and I were rolling about in the long grass, doubled up with the pain of trying not to laugh at my mother's expression, crippled by the agony of not being able to echo the doctor's merriment. Then we heard a loud scream and we turned to see if she had resorted to violence, but the scream was just the beginning of her own laughter and there they were, the pair of them, doubled up over Genevieve's bonnet and howling like a couple of banshees. Several motorists slowed down to view the spectacle and Dr Pritchard straightened up to wave them on with a very Shakespearian flourish. And suddenly I forgot to laugh because the moment was too precious. I stood very still and watched, drank in the sight and the sound of my mother's joy, for I had not witnessed such an event for years.

When we finally got back into the car, she was mopping happy tears from her cheeks and Simon pressed two half-crowns into my hand. I tossed one back to him. 'Easy money, Simon – too easy. She was never going to lose.'

We didn't reach Blackpool until after eleven, because Dr Pritchard travelled the rest of the distance like a tranquillized snail and this unprecedented phenomenon caused even more glee in the back of the car. But by the time we got there, the doctor was calling my mother Nancy and she wasn't calling him anything – not maniac, not Doctor, but not David either, though she had been invited to use his Christian name.

Blackpool itself was not a revelation – we'd all been there at some time or other. But what Blackpool did to us, together and separately, was very revealing. We decided to walk the Golden Mile, but didn't quite manage it, because we stopped to gaze at just about every shop and sideshow. My mother had ten minutes with Gypsy Rose Lee who told her that she had a marvellous future full of travel and money. Dr Pritchard advised a second opinion, so she double-checked with Gypsy Marina May two blocks away and was warned about tall strangers, the number seven and Fridays.

We ate all the things that were bad for us and thoroughly enjoyed them – fish and chips with vinegar dripping newsprint onto our fingers, candy floss, toffee apples, rock, black peas in thick cracked cups. We all had hats. I got the inevitable Kiss Me Quick, Simon had an Indian headdress, my mother sported a blue-and-white-striped cardboard boater while Dr Pritchard, not to be outdone, bought an enormous Stetson with 'Fast Shooter' emblazoned on the band. He was like a big kid. He was first in the cage for the tower, first on the caterpillar, dodgems, big wheel. It seemed that he needed to pack everything into this one day and I found myself wondering how a man with such a pronounced sense of fun managed to cope with his grim-faced wife and that never ending queue of ailing patients.

I also discovered that I was hoping that everyone who saw us in the street would think we were a family, mother, father, brother and sister, a proper family having a day out together.

As evening threatened to end our brief holiday, we walked to the front and sat on a bench facing the sea. We were all exhausted and the almost hypnotic sight of the advancing tide lulled us into temporary silence. On the horizon, the sun was slipping away to make another day somewhere else, to warm another patch of earth's scattered soil. It left in its wake a trail of glorious colours from orange through aquamarine to violet, all beautifully patterned with a lacework of tiny mackerel clouds.

Dr Pritchard was the first to speak. 'Of such visions dreams are made. Isn't that right, Simon?'

Simon glanced sideways at me then muttered quietly, 'He's going to make us play the dream game. He always did this when I was a kid – even got my mother to join in.'

I continued to stare at the sea, feeling that somehow there were only the four of us left in the world, that we had slipped through into an alternative dimension where we could remain untouched and untouchable. My troubles, everybody's troubles were of the past, from another time and place. This was contentment; this was all I ever wanted.

'My dream,' continued the doctor, 'is of a world without pain. Of course, I don't want people to live forever, but I'd like life to be full of joy and empty of war and argument. We should all die in our beds at three score and ten, no doctors, no nurses, no hospitals . . .'

'And no job for you,' said my mother.

'And no interruptions!' After a pause, he went on, 'Every night it would rain enough for us to drink and grow food. The days would all be sunny and full of fun. Silly dream for a grown man, isn't it?'

I didn't think it was silly at all, not now, in this magic place.

'What would you be in a world without doctors?' my mother asked.

'Oh, a mechanic, definitely. I'd have rows and rows of Genevieves to work on and at weekends I'd be a racing driver.'

'That accounts for it,' she answered. 'And you'd soon need a doctor, wouldn't you?'

'Nancy,' he sighed. 'Have you no soul? Your daughter has, I think. What's your dream, Anne?'

I closed my eyes. 'Well, if I can't stay here forever, I suppose I want a lot of children. I'd hate to have just one on its own. In my dream there is no religion and no politics, nothing to fight about. Everybody is equal. There are definitely no nuns and priests, no popes and kings. But the main thing is that my father comes back. I don't see any sense in the way he and the others died, you see. It's all politics and religion. They got rid of the Nazis and now we're getting White Russians and Red Russians – it's ridiculous. So. My dream is just as silly as yours, Doctor. I want the Jews to have peace, the Russians to stop being greedy, the Americans to stop piling up those awful bombs, people to stop hurting one another. Above all else, I want my mother to be happy.'

'I am happy, Annie.'

Yes, she was. In that moment when I opened my eyes after speaking my dream, I saw that her face was glowing with some light that came from within, that she looked about twenty years old. And I knew that I had spoken her idea of Utopia as well as my own.

Simon's dream was an odd one, I thought. I knew he was good at drawing, but when he said that he wanted to paint a picture as good and as meaningful as the *Mona Lisa*, I was taken aback somewhat. Surely he would be a doctor like his father? Wasn't that what usually happened – or was I being as naive as my mother sometimes seemed to be? I sighed sadly as I recalled Simon's homework problems. The rolling tide and the magnificent sky would not put everything right. Simon's talent lay in his hands rather than in his head – he was creative, probably talented, but not intellectual.

My mother took a lot of persuading, but she finally succumbed when the three of us threatened to put her over the rail and into the sea.

'I just want our Annie to do well. Course, I'd like a few other things, little things, but they're not important.'

'They are important, Nancy. All dreams and ambitions are important.' Dr Pritchard reached over and touched her arm. 'You have to tell. We've all done it, we've all made fools of ourselves – it's a matter of honour.'

'Oh well,' she sighed. 'If it's a matter of honour . . . I'd like for her to be a lawyer or maybe a teacher. And I want her to have a happy marriage and some nice children . . .'

'What about yourself, Nancy? What do you want for yourself?'

She paused momentarily. 'If anybody laughs, I'll belt them!'

'We won't laugh, Mother – honestly.'

She took a deep breath. 'A green frock with a matching stole.'

I stared at her in amazement. 'Mother! Whatever would you do with a green frock and a matching stole?'

'I'd go ballroom dancing with some of the girls from the mill. Yes, I think I'd like to learn dancing. It's good for you, you know.'

Dr Pritchard stretched long legs and crossed his ankles. 'A green dress. Yes, that would suit you very nicely, Nancy.' It was obvious that the man was moved, because he turned away as he spoke, his voice gruff and slightly choked.

I felt a huge lump in my throat. She'd never had anything, not for herself. It had all been for the house or for me, yet she never complained about being deprived. And all she wanted now was a dance frock. Yet I knew, felt certain that had she been educated, she would have outstripped us all. I would get a paper round and buy the dress for her. But what would be the use of that? He'd never allow her to go dancing on a Saturday night. And she'd already refused to let me deliver papers. It was something I would remember for the rest of my life, this simple desire for a green frock.

When we reached home that night, I felt that we each knew and valued the others a little better or at least, differently, though Simon was to remain something of an enigma for many years to come. Even when we'd played the dream game, he had held something back. Simon would be holding back forever, but I didn't know that then.

There was no going back to that enchanted time, that small island of contentment in 1953 when I learned so much about my mother, about myself – and about others too, when friendships were cemented between me and Simon, between my mother and Bertha Cullen, when we were free to choose where we went and what we did. And that was a strange alliance too, between my mother and Bertha Cullen, the one so houseproud and exacting, the other seemingly slapdash and fancy-free. But these two women were big of heart and they embraced each other's good points and bad, seemed to complement one another perfectly. The bond between Nancy and Bertha was thoroughly forged that year and Higson never managed to sever it. My mother owed her life to Mrs Cullen and her family – but for them, she might not have survived when her unborn child was beaten out of her, but this was never mentioned between the two women as far as I knew.

We picnicked on the Jolly Brows twice, Mrs Cullen and most of her brood, my mother and I, eating wedges of Hovis and cheese out of waxy bread-wrappings, drinking fizzy lemonade from shared enamel cups. Martin always stayed separate from the rest of us, tagging along with his rusty bike, then snatching his sandwiches before walking away hurriedly. I tried to speak to him several times, but he blushed and mumbled unintelligibly, so I learned to keep my distance from him.

Higson limped home in September. He spoke seldom, simply sat staring for endless hours into the fire, though when he looked at me with those sunken sharp eyes, I knew he was taking his revenge gleefully by refusing to go back on the round for several months, thus forcing my mother to take a morning job cleaning at the Star. For many weeks I watched her shabby little figure disappearing down the road each morning before I left for school, witnessed her exhaustion as she prepared to go out again in the evening for the five o'clock to nine shift. This was my fault. I had dealt him a blow from which, it seemed, he would never allow his wife to recover.

It was Bertha Cullen who set him to rights on Christmas morning when she arrived with my gift. He sat huddled over a roaring fire while my mother and I prepared the dinner. There was seldom any Christmas spirit in the house and this year the absence of festive cheer was even more marked than usual because of the silent figure near the hearth. He hadn't even stirred himself to go out to his brother's house this time and the living room felt chilled in spite of the blazing fire, as if Scrooge himself was sitting in our midst to dampen our pleasure. Perhaps we sensed the atmosphere more acutely because of the brief weeks of freedom we had enjoyed, because we had learned what life was like without him.

I was peeling carrots when Bertha rushed in unannounced as usual and I heard him spit into the coals when my mother and I exchanged seasonal greetings with our visitor. Bertha had a truly amazing capacity for ignoring Eddie Higson altogether, but on this occasion she decided to speak to him. With a broad smile on her face she approached his chair. 'Well then, Eddie – I 'ear as 'ow yer've been given th'all clear fer t' New Year.'

'You what?' He looked up at her.

'Well, I've a friend as works at t' Royal Infirmary, like. She says yer right now – yer can go back ter work in January.'

He shifted uncomfortably in his seat. 'Happen I might,' he said.

My mother's face brightened perceptibly. 'That means I'll be able to give up at the Star!' she cried.

'The money's handy,' muttered Higson.

Mrs Cullen cast a sideways glance in his direction. She had never had much to say to him since the night of the clearout and now she directed her attention towards my mother. 'Never mind t' bloody brass, Nancy. Tha's fair wore out wi' workin'. Now as 'e's right, tha mun stick ter th' evenin' shift an' bugger the Star.' She puffed out her already enormous chest. 'My George might not be up ter much, but 'e's never made me work over the odds. Pace yerself, lass.'

Higson picked up the poker and looked briefly but meaningfully at me before using it to stoke the fire. He seemed shrivelled somehow, as if the 'accident', of which he had never spoken to me, had almost finished him physically and mentally. But no, the anger was still there. I could sense it as he smashed the poker into the coals, could see it in the small sly eyes that sometimes seemed to spit venom in my direction. Had I stopped him? Or had I simply postponed the inevitable . . .?

'Come on, Annie. Open Bertha's present,' my mother was saying now.

'Our Martin chose it,' beamed Mrs Cullen. ''E said as 'ow yer'd like it.' It was a single strand of pearls. 'They're not real, like. Only our Martin said as they'll suit you a treat. 'Ey Nancy – I reckon 'e's got 'is eye on your Annie . . .' The poker clattered noisily into the grate.

'Thank you, Mrs Cullen,' I said.

'Aye well. You deserve nice things, lass. Allers got yer 'ead stuck in a book – yer want ter get out an' enjoy yerself sometimes.'

'She's got to study, Bertha,' said my mother. And Mrs Cullen who, although she did not understand it, now appreciated my mother's need for me to succeed, picked up the large box of crackers I had bought for her family to share, made her goodbyes and beckoned me to follow her to the front door.

''Ey Annie, luv,' she whispered.

'What?'

'I made it up.'

'Made what up?'

'About 'avin' a friend at th' Infirmary. Only I reckon 'e's sat on 'is laurels fer long enough, that bugger.' She began to giggle like a girl. 'Ooh, what am I sayin'? Pity they didn't cut 'is bloody laurels off altogether, eh?'

'Behave yourself, Mrs Cullen.'

''Ey, don't you start laughin' an' all. It were 'is laurels as were the problem – am I right? Does 'e still 'ave ter sit on one o' them rubber rings what you blow up wi' a bike pump?'

'No!'

She wiped her eyes. 'No, listen. I'm bein' dead serious now. I've reckoned 'is number, I 'ave. T' longer as 'e sits there doin' nowt, t' less likely 'e is fer t' get back on t' round. That bloody mate of 'is 'll be buyin' it off 'im next news if we don't do summat. But 'e'll go back now, mark my words.'

And he did. But this proved to be a mixed blessing, because although my mother was able to give up her morning job, he seemed to grow stronger with every passing month and I noticed, gradually, that he was watching me again. But he made no moves in my direction and I managed to stay out of his way most of the time, studying with friends, visiting the Cullens, taking advantage of the fact that I was now old enough to make my own decisions about when I must arrive home and when I must go to bed.

Another year sped by, another Christmas, another birthday – my fifteenth. For eighteen months, he and I had spoken scarcely a word to one another and my mother had by now given up her attempts to enforce an armistice between us. Her own relationship with him was obviously strained and there was little speech or laughter in the house except when he was absent from it. I continued to grow and by the summer of 1955 I was five feet seven inches tall, weighed a good nine stones and was very strong. And he continued to watch, never coming near me, seldom speaking to anyone but watching, always watching.

I threw myself into my work, because I had just twelve months until my GCE examinations; now, there was no time for sitting on walls, little contact with others except fellow students, few opportunities for fun or relaxation. The term drew towards its close. Mother St Vincent remained concerned about me, but she had long since given up on the idea of my confirmation. The 'little chats', which we both enjoyed thoroughly, carried on and she was pushing me gently towards Oxbridge. My mother had been proved right yet again, because the 1950s had indeed opened new doors for the working classes and for women. But although I had decided that I would not leave the North, I did not enlighten the little nun about my intentions. Law and medicine were both available in Liverpool or Manchester and I would go no further from home. To leave my mother alone with him after all her sacrifice would be a crime for which I would never be able to forgive myself. Yet I kept my counsel and agreed with everything the headmistress said.

We spilled out of school on the last day of our fourth year, made our goodbyes, promised to meet sometime during the holidays and went our separate and widespread ways – Leigh, Farnworth, Westhoughton, Affetside, Bolton. The lucky ones would be going away for holidays, perhaps abroad or to Scotland. I had been offered a holiday in Maria Hourigan's caravan, but I could not go. Nothing in this world would entice me away from home, for I would never trust him alone with my mother. He feared me, had good reason to fear me. But without my constant vigilance, he would surely make her pay for what I had done to him. And my mother had already paid enough for me.

As I rode home on the 45, I found myself noticing, as if for the first time, how the world around me had changed during my short life. In the streets I saw girls who no longer looked like younger versions of their mothers, girls with a style of their own – the princess line was slowly making its exit and wide colourful skirts with waspie waists were taking its place. By the side of these girls walked lads with long slicked-back hair, drainpipe trousers, bright socks, deep-soled shoes and knee-length jackets. I realized that something of a revolution had been taking place while I wasn't looking, that young people were demanding attention, seeking a slot of their own in society, snatching a place for themselves, a place that had never been offered or even imagined by adults. They had their own spokesmen too – James Dean, Bill Haley and a new star called Elvis. The music and the words of the Fifties screamed rebellion and I was beginning to notice it.

Everything was changing. Even grown-ups seemed crazy during this decade, entering the throw-away society with enthusiasm as if attempting to deny that there had ever been war, shortages, rationing. Plastic-coated coffee tables with fly-away edges began to appear in the sitting rooms of the nouveau riche, while in thousands of homes a large glass eye called television sat in a corner, often discreetly hidden behind tiny doors. Someone called Fairfield Osborn was warning us that we were using up the world's resources too fast, but nobody heeded him. It was an age of madness, an era of excitement and carelessness. I wondered who they were, these people with money to throw about, because they certainly didn't live in our road. My mother still ran a household on five pounds a week, paid coal and electricity bills, fed three people and managed a mortgage with that paltry sum.

The bus stopped and I got off opposite the library. Martin Cullen, who seemed to have found his tongue when he acquired his first Teddy Boy suit, yelled a greeting across the road and I waved at him. Yes, everything was indeed changing. Now was the time for me to speak out, to join the rebels in my own way. But no, there she was at the gate waiting for me, her hair made fiery by the rays of an afternoon sun. I threw my satchel into our small patch of garden and lifted the tiny woman off her feet, pretending to be happy to have six whole weeks off school. One day, I promised myself, she would be comfortable and my education would buy her peace of mind and provide a passport out of the mill. For now, I must continue to act my part, must keep her as happy as I could manage. This was not the best of our times, but the best was yet to come.

Part Two

. . . is a Whisper to the Living

I

Martin and Simon

On 13 July 1955 Ruth Ellis was hanged for murder. The campaign for the abolition of capital punishment was reinforced by this terrible occurrence and for weeks after the event the newspapers argued the issue. Annie Byrne sat in the reading room of Long Moor Lane Library and wondered anew about man's inhumanity. How far had Ruth Ellis been driven? For how many months or years had she suffered before committing this so-called premeditated crime?

Annie replaced the paper in the rack and picked up her book. They would let you have just one book at a time, so she had been reading a novel each day during the first part of her summer holidays, losing herself in pages of the historical romances which had become something of an addiction now. Every morning she would stand at the library gates waiting for the staff to arrive, an impatient foot tapping the ground if the door remained closed one minute after ten o'clock. On Saturdays, she always chose an extra-thick book to get her through till Monday morning. This was escapism and she knew it. It was exactly what she needed. In a world that hanged desperate women, that forbade blacks and whites to travel together on the same bus, a world that had recently sent six million Jews to a filthy and unspeakable end, one needed to escape before madness set in. There was so much to run from now, because everybody's life seemed to hang by a thread, a slender strand that might so easily be snapped by another Hiroshima. So Annie divided her time into three parts, housework, study and reading. The first left room for thought and she got through it hurriedly in order to engage her mind elsewhere, in a place where she might ignore the Bomb, forget man's current cruelties by reliving those of the past, deny, by burying herself in the intricacies of algebra and Latin, that she might become the next Ruth Ellis.

She stepped out into the sunlight and stood for a moment on the top step to watch her particular bit of the world go by. Did any of these people worry about the atom bomb? Would any one of them care if they knew that in their midst there resided a potential Ruth Ellis, a girl almost grown to womanhood, a young female who might easily commit a premeditated murder any day now? Twice she had struck down her stepfather, twice she had allowed him to remain alive. The next time he might not be so lucky and Annie Byrne could well end up in prison or, if the event should be postponed until she reached her majority, then the gallows would be used again.

From Bryant's corner shop a figure emerged, jaunty and carefree in Edwardian suit, thick-soled shoes and bright orange socks. He called across the road, 'Ho there, a pike – prick me this dog's hide,' thereby identifying himself as a Cullen, harkening back to the time when the seven of them had tried to ruin her performance in a school play. Not that she hadn't recognized him in the first place – anybody who walked about looking like that was seeking attention.

He called again. 'Oy – Freckles – go blind with all that reading, you will.'

She turned to go back into the library, but in a trice he was by her side, a wide grin stretched over his own freckled face, the oily quiffed hair stained a darker auburn by liberal applications of grease.

'D'you like me hair?' he asked, turning his head so that she could see the slick folds at the back. 'It's called a DA – that stands for duck's arse.'

'Thank you, Martin. I always wanted to know that.'

'Anyroad, you shouldn't be reading. You should be helping yer mam.'

'Oh. Why?' Cool green eyes swept over him.

'Well . . . because you should, that's all. All girls help their mams.'

'And boys – aren't they supposed to help in the house too? Or is there some special dispensation that gets them out of it?'

He shuffled uncomfortably. She just wasn't the same any more, was she? She used to be great fun, did Annie Byrne, always up to mischief. Why, Annie and his twin sister Josie used to be the best pair of tomboys going – all the way through the juniors the two of them had plagued the living daylights out of everybody. Annie had always kept up with the lads, roaming the brows on conker hunts, trekking all the way down to Trinity Street to stand on a soot-covered bridge getting train numbers, usually ready for a fight too. Now she talked . . . well . . . posh like, made you feel as if she knew things, as if she was better than everybody else. He'd heard that she still capered on at school and was popular for her sense of humour but at home – well, she seemed as miserable as bloody sin. And it had taken him two flaming years to pluck up the courage to talk to her now she'd gone posh. Oh heck! But there was something about her, something special that made his stomach churn, made him angry and happy at the same time. Was he, Martin Cullen, famous hard case of this parish, smitten with a lass?

'Boys do different things,' he muttered. 'Our Josie and our Ellen help me Mam, do the house and that.'

'And what do you do?'

'I mended the washing line this morning.'

She looked towards heaven before stepping back through the library door and he called after her, 'I fetched the coal in!'

Annie walked past the startled librarian who probably wondered why she had returned so soon. She slammed the door of the reading room and threw herself into a chair. So he'd brought the coal in, mended the bit of rope where Bertha Cullen, on rare occasions, hung her dripping grey wash. Not that Annie wasn't fond of Mrs Cullen – oh she was, she really was, but Martin was becoming a real pain these days, a pain Annie could well do without. He was forever hanging about outside the house with his motley group of Teddy Boy friends, always casting the odd glance up towards her bedroom window where she would sit reading or scribbling.

Yes, perhaps she should go out sometimes for a walk over the Jolly Brows or the top field, get some fresh air and a bit of sun. But Annie only went out in the evenings. During the day she stayed in, emerging only when her mother left for the mill, then walking miles to visit aunts, friends, acquaintances from school. And if she were to come out in the afternoons, Martin would no doubt find her, follow her and regale her with tales of dances at the Palais where he could 'pass himself off as eighteen', or, worse still, he would fill her ears with nonsense about the fights down Folds Road, clashes with rival Teddies. Still, he wasn't all bad, she knew that. Somehow, she realized that his heart was not really in it, that he was out to impress, that he was not truly aggressive like some of the others.

She turned to glance through the window at the little garden at the back of the library where rhodo-dendron leaves gleamed rich and dark while overblown roses tossed their weighty heads in the morning breeze. Because there was no school, Annie had been up since six o'clock as usual, raking out ashes and setting a new fire in the range. By 7.30, she had beaten the rugs, washed, rinsed and mangled the overnight soak and had hung the clothes to dry in the back street. The wash had to be out early so that it might be brought in before the lamp man came or the ragman's pony ploughed through the streets while his master called 'rag-a-bone, donkey-rubbing-stone . . .' By eight she was finished for the day, floors swept, steps scrubbed and stoned, kitch-enette cupboard wiped out, sink bleached, table laid, kettle bubbling on the range. The next two hours had been spent in the attic studying until library opening time. Yes, Annie helped her mother alright. She did what little she could in that deadly atmos-phere to help the poor benighted soul who had brought her into the world. But for how much longer would she be able to carry on? He had recovered now; he was watching, waiting, planning . . .

She jumped up from the table, opened the door and walked past the wide-eyed librarian, then after checking that the coast was clear, she left the library and went down past the doctor's to the Milk Bar where she ordered a coffee. The place was empty, the juke-box mercifully silent. Annie took her book to a corner table and began to read.

Across the road, Nancy Higson carried her husband's breakfast dishes through to the kitchen. She felt tired, bone-weary, worn out after twenty years slaving in a cotton mill and the same number of years worrying about money. But she carried on, filling the bowl, washing and drying the pots, carried on just as always for the sake of peace and for Annie. At least the rows between her daughter and her husband had virtually stopped now. Funny how he'd given over cursing and screaming at Annie since the accident. Something to be thankful for, she supposed. And there were people a lot worse off, weren't there? But oh, she wished things could be . . . different. Annie couldn't bear to be in a room with him for more than two minutes and it was such an uncomfortable way to live, trying to please everybody and finishing up pleasing nobody, least of all herself. But she was a good girl, was Annie – the house fair sparkled of a morning when she was off school. 'Course, she'd be over at the library now, picking a book to read.

Eddie Higson sighed, looked out of the window to assess the weather and took a Woody from a paper packet of five. The room was stuffy and overheated because of the range, but he said nothing. Nancy wanted a better cooker for the kitchen, a safer one, she said – one that wouldn't fight back and spit at her. The range had been good enough till now, so she could sod off for her new cooker. Anyroad, it was likely all down to that daughter of hers putting fancy ideas about because of all that education. Bloody education. The girl should be setting off for the mill any day now and if he'd had his way, he'd have driven her down there with a whip if necessary.

'It's half past ten, Eddie,' Nancy was reminding him now. 'Best of the day'll be gone if you don't get going.'

'Don't start your mithering, woman. I'm on my way.'

He nipped his cigarette and placed the stub behind his ear then shuffled through to the yard for his bucket and leathers. As he steered the newly acquired ladder cart through the gate, he grinned to himself, dragging the feet of the ladder across the bottom of a snow-white sheet. 'That'll show the young bitch,' he muttered, pausing to feel for the cigarette-end behind his ear. He'd have his day with that one as sure as eggs were eggs.

As he walked away, he didn't notice Nancy standing in the gateway shaking her head. After he had disappeared, she painstakingly removed the large double sheet from the line. It would have to go in the dolly for another soak – oh, if only she could afford one of those washing machines! Well, the cold war between Eddie and Annie was far from over – the thick black lines on the sheet were proof enough of that.

'How did that happen, Mother?'

'Ooh Annie, you made me jump!' Nancy clutched the sheet to her chest. 'Eddie caught his ladder on it . . .'

'Again?'

'It was likely an accident, love . . .'

'An accident? He did the same thing last week because he knows I'm doing the washing.'

'I'm sure he didn't mean it.'

'That's a load of rubbish, Mam and you know it. He's mean and spiteful – oh God how I hate him!'

'Now you just stop that kind of talk, Annie. He puts food in your mouth, doesn't he? Do you think you'd be at St Mary's if he'd never worked to keep us all going? He took you on, I've told you before. He took us both on . . .'

'And killed your baby!'

They stared at one another across the small yard, then Nancy, her voice low, said, 'I think we'd better go inside, don't you?'

After closing the outside door carefully, Nancy rounded on her daughter. 'What do you expect, eh? You treat him with nothing but contempt – oh yes, I've seen the way you look at him. He helps us pay our way and don't you ever forget that!'

Annie's laugh, which was not really a laugh at all, made Nancy shiver. 'And you're grateful? Grateful to a lazy lump who should have been out cleaning windows for two hours at least? Grateful because you're forced to scrimp and save while he pours shillings down his throat in the Star? Oh, Mam.' As usual, in her anger, Annie fell back into her old way of speaking, vowels flattened, ends of words missing or distorted. 'You took him on, just you remember that. You took on a murdering bastard! He was fit for nowt when you married him and he hasn't improved over-much.'

'Annie!'

'I'm sorry, Mam. Sorry you have to bear the brunt of it. I'll go upstairs now before I say any more.'

Nancy Higson stood alone in the kitchen, her knuckles as white as the sheet she twisted between her fingers. Yes, she'd taken him on out of pity. Or was it out of fear? Had it been panic that forced her hand, panic because Billy had died and left her with a child to support? Would she have got another chance if she hadn't leapt at Eddie Higson's offer so readily? Or could she and Annie have managed alone? They'd have been re-housed, possibly somewhere nice – and she could have got a grant for Annie's needs. Dear God, why had she married him? He was a cruel man, of that she was sure. His victim had needed no grave, but he had murdered and in cold blood too. Nevertheless, Nancy felt duty-bound to defend her husband no matter what he had done. Marriage, like death, was inescapable and a thing to be endured.

Annie climbed to her room at the top of the house. From her window she watched Martin Cullen leaning on his gate. He took a comb from a top pocket and smoothed his fashionable quiff. A strange lad, that one, she thought as she took her seat and opened the Seton novel. He was brainy but stupid. Briefly, she wondered how somebody could be clever yet daft at the same time, but then she did know others of the same ilk: nuns, priests, teachers who were all clever but as thick as two short planks when it came to common sense.

The angry exchange with her mother had been upsetting, was yet another thing to forget. So she opened the book and immersed herself in the tale of wild romance. The room, the road, the moors didn't exist any more.

Annie had escaped.

She wouldn't look down, he knew that. He was beneath her in more ways than one, her sitting up there like a bloody princess in an ivory-tower, him standing in the street thinking about her as usual. She didn't even care whether he thought about her or not, didn't notice his existence most of the time. Whenever he did manage to engineer a meeting she always treated him as if he was only tenpence to the shilling, a few bricks short of a load, as if he needed another brain cell to qualify as a plant.

If only he'd tried harder. If only he'd passed that flaming scholarship instead of arsing about as if he didn't care or worse still, as if he didn't have enough chairs at home to do the soft test. Well, he wasn't thick – he'd show her that, right enough. Anyway, what difference would it have made if he had got a place? They would still have been separated, her with the nuns and him with the brothers. But she might have looked at him different if he'd passed. 'Naw,' he muttered, kicking a stone into the road. His Mam would never have let him go to the grammar anyway; she wanted him working pretty damn quick with all those mouths to feed.

Martin hated being in their house now. It had been alright when they were kids, it had even been fun living in a midden then, but now he was sick to the back teeth with it. Better out here on the road than in there, nowhere to sit, dirty pots and mucky clothes heaped everywhere, his Mam sitting either pondering or laughing in a corner, kids crawling out of every crack in the walls, muck and stench all around them. He wanted more than that, better than that. He wanted order, quiet, cleanliness and above all, success.

Ah, what the hell – she wasn't going to come out again today; he knew her pattern better than he knew his own. Even if she did come out, he'd likely open his big gob and put both feet in it again, start going on about girls and gangs and fights. And he did know about other stuff, he did! She wasn't the only one who read books and things. They did have common ground, he knew it. But what if the lads ever found out he could discuss Samuel Taylor Coleridge instead of just carrying on about James Dean and Bill Haley? But he wanted . . . oh, he didn't know what! Yes, he did. He wanted to say things. To her. Words he thought of while he lay in that stuffy, overcrowded back bedroom, things his mates would never understand in a million years. How the hell could he approach her? You couldn't walk up to a girl in the cold light of morning and say 'your hair's nice' or 'fancy a walk over the top?' Not with this girl, anyway. She was different and that was why he needed her.

He took a deep breath then gritted his teeth and looked up at her. She was like a statue, never moved except to turn a page or to push a strand of hair from her face. She didn't wear her hair in a pony tail like the other girls did. It hung loose like a silken waterfall down her back and shone in the sun, a mixture of gold and platinum threads – but he could never tell her that. And her eyes, cast down on the book now, were clear and green with long gold-tipped lashes. She was a tall girl, taller than him by an inch or more, but his thick crepe soles helped a bit. Still, she wasn't the type for a Teddy Boy, was she? He couldn't imagine her bopping at the Palais on a Friday or having a bit of fun in a doorway on the way home. He'd never gone all the way yet, but he'd had one or two of them breathing hard, panting for something he still felt too inept to try. He couldn't imagine her like that, giggling and groping in the dark, giving you a feel for the price of a lemonade and a couple of Woodies in the dance hall. One day, he would marry a girl like her, a girl beyond price.

The Hall i' th' Wood bus rattled past and she looked up from her book. Embarrassed beyond measure, Martin jumped up onto the garden wall and, holding an imaginary pole for balance, he executed an impromptu tightrope walk up and down, falling off at the gate and rolling on the ground as if mortally wounded. He picked himself up and began to walk with an exaggerated stiff-legged limp, then, turning to look up at her once more, he made a deep bow. She was standing at the window now, clapping her applause and half doubled over with laughter. He had made her laugh!

He pushed a hand through his hair, waved to her, then walked off grinning like an ape. She liked him, she was laughing at him. And anyway, he was one of the lads, wasn't he? He couldn't be 'in love' like they said in the pictures. But his heart was racing and he couldn't wipe this stupid smile off his face.

Never mind, time was on his side. He was not quite sixteen, only months older than her. But he'd be starting work soon, he'd have a few bob in his pocket. Maybe then, she'd like him more and . . . well . . . go out with him properly, be his girl. He met Lofty going into the Milk Bar. The gang was there, the jukebox was blaring. It was going to be a good day, this was.

'Your dinner's here, Annie,' yelled Nancy from the foot of the stairs. She walked to the range and lifted off the soot-blackened pan of pea and ham soup, setting it down on the metal side-shelf where it could keep warm. She had to get Annie's over with before Eddie came in, otherwise there'd be all that sighing and shuffling at the table again. She ladled a portion of soup into an earthenware dish as Annie came into the kitchen. 'There's fresh bread and marg if you want it.'

'Thanks, Mother.' Annie sat at the square table in the centre of the room and took a spoonful of the thick, scalding liquid. Winter and summer alike, Nancy Higson served at least one hot meal a day, soups, broths, stews, hotpots – 'to line your ribs against the winter,' she would say.

'Have you done all your homework?' asked Nancy anxiously. 'You shouldn't be reading all them stories if you haven't done your work for school.'

'I'm doing a couple of hours study every morning and I finished the essays in the first week.' The school work was no real problem to her. Even the long holiday assignments came with comparative ease – it was just a matter of organization, get the right material, read it, answer the questions . . .

'Just don't be getting too cocky, that's all. Remember you're a scholarship girl and the town's paying for you.'

'I don't need reminding of that.' The nuns reminded them often enough that they were charity cases, financed by the ratepayers and supported by the Church. Yet the scholarship girls were usually the clever ones, the achievers, while fee-paying students tended to lag behind, spoiled brats most of them, pushed along by doting parents with more money than sense.

Nancy stared hard at the girl who had suddenly begun to call her 'Mother' instead of 'Mam', who now washed her hair twice a week and took more baths than Nancy considered necessary or even healthy. And she wouldn't have a bath at night like everybody else did, oh no, she had to be different, had to have her bath in the middle of the day and that often meant two sets of clean clothes instead of one. 'Just don't get past yourself, that's all, Annie . . .'

The loud click of the rusted gate latch, which reached even Nancy's mill-damaged ears, made her stiffen noticeably. He was back and Annie hadn't finished. And anyway, how many windows could he have cleaned in that short space of time? 'Don't start,' she warned her daughter.

'Don't worry, I'm not staying here to listen to him eating. It's like hearing the tide going in and out . . .'

A knocking at the back door prompted Nancy to look out through the side window overlooking the yard. 'It's Dr Pritchard's lad – what's he doing here? I'll bet his mam doesn't know . . .'

'I'll get it, Mother.' Annie ran into the kitchen to open the door. Simon stood in the yard, a school satchel under his arm, his face red with nervousness.

'Is . . . er . . . something the matter?' asked Nancy, peering over the shoulder of her daughter who was now the taller by several inches.

'I just . . . wanted a word with Annie, if that's alright, Mrs Higson.' As always, Simon was the essence of politeness.

Feeling rather snubbed and not quite understanding why, Nancy retreated to the living room. What was he doing here, the doctor's son of all people? Not that he wasn't a nice enough lad, though. And Nancy had never forgotten that great day out with his dad in that daft car – but they'd been kids then, Annie and Simon. Now they were . . . well . . . growing up, like. She was a dark horse, was their Annie, if she was knocking about with Simon on the sly. Apart from anything else, he was a Protestant, wasn't he? That was right, he'd got into Bolton School, but not without a lot of string-pulling. She remembered how proud she'd been when Annie had strolled through the scholarship exams while Edna Pritchard's lad could only squeeze in by the skin of his teeth and because of his parents' standing in the town.

Annie looked into the thin worried face of Simon Pritchard. She hadn't seen him for quite a while and he looked awful, worried half to death.

'You've got to help me, Anne. I'm in a hell of a mess.'

'Why, whatever's the matter? And why didn't you come to the front door?'

His deeper blush was the only answer she needed. His mother wouldn't like it. Of course, that was it. Edna Pritchard with her fur coats and her permed hair wouldn't like to think that Simon was becoming over-familiar with patients and other natives. Having to live in the area was probably bad enough for Mrs Pritchard, though the large corner building that housed both surgery and living quarters was by far the most imposing residence on the road.

Simon pushed a lock of dark hair out of his eyes. 'It's the French and the biology – I'm a bit behind,' he muttered.

'Come in.' She stepped aside and held the door wide.

'Are you sure your mother won't mind . . .?'

For answer she pulled him into the kitchen and slammed the back door behind him.

'We're going into the front room, Mother. Simon needs to borrow some school books – he forgot to bring them home and we use the same text-books, more or less.'

Nancy's hand slowed in its stirring of the soup as the boy and Annie moved through to the front room. By, she'd get her comeuppance would that lady if she had her eye on the doctor's son! Edna Pritchard wouldn't stand for anybody taking a pair of scissors to the apron strings – anybody at all. And she'd been barely civil to Nancy in the shops these past few years since Annie got into the convent right off while Simon had to struggle for Bolton School. Without being aware of what she was doing, Nancy patted her hair, preening herself almost. She would make something, would Annie. She wouldn't finish up with fluff in her hair, noises in her ears and shoulders bent from doffing four machines day in and day out.

Eddie Higson's bucket clattered loudly in the yard and Nancy filled his bowl while he washed his hands at the kitchen sink. She sat in silence as he ate his soup slowly and noisily. Apart from his eating habits, Eddie was a quiet man. Likely something to do with being a prisoner of war, sitting still for all those years, waiting, watching other men wither away. He never really mentioned it. The only thing he'd ever told her, after eight or nine pints in the Star, was of the day they'd woken up to find that all their German guards had fled. 'Some of the lads started walking towards England,' he had said. 'Daft buggers didn't even know which way to go. Then again, some couldn't walk, but they were all for being carried off home there and then. I crawled to the gate and waited for the Yanks. Two days we sat there, but then we were used to it.' Yes, he'd got so used to it, he couldn't break the habit even now. For hours he'd sit on top of the fire, even in this heat, smoking his Woodies or his roll-ups, thinking his own thoughts.

'Cup of tea, Eddie?'

'Aye. I'll have it up to the fire.'

She poured his drink. Like as not he'd sit here now till two o'clock, thinking. Then he might just bestir himself, get up off his bottom and do a few more windows.

'What do you think about, Eddie?' she almost startled herself by saying.

'What do you mean, what do I think about? What sort of a bloody daft question do you call that?'

She stacked the dishes, wishing she'd never spoken. But other people, other married people, surely they had conversations? Surely it wasn't always like this, with one stacking soup dishes while the other stared into the fire?

'I was just trying to . . . well . . . I was just wondering, like, what you think about when you sit there staring into the fire. When I was a little girl, I used to see pictures in the fire and in the clouds too . . .' Her voice tailed away. She expected no reply, got no reply.

Sighing, she carried the pots through to the kitchen and turned on the tap. There was no talking to him, was there? She'd have been just as well off having a word with the coalman's horse. Better shut up, anyroad. She was luckier than most, running hot water, nice bathroom with a flushing toilet and him talking about getting a television set. When he did speak – on rare occasions, like. She leaned against the sink, her hands gripping the cold porcelain sides. She'd give it all up tomorrow for a sight of that baby, the one that never was. Oh yes and she'd tell him where to shove his television set sideways if Billy would just walk in and say, 'I'm back, Nancy. It were all a mix-up . . .' A solitary tear escaped down her cheek and she brushed it away angrily. It was right what they said – no use crying over spilt milk. Or blood, come to that.

Eddie Higson lit his third Woodbine. What did he think about? Stupid cow, what did she know about anything? All she cared about was having a nice clean house and trying to get a new cooker. What did he thing about? Because he did think alright, by Christ he did. Sometimes he lost track of time sitting here, remembering the so-called best years of his life spent in a long hut with narrow planks for beds, sitting, waiting, listening to the sounds of people pretending to be alive. 'Course, some soft buggers had to start digging their way out, but he never joined in their stupid games even when he had his strength. What did they want to get out for? To go tear-arsing round Europe till they found a bullet with their name on it? Oh no, he'd kept himself to himself. Then the bloody rations got cut because the guards had to punish the prisoners for trying to escape. It didn't take the Jerries long to find out that men with no food in their bellies and no flesh on their bones didn't have the strength to escape.

What did he think about? He thought about that one upstairs with her high-falutin talk and her fancy ways. He thought about the weeks he'd spent in hospital, about the agony the young bitch had put him through. He never worried about the others, the little girls he'd given pennies to in the past – they were off his patch, he never saw them twice. But that she-devil was always there, always a temptation. And somehow, he didn't fancy the very young ones anymore. No, he was growing out of that. Now, all he could think of most of the time was Annie Byrne and her fresh young body, a tigress to be tamed.

Could anybody blame him? Look at the shrivelled woman he'd married – she'd never even given him a kid, had she? Oh aye, there'd very near been a kid that time, but not his, never his. He wasn't really sterile – that was a mistake, he knew that now. But she'd gone with another man and he'd never forgive her for it. And look at her now – like a woman of fifty, she was. Not that she'd been like that when he married her. Oh no, she was a fine-looking piece then with good legs and a great figure. And she'd had no trouble getting that daughter off the first one, had she? Ten months married and she'd dropped one, but not for him, never for him. He still blamed her for that. After the operation two years ago, he'd had more tests, hadn't he? And they'd said he could have a kid if he tried hard enough. Tried hard enough? Christ, chance would be a fine thing. She didn't like 'that side' as she put it. It was a quick in and out at the best of times, enough to put anybody off. Had she liked it with him, the bloody war hero? Or with Ernie Bradshaw who was lucky to be alive after that going over Eddie and his brothers had given him?

He cleared his throat and spat into the fire, then grinned to himself. She didn't like him spitting into the fire, though she never said much. Except for her stupid questions and there hadn't been many of them just lately.

Yes, life was one long bloody think, come to that. Up a ladder, down a ladder, window after window, shut the gate, mind the dog . . . Aye, it got boring at times, though he'd copped some sights, by heck he had! Folk still in bed going hell for leather with the curtains open, nice young women half-dressed, one or two having a rinse in the scullery. Happen he could get a good time if he played his cards right, every woman had her price, didn't she? But it wouldn't be the same, wouldn't be her, the one he really had to have. Mind, there might be some sense in taking a look round till he could get her. Because he would in the end, by the hell he would!

Oh, no, he could never tell Nancy what he thought about because what he thought about wasn't right. What he thought about had to be hidden away, out of sight, out of hearing.

But he'd have his own back on that young madam, no danger. He threw his fag-end into the fire and settled back for forty winks. It was hard work, cleaning windows.

'I'm just not going to pass my GCEs Anne, I know it. I'm so far behind now – it's getting to the stage where it's absolutely hopeless.'

'It's never hopeless. Look at the time I've had with the Latin, staying behind for extra lessons because I'm so thick at it. Even if you have to re-sit a few of them in the November, you'll get them in the end if you put your mind to it.' She looked down at the exercise book, wondering how he could have got it all so wrong. None of the adjectives agreed with the nouns, the verbs were barely recognizable . . . 'I think the first thing you must do is to learn the construction of a French sentence. It's not like English, you see . . .' And she heard herself repeating her teacher's words, lessons she'd been taught two or even three years earlier. Bolton School, undoubtedly the best for miles around, could only work with the raw material with which it was presented. Simon was not of the right calibre for such a high-flying establishment. Yes, he was behind. She corrected his work,

234

explaining each step as best she could, unnerved by the look of blank incomprehension on the small worried face.

'Thanks, Anne,' he said after she had outlined the exercise in biology. 'I'll never make a doctor, will I? I think my father always hoped I'd take over after he's retired.' He laughed shakily. 'But he's a sensible chap. He probably realizes that I have neither the ability nor the inclination.'

'And your mother?'

'My mother?' He sighed. 'She just flutters around with her bridge parties and her afternoon teas. She still hasn't recovered from the end of the war, hasn't forgiven the war for finishing. The war gave her something to hang on to, socks to knit, women's groups to organize. It allowed her to be Lady of the Manor, you see, gave her a sense of importance. Now she simply fills in time, bakes fancy cakes for her friends and tells everybody how well her dear boy is doing at Bolton School.' He walked to the window and stared, unseeing, out on to the road.

'I'm sure you could cope if you tried harder, Simon . . .'

He rounded on her. 'Tried harder? For God's sake, Anne – do you think I haven't tried? It's just not for me, I'm not an academic, that's all. But if one more person tells me to try, I'll . . . I'll . . .'

To Annie's surprise and horror, he began to weep noiselessly, a river of tears pouring down his narrow, sad face. Instinctively, she reached and put her arms around him. 'Don't cry – please, don't cry . . .'

The door opened and Eddie Higson eyed the scene coldly. They didn't see him. Simon's face was buried in Annie's shoulder and she, facing the window, had her back to the door. But Higson could tell that the boy was crying because his body was shaking with sobs. Silently, the intruder withdrew from the room. So that was the way the land lay, was it? She was ripe, ripe and ready and he must not think of it for it was driving him to madness.

He swept past a startled Nancy and slammed out of the back door. She didn't know what the world was coming to, really she didn't. The doctor's son in the house and Eddie slamming doors like that. She hadn't told him about Simon, of course. And he never went near the front room, he wouldn't know they were in there unless they'd made a noise and there'd been no noise, had there?

But Eddie Higson had heard what Nancy's damaged ears could not catch from the kitchen, those slightly raised voices, that catch in the lad's tone just before he broke down. The boy was crying, likely begging that one to let him have her. Why else would a big lad like that cry? And Eddie knew what it was like, how it felt to be deprived to the point where you felt you'd burst if you didn't get a woman, preferably a ripe, young one who needed the only education a woman was fit for.

He banged his ladder against a window sill and began to climb. The boy wouldn't get her easily. Eddie Higson knew that better than he knew anything.

Martin Cullen and Dennis Maher, the latter usually known as Lofty because of his height, which had never increased from the age of twelve, made their way along the cobbled entry at the back of Long Moor Lane. They had left the rest of the gang in the Milk Bar listening to a new record. Martin wanted to talk and they wouldn't understand. He could trust only Lofty not to laugh at him, but then Lofty had not the brain to laugh at anybody and Martin, who recognized Lofty's severe limitations, knew that he was using the lad as a sounding board rather than as a comprehending companion. This little weasel-faced lad had always treated Martin as something of a hero, mostly because Martin had watched over him and protected him from bullies throughout the secondary school.

They stopped across from Annie Byrne's back gate and leaned on a garden wall. The houses opposite Annie's, both front and back, were corporation and had gardens. Not that the Cullens' was a proper garden, mused Martin as he cast his eye over Mrs Chadwick's neat square of green. Their own garden was like a jungle, full of waist-high weeds and rusty prams, empty tins, punctured footballs and bits of broken furniture from his mother's famous clear-outs.

The washing had been taken in now, so they had an uninterrupted view of Annie's house, though she would likely be in the front as usual.

Martin glanced down at the small lad beside him. He didn't look more than ten or eleven at the most, a poor thin soul with huge eyes and a forest of curly black hair.

'What's up, Martin?' asked Lofty. 'I knew somethin' were up right off, as soon as you walked into the bar.'

Martin shrugged. 'I just . . . oh, I know this'll sound daft, but I've been thinking, like and . . . and I'm not going in for weaving.'

'You what? You mean you're not comin' with us on Monday an' after we got took on an' all?'

'No. I'm not going.'

Lofty's mouth dropped open as he stared at his best friend. Not going? After an apprentice weaver's job? It was a good job, was that. Lofty himself was going into the spinning rooms, doing odd jobs, a bit of work in the carding shop if he was lucky, running errands more like. But Martin had got took on proper, he'd get learned how to weave, how to make cloth, get set up for life. He was clever, was Martin.

'The mills are finished, Lofty. Oh aye, it'll take a few more years for it to peter out altogether, but they've already started on that rayon and nylon – there's not always going to be cotton mills, you know.'

Lofty thought about this. If there was no cotton, then there'd be no Bolton. Martin must be wrong for once. 'How come you found all that out then?' he asked.

'Something I read in a paper, Lofty. They reckon that foreigners can turn out cotton a lot cheaper than what we can. They'll be importing it by the mile in five or ten years. Then there's all these cheap new materials – I'm telling you now, the mills will close.'

Lofty had never given the future a lot of thought. All he wanted was a couple of bob a week to spend and a few more inches in height then he could get into the pub with his mates on a Saturday night. But he knew one thing – he wanted Martin with him. They'd been together since the nursery and Martin had always been his best mate. Lofty shuffled about uncomfortably. He hadn't the vocabulary to tell his friend how he really felt.

'What are you goin' to do instead, then?'

'I'm going down the *Evening News*, see if they'll

take me on as teaboy, sweeper-up, dogsbody or whatever.'

'You what? Your mam'll bleedin' kill you! They only get shillin's fer that!'

'I'm not thinking about my Mam. Oh, I know she's a good laugh, but she doesn't really bother about me, you know. All she wants is a few more bob in her purse, but I'm thinking about the future, Lofty, planning my future. And the future's a long time to think about. The thing is, you and I have had no education, like.' He looked at his small friend who could scarcely read and write, though he could work out his dad's betting slips as quick as a flash. 'I want a start in life, Lofty and it has to be now. Seventeen or eighteen will be too late.'

Lofty felt lost. He couldn't, for the life of him, work out how Martin could turn down a good job just like that, a weaver's job with a bit of brass and proper learning for a trade. Then a thought struck him and he brightened visibly. 'But runnin' errands is not a good job, Martin. That's the sort o' thing I'll be doin' fer t' ring-spinners. Any bloody fool can run messages, even me. But you could be a weaver, a real weaver. Best I can 'ope for is the cardin' shop. I'll bet I never even get up to doffin'. And they'll always want weavers, won't they? Better a weaver than runnin' errands fer t' paper.'

This was one of the longest speeches Lofty had ever made and Martin smiled at him before saying, 'Even if they do want weavers, they're not having me. And running errands is just a start. They'll likely let me do a bit of office work after a few months, then I could learn how to take snaps and that, go to weddings and christenings.' He couldn't tell even

Lofty what he really hoped, that he'd find a story, a story so good that they'd stop the presses and hold the front page while Martin Cullen typed his piece. That was another thing he'd have to learn – typing. 'We can still get together, Lofty. I can meet you after work and at the weekends.'

'It won't be the same.'

'I know it won't be the same, but it'll have to do.'

Lofty brightened once more. 'They might not take you on.'

'Makes no difference. I'm not going in the mill and that's the end of it.'

Annie's back gate swung open and she stepped out into the street. Martin felt the colour rising in his cheeks and, to cover his embarrassment, he threw back his head and laughed loudly, as if he had just heard a good joke. The laughter died abruptly as Simon Pritchard followed Annie out onto the narrow pavement, a school satchel clutched under his arm.

The street was narrow – just wide enough for the ragman's cart and Lamp Eel's new van, so Martin could hear every word that passed between the two near the gate.

'I'll see you tomorrow then, Simon – if you can get away. In the library at ten o'clock – that should give us plenty of time.'

'Good. I'll look forward to that. Cheerio . . . oh, hello Martin.'

Martin made no reply to the friendly greeting and Simon walked a few paces then set off at a run towards the corner, turning left for the main road.

'Been doing a bit of homework, then?' Martin's voice was mocking and cold. 'I see his mam's letting him out these days – happen she's got him weaned up to Farley's rusks now.'

240

'I wish you'd mind your own business, Martin Cullen. I'm tired of falling over you every time I step out of the house.'

'Ooh, pardon me, your royalness. Tell you what, get the corporation to shift me next time they do the middens and the bins.'

'There's a thought now.' Her eyes darted towards Lofty. 'I'll tell them to scrape your shadow up at the same time.'

'Hecky thump, Lofty. Let's get the riff-raff off the streets, eh lad? Let's keep them under lock and key or chuck 'em in with the pig-swill.'

Annie sighed. 'You know I don't mean it, Martin. I'm just a bit tired, that's all.' She turned towards the house.

'Hang on a minute!' called Martin. He fished a threepenny bit from his pocket and threw it at Lofty. 'Here. Get yourself a comic and a penny lolly.' Lofty caught the coin deftly and made off in the direction of Bryant's shop.

Martin sauntered with studied carelessness over to Annie and, trying to keep his tone casual, he asked, 'Are you . . . going with him?' He stared at his shoes.

'Am I going with whom?'

He suddenly felt choked and reached to undo the top button of his shirt. 'Him. The doctor's lad, Salmon bloody Pilchard, otherwise known as Ole Fish Face. Are you going with him?'

'Going where?'

'Any bloody where.'

'No.'

'Then why was he in your house?' He felt stupid. His voice was high-pitched like it used to be before it broke.

'We were studying together, Martin.'

He took a few paces and leaned against the wall, not looking at her but oh, he could smell her. Like flowers, she smelled, like rain on a summer's day up on the moors . . . oh God, he couldn't look at her.

'I . . . don't want you going with nobody, Annie.' He could feel his cheeks burning.

'That's not right.'

'I know it's not right, but it's how I bloody feel!' He turned away and almost shouted this last part down the street.

'It's "I don't want you going with anybody", Martin.'

For a split second, his hopes soared, then he realized that she was just being superior again, was just pulling him to bits and correcting his English.

'I do know how to talk,' he said quietly. 'It's just that all the lads talk Bolton and they'd think I was a right girl's blouse if I started talking proper, like. I mean properly.'

'I know what you mean. And I'm sorry for teasing you.'

He managed to look at her now, but he could not quite meet her eyes, so he fixed his gaze somewhere in the region of her nose – he was close enough to count the freckles. 'I'm . . . er . . . I'm not going in t' mill.' He gritted his teeth. The mill, not t' mill. 'I'm going to try and make something of meself. It'll take a few years, but . . .'

'Martin! I'm so pleased. What are you going to do?'

He weighed his words. If he said 'I'm going to be a reporter', she might laugh. And what if he didn't make it? 'Office work – to start off with, like.' Oh why did he keep saying 'like' at the end of a sentence?

'Where?' She seemed genuinely interested now.

'Well, I've a few ideas – interviews and that – lined up.'

'Good.' She paused. 'Martin?'

'What?'

'Don't go dressed like that, will you?'

There she was, taking the mickey again. Briefly, he glanced at her eyes and found no mockery in them, only friendliness and what looked like genuine concern.

'I hadn't thought about that,' he said lamely.

'Hasn't Gerard any clothes that aren't . . . well . . . modern?'

She knew! She knew he was wearing his cousin's cast-offs! Christ, Bertha Cullen and her big mouth. Just wait till he got home, he'd tell his Mam off for letting Annie know. 'No, he hasn't,' he answered now.

'What about your uniform? The navy trousers – if you got hold of a decent tie, you might be able to get away without a jacket in this weather.'

'I'll think of something, ta.'

'Good luck then.' She turned towards the house.

'Annie!' She faced him again. It was now or never. He had to say something now. 'Your hair . . . it suits you that way.'

'Thanks.'

'You're . . .' He couldn't say it. Not beautiful, it would sound daft. 'You're a nice-looking girl . . .'

She held the gate wide. 'Look, Martin – I know what you're asking and the answer's yes. But I'm . . . not ready yet. I've a lot to do, you see. But I promise you I won't "go" with anyone else.'

'But you'll . . . go with me?'

'Sometime, yes. When I'm ready. Alright?'

'Yes . . . yes!' He knew he was grinning like a gorilla again.

'Bye, Martin.' She closed the gate.

He ran to the corner. Lofty was leaning in the shop doorway leafing through the *Beano*. Martin picked him up in a fireman's lift and whirled round until they were both dizzy. They flopped on to the pavement.

'Come on, Lofty. I'll read your comic with you.' And he led a puzzled Lofty up to the top field. It was turning out to be a great day, this was.

2

Edna and Simon

Life, for Edna Pritchard, was a constant battle with soot and grime. She would never understand why David insisted that they live here, right on the corner of Long Moor Lane and Enfield Avenue, with all the buses rattling past and the dirt from mill chimneys floating up from the town when the wind was in the right direction. They could have got a nice bungalow up in Bradshaw or Affetside, somewhere pleasant yet not too far from the surgery. But oh no, David had to be on the spot for his precious patients. Mrs Clancy, their housekeeper, did her best, but the rooms were always filled with dust even though they were cleaned every day.

Edna examined the lace curtains at a front bedroom window. Her sharp eyes picked out some small black specks nestling between crocheted roses and, with an impatient tutting sound, she released the curtain wire from its end hook. Twice in a month she had washed these. It was hopeless, absolutely hopeless.

She looked round the room at the rich mahogany furniture which gleamed with many applications of beeswax and hard polishing. She wasn't going to lower her standards just because she was forced to live here. Though what poor Mother and Father would say if they could see her now – well, she shuddered to think. They had been so pleased and thrilled when Edna had taken up with young Dr Pritchard; after all, he was a professional man and the Hulmes, in spite of their wealth, were only too happy to gain a doctor as son-in-law. Their money had been acquired through trade and Edna's alliance with an educated man had been a feather in their caps. Would they still be pleased if they could see that their grandson was being raised in a working-class area?

Edna was the only daughter of the late Richard Hulme, owner of two ropeworks – or ropewalks as the locals called them – and a highly respected Conservative alderman in his time. His wife, Elizabeth, a shy and retiring creature, had been horrified when Alderman Hulme had been elected Mayor, but Edna had revelled in it, enjoying the few functions she had been allowed to attend in her dresses of lace and velvet, waving cheerfully but in a ladylike fashion from her seat in the Mayor's coach as they rode through the town. After all, she'd been educated by a governess, taught the arts that would equip her to be a lady, like embroidery, tapestry, needlepoint and flower-pressing. Her father, a hardened tradesman with two sons to take the reins after him, had doted on Edna, sheltered her from the grim realities of the world, treated her like some rare hothouse plant, educated her to feel and act like a lady. But now, Mummy and Daddy were dead and Edna was left to the mercies of her husband's whims, must survive as best she could in an environment for which she had never been prepared.

'Don't worry now,' her father had whispered on his deathbed. 'That man of yours has his head screwed on. I've left you enough for a proper practice. Get him to Rodney Street in Liverpool – that's where the pickings are for doctors and the like.'

But Edna's inheritance had remained in the bank. David was stubborn. He didn't want a private practice, he had fought for, voted for and was glad of the National Health Service and he cared deeply, too deeply for the snivelling creatures that filled his waiting room three times a day Monday to Friday and twice on a Saturday.

It might be more bearable if they had some sort of social life, she thought as she carried the curtains downstairs. But no, if he hadn't a surgery, then he was out on calls. On Sundays, he tinkered with his car and on the rare occasions when he did take a rest, he would read and snooze in his chair until he was needed yet again by one of his beloved patients. Sundays in particular were dreadful. He was always under his car in the avenue at the side of the house, acting like a common working man, up to his elbows in oil and grease, usually surrounded by interested onlookers who would stop for a chat and stay on to offer advice and opinions about the vagaries of the internal combustion engine.

She could not say that she had married beneath her. Her husband was, after all, a qualified practitioner. But the domestic environment was not what she would have chosen and David had turned out to be rather more . . . enthusiastic and down-to-earth than Edna would have preferred. Their interests did not match. David was not keen on bridge or gin rummy and when he did get a holiday by employing a locum, he would not attend the theatre, refused point-blank to accompany her to concerts in Manchester – could scarcely stir himself to go up to the school and discuss Simon's progress.

And that was proving to be yet another worry. Simon was not doing well. The teachers were all concerned as, indeed, was she. David simply was not being realistic. He believed that Simon was a late starter because of being a premature baby, that he would come on in a year or two, find his own level in time. Edna knew differently. Simon was a dreamer. He had inherited what she considered to be David's weaker traits and showed no signs of repeating his father's academic achievements. The trouble she had had with that boy! Trouble David chose to ignore or not to worry about. She remembered the time a few years ago when Simon had taken up with that Anne Byrne from across the road, a seemingly streetwise and waif-like creature with long plaits and darned socks. That would never have happened if they had lived at the better end of town, Chorley New Road perhaps, where Simon had attended his expensive preparatory school. Simon would have been able to mix with others of his own kind, the sons of doctors and lawyers instead of being stuck here in the midst of slums.

She slammed down the lid of her new washing machine. To be fair, she thought grudgingly, these were not really slums. The terraces on Long Moor Lane were mostly clean and well cared for, though one or two of the council houses, particularly that one of the Cullens', looked unkempt to say the least. And there were worse areas. She should be grateful that David had not, in one of his more pronounced fits of missionary zeal, dragged them all off to the back of Daubhill or Deane Road where the houses were small and poor.

And at least Simon seemed to have stopped associating with the locals. He had used to come in so dirty and unkempt after running amok with Anne Byrne and that drove of Cullens. David had tried to put his foot down, of course, had insisted that their son should be allowed to play outside with the others. But Edna had stopped it, indeed she had. She didn't want Simon getting mixed up with street children, urchins with runny noses and God knew what kind of diseases clinging to their filthy clothes. He might have picked up their habits too and she hadn't wanted her son playing 'knock at the door and run' or chalking hopscotches on the library path. No. Simon was going to be a gentleman if nothing else. And he'd never make a gentleman if he went about with creatures like Anne Byrne.

An infuriating girl, that. She used to be so thin and fragile, yet she always ran wild, always played with the boys. But the most annoying thing about her was that not-quite-politeness, the way she would always greet her betters in the street with a knowing smile that made one's flesh crawl, the way she offered to carry a bag or open a door. It was almost as if the child deliberately set out to mock and deride with her fixed grin that always remained in evidence after the offers of assistance had been refused. She was too clever for her own good. Edna sniffed. By all accounts, Anne Byrne had turned out to be a great scholar, top of her class in most subjects according to David, who seemed to take an unnecessary interest in the girl. Edna had often noticed her going into the library, which building stood on the opposite corner of Long Moor Lane and Enfield Avenue and was, therefore, virtually next door to Edna's house. The girl was beautiful, one had to admit that. And she carried herself with such grace and poise, too much of these for one of her class, in Edna's opinion. Yes, she was glad she had managed to separate Simon from that young madam.

As Edna ran the thick lace curtains through the rubber rollers of the automatic mangle, Simon opened the back door and stepped inside.

'Where on earth have you been, Simon? Fortunately, it's a cold lunch – I've left it on the table in the dining room.'

'I've been to the library, Mum. Just trying to catch up on a bit of studying.'

'Good boy.' She leaned across to kiss him and Simon tried not to notice the face-powder setting in deep grim lines around her painted mouth.

He placed his books on the table. 'Is Dad in?'

'Of course your father is not in, Simon. He's gone to see one of Mrs Cullen's horde – measles again, I expect.' She shuddered. That family seemed to come down with just about everything, each member in turn going through every conceivable disease and taking up a lot of David's time into the bargain. Still, what could one expect of such people when they lived in filth and squalor – the place was probably overrun by mice and cockroaches. Oh dear, she hoped that David wouldn't smell when he came in.

'I saw . . . Anne Byrne in the library,' said Simon, having decided that it would be best to inform his mother rather than have her discover the truth 'accidentally' when peering through the windows. 'We've decided to study together during the holidays – help one another out.'

Edna worked hard to suppress her instinctive anger. Help one another out, indeed! She knew full well who would be teacher and who would be pupil in such a situation and she didn't want Simon learning anything from that girl, anything at all.

'Do you think that's a good idea, Simon?' she asked carefully.

'Why not? Why shouldn't we study together? We're the same age, we're doing the same subjects.'

Edna groped for words, trying to think of a feasible excuse. 'It's not a good idea, Simon, to associate too closely with patients.' She spoke slowly, attempting to keep control of her voice which had a tendency to rise in pitch when she became angry or excited. 'Her family will begin to assume a prior claim on your father, they'll take up more of his time if the girl starts helping . . . I mean, if you and she start studying together.'

'They're not like that, Mum – and you know it. I don't think Mr Higson has ever been to see Dad, and Mrs Higson doesn't come very often.'

Edna took up the curtains and started towards the door. They'd probably get sooty again if she hung them out, but what could she do? 'I just don't think it's right, Simon. The girl is not . . . well, you know what I mean.'

'Not one of us?'

'Exactly.'

'Then who is one of us?'

She turned at the door. 'Your school friends – why don't you telephone one of them? You could meet in the town centre, work in the big library – I'm sure you'd find more reference books there.'

Simon shook his head slowly. As if he could tell any of that crowd that he needed help. Not that they weren't already aware that Simon Pritchard was the class dunce, lagging behind all the way. It was because Anne was different that she did understand. She was succeeding in spite of her background while he was failing in spite of his. Briefly, he found himself worrying whether or not he was as great a snob as his mother. Was he using a member of the working class in the same way as Edna used Mrs Clancy? Was Anne easy to talk to, easy to beg help from because she came from a lower order and therefore didn't matter? He suddenly felt angry. If he was a snob, then who had made him so despicable? He looked at his mother and decided that he would not be like her, he would be strong, defiant if necessary. From somewhere he found the courage to announce, 'No. That would not be convenient. Half of the boys are away on holiday anyway. I shall be working with Anne.' Without waiting for a reply, he left the room.

Edna stood in the doorway, aware that her mouth was hanging open. Simon had never answered back before. Her blood ran cold as she thought of her son consorting with Anne Byrne, learning from her, begging for help, feeling grateful too if her own judgement of Simon's predicament was correct.

In spite of the heat, Edna Pritchard shivered. There was something about that girl, something that had given Edna a strong sense of foreboding ever since she had first met her years ago, on the night when Mrs Higson lost her baby. Hadn't Anne Byrne run away after that, run off to live in an air-raid shelter? She was wild and yet too self-possessed for Edna's liking. No good would come of this, she told herself as she hung the curtains on the line. No good at all.

3

With Premeditation

Eddie Higson had taken the day off. Bugger the windows, a man needed a bit of relaxation now and then. He staggered past the cooling tower and on to the playing field, making his way as steadily as he could manage along the cinder path towards the allotments. There he had left his bucket and ladder with an old gardener who often did him the favour of hanging on to these tools of trade while Eddie took the odd holiday. By, he should never have had that whisky though, not on top of the ale. He reached the small sports pavilion and decided to go in for a rest while the caretaker wasn't about. The green leather-padded form looked welcoming and he sank on to it gratefully, stretching out for a brief snooze to help him sober up. But he didn't get the chance to sleep for long, because it seemed that no sooner had he nodded off than somebody arrived on the open verandah and voices, one of them very familiar, began to drift through the window.

Martin and Annie sat outside on the bench, unaware that every word of their conversation was being overheard.

'What would you have done if you'd never passed for St Mary's?'

Annie looked into the unusually serious face. He'd

made such an effort for this, their first walk together. His hair was free of grease and apart from the thick-soled shoes, he was not dressed in his Teddy Boy uniform. She hadn't meant to go out with him so soon, but he'd begged her to come, said he needed somebody to talk to and that if she could help Simon Pritchard with his flaming homework . . .

'I'd probably do something similar to what you're planning. My mother wouldn't let me go in the mill anyway, so I'd have to find some sort of office job.'

'What about your Dad?'

There was a brief pause while she studied her hands. 'My own father's dead, Martin. I take no notice of Eddie Higson if that's who you mean. No doubt he'd push me in the mill alongside my mother if he could. So I do know what you're up against. Haven't you told your mother yet?'

He shook his head slowly.

'I wouldn't tell her if I were you, not till you've got a job. When you've actually been taken on . . .'

'But I have been taken on, Annie – in the weaving sheds.'

'I know that. But if you can get some prospects, surely she'll see sense?'

'Naw. She'll blow her bloody top.'

'Let her.'

'What?' He stared hard at her. 'By, I never thought I'd hear you telling me to defy my mother, Annie. These last few years, you've seemed to be such a . . .'

'A goody-goody?' She smiled. 'Far from it, Martin. I look at it this way – for a long time we've done what we were told, right? I've had to put up with a rotten stepfather and you haven't had it easy, have you? Well, just glance around you, Martin. Everything's changing. I've never been much of a one for history, but I've picked up enough to realize that for the first time ever, we can do as we like. I've probably known it for a while, because I refused to let them confirm me, if you remember. We're all rebels in our own way, you see. Now listen. My mother, although she's very intelligent, was thrown into the cotton trade when she was younger than I am now. She'd have given her eye-teeth for a chance to do otherwise, but there were no chances then. So. Move with the times and go for it, Martin.'

'And bugger the consequences?'

'Exactly. It's your future, nobody else's.'

He reached out and took her hand. 'You've got guts, haven't you? That's what I always liked about you, Annie, when we were kids.'

'We had some fun then, didn't we?'

'We did that!' He threw back his head and laughed. 'Hey, do you remember that time when you fell in Mrs Stirling's midden trying to get the ball?'

'Would I ever forget? And you pushed me right inside and shut the doors because my mother was coming up the back and you knew she'd kill me for playing in the middens . . .'

'And I'm leaning on the door all casual like – "nice weather, Mrs Higson. No I haven't seen your Annie just lately, Mrs Higson" . . .'

'Then when you finally let me out . . .'

'What a sight! Tea leaves in your hair and a sardine tin stuck to your frock. My, you fair clobbered me that day. I've still got the bruises.'

'You deserved them. You threw the ball in there.'

'You mean you missed it, butterfingers.'

She eyed him with as much coolness as she could muster. 'Rubbish!'

'Aye. That's what I said when you came out covered in it.'

He caught her to him and kissed her gently, first on the forehead and then on her slightly parted lips. 'You're good for me, Annie,' he whispered. 'Still as daft as a brush, aren't you?'

'Yes . . . yes, I suppose I am.' That a first real kiss could be so sweet and undemanding was both a shock and a relief to her. She found herself liking this nuisance of a boy, liking him a lot. Fervently she prayed that he would find what he wanted, that he wouldn't end up following in the footsteps of his forebears.

They wandered home hand in hand, a comfortable silence between them. As he left her at the gate, she laid a hand on his arm. 'Do it, Martin.'

'Oh I will. Now, I definitely bloody will.'

So that was the way the land lay, was it? Eddie Higson swore under his breath as he struggled to his feet. She'd the doctor's lad and Martin Cullen after her now. He stumbled out of the pavilion and into the bright sunlight, his eyes screwed up against its brilliance. His blood was boiling to fever pitch by the time he grabbed the ladder cart from a bemused allotment keeper. He steered it shakily under the railway bridge and past the school, his mind filled by the sight of her kissing that boy. And the things she'd told him too, about her rotten stepfather – he'd show her what rotten meant, by the hell he would.

Nancy had left by the time he got home, but he made no move to get his meal from the range oven. Instead, he ran up both flights of stairs and into the attic bedroom. She wasn't there, of course. He flopped onto the bed and lay there for a while, pondering the situation as best he could through the alcoholic haze which was slowly beginning to lift. Aye, she'd likely be out for the night now, messing about with lads until her mother got home. Then an idea filtered into his befuddled brain and he got up, grabbed a pencil and paper from the table and printed carefully, 'Nancy I've gone up to our Albert's will be back late. Eddie.' He walked down the stairs and pinned the paper to the front door. If the bitch was in the neighbourhood, she'd see it, read it and come inside thinking she was safe. Smiling at his cleverness, he went back up to her room to wait.

When the library closed at seven-thirty, Annie and Simon packed away their books and went their separate ways. Knowing that her mother would not be back for at least two hours, Annie decided to go to the Cullens' for a while – it was too late to start out for Auntie Jessie's now and she didn't want to be carting her satchel all over Bolton. Would Martin be in? Would he think she was chasing him if she visited their house after already seeing him this afternoon? Oh never mind, she told herself. She could not go home yet and there was nothing unusual about her visiting the Cullens once a week.

As she reached Martin's gateway, she looked across and caught sight of the note pinned to her own front door. Quickly, she crossed the road to read it, then, having gathered that Higson intended to be out until late, she went in, glad of the luxury of being able to spend an evening at home. Swiftly she ran up the two flights to her own room, tossing her school bag through the door as she entered.

'Hadn't you best get back down for the poker then?'

She stiffened as a hand came from behind the door and grabbed her hair.

'Scream and I'll bloody strangle you,' he said quietly. He twisted her round then hurled her onto the bed.

'Take your clothes off,' he growled.

She lay frozen and still as he approached her. He pulled her to the edge of the bed and began to fumble with her clothes, his hands tearing at the waistband of her skirt. 'Thought you'd got away with it, didn't you? But I've seen you with the lads, oh aye, I have that. And you didn't finish me with that bloody poker, not by a long chalk. If anybody's having you, it's going to be me, right?' He began to chuckle and she knew then that she dared not fight or scream; if she provoked him, he would surely kill her.

'And you'll tell nobody about this,' he went on. 'Because guess what? I'm going to say you've been after me for years, flaunting yourself, showing me your titties and giving me feels. I'm going to say as how I resisted you for a long time, but you finally got the better of me. Oh, it does happen, you know. Now get your things off before I rip them off.'

Like somebody in a dream, Annie removed her clothes then lay flat and terrified as he threw away his own garments. He eased himself onto the bed. 'You'll like it,' he whispered lewdly, the stench of stale beer and whisky pouring from between his grinning lips. 'I'll get you ready – see . . .' And he began to stroke her body, crooning almost as he lingered over her full, supple breasts.

Annie moved over towards the wall, her hand groping for the edge of her mattress. For how long had she been prepared for this? And wasn't this premeditation? Her fingers closed around the handle of a knife, the weapon that had been concealed beneath her mattress for two years now. He mounted her, his bony knees forcing her thighs to part. Just as she felt his ugly hardness against her body, just before he could pierce her flesh, she managed to pull out the knife.

He grunted his pleasure into her ear. He was there. After all these years, he was there. He found the virgin entrance and began to push gently against her. She hadn't screamed, hadn't given him a bad time, so if she was going to cooperate, then he may as well go at a proper pace, no use ripping her open when he could have her again and again if he treated her right and gave her a bit of fun. A split second before he could ease himself into her, a pain shot through his shoulder and down his left arm. This was quickly followed by another and another and his mouth gaped wide as he watched blood pouring from somewhere, all over the bed and all over her. He drew back as the red river continued to spurt, then he realized that she was stabbing him with a large carving knife, tearing at him wildly and repeatedly.

He rolled onto the floor taking a sheet with him and he used this to try to staunch the flow as he stumbled away from her. She was crouching now like a wild thing on the bed, her teeth bared, the dripping knife pointed towards him as she crept slowly forwards.

'You bastard!' she breathed between gritted teeth. 'You dirty, filthy, smelly bastard. Get out! Get out now or I'll stick this thing in your belly! You die slowly – very slowly – with a knife in your belly. Did you know that?' She walked round him in a slow wide circle. 'No, you wouldn't know that, would you? You don't know anything, because you're so bloody stupid. Did you really think I'd just lie there and let you? Did you?'

He writhed on the floor in agony. The sheet was soaked through and a large pool of crimson was spreading over the lino. But he would have to move – she was coming for him! He crawled out of the room on to the small landing, then fell headlong down the attic stairs, coming to rest on the larger landing below where he blacked out completely, mercifully released.

Annie opened her hand and let the knife slide to the floor. What now? What had she done and what must she do? The haunted face of Ruth Ellis entered her mind and she fled from this image, tearing around the room, stopping only when walls or pieces of furniture impeded her quick, aimless movements. Clothes. She would need clothes. After grabbing the nearest items, she left the room, climbing over his inert body at the foot of the stairs as she entered the bathroom. He looked dead. She was a murderess because she had planned this for years, hadn't she?

As quickly as she could, she rinsed the blood from her face and hands, then stepped into her clothes. She must think. Who would help her now? Where must she go? The doctor, she must get the doctor.

She flew from the house and ran blindly across the road, not caring about the traffic, not hearing when horns sounded. Dr Pritchard, slippers on his feet, newspaper rolled under his arm, answered the door.

'You've got to come,' she shouted. 'He's dead – I know he's dead!'

David Pritchard grabbed his bag from the hall-stand and raced after Annie. When he reached the house, she was already waiting for him at the front door.

'He's at the top of the stairs,' she said, her voice filled with fear and panic.

David took the stairs two at a time and found Eddie Higson stretched out on the landing, stark naked and with a sheet wrapped around a badly gashed arm. He wasn't dead, of course. The bleeding had slowed, David thought, judging from the amount on the sheet and the rate at which the cuts were now bleeding.

Higson groaned and opened his eyes, then let out a faint cry as a needle entered his arm. The bugger was sewing him up and not giving him anything for the pain! He blacked out again as another stitch was inserted.

David Pritchard was a man of strong instincts. He drove the needle viciously into the patient's skin, not caring whether or not he hit another vein, not worrying about the pain he might be inflicting. The lacerations were not really deep anyway and there seemed to be no damage to muscle tissue. Whoever had done this had been defending rather than attacking. Anne, poor Anne. That fine healthy girl could have finished him off if she'd wanted to. For a few minutes he felt heartily weary of being a doctor, sick of the way he was forced to heal the injured no matter what the situation. For David understood this particular situation only too well at this moment. Somehow, he knew what had happened – the girl splattered in blood, the man lying naked at the top of the stairs.

When he was finished, he went down to attend to his real patient, the one who truly needed him. She was sitting by the fireplace as still as a statue, her face frozen with shock.

He cleared his throat. 'I've put him to bed.'

Without moving, she whispered, 'He isn't dead then?'

'No.' There followed a long silence.

'I planned it, you know. Just like Ruth Ellis, I planned it. That knife was under my bed . . . he will be dead next time. There's no way I can stop it happening.' She was staring at the floor as she spoke, obviously to herself, as if she were alone in the room.

He knelt beside her and reached for her hands, trying to rub some life into the icy fingers, but she recoiled from his touch.

'It's alright, Anne – it's me – David. David Pritchard. I'm your friend. Do you understand?'

She nodded mutely.

'Did he . . . hurt you?'

'Yes. Yes he did.' She was talking like someone in a hypnotic trance.

'How long has it been happening – this sort of thing?'

She looked at him now with great sadness, returning from wherever she had been in her nightmare. 'All my life, Doctor. All my life . . .'

Hot anger surged through his veins as he looked at this poor child, because she was a child, in spite of her womanly shape and her adult way of talking. He had never liked the man, had not cared for the shiftless, mean-looking creature. But he would never have believed that something of this magnitude had been going on right under his nose without him, the family doctor, being aware of it. Yet he had known in a sense, known that something terrible was troubling this girl. Why, dear God, oh why had he not forced it out of her?

'Anne. Look at me – that's it. Now. Did he push

himself inside you? Do you understand what I mean?'

'I haven't been raped.'

'Has he ever raped you?'

'No.' She folded her hands in her lap and began to twist them about as if wringing out a dishcloth. 'The last time – a few years ago – I hit him with the poker. He had to go in hospital.'

David began to pace about the room, striding back and forth as he tried to organize his thoughts. 'Have you told anyone else about this?'

'Just a priest. He tried to help me, but he couldn't. Nobody can help me. Nobody.'

He brought a chair and set it down beside hers. 'We have to tell the police about this, Anne.'

She stared at him. 'Because I'm nearly a murderer? It was premeditated, wasn't it? I read that in the paper about the woman they hanged . . .'

'It's not that!' he cried. 'We have to tell the police because he's a child-molester. He's the one in trouble, not you!'

'No!' The ferocity of this response startled him. 'If I've done nothing wrong, then there's no need for the police – don't you see? We can't tell anyone.'

'But he must be punished – he can't carry on – you can't carry on . . .'

'Doctor, for years I've been told what I can and can't do. People think we've no sense because we're young, but I can make decisions . . .'

'This is the wrong decision, Anne.'

'Will you listen to me please? I have to protect my mother . . .'

'No. Your mother must protect you, my dear.'

'Please, Doctor?'

'Alright, I'm listening.'

She leaned back in the chair before continuing and he watched the small beads of sweat pouring down her face as she struggled against shock, fought to find the words with which she might explain herself.

'Dr Pritchard, if people knew – the police, the newspapers and all that – then my mother would suffer unbearably.'

'These cases are not reported and anyway, that's hardly the point . . .'

'That's just a part of the point, Doctor. I would suffer too. I would be removed to a place of safety and the few rights I have as a mere child would be taken from me. I'd probably have to leave St Mary's in order to avoid explanations as to why I had been moved to a council home . . . don't you see? I'd be living in a home with orphans?'

'But that would not happen if he were imprisoned, Anne.'

She half-smiled patiently and with the air of one trying to explain a complicated fact to an infant. 'If he were imprisoned, then my mother would lose the chief breadwinner. She might even lose her home. Do you think I could live with her, look at her every day, knowing I've put her income in jail? And there's another thing too. He swore to tell her that I've encouraged him. What if she believed him?'

David sat very still as he took in the implications of what she had just said. By God, this one had a head on her alright. To think that she'd worked all this out and so accurately too. It was true enough, what she'd said. He wondered how many other intelligent and abused children had reached the same conclusion. How many such children were there, children who endured rape and molestation because they had not the courage or the strength to protect themselves as this one had?

She cut into his thoughts. 'I can't stop you doing what you think is right, Doctor. But please, I beg you – don't ruin what's left of my life.'

He took both her hands in his. 'I'll talk to him upstairs first. Look – I haven't decided what to do yet. Just try to keep calm and I'll bear in mind all that you've said.'

He rose and began to pace about once more. He should report this, he knew he should. But could he really go out now and destroy this child's future? On the other hand, did he dare to leave her to the mercies of a potential rapist?

They heard the front door opening and Annie shot a worried look in David's direction. 'Don't tell her . . . please don't tell her . . .'

Nancy Higson stopped in the doorway, her husband's note in her hand. 'What's going on? Is she ill – is she hurt?'

'Sit down, Mrs Higson.' He looked quickly at Annie, noticing the pleading in her eyes. 'There's been an accident,' he went on. 'Your husband fell over and cut himself . . .'

'But he left a note to say he was at his brother's . . .'

'Yes . . . well.' He coughed to give himself time. 'Before going out he . . . er . . . went up into the roof-space and did a lot of damage to his arm on a rough beam.'

'Whatever was he doing up there?' asked Nancy.

'Looking for somewhere to put an indoor aerial for a television,' said Annie quietly.

'My God!' Nancy sank into a chair. 'Talk about accident-prone. How bad is he? Does he need the hospital again?'

'No, I've seen to him,' said David quickly. The man probably did need hospitalization – possibly even a transfusion. But no. A hospital would recognize knife wounds, would ask questions, too many questions. He glanced at Annie. There, it was done. Rightly or wrongly, Dr David Pritchard was now part of the conspiracy. And he knew only too well that Eddie Higson would be glad to go along with the story.

'I'd better go up to him.' Nancy rose and took a step towards the door.

'No! No, you stay here with Anne. Make her some sweet tea – she's had a terrible shock. There's a lot of blood in her room and on the stairs – Mr Higson used one of Anne's sheets to stop the bleeding, you see. It hasn't been a pleasant experience for her. I've given him the treatment he needed, but I must go up and check on his progress before I go. You put the kettle on, Nancy. I'll be down in a few minutes.'

In the bedroom, David Pritchard shook the patient roughly until he woke, swearing because of the agony in his arm and shoulder.

'Right. You listen to me, you no-good skunk. Stay away from Anne – do you hear me?'

Higson nodded, his face contorted with pain.

'I know all about it, Higson. I know that you almost raped a minor tonight and that this is not the first time you've tried it. But it will be the last, you can be sure of that. If the poor child was not in such a bad state, I'd examine her just to make sure you haven't damaged her. Now.' He took from his pocket an empty envelope which he waved under Higson's nose. 'See this? Anne has made and signed a statement which I have witnessed, so it is now a legal document. Tomorrow, my solicitor will take a fuller

266

account of what has happened and that will be lodged in his safe. If anything, anything at all happens to that child, my lawyer and I will bear witness against you. I'll see you go down if you so much as breathe on her again.'

'She knifed me! You've seen my arm,' mumbled the cowering figure on the bed.

'Yes, but she didn't do a good enough job, did she? She should have stuck you through your filthy black heart – vermin like you should be put down. I'll be back tomorrow to give you an injection and if you're very lucky, I may leave out the strychnine. And don't forget, Higson, you sustained your injuries in the loft while looking for a suitable location for a television aerial. That lie is for Anne's sake, not yours. Understand?'

Higson nodded, then groaned as he rolled to face the wall.

The doctor turned on his heel and left the room, a cold sweat breaking out on his brow. He felt as if he had been in the presence of something truly unnatural, something evil almost. Before going downstairs, he ran as quickly and as quietly as he could up to Anne's bedroom, picked up the bloody knife and shut it in his bag. He shivered as he passed Higson's closed door on his way back to the ground floor. Nancy met him on the bottom step. 'Is he alright, Doctor?'

'He'll survive. Give him rest and plenty of fluid.'

Annie had not moved from her seat by the fire. He walked over to her. 'Remember – he did it in the loft, Anne. Fell over, cut himself, then came into your room for help.'

'Thank you, Doctor. I owe you a lot.'

'Yes, you do. And to pay me back, you will come

to see me tomorrow. We have to make certain legal arrangements – take out an insurance if you like, to make sure that this never happens again.'

'My mother won't know?'

'No. No, she won't.'

He gave her a sleeping draught then stayed with her until she slipped into unconsciousness on the sofa. Gently, he brushed the hair from her face and sighed as he noticed dark shadows under her eyes.

On his way out, he stopped at the bottom of the stairs and called, 'Nancy? Fetch a blanket, will you? She's on the couch and I shouldn't move her if I were you – just let her sleep it off.'

He picked up his bag and left the house, noticing for the first time that he was still wearing carpet slippers. Oh dear, whatever would Edna say about that, he wondered irrelevantly as he entered his house. Suddenly exhausted, he leaned against the front door feeling as if he had aged ten years in this one night. He shook his head wearily. Had he done the right thing?

He sat up well into the night, his mind in turmoil. By two o'clock in the morning he had reached no conclusion. But he knew, as he had always known, that right and wrong were hard to define, sometimes impossible to separate. The child would be protected and that was all that mattered.

4

Tensions

On a cold February afternoon in 1956, Nancy Higson sat in the doctor's waiting room, hands clasped tightly on her lap. The last few months had been hard and no mistake, what with Eddie coming off work for a while over his arm and Annie mithering off and on to leave school and get a job to help out. Now this. She let out a deep shuddering sigh. It couldn't be true, dear God no, not lung cancer. She'd watched her Dad die of that a couple of years back and it wasn't an easy death, not by a long chalk. And it had started the same way too, with a bad cough and then, later on, the spitting of blood into handkerchiefs and towels. Her fingers began to tremble again and she gripped her hands together more tightly until knuckles showed white through work-worn flesh. If only the doctor would hurry up. She had to get it over with now, while Annie was at school, she didn't want Annie worrying over illness in the house, not with her exams coming up this year.

Anyroad, it might not be cancer. Surely you could spit up a bit of blood without it being cancer? She tried to look on the bright side, but no, it had been going on for too long – it must be something serious.

The bell rang for her to go through and for a moment she remained riveted to the spot. This might be her last minute of near-sanity. If it was cancer or something like that, she felt she'd go straight out of her mind, they'd have to lock her up in a loony ward.

She dragged herself to her feet and knocked timidly on the surgery door before entering.

'Hello, Nancy – how are you?' Christ, he was so bloody cheerful she could have hit him. She sank into the chair at the side of his desk.

'It's him,' she finally managed.

'Your husband?'

'Yes.'

He tapped a pencil on the desk. 'Come on, Nancy. Out with it.'

'He's . . . not right.'

David looked kindly at the poor tired soul beside him. Eddie Higson wasn't right? That was the understatement of the century. But what had happened now? Did Nancy know, had she found out? And had that bad bugger touched Anne again? He trod carefully. 'In what way is he not right?'

Nancy tugged at the top button of her coat and cleared her throat before going on, 'He's spitting blood, specially in the morning and sometimes of a night. He's got a bad cough, you see.'

Moments passed, the silence broken only by the tapping of his pencil and the rumble of a 45 as it clattered its way towards town.

'How long has he been seeing blood?'

'I'm not sure, Doctor – a good few weeks at least. He's one as keeps himself to himself, not a great talker. I haven't asked him. He likely thinks I know nothing about it.'

David nodded. Oh yes, Eddie Higson kept himself to himself alright. Too much to hide to ever open up

270

to anybody. Perhaps he'd be answering to his Maker soon enough.

'What do you want me to do, Nancy?'

She shrugged thin shoulders. 'I don't know. He'll not come here to see you. If he thought I'd been across he'd blow his top, tell me off for interfering and mithering again. Oh, I don't know what we must do.'

'Well, I can't make a diagnosis without seeing him. Even then, I'd have to refer him to a specialist at the hospital.'

She suddenly brightened. 'If he's got anything serious, then it's not started overnight, has it? And he was in the Infirmary a couple of years back over his accident – they'd have noticed then, wouldn't they?'

'Not necessarily. Things take time to flare up and anyway, they might not find something they weren't looking for.' He rose and walked to the window, hands deep in his pockets, brow furrowed as he wondered what the hell to do.

'He was in a prison camp, wasn't he?' he asked without turning.

'Yes, he was.'

'For how long?'

'About three years, I think. They put him in hospital when he got home.'

'Was he very thin?' He looked at Nancy now, noticing for the first time that her hair was slightly streaked with silver although she was not yet forty.

'He weighed about seven stone. They couldn't keep anything down him except milk and suchlike. Even now, he doesn't like food with lumps in, rather have soup and rice pudding.'

Or alcohol, thought David, remembering the

times he'd watched Eddie Higson struggling home from the Star using garden walls and lamp posts as guidelines.

'Nancy, I can't be sure, but I rather think it's tuberculosis of the lungs.'

'TB?' She was horrified. Only the poorest and dirtiest of people got TB. 'There's none of that in my house, Doctor.'

He sat down and patted her hand. 'It's everywhere – especially in a big town like this,' he said. 'And his resistance was probably lowered because of poor diet during the war – it's no reflection on you if your husband has tuberculosis.'

Mollified slightly, Nancy relaxed a little. At least there was a chance of it not being cancer. 'What are we going to do then, Doctor?'

'You'll have to talk to him, won't you?'

'Talk to him? He'd go straight through the bloody roof if I mentioned this. He won't come near you, I do know that. He reckons as you treated him bad over that arm of his, says you're a butcher – I think he's terrified of doctors and hospitals.'

David drew in a sharp breath. Here he was, getting enmeshed in a second conspiracy involving the Higson family. 'Then you'll just have to do your best. It's a notifiable disease, but I can't inform the Department until I'm sure. And I can't be sure till we've had it confirmed.' He paused. 'And we can't confirm what we can't examine. Look. Go home and boil the towels – keep yours and Anne's separate from his. It might be a good idea to give him his own set of crockery and cutlery, though boiling water should keep your utensils sterilized. Meanwhile, I'll try to work out a way around this, but it will take time and frankly, I don't know how much time we've got.

After all, I'm just assuming that it's TB – but I'll do my best to find a way of getting him looked at. Alright?'

A sudden thought struck Nancy and, with her hand to her collar she said, 'What about my daughter? What if she's caught it?'

'Even if it is TB, I'm very sure that Anne doesn't have it. She's a fine strong girl – a credit to you, Nancy – she'd make a full recovery anyway.'

Nancy reached into her bag and brought out a greaseproof package which she unwrapped carefully. Inside was a man's handkerchief stained brown with dried blood. 'That's from this morning – he hid it in the dustbin. But I fetched it with me to give you an idea of how much he's bringing up.' Her face brightened once more. 'Hey – can't you send this to one of them laboratory places? Happen they can work out what he's got.'

David smiled grimly. This little woman was not behind the door, was she? With a bit of education, she might have gone far. 'No,' he replied. 'We need X-rays, fresh blood and sputum tests – not to mention a little cooperation from your husband.'

'I doubt you'll get that.' So did he, though he couldn't tell Nancy the real reason why.

'Come on,' he said now. 'Cheer up – things are seldom as bad as they seem.'

'You're a good man, Doctor. You've been a right comfort to me today and I'll not forget it. Ta.' She rose to leave.

'Send Anne to surgery tomorrow evening, will you?'

'What have I to tell her?'

'Tell her she's a guinea-pig – she'll like that. Say I'm running Mantoux tests for TB on a cross-section

273

of the population and that she is to be my example of a typical sixteen-year-old female. And you'll need a test too, Nancy.' The plot, he thought, was thickening by the minute.

'Right. I'll send her in then.'

'Goodbye, Nancy.'

She left the surgery looking, David thought, a sight happier than when she had come in. Now, all he had to do was to persuade a man he hated and who hated him to come and seek treatment. He suddenly knew that he would not, could not do this. As long as the rest of the family was protected, then Eddie Higson could go to hell his own way. He shook his head slowly. Anne's 'insurance policy' was now in the hands of a lawyer, the child was safe at last. But was there a caring God after all? And was this His way of making Higson pay? Unless the man got immediate treatment, his death certificate was virtually signed – nobody who brought up that amount of blood each morning could survive for long without help. But he, David Pritchard, would not interfere in God's plan. Even a doctor could not intrude on divine retribution.

He walked to the window and watched Nancy scuttling across the road to boil her towels. Sighing deeply, he took his watch from the pocket of his waistcoat. Half past four – time for tea. Ah well, it was all part of a day's work, all part of life's complicated tapestry. He walked towards the living quarters, his mind occupied by just one thought. That girl had better be alright. If the brute had given her TB on top of everything else . . . He stood still in the hall for a few seconds. There should be no place in a doctor's heart for such murderous thoughts.

In the dining room, Edna was fussing with the tea as usual, arranging her china in exactly the correct order, milk, sugar and lemon to the left of her, teapot and hot water jug to the right. It was like watching a general planning a military campaign, everything present, in order and accounted for. Simon was sitting bolt-upright in a straight-backed chair, waiting for his mother to pour.

'Was that Nancy Higson?' asked Edna as she passed buttered scones first to her husband, then to her son, in accordance with her concept of doing things right.

'Yes,' David replied curtly, wondering how much longer he would be able to tolerate Edna without resorting to drink – or worse.

'Is she ill?' She stirred her tea slowly, delicately and, as always, in an anti-clockwise direction.

With exaggerated patience, David placed his cup in the centre of his saucer and unfolded a snow-white stiffly starched napkin, spreading it carefully on his lap. 'Could I have some jam please, Edna?'

Pouting in a way that might have been attractive in a woman half her age, she passed the crystal and silver jam pot to Simon, who handed it down the table to his father.

'I was only taking an interest,' she whined in that silly girlish voice.

'Edna.' David spoke with all the forbearance he could muster. 'Most of the people who visit my surgery suffer from some ailment or other. I cannot discuss the condition of patients – I should have thought you would understand that by now.'

Simon shifted miserably in his chair. He could feel the tension in the room and it made him prickly and uncomfortable.

'Stop wriggling at the table,' snapped Edna. 'And remember your manners – use the napkin.'

David looked at his unhappy son and was filled with pity for him. 'Had a good day, Simon?'

'Not bad. I'm getting somewhere with the biology, but the French is a bit much, I'm afraid.'

'He still studies with that Anne Byrne in the evenings.' There was strong disapproval in Edna's tone.

'Good. Glad to hear it – she'll make a good teacher one day,' said David.

'She may not become a teacher, Dad.' Simon glanced quickly at his mother.

'Oh really? What is she going to be then?' asked Edna with unconcealed sarcasm.

'She thinks she might be a doctor, Dad.'

'Really?' David's face beamed a wide smile.

'She'll be lucky,' muttered Edna almost under her breath.

'Then if she's lucky, it won't be before time,' said David, still grinning. 'And if and when she does make up her mind to be a doctor, then she'll be one, just mark my words.'

'What makes you so sure?' Edna's question was fired across the table like a bullet from a gun.

David leaned back expansively. 'Oh, several things. She has patience, humour, kindness – oh and a fine brain too. The latter does come in handy on the odd occasion.' He held out his cup. 'More tea please, dear.'

5

Disruptions

Eddie Higson had spent three months in comparative heaven, so when the trouble started, it hit him doubly hard. It was as if everything was being taken at once – his health, his stamina and most of all, his Dolly.

He had found satisfaction in an unexpected quarter, the last place on earth he would have looked for it. Dolly Nelson was short and fat, had a plain face and frizzled brown hair – to say that she was not attractive would have been a kindness, because Dolly, even on her best days, was little short of downright ugly. He had collected her window money for years and never passed the time of day, never given her a second glance. It was common knowledge that her husband had left her with four kids and that she worked as an usherette at the Odeon, but until the day she called him in and asked him to mend a tap, he'd never had much to do with her.

'Your pipe needs fixing.' He turned to look at her – God, she was fat and all, stood there in her dressing gown with great blobs of white flesh bulging out at the top, nearly meeting her double chin.

'I'll pay you if you can mend it.' There was a knowing look in her eyes. 'Would you like a brew?'

'Aye, go on then.' He walked to the scullery door and she turned sideways to allow him through to the kitchen, giggling and exclaiming 'oops!' as he brushed against her. She made a great fuss of him, gave him a thick wedge of toast which he didn't eat, brewed him a second mug and all the time she leaned over him so that he could look into the deep valley between her breasts.

It was plain what she wanted and he had her there and then on the peg rug in front of the range. She'd no shame, hadn't Dolly, didn't bother when he ripped at the gown to get at her, didn't seem to care about being such a big 'un. She wasn't good-looking by a long stretch, but by hell she knew how to go about pleasing a man. It was like sinking into a feather mattress or drowning in warm cream. Her breasts, too big for his hands, were huge soft pillows and the enormous brown nipples excited him to fever pitch, made him forget her face. And she liked it. He'd never had a woman before that liked it.

As time went on, he visited her two, sometimes three times a day, amazed at his own staying power. Not that she was hard work, oh no. Sometimes he'd just lie there while she did the lot and not always in the usual way. She had imagination, did Dolly and she was always ready for it. She could be up to the elbows in washing or baking and he could just go up to her, open her frock and take what he wanted.

He felt smug, wore the air of a man who has made a voyage of discovery and has stumbled on a secret too precious to impart to any other living soul. Nobody looked at fat women – he'd never have looked at one himself at one time, but now he knew different, didn't he? And the more time he spent with Dolly, the less ugly she looked, partly because he got used to her appearance, but mostly because she seemed to improve, as if she needed a lot of loving. Aye, they were two of a kind, him and Dolly.

But no matter how many times he visited Dolly, it was never enough. Even when he'd seen her twice in one day, he'd wake up at two or three in the morning, ready for more, urging Nancy onto her back so that he could get at her. It wasn't right and he knew it. It was like a fever driving him on, pushing him beyond all endurance.

There was only one thing for it – he'd have to leave Nancy and move in with Dolly, bugger what the neighbours thought. 'Course, the priest would be on him quick as a flash, but Eddie had never been more than a paper Catholic, so he'd tell that lot where to go and all. It would be worth it just to know that Dolly would be there all the time, in the same house, the same bed, ready for him whenever he wanted her.

He'd say nothing to Nancy. He'd just pack his bag and bugger off, wouldn't even leave a note. As for that young cow who'd nearly cut his arm off, well he'd show her good and proper. They'd never manage on Nancy's money. Oh aye, that one would have to leave her posh school and get in the mill like the rest.

Then, just when his plans were laid, the bother started. He'd always had a cough, especially in winter, but this was different. The blood frightened him, but he told nobody – it would likely clear up in a week or two anyroad. But it didn't and the night sweats were getting worse, leaving him drained and useless, so he cut down his visits to Dolly because he was terrified of not coming up to scratch when it mattered. At times, he was back to what he considered normal and he would see her more often, pleased when she complained about missing him so badly. He had to save his strength for the one who would appreciate it.

Just one regret lingered in his sweltering brain and that was that he'd never given it to her upstairs. There was something about her – she needed showing that she was no different to the others. And however good Dolly was, he still hankered after some young stuff, a bit of uncharted territory to explore. Mind, he'd shown flaming Annie what was what, hadn't he? Oh aye, he'd given her some time and attention over the years, got her ready for the one thing a woman was fit for. Now some other bloody sod would be the first to dip his wick. No, he'd no chance now with that bastard Pritchard knowing so much. He should go and see him about this sweating, but he wouldn't, couldn't give him the satisfaction.

Still, he'd get better, wouldn't he? He had to for his Dolly. Christ, you could get lost in a woman like that, sink into her and not care whether you lived or died.

He looked at the dark shape beside him in the bed. Thin mean stick, she was, bothered more about her daughter than she ever did about him. She'd been going on for days now about some tests and X-rays the girl had been for and wasn't it great to know that Annie hadn't got TB. As if he bloody cared. He turned on to his side to try to sleep, but the heat was coming over him in waves, he was drenched with sweat – even the sheets were wet through.

The cough rumbled like a threatening storm deep in his chest, gathering force then rising up suddenly to explode wetly onto the pillow. He knew his eyes were bulging from his head as he fought to breathe.

Blood spurted from his nose and mouth, shooting with great force across the bed and splashing onto the floor. Wildly, he kicked out at her until she woke, then, as light flooded the room, he sank into his own merciful darkness.

Whatever was wrong, it couldn't be her fault, thought Edna Pritchard, self-righteousness outweighing the misery she carried like a solid mass inside her body. She'd always done her best, kept a beautiful home, served meals that were nourishing and well-presented, taken good care of her appearance, brought Simon up carefully and properly.

Her bridge party had just finished and, as always, she felt a degree of dissatisfaction after her friends had left. Olive Mallinson with a complexion to suit her name and more diamonds on her hands than they had in Preston's window. Alice Barton-Bates who, after casting a last scathing glance at Edna's pathetically small front garden, had stepped into the brand new chauffeur-driven Rolls to be whisked back to her country mansion with its semi-circular driveway and acres of formal garden. Lastly, Sarah Pennington, a war widow whose husband had left half a million pounds to help her endure the heartbreaking loss.

Edna whisked lace doyleys from china plates while she nibbled at the last of the cheese straws. She had been eating too much of late, especially when nervous or worried. She would have to cut down, or she might become as fat as that Dolly Nelson woman who had been at surgery this morning.

If only she could put her finger on whatever was wrong; if only Daddy were here to smooth things over like he used to. She sat gloomily at the window, watching the world go by through the lace barrier that separated her from the situation she despised so much. Perhaps David had another woman, someone more earthy and worldly-wise, someone with whom he might discuss politics and medicine, a partner who enjoyed his virility. But no, he had no time for that sort of thing – the practice kept him far too busy. Of course, they hadn't been really close since Simon was born. It wasn't her fault that she was frail. Hadn't she almost died giving birth and hadn't the specialist warned against further pregnancies? David must appreciate that – after all, he was a medical man.

Her pride had been hurt, though, when he had moved into another bedroom. Although she didn't want to be touched she felt, perversely, that he should still find her desirable, should want her even though her condition prevented it. And now, he treated her . . . how did he treat her? Not like a housekeeper, because he always had a smile and a kind word for the woman who came in daily. Not even like one of his patients, that silly flock of sheep who seemed to idolize him and hang on his every word. Oh no. His own wife might as well not be here at all, might be just another piece of furniture for all the notice he took of her. They talked at the table sometimes, but, more often than not of late, he would switch on the Home Service or worse still, read his paper during the meal, a habit Edna considered to be working-class and out of place in a doctor's home.

It was plain enough that Simon was on his father's side. He never said much, but when he did offer a few words, they were usually for David, seldom for her. Yes, Simon would probably turn out like his father, would copy his low-life habits and careless speech. It would happen, she was sure of it. Three times now she'd seen her son walking down the road to that dreadful Milk Bar with Anne Byrne and Martin Cullen. And there was another thing that hurt, though she could scarcely admit it. Martin Cullen and Anne Byrne hand in hand while Simon tagged along like a grateful puppy. Not that she wanted Simon to associate with the girl, but to think that she had the effrontery to prefer that awful boy, that the young madam could pick and choose between the two of them . . .

She gathered the dishes on to a trolley and wheeled it towards the door. She knew how Simon felt about the girl, his face lighting up whenever David mentioned her name. It was humiliating, it really was, she thought as she rinsed translucent china cups and Waterford sherry glasses.

As she was finishing the task, David entered by the back door, a bulky parcel under his arm.

'What's that?' she asked.

'It's a Dansette – a portable gramophone for Simon and his friends.'

She stiffened. 'Which friends in particular?'

'Oh, Martin, Anne, one or two others from the Milk Bar. They've nowhere to go when the bar closes, so I thought I'd give them that large bedroom at the back.'

'No, David.' Her voice was quiet but firm. 'I will not have people of that type in my house.'

He banged the parcel on to the table. 'People of what type? God, woman – we're all the same type. We all have blood in our veins, guts in our bellies, bones in our backs – at least, most of us do. What makes you so different, eh? Come on, you tell me, Edna. I'm sure the answer will be fascinating and very educational.'

She flinched. He had never shouted like this before. She found herself almost whispering in the face of such rage. 'I only want what's best for Simon. He should mix with the right class, boys from his own school. I don't want him wasting his life, David. And yes, I am different from these people.' She began to feel braver, more sure of her ground. 'My father educated me to be a lady. I am not used to . . .' she waved her hand towards the outer door, 'this kind of thing and have no desire to become a part of it.'

'Have you finished?' His voice was quieter now.

'Yes.'

He sat at the table, fingertips pressed together in an attitude of patience that thoroughly infuriated her. 'Simon has much to learn. Your attempts to shelter him from the world – yes, I know your intentions were good – have resulted in him developing into a shy and possibly emotionally retarded boy with a very poor self-image. You are not alone in your guilt. I too have tried to influence him, hoping he would follow in my footsteps. But why the hell should he? I would be indulging my pride were I to push him towards a profession for which he is not suited. You, Edna, are indulging your conceit by trying to turn our son into what you have become – a snob.'

She suddenly realized that he hated her. No, perhaps hatred was too strong a word for what he felt, perhaps contempt or even indifference would be more accurate. In her frustration, she began to weep. 'I'm not having them here. This is my house . . .'

'You can turn off the tap, Edna. And no, this is not your house – it is mine.'

The crying ceased immediately and a look of shock invaded her face.

'It's your home, but not your house. My name is on the deeds and your money is in the bank. Now, if you wish to continue living here, please feel free. If, on the other hand, you would prefer to find another house, one with a better address, I shall not stand in your way. However, I must warn you that in such circumstances Simon would doubtless opt to remain here with me. Meanwhile, I shall have whoever I like, whenever I please, in whichever room is available. After all, you have your bridge parties on my premises – why shouldn't Simon have friends in his own home?'

She was lost for words, yet more angry than she had ever been in her life. She picked up a glass and smashed it into the wall behind his head, then a cup, a saucer, a plate, another cup. When she found her voice, she heard herself using words she'd never uttered before, words she had never had occasion to use. And he was laughing, the bloody man was laughing! Enraged and out of ammunition, she ran to him, pounding her fists against his chest, screaming names, filthy names at him.

He grabbed her wrists and held her easily. 'So the old man did teach you something after all? Do you know what he was, Edna? A snotty-nosed kid with the arse hanging out of his trousers who had the wit and cunning to get out and make good. He broke backs in this town, walked over decent working folk and flogged them till they dropped. And he got rich, very rich. But you must never forget your roots, Edna. That's a terrible mistake. Because your roots will find you in the end and either let you down or pull you up. You can never pull them up, so don't try. You are working-class just like Anne Byrne, Bertha Cullen and the rest. The only difference is a few thousand in the bank. Remember that.'

He pushed her away, picked up his package and made for the door to the hall. 'You know, Edna – I rather enjoyed that. Your vocabulary could be quite . . . extensive if you worked on it.' He walked out grinning widely.

Edna surveyed the wreckage, forty or fifty pounds' worth of crystal and bone china scattered across the floor. Weeping hot silent tears she swept up the fragments, feeling as if she were throwing away her life as she dropped them into the bin. She felt shame and a bitter humiliation when she recalled some of the things she'd said, those dreadful words she'd used.

Well, it was all out in the open now. She wasn't going, oh no, she wouldn't leave Simon with him and that girl. She was sick of the Higson family, sick to the core. All that frantic rushing about the night Eddie Higson had his haemorrhage – you'd have thought the world was ending. And now David and Simon were both running back and forth each day to see how poor Nancy was coping. To make matters worse, David was even driving the woman to the sanatorium once a week to visit her husband, leaving Anne Byrne to get up to no good in the house with that Martin Cullen – and possibly Simon too. Oh yes, she'd seen the Cullen boy going in at the front door bold as brass – and no doubt Simon would be sneaking in at the back. The girl was probably serving the whole neighbourhood, thought Edna viciously as she slammed a cupboard door.

There was nothing she could do. David had put his foot down hard and she'd just have to make herself scarce in the evenings if he was going to allow those creatures into the house.

But she was sure of one fact. Things would never be the same again. Edna Pritchard knew that as well as she'd ever known anything in her life before.

6

Laughter and Worry

In the beginning, when he'd first gone into the sanatorium, Nancy had been beside herself with worry. Now, she was beginning to look happier and healthier than she had for years, though she was working longer hours. It was obvious that the manager at Millhouse didn't want to lose her, because he'd allowed her to work three full days so that she could visit Eddie in the evenings. He'd even hinted that Nancy might be foreman in time and the knowledge that she was so well thought of gave her confidence a boost. A woman as foreman? That would make a few heads turn if it ever came about. As well as doing her shifts, she had taken on the weekend cleaning at the Star, yet she didn't feel tired at all, just . . . well, guilty because half of her was relieved to have Eddie out of the road.

For Annie, it was a blessed reassurance to see him go, though she could never tell her mother that. When she had once more suggested taking a job to help out with money, Nancy had been horrified again. 'No! You'll not end up like me, that you won't! You're at school till eighteen, then college after that. Why do you think we've gone without all these years? For you to end up serving tea and toast in a café? For you to chuck it all away and be a doffer or a shopgirl?'

'I could go to the *Evening News* like Martin did. He's doing well now.'

'Aye. Brewing up and checking the Lost and Found. I know. He's talked to me and all.'

'But it's a start – I wouldn't mind . . .'

'Well I would.' Nancy grinned. 'And so does Bertha. Eeh Annie, I must tell you. She was in the Co-op this after, creating over they'd got her divvy cheque wrong from last week – you know, the big one as goes at the top of your new sheet. Anyroad, she turns round and sees me standing in the next queue. "'Ey Nancy," she shouts. "Come over 'ere an' tell this soft bugger fer t' get a pair o' glasses, will yer?" So we gets it sorted – it was only pennies out – and then she starts in about their Martin. "Eeh Nancy," she says to me, dead serious. "It's awful. I should never 'ave let 'im do that paper round fer Bryant's – it's put ideas in 'is 'ead an' there was 'im down for weavin'," she says.'

They both burst into gales of laughter, 'Oh Mother, you don't mean . . . she thinks the paper round was his downfall?'

'She does that. Happen she's got the idea as the newsprint rubbed off on his hands and got into his bloodstream.' Nancy wiped her eyes. 'She's bloody thick at times, is Bertha. Amazing how she managed to have a clever lad like Martin. Still, I had you, didn't I? But then your Dad was very clever.'

'Was he?'

'Passed all his subjects with flying colours in the army. Map-reading was his speciality – working out routes and roads round things, which bridges to blow up and all that.'

'You never talk about him. I often wonder what he was like.'

'Aye well. It doesn't seem right somehow, living with one man and talking about another. But I've not forgot him, Annie. Not a day goes by but I think of your Dad.'

'You loved him.'

'Yes, I did. Now, shift yourself and get them pots done. I'm going to see Eddie tonight, so I'd best spruce myself up a bit.'

Annie smiled. Although her mother was concerned about Higson, the atmosphere in the house was lighter, happier than it had ever been. A dark cloud had moved and let the sunshine in. And they weren't doing too badly financially either – Nancy's extra hours seemed to be almost replacing the small change that Eddie Higson used to hand over at the end of each week. Nancy even looked different when she came down ready to go out in her new clothes which she'd bought with a Providence cheque. The navy two-piece and spotted organdie blouse with the tiny bow at the neck made her look fresh and young – she didn't seem shrivelled any more. Her face had filled out a little and she had taken to wearing a dab of powder and a touch of lipstick 'to cheer Eddie up'.

'You look nice, Mother.'

'Well, I've got to do my best to lift his spirits. It's awful up there. Do you know, they've only got three walls? The fourth one's all big windows what they keep slid open all day – it's like blinking Siberia. Hey, shall I ask Edna Pritchard for a lend of one of her fur coats?'

'You could try.'

'She'd likely drop dead with shock. Even if she did lend it, I reckon she'd root through the bin so's she could stick the price tag back on.' Nancy pulled on her raincoat and picked up a scarf from the sideboard.

'Listen, Mother – why don't I get a Saturday job? They're always wanting people in the shops in town.'

'No. We're alright. We can manage if we just go careful. Look, leave them pots a minute and sit yourself down.'

They sat at the square table with its green and white check cloth and Nancy studied her hands for a few moments before speaking.

'Now, Annie. You know I'm not one for speechifying, but I'm going to have my say. Look at these hands – go on, look at them.' She held them out so that Annie could study the reddened skin, broken nails, enlarged joints.

'I never, ever want to see a daughter of mine with hands like these. I was but fourteen when I got set on, Annie, fourteen and frightened to death of the noise – I fainted twice in my first week on account of the heat. But there was nothing else, no chance of an education. That was just for the gentry, them as owned the mills.' She paused, her eyes bright with . . . was it anger?

'It's not that long since we got the vote, you know. Women were fastening themselves to railings, chucking themselves under horses' feet, getting force-fed in the jails when they tried to make a stand by starving. Did they do all that so's you'd end up with hands like mine? Oh I know somebody's got to do the factory work, but why can't women have chances to get on in life the same as men? Suffrage wasn't just to do with voting, Annie. It was about women being slaves – slaves to their husbands, slaves to the bosses who paid them in buttons for being female. Vote's not all we want, love. What we want is education. I'm telling you now, this has been a man's world since Adam was a lad and it's up to us women to change it. Your generation can do that. And the first thing you've got to do is educate the bloody men so's they'll recognize you for what you are – people first, women second.' Her eyes blazed with some inner light as she spoke.

'You've got a chance to fight on two fronts. You can lift yourself up out of the bottom drawer, get proper training and stand up with the gentry. And just as important – if not more so – you can get out there and prove yourself as good as any man. It's time for a woman's world. I decided that when you were born, decided to stop feeling sorry for you because you were a girl. Your Dad was a fighter and there's a lot of him in you. So get out, lass and kill them dead.'

Tears pricked Annie's lids and she blinked hard to stop them flowing down her face. Was this her mother, her quiet little mother who had gone along, a blind and uncomplaining servant to husband and employers all these years? How had she hidden all that anger, all that knowledge while she doffed tubes and made dinners? It was for me, thought Annie, she did it all for me . . . Then the tears defeated her and she covered her face with her hands.

'Nay, I didn't mean to upset you, lass . . .'

'But why didn't you fight for yourself, Mother?'

Nancy smiled reassuringly. 'Because it wasn't time, love. But it's time now. I can't let you leave school and if you took a Saturday job, you'd either neglect your books or miss out on your fun. And I want you to have some fun.'

'You didn't . . . you've never . . . had fun . . . oh, Mother, Mam . . .'

'What me? Me have no fun? I've near started a world war, never mind a riot in my time. Dry your eyes and I'll tell you the sort of thing I get up to.'

Annie rubbed her face with the sleeve of her cardigan and once the sobs had subsided, Nancy continued.

'It was Christmas. Foreman, a big daft lad called Tommy Sullivan, was as tiddly as a newt in the office. For once, I was glad of the noise of the machines, 'cos Tommy had been singing "Oh Little Town of Bethlehem" into an empty whisky bottle – he was using it as a microphone – for about three hours all out of tune. I was in charge of both rooms and I kept letting the girls go one at a time to listen at the office door – they were all paralysed laughing. We were getting nothing done – most of the bobbins were so overwound that they looked like giant beehives.

'So I decided we'd all sneak out early and we gets the shoes changed, grabs the bags and the coats and I'm there at the front leading all the girls out on their hands and knees past Tommy Sullivan's glass door. By now, he'd swapped his song – he was going in for "Silent Night" and it was that noisy, I'll swear they could have heard him under the Town Hall clock.

'Now you've got to picture this in your mind, Annie. We're all creeping down the stairs in a line with me at the front. All of a sudden, we come to a dead stop. Now the reason for this was quite simple really – the stair rail had gone up my sleeve – I was wearing that wide-sleeved green coat I used to have. And when this here stair rail reaches my elbow, I grind to a halt with a couple of dozen women behind me all whispering "What's up, Nancy?" Well, I could have told them what was up – the rail was up, right up. But I couldn't say it for laughing.

'Anyway, they all start laughing and all, but they've no idea what they're laughing at – and that makes me laugh even more. Then, to top it all, Tommy Sullivan arrives with his microphone and a couple of spare brown ales. "What's up?" says Tommy. Honest, I thought I was dying. I couldn't breathe for laughing and nobody had guessed what was wrong. I kept pointing to my arm, but with me being at the front, nobody could tell what I was on about.

'Then we got what the French call the piece de resistance. Soft Tommy shouts "Merry Christmas, girls," falls over the back of the queue and right down the stairs, finishes up in the Infirmary with concussion and alcohol poisoning, misses Christmas altogether. He's always blamed me for that, Annie. Mind you, he did give up the drink soon after . . .'

The two of them were helpless with mirth, screaming their laughter into a room that had not heard this sound for many a year. When their giggles began to subside, Nancy reached for Annie's hand and said, 'Never pity me, love. Don't go thinking as my life has been without purpose. I might not be a churchgoer, but I know everything's here for a reason, right down to worms and sparrows. Nay, don't feel sorry for me, lass . . .'

'It's Tommy Sullivan I feel sorry for . . .'

'Aye well, he had it coming. But I laughed all the way home that night on the bus. 'Course, the conductor had to say "What's up?" and that set me off again, I near went hysterical. He looked at me dead funny and I was beginning to think as how they'd send for a black van any minute and a couple of blokes in white coats.'

When David Pritchard walked into the house – because nobody had heard him knocking at the door – he found the pair of them doubled up in pain at the kitchen table.

Annie looked up at him. 'Have you . . . have you got your white coat handy? Only it's my mother, she's . . . she's gone . . .' Renewed gales of laughter followed the unfinished sentence and he joined in their mirth, unable to remain unaffected.

'He doesn't . . . he doesn't even know what he's laughing at! Just like . . . oh God . . . just like . . .' Nancy hid her face in her hands, incapable of continuing.

'But Mother, this isn't fair. If anybody ever asks me what's up, I'll never cope.'

'I know. I've been like that myself for years . . .'

Nancy composed herself with difficulty. When David asked her what the joke was, she said, 'I'll tell you in the car. Good job your driving's improved a bit.'

Annie waved as the car moved off. She'd had happy days before, days when she'd invented a new game, found a good book, days when parcels of goodies from Tom in America had arrived. But this was special. She felt really close to her mother at last. Any barrier had now been removed and even if Higson did ever return, surely this new closeness could not be destroyed.

'Oh, you're wrong, Mother,' she whispered to herself as she walked up the path. 'I didn't get all my little talents from my father.' And Nancy was just one among millions. There must be others, clever women all worn down by hard work and tedious marriages. And yes, it would be up to Annie's generation to redress the balance. She had to make it, must get to the top of one tree or another and take Nancy with her. Only then would the sacrifice be justified. As for him – well, she simply refused to consider him. He had just better not be around, that was all.

As she was about to close the door, she noticed Dolly Nelson hovering on the pavement, obviously in a state of indecision. 'Have you lost something, Mrs Nelson?' she asked.

'You might say that, lass.'

'Can I help?'

'Nay, I don't think so. Were that yer mam goin' off to see Eddie?'

'Yes. The buses to the sanatorium don't run too often, so the doctor gave her a lift.'

''Ow is 'e? Only 'e's cleaned me winders fer years an' I 'eard as 'ow 'e weren't so well.'

'He's got TB, Mrs Nelson. We don't know how long he'll be away, but somebody's going to rent the round, so your windows should get done soon.'

'Aye. Ta then, luv. Tell yer mam ter give 'im me best then.'

'Yes. Yes, I will. Goodnight, Mrs Nelson.'

'Ta-ra, luv.'

A feeling of unease came over Annie as she closed the door. The woman had never been near before – why the sudden interest in an absent window cleaner? She deliberately shrugged the thought away and got on with the dishes. Life was suddenly so easy, so relaxed, why spoil it by worrying about Dolly Nelson? It was great having the freedom of the house, no-one to avoid, no shadows to fear. She stopped suddenly, tea-towel in one hand, cup in the other. Her mother hadn't suddenly developed all this wit and intelligence – it must have been there all the time, hidden, weighted down by the silence that usually swamped this house. Was it possible that a woman of such obvious insight could live here and not realize, or at least suspect what was going on?

She walked into the living room and stood on the rug. Everything remained the same, sofa against the staircase, table in the centre, sideboard along the wall between kitchen and stairway doors. Had Nancy ever suspected?

Minutes passed, filled only by the loud ticking of the mantel clock. During those minutes, Annie, knowing that her mother's life had been dictated rather than chosen, concluded that some things simply cannot be dealt with by the human mind, that sensibility and reason can and sometimes must be poles apart. And during those minutes, Annie matured. She realized that even if Nancy had suspected, then her conscious mind could not have allowed such thoughts to filter through.

If anyone should ever ask Annie where she grew up, she would say 'In a living room in front of a range listening to a noisy clock.' It would be the truth.

Well, this was a pretty kettle and no mistake. Dolly Nelson opened her legs to the fire, heedless of the dark purple mottling on her shins, marks she had acquired over years by sitting too close to the heat. She couldn't even tell him! Three months gone and not a penny to her name – oh aye, he'd told her it was a chance in a million, him fathering a kid. But it was his alright. No use saying it was Eric's – she'd seen neither hide nor hair of him for nigh on a year, he was in a steelworks in Sheffield, never even wrote, just stuck a few quid in an envelope now and again for the kids. Eeh God, what a pickle.

She shifted her bulk and leaned over to roll her stockings down. And she missed Eddie, she really did. He'd never had a lot to say, but he'd kept her company and given her plenty of the other. But he'd given her something else, something she hadn't bargained for. Oh she was regular enough, but she never thought she'd catch, not now when she was but eighteen months short of forty. Mind you, given that she could still have a kid and that Eddie had a chance in a million, was it any wonder? Hammer and tongs they'd been at it, months on end, couldn't leave it alone.

Well, he'd have to be told and that was for sure. He was going to leave Nancy anyroad, so what difference? He could move in here when he got better, same as he would have if he'd stayed well. But it was going to take guts, going up to that place and telling him. If she was any good at writing and such, she could do a letter. Oh heck. She'd have to go up to the hospital, there was nowt else for it. You couldn't say it right in a letter. Face to face, she could tell him she wanted him – and his kid and all. Not that that was strictly true – four was enough for anybody. But he'd never had a kid, not one of his own. It might cheer him up if he knew she had one in the oven.

Aye, she'd kept a watch on Nancy so she could work out visiting times. Nancy had been going of a Monday on the bus and a Thursday with the doctor in his car. Right. She'd go tomorrow, Friday night. He'd get right enough once he knew he'd something to get better for, something a bit more lively than that dried-up stick he'd married. What Eddie needed now was a real woman, one who knew how to go about catering for his needs proper, somebody who enjoyed a glass of stout and a bit of slap and tickle.

She dozed, her slack mouth twitching while she dreamed of herself and Eddie down the registry all dressed up for the occasion. Her eyes flew open as something quickened in her belly. No. She settled back. It was likely wind after that pork pie. Aye, she'd tell him tomorrow. It would all come out right in the end.

7

The Rape

He was going round the bend, he knew that for sure. There were four of them in the room, if you could call it a room – one wall missing half the bloody day and most of the night too. It reminded him of the other place where he'd gone crazy the first time, only then he'd been too weak from lack of nourishment to shout about it. This time he was getting fed and he sometimes had the strength to scream if he had a mind to.

Nights were the worst, because then he would dream about that prison camp, could smell the stink of vomit and dysentery all around him. He would wake moaning and shouting and nurses would run to his bed, rub him down, change the sheets, trying all the while to comfort him with their stupid talk. What the hell did bloody nurses know anyway? They'd somewhere to go after the shift, this was just a job to them. What did they know about being a prisoner? Because that was what he was, oh aye, he was in prison alright – even if there was a wall missing. They might just as well take his photo and stamp a number over it for all the chance he had of getting out of here – and there'd be no time off for good behaviour. He knew whose fault it was. The flaming Jerries had done this to him, hadn't they? God, and he used to think he'd had an easy war sitting it out and waiting for the end.

The other three patients had given up on him. Oh they'd tried the first few days, tipping him off about which nurses would sneak your fags in, where to hide them, how to grab a crafty smoke in the bog or by the window while the nurses were changing shifts. But they'd got the message in the end. They left him alone now and that was how he wanted it.

Nancy came in twice a week to cheer him up. And she did look cheerful and all, better than she'd looked for years, the bitch. It suited her alright, having him locked up with TB. Dolly had faded into the distance, it seemed years since he'd seen her. She wouldn't want him now anyway, not with this rotten disease. And he had his eye elsewhere, didn't he? Not all the nurses were male and that little blonde on nights would do for him if he could just get her on her own. Aye, she reminded him of somebody, did that one. She'd be due on about now, happen he'd have a wander down to the kitchen for his cocoa in a bit. He looked at the other three, all chatting about their families and swapping magazines that their visitors had brought in.

He got up, slipped into his dressing gown and went out into the corridor. Light streamed from the kitchen at the far end – aye, she'd be in there now with the drinks on a trolley. He'd go and have a look at her – looking cost nothing, did it?

She turned from the sink as he entered the kitchen. By the hell, she was a bonny piece, blonde hair, blue eyes, good legs. The buttons fair strained over the top half of her body where the uniform clung so tightly that little imagination was needed to visualize what was underneath. And nurses were supposed to be fair game, weren't they?

'Hello, Mr Higson. Has your wife been in to see you tonight?'

'Aye, she came in for an hour.'

'Good. Here's your cocoa.'

He sat on the edge of the table, his eyes fixed on her round ripeness. He itched to touch her, felt his body stirring in readiness. She handed him the drink and he reached out past the mug, his fingers closing over a warm soft breast.

'Now stop that, Mr Higson.' She sounded cool, as if she was used to it, not a bit put out or frightened.

'I just want a little feel, that's all.'

She slapped his hand away with the air of one brushing off a troublesome bluebottle. 'Come on now. Drink your cocoa and pop back into bed like a good boy . . .'

Suddenly he was filled with a blinding rage. Be a good boy, do as you're told – who did she think she was? She reminded him of . . . yes, that snooty she-devil at home, that runt with the high-falutin voice and the big ideas. He felt strange and dizzy. The room began to recede, everything seemed to be turning dark red around the edges. He grabbed her, turned her round so that her back was towards him and clamped a hand tightly over her mouth. He didn't hear the cup as it clattered to the floor, because by then he was in another time, another place and there was no knife under the mattress. He would show her now. She'd have to be punished for the knife and the poker too. Oh yes, now was his chance to teach her, to use her for the one thing women were fit for.

She was beginning to struggle, but they usually did, didn't they? They were good at that, pretending they didn't want it, didn't enjoy it. Well, she was going to get it at last. He'd give it to her good and proper, make her pay, make them all pay.

He dragged her down and straddled her, punching her hard on the jaw when she opened her mouth to scream. Grinning lewdly into Annie's face, he fastened his fingers round the throat and squeezed until the girl went limp. Quickly, he did what he had to do, ripping into her swiftly, his excitement mounting as she regained consciousness. 'Aye, I've got you,' he whispered hoarsely. 'Where's your knife now, eh? I told you it would be me, I told you I'd get you first.' He slowed his frantic movements and tore open the top of her uniform, pulling away the underwear to expose her upper body.

He was panting hard, ailing lungs struggling for the oxygen he needed to complete his task. He clawed at her trembling flesh, then sank his teeth into a nipple until he tasted blood. There was no end to it, no end. He could go on all night, he knew he could. Feverishly, he thrust deeper, his body slapping against her thighs. Annie Byrne was his, finally his. No matter who had her in the future, she'd never forget this, never, never. He felt power, real power rising in him, driving him on to hurt, hurt this girl, the one he'd prepared, the one who was a woman now. It was so good, just a hair's-breadth from pain when he finally exploded in an orgasm that went on and on until he had emptied himself into this female vessel. When at last he slumped over her, his tortured lungs rasping, he felt a momentary satisfaction he had never known before, as if he had won a prize or killed an enemy.

Then they came in looking for their cocoa, another nurse with them. For a second or two he felt confused as he looked at the girl on the floor. The face was wrong. It was bloody and bruised, but he could still tell that it wasn't . . . Before he could begin to think straight, he was dragged to his feet and out of the room. A man was crying, the stupid bastard, crying like a kid. What for? He'd only had a woman – she'd live, wouldn't she? He'd only done what every man wanted to do.

They carried him up the corridor and threw him into a bathroom. Four of them came in with him, bolted the door, then laid into him. They weren't supposed to be strong, TB patients, but they found the energy from somewhere.

The beating was so brutal that when the staff eventually broke down the door, it took them a while to work out which was the victim. The five of them lay on the floor covered in blood. Eddie Higson's blood. Four stood up and stumbled away. The fifth didn't move.

They sat at the table with the green check cloth, Annie, Nancy and Dr Pritchard. Nancy was numb with shock while Annie sat pale and still, whitened fingertips gripping the edge of the table. David Pritchard felt as if his heart would break for these two women. Yes, she was a woman now, was little Annie. What he'd just told the pair of them was enough to make her grow up.

'What will happen now?' she was asking.

'Well – he's heavily sedated and he's being given some fairly intensive care. He won't be charged until he recovers consciousness. When he did come round last night after the . . . er . . . fight with the other

304

patients, he was obviously unaware of where he was.'

Nancy lifted a shaking hand to her brow. 'But why would he attack a nurse? He's not a violent man . . .' She looked quickly at her daughter. 'He used to hit Annie, but he hasn't for a long time – has he, love?'

'No. No, he hasn't.'

'I think you should leave the room for a few minutes, Anne,' said David quietly. 'I have to talk to your mother in private.'

After a glance at each of them, Annie left the room without question.

'She's a good girl, Nancy.'

'Aye, I know, I know.'

David reached two cups from the sideboard then, after taking a bottle from his bag, poured a hefty measure of brandy into each one. She was going to need it once she'd heard what he must say. And he'd need it too, because he was about to break every rule in his book. He drank deeply while Nancy sipped at the burning liquid, coughing as it caught her throat.

'Drink a bit more, Nancy. It'll take the edge off things.'

She obeyed, welcoming the warmth as it flooded into her, soothing jagged nerves, taking the stiffness out of her hands.

He refilled the cups. 'Right.' He breathed deeply. 'Eddie was found by four patients in the kitchen of the sanatorium. The nurse – a female – was unconscious on the floor. They took him away and gave him a beating – he's lucky to be alive.' He watched Nancy's eyes as questions began to arrive in their grey depths. 'She'd been raped,' he finished, almost in a whisper.

'Raped?' Her jaw dropped. 'Raped?'

'Yes.'

'By . . . Eddie?'

'He was the only other person in the room, Nancy. And . . . well . . . his pyjama trousers were disarranged. There's no doubt in my mind that he did it.'

She remained very still, eyes fixed on him, mouth still slightly agape.

'There are witnesses, Nancy – people who will testify . . .'

'No! No, I don't believe it! I won't believe it!'

He could make her believe it, he knew he could. But how would she take the rest of it? Would she even choose to disbelieve the awful truth which he must, he felt sure, tell her now on this night before it was too late, before she started to become defensive of Eddie Higson, before she could consider ever allowing him back into her life? And into Anne's life too.

'He's a very sick man, Nancy. Some experts in tuberculosis believe that many sufferers display certain symptoms and that one of these can be a heightened libido. That means they want – they need – a lot of sex.'

'But that's not normal. Rape, I mean. It's not normal.'

'No.'

'Then why did he do it?'

'I honestly don't know. He must be very ill indeed – and not just physically ill.'

With trembling fingers she picked up the cup and helped herself to some more brandy. 'Doctor – you mean he's mental, don't you?'

'Possibly.'

She gulped the drink in two swallows, catching her breath as it seared past her throat.

'You're going to have to be very strong now, Nancy. What you said before – about rape not being normal – you were right, of course. Your husband's behaviour has been . . . odd for some time.'

The brandy was beginning to take effect and Nancy stared at the wall behind the doctor's head, speaking, it seemed, to herself.

'She never liked him. My little Annie – she used to say "He's a bad man, he's a bad man."'

'Children are quick to spot oddities. You know the saying – out of the mouths of babes – well, Nancy, Anne was right. And she should know better than anybody else.'

'She was so funny.' Nancy sighed. 'Begged me not to marry him, she did, but you do what you think's best, don't you? I'll never forget the day we . . .'

'Nancy! Listen to me now, my dear.' He moved his chair closer to the table and took her hands in his. 'You know I care a great deal for your daughter. Well, I may hurt her very deeply by what I am about to do, but it must be done, I'm afraid. You see, it's up to you now – you must protect her.'

'Protect her? What from?'

'From him, Nancy. I promised that I would never mention this to you. I'm even violating a patient's confidence – breaking an oath, I suppose. But I care more for you and for that girl out there than I do for my job. A lot more.'

Nancy stared at him for a long time before speaking. What was he saying? What did he know about Eddie and why did Annie need protection? Somewhere at the back of her mind, a warning bell sounded, dull, far away, yet menacing. No, it couldn't be! None of this was true, none of it real. He'd had a reputation at one time, had Eddie. It was likely something from his army days, kept on file, passed down from one doctor to another. He couldn't be a rapist. Annie was safe – she'd always been safe . . .

David read her confusion and tightened his grip on her hands. 'He didn't manage it the last time, Nancy. She coped extremely well. He has the scars on his arm to prove that.'

He watched her face closely, waiting for the impact. At first, she simply looked puzzled, then a dim light invaded her eyes and her cheeks showed twin spots of colour as she suddenly sat bolt upright in her chair. 'You mean . . . oh no . . . it can't be, it mustn't be . . .' She nodded her head towards the door.

'Yes. Yes, Nancy.'

The noise that came from her then was unearthly, something between a howl and a scream, a sound that David had certainly never heard before. She began to rock back and forth, her face nearly hitting the table, the chair almost tumbling backwards each time as she pulled at his hands. 'No! Aw no, Doctor. Not that – tell me it's not true!' It couldn't be, it couldn't be. 'Not my Annie! No, no, please – not my little girl . . .'

He gritted his teeth and hung grimly onto her hands. She continued to rock violently, putting him in mind of certified cases he'd witnessed long ago during his training. Dear God, had he gone too far? Oh he didn't care about himself and some outdated bloody oath – they could shove the practice, but what had he done to this little woman? He should have waited. If only she would cry, she had to cry.

The tears came at last in floods, torrents pouring

from her eyes and nose, while from her wide open mouth she howled her primeval misery.

When Annie ran into the room she found them both standing by the sideboard clinging to one another. Seeing Dr Pritchard crying was a terrible thing. He didn't make a sound, his face was still as a stone; the only movement on it was made by tears as they ran down, dripping unheeded into Nancy's hair. Annie didn't need telling – she knew what had brought this on. Her eyes met David's and found confirmation there.

Nancy turned and opened her arms to her daughter. The three of them wept together, clung together for comfort, each feeling glad that the others were there, that something was over and finished with forever. Annie, her face buried in David's rough tweed jacket, breathed in the medicine and peppermint smell of her saviour, her heart almost bursting with gratitude. Her mother would not, could not grieve forever. As if chains were being tossed aside, she felt her first sense of imminent freedom. Soon, very soon, when Nancy could come to terms with this new shock, mother and daughter could begin, at last, to live.

They were alone now. Nancy had managed to stir herself sufficiently to make a pot of tea and they sat, one each side of the grate, cups balanced on the full-width fireguard. Inch by inch, she had dragged most of the story out of her daughter, her lips tightening into a hard straight line as she listened to the horror of Ensign Street, the nightmare of her present home, the indignities Annie had suffered in this very house, in the bathroom so treasured till now, till all this . . .

She looked at her beautiful child, this precious girl

who had endured so much. 'So you never told me because he said he'd kill us?'

'That's right.'

'Did you never tell anybody, love?'

'A priest. He came up and thumped him.'

'And I'll finish him off, by Christ, I will! I'll go up to that bloody hospital and I'll wring his neck! Holy Mother of God . . .'

'Don't, Mam. Nothing's changed, has it? We're still the same. This went on for eight or nine years – I don't see why you want to do something now, when it's all over.'

'I want him to pay, Annie.'

'It's too late, Mother. Anyway, he has paid.'

'Paid? Has he bloody hell paid!'

'I clouted him with the poker and put him in the infirmary, didn't I? I half-drowned him, I knifed him – there's been enough violence.'

'He's not dead yet. I want him dead so's I can dance on his grave.'

'Mother . . .!'

'Anyway, why didn't you tell me when you got older, eh? I can understand about when you were little and he threatened to kill you . . .'

'He said he'd swear I'd encouraged him. I was afraid he might just be believed.'

'I'd never have believed him, Annie.'

'The court might have! Don't you see – it was the only way. I was so confused – I knew you'd kill him if you ever found out. And where would that get you? Prison – or worse. Dr Pritchard wanted to get the police, but I told him I didn't want to end up in a children's home and I didn't want you to lose the breadwinner.'

'Breadwinner? He's not given me enough for a scrape of marg during the last two years . . .'

'That's not the point! I just did what I thought best and Dr Pritchard backed me up. We got a lawyer to draw up a paper about what Eddie Higson had done to me over the years. We used that to blackmail him and he's never touched me since. Only now, he's done it to somebody else instead.'

Nancy walked across the room, placing her hands on her daughter's shoulders. 'My good brave lass,' she whispered before pulling Annie into her arms. 'We shall never set eyes on him again, I promise you that. The law'll see to him now.'

'Thanks, Mother.'

'What for?'

'Just for being my mother.'

'Nay, lass. If I'd been a good mother . . .'

'You didn't know . . .'

'I knew you hated him. I should have found out why.'

'Never mind, Mam. You know what you always say about spilt milk.'

'Aye, but you're not milk, Annie. You, my girl, are the cream. And never forget that.'

Dolly was puzzled. Frightened too, if she could but admit it. It had cost her one and six and all to get up there, then they wouldn't let her see him, said he was in isolation or summat.

She eased herself onto the bus seat which, though intended for two, managed to accommodate just Dolly and her bag, leaving little room for anyone else. So. It looked as if it were going to be a long job. If he were that bad as he had to be put on his own, then this one in her belly would likely be at school before its dad got out. Still, right was only right at the end of the day. He'd had his fun and she wasn't going to pay his whack as well as her own. Bad enough going through birthing a child, without having him as fathered it out of the road and not tipping up a few bob. Aye, there were nowt else for it, she'd have to call and see his missus, get the cards on the table and demand her rights. Mind, that Nancy were a dark horse. Quiet like, but Dolly reckoned she might turn nasty if pressed. And what about the flaming neighbours? Oh, she'd have to say as how Eric had been back for just the one night, sneaked out in the early hours and left her up the spout.

But she'd best get through to Eddie some road and if it had to happen through his missus, well it was just too bad. She could stick up for herself, could Dolly.

She took a bunch of grapes intended for Eddie and pushed them one by one into her mouth, heedless of the juice dripping down her chin. She'd been partial to a bit of fruit lately, probably summat to do with the kid on the way.

The bus stopped right outside the Higsons' house, so she got off, might as well get it over and done with and she could always catch another for the last two stops. The girl opened the door.

'Is yer Mam in?'

She looked as if she'd been crying. 'She's not well, Mrs Nelson.'

'Oh. Well, I'm right sorry to 'ear that. Nothin' serious, I 'ope?'

'Just a bad cold.'

Dolly felt as if the wind had been taken from her sails. 'Tell 'er as 'ow I want to see 'er – when she's

312

better, like. Ask 'er will she call round one afternoon – I'm off matinees, so I'll be in all week.' Yes, that might be better. Better on her own patch than in Nancy Higson's kitchen.

'I'll tell her,' the girl said.

'Right then, luv. Ta-ra now.'

It was a fine night. She'd walk home, it wasn't that far and she'd a couple of nice green apples to keep her company.

'Who was it, Annie?' Nancy stirred the fire, then set the old blackened kettle on the grid to boil yet again.

'It was Mrs Nelson.'

'Dolly Nelson? What did she want?'

'I don't know.'

'Didn't she say?'

'No.'

They were both bone-weary; this evening had gone on forever. Nancy, after hearing all that from Annie, was almost too tired to care about what Dolly Nelson might want. The initial shock was over, but now the guilt had started to move in, creeping over her like icy fingers as she asked herself why she'd left Annie with him all these years, why she'd never listened, never noticed. She beat her closed fists against the wall. Jesus, Mary and Joseph, if she had him here now, right now . . .

'Don't, Mam.'

Nancy straightened. 'Did she leave a message?'

'She wants you to go and visit her.'

'Visit her? I don't know her. Last time I saw her she was buying tripe in the Jubilee Stores – months ago. We say hello, but we never pass the time. Whatever can she want?'

Annie, whose senses in spite of tiredness were still

313

alert to the point of pain, said, as casually as she could, 'Don't go, Mother.'

'Why not?'

'I'm not sure. I just know you shouldn't go, that's all.'

8

Repercussions

It was a long upstairs room at the back of the house with two mock-Georgian windows, each covered by the lace curtains Mother seemed so taken with. Dad had made it really comfortable, with a carpet square that could be rolled back for dancing, a couple of tables with folding canvas chairs, a dartboard on the wall and a larger table for records and the Dansette.

Simon opened a bottle of lemonade and took a swig, aware of how horrified his mother would be if she realized he had sunk to such depths. She was furious about all this, he could tell, though little had been said. There was an atmosphere in the house, not the usual coldness, but a crackling silence, as if a thunderstorm would shortly break.

He stacked the records, looked at his watch, then went on to the landing. It would be better if he met them out on the road. Mother would consider the felony thoroughly compounded if they were to ring the bell like normal visitors. Her bedroom door was open and he could see right into the flowery girlish room with its frills and rose-pink lighting. She sat by the window in a chintz-covered nursing chair, peering out, waiting for them to arrive. He felt pity for her, so much that he almost ran in and said, 'It will be alright.' But he couldn't. Something in the way she sat, motionless and ramrod-stiff, precluded any such approach – as indeed did reason – he knew she would never approve of Anne and Martin, let alone Lofty and the rest.

He ran down the stairs at speed, opened the front door and waited under a white light illuminating the brass plate that announced his father's profession. They advanced, a tangle of stick-thin legs in drain-pipe trousers, bopping and jiving along the road while the girls, in rustling skirts with layers of net just showing at the hem, followed in a manner only slightly more sedate. Dad was out on call, so his main line of defence was temporarily down. And he wanted it to go well this first time, especially after Dad had said to take care of Anne as there'd been a bit of trouble which must not be mentioned.

They burst in, bringing life and colour into the tastefully drab hall, some of the boys running part-way up the stairs to slide down the highly polished banister several times. Anne and Martin were the last to arrive, separate from the rest, hand in hand as always. And yet although they were outwardly a pair, Simon felt they were incomplete without him. A strange trio, this, he thought. Himself, cherished son of a self-appointed lady of the manor, then Martin Cullen, product of a poverty-stricken home containing no less than seven children . . . and lastly, but never least, Anne Byrne. How to describe her? Daughter of a dead soldier, child of Nancy Higson, doffer and ring-spinner of this parish?

'Hiya, kid.' Martin clapped a hand on to Simon's shoulder.

'Hello, Simon.' She stood under the square chandelier, her hand still in Martin's. No, he couldn't describe her, apart from how she looked, that sad-

316

happy smile, the fall of yellow hair left loose to cover her long back right down to the waist, clear green eyes set wide under a smooth white forehead, the small straight nose with its sprinkling of freckles. Nonconformist might be the word for Anne, who seemed unaware of, or at least unaffected by, the fashion of the day, rarely tying her hair back into a typical pony-tail, never to be seen in a skirt held impossibly wide by layers of crackle-nylon. As usual, she wore rolled-up jeans, white socks and sandals and an over-large sweater with a plain crew neck. But she stood out, for her brightness came from within and she needed no garish feathers to enhance her beauty. Because for Simon, she was beauty – not beautiful, but the very essence of all that was soul-touching. Was empathy, he wondered, akin to love? Yet he felt no jealousy, no resentment towards Martin. He liked him, loved him even, in the way one might love a brother, an older and more worldly-wise blood relation who offered comradeship and demanded little in return.

She placed a hand on Simon's arm. 'I can't stay long. My mother isn't too well – Auntie Jessie's with her just now, but I'll have to get back before she leaves.'

'I'm only glad you came. War could break out at any minute – I may need troops.'

Martin stepped forward. 'Listen, Sime. If she doesn't want us, we'll go – I'll get them all out if this means trouble for you.' The noise from upstairs was deafening, music blaring, laughter and the stamping of feet echoing throughout the house.

David let himself in at the front door and Simon, relieved beyond measure, stepped aside to allow his father into the hall.

'Noisy, eh?' grinned David, his eyes flicking towards the ceiling. He followed them upstairs and into the room, his smile broadening while he watched a pair of rock 'n' rollers whose dancing displayed a degree of athleticism that had to be admired. When the performance had ended, Lofty offered him a lemonade and David sat on a canvas chair sipping at the mug of fizzing liquid. One of the girls, brightly painted and in a dress of multi-coloured glazed cotton, came over to him. 'We want to say ta, Doc, for lettin' us come in your 'ouse.'

'Hello, Margaret – I hardly recognized you! You're welcome, all of you. Now listen.' They waited, respect plain on their faces, for David to continue. 'I'm laying down no rules, but don't go wild. Know what I mean?' They nodded, murmuring their agreement. 'This is a big house, plenty of room for everyone, but please remember that it is fastened to the house next door, that glass is thin and that if you get too loud, you'll disturb the whole neighbourhood.'

Margaret smiled. 'We don't dance all t' time, Doc. Sometimes we just sit talkin' – or listenin' to Annie more like it. Once she gets on 'er 'igh 'orse over summat, she can start a right good thing goin' – interestin' – you know?'

'Oh shut up, Maggie,' said Annie, blushing. 'You give your sixpennyworth and you know it.'

'Aye. But t' difference atween thee an' me is I allers wants fivepence change!'

They all laughed and Lofty broke away to put another record on the Dansette. David slipped out quietly, only to find that Margaret had followed him on to the landing.

''Ey, Doc. Can I 'ave a quick word?'

318

'Certainly. Here or in the surgery?'

'Oh 'ere'll do. It's nowt really, just me Mam – she's gone a bit funny, like. She sits there for hours, starin' into t' fire, there's never no tea when we come in from school. She's like . . . sad, if you know what I mean.'

Poor Margaret, thought David. Not yet fifteen and with the body and mind of a woman already. He thought about Dolly Nelson, knowing only too well the reason for her depression. A fifth child on the way, her husband gone, no sign of the baby's father putting in an appearance or offering support. 'I've seen your mother. She'll get better in time, I'm sure. But you're a sensible girl – there is something you can do to help.'

'Consider it done, Doc.'

Yes, she was a bright girl, this oldest of Dolly Nelson's children. Young people these days had a certain resilience, pondered David, wondering obliquely whether all that cod-liver oil had done some good after all. These war-babies were a tough breed, stronger in mind and body than any previous generation. 'Try to get her to eat the right foods, Margaret. She's overweight . . .'

'I know, she's fat, I've told 'er that.'

'Fish, green vegetables, fruit – those are the kind of foods she should be eating.'

'Aye. She's taken to fruit lately.'

'Well, that's a good sign, isn't it?'

As she went off to join the others, David remained on the landing, his head moving slowly from side to side. Yes, it was a sign. But not necessarily a good one.

Jessie Gallagher sat in the rocker by the living-room range, staring at her sister who occupied the straight-backed chair opposite hers. Jessie's mouth hung open, her jaw slack yet immovable as she tried to take in what their Nancy had just said. And the way she'd told it too, like she was reading it out of a book, like it had happened to somebody else.

'I don't want it spreading, Jessie. I've told you because I trust you and . . . well, I needed to talk to somebody round my own age and it had to be family.'

'Does our Annie know?' Jessie finally managed.

'She knows he went for a nurse – she doesn't need any pictures drawing.' Of course, she hadn't told Jessie about the other thing, about him and Annie . . . Unable to sit still with the thoughts, she jumped up to pour tea.

'Well,' said Jessie. 'Well, I'll go to the foot of our stairs – who'd have thought it, eh? And him such a quiet man.'

'Happen it's the quiet ones that need watching, Jess. Them as makes a noise gets things out of their system. He was a brooder.' Yes, she was talking about him in the past tense and that was right, because he'd gone, gone forever, just as if he were dead and buried.

'Will it get in the papers, Nancy?'

A spoon clattered to the floor as Nancy steadied herself against the table's edge. 'Eeh no – I never thought. Oh my God, how could I forget the papers? Oh no no . . .'

'Now calm yourself. See, sit down while I make the brew. What's done's done and there's nowt to make it different.'

Nancy sat by the fire while Jessie took over the tea-making, stirring a little extra sugar into her sister's cup. 'I wish I'd kept my gob shut now, I do. I'd no intentions of upsetting you, not with what's already on your plate . . .'

'Nay, you're right, lass. It's a consideration, by God it is.'

'Give over. It might never get in the *Evening News* anyroad.'

'*Evening News*? This could make the front page of the *News of the World*, this could. After all, if that poor nurse was hurt bad . . .' For the first time, Nancy found herself really thinking, caring about his victim. She must be in a terrible state. Aye, Nancy knew what he could be like. She felt sick to the core as she remembered the black silent shape hovering over her in the night, his body slick and vile-smelling with all that sweat. Oh, she'd had to put up with it – he was her husband. Even a paper Catholic couldn't refuse. But the other things he'd tried to make her do, unnatural things, nothing to do with making babies, then the anger when she'd refused to allow . . . She fled to the kitchen and retched fruitlessly over the sink while Jessie patted her back and murmured words of comfort.

'Oh Jessie – that poor girl . . .'

'Come on. Have you finished? See, have a glass of water – sip it slow now.'

But she couldn't swallow, her stomach still heaved. 'To think I lived for years with a creature like that . . . oh Jessie, Jessie . . .'

'That's right, love. You have a good cry, it's only natural.'

When Nancy was calmer, they returned to their seats by the fire. Jessie knew she would have to be going soon. Where was that girl? Fancy her leaving her Mam at a time like this. 'Where's Annie?' she asked now.

'With her friends – oh I made her go. If you'd seen the state she was in the other night, you'd have done the same. She's never left my side till now – I had to kick her out. Even then I saw her standing at the corner waiting till she saw you get off the bus. This isn't something she can tell her mates, Jessie. She'll have to put a brave face on and the sooner she starts, the better. Don't you worry. She'll look after me alright. We'll look after one another.'

'Well, I'll have to get the ten past. Eugene wants the last half hour in the Feathers and I'll have to see to the kids.'

'I'll be alright. Anyway, it's only twenty to.'

A sharp rapping at the front door brought them both to their feet.

'I'll go,' said Jessie.

'No.' Nancy rubbed her face with the corner of her apron. 'I'd better do it. It might be to do with what's happened. I've got to face these things, it's my problem, not yours.'

She was somehow not surprised to find Dolly Nelson on the doorstep.

'Can I come in, Mrs 'Igson? Only I've sat in waitin' fer you ter drop by, like . . .'

Nancy stepped aside to let her pass, noticing how the woman's vast bulk seemed to fill the narrow vestibule.

As they entered the living room, Dolly exclaimed, 'Ooh, I never realized as 'ow you 'ad a visitor.'

'It's alright.' Nancy spoke from behind the woman. 'You can go in.'

The two sisters stood side by side with their backs

to the fireplace as Dolly eased herself into a chair at the table. Moments passed while they waited for her to speak.

'It's . . . well . . . private, like.'

Nancy glanced at Jessie. 'It doesn't matter. Whatever you've come to say can be said in front of my sister.'

'I'll go if you want.' Jessie made for the sofa where her coat lay, but Nancy took hold of her arm and pulled her back.

They both continued to stare at the massive female whose flesh seemed to overflow into every corner of the room.

'It's about your Eddie,' she eventually began. ''E's in the 'ospital, isn't 'e?'

'Yes. The TB sanatorium,' replied Nancy.

'Only I've gorra message for 'im. Summat as won't keep.'

Nancy walked to the table and sat down opposite Dolly, wondering what was coming next and how much more she could take. This woman was trouble, she knew it in her bones. And Annie had said as much in her own way, hadn't she?

'What message?'

Dolly studied Nancy carefully for several seconds before announcing, 'I'm carryin'.'

'What?'

'You 'eard – I'm carryin'.'

'A . . . a baby?'

'Aye.'

Nancy's fists curled themselves tight on the green check cloth. A million to one chance, a million to one, thank God it was Dolly and not . . .

'Are you sure it's his?' Jessie was asking now.

'It's Eddie's right enough.' The answer came loud and definite.

A million to one and a million thoughts in her brain. It might have been his own baby he'd kicked to death that time . . . he killed babies . . . he raped nurses . . . a million to one . . . he nearly raped Annie . . . a baby was coming, the nurse was having a baby, Annie was having his . . .

Nancy slumped across the table in a dead faint. The two women leapt up and lifted her, dragging her across the rug towards the sofa.

'Eeh nay,' puffed Dolly. 'I never expected 'er to take on this road. Good God, it's not th' end o' t' world now, is it?'

'She's a lot on her mind,' said Jessie curtly. 'Just lift her legs up then get that tot of brandy off the sideboard – fetch a teaspoon while you're at it.'

Jessie poured drops of brandy between her sister's lips while Dolly patted Nancy's cheeks gently. 'Come on now, lass. Buck up. It's me what's in t' family way, not thee.'

Nancy coughed as the alcohol hit her throat and her eyes flew open, fixing themselves on Dolly's anxious round face.

'Mrs Nelson . . .' Nancy struggled to sit up.

'Call me Dolly. And lie down, fer God's sake.'

'Mrs Nelson.' She gripped Dolly's wrist. 'Were you willing?'

'Willin'? Oh aye, I see what you mean. Yes, I were willin'.' She cast a puzzled look in Jessie's direction. 'Why should she ask that?' she mouthed in a whisper.

Jessie drew Dolly away from the sofa. 'She's confused, I reckon. Not been well, you see, not eating enough. She's gone and got herself light-

324

headed, that'll be why she fainted. Anyroad, she looks to have dozed off now, so come and sit by the fire for a bit.'

'Ooh, I'd never 'ave come if I'd 'ave knowed she were like that,' said Dolly, smacking her thick lips over a cup of sweet stewed tea. 'I mean, it were a case of not knowin' where to turn. You see, I'm up t' spout – t' doctor says so, so it must be reet. I've no man. I've got four kids already an' now Eddie's landed me wi' another bellyful.'

'How long was it going on, you and him?'

'Oh, months. I 'ad 'opes of 'im comin' ter live wi' me. We was proper fond o' one another, me an' Eddie. Got on a treat, we did.'

'Does he know about this baby?'

'Nay, why'd you think I'm 'ere? I didn't come just to make trouble, tha knows. I've been up the 'ospital an' they said no visitors, said as 'ow 'e were in isolation or summat. So I couldn't tell 'im, could I? Is 'e bad?'

'Oh, he's bad alright.' The irony in Jessie's tone passed unnoticed.

'I see. Will 'e not be comin' out then?'

Jessie shrugged her shoulders. 'I've no idea. But if he does come out, it won't be for a long time.'

Dolly balanced her cup on the fireguard. 'Oh 'eck. What the 'ell am I goin' ter do?'

'How far gone are you?'

'Too far fer a bottle o' gin ter do any good, I can tell yer.'

'Well, in that case, I'm as flummoxed as you are. He's not likely to be earning, so if it's money you're after, you've come to the wrong shop. Our Nancy's got nothing to spare and anyroad, she can't be paying for his mistakes – aye, and yours too.'

Dolly stared miserably into the fire. 'I just want 'im told, that's all.'

Jessie measured her next statement carefully. 'Then you'll have to tell him yourself. Nancy won't go near him now she knows he's been getting off with you. She's a proud lass, is our Nancy. The marriage was going sour anyroad. No,' she sighed. 'I don't reckon his chances of seeing her again after this.'

'Oh well. I can't say as 'ow I blame 'er. I just don't know what ter do.' She paused, deep in thought. 'I reckon there's nowt for it but to sell me 'ouse. That's if Eric'll let me – 'e pays t' mortgage. But if I could get a few 'undred together it would see me through till our Maggie's workin' an' till I can get back ter me job.'

Jessie glanced at the clock. 'I think you'd best be off now. Our Annie'll be in soon and the less she knows about this the better.'

Dolly heaved herself up and made for the door. 'Are you sure she's alreet?' She pointed to the motionless figure on the sofa.

'She'll be fine. Go on now, you've enough of your own without worrying over our Nancy. And I'm sorry if I was a bit sharpish earlier on – it was the shock, you see.'

'Don't worry. I'll see meself out. Ta-ra then.'

Jessie walked over to the sofa and stared down into Nancy's wide eyes.

'Thanks, Jess. You did well there, you're a fast thinker. Has she gone?'

'Aye, she's gone.'

'But for how long?'

'For good, love. She's gone for good.'

★　　★　　★

Nancy walked along the green-tiled floor towards large double doors. Why did they always have to paint these places dark cream? The stench of disinfectant pricked her nose and she sniffed to stop herself sneezing. A porter rattled by with a trolley full of bowls and bedpans, the noise of his progress bouncing off close walls.

She wasn't really sure why she was here – impulse, she supposed. But it wasn't something she was looking forward to, she knew that. And she ought to be putting all this behind her for her own sake and for Annie's, but well – you couldn't just leave somebody stuck on their own in hospital now, could you? Especially somebody with nobody else in the world as cared a damn whether they lived or died. No, it was only right and proper, Nancy Higson, she told herself. Get in there and do your duty like you've always preached.

She pushed the doors open. It was a large ward with a row of beds at each side, every bed with a neatly mitred white cover. Some were occupied, but other patients, those almost ready to go home, sat in small easy chairs in the centre of the ward, reading or chatting quietly. A Sister in dark blue came up behind Nancy. 'Mrs Higson?'

'That's right.'

'You are expected. Go to the end of the ward and through that door.' She pointed. 'It's a side ward – a single, for obvious reasons.'

'Yes. I'm sorry you've been caused so much bother.'

'It's not your fault, Mrs Higson. You must never blame yourself for what happened.'

Nancy took the last few steps with hesitation, then braced herself before knocking timidly on the door.

'Just go in,' called the Sister. 'Go on – you'll be alright.'

After taking a deep breath, Nancy opened the door and stepped into the room. Tall windows were shaded by slatted blinds and all the paraphernalia was there, dripstand, tubes, bottles, but no longer connected to the patient, thank God.

'Are you awake?'

'Yes.' The voice was little more than a whisper.

Nancy crept to the bed. The girl's face was purple with bruising on the left side and in spite of the dimness, clear marks of strangulation were visible on her throat.

'It was good of you to let me come, lass.'

'It was good of you to want to come.' The voice was low and hoarse with damage.

'I've brought you some flowers – see?' She held them up.

'Thank you. They're lovely.'

Nancy pulled the one chair over to the bed and looked down into the girl's face. Dear God, she couldn't be much more than twenty – twenty-two at the most. And she looked so much like Annie, even with the bruises the resemblance was plain to see. Hatred for him flooded through her veins yet again, a blind nauseating hatred that made her take in air as she sat down suddenly.

'Don't upset yourself, Mrs Higson – please.'

'You're telling me not to be upset? Good God, after what that bugger did to you! How could any man in his right mind . . . ?'

'He's not. He's not in his right mind.'

Nancy picked up her bag. 'I'd best go, lass. I can tell it's hard for you to talk and it's only a few days since he . . . since it happened. Nay, I don't want to be making you go all through it again in your thoughts.'

'Please don't go. See – you can get me a glass of water.'

Nancy helped the girl to sit up and handed her the glass. It was obvious that she had difficulty in swallowing the liquid.

'You see – I'm alright – just bruised and shocked.' She sank back into her pillows. 'Come closer. I have to whisper because my larynx is damaged – not permanently, so don't start worrying.'

Nancy moved her chair to the top of the bed and leaned over, directing her better ear towards the girl's mouth. 'Hey, we're a pair between us, aren't we? Me with a pair of useless lugholes and you with your croaky voice. Nay, I'm not making light of it, lovey, it's just my way.'

The girl was trying to smile. 'He won't be charged,' she whispered.

'You what? No, you're letting him get away with a crime as near bad as murder as you can get! And it very near was murder – am I right?'

She shook her head. 'He just blacked me out. I don't think he meant to kill me.'

'Aye, I suppose you're right there. I can't see even that bloody swine wanting a dead one – eeh, I'm sorry, lass . . .'

'Don't keep apologizing.' She paused. 'They're going to start tests on him, Mrs Higson. Special tests – on his mind.'

'Is he crackers?'

'They don't know yet. But there are signs of paranoia – he could be schizoid.'

'What does that mean?'

'It means there's a chance that he may be crackers.

At the moment, he doesn't know where he is half the time.'

Nancy shook her head slowly. 'No. I've lived with him long enough to know he's not soft in the head. He'll be acting daft on purpose so he won't get judge and bloody jury. Still, I suppose if he acts mad for long enough, he might even finish up that way. Anyroad, what if they say he is fit to go on trial? Surely you'll press a charge then?'

'I can't,' whispered the girl. 'I can't do it.'

'Why not? Hey, I don't want you worrying over me and mine. If the papers got hold of it, we'd likely survive.'

'It's not that.' She looked directly at Nancy now. 'It's my – I can't do it. Oh, I know they'd keep my name out of the papers, but it would get about, I know it would. And if Pete ever found out, he'd kill him, sane or not.'

'Pete?'

'My boyfriend. He's in the army, stationed in Germany. And . . .' She paused, a hand to her throat as she swallowed. 'He might not want to marry me if he knew I'd . . . well, you know . . .'

'Been raped?'

'Yes.'

'But . . . but it wasn't your fault, was it?' Nancy stood and began to pace the room angrily. 'By God, it is a man's world, isn't it? One of them might not want you because another's had you against your will. They all want sex – well, most of them do at anyroad – wherever they can get it. But they expect a woman to come pure and lily-white to her marriage bed. What I'd like to know is this. If all the men are wandering about having sex and all the women are keeping themselves to themselves, then what the

330

hell's going on? It's double bloody standards all the way isn't it? I'll tell you what – it's a damn crazy world we're living in.' She waved her arms wildly to emphasize the words.

'Some of them think we want to be raped anyway.'

'How convenient for them! Aye well, they have to say that because a lot of them are not up to much and that's their excuse for not coping proper. Yes, I get your drift, lass. My hearing might not be up to much, but I'm all there with me lemon drops. Huh, talk about a man's world? What sort of a world have they made, eh? Full of war and rape and flaming arguments. Oh, I'm not saying they're all bad. Nay, I'm not that daft. But most of them are . . . oh, what's the word? Arrogant, that's it. Arrogant because they've got an extra bit stuck on between their legs. Pity they don't keep their brains in their trousers and all – we might be better off.'

She returned to sit beside the bed. 'Listen to me, Mary Greenhalgh. I got your name off your mate at the sanatorium – dark-haired girl – Brenda, isn't she?' Mary nodded. 'And she told me your Mam's dead and your Dad's gone off to Canada. Aye, she told me a lot about you and I hope she doesn't get into trouble, because I'm right glad I came, I'm pleased to know you, Mary Greenhalgh. If there's anything I can do for you, then phone our Dr Pritchard – see, here's his number and my name and address on this envelope. If you've no voice, get the Sister to ring. Just you get the word to me and I'll come. Aye, I will that.'

Mary smiled wanly through her tears.

'Now, Brenda said as how you're not well fixed with your digs. If you want a bed, there'll be one at our house. And don't worry about him coming back

– I put the deposit down and I've paid the mortgage out of my own wages. Anyroad, after what he's done, there's nobody'll force me to take him back. And there'll be nothing of his left. His stuff's going on the ragman's cart tomorrow. So if he wants anything, he can whistle for it, see if it'll come.'

The girl gripped Nancy's hand tightly.

'Eeh lass, you do look bad. I'm sorry it was my . . . ex-husband as caused it.'

'I hardly knew what was happening,' whispered Mary. 'It was mostly afterwards I felt the pain.'

'Aye. But you felt the fear just before, didn't you?'

'I was a fool. I thought I could manage him. You get a fair amount of that sort of thing from men in hospitals.'

'Then it must be put a stop to.'

'Well, it won't happen to me again – I'm not going back.'

'Just you come to me when you get out of here. You can sort your future out when you're in a better frame. Will you come?'

'I don't know. I'll have to see . . .'

'You'll be safe. He'll not be back, I promise.'

Mary raised herself on to the pillows. 'No, he won't be coming back, Mrs Higson. The disease is rampant and he's allergic to both penicillin and streptomycin.' She paused. 'He'll be dead within the year.'

There followed a short silence, then Nancy picked up her shopping bag and smiled. 'Well then, that's alright now, isn't it?'

9

Confrontations

By the summer of 1956, Martin felt as miserable as sin, sick to the back teeth of his mother forever moaning about him not getting a proper wage, fed up with Annie and her studying, tired of his work-mates' taunts about his dashing off to meet a schoolgirl in his lunch break. After Colin Marlowe spotted them together in Tognarelli's, life became almost unbearable.

'Can't you get a proper woman then, Cullen?'

'Best not have it off with her – we'll be seeing you on the front page.'

'When's her birthday, then? Is it fourteen or fifteen next?'

He'd show them, he would that. He wasn't going to be a junior forever – oh no, not bloody likely. With a couple of little ideas up his sleeve, Martin stormed out of the office one June afternoon, deliberately ignoring wolf-whistles and an enthusiastic chorus of 'Rock-a-bye Baby' as he stamped through the main news room. Aye, his twin sister Josie had had the right idea, clearing off to Manchester, getting digs then a job in a big shop, taking typing lessons at night so she could train for a secretary. At least their Josie had got away from home. And what was he hanging around for? To live in a mucky midden, to get laughed at, to let Annie Byrne drive him mad by keeping him at arm's length?

He jumped on a bus outside Gregory and Porritt's and sat glowering all the way to Breightmet. Yes, he'd show them down the office alright. He'd contacts of his own now, was on his way to meet a ringer from the big Corpy estate and he'd be giving them a story once he'd got to the bottom of these football ticket forgeries.

After his business was completed, Martin stood waiting for the bus back to town, a smile of self-satisfaction on his face. He was ten bob lighter, but with a pocket full of shorthand notes and a printer's plate that should never have seen the light of day, he felt very pleased with his afternoon's work.

'Hiya, Martin!' It was Maggie Nelson in a tight button-up cardigan worn back to front, her large breasts straining against thin nylon.

'What are you doing up here, Maggie?'

'We moved, didn't we?' She turned sideways, hands on hips, to give him a better view of her magnificent hour-glass figure. 'That's our 'ouse over there.' She pointed. 'Come on – they're all out. 'Appen you might fancy a cup o' tea?' Her hands moved slowly up then down over the broad black elastic waspie belt. Martin loosened his tie. God, she must be about 40-22-36, this one. In time, she'd likely run to fat like her Ma, but right now, she was a prize and no mistake.

'Are you working?' he asked as they walked towards the house.

'Off and on, like,' she grinned, tossing peroxide curls.

They had got no further than the hall when she pressed herself against him. 'I've allers fancied you,

Martin. Still goin' wi' Annie? Nay, yer want to forget 'er, lad. I can give yer a good time, a bit o' proper lovin'.' She pulled him into the living room. 'Well, are yer goin' fer t' stand there like 'im outside o' Bowes?'

Martin remained riveted to the spot. Yes, he probably did look like the dummy that used to occupy the pavement outside a tailor's shop in the town centre. But what the hell was he going to do? He loved Annie, he was going to marry Annie one day, wasn't he? But when? If she was going in for a doctor, it could be bloody years. And he'd be a fool to pass this chance up. Slowly, he removed his jacket and tie. If only the damn fools at the office could see him now! Panic and excitement joined forces in his chest, the former winning by a knockout when Maggie stood naked beside him. He'd never done it before! And here was this gorgeous and obviously experienced specimen pushing him onto the wide sofa, tearing off his shoes and socks, pulling at his trousers, fondling, stroking, kissing every straining part of his frustrated body.

In the end, it didn't matter that he was new to it, because she mounted him, guided his flesh until it melted into hers, lifted his head onto cushions so that their mouths might meet each time she rose in her slow, languorous ritual. Then, when he knew that he could not last for one more second, she pulled them both off the low couch and onto the floor so that their positions were reversed. This sudden move broke the rhythm and he found himself able to continue, his pleasure and confidence increasing as he watched her travelling towards climax. Deliberately, he closed his eyes against the sight of those beautiful rose-tipped breasts, determined now to stay the course. When she screamed her final throes of joy, he opened his eyes and, caught up in his first ever sight of female ecstasy, he echoed the sound and gave in to his own urgent need for release.

For a few breathless moments, he lay on top of the girl, his head against the wonderful softness of her, his hand slowly caressing creamy curves. Then he looked up into her face and saw the hard, streetwise expression, noticed the layers of pink foundation and powder, the matted eyelashes with their thick coating of black mascara. His heart lurched, his mind cried out to Annie – oh God, what had he done?

'What's t' matter, Martin? Didn't yer like it?'

He struggled to his feet and grabbed his clothes.

'What's t' matter?' she asked again.

'Nothing. I've got to get back to the *News*, that's all.'

She raised herself to a sitting position. 'I'll bet Annie Byrne never gives yer a good time like that, eh?'

'Annie's different. Leave her out of it.'

''Appen I might. 'Appen I might not.'

He rounded on her. 'What do you mean by that?'

'She'd be right interested ter know about this, wouldn't she?'

Swiftly, he pulled on his trousers. When he was fully dressed, he turned to look at the naked girl at his feet. 'Don't tell her.'

'OK, I won't. As long as you come back, like. We could meet up regular, 'ave our fun an' nobody'll be the wiser. Get me drift?'

He nodded, ready to agree to anything in his desperation to escape.

'Tuesday then? Jolly Brows, near that little 'ill over t' top. Seven o'clock?'

'Right.'

'You'd best be there, Martin. I don't like bein' stood up. I can get right nasty if I get stood up.'

Disgusted with her and with himself, he walked quickly out of the house, slamming the door behind him. How would he ever look Annie in the face again?

But when night came and he lay in his lonely bed, Martin remembered only the pleasure. When he slept, he was tortured by dreams of Maggie and her voluptuous body. When he woke, he knew that he was hooked. No matter how hard he fought the urge, he would be meeting Maggie Nelson, taking what she offered so freely. But his pillow was wet with tears.

It was strange having an emancipated mother, one who did the washing when she felt like it, who loudly declared her conversion to the Labour Party, often going round distributing leaflets for the socialist cause. Nancy Higson, now a fully-fledged foreman with a decent wage, was no longer up and coming. She had arrived, had launched herself on an unsuspecting world with a bang rather than with a whimper. There was talk, of course, what with her poor husband being stuck in hospital for God knew how long and her never visiting him. But Nancy rose above it all, got her hair permed in soft waves, bought a Coty compact of Fair Beauty and took to wearing soft coral lipstick. She also had her ears pierced, an event that led to some discomfort and several interesting expletives until the pain died down.

On Thursday evenings, she attended the Amy Walker School of Dance, for which purpose she acquired two strapless frocks, one in sequined black tulle over taffeta, the other in a figured emerald brocade with a matching stole. At last, Nancy had her green dress.

Annie, her feelings mixed as she watched the butterfly emerging from its grey chrysalis, held her breath, hoping that the wings would dry quickly and that nothing sharp would inflict pain on this reborn creature. It seemed that Nancy's youth had not been missed out, but had simply been postponed until circumstances allowed it to occur.

Mother and daughter stood now in the doorway of the Bodega coffee bar, the older woman still complaining about what they had just consumed in the café's darkened depths. 'I'm sure they make it with Lux flakes. Given a kiddy's clay pipe, I could have blown a fair bubble with that mess.'

'Frothy coffee's all the rage, Mother.'

'Aye well, they should have given us straws – I finished up with a moustache after dipping myself into that cup. And it was cracked.'

They began to walk through the town, pausing occasionally to gaze into shop windows.

'How do you think I'd look in that hat, Annie?'

'Drowned.'

'Shall we go in and try it?'

'Oh, not on a Saturday – it'll be packed in there.'

They stopped on the corner by Timothy White's and Taylor's. 'I'm glad you've got the exams over,' said Nancy. 'But you still seem bothered over something or other. Is it to do with Martin?'

Annie shrugged her shoulders.

'What's up, lass?'

'He's got . . . I think he's got somebody else. Oh, let's go home.'

Nancy trotted beside her long-legged daughter, then grabbed her by the arm. 'Slow down, for goodness sake! Do you think I'm a flaming racehorse? Tell me what's up before I give you a clout. You're not too big for a thump, you know.' She could see that Annie's temper was roused – the two spots of colour on her face were always a dead give-away.

'Margaret Nelson, Mother. That's what's up.'

Nancy stiffened. 'Dolly Nelson's lass?'

'Yes. And she's not a lass, she's a bloody whore!'

'Annie! Will I wash your mouth out with a block of carbolic? What's got into you at all? Oh, bloody hell – talk of the devil!'

Annie was just about to make a remark about the pot calling the kettle black, when she noticed the frozen expression on Nancy's face. She turned from her mother to see Dolly Nelson, pram in front of her massive body, waddling along the pavement towards them. It was too late to take evasive action – the woman was upon them before they could move.

''Ow are you then, Mrs 'Igson?'

'Fair to middling,' Nancy managed.

Annie peeped into the pram. 'Is it a boy or a girl?' she asked as politely as she could, wishing Maggie Nelson's mother would disappear in a puff of smoke.

'It's a boy,' answered Dolly proudly. She turned to Nancy. ''Ow's my little lad's dad, then?'

'The less said about that, the better.' Nancy made to move away.

''Ang on!' screamed Dolly. 'Kept quiet long enough, I 'ave. An' I've 'eard as 'ow yer never even visit the poor sod.'

'He's not fit to visit. He's in a secure wing at the

mental hospital. They can't have him in the TB place because of his state of mind. He's isolated on account of the infection and because he takes bad turns.'

'No wonder, if nobody visits 'im!'

Annie had recoiled from the pram as if bitten by a snake. 'Is this . . . his child?'

'Aye,' said Dolly. 'Your little brother in a way.'

Annie drew herself to full height. 'Eddie Higson is no relation of mine, Mrs Nelson.'

'Or mine,' added Nancy firmly.

'You bloody bitch! No wonder 'e turned ter me! Aye, an' it's me 'e'll come to when 'e's reet!'

Annie, her face ablaze with temper now, stepped forward to stand between her mother and this awful woman. 'He won't be coming out,' she said, fighting to control her voice. 'He's allergic to all the anti-biotics and he'll die soon of tuberculosis. I think they're surprised he's lasted this long. He's incurable.'

Dolly sagged against the pram. 'Dyin'?'

'Yes,' replied Annie.

'And you never even go ter see 'im?'

Nancy stepped forward to her daughter's side. 'We would as soon visit Old Nick himself.'

'Well . . . well . . . you right pair of bitches, you. 'E's better off without you!'

Annie grabbed Nancy's arm and dragged her away, marching her off, picking up speed until they were both running.

'Don't look back, Mother.'

'Don't worry, I won't.'

They reached the bus station and sat on a bench to wait for the 45, Nancy panting slightly after her run.

'Why didn't you tell me, Mam?' asked Annie after a while. 'Why?'

'There was no need.'

Annie sifted through her thoughts for a few minutes. 'Yes, I suppose you're right.' She noticed that Nancy looked downcast to the point of heart-break, so placing her arm about her mother's shoulders, she whispered, 'Hey, you know what annoys me most about you?'

'No – what?'

'You're always flaming well right!'

Nancy shook her head slowly. 'Nay, lass. I'm right when I'm not wrong, same as everybody else.'

Annie's temper still simmered beneath an outwardly cool facade. She stepped on to the bus, her mouth set in a grim determined line. No wonder Maggie Nelson was a whore – she'd followed in her mother's footsteps, hadn't she? And now Annie and Nancy were both suffering, each affected by one generation of that dreadful family. Martin, the damned fool – she would sort him out tonight. It was time now, time to wipe the whole Nelson family out of the picture forever.

Martin rolled away from Maggie, sick to the core for the umpteenth time. And now she was coming on with all the love stuff and about her mate getting wed next year – oh God. That was the trouble with sex, he mused as he fastened his trousers. It was a bit like beer – the more you got, the more you wanted. But he didn't want her, oh no, not a lifetime with Maggie flaming Nelson. He watched her as she pulled down her skirt and fastened the grass-stained blouse. Sometimes, he hated her. And because he hated her, he was beginning to dislike himself as well.

'Lovely evening, isn't it?' The voice came from the top of the mound behind which he and Maggie were supposedly hidden. He didn't need to look. It was her alright. She wore a blue and white striped dress and her hair was coiled into a perfect chignon, making her long neck appear more slender than ever. She stepped down the slope as if she were entering a drawing room or attending a gathering of debutantes.

Maggie hastily finished fastening her buttons while Annie knelt on the grass beside her.

'Tell me, Maggie,' she went on, her tone conversational, 'how long have you been a prostitute?'

'You what?' A look of amazement came over Maggie's painted features.

'Is this something that's passed on from one generation to another – like a legacy? Because your mother's quite generous with her favours, isn't she? Though why anybody should want to touch such an ugly heap of blubber . . .'

'Shut yer gob, Annie Byrne! Just 'cos I've took your lad . . .'

'You've taken nothing of mine, Maggie Nelson. If I really wanted something, there's no way a cheap little slut like you would get her hands on it.' She turned to Martin now. 'How much does she charge, by the way?'

'What do yer mean, 'ow much do I charge? An' mind what yer say about me Mam.'

Annie continued to stare at Martin until he flinched under the coldness of her hard gaze, then she slowly moved her head towards Maggie. 'Your mother had a bastard recently – a boy, I believe. Some man must have a strong stomach. I can smell your mother from forty paces.'

'You bloody cow . . .!' Clawing hands reached out for Annie's hair, but they never attained their target. With a blow that might have felled a sapling, Annie sent Maggie reeling back. The girl lay still and silent, terror plain on her face as Annie rose gracefully to her feet.

Now she turned the full force of her anger on Martin. 'Has it never occurred to you that you might catch something from her? Stay away from me, Cullen. I never want to set eyes on your silly face again. I never did like red hair anyway – not on a man. It's alright for little boys, but you can never be a man, not with a carrot head.'

Then she turned on her heel and walked away.

Martin, heedless of Maggie's pitiful cries, ran after Annie. When he caught up with her on the cinder path, she turned and spat into his face. 'Scum!' she shouted as he wiped his cheek. 'I love you, Annie,' she mimicked. 'Don't leave me, Annie. There'll never be another girl, Annie. And there you are, copulating with a dirty piece of rubbish . . .'

'But you wouldn't let me near you!'

'That's because I don't want you near me! I don't want anybody near me! And even if I told you the reason why, you'd never understand because you're thick. Did you know she was advertising your business with her all over Bolton? Perhaps she's hoping you'll give her a reference.'

'Annie . . . Annie . . .'

'Don't "Annie" me! I'm finished with you. Go away, stay away, don't come back. I'm using simple words for your bloody simple mind, then I can be sure you understand.'

He stood uselessly and watched her walk away. He hadn't seen this side of her before, didn't realize till

343

now what a temper she had. What could he do anyway? She'd told him plain enough to bugger off – aye, that's what he'd do! To hell with her and all of them.

Martin left home that night, taking with him just his clothes, a battered typewriter and one small framed photograph. In his poky back room in Mayfield Street, he placed the picture in the bottom of his suitcase, then pushed the case under the bed. He could manage without her. He had to.

Susan Birchall was a suitable friend for Simon. Her parents were Methodist, but that was a small fly in the ointment and Edna's church wasn't very high, merely moderate in her estimation. Not that Simon was old enough to be considering a permanent liaison, but it was nice to see how carefully he was choosing these days. Those awful people still came on Wednesdays, but, she thought magnanimously, that might be looked upon as charity work. And at least Martin Cullen and Anne Byrne were conspicuously absent of late. Yes, one had to be thankful for small mercies.

Susan was a sweet child, not as mature in appearance as that awful crowd and she didn't have the 'knowing' look that was always so obvious in Anne Bryne's expression. Of course, the Birchalls were quite eminent, the father a solicitor, the mother related to the Partingtons who owned land near Preston. Susan possessed all the ladylike virtues, was a competent pianist, an excellent horsewoman – and her embroidery had to be seen to be believed.

Edna smiled as she arranged some yellow flowers in a rosebowl. It was a lovely day. The muted strains of Vivaldi's *Four Seasons* floated gently down the stairway, so much more appropriate than the raucous sounds that often came from what Edna had decided to call the recreation room. She could picture the scene – Simon at a table with his books, Susan sitting demurely in a chair working on that lovely tapestry she always seemed to bring.

Edna picked up her basket and walked to the foot of the stairs. 'I'm just popping out to the shops – shan't be long,' she called.

'Bye, Mrs Pritchard,' Susan's high girlish voice called in reply. Such a polite girl, such a lady.

The lady in question thrust her small hand down the front of Simon's trousers, eager fingers manipulating his clothing until they found their goal. As her own undergarments had been reposing for some time in her capacious sewing bag, there was no such obstruction for Simon's hand she guided it along her thighs. After a few moments of frantic activity, she pulled away and swiftly removed the rest of her clothes, beckoning him to follow as she went out on to the landing.

In his mother's room, she re-positioned the long mirror so that it would reflect the bed, then she threw herself onto the pink flowered counterpane, small hard breasts thrust upwards like twin cones, one hand working between her thighs while the other reached out for him.

For a split second, he wanted to run, but he knew he'd never face the mocking laughter that would result from such action, so he joined her on the bed. With practised ease, she peeled the clothing from his body, stimulated him to adequate hardness, then pulled him fiercely into her flesh, her head turned all the time towards the mirror so that she could watch their movements. She reached her peak as soon as he entered, the thin body rising from the bed to meet his loins. He followed quickly, shuddering as he spent himself without pleasure inside her hot moistness.

There was no tenderness, no word of affection. She pushed him away, leapt from the bed and began to restore the room to its original order. Methodically, she straightened the bedcover, shook the pillows, moved the mirror while Simon stood, feeling foolish and very naked, at the side of the bed.

'Not much of a gentleman, are you?' she asked coldly.

'Sorry?'

'You didn't pull out. A gentleman always pulls out.' She laughed at the expression on his face. 'Don't worry, dear boy. My fault too – should have brought a towel for Mummy's counterpane. Anyway, it's fine – wrong time of the month for it to be a problem. But you should pull out. Everybody does.'

Miserable and shamefaced, Simon dressed then returned to the recreation room. She followed, pulling on her clothes quickly, attacking her tapestry with renewed vigour as soon as she sat down.

Simon stared at her. This had been his first encounter with sex and he had hated it. Seconds ticked by as a light began to dawn in his clouded mind. He didn't like women, not in that way. He looked back over the last few months, knowing now why he had never been jealous of Martin and Anne. He was different. Yes, he knew what he was and the knowledge made him shiver.

When Edna put her head round the door ten minutes later, he was at the table with his books.

Susan looked up from her needlework. 'Shall I help you put the shopping away, Mrs Pritchard?'

Yes, she was a lovely girl, thought Edna as she went downstairs to make tea. Such a nice little friend for Simon.

Dénouements

Annie opened the front door and steadied herself against the jamb as she stared into her own face. No, not quite, she reassured herself. The eyes were blue and she had to look down an inch or two to meet them. But in spite of the shorter hair and some slight differences in colouring, she might almost have been staring at her own twin sister. The girl looked as if she had been weeping too, just as Annie herself had wept these last few days.

'Is . . . is this Nancy's house?' The voice wavered.

'Yes. But she's out, I'm afraid. Can I help? I'm Annie.'

'Will she be long?'

'Only a few minutes, I think. Come in, please.'

They walked through to the living room where the girl perched anxiously on the edge of the fireside rocker. She stared at Annie, her hands picking nervously at a small clutch-bag in her lap. 'We . . . we look alike, don't we? I noticed that as soon as you opened the door. I'm a bit older than you, mind. But I felt funny then, when I first saw you.'

'So did I.' Annie smiled in what she hoped was a comforting way. 'We're all supposed to have a double, aren't we? I read that once in a newspaper . . .' She forced herself to sit down, determined not to prattle on.

'I'm a friend of your mother's. We sometimes had a drink in Barton's tea-rooms when she was part-time. Only I've not seen her for a while, not since she went back to five full days. We write – she's foreman now, isn't she?'

'Yes.' Annie glanced at the clock. 'She's often a bit late with all the paperwork. And she does take the job seriously – if one of her girls is ill, she goes and visits – does what she can for the family.'

'Yes, she would. She's a great lady, your mother . . .' The girl turned towards the range and rubbed a hand across her eyes.

'I know that.' Annie cleared her throat. 'It's alright, you can cry if you want to.' She felt the need to draw this visitor out, to find out who she was and why she was here. 'I've been doing a lot of that myself lately.'

The girl blew her nose into a small white hand-kerchief then turned to look at Annie. 'Have you, love? Why, what's the matter?'

Yes, she could confide, she sensed that. And such confidences would help this obviously sad young woman to open up. 'Oh, I've let myself down in a big way, lost my temper, lost my boyfriend, clouted a big horrible girl across the mouth. I've got a problem with my temper, you see. I try to carry on like a young lady, the way the nuns have trained me – but you know what they say about silk purses and sows' ears? Well, that's me. You see – what's your name, by the way . . .?'

'Mary.'

'You see, Mary, I told him to get lost and he did.

My boyfriend – he just disappeared. Of course, my mother treats it all as a big joke, probably to cheer me up. She keeps telling me to get the Irwell dragged, then not to bother because if he's chucked himself in there, she says, he'll likely have melted with all the rubbish they pour in. I mean, it wasn't serious, not really, between Martin and me. But he was my best friend and I got rid of him just because he was . . . well, seeing another girl. Have you ever done anything as daft as that?'

'Many a time, Annie. There's plenty more fish in the sea, especially at your age.' She smiled wanly. 'Don't worry, he won't be in the river.'

'No, he isn't. He's at the *Evening News* making a name for himself. But I should never have spat in his face. There I was, all done up in my best dress trying to look like Princess Margaret and what did I go and do? I've never been so ashamed of myself! So don't bother about crying in front of me. I'll probably join in and keep you company.'

They heard the front door opening. 'Annie? Get that kettle on, I'm as dry as a new sock. That Elsie Tunstall took one of her turns in the lav again – she'll have to go in hospital and get it all taken away, she will. Are you there, Annie?'

Annie smiled at Mary. 'Here comes trouble now,' she whispered.

Nancy burst into the room. 'Weeks ago I told her – fibroids, I said . . . oh, hello Mary. Well.' She glanced quickly at Annie. 'What a nice surprise. You've met my daughter, then?'

'Hello, Nancy. Perhaps I shouldn't have come . . .'

'Don't talk so daft. Get that coat off this minute, Mary Greenhalgh. I've told you before and I'll tell you again – my door's always open.'

Annie jumped to her feet. 'Mary? That Mary? The one who . . .'

'That's right, lass. Now do your job and get that kettle on. I've told you – my throat feels like its hand-knitted.'

Annie fled to the kitchen and filled the new electric kettle. Moving automatically, she redistributed the ham salad so that it filled three plates, then, while she cut and buttered bread, she listened to the heart-break as it poured from the next room.

'I couldn't, Nancy. I couldn't. Every time he came home I made excuses. So he's gone and married a German girl . . . I'll never be able to . . . never get married . . . have babies . . . all I wanted, Nancy.'

Nancy's voice cracked as she answered, 'You will. Give it time, Mary. Rome wasn't built in a day, love . . .'

'Terrified of men, I am. Even though I've left the sanatorium and gone over to geriatrics, I go to jelly if some old chap looks at me sideways . . .'

'It'll pass, it will . . .'

'No! Look at me! Look at my hands – I can hardly change a dressing now, let alone handle a hypodermic. I can't talk to anybody about it. Nobody knows except you and the people at the sanatorium – most of my friends have left now, got married and moved away. It's as if I've done wrong, like I'm a criminal or something . . .' Her voice tailed away as she saw Annie in the doorway.

'The only crime you committed, Mary, was that you were born looking very like me.' Annie held back her own tears determinedly. 'It was me he was after, not you.'

'That's right,' whispered Nancy. 'I've known all along, ever since I first set eyes on you, Mary. But it was Annie's secret, hers to tell or keep. He'd been setting about my Annie for years, only I didn't know till the night after he hurt you.'

Mary stared across the room at this taller, younger version of herself. In that moment, a link was forged that would last a lifetime, a friendship born of pain, nurtured by total empathy, bonded through the tiny woman who joined them together now by welcoming them both into her open arms.

'Mary will be living here from now on,' Nancy announced. 'We're going to adopt her, Annie.'

Annie nodded, incapable of speech.

Using her native wisdom, Nancy left the girls together while she finished preparing the meal, wiping yet another tear from her face when she noticed how Annie had divided the food. Aye, this was a blessing alright. Now, Annie and Mary could talk, talk like she'd done with their Jessie. They'd say things to one another that they could never speak about to somebody Nancy's age. It would hurt, aye it would that, she thought as she scalded the teapot. But once they'd got through the hurting, then the mending could begin.

'I'm not condoning anything, Edna! I'm merely encouraging Simon to bring his friends home – would you rather he met them in the street?'

'I'd rather he didn't meet them at all. Especially that one. Her previous . . . arrangement seems to have been dissolved, so now she turns to Simon. And you are allowing them to use a room – an upstairs room – for goodness knows what purpose!'

David flung his newspaper across the room. 'What do you think they're up to in that room? Would you care to elaborate on your statement – or rather your accusation – so that I might assess it, even comment on it?'

Edna stiffened. 'Don't act stupid with me! You know exactly what I mean. There's no need for me to produce maps and diagrams.'

David stared up at the ceiling, shoulders raised in a gesture of frustration as he sighed deeply. He really didn't understand this woman, hardly knew who she was. She certainly bore little resemblance to the person he'd married, the girl whose freshness and naivety had so enchanted him. Those qualities and not a little coercion from both families had led to this . . . misalliance.

He turned on her now, his body rigid and poker-straight on the edge of the sofa. 'Thank God for this generation!' He waved a hand towards the upper floor. 'Independent, strong-minded, adaptable. I can't see them being forced by family into careers or marriages just because such plans are deemed by their elders to be suitable.'

She looked down at her flawlessly painted nails. 'I suppose this implies regret that you married me?'

He took a deep breath. 'Yes, I'm sorry that we married.'

'Nobody forced you!' There was a small catch in her voice and a raising in its pitch as she lifted a lace-trimmed handkerchief to her lips.

'There were pressures.'

'I wasn't aware of them.'

'Really? Then allow me to produce the maps and diagrams. Firstly, your parents set out their stall with you as centrepiece. Secondly, my family came along and bought their pitch, hook, line and sinker. Excuse any mixed metaphor, but this is hardly the time for perfect grammar. Thirdly, you were sent out to ensnare me. Fourthly, I got caught – the bait you used was your virginity.'

Edna's jaw dropped. 'Would you rather I hadn't been a . . . a virgin?'

'I'd have been more pleased had you not used your intact status as a bargaining point.'

He rose now and stood before the fireplace, legs apart, hands clasped behind his back. 'Some women are honest whores. They go on to the streets, use their bodies to make a living. Other . . . prostitutes, for want of a better word, are more astute. They make a man pay for his whole life and with his whole life.' He gazed around the room with the air of a man addressing a large audience.

'These two categories of female have one thing in common – they don't enjoy the sexual act. Streetwomen regard it as a mere commodity, something to be bartered for the price of a meal. Those in the latter and more respectable division tolerate it as part of a bargain, a thing they must endure, a price to pay for a roof, for a life of security and ease.'

She stood, her eyes ablaze with fury. 'And I am one of the latter group, I suppose?'

He nodded, his face expressionless.

'How can you say that to me? You know I've never been strong since Simon was born. If I've seemed . . . distant, it was because I was terrified of pregnancy!'

'You need not have become pregnant again. I could have guaranteed that you wouldn't. As it happened, I was not sufficiently interested in regaining your favours, therefore it mattered not at all that you shut yourself away from me.'

She took a step towards him. 'You moved out of the bedroom!'

'That's true. I saw no point in staying, you see.'

Edna's mouth quivered for a second, then her teeth were suddenly bared into a snarl as she spoke. 'So you've satisfied your lust elsewhere with the other kind of whore?'

'Come come, my dear – don't be crude. Let's just say I've been discreet. After all, my baser instincts – as you no doubt call them – have needed to be appeased occasionally.'

'Oh, my God!' She flung herself into a chair, fingers clawing at the handkerchief. 'What have you done? Suppose my friends were to find out – these things are always found out in the end – how shall I hold up my head?'

'That reaction is exactly what one might expect of you, Edna. You cling to your good name as fiercely as you once shielded your precious virginity! You are a complete and utter sham! Did you imagine that I'd gone without the comfort of a woman for more than fifteen years? How gullible are you, for heaven's sake? But you won't discover who she is, nor will your friends. That is, if you have any friends. I imagined that they were mere callers or bridge partners.'

She wept silently into her hands, her whole body shaking with shock and humiliation.

'And another thing,' David continued. 'I want Simon to choose his own friends, his own career and eventually, his own wife. History must not repeat itself. If I were you, I'd be more selective about the people you encourage to call here.'

She dried her eyes. 'What do you mean?'

'Susan Birchall.'

'Susan? She's a friend of Simon's.'

'Yes. A suitable friend in your book, I'd imagine. Well, her father is trying to marry her off. In fact, she's being put up for auction by all accounts.'

'She's only a child . . .'

'Ah yes, but a child with a problem. The first was the postman, or was it the gardener? No matter. She was discovered with one or the other in what is usually called a compromising situation. There was no question of prosecution – the family name and so on – I'm sure you'll understand that aspect, Edna.' He paused to light a cigar.

'I'm certain none of that is true,' wailed Edna. 'It's gossip – idle gossip. Susan is a lovely girl.' She waited, teeth gritted, while he threw a spent match into the grate.

David looked her squarely in the face. 'More recently, she was found in the summerhouse with four boys. She was entertaining them in a variety of imaginative ways. I understand that the parents are virtually keeping her under lock and key until they can marry her off. So, if she's being allowed to see Simon, he's obviously on the shortlist. And we don't want a nymphomaniac in the family. What would friends and neighbours say then?'

Her mouth opened and closed, trying to frame words that her dry throat could not produce.

'What's the matter, Edna? You look like a gold-fish out of water. Surprised, are you? Surprised that a girl of good breeding can be so disposed? I'll surprise you even further. That girl upstairs, in spite of her "unsuitable background", will not be the one to introduce Simon to the pleasures of the flesh. She has a higher moral standard than you

356

could ever imagine or achieve, because she won't barter her virginity or go under the hammer to the highest bidder for the sake of a wedding ring. And I'd be delighted if she married my son in a few years. Because Anne Byrne will arrive clean – not necessarily virgin, but definitely clean.'

Her eyes, round with shock as she took in the news about Susan, narrowed now at the mention of Anne's name. She rose from the chair and stood stiffly beside it, her hand straying to the edge of a table as if needing the encouragement of its inanimate stability. 'I have several things to say to you.' Her voice shook as she spoke. 'I don't believe all that about Susan. Furthermore, I will not have my standards – moral or otherwise – compared to those of that creature upstairs. And I demand to know the name of your . . . paramour.'

'Why? Would you like a divorce? I'll gladly get you some evidence. Certain women are happy to earn the odd hundred for the use of their names – and a little photography.'

'I will not have a divorce! But I want her name!'

'Really? Will you break all her windows? No, that's too honest a response for you. You might send an anonymous letter – yes, I can imagine you pouring venom onto paper and not having the courage to sign.'

She suddenly felt afraid and powerless. He had shattered her long-term hopes for Simon and Susan. Whether or not he spoke the truth, she could not risk having the girl in the house again. And he was positively nurturing Simon's association with Nancy Higson's daughter. Now, finally, he was admitting that he had another woman, someone he intended to protect.

With unsteady hands she poured a small sherry, swallowing her pride as she gulped down the liquid. She had to ask. 'Do you . . . love this woman?'

The grandfather clock at the far end of the room sang the hour in gentle Westminster chime.

'No,' he said at last. 'I have never loved a woman, never had that rare privilege. I like and respect her, but love – according to what I've read and heard – has always eluded me completely. She is not in love with me either; we simply comfort one another. Now, I've finally found the courage to be as honest with my wife as I've always been with her.'

'Do I know her?'

His eyes travelled from the top of her head right down to her feet. 'You don't know anybody. You measure people, judge them, use them . . .'

'Very well then,' she interrupted. 'Is she among my circle?'

He shook his head slowly then stalked out of the room, slamming the door as he left. In the hallway, he leaned on the banister, his heart racing. She was going insane and she would take him with her. But there had been no need for him to lash out so viciously. It was like kicking a dumb defenceless animal with neither wit nor wisdom to protect itself. Why, after all these years, had he turned on her like that?

He stared up at the chandelier, his eyes narrowing against a thousand shards of reflected light as if he might find a solution in these insubstantial splinters. Dear God, if she ever found out that his source of comfort was part of her bridge four, then her world would collapse. Yet he knew that Edna had not the courage to pursue the issue, that she would nurse it within herself where it would fester like a gangrenous sore.

His friendship with Sarah Pennington had always been easy and necessary to both of them. She, a widow with a young family and a vast inheritance to protect from fortune-hunters, he, with a dead marriage and a son who would surely have suffered had his father found a permanent new mate. For a brief moment, David saw Clive's young face, watched the train pulling out of Trinity Street, heard his dead friend calling 'Look after Sarah.' Clive had become one of the few to whom so much would be forever owed, shot down over Germany. Of course, Edna had soon tired of caring for Sarah and her children. He smiled to himself, knowing somehow that Clive would have approved of his way of 'looking after Sarah'.

But David would never forgive himself for what he had done to Edna this evening. He had behaved stupidly, irrationally, like a spoiled brat. But whichever quality might be required to make him return to the drawing room and apologize, explain, negotiate – whatever he needed to find within himself to put things on a better footing, smooth things over, make some kind of order – eluded him completely. Life, from now on, promised to be completely unbearable.

Meanwhile, Edna sat in a stupor, her second sherry already consumed, a third in her glass. She would, she concluded, do nothing – simply because she could do nothing. She didn't want divorce, abhorred the concept of scandal, was not equipped for 'scenes' of any kind. The name of the woman was not important. Things could continue the same on the surface – nothing would change. And she was far too busy for such trivia. Tomorrow was bridge day, she had baking to do, standards to uphold. She drained the glass. David could find his own way to the devil.

11

Dolly's Lot

The house was situated on a new council estate in
Breightmet, on the hem of Bolton's ever-spreading
outskirts. It was one of many such concrete and
pebble-dashed buildings that were springing up to
replace decaying or bombed-out row houses and to
accommodate the post-war explosion of population.

Dolly Nelson's was an end house, edged on two
sides by open fields, the front facing the blind end of
another corner house across the way. Dolly hated it.
For a kick-off, it was back to front. Whoever heard
of a back kitchen at the front of a house? If she stood
at the sink all day and looked out of the small
window, she could stare, if she chose, at a blank wall
or if she craned her neck to the point of pain, she
could just about see up the avenue. There was
nothing worth looking at, few buses, no cars, no late-
night revellers rolling home from the pub. The
flaming bus came only twice an hour and what with
the pram to push, she'd managed the six-mile round
trip to town just once since she moved in. Aye, and
she'd not forget that in a hurry, meeting Nancy
Higson and her stuck-up kid.

The 'front room' was at the back of the house,
running its full width with two large windows
looking out on to a garden. Beyond the garden were

fallow fields and the only passers-by she'd seen so far were a stray cow and a couple of dogs from the estate. She was bored out of her mind.

Dolly stubbed out her Woodbine in a cracked saucer and lifted Johnny from his pram. He never cried, didn't Johnny, not like the other four little buggers who'd woken up screaming every day and gone to bed in the same state. Their Johnny was an angel, the only thing left to brighten her days since Maggie went off. 'If she thinks t' middle o' Bolton's paved wi' gold, she's another think comin', she 'as,' announced Dolly to the placid child while she fiddled with her buttons. Obediently, the baby accepted the breast, his unwavering deep-set stare fixed on Dolly's face.

He was a bonny lad and no mistake, with peach-tinted cheeks and eyes of a blue so dark that it bordered on violet. Like Eddie's, thought Dolly to herself. Yes, he was very like his dad, quiet and still most of the time. She wondered if Eddie had got the letter she'd finally scraped together on a bit of paper out of their Stevie's homework book. Aye, she'd tried to let him know about his lad. She hoped they'd sent it on from the sanatorium to Prestwich Mental Hospital. Funny, that. She'd never heard of anybody being treated for TB in a loony bin before. Still, that sanatorium had likely driven him daft. Aye, and the bloody Higson woman was having a right good time now by all accounts, going dancing, buying new frocks, taking in lodgers now Eddie was out of the road. Alright for some, it was, made up to foreman, going about with nice-looking fellers, putting shows on with the formation team.

Dolly was in trouble. Any money from the sale of her old house had disappeared now, squandered on cheap sticks of splay-legged furniture, a television set, some gilt-framed convex mirrors, contemporary paper on her fireplace wall and a load of that nice Skaters' Trails carpet that was all the rage. 'Course, things for the baby had cost a bob or two and all.

She shifted the child to the other milk-swollen breast. Aye, there was plenty for him, but what about herself and the other three? Eric's money still came regular, but it was hardly enough to pay for rent and electric and she couldn't do without her fags and her stout, what with her bad nerves and needing fluids to keep the milk coming in. She looked at the dozing infant. Them new doctors down the clinic were on about his development, talked as if there were summat up with him. And she was sick of folk looking in the pram and saying about his unusual eyes. He was beautiful, their Johnny. Nowt up with him – they could all say what they liked.

Still, it wasn't right, none of it. Except for Eddie Higson, she'd still be up Long Moor with her job at the pictures and folk to talk to. Aye and their Maggie would likely have stopped at home instead of legging it hell for leather. She'd been a good help, had Maggie, what with her wages and giving a hand in the house. The oldest of the three boys was but thirteen and lads weren't the same, you couldn't expect them to wash pots and sweep carpets, could you? And the way Maggie had left too, never a note nor nothing, just a postcard a few days after with a photo of the Town Hall clock and a line to say she was alright.

Dolly placed the sleeping child over her shoulder and reached to flick through the pages of an old *Reveille*, the wrapping from last night's chips. Aye, that was a laugh and all, the chip shop ten minutes away and having to warm them up when you got them home stone cold and stuck to the paper.

A car drew up outside, but Dolly remained where she was. It would be nowt to do with her. Then the front door opened and a familiar voice cried, 'Dolly? Dolly Nelson? You in there?'

Dolly hastily dropped the paper, fastened her frock and was just placing Johnny in his pram when Bertha Cullen walked in.

'Tha'd best sit thisen down, Dolly. It's not good news I've fetched.'

'Why? What's up?'

'Come on, lass. We'll sit at t' table.'

The two women lowered their not insubstantial bodies onto frail metal-framed dining chairs.

Bertha leaned forward. As was the custom with most of her generation when speaking of something unsavoury, she mouthed half her words as if the whole world might be listening. 'I've knowed all along as it were summat ter do wi' your Maggie, our Martin leavin' 'ome an' splittin' up wi' Annie. Common knowledge it is now, as your Maggie were givin' our Martin a good time – if yer get me drift?'

'So?' Dolly bristled.

'Well, it weren't just our Martin. An' it weren't just fer free, like.'

'Stop messin' about in t' bushes, Bertha Cullen. Get it spit out!'

'It's not me what's been messin' about in t' bushes, Dolly. It's tha daughter what's been up ter no good.'

'Oh aye? An' what bloody business is it o' yourn?'

'I don't like seein' a young girl puttin' 'erself about. 'Er'll end up in t' courts afore she's much older.'

364

Dolly leaned back on to the chair's yellow plastic cover. 'Like I said, spit it out afore I lose me patience!'

'T' doctor's fetched us – Dr Pritchard. Yer see, Dolly, I caught sight o' your Maggie a few times toutin' fer business outside o' t' wine lodge. I knew I'd never manage 'er on me own, so I got t' doctor fer t' come down in 'is car ter pick 'er up. I 'ad fer t' drag Maggie by the 'air into t' car. It were all done fer t' best, Dolly.'

'Where the bloody 'ell is she?'

'Outside wi' Dr Pritchard.'

'Then tha'd best give over wastin' time an' fetch 'em in!'

Dolly waited in the hallway, arms folded as far as they would reach across her huge chest. As soon as Maggie appeared between the two escorts, Dolly pulled her inside the house. 'Get up them dancers this minute, Maggie Nelson! I'll deal with thee after.'

As soon as the girl had reached the landing, the three adults made their way into the kitchen.

'I'm sorry about all this, Mrs Nelson,' began the doctor. 'Margaret has taken a room in Sherwood Avenue where I have several elderly patients. Of course, I visit regularly and I knew that your daughter was having . . . men calling on her quite frequently. But Mrs Cullen brought things to a head this lunchtime and . . . well, here we are.'

Dolly's eyes narrowed. 'Is she still at Woolworth's?'

'Aye,' replied Bertha.

'Then 'ow come she's toutin' in 'er dinner hour? 'Ow would she get up Sherwood an' back in time fer work?'

David Pritchard glanced at Bertha. 'She uses her

friend's flat near the Lido on Bradshawgate, we believe. Between the pair of them, they've quite a business going. I'm sorry to be the carrier of such bad tidings, Mrs Nelson, but we thought it best to bring your daughter home straight away.'

'Aye. Well you did right. 'Appen you'd best be off now and tend your own business. I suppose yer'll 'ave plenty fer t' talk about now, Bertha Cullen? Yer'll be able ter tell yer mate Nancy 'Igson all about it, eh?'

Bertha breathed in sharply. 'You ungrateful bugger, you! As if I would! There's not a word'll cross my lips. Me and Nancy 'as better things fer t' talk over.'

'Oh aye? Like 'er leavin' a chap ter die on 'is own? Like 'er goin' about dancin' an' takin' boarders in?'

'Now, ladies . . .' began David.

'This is no bloody lady, Doctor,' said Bertha. She turned and stamped out of the room.

'I'll . . . I'll leave you to it then, Mrs Nelson.'

'I reckon you'd better.'

She waited until the car pulled away, then shouted from the foot of the stairs, 'Get thisen down 'ere!'

A shamefaced Maggie entered the kitchen where her mother was arranging mugs and plates on the table.

'We'll 'ave a cup, lass. Sit down, I'll not bite thee.'

'I'm sorry, Mam . . .'

'Nay, never bother. We'll soon be to rights tha'll see.'

They sat at the table drinking tea, Dolly studying her daughter closely.

'So. Yer on t' game, are you?'

'It was fer the rent, Mam. I couldn't manage on

me wages. I won't do it no more – honest.'

''Ow much was you gettin'?'

'About a quid a go.' Maggie, her cheeks blazing, stared down at the stained tablecloth.

''Ow many a week?'

'Ten, maybe more.'

'That's a fair amount o' brass. 'Ave yer spent it all?'

'I've a bit in t' Post Office.'

Dolly stood up and walked to the window. It was dead quiet round here, so quiet that she reckoned the house could burn down without anybody noticing. 'Yer've got to stop off the streets, Maggie.'

'I will, Mam. I will. But I can't live 'ere – there's nowt goes on, nowhere ter go . . .'

'Then we mun make a life, eh?' She turned to look at her daughter. 'Listen ter me, our Maggie. I'm stoney – never been so broke in me life. We could . . . well . . . set up shop, like.'

''Ow do yer mean, Mam?'

Dolly sidled towards the table. 'Get yer gentleman callers ter come up 'ere! I can keep t' lads upstairs, yer can use t' best room – that couch makes to a bed, tha knows. An' if there's any bother, yer'll 'ave yer old Mam ter look after yer.' She smoothed her tangled hair. 'Fact is, one or two of 'em might fancy a bit of older stuff – I could maybe 'elp out.'

Maggie's jaw dropped. 'We'd . . . we'd be runnin' a brothel, Mam!'

'Nay, lass. We'd be stayin' alive best way we can. It's money fer old rope, isn't it? I mean, we could buy a few bottles in, sell drinks on t' side . . . it'd be like 'avin' a party a couple o' nights a week. Come 'ome, Maggie. I'll look after thee. Yer never know what yer might pick up on yer own – yer could get a flamin' murderer or summat. What do yer say?'

Maggie stared at her mother for several seconds. 'Alright, Mam. We'll give it a try. But . . .'

'But what?'

'Well, it seems right funny, does this. I thought yer'd kill me an' 'ere we are talkin' about . . . well . . .'

'About settin' up in business is what, Maggie. Look at it this road – we're 'elpin' out, aren't we? Some women doesn't like doin' it. So their poor 'usbands 'as ter go wi'out. If we give t' men what they want, then they'll likely give over mitherin' their wives.'

'Eeh Mam, you're a bugger!'

'Aye well, 'appen yer've took after me, eh?'

The baby whimpered and Maggie leaned over to look into the pram. 'Is 'e alright, Mam?'

''Course 'e is. 'E's not complainin' 'is 'e?'

'No . . . no. I just wondered . . .'

But Dolly's mind was too full of plans to give heed to Maggie's wonderings. Yes, they had the answer now, a bit of life with money thrown in as a bonus. She took the last Woodbine from the packet and grinned. There'd be plenty more, plenty to go round for everybody.

12

Departures

Eddie Higson, after surviving well beyond the expected span, died in June 1958, just as Annie was completing her advanced level examinations. Nancy, on receiving the news from local police, decided not to tell her daughter yet, then, after making arrangements with the undertaker, she sent word to his brothers. The older man, Bob Higson, arrived at the house and demanded to know why Nancy had never visited Eddie and why she now refused to attend his funeral. So she told him straight, with Mary at her side, both women hoping that any trouble would be over before Annie got back from school.

'He was a rapist and a child-molester,' said Nancy, not prepared at this stage to pull any punches.

'I don't believe it!' came the reply. 'That was all rubbish about him and that kiddy down Emmanuel Street. They proved nowt at all! The child was lying!'

Nancy folded her arms and stood squarely before him. 'That girl and her mother were both killed, weren't they? After your Eddie had gone off to the war. I remember old Florrie Hyatt trying to tell me about that, only I wouldn't listen – just like you, I didn't want to hear bad of him. Well hear me now, Bob Higson. That brother of yours interfered with my daughter, likely affected her for life, he did.' Without glancing at Mary, she went on, 'Then he raped a nurse up at the TB place. Oh yes, he was very generous with his attentions, was your brother. Even got one of his customers pregnant. But above all, he was a . . . a . . . what's that fancy word, Mary?'

'A paedophile.' Mary's voice was quiet.

'That's right. He liked little girls. And you expect me to go to his funeral?' Nancy's tone was bitter and sarcastic.

Bob shuffled about uncomfortably, his face reddened by embarrassment. 'To be honest with you, Nancy, we did know as how he was a queer fish – kept to himself most of the time, then given to odd fits of temper. But we never thought he was one for children and suchlike. Oh heck.' He sank into a chair and sat twisting his cap between his fingers. 'In spite of that business in '39, we never cottoned on, never knew he was that bad.'

'Well he was,' snapped Nancy.

'Anyroad, he suffered for it. Like an animal in a cage, he was . . .'

'We don't need to know all that,' said Nancy firmly. 'I'm convinced he got himself in there so he wouldn't be tried. Then he likely went mad at the finish knowing he'd never get out. You just see him buried decent with his father. I've got my own plot – my bones could never rest easy with his.'

Bob rose from the chair. 'Nancy, lass. I feel awful coming up here on the bounce like, especially after what you've just said. Let us chip in for the burial, give you some money back for Annie . . .'

Nancy held up her hand. 'I'll say this for you – you're a decent sort, Bob Higson and I appreciate your offer. But no, I owe the man one debt and that's to get him safely buried, thanks all the same.'

He left bowed and round-shouldered, Nancy closing the door securely in his wake.

'Right. That's that then, Mary. Pour us both a drop of brandy. Thank God I took a couple of days off – you'd have had his brother to deal with and you on the flaming night shift.' She sipped her drink. 'Daft, isn't it? I get three days' compassionate leave because I've lost a husband I didn't want anyway. Never mind. Cheers – here's to us and our Annie.'

As they raised their glasses, the subject of the toast burst in like a whirlwind, books and papers scattering about her person as she entered the room. 'I've finished!' she cried, tossing a handful of notes into the air.

'Then you shall have a brandy too,' said Nancy. 'After all, you're eighteen – time you got introduced to the booze.'

'Oh give over, Mam,' laughed Annie, lapsing into her old mode of speech. 'I've been pinching the odd drop since I was about fourteen – it would be no novelty.'

Nancy clipped her playfully round the ear. 'Sit down, Annie.'

'What is it, Mother?' Annie placed herself in the fireside rocker.

'He's dead.'

Mary came and squatted on her haunches in front of Annie, this new grown-up little sister whom she had learned to love. 'Yes, he's gone, Annie.'

'Eddie Higson?'

'Yes.' Mary gripped Annie's hands. 'He died two days ago, only we never told you on account of that big exam today.'

Annie's eyes filled with tears.

'Nay,' said Nancy. 'You're not weeping for him, are you?'

'No.' She sniffed hard. 'I'm crying for what he was and what he did. We don't know – perhaps he couldn't help it. He might have been born bad and now he's died all on his own.'

'Honest! She'd see good in Jack the Ripper, she would!'

'Please, Nancy,' whispered Mary. 'He was looked after, Annie. Don't go upsetting everybody, especially yourself. And I'm not waltzing off on nights leaving you in tears.'

Nancy and Mary went to the table and carried on setting places for the meal. Annie sat very still, staring into the grate as she spoke in a voice that was barely audible. 'I read that any man's death is diminishing to the rest of us. It's forever. Death's forever. The only thing we can be really sure of is that we'll die. That's why people write poetry, try to tell us to look at things now while there's still time. I don't like the thought of people dying, no matter what they've done. But I feel so awful, because I'm glad he's gone. Does that mean I'm a bad person too?'

'It means you're bloody human, Annie,' said Nancy.

'Did he die peacefully, Mother?'

Nancy would never tell her daughter the truth, that he had gone out raving and bathed in his own final haemorrhage. 'Yes, he went quiet enough.'

'Good.' Annie rose, deliberately pulling herself together. 'I'll just go and change into some human clothes.'

'Hang on!' called Mary from the sideboard. 'Two letters for you – one's from America, I think.'

Annie took the envelopes and sped to her room, opening Tom's first. His letters and parcels had arrived frequently over the years, providing great pleasure for Annie and her friends with whom she'd often shared Life-Savers, coloured bubble-gums, bright American comic papers and lots of other carefully chosen mementos. Sometimes, he even sent clothing and items of jewellery, things that were not available in England, so that Nancy and Annie often wore things that attracted attention and comment. Always, always, Tom sent his love.

She smiled, noticing yet again how American her Tom had become.

1517 Forest View
Philadelphia, Pa.
U.S.A.

June 1st 1958

Hi Annie,

How are you doing? I've got a good job now in the steelworks, promoted to supervisor just last month. This means I'm in charge of the two P's – paint and people. I don't know which is worse! I wish you would get out here and see this beautiful country. Philly itself is really busy, but there's some cute places around and you would surely love Pennsylvania.

I am busy most days. Everything needs repainting the minute you've done it. We paint everything that don't move and a few things that do! Paint sure spreads easy!

I've saved nearly enough to visit back home

and the guys upstairs are letting me save vacations too so I'll have six weeks in England once I've enough dough. I guess England will seem small. This one state is enormous compared to Lancashire.

I've travelled a bit, went to Niagara a few weeks ago – boy, you should see that water, it kind of makes you want to cry. All that natural power is frightening.

Also I've been to Fort Ligonier, Pennsylvania-Dutch territory. You would love them forests, Annie. This place is full of trees – I guess that's how it came by its name. I'm sending you some souvenirs, Penn-Dutch aprons, tea-towels and the like so you can get the flavor. America has everybody's history rolled into one heap, that's why it's so interesting.

Well, I'm 32 and still not married. Did you wait for me or are you about to marry some college professor?

I'll be seeing you. Best regards to your Ma and hooray for her getting to be foreman.

Lots of love,

Tom.

Annie placed the letter with the others in a drawer of the tallboy. She held on to the second envelope for some time, turning it over slowly in her hand. It bore a London mark and the address was handwritten. She had applied to no colleges in the south and anyway, with her new career decision, she did not expect to hear anything for a while, her late change of mind having made the applications tardy. Slowly, she opened the letter.

113, Sandfield Road,
London EC4

14th June 58

My Dear Annie,

Yes, I'm in London – for the time being. I've gone freelance and already have two assignments lined up. My interest in photography paid off, because I now do the journalism and the pictures, so I don't have to cart a photographer around with me. I'm calling myself a photo-journalist, which sounds a bit posher than tea-boy! I leave for Africa in a day or two, raring to set off on safari.

It seems stupid now, the way we quarrelled. I hope you are happy and that your career will be a success. I write to my mother occasionally, I think she's glad of the pound or two I manage to send at last. She tells me you still visit and keep them smiling like you always did.

Don't you dare forget me, Annie Byrne. You can't write, because I don't know where I'll be, but I'll send postcards and photos from wherever I happen to get to. Look after yourself, kid. I'm coming back one day to see you. I expect you have a boyfriend (or several?) but I'm sure we can get together for old times' sake.

Hope your Mam is well – I hear that your stepdad is not in good health and I'm sorry, though you never did like him, did you?

Will write again and hope to see you sometime soon.

My love to you,

Martin. X

Annie stared for a long time at the single sheet. This was the first time he'd contacted her. Did he want that old flame – never more than a flicker – rekindled? What had she felt for this boy so long ago? Not love. Love was surely something bigger, greater than the childish feeling they had shared. But there had been tenderness, affection, care – and she missed those now.

She walked to the window and found herself smiling as she watched Dr Pritchard struggling to start Genevieve. That car must be as old as the hills. He stood on the pavement, his mouth moving as he spoke to this beloved object, coaxing, stroking the bonnet as if the thing could hear and feel him. She shook her head. Such a marvellous doctor, such a wonderful, lovable and sweet man.

Sighing, she turned away. Tomorrow would be another big day, another hurdle to leap, her final interview with Mother St Vincent. And these letters had unsettled her, had reminded her that there was a great big world out there ready for the taking. But first, she had to get past this tiny but commanding woman who was fighting her every inch of the way. And Annie was going to fight back. After all, life could be short – Eddie Higson's span had covered a mere forty-three years. Again, she wept briefly, praying that she would not waste the rest of her own years hating a dead man.

Then she heard Genevieve leaping to life and she grinned through her tears. 'Hatred is a waste of energy,' she heard David Pritchard saying. He was right, of course. Human, lovable, but right.

They sat in their usual places, the small nun to the left and the tall girl to the right of the window, a tea-tray occupying the table between them. Mother St Vincent, elbows resting on chair arms, fingers tapping together in front of her Cross and Passion badge, stared hard at Annie. Annie played with the fringed end of her prefect's sash, a long red strap that went over one shoulder, tied just below the waist on the opposite side, then dangled down towards the hem of her tunic.

'Annie Byrne! Will you for once listen and pay attention? I have always hoped – no, that's the beginning of an untruth – I have always known that you are Oxford material. Many is the day I have said to myself, "There goes a girl of high academic calibre."'

Annie's mouth twitched. She would miss this woman, really she would. Only Mother St Vincent could put a capital 'I' in the middle of 'calibre' and get away with it in a dignified fashion.

The nun coughed as if irritated by Annie's faint smile. 'And you arrive here now, at the eleventh hour, to tell me that you have the vocation?'

'That depends what you mean, Mother. I'm going to hang on to my legs, that's for sure.'

'Legs? Legs? What have legs to do with it at all, at all? You see? You have me so dismayed I'm sounding as if I just now stepped off the boat with my apron full of potatoes! We are talking about your future, girl. And sit up straight would you, or you'll be getting a curvature!'

Annie straightened her spine, wondering at the power of this frail creature who now rose from her chair, the great wooden rosary with its metal crucifix clanking and clattering as she paced the small area. After muttering and mumbling to herself for a short time, the nun stopped and faced Annie. 'So there you sit, with the world as your oyster, telling me that you're away to get a diploma. Not a degree, mind. A teaching diploma.' She spat this last word as if it were acid. 'And when I give you my opinion, you begin a conversation about legs.' She turned away impatiently and Annie, catching a glimpse of a highly-polished black shoe, found herself assessing the size of Mother's feet. Smaller than a ten-year-old's, they were. Probably a size two – even a one . . . 'I used to think nuns didn't have legs,' she heard herself stating absently.

'Pardon?'

'Sorry, I was thinking aloud. I had the idea, when I was a child, that there were two kinds of teachers, those with and those without.'

'Legs?'

Annie nodded, not daring to meet Mother's eyes.

'And how did you imagine that the Sisters moved about?'

'I'm not sure. Perhaps I thought they floated on a cloud, or had wheels . . .' Her voice tailed away.

'That was a foolish concept, was it not?'

Annie sighed. 'And a sobering one. If you'd known some of them, you would not have expected them to have simple human parts.'

'I know all of them, Anne. And I can assure you

that they are in no way different from the rest of you.'

'I know, I know – I'm sorry . . .'

Mother returned to her seat, pushing away the small table so that cups and saucers rattled, the sound seeming to reflect her impatience and displeasure. She smoothed the heavy black skirt. 'I do not know what to say to you, Madam Byrne. But then I have seldom known what to say, for haven't you always been the difficult one, giving me desperate trouble half the time, then affection and respect for the rest of it? Your teachers here have all convinced themselves that you would be doing the medicine. That's a fine analytical brain you've been blessed with, a mind that could get you into the business of helping the sick, of healing bodies . . .'

'I see, Mother.' Annie's eyes flashed, showing an odd mixture of amusement and anger. 'You'd rather I dealt with bodies and left the minds alone? I've been accused in the past of being a – what was it now? – ah yes, a disruptive influence. Are you afraid that I might cause children to think for themselves, that I won't let them be a herd of sheep guided and forced along against a will they're not allowed to have? Was it St Francis who said "Give me a child until he is seven and I will show you the man"?'

Mother bristled visibly and Annie studied the three perfectly placed round-headed pins which kept a waist-length black square fastened to the miniature head.

'I am not telling you not to teach! Don't be trying to twist the words before they're ever out of my mouth! Get a good Honours, teach a subject . . .'

'No. I don't want to work with older children, those who've already had their indoctrination one way or another.'

'You are impertinent, child!'

'I am eighteen years old, Mother!'

'And I'd surely put you over my knee this very minute, only I'd need a crane to lift the size you are!'

Both women were now perched on the edge of the chairs, each breathing heavily and staring hard at the other. Annie leaned back slowly and deliberately, stretching out her long legs and crossing her ankles. 'We must agree to differ, I'm afraid. I'm going to Manchester. In two years I'll be supporting my mother. I shall be attending college, learning the principles and practice of education with Scripture and Comparative Religion as part of the course.'

'Defiant to the last! You'll need a dispensation from the Bishop to attend a non-Catholic college.'

'No. I am not a confirmed Catholic.'

'And if I refuse you a reference?'

Annie shrugged her shoulders lightly. 'Then I'll have to write and explain such bigotry to the college principal. And you and I would not part the best of friends.'

The ensuing silence was short, because next door in the practice room, someone began to play the piano very badly, like a mouse running up and down the keys. From time to time, the music teacher bawled loudly at the poor sufferer at the keyboard. Unable to contain herself, Annie began to giggle while Mother's shoulders shook with ill-contained mirth. 'Sure, that's nothing,' the nun finally managed. 'You should hear Katie Maher at the violin. I always do school inspection during her lessons, for I cannot bear the agony of hearing a cat being strangulated.'

'Haven't you . . . oh what a din . . . haven't you any earplugs?'

'Indeed I have not. Do as I do, endure it and offer up your suffering for the souls in Purgatory . . .'

'Except for Katie Maher. You don't offer up Katie Maher . . .'

'Anne, there is a limit to every mortal's endurance. Katie Maher's fiddle is my personal limit.'

'Oh, Mother, Mother . . .' Annie cried, reaching for a handkerchief, her face suddenly sober. 'I shouldn't be laughing.'

'Why not? Laughter never did harm.'

'Well, it's just that my . . . stepfather died a few days ago. Laughing seems wrong.' She paused and glanced at Mother St Vincent. 'You see, Mother, I hated him. He was cruel and hurtful – once, he kicked my mother so hard that she lost her baby. I have been . . . filled with hatred for years and years.'

Mother St Vincent stared hard at Annie. 'I thought I detected a note of hysteria. And yes, yes, this explains a great deal about you.' She fingered the edge of her stiff white collar as she pondered, repeating slowly. 'This explains a great deal, Anne Byrne. So. Perhaps you're relieved that he's gone?'

'Yes, I am.'

'No doubt God will forgive you for that. But I'm disappointed that you never told me these troubles. I might have helped.'

'Some things are too bad to talk about.'

The nun sighed deeply. 'I suppose you're right. It's not all of us can do the dirty washing in the street now, is it?' She paused and studied Annie for several seconds. 'Alright then. You can have your reference. I wish though . . . still, no matter. Perhaps you'll come back to the Faith in your own time. I'll . . . I'll miss you, child.'

'And I'll miss you too.'

'Like you'd miss the toothache? Go on with you. Write to me sometimes, Anne Byrne.'

'I shall. Goodbye, Mother.' Annie rose to leave.

'God go with you.'

Annie left school by the front door that afternoon, marching out through the teachers' entrance in a last silly act of defiance. She took the horrible brown hat and flung it into a bush as she walked towards the bus stop. By the time she reached home, her brown and yellow tie was adorning a lamp post in the town centre, while the ribbon with which she had been forced, for seven years, to tie back her hair, was fastened to a used ticket box on the bus. It was over. Over and just beginning.

Simon had scraped by sufficiently to gain a place at the art college in Manchester where he intended to qualify as an illustrator. Annie received one distinction and two credits, thereby ensuring her entrance to teachers' training college in September.

They sat now in Simon's recreation room, talking about their respective futures, though Annie was doing most of the talking. Simon seemed distant, often making inappropriate responses to Annie's questions.

She waved a hand in front of his face. 'Hello! Anybody in?'

He stared at her for several moments.

'What's the matter, Simon?'

He shrugged his shoulders. 'Can't talk about it,' he muttered.

'Oh. Would you like me to go?'

'No! No, don't go – look, I'm sorry. I'm just a bit . . . preoccupied . . .'

'Preoccupied? You're absent without leave, Simon. I've been talking to myself for the last ten minutes.'

'Sorry.'

'Stop saying that! Look, either you tell me what's wrong or I go.'

He jumped up quickly, the flimsy canvas chair falling back as he rose.

'Oh God!' He put a hand to his face. 'She knows!'

'Who knows?' Annie stood and placed a hand on his arm. 'Who knows what?'

'My mother! She saw us . . . in here . . . she saw . . .'

Annie picked up the chair and forced him to sit down again. 'Start at the beginning, Simon.'

'I don't know how. But I can trust you, can't I? It's not really a secret any more, but at least you won't spread it around. How though, how do I tell you?'

'With words, Simon. You can tell me anything – I won't be shocked.'

'Promise?'

'Promise.'

He swallowed audibly. 'Do you know . . . what a homosexual is?'

'Yes, I do.'

Seconds passed. 'I'm one,' he declared finally, his voice deliberately steady. 'I used to wonder why I was never jealous of you and Martin. One time, I saw you kissing and half of me wished I was in Martin's place, but the other half . . . I was so confused.'

She took his hand. 'Oh Simon, Simon . . .'

'I had one experience with a girl – Susan Birchall. It was horrible.'

'But . . . but you may be ordinary after all! This could be a phase because of that bad experience . . .'

He shook his head vehemently. 'No. I have a friend, someone from school. I am fond of him and I believe he cares for me too.'

'But is it so terrible?'

'Yes! Yes, it is! Everyone will expect me to marry and have children – especially my parents. Though my mother . . .'

'What about your mother?'

'Last night,' he said, almost in a whisper, 'she found us in here. She is the last person in the world who might accept. What we were doing must have seemed so awful to her . . .' He broke off, his voice cracking with tears.

'She'd have to know sometime . . .'

'Yes! I suppose she would have to find out that her son is a pervert!'

Annie thought briefly about the real pervert she had known, the one who had been buried some weeks ago. Between Eddie Higson and Simon, there was no comparison. 'You're not a pervert! You'd never inflict pain or force your attentions. You're just . . . different, that's all.'

'Yes – different. I'll be an outcast unless I live some sort of pretended life, force myself to marry and have a family.'

'That wouldn't be honest, especially for your wife.'

'I know! I know I can never be normal.'

'You're still the same old Simon.'

'Yes. Salmon Pilchard, Old Fish Face.'

'I never called you Fish Face.'

He smiled sadly through his tears then went to stand, hands in pockets and with his back towards her as he stared through a window.

'Has she told your father what she saw?'

'I doubt it. They don't communicate. On the other hand, with a thing of this magnitude . . .'

'Don't you think you should talk to him first?'

'I can't. Except for Paul – he's my friend – you're the only one I've spoken to.'

They remained in the room for an hour or more, sometimes sitting silently, often pacing together as they tried to talk their way through to a solution.

Later on, Simon became even more agitated. His father had been out for some time, but was expected back shortly for evening surgery. There had been no sound in the house, no sign of his mother going through her customary tea-making ritual.

'Knock on her bedroom door, Simon.'

'I daren't go near after what's happened . . .'

'Then I'll do it!'

'No!'

'I'm not afraid of her, Simon.'

'That's why she doesn't like you. She calls it lack of respect . . .'

'Well, one of us has to find her.'

'OK, OK, I'll go.' He made for the door.

Annie heard him crossing the landing and tapping gently, then suddenly he was screaming, 'Anne! Anne!' Annie sped across the landing and into Edna Pritchard's bedroom.

The woman on the bed had arranged everything beautifully. She lay flat, her hands clasping a posy of flowers against her breast. The cream-coloured peignoir was of pure silk, her face was perfectly made up and she had even tied a chiffon scarf under her chin and around the top of her head so that she would not die open-mouthed. The pink of painted nails showed fiery red against the whitening flesh of her hands. Beside her, in a perfect copper-plate hand, lay a note.

To Whom it May Concern,

I wish to be interred in Heaton Cemetery with my

385

parents. No undertaker is to interfere with my body
which is to be buried exactly as you find it. Please
remove the scarf once you have ensured that my
mouth will remained closed.

The will is with my solicitor whose details are
known to my husband. I have no reason to live. I
therefore choose my own time, place and method of
dying.

Edna Marguerite Pritchard

The two young people stared in frozen shock at
the figure on the bed, then Annie leapt forward to
feel the wrist, seeking a pulse. But the icy stiffness of
the arm told its story and Annie dragged Simon out
of the room. She felt a strong urge to run – somewhere, anywhere – to find help, but she dared not
leave Simon who was leaning heavily on the banister,
fighting for breath.

Then the front door opened and Annie leaned
over the rail screaming, 'Doctor! Come quickly!'

The man raced up the stairs. 'What is it?' he asked,
his eyes riveted to Simon whose stomach now
heaved. Simon turned, pointed to his mother's
room, then fled to the bathroom.

David entered his wife's bedroom. There was no
need for him to touch Edna; the signs of rigor were
plain to his practised eye. He turned from the bed
and felt Annie's arms around his shaking body. But
he saw nothing, heard nothing except his own voice.
'My fault. I killed her . . . I killed her.'

'Come away, Doctor – come away.' He seemed
not to hear, so she pulled him gently from the room.

'Why couldn't I just . . . what have I done? She
didn't need to know . . . I should have . . .'

Annie quickly worked out the geography of the house and led the doctor to his room. Like an obedient child, he allowed himself to be pushed on to the narrow bed.

'Doctor? Dr Pritchard?' She shook his shoulders.

'What? Anne – where's Simon?'

'In the bathroom being sick.'

'She's dead.'

'I know.'

'I told her . . . things. I shouldn't have done it . . .'

'I'm going downstairs to put up a note cancelling the surgery. If anybody's ill, they'll have to go to hospital. Stay there – don't you dare move.'

She ran down the stairs and found a notepad on which she printed a very shaky announcement. After fixing this to the front door, she sat for several minutes in the dining room, trying hard to hang on to what was left of her composure. But her eyes wandered unbidden over Mrs Pritchard's precious things, china in glass-fronted cabinets, crystal decanters encased in a polished tantalus, the framed tapestry hanging proudly over the fireplace. Simon's mum had stitched that with her own hand, a hand that would never lift another needle, pour a drink, dish out a dinner.

So hard, Mrs Pritchard had seemed, so steely and indestructible. But everyone had a breaking point – even this soul of iron had been worn down, corroded past mending . . .

Reaching out to steady herself on the arm rest, Annie rose from the carver and placed herself in front of the tapestry. 'I'm sorry, Mrs Pritchard,' she whispered. 'Sorry we never tried to understand.'

But there were two still living, two who needed her now. So she turned from what was left of Edna and steeled herself to return to the upper floor. From the landing, she saw Simon sitting at the foot of his father's bed.

'It was my fault,' Simon was saying.

So he had just now told his father! But what a terrible time to have to do it.

Annie could see that even in his state of double shock, David was fighting for control, fighting to shield his son. 'No, Simon. Your mother found out that I'd been unfaithful – in fact, I told her. She might even have discovered that my mistress was a friend of hers. That's why she killed herself.'

'An affair's normal, Dad. But yesterday, she found out . . .'

'No! She would not kill herself because of your preferences! Believe me – she has threatened this for years, but I thought she was being over-dramatic. You must not blame yourself!'

Annie knocked on the open door. 'Shall I get an ambulance or something?'

David nodded. 'Please. Arrangements will have to be made.'

'Mrs Pritchard left very precise instructions, Doctor . . .'

'She would. Oh yes, she would.'

Annie stayed with David and Simon for the whole evening, leaving just once to tell Nancy what had happened. Mary and Nancy brought food which nobody ate, then Annie remained to answer any telephone calls. Edna's body was removed and taken to the morgue. The cause of death would have to be established, so whatever the poor woman's wishes might have been, that final message would be ignored.

At ten o'clock, Annie unlocked the medicine

cabinet and took out four sleeping pills, forcing the men to swallow two each. When they finally drifted off into restless sleep, she took the phone off the hook and went home.

'Eeh, Annie,' cried Nancy. 'Why?'

'Because she couldn't face life any more.' Annie allowed her tears of shock to flow now. 'Oh Mam, it was awful . . . awful . . .'

They gave her a hot toddy and put her to bed. Mary sat the whole night in Annie's chair by the window, watching the lights going on and off in the doctor's house. Each time Annie moaned in her sleep, Mary leapt up to stroke her head and soothe away the nightmare.

This child, this eighteen-year-old girl, had experienced more in her short life than most people did in a full three score and ten. Sighing, Mary resumed her seat and watched the dawn break over Bolton. Edna Pritchard would never see another dawn. Others had been left to face many such mornings.

Part Three

Anne

1960

I escaped from college in late June with a cartload of useless books, distinctions in some final exams and a marked dislike for certain educationalists. The system was changing and loud voices were proclaiming the benefits of 'learning by discovery' which, roughly interpreted, meant let the little beggars do as they like. I tried these methods once during a teaching practice in Stockport, found myself reading a story to three children while the other forty-six did interesting things like throwing paint, eating jigsaw puzzles and getting up to no good in the boys' toilets. I therefore gained one of my distinctions by writing a thesis on this load of progressive rubbish and emerged with an undeniable suspicion that the three Rs still had a place in our schools.

I threw off the student garb which included shocking-pink stockings, bright tartan skirts and two college scarves sewn together to make one long enough to go round Manchester Town Hall. It was like getting rid of another uniform.

The courses had proved disappointing, though scripture fascinated me because I discovered that the Old Testament was so crammed with anomalies and improbabilities that it was either a pack of lies or a collection of interesting errors. Comparative religion sessions were another eye-opener; Islam was too weird and wonderful for me, while Buddhism proved unacceptable as I had no desire to return as a spider or, worse still, as another human seeking Nirvana. This, apparently, was on offer to those who did nothing at all apart from following some odd eight-point plan in their minds – I never did get to grips with it. So I left poor Buddha sitting under his tree and decided to be a Christian after all.

As the college was in Manchester, I was able to come home each weekend. I received the full grant of £25 a term, a total of £150 throughout the two years. This laughable amount forced me to take a Saturday job in Marks and Spencer on Deansgate where I thoroughly enjoyed selling stockings from ten till six, for which service I earned a guinea a day, a wage that compared favourably with the pittance I would eventually receive as a qualified teacher.

During what was left of my weekends, I spent time with Simon, who also came home each Friday and with his father who taught me to play a mean backgammon and a passable game of chess. Simon saddened me. He remained quiet and withdrawn; I knew that he would always blame himself for his mother's suicide.

I had just two boyfriends during my time in college. The first, Mike Stewart, hailed from Bradford and I soon learned to imitate his fascinating accent. We were never close – merely part of a group – and we drifted apart when he met a stunning girl from the university who enticed him to her lair from whence he would emerge dazed and unshaven to take in the odd lecture.

My second encounter, with John Beresford, was slightly more intense. For a whole term we mooned over one another, passing love-notes and poems across lecture halls while the Philistines around us sniggered at our pure and beautiful romance. When John suggested that our relationship should become less than pure and more than beautiful, I lost him too because of my blunt refusal. John went off in a huff to comfort himself with a florist's assistant from Wythenshawe. I retired to a corner and licked my shallow wounds which healed after a fortnight because I was invited to write the lyrics for our revue, an exciting honour given only to the favoured few.

And now it was over. For all my pains, I would soon be receiving the princely reward of £32 each calendar month, for which sum I must take charge of and educate a class of no less than forty-five infants.

My mother was very proud. 'You'll be able to save up.'

'For what?'

'For the future, for holidays and nice clothes.'

'I'll pay my keep like Mary does.'

'We'll see. I'm alright now, you mustn't worry over money.'

She didn't need my salary, probably didn't really need me any longer. She loved me, I was still her favourite girl, but Mary was there now to keep her company and although I felt no jealousy, I sometimes had a sense of being surplus to requirements. This was all a part of my mother's plan for me. She had given me the wings and now she wanted to see me fly.

Then, during the long break between college and my first term as a teacher, life suddenly went completely mad. Tom and Martin returned almost simultaneously to colour and disrupt my existence to the point of exhaustion. I was not surprised when Martin pursued me relentlessly – after all, we had had some kind of relationship in the past. But when Tom began to press his suit, I was amazed.

Tom was the kind of man who might sweep any girl off her feet – tall, bronzed, muscular and with a slight American accent that lent him a film-starrish air. But it was plain from the start that he had come home with the intention of taking me back with him.

'You'd love it, Annie. Remember how you begged me all those years ago to take you with me? Well – now's the time! You could have a real good look around, then if things worked out – who knows? We might even get married once you know me better.'

I sat in the passenger seat of the large hired car, squirming because I didn't know what to say. The Tom I knew from his letters was not the same as this powerful person who sat by my side.

'What d' you say, Annie?'

'I . . . don't know. I have to get through my probationary year . . .'

'You can do that back home!'

'This is home, Tom.'

'Yeah. Well I guess I have two homes now. Think about it, Annie. I've saved all the photographs and letters over the years – I knew my Annie was growing up to be a real beauty. And when the guys hassled me about not being married – well, I'd tell them straight – "I'm going home and get my English rose", I'd say.'

His arm crept along the back of the seat and he pulled me as near as the gear lever would allow. The kisses were sweet and tender at first, then, as his tongue began to probe, I pushed at his chest. I liked him, really I did. But there was something missing, something I knew about. Whatever this something was, I had met it before and let it pass me by. But I couldn't remember where or when.

Martin was a different matter altogether. His confidence was unshakeable from the start, that very first day when he walked into our house and swept me off my feet, not caring who was watching.

'Eeh, Martin!' cried my mother. 'Put that woman down this minute!'

Then I stood and watched as he kissed my mother and introduced himself to Mary. He was taller than I remembered and his voice was cultured and controlled.

He turned to me now. 'Am I welcome, Annie Byrne?'

'Of course you are.'

'Then I shall be escorting your daughter this evening, Mrs Higson.'

'Nay, don't tell me, lad. She's her own mistress now – not that she's ever been any different, come to think . . .'

'Will you come?' he asked me.

'Yes.' Perhaps he was whatever I'd been missing. So I went and listened to him talking over dinner, spinning tales about his exciting life and how many pages of his passport were full. No, I wasn't bored, I told myself firmly. I was tired, that was all.

Fighting him off was not easy. He was strong and determined to have his way. Not that there was room in his little two-seater sports car, but he had parked right out in the country and escape would not be easy.

'Come on, Annie. You know I've always loved you . . .'

'For goodness sake – grow up, Martin! I wasn't

397

born yesterday and neither were you! I haven't seen you for years – what do you expect? I'm not going to give in just like that! So, if you're determined to carry on with this, you can do it alone.' I reached for the door handle.

'I'm sorry – look, I'll slow down, I promise.'

'You will grind to a complete halt, Martin Cullen! But the car will move! Now – this minute!'

He started the engine.

'Move!' I shouted.

The car leapt forward. 'I didn't mean to upset you, Annie. Your picture has been in my wallet right next to my heart for a long, long time. I just got carried away. You're more beautiful than ever – it's not easy for me. In a few weeks I'll be gone. Come with me, Annie.'

I gritted my teeth. Not again, not another one. Everybody suddenly wanted to take me away!

'I'm not going anywhere, Martin. I'm a Bolton girl and Bolton's where I'll stay.'

'And marry a boring Bolton man and have boring Bolton kids?'

'Probably.'

'Think about it, Annie.' He pulled up outside our house. 'And by the way, who's this American I'm hearing about?'

'He's an old neighbour from the other side of town. He emigrated and has come back to visit family.'

'Spends a lot of time with you, doesn't he?'

'That is my business!'

He grinned in that boyish way I remembered so well. 'You're going to marry me one day, Annie.'

'Really? Then drop me a line so I'll remember to go to the church!'

I stamped into the house and banged the door.

These two situations continued for weeks. I juggled with them, divided the hours and days as fairly as I could between the two of them, hung on grimly to my virtue as I tried to decide which, if either, was the right one for me. I was pulled this way and that, persuaded, cajoled, bribed almost . . . then, finally, I had had enough. Arrangements had somehow become muddled, I knew that the two of them would arrive this evening – dear God! I couldn't even live in my own house anymore! Every time I opened the door, one or the other would be there complete with chocolates, flowers and an inane grin. But both together? That I could not face.

So I simply walked out and went across to see Simon. He would listen. He would understand. But David opened the door to my frantic bell-pushing.

'What the hell's happened to you, Anne? You look . . . rather flustered to say the least.'

'Just hide me! Put me in a cupboard, lock me in the lavatory – where's Simon? He'll help me.'

'He's out for the evening.'

I glanced over my shoulder. 'Then . . . give me an injection, send me to hospital, say I'm in a coma . . . anything! I'll even play backgammon. Please?'

He took my arm and led me through to the drawing room. The minute he touched me I knew what had passed me by, knew all about that missing something. It was terrifying, like an electric current running up my arm and right through my body. All I was aware of was him, that peppermint and medicine smell, the tweed jacket, a hint of cigar smoke. We stood in the doorway of the room, an untidy room now with no wife to care for it. And I looked at my darling scruffy saviour from the past, with his over-long hair and not quite clean shirt.

'David!' I heard the second syllable as it rose like an alarm, a warning to myself.

'Anne?'

I stood to one side then and watched this girl, this terrible wanton creature as she put her arms around the man and kissed him. But I did not remain an observer for long. He was shaking just as he had on that awful night two years ago when his wife had died. We had to lean against a wall because I too was trembling violently.

So, having come to this place to seek refuge and protection from virile suitors, I found myself in the hands of a truly experienced man, one I had loved forever without quite realizing the fact. It was so natural, so perfect and beautiful. He wiped out all the pain and confusion, eliminated every fear, treated my body with a reverence that shook and delighted me. I didn't care in those moments whether or not this would be forever. Now mattered. Now was all that mattered.

'Oh my darling girl. I am so sorry . . .' he murmured afterwards.

'Don't be. Can't you see what you've done? Don't you realize how terrified I was of all this? I didn't know it could be so wonderful.'

'Yes, it was. But it shouldn't have happened – apart from anything else, I'm your doctor.'

'Then I'll get another – I've been thrown out of better surgeries than yours. Please don't be sad . . . please?' I stroked the head that nestled between my breasts. 'I love you, David. I think I've loved you since I was fifteen.'

'That was gratitude,' he answered, his fingers

gently tracing the contours of my upper body. 'Never confuse gratitude with love.'

'Then what do you feel for me, Dr Pritchard? Is this lust?'

'No,' he said quietly. 'I have the temerity to love you, though God knows I'm too old for you. But I've been a member of the Total Idiots' group for some time now.'

'Tell me how you qualified.'

He lifted his tousled head and looked into my eyes. 'I've wished you were older. I've imagined how it would be if I were twenty years younger . . .'

'But you're not. What does age matter anyway?'

'It matters. I think you should get dressed and go home, my dear.'

I moved away from him and began to pull on my clothes with furious haste. 'Get dressed and go home, my dear,' I mimicked viciously. I dragged my fingers through my hair in an attempt to restore it to some kind of order. 'I don't suppose there's a comb in this dump, Dr Pritchard?'

'On the hallstand.'

I stamped through into the hall and stared at the mirror. I didn't look any different, no matter how many angles I tried and this disappointed me beyond measure. That he would follow me I did not doubt for a moment. Where had I got the wisdom, the certainty that this was what magazines called 'real love'? From him, I supposed, from this thing between us that was a fact, a thing that belonged to neither and yet to both of us. He came up behind me and our eyes met in the glass.

'You're angry,' he said flatly.

'Angry? Why the hell should I be angry? Nothing's

happened, nothing real. It obviously meant little to you when I said I love you. No, I'm not angry, Doctor. I'm bloody furious!'

Then he started to laugh, that awful infectious guffaw that made you either join in or thump him, so I thumped him good and hard, swinging round from the mirror and delivering the full force of my clenched fist, which was not inconsiderable, onto his chest. He coughed, stepped backwards, then grinned broadly.

'Right,' he said quietly. 'I suppose you're going to insist on making an honest man of me. Because you hold all the trumps and you know it, Anne. But it won't be easy. I had to give you the chance to walk away from it. What we're going into will take some explaining.'

I tapped my foot. 'What would you have done if I had walked away?'

'I'd have come after you.'

'It's a good job you said that, David Pritchard!' I reached for him and we clung together saying all the silly things that come with new-found love. And all the time part of my mind was wondering what might or might not have happened if Simon had been at home, if I hadn't got into that dreadful mess with Tom and Martin, if . . . But no, this would have found us sooner or later.

So it was all arranged, mapped out within the hour, at the end of which time we made love again. I had never imagined such happiness, not for myself. For years I had kept my distance, denied my sexuality, indulged my fears. This was not just compensation, it was liberation too. There must be a God, there must be a plan.

We dressed, then hand in hand for all the world to

see, we walked across the road to tell my mother. Just as we reached our gate, he began to chuckle again.

'What's the matter now?' I dug him in the ribs. 'Pull yourself together – this is a very solemn occasion!'

'Remember Blackpool?' he asked. 'She's no easy opponent!'

'She's only little.'

'Yes, so is a bottle of poison. Do you realize – I'll be the same age as my mother-in-law? She'll never buy this.'

'David!' We stood on the pathway facing each other. 'You'll just have to trust my salesmanship.'

My mother was seated at the table with Mary and Bertha Cullen when we entered. They all looked startled when they saw David, but I quickly beckoned to my mother to follow us into the kitchen. I closed the door, took David's arm, then faced her.

She stared at us for some moments. 'What the hell's all this?' she asked eventually.

'Nancy . . . I want to ask for your daughter's hand . . .'

Her jaw dropped. 'You what? You bloody what?'

'We're getting married, Mother.'

'You're . . . you're . . .? No such flaming thing! Still a kid and wanting to chuck your life away – not likely!'

'I love him, Mother.' I squeezed his hand. 'And he loves me.'

There followed a deafening silence during which I could almost feel the straining ears in the next room. Then in she waded – at the deep end as always. 'When you're forty, he'll be sixty bloody odd! Are you daft, lass?'

'No and I'm not a kid. I'll be twenty-one in five months.'

'Don't you come the clever lip with me, our Annie!'

David coughed. 'She'll be well looked after, Nancy.'

'Aye. So will you, eh? Specially when she's shoving you round in the wheelchair.' She turned her venom on me again. 'Years we went without. Now you've got the training and a good job – what the hell do you want to go getting wed for? I've fetched you up to know you don't need a man. But if you've got to have one, why can't you pick somebody your own age? There's Martin – and Tom's only in his thirties.'

David's tone was quiet but firm. 'She doesn't want them, Nancy. She wants me.'

I straightened my spine and looked down on my angry mother. 'Either you accept this or I leave home. That way, I'll be able to do as I please. You can't boss me around forever! I thought it was bad enough when I was a child, you, the nuns, the priest – but we've reached the end of that particular line now. Would you rather David and I lived over the brush as they call it? Because I'm going to live across the road whether I marry him or not.'

She glowered and opened her mouth to speak, but a tapping at the door to the living room put a stop to whatever she was about to pronounce.

Mary opened the door an inch or two. 'Tom and Martin have both come back,' she whispered. 'They're sitting in the front room looking daggers at one another. And we can all hear what's going on in here.'

My mother followed Mary into the living room.

David drew me into his arms. 'Perhaps she's right, darling.'

'No!' I mouthed fiercely. 'She can't take away what's happened between us. I won't let her spoil it, I won't!'

We walked into the living room just as Tom and Martin arrived through the other door. My mother stood at the far side of the table, arms folded, one foot tapping on the floor.

'Well, Tom. Well, Martin. Lady Annie's led you both a dance, I'm afraid.'

'Now, Nancy,' said Bertha. 'Don't go so 'ard on t' lass. She's nobbut doin' what she thinks is reet. Just leave 'er be.'

'Please, Nancy,' begged Mary. 'Let's not have a scene.'

Tom stepped forward. 'What's going on here?'

Martin tried to push his way into the crowded room 'Yes – what's all this about?'

David placed himself in front of the sideboard, leaving me to stand by the kitchen door. He was obviously preparing to fight alone for the cause. He cleared his throat. 'Anne and I want to be married. Obviously, Nancy is under the impression that I'm taking out some kind of insurance policy, getting myself a young wife who will see me through my dotage. This is not the case. Anne and I belong together.' He reached out an arm and I ran to him gladly. 'We didn't plan to fall in love, Nancy. And please, please don't turn away from your daughter now. She loves you. In the past, she has proved how much.' My mother flinched slightly as she took in the meaning behind his words.

Tom shook David's hand vigorously. 'I won't

405

pretend I'm not disappointed, but you sure got a great girl there. Congratulations.'

Martin turned and left the house, slamming doors as he went.

'Tek no notice to 'im,' said Bertha. ''E'll likely get over it.'

My mother, her face white with fury, stormed out of the room and up the stairs.

'Well,' Bertha struggled to her feet. 'I'll . . .er . . .I'll just go an' see ter me . . . me ironin'.' She waddled out, leaving Mary, Tom, David and me standing uncomfortably about the room.

Tom looked at Mary. 'We could . . . go for a drink, you and I . . .'

'Yes . . . yes, I'll just get my coat.' She fled from the scene.

'I'll . . . I'll wait in the car.' The door closed behind Tom.

David shook his head. 'We've upset everybody's applecart, Anne.'

'I don't care! We've got one another and that's all we need.'

The next morning I lay in my bed and waited for the inevitable. She hadn't come downstairs again after that dreadful scene the previous evening, but I knew she hadn't finished with me, not by a long chalk. Somewhere inside myself, I felt torn in two, yet I realized that my love and need for David would win hands down if it came to actual warfare. And the opening salvo was about to be fired, for I could hear her coming up the attic stairs.

She entered my room quietly, which was an ominous sign, walked past the bed and opened the curtains at my three-sided window. With her back towards me, she began to speak, her voice almost a whisper.

'You're not asleep, Annie. I'd know if you were asleep. Likely you've been awake for hours.' She paused as if deep in thought. 'Twenty years I've watched you grow, cared what happened. I've not done it all right. If I'd done it all right, things would never have got so bad for you.'

'Please, Mother . . .'

'No, lass. I'm up on the horse now and it's taken a fair climb. I shall get off when I'm ready.' She cleared her throat as if embarrassed. 'Before I start, I've got to say I'm sorry over what happened last night, me kicking off like that in front of everybody and showing you up . . .'

'That was my fault. David and I should have waited until . . .'

'Shut up, Annie, will you? Let me say my piece, because I've been up all night practising.'

She lowered herself into my chair at the window and shook her head wearily. I couldn't see her face, but I could read its expression from her tone. At first, it was almost as if she were talking to herself.

'When they came with that telegram, I thought my world was over and finished with. I loved him. We fought like cat and dog, but that was part of it, you see. It was like we enjoyed the fighting for the sake of making up. Eeh, when I think back . . .' She disappeared for a while inside her own precious memories and I lay motionless, waiting for her return.

'He was a daft lad, was Billy Byrne. First off, when I said I wouldn't have him, he sent me a note to say he was going up Dawson's chimney with four butties and a bottle of tea. It said "If you don't come and shout yes, I'll starve to death." So I went and there he was, top of the mill stack and all I could think was he'd either fall off or get covered in soot. It was Sunday, so he never did get dirty, because I shouted and he came down fast as a monkey. I married that lad and I thought it was forever. Only it wasn't. Nothing ever is.' She bent her head for a few minutes and I longed to run to her, but something about the way she sat, so stiff and still, made me stay where I was.

'After Billy had died, I put his things – letters, the wedding ring and all that – in an old biscuit tin. I gave it our Jessie to hold for you – I couldn't keep it in the house while . . . while the other one was here.' She sniffed audibly. 'Ever since the day we got the news and you ran to the lions, you've been looking for Billy. I don't mean you've walked round expecting to find him, but inside, in here,' I heard her strike her breast with a clenched fist, 'you've been searching. So now you've found him. But a husband can't be a father, Annie. You're making a terrible mistake that can't be undone easy. So there. I've had my say. Now it's your turn.'

She dried her eyes and faced me and I saw the depth of her sadness and confusion.

'It's not like that, Mother – I promise! I love David. I want him like . . . like a woman wants a man.'

'Aye well. You can want a lot of men in that way. It doesn't mean you love them.'

'I know, I do know that!' Oh what could I say to make her understand? 'It has to be him, Mam.'

'Well, I shan't agree to it.'

'I don't want to hurt you, Mother. If only you knew how much I don't want that. But if I have to, then I must. He's mine. I already belong to him and there's nothing I can do to change it.'

'You don't want to change it, do you?'

'No, I don't. And I won't allow anyone else to spoil it either.'

She walked unsteadily across the room and sat on the edge of my bed. 'We're going to fight, Annie, you and I. And there's neither of us will fight clean.'

'Then that's too bad, Mother! If two grown women can't talk this thing out properly and sensibly . . .'

'What's it got to do with bloody sense?' Colour rose in her cheeks and her voice grew louder. 'What's the sense in getting wed to a man twice your age? And he's a Protestant too . . .'

I heard myself chuckling grimly. 'You can jump off that wagon, Mam. I'm hardly a Catholic and you've not seen the inside of a church for years.'

'That doesn't matter,' she shouted. 'A Catholic is always a Catholic!'

'And that's what you call a sensible argument? If you can't think of anything better . . .'

'Ah, but I can, I bloody can that! His first wife poisoned herself, didn't she? Took a load of pills and a gallon of sherry by all accounts . . .'

'Yes, but . . .'

'Never mind but! Never mind all the flaming buts, Annie! Something drove her to that. Do you want to end up the same road as her? Well . . . do you?'

I sat bolt upright in the bed. 'That is unfair, Mother!'

'Aye, lass. I warned you it wouldn't be fair boxing, didn't I? A man whose wife does herself in has a few questions to answer. Maybe I can answer for him, eh? He's out on his blinking rounds all the time or sitting in that surgery of his. Them two never had more than half a marriage. Poor woman didn't have a husband!'

'Poor woman? Oh Mother, what a hypocrite you are! You'd no time for her when she was alive, we were always cracking jokes about her . . .'

'That's as may be. Only the joke's over now, specially for her! How do you know what he's like to live with, eh?'

'I don't. But I know him, he's a good man.'

'A good doctor, I'll grant that. But how can you be sure he won't push you into doing what she did?'

'That, Mother, is mean, spiteful, despicable . . .' I groped for words then leapt angrily from the bed, grabbing my folded clothes from the top of the tallboy.

'Aye, but you've no answer to it, have you?' she screamed.

'I don't owe you or anybody any answers! How dare you – you of all people? Did you know what Eddie Higson would be like to live with? And even if we leave your mistakes out of this, Mother – and I'm quite sure that we should leave them out – who are you to judge David, to undermine him? And isn't it time you credited me with a bit of intelligence? Do you think I'd go off and marry a dangerous man? Can't you get it into your head that I, Annie Byrne, have seen danger at close quarters and can now recognize its stench from a mile away? Are you implying that I'm so bloody stupid?'

She stood up and glared hard at me. 'Right then, Annie. On your head be it.'

'Mother . . .' But she was already out of the room.

I ran to the top of the stairs and called after her. 'Mam, you are hopeless! You talk about liberation and freedom of choice, about it being time for a woman's world – then you say I can't choose. I am just about sick and fed up with you! You're like a book that's been written back to bloody front!'

She turned at the foot of the attic stairs. 'Don't you take that tone with me, lady. I'm not having you losing your temper just because I stick to my guns in my own house! Anyroad, I'm off to our Jessie's for a week or two, give you time to come to your senses.'

I heard myself gasp. 'You . . . you won't be at my wedding then?'

She stuck out her chin. 'Bolton Wanderers could be at home. Happen I might call in at the match instead.'

I sank on to the top step. 'But . . . you've always hated football.'

'Exactly.'

'You are so stubborn!' I jumped up and threw my handful of clothes at her head and she sidestepped quickly to avoid these flying items.

'I'm not as stubborn as you are, lass,' she said quietly.

Then she was gone. She took her packed suitcase to work and did not return home that night. When she had been gone for a week, we had a meeting, Mary, Simon, David and I, all sitting round the table with the green and white check cloth.

Simon scratched his ear thoughtfully. 'I suppose we have to look at it from her point of view.'

'Fire away,' I said. 'If you can work out her point of view, you deserve a medal.'

'Well,' Simon went on slowly. 'Say I came home with a forty-year-old woman – I know it's not likely, but say I did – what would you think, Dad?'

David gazed steadily at his son. 'I can't answer that. It would depend who she was.'

Mary sighed loudly. 'There's nothing to be gained from this, Simon. We've tried just about everything now. I went up to Jessie's and tried to make Nancy listen . . .'

'You were lucky,' I snapped. 'At least she opened the door. When David and I went . . . oh, I'm sorry, Mary. I didn't mean to bite your head off.'

'Perhaps you should go alone, Anne,' said David.

'I will not! That's exactly what she wants me to do!'

'Then you're just as bad as she is!'

I shook my head slowly. 'You don't understand, any of you. She's made up her mind and so have I. Talking won't do any good. I think we'll just have to go ahead without her.'

David looked quickly at Simon and Mary. 'Would you two mind? I'd like to talk with Anne for a little while.'

After they had gone, he reached for my hand. 'Look, I don't want you to regret this. In years to come, you may well blame me – or worse still, blame yourself for this rift. I'm lucky, I suppose. If Simon had been opposed, I would have had a similar problem. Are you sure you want to go on without her?'

'Absolutely. She'll come to terms with things after the wedding.'

'How do you know?'

'Because she's my mother and we're very alike. She won't punish me for long, David. You don't know her – it's hard to explain. But we'll have to get married without either her blessing or her presence. She'll come back, believe me . . .'

Mary came. And Bertha and Tom, though the latter was due to fly back to the States the same evening.

We had chosen a tiny chapel on the northern edge of the town, so many centuries old that I had to stoop to get through doorways, bending my head to match the height of those who had built it of huge stones and solid dark oak.

Tom was to give me away and I felt that this was appropriate because he'd helped me to survive twenty long years earlier – I owed my life to him.

We stood at the altar while the vicar intoned the service, David holding my hand throughout. When it came to the words 'Who gives this woman?' and Tom stepped forward to do the honours, there was a sudden pushing and shoving aside and there she stood, resplendent but breathless in a pale green suit with white trimmings.

'Hang on a bit,' she said to the disconcerted vicar. 'Only I want a word.'

David hid a smile behind his hand, but I was used to this. Hadn't she always been there in the right place though not necessarily at the right time? Only my mother would dare to cause such a commotion during a marriage ceremony. She pulled me into her strong little arms then reached across to pat David on the shoulder. 'I had to make sure she was sure. If she'd taken any notice of me, I'd have known you were wrong for her. You have to test her at times. You'll find that out once you're wed,' she said, paying no heed at all to the small congregation who gasped at this interruption.

Then she turned her attention to the poor clergyman. 'No disrespect to Tom,' she announced, 'but this here is my only daughter. I gave her life and she owns herself, always has and always will. So nobody gives this woman. My daughter gives herself.'

The vicar, a man of about six feet in height, stared open-mouthed at this tiny intruder.

She looked him up and down. 'It's alright,' she said. 'I've finished now. You can carry on when you're ready.'

She stood by my side throughout the rest of the service, her little head held high and proud while I married David Pritchard. After the service, she pursued us into the registry then out into a bright August sun.

'I'm a daft old bat,' she said, her hat askew after hugging me and David. 'But I'll never be any different, will I?'

'No Nancy,' answered my husband. 'You're incurable, thank God.'

She took me aside. 'Nay lass. I couldn't let you get married without me here, could I? There's no show without Punch.'

'Or Judy, Mother.'

She smiled broadly. 'That's right. Let's never forget Judy.'

THE END

Author's Note

A very special thank you to those men and women who, in spite of some distress, managed to share their experiences with me. The help they gave was invaluable. In all these new friends, I found an unquenchable thirst for living, an unusual tenderness of heart and actual proof that meaningful life can and does continue after damage.

None of us can condone my Annie's way of coping, but, taking into account the era in which this author placed her, we should at least understand her great dilemma. Even in these more enlightened times, situations like hers do exist, cries for help are not always heard.

My prayer is that all our Annies will find the courage to speak out, the strength to persevere and, eventually, the ability to forgive a society which often fails to notice. If this novel helps to save just one child, then it will have done its job.

Ruth Hamilton

PARADISE LANE

Ruth Hamilton

This one is for Mrs Florence Allen of Southsea,
who has been my stalwart supporter from the start.

God bless you, Florence.

A very big thank-you to my editor, Diane Pearson,
who copes with me so well!

ONE

There were only four houses in Paradise Lane, and they were all on one side of the street. The front 'parlour' windows of numbers 1 to 4 inclusive enjoyed an uninterrupted view of Paradise Mill, while the backs of these dwellings overlooked the Paradise Recreation Ground. Those lucky enough to have a cottage in the tiny lane had rear gardens too, long and narrow strips of land whose main feature seemed to be a total antipathy towards anything approaching cultivation, though weeds from what the locals called the 'Parry Rec' grew in abundance all the year round.

Ollie Blunt and his wife Rosie lived at number 2. This childless couple had moved into the cottage a few years before Ollie's retirement from the mines, and Ollie Blunt's battle with barren soil had continued for two decades. Even now, at the age of eighty, the robust ex-miner, who had left Blackburn to finish his working days on the surface of a Westhoughton pit, was wont to express his disillusionment with the town of Bolton. 'It were nowt like this i' Blackburn,' he was heard to say with a frequency that was monotonous. 'We'd good soil over yon. I were known all over for my leeks and cabbages in my day.'

His wife, who also hailed from Blackburn, owned several answers to Ollie's moanings. 'Yer've never grew a leek in yer life – it were your dad had the green fingers,' was one, though her favourite was longer and usually louder. 'Get thissen back 'ome, then,' she would yell with all the vigour of an exceptionally lively seventy-plus-year-old. 'Nigh on twenty year we've been i' Bowton. If tha

9

wants t' pack up an' go 'ome, get gone afore I clock thee wi' me posser.' Her posser, a circle of wood attached to a long pole, was always on guard just outside the scullery door. Only when clothes were battered in a dolly tub was the posser used for its original purpose.

Rosie Blunt was a tiny, apple-cheeked woman whose previously dark locks had bleached themselves silver with the passage of time. What she lacked in height, she made up for in what her husband called 'nowtiness', and this tendency to quick temper had resulted in a collection of armoury stored in the kitchen, under the stairs with the coal and in the back yard. Armed with shovel, clothes prop, posser or yardbrush, she had clouted Ollie, chased dogs, seen off gypsies, children and tramps. But she never went too far. Those who had suffered a 'possing' or a 'shovelling' had come out intact, more or less.

Sally Crumpsall, the youngest resident of Paradise Lane, would sit on the back doorstep of number 1, partly to escape the unhappy situation in her own neglected home, and partly because she enjoyed listening to the Blunts' many arguments. This was one of her few escapes, though her favourite times were spent in the company of a man and some pigeons whose address was 4, Paradise Lane. There wasn't much in Sally's life. School was all right, she supposed, but no-one wanted to be her friend. Although the area was far from rich, few children chose to play with a child as ragged as she was. So her pleasures were few and mostly solitary.

'Sal?' wheezed her father.

Sally picked herself up, turned reluctantly towards the scullery of her home. Dad was dying. He'd been dying ever since a year after the end of the Second World War, since round about Sally's sixth birthday.

'Sal?'

'Coming, Dad.'

She hurried through the scullery, almost fell over the cat. What would happen to Gus when Dad died? she wondered. She seldom thought about her own future, because it seemed too terrible to contemplate. Gus shot outside, bounded over the fence, across the Blunts' garden, into Maureen Mason's. Sally could hear Maureen shouting, 'Come on, Gus, I've a bit of fish for you.' But Gus wouldn't stop in Maureen Mason's garden, oh no. Because Gus would be on his way to see Mr Goodfellow's pigeons . . .

Dad looked awful. At the age of thirty-three, Derek Crumpsall was a doomed man. Doctors and hospitals had done all they could for him, and Derek had come home to die in the company of his family. He gulped painfully, realized, not for the first time, that apart from his ageing mother, this little ragged child was his whole family. He could not lie there and allow her to watch his steady deterioration. Any hope of rekindling the ashes of his marriage was long shattered, so he must now take steps to protect his beloved baby from what was to come. 'Get your gran, love.'

Sally hesitated, one hand straying to her mouth. Mam couldn't stand Ivy Crumpsall. Granny Ivy was a big, tall woman with a stoop which had caused her to lose a couple of inches in height, though her vocal power showed little sign of diminishing with the passage of years. The child swayed from side to side, the movement betraying inner turmoil.

'Go on, Sal.'

She continued to shift her weight from foot to foot. 'What about Mam?'

He stared at her, the over-large eyes burning in their sockets. Every bit of him was sore. Soon, too soon, there would be a daily visit from the doctor. A cocktail of drugs would be administered, its components varying and intensifying in strength until the patient's senses had been removed. Derek was a moderately well-read man, and his depleted brain scuttered about now among a mountain of half-remembered phrases. 'One may have good eyes and see nothing.' Was that from some Italian writings?

'Dad?'

He no longer had good eyes. They were huge in his face, because his flesh was disappearing, but nothing functioned adequately any more. Who had looked after this child between '40 and '45? he wondered. 'Who looked after you while I was away fighting?' he asked.

'Mr and Mrs Blunt and Maureen Mason.' The old couple from next door and the Irish lady from number 3 had cared for Sally. They had looked after Gus, too. Sometimes, child and cat had slept in Maureen Mason's spare room at number 3 while Mam had been out with her friends. Often, Sally, Gus, Maureen Mason and the Blunts had spent the night trying to rest in an air raid shelter. It had been cosy then, Sally thought. Cosier in the shelter than it was in number 1, especially after Tom Goodfellow's arrival at the end house. The war had been almost finished, and there had been no more bombs. But Mr Goodfellow had limped to and from the shelter, his legs infirm as a result of an accident in an aeroplane. Sally was dreaming, remembering, because she didn't want to fetch Granny Ivy, didn't want her mother to come back angry and shouting . . . But poor Dad needed somebody.

Derek closed his eyes, felt as if he were literally sinking lower and lower into the mattress of uncomfortable flock. Lottie. Aye, she'd be back shortly, would Charlotte Crumpsall. He seldom spoke to her these days, preferring to wait for help until a neighbour came in. Tom Goodfellow had turned up trumps, took bedpans and soiled linen in his stride. But Derek needed nursing during the nights now. He couldn't ask Tom to do even more, didn't want to place a burden on the Blunts or on Maureen Mason. And as for Lottie – well – she was often the worse for drink at night, and she couldn't bear to touch her dying husband. 'I need you to run down to Worthington Street for Gran,' wheezed Derek. 'Tell her . . .' Tell her what? That his time had come? 'Tell her your mam's out and I need some shopping. Then come back with her.'

Sal backed out of the kitchen and into the small scullery. Mam would be back in a minute. She'd only gone to the post office to send a letter to New York. What would happen if Mam and Granny Ivy came face to face again? Another big row, another lot of yelling and bawling? Mam hated Granny Ivy Crumpsall with a ferocity that was overwhelming for a child of seven.

She always wrote back to America straight away, did Mam, always scuttered off to post her reply before the ink had dried properly. She'd been at the mirror today for half an hour before setting off for the shops. While Derek Crumpsall waited for his end, Lottie had preened and pouted, had spat on her fingers to wet the kiss-curls and make them more firm.

Little Sally Crumpsall leaned against the slopstone. Had she been able to see herself, the child would have noticed much of Granny Ivy in her own stance. Ivy Crumpsall, a great thinker, often stood staring into her own slopstone when cogitating. 'I don't know what to do,' mouthed the child. 'They'll only fight.'

She lifted her head, looked through the window at a sky dulled by filthy glass. Mam didn't love her, didn't love Dad. Mam loved a man in America, a big, loud person with red cheeks and greased-down hair and a laugh that didn't sound real. There was a letter every two weeks from America. Mam always giggled when she read those letters.

Sally scraped the toe of a clog against the floor, swallowed a bubble of pain, grimaced against the echo of a stomach whose sole occupant was guilt. 'She'd like me if I were good,' she whispered to herself. Lottie Crumpsall had been Sally's mam for seven years, but she showed no love for and no patience with her daughter.

The little girl drew a hand across her face, then skimmed an unclean flannel over tear-stained cheeks. Mam had chosen an awful boyfriend. He was too old to be a boyfriend, really, because he was a great big grown-up lump of a man. But all of Paradise knew about Lottie Crumpsall's American bloke. Folk who didn't like Lottie – and there were many of those – would sometimes call after her, 'Oy, how's yon Yankee boyfriend, Lottie?' and 'Got any gum, chum?' There shouldn't have been a boyfriend at all. Married people were supposed to look after one another, were supposed to have no girlfriends and boyfriends. It was all a mess and it made Sally ashamed, especially when the letters came and Mam read them and laughed in front of poor Dad.

Mr Goodfellow got letters too, mused Sally, her thoughts expanding to encompass the lovely man from number 4. Every four weeks, a big white package was delivered to number 4, with GOODFELLOW printed above the address, and a fancy blue drawing on the back of the envelope. Nobody else ever got much mail, but numbers 1 and 4 were visited regularly by Henry Chaucer, who had a red bike and a funny moustache. Henry Chaucer said Mr Goodfellow's letters had all been redirected from a London address and that the blue drawing on Mr Goodfellow's letters was a crest, but it had never looked like a bird's topknot to Sally.

The child drew breath as if steeling herself against her mission. Granny Ivy must be fetched, then the consequences must be endured. There was no time to be standing here thinking about the man of mystery who lived at the end house.

She slipped through the back gate and along a narrow dirt track that separated the Paradise houses from the Rec. A few children played on the field, but none called to Sally. At top speed, she flung herself towards Worthington Street and Granny Ivy Crumpsall.

Ivy was holding court in the midst of three spellbound neighbours. She was famous for her opinions, was Ivy. '. . . and that there Jimmy Foster's got extra tinned fruit and tea and toffees, I saw it all being delivered to the shop

Tuesday last. Fancy rationing and shortages still going on in 1947. Who'd have thought it would last, eh? Aye, he'll be stashing all the good stuff for the Worthingtons. Pigs, the lot of them.' The last five words were stained with bitterness towards the man whose family had built Paradise Mill and most of the cottages that flanked the massive structure.

'Easy for him, eh?' Ivy waved a hand towards her small audience. 'Gets his dad's money, throws these houses up and sticks a bloody great mill on top of us. Oh aye,' she nodded vigorously. 'But for Joseph Heilberg, yon Worthington would have used the Rec for another mill. Good job we've got folk like Joe looking after us.'

A thin-faced woman at the table spoke up. 'Worthington tried to get his hands on Heilberg's land during the war, while that lovely man were interned.'

Ivy exploded with rage. 'Aye, and there's another injustice for you.' Her eyes, which were so like her only son's, blazed in triumphant praise of her own oratory. 'Interning a Jew – I ask you. What were the point in locking up a bloke who came over here years ago to get away from bloody Hitler? He's a good man, is Joseph Heilberg. Not a penny rent did he ask when he came back. All them in Paradise Lane lived rent-free for the duration.' She sniffed deeply, eyed her granddaughter. 'And that's just as well, because my poor son's rotten wife would have had to increase her turnover if she'd needed rent on top of perfume.' It was no good being ashamed, she had decided wisely. Everybody knew what Lottie was, no-one better than the mother of the man she had married. 'Hello, our Sal,' she muttered belatedly.

Sally bit her lip, which wasn't an easy task, as most of her infant incisors had vacated their place of residence. 'Dad says you've to come, Granny Ivy.'

The thinnest of the trio of visitors blessed herself hurriedly.

'Eeh, whatever next?' The rhetoric was ignored while

15

Ivy Crumpsall reached for her shawl. Summer, winter, boil or freeze, the good woman never set foot outside her house without her pinny and her shawl. The black skirt swept the floor as she approached Sally. 'Right, our Sal. Let's go forward into the fray.' She had looked at one or two of her son's books in the past, liked to think she had picked up a smart turn of phrase. She was very proud of her lad. Her lad had been born when she was over forty and 'on the turn'. Everybody knew about 'on the turn' babies being special.

When her neighbours had left, Ivy looked around the sparse home to see if she could find something for her dying boy. With the fringe of her dark shawl, she dashed a tear from a cheek and picked up a couple of old newspapers. 'That should keep him happy for an hour,' she mumbled to herself.

'Me dad can't read,' said Sally.

'Course he can . . .' The dim light of anger that always glowed in Ivy Crumpsall's eyes was suddenly fully rekindled. 'Blind?' she asked.

'Nearly. And he can't get out of bed no more, Granny Ivy. Mr Goodfellow's been seeing to him.'

The old woman hung on to her composure as best she could. No use falling apart in front of the little lass. 'Aye, he's Goodfellow by name and a saint by nature, is yon.' She moved towards the door. 'Where's your mam?'

'Post office, I think.'

'Huh.' She grabbed the child's hand and marched across the street into Paradise Lane, stopping for just a moment outside the open door of number 4. 'Mr Goodfellow?'

'Yes?' enquired an unusually cultured voice from somewhere within the house.

'It's Ivy. Ta for looking after our Derek. I'll see you later.'

They passed Maureen Mason's and the Blunts' house, walked through the front door of number 1. Ivy stopped short when she saw the empty shelves near the parlour fireplace. 'Where's his books and papers?' she asked.

Sally shivered. 'I don't know where the books are, Gran. We don't get papers no more.'

'Does he know his encyclopaedias is all gone? Does your dad know?'

Sally shook her head, blushed on her mother's behalf. 'He stops in the kitchen all the while now, Granny. Me mam said he couldn't read no more, so—'

'He could still hold them. He could still touch the pages and remember how much he loved reading.' Ivy squared her shoulders. 'Don't say owt to your dad about the books.'

'I won't.'

Ivy Crumpsall squatted down and stroked the child's thin cheek. 'I wish I had a few bob, love. If I had a bit of money, I could feed you up and get you a decent frock. I don't get much for cleaning the pub, you know. Still.' She stood up and made her face fierce again. 'We must make best use of what's to hand, as my old mother used to say.'

Sally followed Granny Ivy into the kitchen. It was sparsely furnished, with flag floors, a black grate and a tattered rug in front of the hearth. The mantelpiece was not bare, though. Across its length lay pots of rouge and powder, two dark blue bottles of Evening in Paris and a stick of eau de Cologne, then a confusion of combs, brushes, curlers. Lottie Crumpsall's mirror was propped behind a broken clock, and the rest of the shelf was taken up by hairnets and pins. 'She wants whipping,' breathed Mrs Crumpsall Senior.

'Hello, Mam.'

The bed was under the window, its sheets crumpled and torn, the top quilt stained and ragged. His hands clawed at the fringe, while large, uncertain eyes blinked in the direction of his mother's voice. 'We'll get you sorted,' said Ivy with a cheerfulness that was tailored to hide her distress. 'I'll borrow bedding, lad. I've good neighbours down Worthington Street. If yon fancy piece had let me in here more often, we'd have had you sparkling – wouldn't we Sally?'

Sally made no reply, as her gaze was fixed on the fancy piece who had featured so recently in Ivy's words.

'Get out,' said Lottie Crumpsall.

'No.' Ivy planted her feet wide, knew that she looked quite terrifying in the long black clothes. 'I'm stopping. This time, lady, you'll not see me off, because my lad needs me.' She unfolded her arms, waved a hand in Sally's direction. 'And our little lass could do with a bit of looking after and all. Look at her. She's all rags and bones, not a pick on her and the clothes in bits.'

Lottie made a noise that sounded like 'pshaw', picked up a lipstick, pushed it into her bag. 'I've somebody to see,' she said. 'When I get back, you'd best be out of here. If you've not gone, I'll pack my bags and leave.'

'Oh aye? Are you making that a promise?' Ivy leaned her head over to one side, put Sally in mind of a rather tall bird looking for worms. 'It's nice when you've bags to pack, Lottie Kerrigan. It's nice when you've summat to shove in the bags. How many pairs of silk stockings did you collect, eh? And underwear and fancy scarves and bottles of scent? You could happen fill a trunk out of your earnings, 'cos you're nothing but a cheap whore. Your mam were the same, only she kept her business away from the Yanks. I suppose there were no Yanks then.' She nodded. 'Now as I think back, Nancy Kerrigan would have entertained a battalion for some stockings.' She looked her daughter-in-law up and down, was glad of the distraction. Because while she was attacking Lottie, she wasn't looking at the haggard face of her son.

'Shut up, you old bag.' There was no energy in the words, because Lottie didn't care any more. In a matter of days, she would be gone. Morton was waiting for her in New York. He'd found an apartment and a job, knew somebody who knew somebody who wanted English hostesses in a club. 'Do what you want,' she said while studying a chipped nail. 'It's all the same to me.'

Sally had had enough. She crept out of the room, through the scullery and into the garden. The noise still reached her, though. Granny Ivy was going on about Mam being a bastard, about nobody knowing who Mam's dad was. 'There were that many candidates, they were thinking of calling a general bloody election,' screamed Ivy Crumpsall.

All that shouting would do Dad no good at all, thought Sally. But Mam and Granny Ivy were only carrying on like they always did, so happen Dad would fail to hear the racket. There was nothing wrong with his ears, but Derek Crumpsall had stopped listening years ago.

The little girl walked through the gate and down Back Paradise Lane until she came to number 4. Without hesitation, she pushed her way into Mr Goodfellow's garden and walked to the pigeon cages. Gus was curled up between Scarlet and Beau, a breeding pair who were not in the slightest way perturbed by the grey cat's presence in their loft.

'He's in the birdhouse again,' said a male voice.

'They're supposed to kill birds,' replied Sally. 'I never knew a cat who guarded birds.'

'Always a first time, me dear.' Tom Goodfellow turned away and shook his head. She was as thin as a rake. Her clothes were probably held together by the filth they had collected over several days. 'Come inside for a sandwich, Sally,' he said.

Sally loved Mr Goodfellow's house. It was filled with shining silver cups and pictures of pigeons. There was always a fire in the grate, even in summer, and Mr Goodfellow made lovely cakes and scones. 'Thank you,' she said when her plate was loaded. She was careful to eat slowly, did not want to look greedy. Her stomach moaned with pleasure as the food occupied its cavernous emptiness.

He sat on a chair, sat on his anger, worked hard to keep a smile on his face. 'How is your father today?'

'Very ill.' Her dad was ill and her mother was going to America and here she sat eating butties. No, they were sandwiches, she told herself. Sandwiches were thinner than butties and sometimes, the crusts were cut off. 'Thank you,' she said when the plate was empty.

'And your mother?' he asked casually.

She could have told Mr Goodfellow anything, as the man was completely trustworthy. When Sally had been left alone during the death throes of a world war, this man had come for her, had fed her and installed her at Maureen Mason's house. During evenings in the shelter, he had sung nice songs to lull her to sleep. But she didn't want to find the words, made no effort to frame a proper answer. Dad was going to die and Mam was setting her sights on a future at the other side of the world. 'I'll talk him round,' Lottie said whenever she remembered the small hiccup who was her daughter. 'Morton doesn't want children, but you'll be sent for, don't worry.'

'Sally?'

She shook herself out of the gloomy reverie. 'She's been to the post office.'

'Another letter?'

Sally nodded. 'Same day as yours, Mr Goodfellow.' Everyone in Paradise Lane, Worthington Street and Spencer Street gossiped about Tom Goodfellow. He got queer letters, envelopes with a piece of paper hiding another address, packages bearing more than one set of stamps. Where had he come from, why did he talk so posh? How had a grown man learned cooking and washing, where did his money come from? But Sally accepted him gratefully for who he was now, occasionally wondered who he used to be. 'And she wrote back last night.'

Tom cleared the small tea table, picked up a blue-rimmed jug and opened the tap on the copper. 'I'll let you wash up,' he said.

In the scullery, Sally caressed bone china cups and silver knives, made up a story in her head about living in a beautiful house with roses in the garden and roses on the plates. She had never broken a single piece of Mr Goodfellow's dinner and tea set. To smash even the smallest item would have been a crime, because everything matched, right down to salt, pepper and a sugar bowl from whose handle a tiny spoon was suspended.

He watched her, knew her thoughts. What could he do for her? When was that dreadful woman going to leave the country? After Derek's death, little Sally would probably live with Ivy Crumpsall. Ivy was a good woman, rather firm in her views, but sound enough. So the child was going to move from one poverty to the next, from one empty larder to another. Though she would doubtless get love from her grandmother, and love was worth a lot.

'I've finished, Mr Goodfellow.'

He sank to his haunches, fought back a groan when his game leg creaked. 'Why don't you call me Uncle Tom?'

She blushed, put a finger to her lips. 'I've got no uncles.'

He nodded grimly. She had been visited by several 'uncles' during the latter years of the war. In addition to some with ordinary names, there had been Uncle Buzz, Uncle Dwight, Uncle Morton. Tom had explained, when asked, that uncles were brothers to a child's parents, and Sally had stopped saying 'Uncle' when addressing her mother's consorts. For that sin, she had been beaten and sent to bed for two days.

'Let me be your uncle,' he said again. There was a basket and a rope under the child's bed these days. Whenever she was locked upstairs, she would raise the sash window and lower this container to the ground. The Blunts, Maureen Mason and Tom Goodfellow had been feeding her for some time by placing what they could spare in the empty basket as soon as Lottie Crumpsall had disappeared up the street. Lottie seldom used the back garden, never attempted to clear the waist-high weeds, hung out precious little washing beyond the odd pair of stockings and some French knickers in pink and blue satin. Only when the lavatory was needed did Lottie Crumpsall venture out along the whole length of the rear garden.

'You can be my uncle, then.'

She was thinning towards transparency, he mused. Fine blond hair hung in greasy rats' tails about the narrow face, while enormous blue eyes expressed all the feelings she refused to verbalize. In the depths of Sally Crumpsall's pupils, Tom read poverty, pain, bewilderment. Above all, he saw an aching need to be loved. Ivy was getting on. Some days, she was as straight as a die, bold to the point of belligerence. But in the twilight of her own life, Ivy's heart was about to be broken by the death of her only son. Would the pale waif be enough to keep Ivy Crumpsall on this side of the frail curtain that divided the living from the dead? Only time would bring the answer to that question.

'Shall I get Gus out of the loft, Mr . . . Uncle Tom?'

Her smile cut right into him, because it was clear that she would have had dimples had her face been fully fleshed. 'If he's happy, leave him where he is. Mrs Mason has some fish for him, I believe.'

'She likes you, does Mrs Mason.'

'And I like her.'

Sally thought for a moment. 'Yes, but she likes you the same way as she liked Mr Mason till he got blew up in France.'

He laughed. 'I'm too old for all that nonsense, child.'

Enlivened by the food, she decided to ask a question. 'How old are you?'

'Somewhere between forty and fifty,' he said with mock gravity.

Her jaw dropped. Nobody except Granny Ivy was as old as fifty. Yet Mr Goodfellow – Uncle Tom – had dark brown hair, light brown eyes and skin that looked young. 'But you don't look old,' she exclaimed.

He threw back his head and chortled. 'And the reason for that, Sally, is that I have avoided the female predators of this world. No woman has managed to ensnare me.'

She sniffed, pondered. 'Scarlet's a woman bird, isn't she?'

'Yes.'

'And she lays eggs for you to have more pigeons and she's Beau's missus. So you have got some fee . . . some females, 'cos they're out there in cages.'

He laughed again. 'Where they belong, isn't that the case?' If he could just shut Maureen Mason in a cage, then his life might become a little easier. No, no, he was surely being uncharitable. And Maureen was extremely gentle and pretty . . . But the good Irish lady had taken to wearing powder and paint, had started simpering whenever she found a reason to visit him. The reasons had deteriorated, had become mere excuses. And now, the excuses were so feeble that most showed signs of rigor mortis as soon as they dropped from Maureen's reddened lips. 'Could you lend me a couple of spoons of sugar, Tom?' This after he had seen her coming out of the Co-op with the tell-tale blue package perched on top of her shopping. He had 'mended' bedsprings, doors and window catches. He had almost choked on air redolent with California Poppy, had been plied with enough tea to refloat the *Titanic*.

'You can get married if you want,' advised Sally. 'Then you won't have to do the cooking and polish your cups.' She pointed to the rows of trophies. 'What's that one for?'

He shrugged. 'Tennis.'

'Oh.' Her eye followed the line of trophies. 'That big one?'

'Yachting.'

She looked hard at him. 'Boats?'

'Yes, boats.'

He was a lot more interesting than she had thought, then. 'What's the round plate for?'

'Golf.'

Sally wasn't one for questions. Because few of her peers spoke to her and, since her mother seldom noticed her, Sally had failed to master the basic arts of conversation. Also, she worked hard at being inconspicuous. When near invisibility proved impossible, she tended to opt for silence or total acquiescence. But curiosity overcame her on this occasion. 'Was them all won before you lived here, like?'

He nodded.

'Where did you live, Uncle Tom?'

'Hampshire, then Surrey. A year or two in Plymouth.'

'Oh.' She mulled over this information. 'Is them places down London way?'

'Most of them are in the south, yes.'

She smoothed the tattered dress and made for the door. Everything had been explained now. Folk from London were different from folk round here. They had loads of money, cigarette holders, nice frocks, motor cars and a lot of time for games like tennis. After thanking her host for the meal, she made for the door, stopped, turned round, this movement fuelled by sudden impulse. 'Why are you here?'

'I arrived and I stayed,' he said softly.

'Can you not go home no more?'

He put a hand to his clean-shaven chin. 'I could, I suppose.'

Sally's eyes were like saucers. 'Do you stop here because you want to, then?'

'In a way, yes.'

She allowed her gaze to wander round Mr Goodfellow's house. It was nice, she supposed. Clean, better furnished than most. But it still had the mill blocking out the light at the front, then an outside lav shed at the back. He talked like . . . like the man whose voice came out of Maureen Mason's wireless set. When she'd been only five or six, Sally had peered for hours through the tight mesh of the set's speaker, had never seen the tiny people inside. Of course, at the grand age of seven, Sally knew that those men and women were full-sized and from London, though she hadn't managed to work out how they shouted loudly enough to be heard from so far away . . .

'Sally?' He loved to watch her face, enjoyed its mobility. Females with expressionless features were judged to be the most attractive according to something he had read recently. That might well explain the vacuous ladies portrayed in so many paintings. Ah, she was going to speak again.

'But it's dark here, Mr—' She grinned in response to his deliberately fierce expression. 'Uncle Tom. It's poor. Everybody's poor. They all work in Paradise Mill or down the pits. And you're . . . not the same.' The difference was impossible to verbalize, but she was certain of its existence.

He raised his hands, pointed to various portions of his body. 'Two arms, two legs, two eyes. I am made of flesh and blood and bone. How am I different, Sally?'

'You just are.' Why did he never go to work? she wondered. Everybody else clattered off at the crack of dawn, but Mr Goodfellow just messed about with books and pigeons all day. No, she wouldn't ask him about work, because that might be rude, like accusing him of laziness. He wasn't lazy. He helped her dad, washed him, lifted him on and off the potty chair. 'Ta-ra,' she said.

Ivy Crumpsall stood in the parlour of number 1, Paradise Lane, a bunched and white-knuckled fist clamped hard against her mouth. There was neither rhyme nor reason to any of this. He'd always been a good lad, had their Derek. Born at the start of a war that had taken his dad, Derek had remained in good health long enough to defend his country against the Third Reich, yet his reward was . . . She stifled a sob. Derek's reward was cancer.

It was the pit that had done for him, she thought. Not

one man emerged from the bowels of the earth unscathed. Each and every miner she knew was older than his years, seemed to be starved of air and sunlight, deprived of most sensory perceptions for eight or more hours of every day. Coal was killing her boy.

She sank into a chair whose stuffing had exploded through several cracks, eased herself off a protruding spring and wondered what was going to happen next. Lottie had been and gone, the doctor had been and gone for medicine, Sally had simply gone. She would be with Goodfellow, no doubt. The poor child was escaping at every opportunity, because she had no mam, no dad . . . Ivy was determined not to cry. She'd cried enough already, had wept a river during recent months.

Still, at least Derek had been lying in clean linen when the doctor had arrived. The sheets weren't Derek's own, but they were spanking clean. 'You're doing a good job, Mrs Crumpsall,' the medic had said. Well, the smart-mouthed Lottie was not going to get her own way this time. Ivy intended to stay, as it was plain that Derek was nearing his end.

She leaned back and closed her eyes, was once more in Worthington Street with the newborn Derek. Her husband, almost ten years her junior, had set off for the trenches a few weeks earlier. Sam never saw his son. Her mind rushed forward, endured the pain of the lad's first day at school, the weeks spent at his bedside during measles, mumps, the whooping cough that had nearly taken him. But she had hung on to him. She had hung on until Lottie.

Ivy's eyes flew open. Lottie Kerrigan. Lottie Kerrigan, daughter of a nasty piece of work, another nasty piece in the making. How Ivy had pleaded with her son. But Derek had begun to fear his mother's over-protectiveness, had run straight into the arms of a woman who had removed him from his mother's apron strings. For years, Ivy had seen little of her son, then the family had moved back to the Paradise streets. Paradise. She made a tutting sound, looked through the front window and saw nothing but red bricks and mill windows. If this was Paradise, most gradely folk would opt for the other place any day of the week.

She crept through the room, peeped into the kitchen, reassured herself that he was sleeping. Back in the uncomfortable chair, she mused on the choices of names for these streets, tried to keep her mind busy. Paradise was a newish mill, just about sixty-odd years old, she thought. Worthington owned it, and a bad bugger he was, too. His dad had built the factory, had set out the capital H that formed this far from godly creation. The mill sat in the top of the H, the recreation area in the lower half. Ivy's street formed one of the uprights, then Spencer Street ran parallel. Between Worthington and Spencer, the horizontal was created by Paradise Lane. Andrew Worthington and Prudence Spencer's marriage had been made in heaven, so the cobbled way that connected the two longer streets had been christened appropriately.

In spite of herself, Ivy allowed a faint smile to caress her worn features. The Worthington-Spencer alliance had been hell for both parties, though few knew the truth about the mismatch. Ivy's information had come from a reliable source, as one of her friends had once been cook at Worthington House. And from personal experience, she had learned about Andrew Worthington . . . she'd be better not thinking of that. Yes, the old swine had failed twice, because his marriage was miserable and Joseph Heilberg had refused to sell the Paradise houses and the recreation ground. Paradise Mill Number Two was still on the drawing board, was a mere phantom created by architect and draughtsman. And so it should stay for ever, if Ivy Crumpsall had her way.

'Granny Ivy?'

The old woman came out of her reverie. 'Hello, our Sal. Have you been to Mr Goodfellow's?'

Sally nodded. 'He's from London way. That's why he talks like the wireless. All them cups and things is from golf and tennis. And a boat, too. Why is he here?'

Ivy shook her head slowly and placed a finger to her lips. 'Hush, love. Your dad needs his sleep.' Soon, too soon, he would have all the sleep he needed. 'Have you eaten, lass?'

'Yes. Sandwiches.'

'Crusts cut off?'

'Yes.'

Ivy's head dropped, because she could scarcely bear to look at the poor ragged child who depended on neighbours for sustenance. But when she saw the state of the floor, she raised her head again sharply. Dirt and Ivy were not on good terms. The child would have to move to Worthington Street. If Ivy could get a couple more hours' cleaning work, they would manage.

'My dad's going to die, Gran.'

What could she say? How was she going to comfort a child whose parents were about to make an exit from her life? 'Aye. Well, I suppose it's God's will.'

'That's what you said last time,' replied Sally, her voice devoid of emotion. 'I've stopped going to chapel, because God's let my dad be very ill. He hurts. Sometimes, he cries when he thinks I'm not looking.'

'I know, lass.' At least she was talking, was saying something. A hint of pale-rose in Sally's cheeks proved that she had eaten. 'Look, I'll see to you, Sal. There's no way you'll be on your own as long as I'm alive.'

Sally studied her grandmother. She stooped a bit, did Granny Ivy, almost had a hump on her back. Granny Ivy was probably the oldest person in the whole world. No – not quite. There was often a huddle of shawlies at some street corner or other, women who, like Gran, were always dressed in black. Some of them were smelly. The snuff-takers ponged of tobacco, the pipe-smokers reeked of tobacco, and most carried the aroma of unwashed flesh.

Gran wasn't like them. Gran was always having baths and all-over washes. But a lot of shawlies had lived for years in houses without coppers and inside taps, and they had grown used to the scent of dirt. So there were other old folk like Ivy Crumpsall, people whose lives had spanned the end of one century and the start of another. 'Thank you, Gran,' she said at last. 'Because Mam won't be here, you know. I can stay with you till she sends for me.'

Ivy made a strange noise, but said nothing. That bold strumpet would never send for Sally. Even if she did find time and energy to persuade the Yank with the daft name, Lottie Kerrigan wasn't going to saddle herself with the child. 'You can come and stop with me soon,' she promised. 'And Mrs Hargreaves will happen make you a couple of decent frocks.' She nodded sadly. 'I'd have got you some clothes before now, Sal, but I thought . . . well, you know how things are.'

Sally knew how things were, all right. 'Uncle' Morton, who had been good at getting his hands on things, had bought a beautiful outfit for Sally one Christmas. She remembered it now, could see it if she closed her eyes. A red coat with white fur trim, a hat to match, then little red boots. It had been put away in a cupboard, though Sally had sneaked outside in it once or twice. After Morton Amerson's departure, the clothes had disappeared into Mr Heilberg's shop. Mam had never mentioned the outfit and neither had Sally. But she'd seen it again, oh yes. A girl at chapel had flaunted it. Sally, in worn clogs and too-small coat, had been forced to listen after the service while the congregation made comments about the red coat.

'It'll get better, love.'

'Yes.'

'Try to buck up, Sal.'

'Nobody liked it anyway. They all said it were too bright for chapel.'

Ivy had no need to ask any questions. She recalled the occasion, had sat with Sally until the tears had dried. The books would likely have gone the same road and all. She would have a word with Joe Heilberg when she got the chance, see if he'd hang on to Derek's books so that Sally could have them one day. 'It were a very common colour, that red,' she said, her voice gentled by love. 'He'd no taste, yon Yankee man. A pretty little lass with your colouring should wear blue. Now, you'd look lovely in a navy velvet frock with a bit of lace. One day, I shall take you to our chapel and you'll look like a little princess, love.'

Sally, who had asked several questions that day, suddenly found her lips framing another. 'Why do you always wear black, Gran? Is it 'cos Grandad died? And all the other shawlies – why do they never wear colours?'

Ivy Crumpsall put her head on one side. 'Well, it were this road, pet. Our mams wore black when they got to forty. It were always a black skirt, dark stockings, grey shawl.' She opened the shawl, looked down on her blouse. 'It's nice, is black, as long as you're old enough to carry it. But my blouses is always nice because I look after them proper. I starch them, see. I boil, bleach and starch every Saturday. This used to be a good blouse when it were young.'

Sally walked across the room, placed a hand on her grandmother's knee. 'Black's sad.'

'And sensible.'

'Yes, but it would be nice to have a change.'

Ivy sighed. Change was coming. Derek had done well at school, she thought suddenly. If she'd had a bit of money, a pinch of clout and a lot of cheek, she might have got him educated. If she'd got him educated, he wouldn't have gone down the pit. If he hadn't gone down—

'Gran?'

'What, Sal?'

'Don't be sad.'

Yes, change was coming. Lottie Kerrigan-as-was would no doubt make a run for it any day now, would take off into the wide blue yonder with her French knickers and her Yankee fancy man. Derek would die soon, please God. She sat as upright as her stoop would allow, realized with a jolt that she was wishing him gone, wishing him past pain. 'We must both try to cheer each other up,' she advised her granddaughter. 'See, here's a ha'penny. Go up to Florrie Dent and get yourself some cocoa and sugar.'

Ivy stared blankly into the empty room, listened as Sally's footsteps grew fainter. If he hadn't gone down the shaft, he wouldn't have got cancer. She rose, tightened her apron, waited for Lottie's return. She decided to do a bit of cleaning, use up some anger. If she got busy, then she might just keep her hands away from Lottie's throat. When the sleeves were rolled, she mopped, scrubbed and tidied, but in spite of all the work, she remained ready for the fray. Lottie was out of order, and Ivy simmered as she spoonfed her precious son.

'You only came to live round here once you were pregnant,' said Ivy softly. She was not averse to street-fighting, had even been hauled up before the magistrates for brawling with a woman who had pinched a good woven quilt off the line. But this was family business. Her lad had listened to enough for one day, so this particular alter-cation must take place out of doors, and as discreetly as possible.

'We'd never have come at all if I'd had my road,' replied Lottie. The wind was freshening, and she'd only just had her hair done. It felt like rain, too, and she didn't want to waste the half-pint of setting lotion she'd not long paid for. Her hair was her best feature, and she intended to look after it. 'I'm going in.'

Ivy grabbed the front of Lottie's coat, twisted the lapel into a tight ball. 'Stop where you are, lady, or I'll shove you through yon window. Aye, your hair's a picture.' She allowed a smile of mockery to touch her lips briefly. The intricately sculpted style did little to enhance Lottie's rather ordinary features. 'You came to Paradise Lane so's I'd be handy. You thought I'd step in and rear yon kiddy, didn't you?'

'Me rolls are coming down.' Lottie patted a sweep of hair that threatened to tumble. 'I've been invited to a mill do at the Empress tonight.'

'Oh aye? And who's looking after our Sal?'

The younger woman tried to shrug, was stopped by the iron grip on her coat. 'This coat cost seven and six,' she snapped. 'And Maureen'll see to Sally.'

'And Derek?'

'Look, I can't stop in all the while. I'm only thirty-three. Me life'd be over if I sat in there all day and all night long. Any road, it's none of your business.'

Ivy's mouth stretched itself into a snarl that was made fiercer by all the gaps in her teeth. 'I'll bloody swing for you yet,' she whispered. 'And when that rope cuts into my neck, I'll still think I've done the right thing. You're scum, you are. Your mother were a cheap piece and all, still chasing men right till the day she choked on her own gin-soaked vomit.'

Lottie's patience was fully extended, not because of Ivy's taunts, but on account of the expensive hairdo. She raised both hands, raked ten red-painted nails down Ivy's face. 'I hate you,' she screamed as her mother-in-law backed away with scarlet rivulets decorating her cheeks. 'You're an ugly old bag, and you're jealous because I'm still good-looking enough to get a decent bloke.' She jerked a finger towards her own front door. 'As for him in there, he were no use when he were right. I'm not stopping in with him coughing his filth all over me and—'

Ivy's balled fist made hard contact with Lottie's nose. Both women stood motionless for a few seconds, the elder fascinated and stunned by all the blood, the younger struck dumb with shock. 'If you've broke my nose,' she managed eventually, 'I'll kill you. And when I've killed you, I'll stamp on your horrible mug.' Pain arrived then, a horrible throbbing ache that spread the width of her face and up into her skull.

'Try me. Go on, try.' Ivy's fists were raised in the fashion of a prize fighter, the left punching air, the right defending her face. The hump seemed to be disappearing as she rose to full height. 'Come on, you daft bitch, take me on.'

'Sod off.'

'Aye, I thought as much. All wind and water, you are. Now just you listen to me. I'm stopping in this here house till my son's laid to rest. If you so much as show your face round these parts when we take him to our chapel, I'll set all my mates on you. See, the difference between me and you is I've got friends, good friends as'll stand by me come all weathers. If anybody catches sight of you when Derek goes under, you'll have more than a broken nose.'

'Mrs Crumpsall?'

Ivy glanced over her shoulder, nodded in the direction of Tom Goodfellow. 'I'm all right, lad. Unless poison sets in from them claws of hers.'

Lottie's nose was hidden beneath a white handkerchief. 'She's god ad broke by dose,' she muttered with difficulty.

Tom eyed Lottie Crumpsall, thought about the poor man inside number 1. Derek Crumpsall had lost all his dignity, needed to be toileted like a newborn. The pain showed in the good man's eyes, yet he never flinched while he was lifted and turned, while bedsores were treated with lotions that seemed to serve no purpose. 'A broken nose is nothing compared to a broken heart,' he said in perfect English.

'Why dod't you bugger of ad all?' spat Lottie through the makeshift face mask. I were goig to the Ebpress todight. Dot dow, though. Dot with a sbashed dose.'

'What about that poor child of yours?' asked Tom. 'She's in my garden now playing with the cat. Don't you ever think about her? Aren't you concerned for her future?'

Fierce hazel eyes burned at him above a crumpled square of cotton.

Ivy chipped in. 'You see, she's no brains. Most folk grow out of dance halls and the like once they've got kiddies. But this one wants to carry on like a girl of eighteen. And there's money in it, too, because she'll drop her knickers for anybody with a couple of bob. She got that off her mother, of course. Her mother were a bit on the stupid side and a right trollop.'

'Shut your bouth, you.' The younger woman positively bristled with anger. This was too much, she thought. She had all her papers, a ticket for the boat, the money sent by Morton – and a sore nose. She would clear out of here now, today. 'I'b goig,' she announced with a sudden burst of energy that propelled her into the house. She hurled herself at the door's inner side, pushed the bolt home. Ivy pounded with both fists, but the door remained closed. 'Get round the back,' she told her companion. 'Hurry up.'

She waited for several minutes, tried to ignore a small gathering that had begun to form at the Worthington Street end of Paradise Lane. As soon as Tom appeared, Ivy ran to him. 'Locked?' she asked breathlessly.

'Bolted.'

Lottie's head poked itself through the lower half of a bedroom window. 'What are you goig to do dow?' she yelled.

'How will Sally get in?' asked Tom Goodfellow.

'She wod't.' The handkerchief was dropped for a moment while Lottie addressed the congregation. 'Look what she's dod to by dose,' she yelled.

'Aye, what about the scratches on her face?' replied a neighbour of Ivy's. 'She's nobbut an old lady.'

'Lady?' screamed Lottie. 'She's a bloody bitch.'

Ivy took Tom on one side. 'Get home and see to our Sal,' she advised. 'And leave the rest to me.'

TWO

Rosie Blunt's posser had never looked so menacing. The owner of the implement claimed first place in the line, though Ivy Crumpsall was hot on the heels of the small, silver-haired woman. Behind Ivy, a pair of hefty girls from Worthington Street brought up the rear, faces almost splitting in two at the hilarity of the situation. 'Rosie?' yelled one.

'What?' Rosie was running out of patience with a lot of things. Had she been required to write a list of the banes of her life, Lottie Crumpsall and Ollie would have shared the top place. Ollie Blunt was a bloody great moan from dawn till dusk, and Lottie deserved the death penalty for neglecting that child. Rosie would have loved a little girl. 'What?' she called again, temper spilling into the words.

'Are you fit for this?'

Rosie left her end of the posser and walked down the short line. 'I've fettled for yon daft husband of mine for over fifty years,' she snapped. 'There's no door thicker than yon man's head.'

The girl stopped laughing. 'Right,' she said meekly. 'You shout, then we'll run.'

Ivy relaxed her hold on the pole, gave her daughter-in-law one last chance to open the front door. 'We're breaking in now,' she shouted. 'When I've counted to ten, we'll be giving you no more chances.' She bent, pushed an ear against the letterbox. Not a sound came from within number 1.

'We might make our Derek worse,' she said to Rosie Blunt. 'All the noise'll fret him.'

Rosie nodded quickly. 'All that blinking hunger and thirst'll fret him more, Ivy. Are we ready?'

'Yes,' chorused the invading force.

They walked to the other side of the cobbled way, stumbled in the ruts between stones. As they waited for Rosie's command, a voice reached their ears. 'Ivy?'

They all swivelled and saw Tom Goodfellow emerging from his house. He stood still for a second, wondered how on earth they expected to break down a door with a dolly posser. 'No need,' he advised them. 'She's just gone across the Recreation Ground carrying a couple of cases. She allowed Sally into the house, then bolted the door again until she left. Sally's all right – she waved to me from her bedroom window.'

'All well and good.' Ivy motioned to the other women until they had laid down their battering ram. 'Only we've not done, girls. We'll happen give her a good send-off. Tom, if Lottie's gone, I know the back door's open, 'cos there's no key. It can only be bolted from the inside, and Lottie must have opened it to scarper. So get in that way and see to Derek, will you?'

'Certainly.'

Satisfied that Tom would also be keeping young Sally occupied, Ivy faced her fellow soldiers, rubbed her hands together, then beckoned towards a gathering clutch of onlookers. 'She's done a bunk,' she said loudly. 'Took her cases and every penny in yon house, I shouldn't wonder. I think we should give her a nice little ta-ra party to wish her well. We need a few bits and pieces, though.'

'Good idea,' called a younger woman.

Ivy nominated search areas. 'Jimmy Foster's shop's your best bet,' she announced. 'Root through his back yard, then make your way to the Rec. The rest of you split up and cover Worthington and Spencer. Five minutes, that's all. We meet on the Rec as soon as we've collected enough ammunition. Are we all game?'

'Yes,' came the spirited response.

'Right,' ordered Ivy, every inch the Sergeant Major. 'On your marks – get gone!'

A short time later, a dishevelled group gathered on the Parry Rec, each woman breathing hard and carrying a miscellany of putrid vegetable matter. 'You want to see what's in some of them Spencer Street middens,' complained a fat housewife with sweat streaming down reddened cheeks. 'Fair turns your stomach, it does.'

'Shut up, Molly Hargreaves,' snapped Ivy. Her hair had tumbled down, and a few streaks of dirt mingled with caked blood on her cheeks. 'This is serious business. Right. Are you all listening?'

They all listened.

'Remember when Cissie Burns-as-was left her children in the house all night? Remember what we did to her when she showed up next morning?'

'Aye,' replied Rosie Blunt. 'That were a right good do. Eeh, I did enjoy it.'

'Well, we want more of the same.' Ivy knew she looked fearsome. Various substances had clung to her skin, giving her the appearance of a Native American painted in readiness for battle with white intruders. 'Follow me,' she commanded. 'Her won't have got far, not with two cases.'

The women crossed the open ground, turned into Wigan Road and made a beeline for Trinity Street Station. As they walked past the market, several members of the group stopped to pick up bits of discarded fruit and veg. On Newport Street, passers-by gave Ivy's army a wide berth, as the smell of putrefaction was becoming far too strong for most noses.

They turned into Trinity Street, Ivy still in the lead. She stopped abruptly, causing a slight pile-up of breathless females in her wake. 'I can see her,' she said. 'Stand still a minute, keep out of the road where she can't catch sight.'

She stood alone on the corner, watched while Lottie Kerrigan teetered across tram tracks on thick wedge heels.

The suitcases made her weight uneven, and she was plainly struggling to carry all the luggage.

'Well,' said Ivy. 'Poor lass needs help. She can't manage all yon packages, so we'd better go and give her a hand, eh?'

With a whoop of joy, nine women dashed into the road, each pushing and shoving her neighbours in an effort to be the first on the scene. Ivy simply stood under the station clock, arms akimbo, head to one side as she studied the scenario.

Lottie was soon separated from her bags. Lids flew open, clothes were grabbed, torn, fought over. 'I allers wanted some of these fancy keks,' cried a woman from Spencer Street. She waved a pair of satin knickers above her head. 'I reckon I might even stir the owld man back to life if I wear these.'

Within a matter of seconds, Lottie stood alone. The empty cases lay on their sides, and not one item of clothing was intact. Ivy's gang began to circle the traveller, each tossing a tomato or a rotten cabbage in her hands. Ivy came forward at last. 'Girls?' she asked.

Money was passed from hand to hand, each member coughing up every last penny culled from the luggage. Ivy nodded just once, and the two battering-ram bruisers stepped towards the terrified Lottie, waited for the order.

'Right,' shouted Ivy. 'Tilt.'

They tilted. Lottie's head was where her feet had recently been, while the silk-clad and inverted legs were parted in mid-air. 'Hey,' yelled one of the large women. 'She's got nowt we haven't got.' First a purse, then some loose coins were passed into Ivy's hands. She pocketed the latter, opened the former. 'Here's her tickets for the trains, and here's her passage for the ship.' These were placed in Lottie's hands once she had been righted. 'I hope she bloody drowns. Let her go now.'

When Lottie had straightened her rumpled clothing, she stood red-faced and sweating with shame and temper.

'I'll bloody get you for this, Ivy Crumpsall,' she snarled. 'Nobody shows me up and gets away with it.' She touched her swollen nose, tried to arrange her hair into some kind of order.

Ivy grinned. 'From America? What can you do to me while you're stuck in New York?'

'Morton's got friends—'

'Very nice,' replied Ivy. 'Right, girls. Ready, aim . . . fire.'

A barrage of stinking vegetable matter was thrown, most of it spattering the victim. When a police whistle sounded, the attack stopped with a suddenness that was not far short of miraculous. Nine pairs of legs beat a swift retreat towards the centre of town, but Ivy stood her ground until the policeman was almost upon her. 'One word out of you, Lottie, and I'll have you in prison,' she whispered. 'Remember, I know things about you. There's been a fair bit of stolen and black market stuff through your hands.' She did her best not to worry about Rosie Blunt. Rosie was getting on and – Ivy stopped mid-thought, remembered that she was two years older than Rosie. In that case, she told herself severely, it was every woman for herself.

The policeman ground to a halt, looked at Lottie, at Ivy, at the tomato-spattered pavement. 'Well?' he asked.

'Nice of you to ask,' said Ivy. 'Yes, I'm well enough, fair to middling as you might say.'

He frowned deeply. Ivy was a legend in her own lifetime. She'd had many a cup of tea in the police station, had Ivy Crumpsall. If she'd been a bit younger, she would have been dangerous, he mused. In fact, he thanked his lucky stars that he hadn't been in the force during those years when Ivy had been truly powerful. 'How's she got in that state?' He jerked a thumb in Lottie's direction.

'I were wondering that myself,' said Ivy sweetly. 'She's my daughter-in-law and—'

'We know who she is, Mrs Crumpsall.'

Ivy nodded, folded her arms. 'There's nowt as queer as folk, lad. See, she were a bit on the friendly side when it came to the Yanks, so—'

'We know that and all.'

'Neighbours took umbrage, like. She's off to America to start a new life, see. And when the women from Paradise heard about it, they were upset, like, 'cos her husband – our Derek – is very ill. Then there's the little lass. Lottie here is setting off for New York without even saying ta-ra proper to our Sal. So all the girls followed her down here. I did what I could, but—'

'Names?' He pulled a black book from a pocket.

'Eeh, I don't know,' answered Ivy. 'They had masks on, didn't they, Lottie?'

Lottie growled what sounded like a 'yes'.

'And how did you get hurt?'

Ivy remembered her face, put a hand against the crusted blood. 'Well, I were sticking up for her. See, we know she's no good, but you can't just stand there and let people get away with assault in broad daylight.' A few more policemen had appeared at the Manchester Road junction, but she was confident that the contingency from Paradise was well out of danger.

'That blood looks old and dry,' he said sharply.

'I've thick blood,' she answered. 'It sets quick. I remember when I near took my finger off with a breadknife – I were as right as ninepence within five minutes. They're always saying in the Paradise streets as how they wish they could find jelly crystals that could set as quick as my blood. Once, oh a few years back, I were stood in the middle of town minding my own business—'

'Shut up, Ivy,' he said resignedly.

She turned to Lottie, handed over a ten shilling note. 'Here you are, lass. This should keep you in grub for a while. And if you get a bit short, you know how to earn a few bob. Sailors is always ready for your sort.'

'I've no clothes,' managed Lottie.

The constable studied the victim's face. 'What's wrong with your nose?' he asked.

For answer, Lottie spat in the road, wiped a few bits of vegetation from her jacket and staggered off towards the station.

'She's left her bags,' said the policeman.

'Aye, and her husband and her daughter.'

He watched until Lottie had disappeared. 'Never mind, Ivy,' he said. 'It looks like you've done a good enough job on her.'

'I wonder how she'll travel in that state?' asked Ivy.

He shrugged. 'She'll come up smelling of roses. That sort always does.'

'Rotten cabbage, more like.' Ivy smiled at him, then started back towards a dying son and an abandoned child.

'Ivy?' He had followed her, was pushing a half-crown into her hand. 'For the little girl,' he said before marching off to speak to his colleagues.

She lingered for a moment, weighed the coin in her palm. For the first time ever, she had seen tears glistening in the eyes of the law.

The front parlour of number 3 Paradise Lane was very interesting, because Maureen Mason collected things. She wasn't an organized collector, kept no books of stamps, no collages of dried flowers. Maureen simply bought anything that took her fancy, kept it for a while, then sold it on. She had a sweet face, a pleasant temperament and an ability to negotiate that might have been useful in the making of international treaties.

Sally gazed round Maureen's 'best room'. 'What's that?' Everything had changed in a matter of days. She pointed at a monstrous plant in a blue-and-white container.

'Aspidistra. Belonged to Betty White's mother when she was alive. Betty White didn't want it, so I brought it here. It was a lovely funeral, too—' She cut herself off, because funerals should not be on the menu when the child's dad was dying. 'I found a good home for the Chinese figurines, made two shillings. Remember? That Buddha with the gold trim – he was one of them. That's a snuff box, Sally, worth a bob or two. Be careful, there's a bit of inlay coming loose. Now, where's my glue?'

While Maureen went in search of what she called her 'mendings', Sally had a good look round. There were figures under domes, without domes, then there were domes without figures. A large dog sat on the mantelpiece, but his nose was on a small table waiting for glue. On the floor, a one-legged shepherd leaned on another dog. Sally smiled. If the dog went off to round up sheep, his master would fall over. She searched for the man's leg, gave up when she found a dead tiger behind a chair.

'That's Sinbad,' Maureen told her when she returned with her repair kit. 'He was going to the ragman, but I rescued him. He'll be all right once I find an eye to match.' She lifted a brush from a pot, dripped glue all over the place. Maureen Mason was known as a good-hearted woman who was dangerous with glue. 'Don't go near on a mending day,' the neighbours often said. 'Or you might finish up stopping there for ever, stuck fast to a chair.'

'Shall I help?' asked Sally, her eyes fixed to a beautiful glue-ravaged carpet.

'No, I'll manage, love. Go through and put the kettle on. Not the copper one, there's a hole in it.'

Sally wandered into the kitchen, set the grill across the fire, put the kettle in place. In spite of all the chaos, Maureen Mason's home was a thing of beauty. The shine on the black grate was almost like glass, and a pair of old chairs had been rejuvenated by the simple act of throwing quilts over their war wounds. A flowery tablecloth spread its knee-length skirt over a table whose shins boasted many applications of beeswax. All around the walls, holy pictures in gilded frames punctuated distemper of a colour that Maureen had invented herself by mixing green and white.

'You all right, love?' called the voice from the parlour.

'Yes, thank you.'

After a small pause, Maureen spoke again. 'I think I've stuck this man's leg on back to front, Sally. My hands are covered in glue, so can you help?'

The child managed not to laugh. Maureen squatted on the floor with a brush in one hand, a glue-pot in the other. 'I daren't put these down,' she explained. 'Last time I put them on the floor, they stuck. Can you pull his leg off?'

Sally did as she was asked, stayed with Maureen until the shepherd's limb conformed with nature's design.

'I liked him wrong, though,' said Maureen thoughtfully. 'He'd a bit of character when he was wrong.'

The little girl perched on the edge of a chair while this wonderful Irishwoman continued with her mending. She tackled the snuff box, a cake stand and a milking stool. 'Ah well,' she sighed when the last job was completed. 'Sure there's one leg a bit longer than the other two, but that's a never-mind, for it reminds me of home.' She rose, looked at a photograph on the mantel. 'He loved England,' she said to herself. 'Enough to die for.'

Sally heard, kept quiet. The sad thing about Maureen Mason was that her husband was dead. Patrick Mason had been born to an Englishman and an Irishwoman. He had lived half his life in Bolton, until the death of his father, then had returned to Mayo with his mother. Patrick and Maureen had married in Ireland, had returned to Bolton only months before the beginning of the war. It was awful, Sally thought, because Maureen Mason enjoyed looking after people. She wanted to look after Mr Goodfellow, but Mr Goodfellow wanted females kept in cages . . .

'What are you thinking of, Sally?'

'Mr Goodfellow. I've to call him Uncle Tom.'

'That's a marvellous man, Sally.'

'Yes.'

'Always very kind to me, you know.'

'Yes.' Should she say something? It was wrong that Maureen should go on hoping. It would be better if she went to the Empress where all the mill dances were held. Or the Aspin, or the Palais, or the Floral Hall. Maureen might get a new husband at the Palais. 'He says ladies should be in cages.'

Maureen stood still, her head on one side. 'Who did?'

'Mr . . . Uncle Tom. Said they should be in cages like Scarlet.'

'Ah, you must have got him wrong there, Sally. The man would not even harm a flea. See, come away now till I get you a nice slice of soda bread. Did I ever tell you about the day my daddy was attacked by the bull?'

'Yes.'

It didn't matter, because Maureen would tell the tale anyway. She believed in keeping a child's mind occupied while trouble was afoot. The tale changed, of course, just as all Maureen's tales did. The main thing was to keep talking. If the poor little girl were allowed to think, her mind might be filled by all kinds of gloom. 'So we sold him,' she announced.

Sally nodded. The last time, the bull had run away never to be seen again the length and breadth of three counties. The time before that, he'd been given to a passing leprechaun with a limp. The leprechaun had tamed the animal to the point where it wore a saddle. From that day on, the crippled leprechaun had saved his bad leg by riding through Mayo on the back of a bull.

'And there's a bit of shortbread for you.'

Sally munched and thought. Sometimes, not very often, Maureen Mason got on Sally's nerves. She was like a toy that got wound up and just rattled on until its spring ran down. Except that Maureen's spring never reached its end. But this lady was the soul of kindness. Perhaps she might have a few answers to the questions Sally had never dared to ask. She swallowed, took a sip of tea. 'Mrs Mason?'

'Yes?'

'What'll happen to me and Gus?'

Maureen sat in the chair that faced Sally's. 'Well now, I'm not entirely sure I understand what you mean, Sally.'

The little girl took a deep breath. 'See, my dad's going to die. It's something to do with coal, Granny Ivy says. And my mam's getting ready to go to New York. Morton doesn't like children. Mam says she'll send for me, but she won't. Granny Ivy is very old. Old people always die, don't they? So when she dies, there'll be just me and Gus.' She looked straight into Maureen's green eyes. 'I can't pay the rent. I don't want to go in the . . . orphan place. There is no orphan places for Gus. What's going to happen, Mrs Mason?'

Maureen had no idea. 'Ah, something will turn up.'

'What, though?'

'I don't know, child. But you're such a lovely girl – somebody will surely . . . We can only wait and see.'

Sally nodded. 'Why does my mam not want me? If she wanted me, she'd stay here. There's other children with no dads, because their dads died in the war, but their mams don't go to America, do they? No, they stay and look after all the children.'

Maureen had never heard Sally say so much in one go. She hadn't realized how pensive the girl really was, because replies from Sally were few and far between. As for questions – well – Maureen was not ready for any of this. 'Your granny will be back soon, child. Will we go up and see how your daddy is?'

Sally sighed. 'All right.'

Maureen prettied herself in the mirror, dabbed on a bit of powder, smeared a dot of lipstick over her mouth. She didn't believe in going over the top, because Mr Goodfellow saw inside a person. Satisfied that she was neat and tidy, she took Sally's hand and walked towards the door. 'Sally?' she said, a hand resting on the shiny brass knob.

'Yes?'

45

'You'll not starve while I'm alive. And, God willing, I've a way to go yet.'

Derek's eyes had bucked up a bit, partly because he was enjoying Tom Goodfellow's company, mostly because Lottie had gone. Also, strange as it seemed, a couple of brandies seemed to have knocked the pain out for a while. 'I feel good,' he told his companion. 'For the first time in months, I'm a bit better.'

'That's the spirit.' Tom laughed as he pointed to the bottle. 'In more ways than one, wouldn't you say?'

'I would.' Derek rested, thought for a moment. 'I wonder what they did to her – Lottie, I mean.'

'Oh, I imagine they've allowed her to carry on alive, just about. But I wouldn't have been in her shoes, Derek. Not for any price.'

The man in the bed found himself very near to laughter. 'That's if they've left her any shoes. Can you picture her arriving barefoot in New York?'

'She'll be clothed and shod before she's out of Manchester. That's a very wily woman you married. She's astute, and she's not averse to doing whatever's necessary to get her own way.'

Derek frowned. 'You don't think our Sal might turn out the same road, do you? I mean, Lottie's mother were on the game for years. Aye, and I wouldn't listen when my own mother warned me. But Lottie took after her mam—'

'No. Sally has a mind of her own. She may not say much, but it's unlikely that seven years with her mother will have much effect. Sally's sensible.'

Derek's face clouded over. 'What's going to become of her after I've gone, Tom? Mam's well into her seventies, too old for getting landed with a young one. How will I rest when I've nobody to take over? I'll be haunting these streets looking for my daughter. Any idea what I can do?'

Ivy clattered in at the front door. She shouted, 'It's only me,' before dashing through the parlour and into the kitchen. Tom sank into a chair, grateful for the old woman's timely arrival. Derek's unanswered query would no doubt crop up again, but at least Tom could take some time to prepare his reply.

Derek peered at his mother. 'What happened?'

'She scratched me face. Any road, she's gone on that train like a salad on legs, coated in muck, she were. I had to hang on for the bobbies so the others could get home. Has Rosie Blunt come back?'

Tom nodded. 'About ten minutes ago.'

'Good.' She walked to the mantelpiece, noticed how empty it was without all Lottie's creams and lotions. But the mirror was still propped behind the broken clock. Ivy picked it up. 'Bloody hell,' she said. 'I look like the loser in a boxing match. Any road . . .' She looked at her son, gave him a smile. 'We'll be all right now, lad. I can fetch a few bits and pieces across, no danger of them getting pawned. We'll feed you up in no time.'

The back door swung inward and clanked against the scullery slopstone. Maureen Mason and Sally entered the room, the former looking flustered in the presence of her hero, the latter smiling tentatively when she realized that Mam wasn't in. When Mam and Granny Ivy were in a room, sparks flew.

Maureen raised her eyebrows at Ivy; Ivy responded with a single nod. So. Charlotte Crumpsall had gone. 'We'll stay a minute, Sally and I,' said the Irishwoman. 'Then I'll give her a bite to eat at my house. We've had a lovely time mending a shepherd.' She smiled at Tom Goodfellow. 'Go now, Tom. Ivy and I will sort things out.'

Sally looked at her father, at Uncle Tom, at Maureen, at Granny Ivy. 'Mam might be back in a bit,' she said.

'No she won't.' Derek's voice was unusually powerful. 'She's gone to America.'

'I saw her with the cases,' the child said quietly. 'But I thought she might have been going to the pawnshop.' Every adult in the room was dismayed when Sally began to cry. She cried not because her mother had gone, but because no goodbye had been said. Feeling sure that everything was her fault, Sally buried her face in Granny Ivy's long black skirt.

'Well, who'd have thought?' asked Ivy of no-one in particular. 'Shut in her room for hours on end, never a decent meal unless she ran to me or a neighbour, yet here she is breaking her little heart.'

Sally sobbed. They didn't understand. None of them seemed to realize that if she'd been a good girl, Mam would have been different. There would have been a fire in the grate, meals on the table, clean clothes. But all these things had been neglected because of Lottie's need to get away from her terrible daughter.

Ivy shook the child gently. 'Come on, our Sal. What's up with you? You knew it were going to happen.'

The child lifted her tear-stained face. 'She were my mother, but she didn't like me. It's with me being so thin and ugly. I can't sing and I can't dance and I'm not clever at school. If I'd been nice, Mam would have stayed and looked after me.'

Ivy clicked her tongue, seemed lost for words.

Tom, who had never known Ivy not to have an answer, decided to leap into the breach. He squatted low, pulled Sally away from her grandmother. 'Sally, look at me.'

Obedient as always, she turned her face up and tried to stop the tears. Uncle Tom. He'd told her that no-one could be an uncle unless he was related, yet he'd said she must call him 'Uncle'. Adults, even nice ones, got a bit mixed up.

'You are beautiful,' he said. 'It's just a matter of time, then you'll leave every girl in England at the starting post.' He touched her face, traced the fine lines with a gentle finger. 'Your bones are perfect, Sally. Your eyes are large and well-spaced, you have good, visible eyebrows, dark lashes, blond hair. Women would kill for a skin as soft as yours. Flesh is all you lack.'

Maureen Mason blinked rapidly. Oh, if only he would speak to her like this! If only he would compliment her . . . She crushed the thought, hated herself for almost resenting a little waif who needed every ounce of support from every source. 'Sally,' she said quietly. 'I'll eat my Easter bonnet in 1960 if you're not the belle of the ball.'

Tom turned, looked at his next-door neighbour. In spite of her unwanted approaches, Tom had always judged Maureen Mason to be a good woman. But now, with a suddenness that was almost frightening, he was struck by her beauty. Like many Irish people, she was blessed with pale skin, hair that was nearing black, eyes of a green that managed to be soft. But he was in no position to . . . He glanced from Maureen to Sally, back to Maureen.

Ivy, who was old enough to read the thoughts of most people, could almost hear the man's brain slipping into gear. If he married Maureen, he could take Sally into his house and . . . Oh, this was a good man. She busied herself by tidying up Derek's bed. 'You always were a messy sleeper, our Derek. Used to tie all the bedclothes in knots, didn't you?'

He was becoming tired again. 'Yes, Mam.'

She couldn't go on for ever. Her bones complained while she bent to tuck in a sheet, the room spun when she lifted her head. Most mornings, her extremities were numb, as if her heart had slowed to a point where the blood was scarcely moving. But oh, she could go gladly to her Maker if Maureen and Tom could just be there for Sal. 'Cup of tea?' she asked her son. At least Sally had stopped weeping. If only Derek would eat, if only he could fool the doctors by pulling round . . .

'No, thanks. I think I'll have a doze now.'

Ivy ushered everyone into the parlour, closed the door to the kitchen. 'Right,' she said. 'We can all set to, now. Would you two lend some pans, towels and bedding?'

The neighbours answered in the affirmative.

'I'll get some bits and pieces off Rosie Blunt, then

49

there's my own stuff. I want . . . I want them to have a proper home till . . .' She glanced at her granddaughter. 'We can fix them up between us. But I want to say ta to both of you. Without neighbours like you and the Blunts, I don't know how we would have managed.'

Tom Goodfellow put his arms round the old lady who was frail in body, powerful in spirit. 'Anything, Ivy,' he whispered. 'Maureen and I will do all we can.'

'I know.' Ivy pulled away from him, was surprised to feel the heat in her face. 'Stop chasing after me, Tom Goodfellow,' she said jauntily. 'I'm not in the market for a man. Fact is, I'm too clever and good-looking for any of you.'

She left number 1, dragged Sally to the house in Worthington Street, sorted out some essentials, piled them on the floor. 'Sal,' she said when the task was nearly done. 'Don't cry for your mam. No use getting yourself in a state over her. What's done is done, and it can't be undone.'

'I won't cry,' the little girl replied. 'From now on, I'll hardly think about her at all.'

She did, though. All through the night, she was plagued by dreams whose central character was always Lottie Crumpsall. Most of the time, Sally was chasing her mother, trying to catch up with her. But the further she ran, the further away her mother moved. Sally's dream legs were like lead, holding her back, making her too heavy to run properly.

'Go away,' called Lottie. 'Morton doesn't want you, doesn't like children. I'll send for you.'

'You won't.'

Even from a distance, the grin on Lottie's face was visible. 'I will if you're good. If you're not good, you'll have to stay upstairs. I know about the basket. There'll be no more baskets.'

'I'm hungry.'

'You're always bloody hungry.'

Towards morning, Sally stopped running. The next dream was calmer. She was living in a house with a proper garden and a neat front door. Inside, everything was beautiful, right down to salt and pepper pots with flower designs and little silver tops. The chairs had real covers with no rips and no bulging springs. Gus lay on a red rug in front of the fire. He was purring so loudly that the sound filled the whole house . . .

She woke. Gus had his nose in her left ear, and his engine was running. Dad always compared Gus's purr to a motor. She stroked the grey fur, wondered whether she would manage to feed him today. Yes, of course he would be fed, because Granny Ivy was asleep next door in Mam's bed. Anyway, Mrs Mason was forever feeding this lovable cat. 'You're nice,' she told him. 'You never scratch and you never bite and you like pigeons.'

By way of an answer, he licked her face, his sandpaper tongue making her shiver.

'Sal?'

'Hello, Granny Ivy.' The old woman looked really strange. Her iron-grey hair, which was usually dragged off her face into a bun, hung down her back. She was dressed in a long white nightie that billowed out all around her sparse frame. 'You don't look like you,' said Sally.

'Who do I look like, then?'

Sally couldn't tell the truth, dared not express the opinion that her grandmother reminded her of a good witch. 'I don't know,' she answered lamely.

'Well, get yourself up. We've sorted out something for you to wear, then when you've had a wash, go round to Maureen Mason's for your breakfast.'

Sally stared at Ivy. 'Why?'

'Because I said so.' She had such beautiful eyes, thought Ivy. They were a bit like Derek's used to be before . . . 'Just do as you're told, love. I'll bring the washbowl and jug up, then you go out the front way, because your dad's had a very bad night.'

When Sally was washed and dressed, she didn't know herself, either. She sneaked into the bedroom where Ivy had slept, looked at the vision in a pock-marked mirror. Where had these clothes come from? she wondered. There was a proper gymslip in grey, with box pleats going right up to a square yolk. The blouse was so white that it almost hurt her eyes, and she had lovely new socks, a belt with a buckle, a navy mac, black shoes and a navy beret.

'Tom Goodfellow's had them clothes for weeks,' said a voice from the doorway. Ivy smiled at the expression of wonder on her granddaughter's face. 'Even went into the cloggers for your shoe size. There's another set too, in different colours. I think there's a navy gymslip with a blue blouse.'

'Oh.' Sally was so choked that she didn't know what to say. Her mother hadn't loved her, hadn't even liked her, but there were lots of other people who cared.

'He couldn't have given you them before, love. They'd only have ended up in Mr Heilberg's shop. Though I think he'd started refusing stuff off your mam, but she would have pawned them or sold them somewhere in town.'

'I look nice.'

'You look lovely, our Sal.'

The little girl swallowed a bubble of gratitude that threatened to spill its wetness down her cheeks. 'Why are they helping us, Gran?'

Ivy thought for a moment. 'There were a time not that long ago when folk always helped each other. That time had a name, Sally, and its name was war. We pulled together and fettled our way through it as best we could. Them as wanted toffees swapped points with them as wanted tea and sugar. Your door were always on the latch in case a neighbour ran out of summat vital like milk.'

Sally turned from the mirror. 'Where has that time gone?' she asked.

'To peace and to bloody pieces,' replied the famous

orator. 'Same last war and all, the Great War. We all huddled together for comfort, kept one another's body and soul together. Mind, even when that were over, I suppose we still helped one another. Eeh . . .' She sat on the edge of the bed, a wistful look on her face. 'You know, life were good when I were a child.'

'Was it?' Sally loved her grandmother's stories.

Ivy nodded. 'We moaned because we had nowt, but there were a lot of fun. Bruised fruit, a pinny full from the market at closing time, apples, oranges, pears, all for a ha'penny. Ten jam jars and you could get in the Theatre Royal without paying. Aye, they were good old days.'

'Who's downstairs?' asked Sally.

Ivy's features rearranged themselves into a facsimile of serenity. 'Only the doctor, love.'

Sometimes, Sally could read Granny Ivy like an open book. This was one of those occasions. The old lady was doing her best to be chatty and pleasant because something awful was happening. Dad must be worse, she thought. Perhaps this was the day when her dad would finally go to the angels. Granny Ivy always said there was no pain in heaven, just God and Jesus and angels with wings and harps. Sally swallowed. She didn't want him dead, but she didn't want him hurting, either.

'Go on, love. Have a nice day at school.'

Sally went. There was nothing she could do for her father, so she took the line of least resistance and obeyed.

'Who got you ready, then?' The big lad pushed Sally against a wall, reached out and ruffled her hair. 'All dressed up, eh? I bet you've still got nits, though. Let's look in her hair,' he yelled to a gang of followers.

Within seconds, there seemed to be a dozen hands pulling at her pigtails, while several voices were raised, some in encouragement, others in mockery. 'Thinks she's somebody now, I suppose,' said a girl from Standard

53

Three. 'Go on, pull. She'd be better without that mop of string.'

Then someone made the mistake of tugging at the collar of Sally's new raincoat. Although she was terrified, she opened her mouth and screamed so loudly that several of her attackers stepped away. But the big carrot-haired boy who had started the trouble remained, strong fingers crushing the navy gaberdine.

Sally had amazed herself with the sheer force of her lung power, yet the noise she had made seemed to create a chink in the shell behind which she had hidden for most of her seven years. During a couple of very long seconds, she studied her tormentor and judged his appearance to be as unfortunate as his attitude. Then, she bent her knee, drove it upwards and watched in horror as he collapsed in a heap. He writhed on the floor, his hands clutching the front of his trousers. Several children turned and ran away. Arthur 'Red' Trubshaw was not a man to be trifled with. That scraggy girl out of Standard One had hit him in a sensitive place, and he would no doubt be dangerous when he recovered.

She stared down at him, fascinated by the various contortions that further disfigured an already disastrous face. 'If you ever come near me again,' she said plainly, 'I'll set our whole street on you.' The street loved her. Its inhabitants fed her, clothed her, minded her dad and her cat. 'Paradise Lane and Worthington Street'll cripple you, Arthur Trubshaw.' She straightened the collar of her coat, walked away, stood in line as soon as the bell rang.

From the corner of an eye, she watched as Standard Four lined up. They were ten and eleven, the children in Standard Four. He must be a coward, she decided, if he had to pick on somebody from a lower class. Until today, she'd been ignored. But now, because she looked a lot better than usual, he had chosen her. And she wasn't going to be all dirty again just so that Red would leave her alone.

The top class marched past first, and she noticed that the boy was looking at her. There was no anger in his face. In fact, had Sally been older and wiser, she might have recognized a grudging admiration in those pale blue eyes.

Craddock Street Junior Mixed and Infants was a cheerless place with tall railings round the flagged playground and an elaborate Victorian frontage that belied the squalor inside. In the junior department, the classrooms were positioned round a hall with a wooden floor that had donated many an unwanted splinter. Windows were high, beyond the reach of most children, so the only view was a patch of sky or, occasionally, a glimpse of sun.

After assembly, Standard Four filed out, its members subdued not only by a tyrannical headmaster, but also by the knowledge that the 'cock' of their class had been flattened by a thin girl from Standard One. Red Trubshaw caught Sally's eye on his way out, winked at her. She tried not to shiver in her new black shoes. That flickering eyelid had meant WAIT TILL PLAYTIME. The thought of playtime terrified her, not because of the usual isolation, but because she knew that she had no more than two hours to live.

The situation was not improved by the fact that Miss Irene Lever pounced on Sally as soon as she entered the classroom. 'Don't you look nice?' beamed the kind lady. 'I'm so glad to see that your mother has managed to get some lovely school clothes for you.'

A hand shot into the air. 'Miss?'

'Yes, Jean?'

Jean stood up. Jean Irving lived on Worthington Street. Jean Irving was one of those people who seem to know everything. 'Miss, her mam's not there. She ran off, miss, to America, miss. And all the other women went to see her off, miss. They bashed her and turned her upside down, miss and took all her money and threw tomatoes at her, miss and—'

'Thank you, Jean.' Miss Lever patted Sally's hand, asked her to take her place.

Sally glared at Jean Irving. A terrible coldness seemed to enter her bones as she looked at the grinning girl. 'Jean Irving is telling lies, Miss Lever,' said Sally clearly.

Nonplussed, Miss Lever pushed the spectacles along the bridge of her nose and closed her mouth with a snap. Never before had she known Sally Crumpsall to speak without being spoken to. The teacher was so shocked that she had to sit down rather quickly. 'Sally, I—'

'Miss, I know all about Jean Irving, so does my granny. She's always telling lies. All the Irvings tell lies.' The iciness was melting, as if speaking up warmed her, made her comfortable.

'Sit down, Sally.'

Sally walked towards her desk. 'And you can shut your mouth,' she told Jean Irving, her tone conversational. 'Because all of Paradise knows about your mother and the gin.'

Jean Irving clenched fists and teeth. 'I'll get you at playtime,' she mumbled.

Sally sank into her seat. It was plain that there was going to be a queue in the yard later on. The thought of Red Trubshaw took away all the false courage, made her shake so much that she could hardly manage to hold her pencil.

Irene Lever watched her charges closely that morning. She was a good and fair woman, the exception that proved the rule in Craddock Street. Miss Lever wielded no cane, slapped no legs. She sensed that trouble was brewing, because never before had she known little Sally Crumpsall to be cheeky. When the register was marked, Standard One's mentor made a vow to keep her eyes open at playtime. Unless she was mistaken, there was going to be a showdown.

Hiding in the toilets was no fun, because the toilets stank. Girls' toilets weren't as bad as boys', but they were foul enough to make any sitting tenant vacate her place as quickly as possible. Sally had often wondered why the smell from the lads' lavatories was so strong that it spread its tentacles across several corridors but, for the moment, her chief concern was to stay in one piece.

Jean Irving's face appeared in the gap at the bottom of the door. 'Scared of me, are you?'

'No.'

'Then why are you stood there like a lamp post?'

Sally decided not to answer such a stupid question. 'Why are you lying on a floor that smells?'

Jean Irving snorted. 'You should know all about smells, Sally Crumpsall. Nobody ever wanted to sit next to you 'cos your clothes were that rotten – we could tell when you were about a mile off. And the Paradise women did bash your mother, it weren't a lie. And I'm going to wait here till you come out, then I'll bloody well—'

'Jean Irving, stand up at once.'

Sally almost died of relief when she heard Miss Lever's voice. Miss Lever was the owner of several voices. She had a kind one, a teaching one and a woe betide you one. This was the woe betide. But not even a woe betide carried the ultimate threat for a Craddock Street schoolchild, because nothing on this earth could have persuaded Irene Lever to send one of her charges to Basher's office. Ernest Bates, commonly known as Basher, had one talent. This solitary gift involved a cane or a strap, sometimes both.

'Who's in there?' Miss Lever asked of Jean Irving.

'Sally Crumpsall, miss.'

'Then what were you doing on the floor, Jean Irving?'

'Well . . . I were seeing if she were all right, 'cos she's been in there ages, miss.'

'Out. Get out this minute, Jean, and stand at my desk until playtime is over.'

Sally breathed more easily when she heard Jean's clogs clattering their way through the outer door.

'Come out, Sally.' It was the kind voice this time.

She came out, stood staring down at the floor.

'Has your mother gone, dear?'

Sally nodded.

'Ah.' This was such an unsavoury place, yet Irene Lever continued, grateful for a moment's privacy. 'I shall visit your father.'

'He's dying.'

The teacher fought a moment of nausea, decided never to spend more than ten seconds in the toilet shed again. 'I am so sorry.'

'Can I go now, miss?'

'Yes.'

Sally walked into the playground, waited for the world to tumble in great lumps about her ears. A heavy hand fell on her shoulder, and she suffered an acute thrill of pure panic that almost riveted her to the floor. She kept telling herself that Miss Lever was just behind her, that everything was going to be all right, but Arthur Trubshaw was bigger than Miss Lever.

'Sal Crumpsall?' said a male voice.

She nodded, waited for the blows to begin.

'I'll see to you,' he announced.

Her heart sank. He wasn't going to kill her now, was promising her a 'seeing to' at some unspecified time in the future.

'There's no need for you to fear owt from now on, Sal. Anybody as can gut a lad like you gutted me wants praise.'

She lifted her head, saw smiles of encouragement on the faces of Red Trubshaw's cohorts. 'Sorry I hurt you,' she said. 'Only it's a new mac. It were just the mac.'

The red-headed boy inclined his head. 'I knew that,' he said. 'But nowt'll happen to you from now on. If you want help here or at home, just yell "Red". You've a gob on you that'd do for a rag and bone man. I reckon they must have heard you shouting down Manchester way. We could do with somebody like you as a lookout when we're playing knock-and-run.'

Irene Lever slipped away unnoticed. At least Sally had a champion of sorts. The teacher entered the staffroom, listened while the headmaster regaled the audience with tales of this morning's whippings.

Irene poured out her tea and sat near the window. Sometimes, she knew she was working in a prison. Always, she knew she was working for a sadist. In her mind's eye stood a little girl in new clothes. How was poor Sally Crumpsall going to survive in this hell?

'. . . said he'd set his dad on me,' announced Bates to his small congregation.

'I hope he does,' mouthed Standard One's Miss Lever into her cup. 'Something has to change.'

THREE

Joseph Heilberg lingered in the doorway of his Derby Road shop. Several passers-by greeted him during their swift escape from Paradise Mill, and he waved to them, smiling sadly as he watched the sparks flying from clog-irons attached to feet that rushed homeward. Only this morning, Joseph had lain in bed next to his wife, had listened to work-bound feet dragging slowly along the pavements, as if each man and woman wanted to be on time but not early.

Most of these people hated their jobs, despised their employer, carried on simply to buy bread, coal, clothes for their children. Joseph knew many of them, knew the shape of a clock, the cut of a suit that would be pawned on Monday morning. The silver teapot woman passed by, then another lady who pledged her dead father's watch at the beginning of each week. Joseph kept that item ticking, made sure it was safe and healthy every Friday when its owner redeemed it.

He pulled out his own watch, noted that closing time was almost upon him. This was Tuesday. Tuesdays, Wednesdays and Thursdays were often quiet except for a few sales of unredeemed pledges and some visits from totters. The rag and bone merchants were a wily lot, often extracting items of value from waste, then trying to sell them on to pawnbrokers. Today's totter had been particularly difficult, as he had arrived in a good suit. But Joseph had looked not at the diamond ring, but at dirt ground into the huge, outstretched palm on which it rested. 'Your mother's, you say?' Joseph had asked pleasantly.

'Aye.'

'She died recently?'

'Aye. Sad loss.'

Joseph had carried on as usual, had studied the ring. He was no jeweller, but he understood marks. 'Her engagement ring?'

'Aye.'

'So this is quite old, then?'

'Aye. Married nigh on fifty year, she were.'

The pawnbroker had handed back the item. 'That ring is new. Did you find it on your rounds? Can't you remember where?'

The totter had held his ground. 'It were me mam's. The owld man bought her a new one when she lost the other. See, I'd forgot till you said. She can't have had this one more than ten year, happen twelve.'

'More like five or six.'

The man had picked up his find and dashed from the shop. His round was probably out of Bolton, because Joseph recognized most Bolton totters. Somewhere, a heartbroken housewife was looking for a mistakenly discarded token of her husband's love.

He put up his shutters, went inside, locked the door with three separate keys. Although the Reich was defeated, he did not forget. In spite of his best efforts at reasoning with himself, the fear of being targeted as a candidate for persecution stayed with him. Ruth often got cross with him. 'This is England,' she would say in German. 'It will never happen here.' Ruth was a clever woman with a simple soul. She was, he thought now, an enigma. Well-read, a good conversationalist, an excellent organizer, Ruth Heilberg saw only the good in people.

Joseph stood behind his desk, rooted about in the recent memory compartment of his mind. Ah yes, the books. He would carry one or two of Derek Crumpsall's books round the corner, would visit the poor man. How on earth had that wife of Derek's managed to carry such a weight from

Paradise Lane to Derby Road? With determination, he answered himself. She wanted, she got. Then, of course, she left the man to die. Since the books, Joseph had refused to lend money to Lottie.

He called up the stairs, told his wife of his intention. She poked her head round the top of the stairs. 'For a businessman, your heart is almost gentle,' she chortled.

'Your English improves,' he replied. 'So try with the cooking.'

He walked down Worthington Street, counted his blessings. He had three successful shops. His son ran and lived above one, Maureen Mason ran the second, and he and Ruth looked after the third. He worried about Maureen's shop, because it was a lock-up with no accommodation, but all had been running well for several years now. Even through the war, Heilberg's had ticked over with the help of friends and neighbours.

Joseph was happy in England. His understanding of the British dilemma had nursed him through internment. Even then, he had been fortunate, had worked alongside his wife right through the war. His hands twitched as he remembered all that sewing of Land Army uniforms, and he almost felt the old pain in his fingers. Strange times, those had been. A hundred German and Austrian Jews had watched the war, had flown the Union Jack at the end. Whenever he thought of his and Ruth's families abroad, he closed his eyes in prayer. After two years, no word of any survivors had reached England.

Ivy Crumpsall opened the door of number 1 Paradise Lane. She stepped into the street, held a finger to her lips.

'How is he?' asked Joseph.

She shook her head. 'Not long now.'

'The books.' He pushed them into her hand. 'You will get them back, all of them. These were all I managed to carry.'

She lifted her head. 'You're a good man, Joseph. I don't

know a right lot about your religion and your way of doing things, but I think we've the same God.'

'There's only one,' he said softly. 'Christians and Jews share Him. Keep your faith, Ivy.'

'Aye.'

Her eyes had begun to cloud with age, and rings were appearing round the irises. He saw the fear behind the calm exterior, felt so much sympathy that it almost cut through him. 'May He be with you now, Ivy.'

'I need Him, Joseph.' She loved this man. Everyone who knew the Heilbergs felt affection for them. Unlike many in his trade, he cared about the folk who pledged with him, often went out of his way to visit a house before selling on an item that had outstayed its date.

'Can we do anything for you? Ruth will come down if you wish.'

'I know, lad. I'll send for you if I need you.'

He stepped back, cast an eye over the frontage of Derek Crumpsall's house. 'How many times did she come to my shop?'

He had spoken no name, but she knew he referred to Lottie. 'Just before the war were over, yon daft Yankee bought an outfit for our Sal. Red, it were, with a fur trim. Lottie marched it off quick smart to that shop of yours, never let our Sal go out in it. Peter Quinn looked after your shop while you were away, didn't he?'

Joseph nodded. 'An honest man. I trust his soul is resting.'

'Well, he took the outfit and gave Lottie money. Next news this other little lass is at chapel in our Sal's coat. Eeh . . .' She shook her head. 'Lottie Kerrigan were bad through and through.'

Joseph remembered Ruth's words. 'No-one is completely bad, Joseph. Everyone has a little of God in his heart.'

'What about Hitler?' he had asked his wife.

'That was a sick man,' she had replied.

Had a whole country followed a maniac, then? Were all Germans blind and stupid? Ruth had even found an answer to that question. According to Ruth Heilberg, the Germany of 1930 had been desperate. In desperation, the people had followed the only star in its ascendency. As that particular star had not been David's, the Reich had wiped out several million Jews. One question that had never been answered by Ruth was, 'Why the Jews?'

'Joseph?'

'I beg pardon, Ivy. I was thinking.'

'I asked did you want to see Derek.'

He nodded. 'Yes. I shall come and sit for a moment.'

Joseph Heilberg took one of Derek's books and sat by the bed of the dying man. He allowed the volume to fall open at random, read out a paragraph about African animals.

'Bigger than the Indians,' breathed Derek.

'I beg your pardon?'

'The elephants. Can't be trained as easily. A rogue on his own can do a lot of damage.'

Joseph smiled, took hold of Derek's emaciated hand. 'When I go to Africa, I shall not talk to a lone elephant. I shall talk only to elephants who have company.'

Derek's features stretched into a smile that made a death's head of his face. 'If you do ever go, bring some photos for our Sal.'

'Ah, this I will do, Derek. I most certainly will.'

Ivy went into the back garden, looked over the fence at her old friend Rosie Blunt. 'Is our Sal all right, Rosie?'

The small white head nodded. 'Playing snap with that daft lump of mine. She thinks he's letting her win, but he's not. Twenty-odd year that man's needed glasses, only he won't admit it.' Rosie glanced over her shoulder, approached the fence. 'How's Derek?'

'Morphine,' replied Ivy.

'Eeh, lass, I'm that sorry.'

'So am I. Joe Heilberg's with him. Doctor's coming

again later on. I think . . .' She drew an unsteady breath. 'I think you'd best find some excuse to send our Sal round to see her dad before bedtime. Derek might not be here come morning. And ta for letting our lass stop with you tonight while Maureen's at her evening blessing.'

'She'll be praying for Tom Goodfellow to see the light and marry her. And she'll say one or two for your Derek, love. Any road, Ivy, I'll send Sally across to you for sugar. Do you want me to come and sit the night with you after I've settled Sally in bed?'

Ivy gazed sadly at the little woman. 'If you're well enough to miss a night's sleep.'

'I'll bring me knitting. And some stout. It'll be a long night, Ivy.'

'Not long enough, Rosie. Not long enough . . .'

'I think she knew,' pronounced Ivy. 'She's deep, is our Sal, takes it all in and says nowt. Only the last thing she said to her dad were about hoping he weren't in any pain, like.'

Both women turned from the fire and looked at the still figure beneath the window. Apart from some slight movements in the region of his chest, he looked as if he were dead already. 'Last time he spoke were to Joseph Heilberg,' continued Ivy. 'Joe told me after – they'd been talking about elephants.'

'Eeh, this lad of yours has always loved animals,' said Rosie. 'Dotes on that cat, he does. He'd have had a dog but for yon Lottie. You know, it makes no sense to me at all, this. His wife's beggared off, he's not long to live, and there's Sally to think about. Where's God been while all this were going on? On His holidays in blinking Blackpool?'

Ivy, mellowed by the stout, nodded sleepily. 'The road I see it, Rosie, is that we gets born and we puts up with it. God's there, you know. He's give us all these things to use like coal and gas. But He never tells us how to go about getting our hands on these things, like. Same as the

Garden of Eden. Eve sees this apple, thinks it looks good, has a taste. God put it there. All God's gifts has a dark side. If we want coal and gas, we've got to find a way of getting it, a way that doesn't kill people like it's killing our Derek. God's give us the brains, so we've to use them.'

Rosie stared admiringly at the Speaker of Worthington Street. If only Ivy Crumpsall had been a bloke. If she'd been a man, she'd have sorted Westminster out right down to washing, ironing and telling the Germans they'd best not try again or else. 'What time did the doctor say, Ivy?'

'Midnight.' She glanced up at the newly mended clock. 'I gave him that clock, you know. When it broke down, he had it mended, then it stopped again. Three or four times it's been back to the shop. Then he realized as how Lottie were overwinding it on purpose to spoil the spring. She told him once that having my clock in her house made her feel as if I were supervising her all the while. Mind, if I'd been in charge of her, she'd happen have changed some of her mucky, slapdash ways.'

The front door opened, causing a draught to enter the kitchen. 'In here,' called Ivy.

Maureen Mason entered the room. 'I couldn't sleep, girls. Is Sally next door?'

Rosie nodded. 'Fast asleep in our back bedroom, cat and all. Is yon clock right, Maureen?'

'Yes. Going on midnight.' As Maureen finished speaking, the Town Hall chimes drifted through the night and into Paradise Lane.

'Doctor'll be here in a minute,' said Rosie.

Another draught announced a second caller. Tom Goodfellow walked in, stopped for a split second when he saw Maureen, then stepped over to the bed. 'Still asleep, I see. Has he woken at all?'

'No,' chorused Ivy and Rosie. Ivy blinked, wondered which invisible force had prompted her neighbours to leave their homes in the middle of the night.

'His breathing's very shallow.' Tom pulled a chair to the

66

bedside, lifted a waxy hand from the coverlet, felt for a pulse. 'His heart's failing, Ivy,' he said. 'I think he's slipping away.'

Derek's eyelids flickered, then he drew in so much oxygen that it had to rattle its way down into clogged lungs. 'Thank you,' he murmured. 'All of you.'

Ivy, Rosie and Maureen joined Tom at the bedside. The man from number 4 rose and gave his seat to Derek's mother.

'Derek, lad,' she whispered. 'I do love you. You've been the best thing in my life.'

He smiled, and there were no lines of pain above the large blue eyes. 'Mam. See to her. You're old . . . soon be with me.' He sighed, coughed weakly. 'Tom, Maureen, Rosie. Keep her. Whatever . . . keep our Sal. She's a good girl. Lottie. Keep Lottie away from Sal. America. No, no. Sal stays here. She's your Sal now. I'm giving her to you.'

Ivy's body was racked with sobs. She clung to her son's fingers, tried to hold on to him, even though she wanted him to go into peace. 'I love you,' she kept repeating. 'We all love you.'

Tom turned away, dabbed at his face with a large handkerchief.

Rosie, who could bear no more, carried the kettle to the scullery and turned on the single brass tap. Thirty-three, that lad was. And here she stood, well gone twice his age, filling a kettle at the slopstone. Never before had she known all the neighbours to gather in one place at midnight – except during the *Luftwaffe*'s little expeditions, of course. It was as if God Himself had reached out to draw Maureen and Tom into this house, as if they had to be there. She raised her head to the ceiling. 'Back from Your holidays, then?' she mouthed. Yes, God was here, all right. He was the love that still emanated from what was left of Derek Crumpsall.

Maureen Mason fixed her eyes on Derek's stilled hands, allowed the tears to flow unchecked down her lightly rouged cheeks. She had prayed for him in church. She had begged God to take this man into His arms. Soon, his spirit would fly away into everlasting glory. Maureen wept not just for Derek, but also for his mother and his daughter. A hand grasped her shoulder. 'Buck up, old girl,' said Tom Goodfellow.

'I will,' she promised. 'In a minute, I'll be all right.'

Tom studied her face, found her vulnerability touching. With furrows in the thin film of make-up, she looked childlike, innocent. 'We'll have to do our best for Ivy and for Sally.'

She nodded.

'And for ourselves, too. We must build a wall of support and take strength from each other.'

'I know.'

A terrible sound filled the room, a crackling groan that came from the man in the bed.

'It's the death rattle,' whispered Maureen. 'Stay here, Tom. Let his mother see him out.'

He pulled her into his arms, placed a hand behind her head and drew her in to his shoulder. Her whole body shook as the dreadful noise continued. She could hear Ivy, too, tried not to listen as the old woman sobbed her sorrow while this beloved son made his final exit. It never occurred to her that she was being held by Tom Goodfellow. He was just a shoulder, just a warm place where she could hide safely for a few moments.

Rosie stood behind Ivy, age-gnarled hands resting lightly on her friend's trembling back. 'Let go, lass,' she whispered. 'There's nobbut pain for him this side. He'll cross over now.'

And he did. A final whisper of air left his lips in a small sigh, then it was all finished. His face relaxed, looked nearer to normal than it had in months. Ivy stood up, folded her boy's arms across his chest, intoned the Lord's Prayer.

The doctor came in. 'Am I too late?'

Tom nodded, pulled himself together. 'Only a little. He's been gone just a matter of seconds.' Unlike the cavalry in the western films, this poor, tired doctor had failed to save the situation. 'There wasn't a great deal you might have done, doctor.'

'I know. I came just to ease the pain. But he's out of it now. Mrs Crumpsall?'

Ivy swivelled on the spot, stared at the man as if he were a stranger. 'Oh, doctor,' she said eventually. 'Rosie were just about to make a pot of tea. I'll find you a nice cup and saucer, because I brought some of my own, you see. Been a funny day for this time of the year, hasn't it?'

The doctor nodded, recognized the signs of shock. 'Will you take a little tablet for me, Mrs Crumpsall? It's only a tonic.'

She thought for a second. 'Yes, I reckon I might. Been run down a bit just lately.'

While the doctor checked Derek for signs of life, Ivy sat staring straight ahead into the fire. 'She shouldn't have done it, you know,' she announced after a minute or so.

'Who?' asked Rosie.

'Lottie. She shouldn't have broke my clock. Our Derek just died, you know. With having no clock, I can't mark the minute. He were born at twenty-two minutes past four in the morning, a Thursday, it were. In 1914. You should know the minute when your son dies. But I don't, because Lottie broke my clock.'

'But the clock's all right now,' said Maureen. 'It's mended, Ivy.'

The doctor drew Tom to one side, told him how to organize the funeral. There was nothing wrong with the clock, though the old woman's mechanism was becoming a source of worry. 'Watch her,' he said, a thumb jerking towards Ivy. 'She's not a well woman. Nothing specific, just wear and tear. Keep an eye on the old girl, please.'

Ivy took her tablet, snored on a ragged horsehair sofa while Tom, Maureen and Rosie washed the body. They dressed Derek in his demob suit, pushed a snapshot of Ivy and Sally into the breast pocket. Rosie paused to make yet another pot of tea, saw dawn approaching over the Parry Rec. It was only then that she thought about all that had happened during the last few hours. At the time, she'd ignored it. But now, as plain as the daylight behind the horizon, she remembered that Tom Goodfellow had wept noiselessly while Derek was being prepared.

She emptied the teapot, poked old leaves down the slopstone drain, rinsed three cups. Ollie had cried on several occasions. She could see him now weeping over every dead child she had borne. He was a bloody nuisance in many ways, but he was very much a man. Sometimes, when she was threatening to batter him for drinking or for going on about leeks he had never grown, she had to fight a strong urge to forgive him.

She opened the caddy, found a spoon, wiped the wetness from her face. There was something about men who cried. It was because they'd nothing to prove, she thought. The majority of males would rather die than be seen weeping, but Tom Goodfellow and Oliver Blunt were members of a blessed minority.

Rosie entered the kitchen, warmed the pot, brewed. Ivy would wake soon, would face the first day without her son. But at least Tom Goodfellow had stopped weeping. He would be here, no doubt, when Ivy woke. Yes, he would be here.

The Spencer Street Methodist Chapel was full. Everyone had heard the story about Derek Crumpsall. The whole of Paradise was represented; even members of other churches had come along to say goodbye. Elsie Bicker-staffe and Mary Dawson from Spencer Street sat at the back among a clutch of Catholics, every last one of them counting prayers on rosary beads. Several of St Augustine's C of E had turned up in the company of three Anglican nuns. But the most noticeable presence was that of two

Jews, Joseph and Ruth Heilberg. They sat not at the back, but just behind Ivy, Sally and the other residents of Paradise Lane. Never before had Joseph been seen to enter a Christian church.

Ruth nodded and smiled sadly at other members of the very mixed congregation. Ruth knew her bearings, because she was an avid attender of jumble sales and beetle drives. Nevertheless, her presence caused a slight stir among the various Christians who packed the small building.

The minister beamed over wire-rimmed spectacles, spread out his arms in welcome. 'There are good men in the world,' he began. 'And Derek Crumpsall was one among that category. Even now, he has brought together people of differing opinion and culture. Even now, Derek's love is strong enough to reach the heart of each and every one of us.'

Sally stared at the shiny wooden box that contained her father. It was so small, far too small for the Dad she remembered. Although he had been at war for most of Sally's life, he had made up for his absence during the first year after his return. If she closed her eyes, she could see him now, all black and shiny about the face, the darkness of coal tattooing itself into laughter lines, into the small creases below his eyes. The bath would be dragged in, the copper and kettle filled. With a tall, white enamel jug, he had mixed hot and cold until the temperature was just right. 'Go out now, Sal,' he used to say.

In the scullery, Sally would wait with the loofah, then, when Dad had submerged himself, she would go into the kitchen and scrub his back. For a year, that had happened almost every day.

She opened her eyes. The second year had been different. Dad had gone very thin, had started to refuse food. A short walk across the Parry Rec became too much for him. One night, she had overheard Mam talking to Mrs Blunt. 'Cancer,' Mam had said. 'There's nowt more they can do for him.'

Mrs Blunt hadn't answered, but the good woman had slammed her back door very hard. Sally had never been completely sure, but at the time, she might have heard something like a laugh. But no. Even Mam wouldn't have chuckled about Dad having some terrible illness. Would she?

The man at the front continued. 'He never shirked his duty. He devoted his life to working and caring for his family.' He smiled at Sally. 'His dear daughter was the very core of his existence. This was a man who was near to God in his daily routine, who worked in the earth's belly to bring warmth and comfort to many. Let us say our own private prayers now. Let us offer up our thanks for the privilege of having known such a man; let us also ask the Lord to give strength to Sally and Ivy Crumpsall.'

A few people shuffled about, gave one another knowing looks. There had been no mention of a wife, because the bad creature had upped and left her husband knocking on death's gate. Some dabbed at their eyes with handkerchieves, many bowed their heads and prayed as hard as they could for the welfare of the poor orphan child.

At first, Sally couldn't imagine what to say in her mind. She knew about silent prayers – it was like silent reading – no need to say the words out loud. What could she say to God? God shouldn't have taken Dad. It would have been better if He'd taken Mam, because everyone said that Lottie Crumpsall was no better than she ought to be and a damned sight worse than most. Damned. She shouldn't have thought 'damned', not in chapel.

She decided to pray to her father. Her father was a good man. Being a good man meant he was still alive, but in heaven and without a body. She glanced at the coffin and an idea struck. Perhaps when the piece of Dad that was his soul had gone, the man had somehow shrunk even further. That could be the reason for such a little box, then. 'Dad,' she said in her head. 'What's going to happen to me and Gus? See, he's only young, about two and a bit, so he can't manage on his own. Uncle Tom would have him, I suppose, but I want Gus with me.'

Sally glanced sideways at Granny Ivy. She was very, very old. If old people who were only as old as Dad died, then what chance was there for Granny Ivy? The little girl's chest hurt when she thought of losing her gran. There would be nobody once this lady was gone. 'Dad, please make Uncle Tom marry Maureen Mason. I could go and live with them. Me and Gus could stay in Paradise Lane if they got married. And—'

'Come on, lass.' Ivy pulled at her granddaughter's navy mac. 'We have to go now.'

They walked behind the coffin, looked at all the weary faces in the chapel. Sally didn't want to watch the sad people any more, so she fixed her eyes on Dad's coffin. Uncle Tom and five other men in black suits were carrying Derek. She kept pace, kept her grip on Ivy's hand. Outside, the chief mourners waited until the coffin was in its hearse.

Then two things happened. First, a man appeared at the Spencer Street end of Paradise Lane, marched across the road and stood against the chapel wall. In his hands, he held a notebook and pencil. Several mourners rushed back into the chapel when they saw the man, though most simply stood with their heads bowed. 'What's going on now?' whispered Rosie Blunt to Ruth Heilberg.

Ruth's lips curled into a sneer of disgust. 'Worthington's sent that man to see how many have left their work to attend the funeral. He's taking names. They'll lose their jobs, I dare say.'

The second event was caused by Sally. She opened her mouth and screamed. She didn't know where the scream had come from, did not connect it to herself at first, yet her mouth was wide and the noise was definitely coming from somewhere inside her. 'Dad!' she shouted. 'I want my dad.' She forgot all about bodies and souls, wanted to be with whatever was left of Derek Crumpsall. Knowing that she was in the wrong, she tried to clamber inside the glass cage that held the coffin, but the men in black held her.

'You're not taking him, you're not. He's my dad. He can't go in the ground. He was always under the ground in the pit and he hated it. My dad can't go back down there, so get him out now.'

Ivy took Sally away from the undertaker's men and shook her. 'Come on, Sal. You've been a love up to now. He'll be nobbut six feet down, lass. This is just something we have to do, child. See, in that coffin, that's not your dad. Them's just what we call his earthly remains. Your dad's watching us now. Look up there.' She pointed to the sky. 'He's an angel, is our Derek. He's just behind them clouds and he's wanting you to be strong. Please, Sal.' The old lady's voice cracked and she wept copiously into one of her dead son's ragged handkerchiefs.

Sally gulped, tried to compose herself.

'Leave her to me,' said a new voice.

Ivy turned to her left, noticed a red-haired boy with a torn jumper and concertina socks. 'Who are you?'

'Red Trubshaw,' he replied. 'And I'll look after her.'

'Shouldn't you be at school?' asked Maureen Mason.

The lad nodded. 'Aye, but I wanted to see if she were all right.' He focused his attention on Sally. 'Come on with me,' he said. 'I'll take you home and we'll sit quiet till everybody comes back.'

Sally stared at Red and nodded. She didn't want to watch her dad going in a hole.

'He may be right,' said Maureen. 'Sure, she's a bit on the young side for a graveyard service.' Maureen squatted down, made herself level with Sally. 'Look.' She took a package from her bag. 'I know you're not a Catholic, but I bought you a nice little rosary. You can use it for counting with. And I've left a banana cake in the scullery. Go to my house, but don't eat any sandwiches until the grown-ups

74

get there.' Out of the goodness of their hearts, the folk of Paradise had prepared the funeral tea.

Red took Sally's hand, started to lead her across the road. But before they had reached the corner of Paradise Lane, another commotion began. Sally lingered in the care of Arthur 'Red' Trubshaw and saw, for the first time ever, that Mr Heilberg had a temper.

He accosted the man with the notebook, pushed him hard against the wall. 'Well, now. And here we have the hero,' said the tiny Jew. He squared up to the larger man. 'You don't know nothing from nothing,' spat Joseph. His anger was fuelled even further, because he became impatient with his own tendency to use poor English whenever he became heated, and Joseph was extremely proud of his command of the language. He was furious with Worthington's spy, livid with himself, heartbroken because a good man lay in a coffin just feet away.

'Hang on,' said the flat-capped man. 'I'm nobbut doing the job I'm paid for.'

Sally pulled Red's jumper. 'What's wrong?'

Red bent his head. 'See them women near the back? That lot over yon, near the chapel door?'

'Yes.'

'Well, if you look close, you'll notice they're not got up proper for a funeral. They've dark coats, but can you see the mill pinnies hanging down? Them coats is likely borrowed. Look – that one with the blue scarf on her head – her black coat's never hers, 'cos it's miles too little. That's a mill overall showing where the buttons won't fasten.'

'Oh,' said Sally, who didn't understand.

'They're on the 'ook,' he whispered.

'Eh?' Which hook? she wondered. Their clothes weren't on pegs, they were on their backs and—

'They should be in work. They've sneaked out for the service. Their mates'll be covering up for them, like, but it looks as if Worthington's on to them.'

The two children watched while Joseph Heilberg tackled the situation. 'He was a good friend to these people. Ten minutes is too much for a good friend? One funeral is all we get. And Worthington cannot afford to lose half a dozen workers for a few moments? He is a poor man, then. For him, we should feel sorry.'

The man brushed away the small body as if dealing with an annoying and persistent bluebottle.

'Your mother is alive, I hope?' asked Joseph.

'No.' The man scribbled on his pad, counted heads, wrote again.

'Were you at her funeral?'

'Aye, but she were family.'

Joseph removed his black hat, handed it to Tom Goodfellow. 'For this I came to England?' he shouted. 'For this I brought my Ruth out of Austria?' He inhaled deeply, looked the intruder up and down. 'I am a Jew,' he said with the air of one who imparts new information.

'I know.' Another name was scribbled on the page.

'So I know from persecution. I know.' He beat his breast dramatically. 'My family all died,' he announced. 'And a few million others, too, many of whom I did not know. For this, I grieve. For all the funerals I never attended, I feel sorrow. My shop is closed and shuttered; my wife is here. Maureen Mason who runs my other shop is also here. Business is suspended, business I have lost. I cannot bring back those who would buy in my shop today. I cannot chase them down the street and make them pay me. He . . .' Joseph waved a hand at the hearse. 'He cannot be replaced. Tomorrow, other customers I will have. Tomorrow, more cotton will be spun. But the man inside that box is gone for all eternity.'

Sally sighed. Mr Heilberg was wonderful, much better than the preacher. Mr Heilberg had said all the things in Sally's heart. 'Red,' she mumbled. 'Let's go to the graveyard.'

He frowned, making many of the large freckles on his

forehead join up until they looked like maps of countries. 'You sure?'

She nodded.

Joseph Heilberg stepped away from Worthington's spy, was plainly limbering up to land a punch.

But the flat-capped man nodded, removed his headgear, tore off a sheet of paper. 'All right, Mr Heilberg. I'll face the wall while they go back in, then I'll say I saw nowt. I mean, I weren't close up, were I? From this distance, a woman is a woman. So when I turn round again, there'll be nowt for me to see.'

'May you have long life and happiness,' replied the little pawnbroker.

A flurry of women shot along Spencer Street and into Paradise Lane. 'All gone,' announced Joseph.

'Right.' The cap was replaced, the notebook and pencil tucked into a pocket. 'I'll be off, then, Mr Heilberg.'

Joseph shook hands with the man who had so recently been an enemy agent, then ushered the mourners into a semblance of order. They were strange, these Christians. They left their dead to lie for days before burial, ate any old thing that appeared on a butcher's slab, served meat and milk at the same meal. Well, they were good-hearted for all that, so he stood in line with the others and followed Derek to his final resting place.

Maureen and Ruth, both social animals, were in charge of arrangements. The kosher side of the funeral meal proved very popular with everyone except Red Trubshaw. He scowled when offered lox, said he wasn't going to eat no funny-looking fish, not for nobody, even if this was a funeral. But most were begging Ruth for pâté and bread recipes, and everybody had a comment to make about Ruth's German porcelain.

Maureen, whose house was being used, made much of Sally and Red, kept saying what a wonderful thing it was for Sally to have a young man all to herself. Red shrugged this off, said he was nobbut minding a girl who used to be a victim of bullying. The fact that he had been an offender had apparently been erased from his very selective memory.

Sally spent most of the afternoon staring at Granny Ivy. She didn't know where they were going to live. Would Ivy come to Paradise Lane, or would Sally move to Worthington Street? If Worthington Street was to be their address, would Gus settle? Gus loved pigeons, and no-one in Worthington Street kept them. And Gran looked older, wearier than ever. Living with her was going to be a terrible worry, because if Gran got ill, Sally would have to be in charge.

Rosie Blunt bumbled across the room, a glass of stout in one hand, a sandwich in the other. 'How are you, Sal?'

How was she? Lonely, frightened, missing her dad. 'I'm all right.'

'Ivy'll look after you. Your gran's a good sort.'

'She's old,' said Sally. 'She might get ill.'

Rosie understood. 'We're all here for you, love. Your dad said we'd all to have a hand in looking after you. Me, Ollie, Maureen and Tom. Then there's the Heilbergs. You don't think they'd let anything happen to you, do you?'

'I don't know.' She was tired, wanted her bed, wanted her father. 'I'm not anybody's, Mrs Blunt. I was my dad's girl. Mam doesn't want me. She didn't even stop to help with Dad. So it's . . . it's like there's just me on my own.'

Rosie nodded wisely. The poor child had lost all her framework in a matter of days. Whatever Lottie had been, she had figured in the centre of Sally's universe. Now, the little girl had no security, no way of knowing what her future would be. 'Your gran's moving into number one. She says that's what Derek would have wanted.'

Sally tried to feel relieved, because one of the problems had been sorted. But she was still alone.

Red came over, half a pasty clutched in an unclean hand. He grinned at Sally, told her that this was the best feed he'd ever had. 'Come on,' he said. 'We'll sit on the doorstep.'

Sally fixed her eyes on Paradise Mill, wondered what this great big lad was doing here. His mates would laugh at him for hanging about with a girl from Standard One. No, they wouldn't. Not to his face, at least, because Arthur 'Red' Trubshaw was cock of the school. But they might smile behind his back. So why was he here?

'She were just like you,' he muttered through a mouthful of pastry and potato.

'Who was?'

He swallowed noisily, took a swig from a lemonade bottle. 'Our Alice. She were nine.'

Sally waited, knew he would carry on at his own pace.

'I were chasing her one day and she kicked me. Same place as you clobbered me with your knee.'

'Oh.'

He devoured another wedge of pasty, spat out a bit of beef gristle, wiped his mouth with a cuff. 'She had a white coffin, our Alice. It were last year, just after her birthday. Our Alice were on the thin side like you, but she packed a punch.'

Sally turned her head slowly and stared at Red. 'Only nine?'

He nodded.

'I thought you had to be old to die.'

He shook his carroty head vigorously. 'No. We've a woman down our way past a hundred. Mam says when your time comes, you just die, doesn't matter whether you're three or three hundred.'

'So can my gran live till I'm grown up?'

'Course she can.' He finished the lemonade, grinned at her. 'She were the only girl, our Alice. Rest of us is lads. You remind me of her. I'll tell you summat now, eh?'

'If you want.'

'Well, you just say your name very fast. Say it about ten times.'

79

This was daft, Sally thought. 'What for?'

'Just do it.'

Sally shrugged. 'Sally, Sally, Sally, Sally,' she said.

'Faster,' commanded Red.

'Sallysallysally—'

'Can you hear it?' His cheeks glowed. 'Can you? When you say "Sally" fast, Alice is in it. And that were me sister's name.' Pleased with himself, he jumped up and dragged Sally to her feet. 'Shall we go and swing on yon lamp post?'

Sally nodded, followed him to the corner. It was no use worrying. She was Sally/Alice and Gran might live for years and years. And swinging from the lamp post was good fun.

FOUR

Ivy opened the door of 1 Paradise Lane. She could hear a commotion of some sort, and she wasn't one to miss out when an event of import was afoot. Sally was at school. That odd-looking lad with the red hair and freckles had walked up with her this morning. Ivy knew the Trubshaws only vaguely, but she remembered the little girl dying about a year ago. Arthur seemed to have taken Sally under his wing, so at least the child wouldn't get teased at school any more, because Arthur Trubshaw was a bruiser, as big as many thirteen-year-olds.

She craned her neck, tried to see what was happening in the mill yard, but the gatepost was in her way. Ivy was not the sort to be overcome by an obstacle as frail as a few hundred bricks and a bucket of mortar. She slammed the door, crossed the cobbles, stood in the gateway.

Andrew Worthington had gone a strange shade of purple. His eyes seemed to bulge from their sockets, put Ivy in mind of a very large, dead and extremely unsavoury fish. He was screaming at a group of women. 'No more excuses.' He pulled at his collar, turned towards the mill, swivelled again. 'If I let people out every time there's a funeral, I'll be in the bankruptcy court within weeks. So get out, the lot of you. There's no excuse for what you've done.'

Rosie Blunt came across and stood beside Ivy. 'Hey, do you reckon yon man with the pencil did give names in?'

'Might have,' said Ivy. 'The lad's got a living to make. But it makes no difference in the long run, because yon owld bugger has eyes in the back of his head.'

Rosie nodded thoughtfully. 'Them at the front of his head are bad enough. They look ready to roll across the floor any minute.'

Ivy decided to step into the arena. She shook off Rosie's attempts at restraint, strode across the yard with a vigour that would have surprised her doctor.

'What do you want?' asked the mill owner. He remembered Ivy Crumpsall. Ivy Crumpsall had made his life difficult for many years. When the harridan had retired, Andrew Worthington had breathed a sigh of relief before treating himself to several brandies and a roll in the sorting shed with some girl or other . . . No, he didn't seem able to remember the name of that one.

'Have you sacked this lot?' she asked.

'Is that any business of yours?'

The old woman straightened her spine as best she could, cursed the slight curvature that had become more pronounced of late. Being bent over all the while made her look weak, submissive. 'Course it is. It were my lad we were burying. And yes, you would be bankrupt if you let folk out for every funeral, because you're killing us by the bloody thousand. There's undertakers lining pockets and coffins every minute of the day.'

Ivy looked the women up and down. 'Listen to me.' Her voice was confident, strident. 'This bad swine wants stopping. Don't listen to him. Go and get your bloody union sorted out, get yourselves affiliated. Terrified of unions, he is. He's sacked more good spinners and weavers than any other mill boss in this town. Your working conditions stink and you've got to keep your daughters locked up in case the evil beggar takes a fancy to them.'

'How dare you?' he spluttered. His heart leapt about, just as it did every time he heard the word 'union'. Most other mill owners had thrown in their hands, had given in to the concept of organized labour. But Paradise was still a proper mill, a place where folk knew their place and kept their place. 'How dare you?' he repeated, his tone quietened by the expression on Ivy's face.

'Easy,' she snapped. 'I just open me gob and let the truth float out. You've cottages for kept women on Halliwell Road, Blackburn Road and Vernon Street. There's been big bellies of your making since I were a lass.'

'Prove it,' he said.

'Right, I will.' She squared up to him, arms akimbo, feet planted apart. 'In 1921, Rita Eckersley from somewhere down Darcy Lever way had a boy of yours. You paid her to keep her mouth shut, only you didn't pay her enough. Shall I go and fetch her? That lad's twenty-six now, and he's fought in a world war. Last time I saw Rita, she reckoned as how her lad were just waiting for a chance to give you a hiding. Then there was Mary Shaw's girls, Tilly Saxton's lad . . . no, that were a girl and all. And Phyllis Caldwell had twins, one of each. Aye, you hit the jackpot that time, eh?'

'This is slander,' he hissed.

'It's the bloody truth, you owld swine. And the state of you – it's got to be rape. No woman in her right mind would lay down with that physog on the next pillow.' She moved forward until she was so close that she could smell his breath and almost taste his anxiety. 'I'll get them to speak up. There's others, too, girls who ran home with a ripped frock and a fistful of half-crowns and two-bob pieces. But there's power in numbers. You've forced yourself on too many women, you see. One or two would have stayed quiet, but when I get all this lot together, you'll be in court so fast you'll need clean underwear.'

The group of women backed away. They knew all these things, had heard the rumours, had even met the offspring. But nobody ever bested Andrew Worthington.

'You can get out of my house tonight,' he said.

'No.'

'Then I'll have you thrown out.'

'No.'

'Just you wait,' he whispered.

'No.' She smoothed her hair, bared the few teeth that remained. 'I'm living in one of Mr Heilberg's houses now. You know the ones I mean – Paradise Lane. It's that little street there, the one that joins Worthington and Spencer in unholy matrimony. She's a sensible woman by all accounts, your wife. I hear she kicked you out of bed within a fortnight because of your . . . strange way of doing things. Any road up, I'll be living on the street you tried to buy. No way will Joe Heilberg ever let you get your mucky paws on that piece of Paradise. He bought that with the bit he smuggled out of Austria, and we're all grateful to him for keeping you in your place. And shut your cake-hole, there's a number three tram coming, might stick in your ugly gob and choke you.'

Silence hung over the yard like a thick, black cloud. Even the sounds from the mill seemed muted. He stared at her with a loathing that was almost tangible. She had returned to haunt him again. Ivy Crumpsall hadn't always looked like this. She had been a thing of beauty in her time . . .

'I'm on that list, Worthington,' she said, her voice clear enough for all to hear. 'I might be a good fifteen year older than you, but you had the blouse off my back, didn't you? You chased me the length and breadth of this yard.' She turned round, her eyes sweeping the walls. 'Over there.' She jabbed a finger towards a pile of skips. 'Just outside the carding shed. And a miner coming off shift saved me, remember? He were that covered in coal dust, he weren't recognizable. Blacked your eye and thickened your lip, he did.' She laughed, but the sound she made was menacing. 'Fastened your trousers quick enough that time, didn't you? Mind, as I look back now, you'd not a great deal to hide in that department.'

He backed away, a hand to his throat. All his life, he had been sure that none of his prey would speak up, that

84

each one would be too ashamed to talk about him. Yet he had always feared this one. She had been the exception, older than his usual targets, widowed. And now, thirty years on, she was punishing him. 'Take them back,' she ordered.

'What?'

'You heard me. Or are you deaf as well as pig flaming ignorant? Give these girls their jobs back, or I'll organize a lynch mob. You know I will. You know my threats are never empty.'

He blinked a few times, seemed uncertain of what to do next.

'Take them back,' she repeated.

Andrew Worthington drew the watch from his pocket, looked at it for several seconds. 'These people are not dismissed,' he said carefully. 'It was my intention to suspend them until tomorrow.'

Ivy inclined her head. 'Very nice, I'm sure. I wish you could be suspended till tomorrow, Worthington. By the neck, with a nice thick piece of rope. Happen I'll nip round to the rope walk, see if they've any seconds. All you're fit for, seconds.' She turned and walked out of the yard, alarmed by the weakness that suddenly invaded her body. She had to make it, had to walk out of this yard with dignity. She paused, fiddled with her hair, gave herself time to breathe.

Rosie took her arm. 'He'll have you, Ivy.'

'Nay. He tried once and didn't get so bloody far. And this time, I'm ready for him.'

The woman hammered on the door of number 1, pushed it open impatiently when there was no reply. 'Hello?' she shouted. 'Anybody in?'

'They're out.'

The intruder turned and faced Rosie Blunt. 'Where've they gone?'

'Lass is at school and Ivy's doing her cleaning job, then

going down the fishmarket buying finny haddy for their teas. Any road, who are you?'

'I'm Lottie's sister, Sally's auntie.'

Rosie sagged against the wall, made a great effort to remain composed. Lottie's mother had birthed three or four, Rosie seemed to remember, every one with a different father. But they'd never been near. As far as Rosie could recall, no sister of Lottie's had ever visited Paradise Lane. So what did this fancy piece want?

'Will they be long?'

'I don't know.' Lottie Kerrigan-as-was's sister was a right mess in Rosie's book. She wore a frock of emerald green crêpe, very skimpy, plus wedge shoes and a black hat with a veil covering the front of improbably red hair. All of which might have looked all right on a thin woman, but this one's backside was spreading faster than gossip, and her belly had never been introduced to a corset. According to Rosie, any female who didn't wear whalebone was a disgrace.

'I thought I'd see how they were getting on. Lottie sent me a letter.' She waved a bit of paper under the old woman's nose. 'Said I'd to come round when Derek died. So I've come.'

'Aye, I can see that.' You'd have to be blind not to see such a woman, thought Rosie. This creature could get noticed from a mile off, enough slap and rouge on her face to paint the *Mona Lisa* including background. 'This your first time round these parts, like?'

'No. We live up Derby Road, next corner to Heilberg's shop.'

'Not far to come, then.'

'No.'

'But you never came while your Lottie were here.'

The woman blushed till her heavily rouged cheeks clashed loudly with the orange hair. 'We didn't get on, me and our Lottie. I never approved of the road she carried on. But a niece is a niece.'

Rosie's head leaned itself to one side. There was something not quite right about this person. It wasn't just the way she was dressed. There was a deep sadness in her, an old grief that sometimes rose to fury behind the greenish eyes. 'Have you any kiddies?'

'No, we've not been blessed.'

So, that was it. Rosie had seen the same expression many times in the mirror while combing her hair. As a childless female, she recognized the resentment in the intruder's face. The woman had come for Sally, then. Rosie's chief concern was to get to Ivy before this one did. 'What's your name? I'll tell Ivy you called.'

'Gertrude Simpson. Most call me Gert. It's a scream, because my husband's Bert. Gert and Bert – funny, isn't it?'

Rosie, whose concern for Ivy and Sally was the burning issue, found the small quip almost as amusing as the skin off yesterday's rice pudding. 'If you want to come back tonight, I'll tell Ivy to expect you. Once she gets roaming round Bolton market, she can spend up to two or three hours. She knows everybody, see. Has a lot of friends.'

'Oh.'

'And she's busy now, what with her job, then Sally to care for. She loves her Granny Ivy, does little Sal. It's a good thing Ivy were here to pick up the pieces after your sister ran off. If it hadn't been for Ivy and the neighbours, Derek would have been left to die with Sally watching.' She looked the stranger up and down. 'She were a very tarty woman, your sister. Always dyeing her hair and carrying on like a kid, short skirts and daft shoes.' With deliberation, she allowed her eyes to move from short skirt to daft shoes.

Gert Simpson bit her lip. 'It's work, you see. I'm on toffees. They like you to dress nice at Woolworths.'

Rosie pondered for a moment. 'Haven't they started giving you overalls to wear? Like a coat that covers all your clothes?'

Gert realized her error, lifted her head until the light of

defiance shone in the direction of the door. 'It's morale,' she explained. 'They tell us to wear something nice underneath for our morale.'

Determinedly stupid, Rosie spoke up again. 'Moral? Eeh, I wouldn't call your frock moral, love. It's stretched that far across all your bits and bobs that I can nearly see straight through the front as far as your backbone.'

Gert, who could see right through Rosie, stepped back. There was going to be trouble here. But Lottie had left the girl to Gert and Bert, and this would probably be Gert's only chance of rearing a child. She wanted Sally, wanted a little girl so badly that it hurt. 'Tell Mrs Crumpsall I'll be round just after seven. And Bert'll be with me.'

'Right.' Rosie followed the woman into the street, closed Ivy's door, watched while the creature stumbled over cobbles. Ivy was going to go straight through the roof like a blinking rocket. No way would Ivy Crumpsall let Sally go without a fight. And once Ivy saw the state of Lottie's sister . . . well, it didn't bear thinking about, especially on an empty stomach.

Rosie entered number 2, closed her door, went into the kitchen with the intention of preparing a meal.

'Where've you been?' Ollie was fiddling with four failed potatoes that sagged on newspaper in the middle of the table. 'Spuds should grow anywhere,' he grumbled. 'But they'll not grow in Paradise.'

She touched his shoulder, smiled at him. 'Thanks, lad,' she said.

He jumped to his feet. 'What the bloody hell do you want now? You're only nice to me when you're after summat.'

'No. I just wanted to say ta before it's too late. You've minded me and kept me safe for a long time, Ollie.'

'That's all right.' He watched her as she walked into the scullery, tried to judge whether she might be ill in mind or body. 'Are you sickening for summat?' he asked.

Rosie leaned against the slopstone, thought about all the

children she'd never reared. She wasn't ill, just tired. But Ivy was more than tired. Ivy was worn out and heart-broken, too exhausted for the kind of trouble promised by Gert Simpson. Rosie filled the jug, carried it to the kitchen copper. 'Take them things off my table, Ollie Blunt. And if you've walked anything in, I'll sort you out and no messing.'

He smiled to himself. His Rosie was all right after all.

Tom Goodfellow picked Gus out of the cage, placed him on the floor next to a plate of flaked fish. 'I'll never understand you,' he said to the cat. 'There are mice to chase, yet you come in here and nest with a pair of birds. Here, eat that.'

Gus sniffed at the cod, sat down, fixed his suspicious eyes on Tom. This fellow was going to let the birds out again. They were warm and comfortable, and Gus would miss them. He watched while the man held a bird, listened to the cooing. After a quick flurry of wings, the pigeon rose into the sky. The whole process was repeated, then the box belonging to Beau and Scarlet was empty. Gus ate his fish, lay down to wait. He'd tried being friendly with some of the other birds, but only Beau and Scarlet accepted him for what he was – a docile creature who liked soft feathers and enjoyed being groomed by thorough beaks.

Tom entered the scullery, picked up the letter, read it again. He would bank the cheque later, but he needed to read through this wretched thing once more. His presence was requested in Regent Street, London, as soon as possible. He was to make an appointment with Matthew Marsh of Marsh, Marsh and Fotheringay. So, he was summoned by a senior partner. Which was a shame, he told himself in a small moment of levity. Fotheringay was a wonderful name, quite Shakespearian. It would have been fun to spend another hour in the company of Peregrine Fotheringay, as that splendid man failed completely to live up to his elegant name. But today's message had been signed with a flourish by no less a personage than Matthew Marsh himself, so Tom would respond immediately.

The pigeons would be cared for in his absence by Maureen Mason, Gus and Sally. Maureen would feed them, Gus would watch them and Sally would clean out the cages and lofts. London. He disliked London with a passion, hated the noise, the bustle, the almost total lack of human contact.

He went inside, stood deep in thought. 'I could have lived in the country,' he eventually told the cat who had followed him in. 'But I'm so glad I didn't.' Tom pointed to his 'reason' for living here, a pile of papers and folders on the dresser. The doctorate in sociology would never materialize, because he was too busy enjoying the company of those he was meant to interview. 'Lancashire, A Social History, Industrial Revolution to Present Day', was curling at the edges. He'd coped with the Industrial Revolution, had decided to remain in the present day. Though Andrew Worthington might be a suitable candidate for close questioning, he told himself. Andrew Worthington was as Victorian as the Albert Memorial, a man whose views were so definite as to brook no discussion. Perhaps silent vigilance might be preferable to interview, then.

'Sociology is an inexact science,' he informed the feline audience.

Gus stuck a rear paw in the air, began to wash his behind. They did go on, these two-legged ones. Birds went on too, but that noise was softer, gentler.

'I'm off to hell tomorrow,' he informed the furry contortionist. 'It may be that the money is about to dry up. If so, I shall be forced to join the labouring classes. In which case I shall, no doubt, gather sufficient material to write a tome rather than a thesis.'

Gus remained unimpressed.

'Talking to that cat again, Tom?'

Tom grinned. 'Hello, Rosie. Do come in.'

'I already have. Make a brew lad. My daft bugger's sat at the kitchen table having a conversation with four King Edwards. I've stuck a tater pie in the oven and left him moaning.' She sank into a chair. 'At least the cat's breathing, so you're one up on Ollie.' She watched as he made the tea. He was easy on the eye, was Tom Goodfellow. In spite of a slight limp, his movements were fluid, sure and relaxed. Tom didn't go mithering on about poor soil. He just cut the weeds and let the garden take care of itself, but at least it looked like a lawn when it was short. 'We've still not worked out why you're living here, lad.'

'You promised not to ask again,' he told her mildly.

'I know, but I'm a liar.' She took a noisy slurp of tea, waited hopelessly for some information about the man's origins. 'There's bother, Tom.'

'Oh?'

'A woman's just been hanging round number one. Gert Simpson, says she's Lottie's sister. I think she's after taking Sally to live with her.'

Damn, he cursed inwardly. 'Why must every problem float to the surface at once?' he asked the cat. He smiled ruefully at Rosie. 'I do hope there's no trouble, because I have to go away for a day or so – something's come up. It's business in London. It might take only twenty-four hours, or it could use up a week. But I'll get back as quickly as possible. Now, stop eyeing me expectantly, Mrs Rosemary Blunt, because as I've told you before, you must take me as I am now, not for who I used to be.'

She cocked her head to one side. 'Have you been thrown out, Tom? Did your dad chuck you to the four winds with one of them "never darken my door" looks on his face?'

How near the mark she was! 'No. Now, there's no immediate danger to Sally or to Ivy. I'm fairly sure that the system would decide to leave Sally with her paternal grandmother. I should be very surprised if any so-called welfare committee moved the child into the home of a stranger whose sister deserted a young girl and a dying man.' He got up, paced about. 'Look, I'll go and see somebody. I've a Bolton lawyer – he negotiates with London, keeps my finances in order. In an hour or so I'll pop down and have a word with him.' He rooted in a drawer. 'Here's his card. If Ivy has any trouble with the woman while I'm away, send her to my lawyer.'

Rosie took the card. 'It'll be all right for now, Tom. But Ivy's not well, you know. I mean, she's good enough some days, worn out the rest of the time. Something tells me her system's getting a bit tired.'

'I know. But I still think she'll fool us all by reaching ninety – even her century.' He walked about, pondered. 'When is this sister of Lottie's going to call again?'

'After tea. She's fetching her husband with her. Gert and Bert Simpson – did you ever hear the likes of that?'

'No,' he answered absently. 'Though Peregrine Fotheringay's a name to conjure with isn't it?'

'Eh?'

'I beg your pardon?'

'Who the hell's Peri-green Featheringay?' She knew she'd got it wrong, but it was a mouthful, all right.

'Sorry, I was dreaming. A chap I used to know. Go home, Rosie. Wait for Ivy, sit on her if necessary. We must all be there when Lottie's sister returns. Myself, you and Ollie, Maureen, Ruth and Joseph. Let her try to take Sally then. It will be as well if we make it plain that there will be a fight. That man's dying wishes were for us to act *in loco parentis*.'

Her face shrivelled into a frown. It was no use saying 'eh?' again, because he was of an educated turn of phrase, was Tom Goodfellow. 'Right. I'll go and wait for her then.' She walked to the doorway, paused. 'Is there summat bothering you, lad?'

He nodded. 'You know I've a private income?'

'We guessed as much. I mean, nobody manages to eat as

well as you do without the odd copper coming in. But what's wrong with your face, eh? You look like you've lost a bob and found a tanner. I wish me and Ollie had a private income. We're living on savings, hoping we'll peg out before the money does.'

Tom smiled at her. 'Money isn't everything, but it helps. My source of income may be about to dry up – I shan't know until I get to London. If necessary, I'll get a job when I return.'

'What were you in the war?' she asked sweetly.

'A trainer of pilots.'

'In the Air Force?'

'Yes. Fighters, mostly.'

She remembered him arriving here with a bad leg and a brass-headed cane, remembered Joseph Heilberg's solicitor bringing Tom for a look round number 4. Going on three years Tom had been in Paradise Lane. He was a man of mystery with a heart of gold. 'You'll tell me when you're ready.'

Tom inclined his head, then in perfect Lancashire he said, 'Aye, an' 'appen ah will an' all, lass.'

When he was alone, Tom picked up his notes, looked through them. It seemed stupid now, downright mad to start studying for a doctorate at his age. What on earth had he intended to do with it? Go back to Oxford and lecture callow youths on the subject of northern life?

Goodfellow. Wasn't that a name to conjure with? He wondered yet again why he had hung on to it – after all, there were other family names he might have used. Was he trying to live up to it? Was he aiming to become the first decent Goodfellow within living memory?

Smiling to himself, he shook his head. No. He had stuck to the name out of habit or laziness, had grown in to it like an item of clothing that had been passed down through a family. One day, given a good enough reason, he might just do something about it . . .

He read some of his work, spoke it into the empty room.

'The most distressing and annoying factor in this field is the apparent blindness of cotton factories. Few mill owners are developing or diversifying. While machinery improves, attitude remains unchanged. There is a markedly severe and blinkered structure to the cotton industry and it will die a natural death within two or three decades. Overseas markets will not be sustained; cheaper fabrics will infiltrate from Eastern countries.'

He riffled through the pile, found more words of pseudo-wisdom. 'However, what is remarkable is the continuing importance and vigour of the family unit. Beyond that, a social stability has been achieved by the almost accidental creation of interrelating aid groups within the community. A strong sense of local culture makes these people some-what insular, yet they absorb with ease migrants from other Lancashire towns.'

He tore the pages into four pieces, placed them on the fire. Bolton had also taken to its bosom a man who was so markedly different that he should have stood out like a boil on the face of a baby. How would they react, he wondered, if they knew the truth about him? What could a member of the landed and titled gentry expect from these proud working people?

He watched the dancing flames, answered himself. 'They would still care for me,' he told the heat-curled notes. 'There are more similarities between classes than there are differences. So, "Dr" Goodfellow, you will remain a simple MA Oxon. And your main job, after seeing Matthew Marsh, will be to keep safe Derek Crumpsall's daughter. After all, aren't you the one who always saves females in distress . . . ?'

Maureen Mason was putting her face on. She never went over the top with her make-up, was not in the same league as the dear departed Lottie Crumpsall, but she liked to make the best of herself. At thirty-five, she was still an attractive woman, with near-black hair and eyes of a startling green. The Irish skin had remained fine, but it never reacted to the sun. So Maureen helped nature a little by applying mascara to lashes, plucking brows that had a tendency towards thickness, stroking a little rouge along cheek-bones.

She pouted, then stretched her lips, smoothed on a mere fingertip of rose lipstick. It probably wouldn't make any difference, anyway. He would be too engrossed in Sally Crumpsall's problems to notice an Irish flower in full bloom.

'I could go home,' she told her reflection. 'I could go back and get me a fine Irish farmer. But I'm stupid. I like my job and I love the man next door. Above all, I want to keep that baby out of reach of the Kerrigans.'

She pulled on a navy skirt, looked over her shoulder to judge the straightness of stocking seams. A pretty white blouse completed the picture once a small cameo was pinned at the neck. 'It's himself is the fool,' she told herself jauntily. 'Because I'm a woman in my prime. If he can't see that, then the man needs a white stick and help to cross the road.'

'Hello, Maureen?'

Oh God, it was Tom! 'Come in,' she said, her tone carefully controlled. If he'd arrived a minute earlier, she would have been undressed and talking to herself. Talking to herself about him. The thought of being semi-naked in the presence of Tom Goodfellow made her cheeks glow naturally beneath the film of applied colour.

'I want a word with you,' he said.

She carried on brushing her hair, looked at his image in the mirror. 'Yes?'

'I'm going away.'

Her heart sank. She felt sure he must have heard it hitting her diaphragm with a sickening thud. 'I see.'

'Just a few days, that's all. Rosie and Ollie are old, Maureen. So is Ivy. I wondered if you would keep a weather eye on the situation while I'm in London.'

Ah, London, was it? Did he have a family there – brothers, sisters . . . wife, children? 'I'll do my best, Tom. Mind, I do have to work, you know. Mr Heilberg's a splendid man, but I don't think he'd pay me for staying at home. Also, I'll be away to visit my family in a couple of weeks.'

'Joseph will help. I've spoken to him. Sally has a few days' holiday from school next week. Ruth will fill in at your shop in the mornings, then she'll watch Sally till Ivy gets back from work. Between you and Ruth, you can cover both situations. According to Rosie, this Gert person seems quite capable of kidnapping Sally. I've spoken to a lawyer, and there is little we can do unless a crime actually occurs. However, we must be watchful.'

Maureen laid down the brush, pushed her feet into navy court shoes. She had nicely turned ankles, and she felt his eyes brushing her legs as he spoke again. 'I really don't like the sound of Gert,' he continued. 'She is, after all, Lottie's sister.'

'And a Kerrigan,' she replied. 'That mother of hers was the biggest disgrace ever to come out of Ireland. I mind she went once to the doctor – she was pregnant, I think – and the doctor sent her home, told her to have a good wash before he would touch her. So she must have been entertaining some men of poor taste if they didn't mind the smell of her. Blood will out, Tom. They're bad daughters of a bad mother. Mind, Sally will be all right because she has a lot of her father in her.'

He stood in the doorway while she pulled on her jacket. If only he were free to ask this sweet woman to walk out with him. On the moors, she would look perfect, because looks as Irish as hers wanted wind, sun and space. With a breeze in her hair, she would be truly beautiful. Her attentions and excuses would not have become a problem if only . . . If only what? He needed to stop thinking, conjecturing. After all, things might change once he'd been to London.

'I've left my bag upstairs.' She squeezed past him, gave him the benefit of the subtler perfume she had bought for an occasion such as this one.

Freedom. Just a couple of syllables, yet he couldn't afford it. 'You're not married,' he whispered to himself. But he could not be convinced that a normal life was within his reach. 'You are fastened to a secret,' he murmured. Tom would never be able to marry unless his bride knew the whole truth. He was a man whose crime had not been a crime, yet the disgrace hung heavily about his shoulders. In order to contemplate marriage, he must force himself to pass on the burden. A woman like Maureen would take the problem on board, he felt certain of that. But could she or any other working woman consider a man of his so-called class?

She came down the stairs, handbag looped over an arm.

'Why do women always carry a bag?' he asked. 'After all, you aren't going far.'

She laughed. 'It's a symbol, I suppose. If I were going to ask for a loan of some butter, I'd leave my bag here. But it's a sign of . . . of formality, I'd say. When Sally's so-called auntie and uncle see how I'm dressed, they'll know we mean business.'

Tom stood back, allowed her into the street. He had learned the answer to another of life's small mysteries. A handbag was a statement of intent.

The parlour was cramped, even without Ruth Heilberg. That good woman had been sent off with Sally, because none of those present wanted the child to worry about what might happen here tonight. Ivy gazed across the small room, decided that Maureen Mason was definitely setting her cap at Tom. And so she should. They were both lovely people, both alone. She didn't want to think about losing Sally. If she kept her mind busy for these few minutes, then she might just hang on to some control.

Anyway, the Simpsons could be visiting their niece, no more than that. But then again, they'd never shown an interest before . . .

'Are you all right, Ivy?' Rosie, squashed on a horse-hair *chaise* between Tom and Ollie, looked smaller than ever.

'I'm ready for anything,' answered Ivy calmly. She noted that Tom had just risen and was moving to position himself behind Maureen's chair. He looked like a knight preparing to protect his damsel. So he was receiving Maureen's unspoken messages, then. Joseph Heilberg sat in a straight-backed chair against the wall. His eyes were closed, as if in prayer.

'Half past,' announced Maureen. 'Will they come?'

'They'll be here.' Ivy smoothed her hair, spread the skirt of her brilliantly white apron over her knees. 'Joseph knows them.'

Joseph Heilberg's eyelids flew open. 'I do indeed,' he said. 'The woman's a loud-mouthed person. She dresses to look like a girl of twenty. For her I feel sorry, because her man has a thirst. Him – well – that I should ever meet such a man again!' He shook his head. 'He drinks straight from the barrel, I think. We hear him coming home, Ruth and I. Such songs he sings, words I would never wish my Ruth to hear.'

Maureen leaned back in her chair. She could feel Tom's warmth, as if his aura reached out to caress her. 'There are too many of us,' she said. 'I can't imagine the Simpsons getting past all of us.'

'Not while Ivy's alive.' There was a sombre note in Tom's voice, as if he had edged the words in funereal shades. 'We expect you to be among us for some years,' he added hastily. 'But should you die before Sally comes of age, the Simpsons' claim may be validated. After all, the woman is Sally's aunt.'

Ivy nodded slowly. 'She's an Aunt Sally, more like, summat to chuck things at. Her sister were the same, and we Aunt Sallied her all over Trinity Street.' She looked at Rosie. 'Got your posser handy, love?'

'I have.'

'As usual,' moaned Ollie. 'And don't I know it.'

Rosie gave her husband a look that was meant to be mild. 'It's the running away from me and the posser keeps you alive, Ollie Blunt. Gives you plenty of exercise.'

Tom smiled. 'There must be no violence,' he told them. 'If any one of us hits out, then Sally might be taken away to an orphanage. The welfare people would have a case.'

'Never,' said Ivy, her hackles preparing to rise. 'I've never laid a finger on that child.'

'Behave yourself, Ivy.' Tom Goodfellow was one of the few who could frame such an order without fear of recrimination. 'We shall be calm and collected.'

They remained outwardly composed for several further minutes, then Mr Heilberg spoke up again. 'He'll be in the public house,' he declared. 'Sober, he is quiet, but in drink – ah.' He waved a hand downward to express his opinion of Bert Simpson. 'Yes, he will be drinking beer. She, also, may need what people call the courage of the Dutch.'

'Dutch courage, Joe,' advised Ivy wearily. She wasn't correcting him, but she had played no small part in Joseph's mastery of the English language, which fact had, in its turn, played no small part in the man's tendency to pepper his speech with colloquialisms. 'I wish they'd hurry up.'

'So do I,' grumbled Ollie. 'My stomach thinks my throat's cut.'

'He's had near enough half a plate-size tater pie with peas and onion gravy,' snapped his wife. 'There's no road he'll starve – unless we start depending on what he grows in that there wilderness he's made at the back of our house.'

Ollie bridled, but refused to be drawn on this occasion.

It was no use arguing among themselves while adversaries were about to knock at the door.

Maureen checked a hand on its way to her mouth, told herself she'd stopped nail-biting years ago.

'Happen they're not coming,' said Ivy. 'Happen seeing Rosie once was enough.'

'There's no sense in that,' muttered Ollie. 'Rosie is only dangerous when she's armed. Happen she didn't have the posser with her.'

Someone clattered a fist against the front door. Tom glanced at Ivy, saw nervousness lurking beneath a mask of bravado. 'I'll go,' he said. He strode out of the room, threw the outer door wide.

Each member held on to his or her breath, listened while Tom said, 'Yes? May I help you?'

'It's about the kiddy,' announced a second male voice. 'Come this way, please,' said Tom, his accent sounding as if it had been cut with great delicacy from lead crystal. He was followed into the room by Gert and Bert. The intruders ground to a halt when they saw the gathering. 'Oh,' said Gert feebly. 'We've only come to see our Sally.' Pale eyes scoured the room. 'And her's not even here,' she added.

Bert lingered in the doorway. He was small and plump with colourless piggy eyes and dark brown hair. 'Where is she?'

Ivy scoured the couple thoroughly, taking in as many details as her mind was capable of collecting. Gert was dismissed fairly quickly as a sight not worth looking at, all make-up, henna and too-tight clothing. But Bert was something . . . different. He carried a lot of spare lard, probably due to over-indulgence in beer, looked like an idle swine. Yet Joseph Heilberg had declared this man to be a labourer, a carrier of bricks, a mixer of mortar. His hands had signs of wear ingrained in the flesh, yet they were wrong. The wrong hands, thought Ivy. Aye, they were small, like the hands of a woman. He was weak, she decided. Weak, easily led astray, yet wily.

'Shall we come back another time?' ventured Gert.

'No.' The woman looked like a circus clown. Ivy folded her arms, leaned back in her chair and hoped that the palpitations would slow down in a minute. 'All I want to know is why you've never been before. I mean, they needed help. Your sister were about as much use as a dead dog, wouldn't fettle for nobody. As for our Sal, she were in rags till the day her mam buggered off.'

Gert cleared her throat. 'She's no good, our Lottie. Only she asked me and Bert to have Sally, like. We have seen the lass before, you know. We've seen her on the road after school. Only I've never spoke to our Lottie for years. This letter came out of the blue, from me sister, asking us would we mind Sally till Lottie sends for her to go to America.'

Ivy nodded. 'Lottie asked you to take our Sal just to spite me.' She moved her head, looked at all her neighbours. 'Tell this woman our Derek's dying wish,' she instructed the company.

Tom took up the cudgels. 'Derek asked us to look after Sally.'

Bert decided to have his say. 'Aye, well Derek's dead and Lottie isn't. It's what the living wants as matters. So we'll be taking her to live with us.'

Ivy's heart did a somersault, though her demeanour did not alter. 'What's the point of moving her up to Derby Road?' she asked. 'It's nobbut a spit from where she is now.'

Rosie was bridling. Ollie held on to his wife's arm in an effort to restrain her. 'Shush, love,' he whispered.

'We might not be stopping,' announced Gert. 'We've a chance of living-in jobs in a big house at the top of Wigan Road.' She glowered at Bert, hoped he'd have the sense not to mention the family for whom they'd be working. Andrew Worthington was not a favourite with the famous Ivy Crumpsall. 'The lass'll get plenty fresh air up yon, away from all the chimneys.'

Ivy rose to her feet, rested one hand on the mantelpiece. If these Simpsons had bothered to visit Sally in the past, they would have noticed a change in the place. In the centre of the shelf against which Ivy was leaning sat the clock from the kitchen. It was ticking happily, had been given yet another overhaul by a friend of Joseph Heilberg. There were clean lace curtains at the window, new rag rugs, a polished table with Maureen's aspidistra as a centrepiece. 'I'm Sal's granny,' she said softly. 'And she'll stop here with me. She's at Craddock Street School, and I reckon she should stop there instead of piking off to another school up Wigan Road.'

Gert and Bert looked round at all the faces in the room. There was Joseph Heilberg from the pawnshops – he was worth a penny or two, might have a bit of influence. Ivy herself was forbidding in the long black skirt, while the little woman on the couch was plainly ready to burst a blood vessel at any minute. Her husband was glaring at the Simpsons, as if he blamed this pair of intruders for Rosie Blunt's anger.

'Have you anything more to say?' asked Ivy, sarcasm trimming the words.

Gert glanced at Maureen, was immediately jealous. Maureen had the sort of beauty that needed little help from jars and bottles. She saw that Bert was looking in the same direction, felt like clouting him with her handbag. 'We've no kiddies of our own,' she said lamely.

Tom cleared his throat. 'I have no car, but I would not consider stealing someone else's.'

Gert could not help answering this posh bloke. She'd heard about him with his airs and graces, was determined not to be taken in by his patronizing manner. 'Who said owt about cars?' she asked snidely. 'We're not after a car. All we want is to carry out the wishes of my sister.'

Tom nodded. 'Would you consider your sister to be a woman who makes all the right decisions in life?'

Gert and Bert glowered at the speaker.

'Well?' asked Tom.

'No,' replied Gert begrudgingly. 'She's one for the men, I'll give you that. But she's Sally mother and—'

'The woman were never a mother,' snapped Rosie. 'She were more of a bloody liability.'

'We cared for Sally all through the war,' added Maureen. 'Especially once the Americans were here. Weren't we the ones who took her in after the sirens went? Weren't we the ones who fed her? So don't be coming here to tell us about motherhood. And I never noticed you around here when Sally wanted a bit of bread and jam.'

Bert pulled at his wife's arm. 'That one's old.' He nodded his head in Ivy's direction. 'She'll not reign long, Gertie. We'll get what's rightfully ours in time.'

Ivy all but exploded. 'Rightfully yours?' she shouted. 'You make our Sal sound like something that's been left in a will, an ornament or summat. This is a little girl, not a bloody set of pots and pans.'

Tom held up a hand, spoke quietly. 'Sally is no-one's property,' he said. 'She is a seven-year-old girl who needs her grandmother.'

Bert dragged Gert to the door. 'Come on,' he begged. 'Our time'll come.'

But Gert wanted the last word. 'When you die, Mrs Crumpsall, that kiddy will go to her nearest. And that's us.'

'In that case, our Sal is poor in more ways than one. Shut the front door behind you.' Ivy felt sick, but she maintained her dignity.

When the Simpsons had left, a dense silence hung over the meeting. Each member present felt uneasy, worried about Sally's future. It was Ivy, of course, who summed up everyone's mood. 'He's a queer feller,' she announced. 'And his wife's a bloody fool.'

All were in agreement, though no-one said a word.

FIVE

Two things kept Prudence Spencer-Worthington alive.
One was her love for Victor, the thirty-year-old product of
her marriage; the second was the hatred she felt for
Andrew Worthington. Her daily encounter with each end
of the emotional spectrum often left her drained, yet she
continued doggedly as mistress of Worthington House, a
detached piece of Victorian ugliness that squatted at the
top of Wigan Road.

Deep inside Prudence's heart there lingered two hopes.
She wanted Victor to be happy and successful, longed for
the day when Andrew would be brought down. For these
ends, Prudence remained alive, healthy in body if not in
mind, and extremely lonely. Worthington House entertained few visitors as its atmosphere was often repellent.

She lingered over the piano, could still feel reverber-
ations from the series of dissonant chords she had just
played. She was a good pianist, had been an adequate
singer, but sometimes, she took her anger out on the
keyboard. Another girl at the door today. Another child
with a child in its belly. The girl's father had twisted his
cap in fretful hands, had shed a tear or two. 'We've spoke
to Mr Worthington,' he had said, his voice trembling with
a mixture of emotions. 'And he told us to go away. My
little girl – she's nobbut sixteen – what am I to do? He
swears blind it weren't him, missus, says it were likely one
of the carders. It'd be our word against his, you see.'

Andrew Worthington's wife crossed the room and
studied herself in the overmantel mirror. At fifty-four, she
remained a remarkably attractive woman. The ash-blond

hair was greying, yet the threads produced by age were not thick and wiry, but fine, silvery. She was a rounded woman, had always tended towards plumpness, but she had maintained a definite waist and firmly rounded breasts and hips. Love was supposed to keep a woman young, she thought. In her case, all affection was aimed not towards her spouse, but in the direction of another man. That other man was twenty-four years her junior, and she was his mother.

She hadn't needed to ask the whys and wherefores today, hadn't needed to ask for years. The girl on the doorstep had been bullied or bribed, was yet another of Andrew Worthington's victims. The story was so old that it had engraved itself on Prudence's heart. Girls who appealed to the beast were often young, sometimes as young as fourteen or fifteen, usually thin. He would take one at a time 'under his wing', would get the chosen one to do a bit of shopping for him after her shift. At the end of a working day, he would pounce. No-one had ever charged him. No policeman had been brought in, as all the girls, thus far, had refused to talk. 'Soon,' she prayed aloud. The answer would arrive in the form of unionism, she knew that full well. The unions were spreading, would reach Paradise eventually.

Prudence sat down, folded her hands, dreaded another evening in this house. Once Victor had moved out, she had tried to leave, had yet to manage the move. The younger Worthington had not followed his father into the factory, yet he was employed by Paradise, among other companies, as accountant. Victor had his own small accountancy firm in town. He handled the financial affairs of several businesses, including his father's, and was therefore detached from the filth and noise that was cotton, from the filth and noise that was his father.

She had given money to the waif on the doorstep. The poor little thing's father had been pathetically grateful. Andrew Worthington was a shrewd man, chose his targets carefully. The girls he used were from poor families with limited education. Some were orphans, others lived in houses owned by Worthington, a few parents accepted what happened to their female children as part and parcel of keeping a job in the Paradise Mill.

Prudence smiled grimly. Times were changing. The blustering buffoon she had married was still a piece of Victoriana, was still clinging to a life that had died a natural death before the end of the Great War. He had even denied his own contempt for womankind by insisting on naming his son after the queen who had occupied the throne until the century's turn. Now, Andrew's come-uppance must be due, Prudence mused. The workers of the 1940s were more vigorous, more outspoken. Soon, the spinners and weavers would unite in spite of the ogre's objections. Soon, soon, he would fall from his own self-made throne.

Today's child had been a sad, shy thing. Tomorrow's might just fetch the law. As for the shame of it all – Prudence had given up on worries of that sort thirty years ago. No young wife wanted the world to learn of her husband's bestiality, yet she had been forced to accept long ago that she was married to a creature that defied description. Everyone knew about him; everyone feared and hated him. All she needed was for one voice to be heard in court and he would be gone for ever.

She picked up a book, flicked pages, could not immerse herself in Charles Dickens just now. Dickens was a bit wordy for an unhappy and preoccupied woman, so she turned to *Good Housekeeping* and read an article about fashions in the nursery. Victor would probably get married soon. He had been courting the very correct Miss Margaret West for some four years, had brought her home several times. The piece about infants' clothing made Prudence realize how near she was to becoming a grandmother. Perhaps Margaret might improve in time, become approachable, less starchy. Perhaps Margaret might invite her mother-in-law to live with . . . No. That would never happen.

She tossed aside the magazine, closed her eyes and remembered Victor as a child. He had been so round and plump, pretty, funny, warm. He wasn't like his father, she told herself firmly. All those little escapades were in the past, surely? She would not consider the difficult times. Instead, she conjured up in her mind's eye memories of Bournemouth, Southport, Morecambe. His little fat legs running in the sand, tears when he had been urged to leave behind a favourite beach donkey, a tantrum when the tide swamped his castle . . .

The particular girl who had tried to destroy Victor had been a loose type, had been asking for trouble, she told herself determinedly. That female had not been comparable with Andrew's collection of victims. Oh no, the little madam who had accused Victor had been trying to get her hands on the Spencer-Worthington fortune. Victor was not a bit like his father, not at all. Andrew Worthington's face had blazed with a mad triumph when the girl's father had appeared. 'Your son tried to force himself on my girl,' the tobacconist had roared.

Prudence opened her eyes and stared into the grate. Two thousand pounds had changed hands when the tobacconist had threatened to bring charges. Not one of Andrew Worthington's casualties had spoken up. But poor Victor, who had made just one or two mistakes, had almost been brought to book. That fire at school – surely the other boys had goaded him into playing with chemicals? And didn't all young people get involved in stealing apples? No, no, he wasn't like his father, could not possibly be another monster. She had brought him up so carefully. Best to concentrate on happier times, she thought. Victor was a good boy, a lovely man. So she dreamed of grandchildren and of happy times. Because Victor was a good boy, really . . .

*   *   *

The line seemed endless. Tom Goodfellow stood in the middle of the road and watched Londoners queuing for potatoes. It was 1947, and there wasn't a spare halfpenny in sight. This was victory, thought Tom. This was a sure sign that the Allied Forces had won the war. After all, wasn't there food aplenty, weren't people showing signs of health and vigour? The only symptom of life in the placid line of humanity was a squabble between two women. 'I was here first,' shouted a tall, fat female with a child clinging to her tattered coat.

'No,' yelled her opponent, a spare creature with very little hair. 'I been standing here since the crack of dawn.'

The untidy crocodile of people waited not for tobacco or some exotic fruit from overseas. No. They hung around and argued over the humble potato. He considered separating the two warriors, changed his mind. Only once had he come between Rosie Blunt's temper and her intended victim. After that unhappy occasion, he had avoided intervention between people of the female persuasion – unless blood actually flowed. Women were angry and in pain. They had lost their men, or were nursing husbands and sons through wounds physical and mental. Most of the former scars would have healed, though psychological damage lingered, no doubt.

Tom took a bus across the city, then walked down Regent Street. Things looked a bit better here until he looked closely. Navy pinstripes and bowlers were dotted about but, in doorways and alleys, a few shabby figures lurked. These were not young men, were not the immediate casualties of the second war. A one-legged chap on expertly balanced crutches bared his gums at Tom, held out a hand. 'Penny for a cuppa rosie, mister? Lost all three of me sons, I did. Died in France.' So the second war had brought to the surface the poor who had survived the earlier abomination.

Tom jangled some coins in his pocket. The beggar was chattering on about battles he had fought almost thirty years earlier. 'Who's looking after you?' Tom asked.

The toothless grin spread across skin that was prematurely aged – surely this man could not be much older than fifty? 'The gel next door looks in most days. Got a flat, I have. Me house was flattened, see. They put me in a new place, but times is hard. Just a couple of pennies, guv.'

Tom handed over a shilling, hurried along. The beggar had probably been forced out of his new, custom-built home by boredom, he thought. Here, in the city, the middle-aged man saw and heard all the bustle he had lost when his house was razed. And, if his sons had lived, he would not have suffered such dreadful loneliness.

Another group of men chatted on a corner, their ageing cleaned-and-pressed-for-the-occasion coats festooned with medals from the First World War. From snatches of conversation, Tom gathered that the company was preparing a celebration of some kind, a few drinks to mark earlier empty triumphs in fields of blood and clay. How many of them had been deprived of sons and homes this time round? Proudly, they displayed the shining proof that they, too, had fought for freedom. Tom smiled at the veterans, crossed the road and walked towards the lawyers' offices, his head full of memories that were not all savoury.

An unfamiliar anger bubbled in Tom's breast. He had lost so many friends, had visited men without legs, men whose faces had been destroyed, whose bodies had been seared in burning cockpits. His own crash during one of many training flights had been a mere hiccup compared to some disasters. This morning, Tom had read the news. The Chancellor of the Exchequer was telling parliament that rations must be reduced even further. Twopenceworth of tinned meat a week was the new allocation, though a little more sugar was being sifted through to the populace, and each holder of a ration book was now allowed five ounces of sweets each week.

'Is that Group Captain Goodfellow?'

Tom ground to a halt, swivelled and saw a man whose features rang a slightly muffled bell. 'Hello?' he said uncertainly.

'Bombardier Clarke, sir. Known as Nutty in common parlance, because I—'

'Because you would have bombed the whole globe for a bag of peanuts. Good to see you, old chap.' The 'old chap' was about twenty-five. He had no hair, as it had been removed by fire. Gloves hid heat-scarred hands, while Nutty's baldness was covered by a bruised trilby-type hat of indeterminate colour.

'Battle of Britain hero, eh?' remarked Tom. 'I seem to remember visiting you in hospital. What are you doing these days?' He needed no answer, had noticed the barrow parked at the edge of the pavement.

'This and that,' answered Nutty. 'Me hands isn't up to much, but I'm being retrained. Used to be a carpenter, sir. They're teaching me how to use the tools again, only it's a slow job, so I sell a few bits and pieces between classes.' He nodded towards his cart, then faced Tom once more. 'The wife's just had twins and my mum's fading fast. Had a rough war, my mother. Got bombed out and lost Dad in the blitz. How's the old leg, sir?'

Tom straightened his spine. 'It aches in the rain, that's all. They should have let me stay on, but they pensioned me off as disabled.' He felt something akin to shame when he considered his own accident, because many others were scarred beyond measure. 'Will you accept a gift for the babies?' he asked. Nutty Clarke. Of course. The full memory flooded back in glorious colour. Nutty had been the madman, the one who would have flown solo to Germany with a single bullet in his gun. 'Just let me at 'im,' Nutty used to curse. 'Bleeding 'Itler? I'll bleeding do for him.'

Nutty pondered, nodded. 'That's very kind of you, sir.'

Tom smiled, saw the tic at the corner of Nutty's mouth, noticed a slight tremor in the young man's hands. This chap's nerves were stretched to breaking point. The airman had coped with the war, with his wounds and his scars, but now, reaction had set in. Would he ever plane wood again? wondered Tom. 'I'll be back in a few minutes,' he told his companion.

Tom sped up some stairs to his solicitors' office, pushed open a door, demanded to see Peregrine Fotheringay.

'Name?' asked a woman with tight lips and a ploughed forehead.

'Goodfellow.'

She pored over a tome. 'Your appointment is for ten-fifteen.' She made much of looking at the clock, referred to her watch for confirmation. 'You are early and your appointment is with Mr Matthew Marsh.'

If she would only keep her eyebrows in their proper place, the skin above them would be less furrowed, he thought. And she had been over-enthusiastic with the tweezers, had left two very thin lines of hair that did nothing to enhance her unfortunate appearance. He leaned over her desk. 'Perry is a friend of mine,' he said sweetly. 'If he isn't busy, please tell him I'm here.'

He sat down in the waiting area, thought about the human tragedies hidden behind Chancellor Dalton's words. More than half the money loaned by America had been spent, and there was little hope of repayment. The British had been warned that a further period of austerity could be expected, that the months to come might be worse than the war years. A worldwide shortage of dollars was leaving soldiers, sailors and airmen with precious little beyond the training schemes thought up by the Labour government. Attlee was under threat of being ousted by Bevin, and many older members of parliament had collapsed into illness under the strain of running a bankrupt country. Germany, Tom decided, had done very well . . .

'Tom!'

The two shook hands, clapped each other on the back. 'I'm here to see the bigwig,' said Tom. 'Have I been cut off for ever? Have they found a way of depriving me of Mother's money?'

Peregrine laughed over-heartily. 'Nothing like that.' He glanced at the receptionist. 'Make yourself scarce for a few secs, Joyce. Go and have a cup of tea.'

Tom looked his friend up and down, decided that Mr Fotheringay's dress sense had deteriorated even further. Peregrine was an oddity, probably felt forced to be different because of his name. Tom grinned, sympathized. Goodfellow was not a handle he would have chosen, either, though he'd never bothered to change it. 'Have you a few pounds?'

Without hesitation, the lawyer rooted in various pockets of a suit that might have fitted a man twice his size, came up with a squashed sandwich, two bus tickets and a five-pound note. 'This do?' he asked.

'Thanks.' Tom dashed down the stairs, gave the fiver to Nutty. 'My address.' He thrust a bit of paper into Nutty's hand. 'Don't hesitate to get in touch. Let me know how you and your wife are faring, and the little ones, too. Go home now. Go and look after your family.'

Nutty gulped, folded up the money and the scrap of paper. 'You always was a gent, sir.' Despite the fact that neither man was suitably dressed, the rear gunner saluted the officer. 'Thank you.'

To save further embarrassment, Tom said goodbye, then went back inside. It would have been dreadful if those wet eyes had spilled into Regent Street. Nutty could go and cry in dignified solitude now.

Peregrine was on the landing. He reached out a hand to impede Tom's progress. 'Hang on for a sec. I shouldn't tell you, but it might save you a shock when old Matthew sends for you. Matthew's bedside manner is non-existent. Take a deep breath.' He paused for a second. 'There's no way of saying this gently, so I'll come straight out with it. Lady Sarah is dead.' He reached out again and steadied his friend. 'She took her own life, Tom.'

112

The world was going completely mad, then. Sarah had been a wonderful girl, a credit to her family. Until . . . Until Tom's brother had altered her life beyond repair. 'I'm still not sorry,' he told his friend, though the timbre of the words betrayed a degree of uncertainty. 'I . . . did the right thing.'

Perry nodded. 'Of course you did. Anyone decent would have acted in exactly the same way. The fact that you didn't manage to save your brother is irrelevant. You saved Lady Sarah.'

'Yes. And she killed herself.'

The receptionist poked her corrugated face on to the landing. 'Mr Marsh will see you in ten minutes,' she told Tom.

Perry glanced at the clock. 'I must leave you now,' he said. 'Stop feeling guilty, Tom. I'll try to catch up with you later. Things to do,' he muttered vaguely before stumbling towards his own door.

Had the situation been different, Tom might have laughed out loud at Peregrine's caperings. How on earth did such a scatterbrain manage within the strait-laced architecture of British law?

The view from the window was dull, just some courtyards and an expanse of dirty sky. He picked up a 1945 magazine, a ragged piece of literature whose skeletal construction spoke volumes about the paper shortage. On the cover, thousands of people waved flags and shouted words that were frozen for ever by the camera's lens. Sarah. No, he would not think of that . . . He sat down, stared at the photograph.

Jon stood at the foot of the stairs. 'He did it,' he screamed at the governess. 'He wrote those words on the blackboard, Miss Simms. He tore up your papers and locked the cat in the cellar.'

Miss Simms was no fool. She wore small, wire-rimmed spectacles and sensible black skirts. 'Thomas would not do such a thing,' she replied. Miss Simms had little time for the wayward and stubborn Jonathan.

'I hate you,' screamed the son and heir of Goodfellow Hall.
'I hate everybody.'

Joyce entered the room via a squeaky inner door, her brow smoother, as if she had been comforted during her brief absence. 'Are you all right?' she asked, the tone almost kind.

'Yes.' He wasn't all right, though there could never be any help for him, could there? Could there? He must not give up hope.

Jon went through infancy, childhood, puberty and young manhood with the same attitude, the same contempt he had shown to that long-ago governess. At school, he even organized a gang of youths who stole property and frightened people just for fun. 'Expelled?' roared his father. 'Expelled, you say?'

As if disturbed by that blustering echo from long ago, Tom jumped and looked across at Joyce. She was typing, one eye on him and the other on her work. He had killed his brother. No, no, he had simply failed to save him. Whatever, this ugly woman was right to watch him. Something was happening to him, because he was reliving times long gone, events that had been buried with Jonathan. Sarah now. Poor Lady Sarah had been returned to the soil from which mankind had supposedly risen. Tom tried to smile at the secretary/receptionist, managed, just about, not to scream with the pain and noise inside his head. Watch over me, he said silently. I think I'm going mad.

No-one ever knew how to handle Jonathan.

The boys' mother, Lady Goodfellow, died after years of abuse from the fool she had married. Although she was never physically beaten, she was a victim of a different and slightly more subtle cruelty. Lord Goodfellow had an eye for the ladies, and his paramours, with or without their legal spouses, were often flaunted at dinner parties and weekend shoots. Tom's mother simply faded away, as if she had shrivelled and dried into non-existence beneath her husband's contemptuous gaze.

'Did you hear me, Mr Goodfellow?'

There was tenderness and concern in the woman's face.

He reached out and touched a dry, sandpapery hand. Many females had hands like these, because decent soap was still hard to find. 'Sorry,' he mumbled. 'Miles away.'

'Coffee?' she repeated.

'No. No, thank you.' He needed her to stay, didn't know why he needed her. 'Life has a habit of catching up, doesn't it?' he remarked.

She folded her other hand over his, held on tightly. 'I know,' she whispered. 'If you want anything, you only need to ask.'

Tom leaned back into the chair, gripped the edges of the seat with fingers that were suddenly cold and stiff after being deprived of Joyce's touch. He watched her as she returned to her tidy desk, breathed a sigh of relief because she was staying. She was strong, he thought.

Lord Goodfellow exercised his droit de seigneur many, many times, laughed when his older son followed suit. 'Bloody buffoon,' he roared at Tom. 'Stop complaining about your brother. At least he has some spunk. Somebody's got to break in these damn fool women.' Tom tried to comfort the weeping girls, the anger-crazed parents. He never quite managed that, though. The young creatures were usually married off quite swiftly to some suitable lad on one of the estate farms.

'Shouldn't be long now, Mr Goodfellow. Just a couple of minutes.' There was misery in his face. It was as if he were in two places at once, as he seemed not to hear the words.

Tom looked at her without seeing her.

It was drink that finally pushed Jonathan Goodfellow over the edge. Sober, he was unpleasant. Drunk, he was positively dangerous. Right from the start, Jonathan Goodfellow had reacted strangely after stealing wines from his father's cellar. In drink, he was wild, uncontrollable and unnaturally strong.

On that fateful day, Jon had consumed two bottles of very old Mouton Cadet. Tom, who was often a victim of his brother's cruel jibes, decided to absent himself. Goodfellow Hall was a large building, but nothing was big enough to contain the heir when he was drinking. There was no hiding place inside the house, so Tom made for the grounds.

Joyce licked an envelope, sealed the flap, applied a stamp. The man in the chair had gone white beneath a layer of tan. Any minute now, he would surely slump to the floor in a dead faint.

As if reading her thoughts, Tom spoke. 'Make my apologies . . . I need . . . some air.' He stumbled to the landing.

The frenetic pace of Regent Street gave Tom no comfort, but that poor woman did not deserve to see a man torturing himself in this way. He missed her, felt totally alone, but he leaned against the wall and allowed his mind to open fully.

He came through from the kitchen garden after a short conversation with a groundsman. The balustrade was on higher ground, and he climbed the steps, stood facing a wide sweep of lawn. Beyond the small and carefully sculpted maze, he glimpsed a flash of colour, imagined a shriek. No, no, someone really was screaming. Tom's temper finally snapped. His brother, drunk as the lord he aspired to be, was no doubt committing another foul crime.

Tom ran, skirted the maze, ground to a halt a few yards from the lake. 'Jon!' he yelled. 'Jon!'

The woman's clothes were torn. Her upper body was naked and her face was a mask of terror. As if mesmerized by the horror of it, Tom froze. He watched while his brother picked up the woman and tossed her like a broken doll into the lake. The water was deep, full of giant carp and underwater weed.

It was then, just after the water broke loudly to receive the victim, that Jonathan's wine-soaked body stumbled into the lake.

Tom was not a strong swimmer. Anaesthetized beyond rational thought, he jumped absently into the icy mass, his heart suddenly beginning to pound with panic. What was he doing? He could scarcely save himself . . .

Her arms circled his neck as he turned and looked for land. A fish brushed past his face, seeming to mock his inadequacy. With lungs like saturated sponges, Tom fought for life, dragging behind him and often beneath him the inert body of a woman who might already be dead. She no longer clung to him. He felt her essence draining away, as if the lake were actually feeding on its human sacrifice.

She wasn't dead. While water poured from his own throat, he pummelled her torso until she heaved and coughed. It was only afterwards, as he thanked his lucky stars, that two facts hit him hard. The half-naked woman was Lady Sarah Collingford, and the lake's surface was glassy smooth. Jon could not swim at all.

Help arrived. Lady Sarah was covered and carted back to her home. The water was dragged until Jon's body lay exactly where the daughter of an earl had recently come back to life. But Jon never breathed again.

A grim silence emanated from the Collingford estate, and no representative of that family attended Jon's funeral. Tom's father, after burning out his temper by turning on his one remaining son, took refuge in the very substance that had killed his heir. Lord Goodfellow's anger was fuelled not by guilt and sorrow, but by impatience and malt whisky. His older son had committed three unforgivable crimes. Jon, while in his cups, had mistakenly raped a lady rather than a labourer's daughter, had been caught in or after the act, had died carelessly and needlessly.

After a while, Tom Goodfellow simply left home.

'Are you ill, sir?'

Tom shook himself into the here and now, looked into the face of a bowler-hatted city man. 'I'm better now, thank you.' Strangely, he was better. Perhaps he had purged himself, perhaps the memories had paid one last, brief visit before leaving him in peace.

The man pointed a folded umbrella towards the pavement and strode away.

Yes, Tom was all right. Sarah, too had been settled for a

while, had married, he understood, had borne children. But something had died in Sarah that day. Tom had saved her body, but the emotional damage had persisted. Tales of declines and rest cures had been whispered round the Hampshire dinner tables. And now, the poor woman had taken her life.

Careless of the time, Tom wandered about until he found a Lyons', then sat nursing a cup containing what tasted like mud. He nibbled at a margarine-smeared scone, returned with flagging feet to Regent Street.

Joyce looked up, smiled encouragingly. Perry appeared, an expression of concern lengthening his usually cheerful features. 'Are you up to seeing the old boy, Tom?'

Tom nodded, surprised to find himself feeling almost cheerful, almost cleansed. 'Yes, I'm fine, thank you.' He allowed himself to be guided to the senior partner's door. 'Thanks,' he said to Perry. 'For trying to prepare me.'

When Tom entered Matthew Marsh's room, he thought he was alone in a recently abandoned battle zone. Then a minuscule creature leapt into view and peered over a pile of books. 'Sorry,' he said before sweeping the tomes to one side. 'Research, precedents et al. Briefing the bar. Old Bailey. Good chap, innocent.'

Tom realized within a very short time that he was in the presence of yet another extremely untidy and scatter-brained genius. But this one's words were so valuable that he did not speak in sentences. Tom refused a cigarette, sat in a chair that was deliberately low. He suspected that the legs of the man opposite were dangling about a foot from the floor, as the lawyer's chair was a tall one. Sarah. He was going to get the details any minute now.

'Still living up north?'

'Yes. Cheaper, you see. Can't afford much.' He might as well play the same staccato game. 'Bolton.'

'Quite.' Papers were shuffled for a second or two. 'Lord Goodfellow. Hampshire.' He searched the table for Tom's father, failed to find him. 'Wants to see you.'

'Why? There's no love lost.'

'Quite. Nevertheless. Papers, papers. Ah. Well. Inheritance, so forth. Brother dead, sister gone abroad. Just you left. Wants to see you.'

'Is he ill?'

'No idea. Instructions, you see. Client of . . .' He threw a pile of books to the floor, extracted a crumpled leaf of fragile paper. 'Here. Chatworth and Chatworth of Mayfair.'

'Yes, they are my father's lawyers.'

'Quite.' He pushed the letter across the table, almost fell off his perch, wriggled back to safety. 'Read it. Might as well.'

'Quite,' said Tom with all the sarcasm he could muster. If this chap said 'quite' again, his client would probably scream.

The letter asked Marsh, Marsh and Fotheringay to convey to their client . . . 'Lord Goodfellow wishes to see his son Thomas . . . the regrettable past . . . Thomas is next in line . . .'

Tom threw the letter back in the direction of Matthew Marsh. 'Why didn't Fotheringay deal with this? He is my personal solicitor.'

'Friend of yours, young Peregrine. This needs . . . er . . . detachment. Go home, Goodfellow. Father needs you.'

Tom shook his head. 'Not yet. I'll go when I'm ready.' And that would be never.

Another document saw the light of day. 'Ah,' mused the tiny man. 'Collingford's legacy. Three thousand pounds.' He peered across at Tom. 'Lady Sarah . . . very sad. Took her own life. Collingford died. He was her father, don't you know. Shock of daughter's death finished him. Legacy by way of thanks to you for . . . services rendered.'

Tom Goodfellow closed his eyes, saw his brother throwing the daughter of an earl into the lake. But this time, the pictures did not hurt. He thought about Andrew Worthington, compared him to Sir Peter and Jonathan Goodfellow. The gentry, he mused, had as many black sheep as—

'Goodfellow?'

Tom tried to ignore the interruption, sought his train of thought, caught a different one. He hadn't wanted thanks from Sarah's father, hadn't wanted anything. And he needed to get back to Bolton, longed to be at home in the place he had made for himself.

'Goodfellow?'

'I suppose the old man wants me to apologize for saving Lady Sarah Collingford instead of Jon. Jon was a brute. Do you know what my father said when he learned what had happened?'

Matthew Marsh made no reply.

'After telling me that I should have let the girl drown, he informed me that my brother had been a fool. Jon was a fool because he had attacked a woman of breeding instead of sticking to his usual prey. Had Jon killed a housemaid, that would have been acceptable. But my father's biggest worry was not the loss of his elder son, oh no. He was not concerned about the dead. The fact that I had allowed Sarah to live was my biggest sin. Sarah Collingford might have brought trouble to our door, you see.'

Tom pushed back his shoulders. 'As you are well aware, when Mother died, she left a small amount of money in trust for me and for Jon. Both portions are now mine. At twenty-one, when my fund became available, I left home. That was many, many years ago, Mr Marsh. For all those years, your firm has handled my monthly income. You have also forwarded to me each month a letter from my father, and I have burnt the lot without opening a single one. I have no intention of returning to Goodfellow Hall.'

Matthew Marsh mopped his forehead with a white handkerchief. 'Did my best,' he remarked. 'Did what was asked, good day to you, sir.'

Tom rose, picked up his hat, made for the door. His whole life had been ruined by that one day when Jon Goodfellow had slaked his lust from the wrong barrel. Tom had never married, had wanted no children, because Goodfellow blood was tainted. His father had been a rake in his youth, and his brother had been a swine since birth. The only saint in the family was Patricia, his only sister. Patricia was also in disgrace, as she had run off to Africa with a group of missionaries. She, too, had remained single.

Lady Sarah had married, though. Would she have been happy and sane if Jon hadn't touched her? Were her children well and cared for? he wondered. Was Sarah's husband still alive? She would have been into her middle years. Why had she waited so long before making an exit?

Perry lingered in the reception area. 'All right, Tom?'

'I suppose so. Father wants me home.'

'Yes. He guessed that you weren't reading his letters, I'm told. Poor old chap has gout, don't you know. Gout and a troublesome heart.'

Tom shook his head. 'No heart at all, Perry. He killed my mother, you know. Drinking, gambling and fornicating his way all over Hampshire—' He cut himself off, because poor Joyce, her face bowed towards the desk, had turned an interesting shade of magenta. 'I'm going back to my real home,' he said.

Peregrine Fotheringay looked at his watch. 'I've a client in five minutes. Won't you stay for lunch?'

'No.' There was nothing for Tom here. There wasn't much up north, but at least he was settled with his pigeons and his little bits of writing. 'Three thousand pounds,' he said. 'From Sarah's father. I know exactly what I'm going to do with it.' He smiled. 'I'll use it to save some other little girl.' He gripped his friend's hand firmly. 'Tell me – why did Sarah kill herself?'

Perry had never lied to Tom. 'All her life, she was plagued by dreams, memories—'

'Of my brother?'

Perry shrugged. 'Who knows? But her sanity was in question for a long time. Before the . . . incident with Jon, she seemed perfectly all right, but one can never tell. The mind is a strange machine, Tom. I know—'

The door to Matthew Marsh's office flew open. 'Goodfellow?' yelled the senior partner. Without his high chair, he looked too small to be in charge of anything. 'Yes?' enquired Tom.

'Telephone.' He waved a hand towards his office. 'For you. Come.'

Tom wavered for a moment, was tempted to simply run. But he followed obediently, picked up the phone and spoke into it. 'Hello?'

'Thomas? This is Dr Fowler, your father's physician. You may not remember me after all these years, but I was your doctor, too, a long time ago.'

Tom paled, flopped into Matthew's high chair. What now? Was Father going to make another impassioned plea via the doctor?

'Your father died at nine-fifteen this morning. I contacted his lawyers who told me where to find you. I suppose . . . well . . . you are Lord Goodfellow now, Thomas.'

'I see.' He didn't know why he was trembling. No-one had loved Lord Goodfellow. But Tom quickly concluded that every human must be affected when a blood relative died – it was probably instinct.

'You will be coming home, sir?' asked the disembodied doctor.

'I think not,' he replied carefully.

The ancient doctor coughed, sounded chesty. 'There are a few small debts, you understand, then the funeral. We need a family member here. Lady Patricia gave up any rights she might have had, asked to be left out of your father's will. The fact is, none of us knows where she is. There are tenants here—'

'I have to be elsewhere,' muttered Tom. Good God! The implications began to home in. He had no intention of sitting with the Lords temporal in the upper chamber in his dead brother's place. He took a few deep breaths. 'Look, doctor. What do you expect of me?'

'Thomas, someone must attend to the details. There are thousands of acres of farmland, dozens of cottages, many tenants who will need attention. And I suppose you understand that there must be a burial?'

Tom sagged against the desk, felt hopelessness sweeping over him, darkening his soul. There was nothing else for it. He would have to go to Hampshire to clean up his father's mess. The doctor prattled on meaninglessly into Tom's inattentive ear.

Goodfellow. That was who he was. 'Gooders' at school, 'Good Egg' at college. He had grown used to it, yet wanted rid of it . . .

It was all the fault of Henry VIII anyway. A distant ancestor called Marchant had ridden with the king through the New Forest in pursuit of wild boar. After the long journey home, an evening meal and a lot of wine at Marchant Hall, old Hal, in festive mood, had dubbed some poor drunken soul Earl of Goodfellow. Folklore had it that the king, in his cups, had declared Marchant to be a French name. Thus the family decided to strip itself of a perfectly decent name, only to take on the silly-sounding 'Goodfellow'.

Tom replaced the receiver, looked at Matthew Marsh. 'Goodfellow isn't even a real name,' he informed that miniature person. 'We are Marchant, but a fat old chap with more wives than chins announced that we were good fellows, wonderful horsemen, too good to be saddled with a foreign name which translates into 'walking'. My dim and distant ancestor went down on one knee and had his name amputated. Still, I suppose he fared slightly better than Anne Boleyn. Good fellows all from Goodfellow Hall. And I can't even ride a wretched horse.'

When Tom had left, Matthew Marsh settled into the high chair and resumed his proper position in life. Things he had heard about titled people seemed only too true. Inbreeding, he decided, was a bad thing. Tom Goodfellow's brain had plainly turned to sawdust.

The year wore on while Maureen waited for the man of her dreams to return to Bolton. Many letters had arrived, some for her, some for the Crumpsalls, the Blunts and the Heilbergs. But none of these missives had carried an address until lately. At least there was now a poste restante to which replies might be sent. Hampshire. Maureen tapped the pen against her teeth, tried again to put down on paper some sensible words in sensible order.

In the end, she simply wrote what came into her mind. She advised Tom that Ivy was ill but improving, that the Blunts, the Heilbergs and Sally were well, that the pigeons thrived. 'I go to Ireland soon for my yearly visit,' she wrote in her best hand. 'As you know, everyone else here is old or busy – often both – so I do not know who will mind Sally properly while I am away.

'But I must go, as members of my family look forward to my holiday and I do not wish to disappoint them. However, my mind would rest better if you would come back to Paradise Lane for a week or so while I am away. Ruth Heilberg will be running the Wigan Road shop in my absence, so she will not have the opportunity to watch Sally.

'Rosie Blunt has enough to do looking after Ollie. He is becoming a little vague, has started to do his gardening in the night or at dawn. Ivy is recovering from a bad bout of bronchitis. There is little money left in number 1, so we are feeding the Crumpsalls, while Joseph Heilberg contributes by not charging rent.

'I trust that you remain in good health and that the family troubles you mention will soon be over.

'I remain your sincere friend,
Maureen Mason.'

She pored over her letter for several minutes, knew she might have written it better, decided that it would have to do. When the envelope was sealed, she went out straight away and posted it.

On the way back, Maureen called in at the Crumpsall house. Ivy had taken her son's place under the window, lay in a bed brought down by several hefty fellows from the Paradise breaking sheds. Arthur 'Red' Trubshaw stood at Ivy's head, mopped her brow with a damp flannel. He was a grand boy, thought Maureen. 'Where's Sally?' she asked.

'Gone for medicine,' replied Red.

Ivy grinned. 'Don't worry about me, lass,' she ordered. 'Get yoursen home to Ireland and have a good rest. I'll still be here when you get back, only I'll be hanging washing out by then.'

Maureen smiled. 'I hope so.' Hope cost nothing, she said inwardly.

'And I'll see to Sally,' said Red, his colouring suddenly matching his name. 'She'll catch no harm while I'm in charge, Mrs Mason.'

Maureen compounded Red's embarrassment by giving him a loud kiss on his forehead. 'You don't look the part, son, but you are an angel if ever I knew one.'

Red brushed away what he considered to be an assault on his person, tried at the same time not to smile. Somebody liked him. If he thought about it, quite a few folk had taken to him lately. When his skin had cooled, he spoke up. 'Don't tell nobody,' he begged the Irishwoman.

'Never.' She wet a finger, made a cross over her ribs. 'I hope to die should I ever betray you as a decent boy,' she said seriously.

'Thanks.' Being cock of the school wouldn't count if all the lads found out he was doing good deeds on the sly.

'Ollie will see to Tom's pigeons,' said Maureen. 'Red, you must take care of Gus. There's money for fish at my house. You come down and get it later, because I'm away home tomorrow.'

Ivy sighed. 'Eeh, I wish we could come with you, lass. Country air would do me and our Sal a lot of good. Never mind. Somebody's got to stop here and mind the fort.'

Maureen left number 1, used the key to enter Tom's house. She had kept his home clean and aired during his absence, had taken money from a cigar box to buy pigeon food. One of those crested envelopes had arrived just after Tom's departure, two lots of stamps on it. The small piece of paper that bore the Paradise Lane address had peeled away at one corner, allowing her to see that the letter's original destination had been in Regent Street, London, some firm of lawyers.

She picked up the letter yet again, weighed it in her hand, wondered where all the others were. Tom must have received at least two dozen of these. No, no, she must not give in to curiosity. Curiosity did kill, had almost killed the cat when Gus had got up onto the roof of number 1 some months ago. It had taken half the members of a mill shift and two ladders to get him down. Anyway, reading another person's mail was a sin. Against which commandment? she wondered. Probably 'thou shalt not steal'.

Maureen Mason let herself out of Tom Goodfellow's house, went home and finished her packing. Tomorrow, she would sail out of Liverpool and across a cruel sea that often showed its Irish temper. Yes, the stretch of water between England and Eire was aptly named. As was Tom Goodfellow . . .

She sat on the edge of her bed, wondered who on God's good earth Tom Goodfellow was. He was educated, well-spoken, a reader of books, a scribbler. Her conscience had not pricked when she had read some of his notes on the Industrial Revolution, as these had been on display for all to see. The pages had been numbered and some were missing, others simply torn. What was he doing up here when he was plainly a member of another class?

Maureen rose and went to the mirror. It would be as well if she looked for a husband in Ireland, because Tom Goodfellow might never return. Even if he did come back, he would still be well beyond the reach of an ordinary woman who worked in a pawnshop and collected oddities. Her eyes strayed round the room, lighted on broken dolls, a scratched table, some old books whose pages were deciduous.

Yes, she had better find a man at home.

Tom Goodfellow entered the house without knocking. He walked straight into the kitchen, found Ivy up to her elbows in flour. 'Oh, I'm so glad you're better,' he said. 'Where's Sally?'

Ivy threw down the rolling pin. 'Where've you been?' she asked. 'Ollie's halfway out of his mind – no – more like three-quarters by now, soft beggar. He keeps losing your bloody pigeons, running round after them. Even when they're not lost, he's stood outside his back door every night making funny noises, trying to sound like a bird. Rosie's shoes don't need her feet in them no more – they're that used to chasing him, they can do it on their own. And . . . and it's good to see you, lad.'

He smiled broadly. 'I can hear the improvement,' he remarked. No bronchitic woman could possibly make such a noise. 'But there's no time, Ivy. I want you to pack your bags – Sally's too – and come with me to Hampshire.'

Ivy's chin all but joined the rolling pin on her table. She closed her mouth with an audible snap. 'Don't talk so daft, Tom. Our Sal's got school. We can't go traipsing off to some highfaluting place . . . where did you say?'

'Hampshire. There are schools there, you know.'

'Never heard of it,' she said, almost truthfully. 'What's in Hampshire? What would I be doing at my time of life?'

'Having a rest.' His tone was firm. 'There's plenty of open land, a cottage if you want it. Or you can stay with me.' He could not imagine Ivy fitting in at Goodfellow

Hall. He could not imagine anybody fitting in to a place that was so unwelcoming. 'But if you do stay with me, no cleaning up, no mopping or washing or ironing.'

'And what would I do with meself?'

'Enjoy life,' he replied. 'Now listen. I've important business to attend to – my father has died.'

She shook her head sadly. 'Eeh, I'm sorry to hear that, lad.'

'Thank you.' He would tell her the full story when there was more time. 'I've brought a basket for Gus and some crates for the pigeons.'

Ivy gulped. 'Would we not be coming back, then?'

'Of course you'll be coming back.'

She studied him for several seconds. 'And you?'

He nodded. 'In time, I'll come. But it could be months, even years. There are a lot of things I need to do. And you must pack yourself up and get ready. We leave tomorrow morning.'

Ivy pondered. She had never allowed anyone to tell her what to do. At her age, she wasn't intending to change her colours and walk meekly behind a bloke. Even if he was a nice bloke. Also, deep inside herself, a feeling akin to fear was bubbling its way nearer the surface. 'I'm stopping where I am, Tom. So's our Sal. She's had a fair few shocks lately, so she wants settling.'

'She needs a holiday. So do you.'

Ivy picked up a dishcloth, flicked some flour from her person and onto the table. 'I'll think about it. Sally's round at the Heilbergs' doing sabbath with them, they'll all be sitting there waiting for the sunset.' She walked to the door, looked at her clock. 'I told her to come back once the candles were lit and the prayers had finished. Maureen said Friday night at the Heilbergs' is a bit like the Catholic mass – breaking bread and praying over wine, all that sort of stuff. Shall I go and fetch her?'

Tom chuckled inwardly. Nations had gone to war over the so-called differences between Gentile and Jew. The politicians and religious leaders should have visited Paradise for a word with Ivy, whose ecumenism catered for all-comers, not just for Christians. 'No, let her have her sabbath bread, Ivy. I'll go up for her later. Are you going to make me a cup of tea, or have you forgotten your Lancashire manners, Mrs Crumpsall?'

She flicked him with the tea towel. 'Listen, you. You've come right in the middle of me bacon and egg pie. Sit down and I'll put the kettle on.'

He hesitated, remained standing.

'What's up with you now?'

'I've someone with me. It's the chap who's taking the pigeons to Oakmead on a truck. He'd be very grateful for some sustenance.'

'Oh, wheel him in,' she said. 'I hope he likes ham butties.'

Bill Yeats did like ham butties. He did justice to three, washed them down with four cups of tea and most of Ivy's sugar. 'Thanks,' he said. 'Shall I get the birds now, M'lord?'

Tom could hear the clock ticking in the next room. He laughed over-loudly, clapped his companion on the back. 'Now, stop calling me names, Bill.' Ivy must find out the truth soon, but Tom didn't want to put her off by telling her now. She might just go away with a chap called Goodfellow, but a lord could merit very short shrift. 'Go and get them loaded,' he said. 'And you can sleep in number four tonight if you wish, or you can start back. Take plenty of food for the birds.'

Bill touched his forelock. 'Right you are, sir.'

Ivy Crumpsall stood in the middle of the hearthrug, a frown creasing her forehead. 'What's this "lordship", then?'

Tom shrugged. 'It's probably because I talk posh, as you so politely informed me a couple of years ago. A rose by any other name? Take no notice.'

She pondered, put down her cup, walked to the door. 'We've no suitcases,' she announced. She was beginning to admit to herself that a few weeks away might do Sally some good. And Ivy was tired, had worn herself out coughing for over a fortnight. Perhaps this was the time to give in gracefully. Well – perhaps not with complete grace . . . 'We'd look well arriving with brown paper parcels, eh?'

'I've cases outside in the car,' he told her.

Several moments passed while Ivy went outside. She re-entered the kitchen, a look of surprise on her face. 'Isn't that one of them there Rolly-Roycers?'

He kept his laughter in check. 'Yes, it's a Rolls-Royce Phantom. Used to belong to my father. Did you find the cases?'

She waved a hand behind her back. 'They're in the parlour.' She circled him, her eyes seemed to bore through his skull. 'You're gentry, aren't you? Not just educated, not some feller from a good school and college and all that. You're from money, eh? Old money?'

He nodded. 'Don't hold that against me, Ivy.'

Her eyes twinkled. 'Nay, no fear of that, lad. If you've money, there'll be plenty for our Sal to eat.'

He should have known that Ivy would put Sally first. 'You'll come, then?'

'I'll think about it, like I said before,' came the reply. 'I've never had a holiday, so it's time I did. And time our Sal did and all.'

Tom heaved a sigh of relief.

Ivy smiled at him, drained her cup, then went upstairs to sort out her things.

Sally was spellbound. Mr Heilberg wore a cap on the back of his head. Well, he wasn't so much wearing it as walking about in front of it. The small black circle was fastened to his hair with some of Mrs Heilberg's hairgrips. And he was talking in a funny language, too.

After a few moments of silent prayer, Mr Heilberg picked up two loaves and talked to them, then he broke bits off and passed some to his wife, some to Sally. 'Eat,' he said, a smile stretching his face. 'This is a sign of rejoicing, because we have food enough.'

Sally bit, chewed, drank some lemonade. 'What's a Jew?' she asked.

Ruth burst out laughing. The candlelight made her so pretty that her husband kissed her hand. 'Look at my Ruth,' he said proudly. 'The mother of my son and the mother of my house. Sally, take some fruit. Fruit is good for you.'

Sally chewed on an apple.

'We Jews have our own country,' explained Joseph. 'But Ruth and I are also Austrian and English. Soon, we will be citizens of England.' His face grew serious. 'Sally, a Jew is a person who lives with God all the time. Whatever we do, we do for God and for our families.'

'Same as us, then.' Sally took some more bread and ate it with her apple. 'We're supposed to be good. Preacher says God can see us all the time.'

'This, my young friend, is true,' agreed Joseph. 'Our actions and our words have God in them. Well, if we listen to God, that is. Some don't. Some wait till a man is unjustly interned, then they try to take his land and—'

'Joseph!' Ruth's eyes were round. 'Not now, not on the sabbath. Hatred is bad for the digestion.'

'Then Worthington should have an ulcer.'

Ruth patted Joseph's hand. 'That you should talk of this now when our candles are lit, when our guest visits our home to see the beginning of sabbath. Also, there are crumbs in your beard.'

But Sally had not been listening properly, because she had another problem in her mind. 'Well,' she began carefully. 'I don't want anybody looking at me all the time, even God. Like when I'm having a bath on a Saturday and . . . and other times when I want to be on me own.'

The little woman at the other side of the table giggled. 'This I understand, Sally. But God is never embarrassed. He loves us just as we are.'

'Good,' said the child. 'But I'd still rather be on me own when I go down the garden.'

A knocking at the door downstairs ended the conversation. Joseph bustled down to answer the door while Ruth found sweets for Sally. 'Do not eat these all at once.'

'Thank you. I won't, I'll save some for Red.'

'Ah.' The dark-haired woman came to sit next to this little blonde waif of whom she was extremely fond. 'This is your young man? This Red person? He is the one with the strange hair, very bright in colour.'

Sally placed the core of her apple on her side plate. 'We don't have boyfriends at my age,' she said wisely. 'I think you have to be in the mill before you get a young man.'

'Ah.' Ruth pondered for a while. 'You will go into the mill, Sally?'

The child shrugged. 'I suppose so. That's what happens. People go to school, leave school, go in the mill. Then they get married and the girls look after babies. When the babies get grown up, the mother goes back in the mill. Sometimes, the dad goes in the pit.' Her face clouded. 'My dad was in a pit.'

'Yes.' A change of subject might be a good idea, Ruth thought. 'Maureen is in Ireland. Soon, we should get another letter from her, because it is almost the end of her holiday.'

The door opened to reveal Tom Goodfellow. He smiled, came right inside and picked Sally up. 'Come along with me, young miss,' he said.

Joseph could not contain his excitement. 'They may go to Hampshire, Ruth,' he said. 'Ivy also. For a holiday and a nice rest.'

Sally touched Tom's face. 'Where's Hampshire?'

'Oh, Sally.' He shook his head. 'Not you as well. Tomorrow. I'll tell you tomorrow, because I've come a long way today.'

'Have you petrol?' asked Joseph.

Tom nodded. 'There was some stored. I'll write to you,

Joseph. There are things I need to explain in time.'

Joseph Heilberg touched his friend's shoulder. 'I wish you well in all you do. Come back to us, Tom. We'll be waiting.'

'I know.' He knew they'd be waiting. And he knew that he would be back. The burning question was when.

SIX

Andrew Worthington leaned back in his leather chair, thumbs hooked into a tailor-made waistcoat, eyes bulging even further than usual from beneath shaggy, grey brows. He was waiting, and he was not used to waiting.

He released one hand, used it to bring a gold watch from a pocket. It was three minutes past ten. Just to make sure, he looked at the clock on the wall, then walked across and opened the door, checked the time in the general office. It was now four minutes past ten. 'Nothing to do?' he roared at the nearest worker.

The woman looked at him, bowed her head and typed some nonsense. She had read the mail and now needed the boss's instructions. All the day-to-day letters had already been typed, but Mr Worthington should be dictating many replies this morning.

The mill owner's eye fell upon the general clerk-cum-teamaker, sweeper-up, dogsbody. 'Three teas, lad,' he roared. 'With matching saucers, but not the best china, on a tray, no spills, and half a dozen plain biscuits.'

'Yes, sir.' The boy ran off to do the master's bidding. It was usually like this when someone missed an appointment. Worthington's bad moods were legendary, but he was always particularly devilish when kept hanging about.

The much-hated man re-entered his office and stood at a window. Across the yard and through open gates, he could see the Paradise houses. As the owner of Paradise Mill, surely he should have Paradise Lane as well? His family had named the bloody street, yet he hadn't been able to get hold of title deeds, because a Jew-boy was holding on as tightly as any bulldog. Aye, and the man was a real foreigner, from Austria or some such highfaluting place.

Behind the houses lay the stretch of land that really annoyed Worthington. It was as well that it was hidden from view, because the failure to acquire the Paradise Recreation Ground was the biggest disappointment of his life. With the possible exception of his wife, he told himself. That wretched mare was more than a disappointment – she was a flaming disaster.

The tea arrived, stood cooling on his desk. Eight minutes and forty seconds past ten. He sat, drank his own tea, left the other containers to go cold. Perhaps Bert and Gert had not been such a good idea after all.

A timid tap at the door elicited no response. He waited for a firmer knock, boomed a reply. 'Come in, damn you!'

Bert Simpson entered, his wife two paces behind him. And that, thought the man at the desk, was a woman's correct position in life. He did not invite the visitors to sit. He simply stared at them for a few seconds, then went through the watch and clock ritual all over again.

'Sorry,' exhaled Bert. He was out of breath, anxious. 'We've been all over, sir,' he managed. 'Run all round the shops, Derby Road, Wigan Road. Paradise Lane's empty except for number two. So we didn't get to visit Ivy Crumpsall, 'cos she's gone and done a bunk.' He rubbed his arm. 'The old woman from next door – number two – chased me with a brush or summat, pretended she thought I were a gypsy or a tramp. And she knows me. There's no way she thought I were a gypsy, Mr Worthington. Any road,' he appended lamely. 'We can't get hold of Gert's niece, because she's not there no more.'

Gert stepped forward. 'There's furniture in number four,' she said. 'No sign of a flitting. But the posh feller's been gone a while and the Irishwoman's not at work in Heilberg's Wigan Road lock-up. Heilberg's wife's running it, but she said nowt when I asked her where everybody had gone. All the doors in Paradise are locked, except for the Blunts'.'

Worthington tapped his teeth with a pen. Nobody ever locked a door round these parts. If they went out, only a latch kept the door closed in case the milkman or the insurance man came for his money. Neighbours flitted in and out of one another's homes, left notes like 'Borrowed two spoons sugar, will give it back tomorrow'. What the hell was going on?

'Did the Blunts say anything at all?'

Gert shook her head. 'The man were stood at the front door making funny noises when we got there. Then his wife come to the door and told him off, said all the pigeons had gone away to live with Tom down south. Tom's the posh bloke from number four.'

'The man of mystery,' said Worthington. 'So. What do I do with the pair of you now? You understand the conditions of our agreement?'

'Aye,' replied Bert. 'But what can we do about our side of things? I mean, it's not our fault if they've all upped and buggered off.'

Worthington's massive fist made sharp contact with the desk, caused inkwells to shiver and pencils to roll. 'You get that girl away from Ivy Crumpsall, right?'

Gert shifted uncomfortably from foot to foot. What did Worthington want with a seven-year-old kiddy? She'd heard tales, of course, knew that the man was interested in tender flesh. But a girl of seven? And she didn't like this bloke, was uncomfortable in his presence. She wanted a child, yet she didn't hold with kidnapping Sally and tormenting Ivy Crumpsall. Any road, whatever did Andrew Worthington have against a woman who was long retired?

As if he read her thoughts, Worthington continued. 'Ivy Crumpsall caused a lot of trouble when she worked for me. Even after her son's death, she brought my workers out of the sheds for the funeral. She's a nuisance.' Yes, and he would have bet his last fiver that Ivy was behind the workers' whispers about joining a union. Many mills had become unionized, so it was only a matter of time now. He sniffed. Over his dead body would Paradise folk organize themselves.

'We've done all we could,' said Bert.

Protruding eyes rolled in their sockets until they settled on Bert. The best way to punish Ivy would be to remove the granddaughter from her care. He'd paid Lottie Crumpsall twenty pounds to write that letter to her sister before swanning off to America. 'Get that child for me,' he muttered, his tone low and menacing. He pulled himself up, decided to rephrase the instruction. 'You want Sally. I made sure Lottie left her in your care. So sort this bloody mess out.'

Gert swallowed. 'What about our jobs, Mr Worthington?' He had promised them a nice little cottage up Wigan Road, a job as daily help for her, some gardening and chauffeuring for Bert. She swallowed, noticed that her throat was dry. In a way, she didn't want to work, not for this man.

Worthington tapped his teeth with a pencil, pondered for a moment. He needed these two on his side. Ivy couldn't have gone far, not in her condition. Only last week, he'd overheard a lunchtime conversation between carders. Ivy's bed was in the kitchen. Was she dying? He wanted Lottie's sister and brother-in-law to remove the child before Ivy died. Afterwards would be no good, because his main aim was to see the woman suffer. She was the only one who had ever spoken out against him. Others had made noises, had hinted at blackmail, but the Crumpsall woman stood alone, as always.

'Mr Worthington?' Bert's tone was suitably quiet and humble.

'I'm thinking.' Where had everyone gone? 'The Irishwoman visits family every year,' he said aloud. 'And Goodfellow's travelled south, I believe. But where's Ivy Crumpsall?'

They didn't know, so they remained silent.

Worthington threw open the door. 'Boy?' he yelled. 'Get in here this minute.'

The general dogsbody followed his boss into the office, closed the door quietly. He stood shaking from head to foot, his mind chasing round in circles looking for possible sins. Had he forgotten the sugar? No, no, it was on the desk next to two full cups. Had the tea been too weak, too strong, too cold?

'You live in one of my houses in Spencer Street, don't you?'

'Yes, Mr Worthington.'

'Sir will do.'

'Yes, sir.' Had Mam paid the rent?

'Do you know anything of the whereabouts of Ivy and Sally Crumpsall from Paradise Lane?'

The lad shook his head. 'No, sir. Nobody knows where they've gone, but there were a great big car and a motor truck. The motor truck took Mr Goodfellow's pigeons. Then Sally and her gran went in the big black car with Mr Goodfellow. They had cases and boxes and all kinds of stuff. But they never said where they were going. They've took the cat and all, sir.'

Worthington glared at the Simpsons. 'And you say they haven't flitted? Why else would they take cases?'

'Furniture's still there,' insisted Bert. 'They'd not have gone off without chairs and that. Happen it's a holiday.'

Worthington settled into his capacious chair, dismissed the office boy with a wave of his hand. When just the Simpsons remained, he lit a cigarette, ignored the look of expectancy on Bert's face. If this rat wanted to smoke, he could pay for his own Players Weights. 'I shall honour my side of the agreement,' he said. 'You will take the Wigan Road cottage and you will work at Worthington House. For now, your brief will be to keep an eye on my wife. She . . .' He couldn't tell them that Prudence hated him. 'She's difficult, a bit unpredictable. Watch her movements, make sure you report any odd behaviour.' He would get the bitch committed to an asylum one way or another. She was as daft as a scalded cat, anyway, couldn't get past the front door some days. Panic attacks. He stubbed out the half-smoked cigarette. 'You might as well get moved in.'

Bert picked up the keys to their new home. 'Shall we start work right away, sir?'

'Tomorrow will do. Moving furniture and so on will keep you occupied for the rest of today.' He dismissed the pair with a wave of his hand, then reached into the top drawer of his desk. When four five-pound notes had been folded and placed in his pocket, he took his hat and Burberry from the stand and made for the door. Twenty pounds should be enough to loosen somebody's tongue. That Tom Goodfellow must have told some bugger what was afoot.

'Get back to your desk,' he roared at his hovering secretary.

She blinked rapidly, stood aside to let him pass. Tomorrow, he would scream at her about unanswered mail. With her head moving slowly from side to side, she returned to her chair. At least he had gone out.

When the office door closed, each pair of shoulders relaxed, while a corporate sigh of relief filled the room. They all despised him, but their fear was bigger than the hatred, and their need to work and feed families was the most compelling factor in their endless silence.

The posser was nearly as tall as she was. She stood it on its head, one hand clasped about its steel. The number of sheets, towels, pillowcases and shirts she had battered with the implement did not bear thinking about; nor did the several dozen strangers she had seen off with this weapon in her grip. But she was getting sick and fed up of using it to prod Ollie back to normal.

With a sigh of resignation, she walked to the back gate

of number 4, saw her husband gazing at the empty cages.

'Ollie?'

He turned, looked at her, looked lost and confused.

Rosie suddenly knew that Ollie was beyond a possing. 'Come on, lad,' she said gently, her tone belying a feeling of terror that seemed to be chilling her bones right through to the marrow. 'Come home and have a nice plate of tatie pie.'

Ollie fixed his eyes on her. 'Rosie?'

'That's me.'

'They've all gone.' He waved a hand towards the cages and lofts. 'I don't know why, 'cos I can't remember, only I'm supposed to be looking after some birds. And they've all flew off while I weren't looking.'

'They've gone to Hampshire, Ollie. I told you last night. Remember Tom and Ivy bringing little Sally to say ta-ra? We've three houses to mind now, love. Four if we count our own. Come on, don't be standing there like a lost soul.' Inside, she was crying. Something had happened to Ollie these last few weeks. He'd stopped moaning about the garden, was eating little, was wandering off all the time. It was as if he were becoming a kiddy all over again, because he needed constant watching.

He walked towards her, his gait rather one-sided and unsteady. Sometimes, his words got all mixed up. He wanted to tell her things, but his tongue didn't work properly any more and he kept forgetting. Not Rosie, he'd not forgotten her. But things he should have known were beyond him. Like in the house. He couldn't find his collar studs, his socks, his shoes. He kept searching for things and forgetting what those things were. 'I'm not right,' he managed.

'I know, lad. Come on, let's get you fed and watered.'

When she got him home, she guided him to his chair, set a plate of pie and peas before him, watched while he struggled to eat. It was his right side that failed him, as if the arm had gone stiff and stupid overnight. Yet this hadn't happened overnight. No, the process had been gradual, which was why she'd dismissed the early symptoms. They were both getting on in years. Folk slowed down a lot when they grew older.

She would have to get the doctor, though she believed that she already knew the answer. Things were happening inside his head. Her mam had gone like this, something to do with little blood vessels giving way in her brain.

When Red Trubshaw arrived after school, her relief knew no bounds. 'Eeh, love, I'm that glad to see you.'

Red blushed to the roots of his carroty hair. 'I told Mrs Crumpsall I'd keep an eye on you,' he said. 'So I've come.'

'Nip up and get the doctor, son. Go on. Tell him our address and that I don't like the looks of my husband. He's down on the list as Oliver Blunt. Hurry up, now.'

Outside, Andrew Worthington watched the boy running towards Spencer Street. After a day spent making enquiries elsewhere among the Paradise streets, then a long and beery lunch in town, he had decided to come here to see Rosie and Ollie Blunt. They would know. They'd have the answers, all right. Borne along on a tide of Dutch courage, he made his way towards the cottages.

Andrew Worthington crossed the cobbles, knocked on the door of number 2, towered over the tiny, white-haired woman who answered. 'Mrs Blunt,' he began.

But Rosie had his measure. 'Bugger off,' she said smartly. 'There's nowt I want to say to you. My husband's been took bad, so me hands is full.'

'I won't keep you, but—'

'No, you won't. Just like you couldn't keep Ivy in the yard that day when yon miner come and sorted you. There's nowt here for your sort, so get yourself gone and . . .' Her eyes rested on the large, white five-pound notes that he was counting.

'Ten pounds would help,' he said softly. 'This could pay for a few doctors, Mrs Blunt.'

'Hang on a minute while I see to Ollie.' Rosie walked

through the house and into her garden, picked up the implement, retraced her steps. She opened the door and thrust the business end of the posser into Andrew Worthington's not insubstantial stomach.

She was not a powerful woman, but the attack had been unexpected. The master of Paradise Mill lay sprawled on the narrow pavement, his face purple with rage. Muted laughter drifted out of the breaking shed, and he even heard a man's voice calling. 'Give him another one for us, missus.'

'By Christ, you'll suffer for this,' he mumbled.

Rosie pulled herself to full height, achieved at least four feet and eleven inches when her spine was stretched. 'Threaten me and I'll have you bloody tarred and feathered,' she shouted. 'There's many a woman round here would join me. Now, see that mill?' She pointed to the huge building. 'Get back there and weave yourself a shroud. 'Cos you'll be needing one if you don't shape.'

When the door had been slammed home and bolted, Andrew Worthington heaved himself up and turned towards the mill. Not one worker lingered in the yard. Still, never mind. He would wander across in a minute and find some fault or other, some excuse to drop the breakers' pay. Nobody crossed Andrew Worthington. Unions? He coughed, dabbed his heated face with a large handkerchief. He'd see the lot of them in hell before allowing any card-holding member cross the threshold of Paradise. Yes, they'd soon learn the difference between hell and heaven if they didn't shape up.

Well, he would sort them all out in a minute. Once he'd got his breath back . . .

Sally had slept for most of that first day on the road. Uncle Tom was taking it slowly, because Granny Ivy hadn't been in a car before and was a bit frightened. Gus had travelled with the other man and the pigeons in a big motor wagon. Uncle Tom was pleased about Gus, because the cat might persuade some of the birds to stay in . . . in Hampshire? Was that the right name? 'Is it Hampshire, Uncle Tom?' she asked the man at the wheel.

'Yes. A place called Oakmead, on the edge of the hills. You'll like it.'

'Will I?'

'Oh, yes.' She hadn't seen anything of Derby, had been carried flat out into the guest house. But Ivy had seen, tasted, enjoyed. He smiled as he remembered the old woman's face over a plate of lamb. 'Are we still in England? Is there no rationing round here?' she had asked.

Tom glanced over his shoulder, saw that Ivy was asleep. 'Sally?'

Sally was twisting and turning in the front passenger seat, her eyes all over the place. 'Trees, hundreds of trees. Millions,' she said. 'There's a lot of room, isn't there?' They passed through a hamlet in the twinkling of an eye. 'Only about ten houses there,' she remarked. 'And no mills.'

'But you remember the potteries, don't you? When we came through Stoke-on-Trent, all those kilns? Different things get made in different places.'

She nodded her agreement. 'Yes, that was dirty, that place where they do the pots.'

He negotiated a bend, checked to see whether Ivy was still asleep. 'Sally, I have a very big house,' he began. 'It's falling to bits, but it's enormous.'

'Like Buckin'ham Palace?'

'A bit. Not as big as Buckingham Palace.'

'Oh.' She didn't care about his house; she was too interested in the sheep. 'Millions,' she said again. 'And no black ones.'

'Sally, I'm a lord.'

She turned her head and gave him her full attention. 'Like Jesus?'

He tried not to laugh. 'No. Jesus is a different kind of lord. I'm just an ordinary one. A long time ago, when my family was very rich and important, the King of England turned one of my ancestors into a lord.'

She was not getting a grip on this at all. There were stories at school and in picture books, fairy godmothers changing pumpkins into coaches. But not in real life, surely? 'Did he use a magic wand?'

'I beg your pardon?'

'The king. Did he do a spell with a wand?'

He shrugged. 'He used a sword.'

'Oh.'

'I'm Lord Goodfellow, Sally. Not for much longer, though. Our real name was Marchant and I'm changing my name back to that.' And he wouldn't be parading about in ermine and velvet, either. Poverty had not exactly suited him, but he had enjoyed being an ordinary man. For over twenty years, he had been a plain 'mister'. 'When we reach Oakmead, you will hear people calling me 'My Lord'. I'll soon stop them. In fact, most of them have begun to learn already. But your grandmother may feel uncomfortable.'

'Why?' Grown-ups always made things hard for themselves.

'Because I'm a lord.'

They were back to the beginning again and she was still no clearer. She didn't know what to say to him, because too much was happening. There were fields and animals flashing past the window, and here was Uncle Tom going on about some dead king and changing his name with a sword. It was all beyond her.

'Make Ivy stay, Sally. Persuade her. She needs the rest and she needs a change.'

'I'm stopping, your blinking lordship,' said the voice from the back seat. 'Don't be setting our Sal on me. I can make me own mind up on me own by meself with no help from nobody.'

'Sorry,' mumbled Tom. Ivy was great at putting people in their proper place.

144

'And you're not telling us nothing we didn't already know, 'cos we'd all guessed as how you were summat unusual. Will you stay away from these hedges, Tom? They're scratching at the window. Any minute now, you'll be in the ditch. And don't expect me to treat you different just 'cos you're next to royalty.' She sniffed. 'I've a lot of time for the king, but I can't be doing with all them hangers-on.'

Tom grinned. He might have known. Whatever he said or did, there would be no shocking Ivy. 'We're nearly at our next stop,' he told them.

Ivy sighed, muttered about her bones being jangled in this bloody car, stopped mid-sentence when she saw the view ahead.

Sally's jaw dropped. 'Fairyland,' she whispered.

Tom stopped the car. 'You're right in a way, Sally. I spent the happiest years of my life here.'

'Look at that,' exclaimed Ivy. 'That is the bonniest place I've ever seen in my life. Where are we?'

The Earl of Goodfellow Hall wiped some wetness from a cheek. 'Oxford, Ivy,' he said. 'This is where we'll sleep tonight.'

Ivy was all agog. She had travelled to Oxford in a Rolls Royce, had seen more wonders than she'd experienced in her many years on earth. 'All them books,' she kept saying when they drove through the city on the last leg of their journey. 'There's more books there than in the rest of England put together. Scotland and all, I bet. My Derek would have loved Oxford. What was that last place called?'

'University College.'

Ivy turned for one last look at the spires. 'Well,' she began. 'You live a long life, you fettle as best you can, and you still know nowt. All them men in black coats. Gowns, I mean. And folk walking about with their heads stuck in a book. That's all been going on while I've been living in the same place with nowt new to see.'

He nodded to himself. Ivy had wisdom and common sense. Some of those in gowns could well finish up under the wheels of a motor car, because they hadn't the wits to glance up from the written word to look out for themselves. 'It's just another way of life,' he told her. 'And I am a student of the way people live.'

Ivy laughed. 'A student? At your age?'

'Oh yes. You're still learning, aren't you? You've been inside a hall of residence, a refectory and a library. I'd never been inside a factory until I came to Bolton to write a thesis. My learning continues. Everybody learns constantly, from birth to death.'

Ivy looked through the window, saw ordinary people going about their ordinary business. 'They're not all students, are they? Look at her, that one in the green coat. See, she's three children getting under her feet.'

'Town and gown,' he told her. 'There were riots in the past between townsfolk and gownsfolk, but they've settled for ignoring each other. That woman's possibly a jam maker. They specialize in marmalade, you know. Then there's publishing, some engineering – it's not all degrees and end of term celebrations. Like any other place, it's a mixture.'

'Eeh, we live and learn – don't we, Sal?'

Sally had little to say, simply because she had been overwhelmed by all the sights and was organizing her thoughts. She had run around a big square called a quad, had dashed in and out of archways, had been given a mint by a very old man with colours on his black gown. And she'd looked up and up into the sky until she'd got dizzy, had tried to count all the steeples, had listened to many kinds of bells, had seen great big paintings that would never fit on a wall at home.

'Sal?' Ivy leaned forward, touched the child's shoulder. 'Did you like Oxford, love?'

Sally nodded, let it all spill out. 'I'm going back there,' she said. 'I'm going to read all them books and have a bike and a black gown. They were nearly all men, but some were ladies. I'm going back,' she said again. 'And I'll have a straw hat and go on that river Isis in a boat with a long pole and have my dinner in that re-flectory place at a big long table.'

Tom grinned to himself. Sally had fallen in love with Oxford. That was a very easy thing to do. 'It's not out of reach,' he told her. 'Work hard at your lessons, and you'll be halfway there.'

She looked at him. 'Why did you leave? Couldn't you have stayed there? Bolton's horrible and dirty.'

Tom slowed down. 'No. Bolton's a lovely town, but its beauty is different from Oxford's. The moors are wonderful and the people are splendid.'

'It takes all sorts,' pronounced the oracle in the rear seat. 'And somebody's got to spin the cotton, eh?'

Ivy stood in the middle of a huge lawn. 'I don't understand,' she said for the fourth time. 'Why, Tom?'

He shrugged. 'Family trouble. I just had to get away. I'd fought in the Great War when I was just a boy – ran away to join the forces – and I couldn't seem to settle when I got back. Then there was Oxford. After that, I came home very reluctantly and . . . and the trouble between my father and myself began.' He coughed, seemed ill at ease. 'My older brother died, and my sister went abroad to work with missionaries. So I simply disappeared.'

She stared at the house. It was nearly as broad as Paradise Mill, and she'd counted forty-odd windows in the front.

'My mother left me money. I reached twenty-one while at Oxford, got the inheritance, but my spending spree began some years later. Sailing, tennis, golf, gambling on the horses and—'

'And you spent it all and ended up in Bolton.'

'To study.'

She winked at him. 'Aye and to live cheap and stop away from your dad.'

'Something like that, yes. The old chap wrote to me every month through solicitors, but I never read his letters. He was an unpleasant man, another Andrew Worthington, I suppose. My mother died of a broken heart.'

'And your brother?'

'Drowned.'

She gripped his hand tightly. 'Tom, what are you going to do with this lot, eh? I mean, look at it, lad. Just take a good, long look. It's . . .' Words failed her, but not for long. 'It's beautiful.' She hadn't been inside yet. But here she stood, on a park-sized patch of green with weedy paths, a dried-up fountain, statues, urns. 'This is all yours, Tom. It's a responsibility. I mean, yon chap who chased wild boar with that fat King Henry – he owned this and all. It goes back to Adam, does this place.'

He inclined his head. 'Ivy, it means little to me.'

'Why?' she asked. 'You're gentry, aren't you? Take me, now. I'm from a cotton and mining family. It were like a tradition. Boys down the pit, girls in the spinning. Your history's longer than mine. It's important, is history.'

'So is progress.' He watched Sally cavorting about with a couple of daft spaniels, saw that the child was inhaling good air for the first time. 'The house wants children.'

'Then get some,' Ivy answered. 'I don't need to tell you how to go about that, do I? Bring the house back to life.'

He nodded. 'Oh, I shall.'

Something in his tone made her face him full on. 'You're not planning on stopping here long, are you?'

'No.'

'But—'

'Don't ask, Ivy. When I'm ready, I'll tell you precisely what Goodfellow Hall signifies for me. Meanwhile, I'll take you and Sally to look at the cottage. One of the servants has prepared it for you. Then, after a cup of tea, we'll go into the big house. You may choose where you live. There's space in the house, but if you want a bit of time to yourself, you can use the cottage.'

She grinned broadly. 'I'd not know how to talk to a servant.'

'Oh, but you would,' he told her. 'Because you'll talk to my friends here just as you talk to me. The people who work here are no different from the rest of us.' He became pensive for a moment. 'Have you ever talked to Joseph Heilberg about Judaism?'

'Not really, no. He's told me about what they do on a Friday night and why he shuts his shop on a Saturday. Mind, he leaves Maureen's shop open so that she can have her Sunday off instead.'

'That's a very old religion and it's packed with common sense. Like, "therefore, but a single man was created . . . that none should say to his fellow, 'My father was greater than thy father.'" All equal, Ivy. Those who work here do a job and I pay them, but we remain on equal terms.'

'Different from your dad, I bet.'

'Very much so,' he said softly. 'Thank God.'

They climbed into the car, this time with the two dogs. The animals squealed and panted a lot, steamed up all the windows. Ivy, squashed beneath the weight of a golden-coated hound, grinned ruefully at Tom when he turned to look at her. 'I'll be all dog hairs,' she complained. The dog licked her face, gave her a thorough going over with its gentle tongue, made her giggle like a child.

She looked better already, thought Lord Goodfellow. There was colour in the old woman's face, while some of the wrinkles seemed to have been ironed out, particularly round her eyes. Hampshire would be good for Ivy, he decided.

They drove a few hundred yards, stopped outside a cottage that seemed to have been picked out of the pages of a story book. It had roses round the door, sweet little windows with bottle-bottom swirls in some of the panes, a tiny garden filled with flowers. Sally looked through the car's windscreen, her hand fastened to the collar of the second spaniel. 'It's what I dreamed about,' she said. 'This and flowers on the cups, too.'

Tom opened his door and a dog bounced away from Sally and followed Tom out at the driver's side. Sally swung round and looked at Granny Ivy. 'I want to stay here for ever,' she said.

'What about Oxford?' Ivy was still being assaulted by the larger dog. 'I thought you wanted to read all them books. Get off me hat, you bugger,' she told the wayward canine.

Sally shrugged. 'This is nicer than Oxford, Gran. This is a special place where we could live, just the two of us.'

Ivy thought about that. It wasn't what she wanted. Funny, she said to herself. Sometimes, you had to have a look at the nice things before realizing that they weren't important. This was the most beautiful little house she'd ever seen, and a holiday round here was going to be lovely. But when she studied the situation, all she could think of was home. At home, there were the Blunts and Maureen Mason, there was the corner shop, the Co-op, the market. When she pictured the giant H that formed Paradise, she suddenly realized that she knew dozens of people and that she needed them. Especially now, when she was becoming less robust.

The dog yapped, got a cuff from Ivy, was dragged from the car. Ivy stepped out, opened the garden gate, walked up the path to Rose Cottage. Its name, written over the door, was only partially visible because of a profusion of the blooms after which the building had been christened.

The door swung inward, was pushed all the way open by the dogs. There were two rooms downstairs, just a parlour and a big kitchen. 'Two bedrooms and a bathroom upstairs,' said Tom. 'And a big garden at the back.'

Sally was in heaven. The back door was in two halves, and she slipped through the bottom part in pursuit of the

150

golden spaniels. Then she remembered Gus, flew back into the house. 'Where's my cat?' she asked.

'At the hall,' replied Tom. 'He'll be in the kitchen with butter on his paws. The cook always butters a cat's paws to stop him from straying.'

Ivy was going to make a comment about margarine being good enough, but she held her tongue. If there was butter in the country, then she'd be taking advantage of it, so sarcastic comments had better stay put inside her head. 'Lovely cottage, Tom,' she said. 'But whose are them bloody dogs?'

He frowned. 'Mine, I suppose. They were my father's and, according to what I've been told, he acted in character and treated them unkindly. Spaniels tend to sensitivity, which means they become nervous when handled badly.' He paused for a moment. 'My father, too, regarded everyone and everything the same, no favouritism. He was bad to man and beast alike. We'll settle the dogs eventually.'

She walked into the kitchen and looked out at her granddaughter. Sally was outside again, was rolling about in a bundle of golden fur with ten legs – counting the child's – three heads and two pluming tails. 'You've lost your dogs, Tom. We'll have a terrible time getting yon lass back to Bolton without them spaniels.'

He glanced sideways at the black-clad woman. Her only concession to long-distance travel had been the leaving off of her white apron. She was one of the last remaining pieces of Victoriana, in black from head to foot and with a ridiculous veiled hat perched on top of the iron grey hair. 'Ivy, black's hot in the summer. Won't you let me buy you a couple of lightweight dresses?'

She fixed him with her gimlet stare. 'Tommy Goodfellow, you might be a lord, but I'll have you know I'm a lady. I don't hold with folk dashing about with all their bits showing. I like me black. You know where you are with black. Put me in lilac and I might go on a manhunt down the road. Aye, I'd be in that pub in . . . what's that little place called?'

'Oakmead. There are a few grand gentlemen who'd be glad of your company if—'

She clocked him across the head with her dorothy bag. 'I've still got all me facilities, you know. I'm not letting you marry me off to somebody in a bloody smock.'

He rubbed his scalp. 'The farmers don't always wear smocks any more, Ivy. And only women in mourning or in service are clad in black.'

Ivy grinned at him wickedly. 'Well, they don't even talk proper. Sound a bloody soft lot to me. When we went in that shop, I couldn't tell a word they were saying.'

Tom didn't bother to tell her that no-one would fathom her Boltonese for at least three days. He was just glad that they were here, that Sally would be safe from those prowling Simpsons, that Ivy would not become heart-broken just yet at the possibility of Lottie's sister claiming Sally once the poor child's Granny Ivy had shuffled off the coil.

'Uncle Tom?'

Sally's face was rounder already. The dimples were slightly deeper, less of a hint and more of an actuality. 'Yes, Sally?'

She bit her lip with the almost-grown adult incisors. 'Are you really, really rich?'

'I suppose so.' In the grand scheme of things, he was not particularly wealthy. But compared to the Crumpsalls, he was Croesus.

Sally glanced at her grandmother, swallowed, cleared her throat. 'Can we rent this house for ever? We could come in the Bolton holidays, then I can live here all the time when I'm grown-up. I'll keep it clean. Ask Mr Heilberg – number one's been clean since me and Gran had it.'

Tom crossed the room, ruffled Sally's pale blond hair. 'Rose Cottage is yours for life, Sally,' he said thickly. 'And no rent to pay. When I've sorted everything, the deeds will be yours.'

Ivy tutted. 'You're spoiling her, Tom.'

'It's time somebody did,' he replied.

For once, Ivy Crumpsall was lost for words. Little Sal had never had much, had been blessed with a mother whose few coppers went on fripperies, with a dad who had died young. And here was a man who was no kin to Sally, a man who had just given the child a house and a couple of dogs. More than that, Tom had made Sally smile. 'I'll just have a wash,' said Ivy gruffly when she found her tongue. 'Then I'll make us all a nice cup of tea.'

'I can't take no more of this,' said Ivy. 'I don't know whether I'm coming or bloody going.' How many rooms had they been through? 'It's like your first day in the mill, too much to take in.'

Sally and the spaniels were in their element. It had been daunting for the little girl at first, especially when they had stood in the great hall. That room had not just been wide and long – it had climbed up and up right to the roof and beyond. The far-away ceiling held a circular window with patterns in multi-coloured glass, and she had gone dizzy again while twisting about to look at all the pictures near the sky.

But she'd got used to it within half an hour, had made acquaintance with below-stairs staff in the cellar-level kitchens and service rooms. She had taken in the red and gold Inigo Jones dining room, chandeliers, tapestries, marble fireplaces, polished wood floors. There were four-poster beds, one of which sat in a Chinese room with black chests and cupboards lacquered in gold. She'd been in a withdrawing room filled with huge Tudor chairs and massive silver candlesticks, then into a second sitting room with floor-to-ceiling pillars and arches that held rude statues of naked men and women. After a while, it had become just another place like Oxford, something that was not quite real, not quite reachable.

Ivy tutted into a black marble bath. 'It'd take three weeks to fill that,' she said. 'And this room's that big, you'd be froze over in winter before you could get dry.'

'There are smaller ones,' the host informed her.

Ivy shook her head. 'How many?'

He shrugged. 'Ten, twelve – I'm not sure.'

They retraced their steps, reached the massive front door, stood outside on an open terrace edged by a long balustrade. 'You don't like it here, do you, Tom?' said Ivy.

'There's no communication in a house this size. When we were small, Jon, Patricia and I could rely only on the staff when we needed help or comfort. Had we looked for our parents, the problem we wanted to solve would have disappeared before we'd found Mother or Father. It's too big, far too big for me.'

She understood. Tom had gone from trenches to small rooms in Oxford, had lived in spaces that had been confined. During his spendthrift years, he had probably lived in flats or hotels. Now, after an absence of almost thirty years, he was Lord Goodfellow of this huge country seat. 'What'll you do with it?'

He shook his head. 'Not sure. I'm mulling over a few ideas. First, I want to get rid of my title. To do that, I must find Patricia and see if she has any children. Whatever, I'll change back to Marchant. Then, unless Patricia wants this heap, I'll find a use for it.'

'You could sell it to some other lord,' she suggested.

He heaved a great sigh. 'Ivy, if it were only as simple as that. There are tenant farms, crops, animals, families whose income depends on me now. My land cuts a jagged swathe almost all the way from Aldershot to Winchester and beyond. People, Ivy. Hundreds of people.'

'Aye, that's a tough one, Tom.'

'There should be no one person in charge of all this. There are dairy and crop farms, we grow hops, most vegetables, maize . . .' He ran a hand through his hair. 'A lot of thinking to do.'

'Yes.' Ivy spread her hands along the balustrade, looked along the weedy path that divided into many patterns what had once been formal gardens. 'Everything's neglected, Tom. Furniture's showing signs of wear, some ornaments are cracked. Mind, them paintings and stuff might be worth a packet.'

'They are,' he said. 'And all I want is to be rid of the lot.'

SEVEN

Prudence closed the door quietly, left him to get on with it. For years, she had avoided eating with him, always had a tray brought up to her room by their one servant. Mrs Miles, from a small street just off Wigan Road, arrived at Worthington House at 7 a.m., prepared breakfast, cleaned the house, then went home at about 1 p.m. Prudence always got her own lunch, then Mrs Miles returned at 5 p.m. to cook and serve the evening meal. The woman came in six days, then had Sundays off. Sunday was a nightmare for Prudence, as Victor visited and things had to look normal while Margaret West, Victor's fiancée, was in the house. 'Normal' meant everyone sitting in the dining room eating a meal prepared by Prudence and indulging in small talk created by the presence of an outsider.

She walked up the stairs to her bedroom, was intending to collect her used tray. But just as she reached the landing, the front doorbell sounded. Mrs Miles would be busy in the kitchen, was probably starting to wash all the dishes, so Prudence retraced her steps, opened the door.

The woman smiled. 'I'm Gert Simpson,' she announced.

The name meant nothing, and Prudence worked hard to shift the look of surprise that was visiting her face. Was this another of Andrew Worthington's injured flock, was she a mother of some deflowered child?

'I work here,' said the scarlet mouth. 'Me and Bert. We've to help somebody called Mrs Miles and do the garden and drive the car when you want to go out and—'

'I haven't employed you,' said Prudence, unable to steer

her eyes away from the crimson gash from which this female's words had fallen. 'Would you wait here for a moment, please?' She closed the door, left the would-be intruder outside. What a vision that had been! Red lipstick, red hair, red skirt, red shoes, each red clashing loudly with its next-door neighbour.

At the dining room door, Prudence stopped, breathed in, organized a speech. But when she entered, everything seemed to go out of her mind. It was his eyes. She shuddered, remembered yet again the few occasions on which he had forced her to succumb to his perverted will. 'There's a woman,' she said softly.

He looked up from the evening paper. 'Speak up,' he barked.

'On the doorstep,' she said. 'A woman in red. She's horrible.'

Andrew Worthington studied his wife and chewed on a bit of gristle. Mrs Miles's steak and kidney pies weren't what they used to be, but with the war, rationing and so on . . . 'What do you want me to do about a woman in red?' he asked scornfully. 'I haven't even started on my pudding.'

This was Worthington to a T, his wife thought. His belly betrayed one of his appetites – two if she counted the beer – and his third dreadful excess had shown itself many times in the form of weeping girls and their families. 'She says she works here,' she said with as much courage as she could muster.

'Then she does. It'll be Gert Simpson. She and her husband are due to start here tomorrow. I had intended to start them earlier, but the woman had to work her notice at Woolworths, so they're a few days late.' He sucked loudly on his teeth before continuing. 'Mrs Miles is getting no younger.'

Prudence ventured a little nearer to the table. 'You've never worried about Mrs Miles before.' He had never worried about anyone, she supposed.

He put down his knife and fork, snatched the napkin from its place beneath his chin. 'Must I do everything myself?' he roared, tossing the square of linen into a dish of carrots. 'Can't you even answer the door without a bloody song and dance? Look, we need more staff, somebody to put the garden right and do odd jobs about the house. The woman can help in the kitchen and with the heavier cleaning work.' He sneered at her. 'This is my house and I say who works in it.'

Prudence nodded, turned, walked into the hall. Several seconds ticked by before she opened the front door. 'Come in,' she managed. 'Is your husband with you?'

'No.' Gert placed the red handbag on the hall-stand, preened the dyed hair in a mirror. 'We were supposed to start a while back, only there were me notice at the shop, then Mr Worthington had another little job for us.' That other little job had been to hang around in all the cafés and pubs to see if anyone mentioned the whereabouts of Ivy and Sally Crumpsall. It had been a cushy number, beer money thrown in, plus enough to buy the odd round to loosen tongues. But the Simpsons had gleaned nothing. The Crumpsalls had gone off with Tom Goodfellow, but he could have dropped them at any of the local seaside resorts before proceeding south.

'My husband is eating.'

Gert studied her prospective employer, decided that Mrs Worthington was good-looking in a pale sort of way, that she seemed to have what the toffs might call breeding. 'I could do your hair for you,' offered the unwelcome visitor.

Prudence tried not to look at the thatch of henna. 'No, thank you. I go to a hairdresser in town once a week.'

There seemed to be nothing else to say, thought Gert. She was a boring type, this Prudence Worthington. No wonder the old man strayed from the straight and narrow now and then. 'Can I look round?' she asked. If she stood here much longer, she'd be rooted.

'Feel free. My husband has employed you, so you must do as he wishes. Excuse me. I shall leave you now.' Prudence walked upstairs, left the strange creature clattering her way into the kitchen in shoes that looked unready for any kind of toil.

In her sanctuary, Prudence locked the door and perched on the edge of her dressing stool. In the mirror she saw a sad and serious face with questions in its eyes. All the whys of her life were burned deep into irises of a colour approaching china blue. These orbs were the feature that kept her looking young, because they were startling and startled, like the eyes of a child who is filled with wonderment at the sights before her.

She picked up a brush, smoothed it through pale blond and silver hair. If she'd had any pride at all, she would have left the brute long ago. There was enough money salted away, cash she had inherited from her parents. If she could get to the bank, she would be able to buy a house, perhaps a car, some small furniture. She placed the brush on its tray, looked round her room. This was the only dainty furniture in Worthington House. Everything else was huge, ponderous, Victorian. Tables had great, bulbous legs. Sideboards and cupboards were heavily moulded – even some of the ornaments were hideous. But here, in her own part of the house, Prudence had created a haven of pretty tranquillity.

She had installed a cream dressing table and wardrobe with a small Greek key pattern gilded round doors and drawers. Mirrors were small and oval, edged again in cream and gold. Curtains as light as morning floated inward on a breath of breeze, and the floor was covered in a carpet of plain blue. Pretty, she thought. Pretty, functional and peaceful.

Where would she go? If she could, where would she travel to? She lay on the bed, faced the wall and brought up her knees into a position that seemed to comfort her. No, she was not mad. Being unable to step outside this dreadful house did not mean insanity, surely? When had she last been out? And why had she lied to that horrible woman called . . . called Simpson? Yes, Gert Simpson. A hideous name for an odious female. Why had she lied? 'I go to a hairdresser in town once a week.' Town was fast becoming another planet. The hairdresser, a nice little lady called Sheila Dawson, visited Worthington House on Thursdays.

Prudence curled herself into a tighter ball. He never tried to touch her any more. For years, she had lived in terror, had pushed her bed against the door to prevent him entering her room. Then, about ten years into the marriage, he had fitted the door with a lock and two bolts. 'Just so that you will sleep better,' he had said. But before he had left the room, he had paused in the doorway, as if struck by an afterthought. 'By the way,' he had said jovially. 'If there's ever a fire, you won't get out, because I'll make sure you're left to fry in your silly little room.'

She shivered. The evening was warm, yet her bones felt iced and brittle. Fire? Even death by burning would be preferable to the feel of his hands, the sound of his breathing, the ferocity of that final attack when all sense seemed to elude him. He was the insane one. He was the deviant.

One day, she told herself. One day soon, when she felt strong enough, she would visit the Crumpsall woman. Oh, she'd heard her husband talking on the telephone, had eavesdropped while he'd told some unseen person about Ivy Crumpsall and her 'allegations'. 'She says she can name my illegitimate children,' he had boomed into black Bakelite. 'Nonsense, of course. No, no, I can't sue. They'll all say there's no smoke . . . quite, quite. But I want her silenced.' Of late, Prudence Worthington had begun to worry about the safety of a woman she had never met.

And now, there was this Simpson person and her husband. Gert had all-knowing eyes and a face that had hardened too early. Why were they going to be here? Worthington House had managed, just about, with only Mrs Miles for many years. What was he up to this time?

A knock on the door made her spring from the bed like a cat. 'Who's there?' she finally managed.

'It's me, Mrs Worthington.'

Prudence's heart slowed. She was not on close terms with Mrs Miles, yet the good soul was no threat. When the door was open, Mrs Miles marched inside and took her mistress's hand. 'I'm leaving, madam,' she said, her face working its way through a maelstrom of emotions. 'There's no way I'm stopping here with that . . . that piece downstairs.'

Prudence, uncertain about what to do or say, patted Mrs Miles's arm. 'There, there,' she muttered. 'Please try to be calm, Mrs Miles.' This was ridiculous. 'Isn't your given name Cora?'

'That's right, madam.' The eyebrows had raised themselves in surprise. 'I just came to tell you because it isn't right. I couldn't walk out without seeing you.'

Prudence dropped her servant's hand. 'Cora.' The name came clumsily from her lips, sounded strange, rusty. 'You must not leave me. Have you told Mr Worthington of your intention?'

A hybrid sound came from the servant's mouth, an improbable cross between a cough and a 'pshaw' of impatience. 'No. I've not talked to him, madam. I never talk to him unless he asks a question. Can I sit down?'

'Of course.'

The housekeeper sat on the bed, her hands twisting together as if wringing out a mop. 'Twenty-odd year I've been with you,' she said. 'And I stayed for you, not for him. It were you I wanted to fettle for, you I liked. I still like you, madam, but I'm telling you here and now that I can't work with that trollop.'

Prudence nodded slowly. 'You know her?'

'I don't need to know her, Mrs Worthington. I can see what she is just by looking at her. And her husband's arrived and all, he's sat in my kitchen like the King of England. Piggy eyes, he's got. Piggy eyes and a woman's hands. And he smells like a brewery.'

The lady of the house sat on the bed next to her servant. 'Mrs Miles – Cora – if you like me, you must stay.' She swallowed a bubble of fear that felt like a fruit stone in her throat, huge, dry and difficult to absorb. 'I'm afraid, you see.' What was there to lose at this point. Her dignity? She had been robbed of that eons ago. 'I feel sure that the Simpsons are spies.'

Cora Miles said nothing.

'This isn't a persecution complex. He . . . he really hates me, you understand.'

'Oh aye. I understand, all right. I've understood for years how things are for you. He's took your confidence away and you stay in this house hiding like a frightened rabbit. I've said nowt, 'cos I know me place, but I've took it all in. But, madam, that there Gert is more than I can stomach. She's sat at me kitchen table filing her nails all over me clean cloth. And her husband's got his feet up on the draining board.'

Prudence inclined her head. 'They will have been told to behave like that. They have probably been ordered to make your life so difficult that you will go and never return.' She swallowed again. Her parched throat seemed to rasp like sandpaper. 'If you leave me, these two will start tricks. Eventually, I shall be put away into an asylum.'

Cora Miles pondered for a few moments, made her decision, sighed. 'In that case, we mun help one another.' She stood up, looked down on the lady she had pitied for so many years. 'I want you to come into my kitchen and tell them off. If you can do that, we might just manage between us to carry on, you and me. I can't do nothing about them, you see. Mr Worthington hired them, and there's no way I can put me foot down. You can. And I'll tell you summat else and all, Mrs Worthington. If you come down them stairs with me now, your life will change. Once you've acted as if you rule the roost, you'll get a bit of that confidence back.' She paused, got no answer. 'Confidence is all pretend, you know. There's none of us certain sure of owt these days. But once you start speaking up, you'll respect yourself, like.'

Prudence weighed each awesome prospect. The idea of bursting into the kitchen and shouting the odds was appalling. But the concept of life without Mrs Miles and with the Simpsons was by far the worse possibility. She got up, made for the door. Whatever it took, she would keep Cora Miles by her side.

The housekeeper remained in the hallway, smiled encouragingly as her mistress entered the kitchen. Prudence, alone and afraid, faced the couple at the centre table. 'Take your feet down from the draining board, please,' she said softly to the man. 'As you will notice from the name, a draining board is a place where clean dishes are left after washing and before drying.' At last, she managed to clear her throat, thereby strengthening her tone. 'Dirt from your feet would not go well with the Crown Derby.'

Bert blinked twice, brought his feet down very slowly and placed them under the table.

While the going was good, the mistress of Worthington House continued. 'Mrs Simpson, my housekeeper prepares food on that table. You will not file your nails, comb your hair or apply make-up in the kitchen.' Her breathing was quickening, but she continued anyway. 'My cook-housekeeper is a woman of great value and talent. You will obey her at all times. I know that my husband has employed you, but I would remind you that he is away at business for much of the time and that I am mistress of this house. You will obey me and you will heed Mrs Miles's instructions.' She lifted her head defiantly. 'Whatever he has told you . . .' She nodded in the direction of the dining room, 'I assure you that I am capable of making your life extremely difficult.'

'No offence intended, I'm sure,' said the man.

The moment she heard his voice, Prudence hated Bert Simpson. Like his hands, the tone was disproportionate to the body, lightweight, fawning, boyish. 'You will not smoke in here, either,' she went on, emboldened and calmer. 'One false move from either of you, and I shall send for my son. Victor is not a man with whom you should trifle.'

The woman sat bolt upright, patted her hair, tried to smile at Prudence. 'We didn't mean nothing, missus.'

'Madam,' corrected Prudence. She gave her attention to the man. 'There's a rather nasty patch of nettles at the bottom of the garden. You will clear that tomorrow. The fish-pond needs cleaning, and the rockery must be weeded by the weekend.'

'I'm not used to gardening,' he mumbled.

'Then you must learn,' advised Prudence before directing some words at Gert. 'You will clean the oven and clear the pantry shelves. There is new shelf paper in a box under the vegetable racks. Then I want to see all the windows and mirrors sparkling clean by this time next week.' She nodded, was satisfied with herself. 'And I suggest you tone down the colour of your hair, Mrs Simpson. Such a raucous shade is not in keeping with a position of service. Good evening.' She stalked out of the kitchen and fell into the arms of Cora Miles.

Cora led the mistress back to her room. 'I'm that proud of you, I could sing,' she declared. 'Between us, we'll beat them two buggers.'

'We shall indeed.' Prudence shivered her way through the shock, then began to feel better than she'd felt in ages. She smiled broadly at the woman who had served her for years. 'You and I will make an excellent team,' she said.

*　　*　　*

Bert was brooding. 'He never said owt about this lot, did he?' He waved a hand towards the closed door. 'Never told us we'd be answerable to some bloody housekeeper. He said we could have the run of the place because his wife's doolally. Well, she looks as if she's got a full set of roof slates, doesn't she?'

Gert jumped up, pushed the manicure tools into her crimson bag. 'Happen we should go and talk to him.' Really, all she wanted was to put a lot of space between herself and this oppressive house. But they were trapped here, caught in Worthington's web. 'I don't like this place, Bert,' she moaned. 'I don't like him and his wife can't stand the sight of me. Let's go and talk to the boss . . .' Her voice tailed away. The sack would mean nowhere to live, no money coming in because she'd left Woolworths.

Bert shook his head. 'Nay, that'd be like saying we can't manage, like. If we go running to him after half an hour in this house, he'll show us the way home. And the way home'd need a map, lass, 'cos our new house goes with the job and we've give up our place next to the Dog and Gun.' Aye, and he would miss his pub. It had been near enough for him, just a few stumbles from bar to bed. 'We can't go to him yet, Gertie. If we can't find the Crumpsalls, we can happen help him to get rid of yon wife of his.'

Gert reclaimed her seat, thought for a few moments. She hadn't taken to Mrs Worthington, but the idea of getting her locked up didn't seem right. She lowered her voice, spoke in a near whisper. 'Bert, she might be a bit of a la-de-dah, but it all seems very queer to me. I mean, he's the one who goes about attacking folk. Whereas Mrs Worthington—'

'She likes being called Spencer-Worthington,' he interspersed.

'Aye, and I don't blame her, neither. Even after what she said about me hair.' She fingered the carefully cultivated shock of orange that framed her face. 'That's a lady, a real lady. I could learn things from her.' She pondered for a moment. 'I reckon we're on the wrong side, lad.'

'Eh?' He sat bolt upright, wondered whether his wife had suddenly lost a few of her marbles.

'Well, her's the one in the right. I mean, it must be awful sitting in here every day knowing he's chasing girls all over the place. And he's no manners, you know. He doesn't ask before taking what he wants, oh no. He just whips their knickers off and gets on with it from what I've heard.' She nodded pensively. 'It'll all come to a head one of these days. Aye, he'll go down, he will. Then we'll look bloody daft, won't we? I say we try to get in with the missus and pretend to be on Worthington's side. Then, we should win both ways.'

'You can do what you like,' said Bert. 'I'm stopping where there's thickest butter on me bread.'

Gert stuck to her guns, but said nothing. Bert could do as he pleased, but she intended to make an ally of the woman upstairs. All that rubbish about going to the hairdresser's – Gert was almost certain that Prudence Spencer-Worthington had been stuck in this bloody mausoleum for years. She would get Prudence through that front door. Whatever it took, Gert would be the one to cure Prudence Worthington. And if the boss had anything to say, Gert would convince him that she was forcing the woman outside to make her nerves worse.

'What are you thinking about?' asked Bert.

'Nowt. I agree with you. It's a shame, only she's not ours to worry about, is she? No, you're right, Bert. If Worthington wants his wife put away, he must have his reasons. I'll make it my business to get to know her – if she'll let me. Then I can find out what's best for us to do. Don't worry, I'm on your side.' As she spoke the lie, she crossed her fingers under the table and made two wishes. She wished for Sally to become her adopted daughter and for the po-faced Prudence to win the war in Worthington House.

★　　★　　★

The owner of Paradise Mill was livid. He had rampaged about the offices all morning, had reduced his secretary to tears and was now berating the poor lad who always took the brunt when Worthington was in one of his moods. 'Call this tea?' he roared. 'Cats' doings, this is. What the hell do I pay you for?'

The boy, who was on just a few shillings a week, shook from head to foot as if he had the ague. All he wanted was a chance to become a weaver. The position he held was supposed to be temporary, had been temporary for months. 'I'm sorry, sir,' he muttered, the words clouded by chattering teeth.

'Sorry? It's my turn to be sorry, sorry I ever took you on. What sort of an office boy are you?'

It was no use. He was probably going to get the sack anyway, so he forced himself to speak up. 'I wanted weaving, sir. You said I could go in the sheds when—'

'When you'd proved yourself. All you've proved is that you can't make tea.' Worthington thrust the cup at the boy. 'Here. Take the bloody stuff away, then report to number two shed. You'll be on the brush for a while, but somebody will take you on as apprentice. See the foreman.'

'Th-thank you, sir.'

'What for? I'm only giving you a chance to prove there's another thing you can't do. Go on, bugger off out of here.'

Alone, Worthington paced up and down, his temper cooling slightly towards a steady simmer. Nobody. Nobody knew where that bloody Ivy Crumpsall was. And he'd planned it all so carefully, had been to the Welfare Committee to express his concern about young Sally Crumpsall being left with an old woman.

He walked to the window, looked across at Paradise Lane. The Irishwoman would be back soon. She was a tasty piece, a bit old for his taste, but a good-looker. She might know where the Crumpsalls had gone. He rubbed his abdomen, remembered Rosie Blunt's posser. They were all in it together, the Paradise lot. And the ringleader was their landlord. Joseph Heilberg.

Seated at his desk, the large man leaned back and closed his eyes. There should have been two Paradise Mills by now, two sources of income. He had fought tooth and nail throughout the war, had explained to the authorities that two mills could make twice as much cloth for the war effort. No joy there. The recreation ground and the four houses were the property of Mr Joseph Heilberg who had been interned for the duration. And that had been a piece of positive discrimination, thought Andrew Worthington. Everyone had been so embarrassed about the internment of German Jews. If the land had belonged to any other man, its acquisition might have been assured.

Heilberg. His hatred of Joseph Heilberg was something he fed regularly. The hatred, in its turn, fed its master until his whole being had become a shrine to the animosity he nursed. One day soon, he would have his revenge.

His eyes flew open. Why did that one day never arrive? Why was he just sitting here when the tools were at hand? Bert Simpson. For fifty pounds, Bert Simpson would not be averse to blowing up Westminster. He lit a Navy Cut, spat some loose tobacco from his tongue. As the match dwindled, he set the tiny flame to some paper and placed the small conflagration in an ashtray. It would be wonderful if he could destroy Joseph Heilberg as easily as that. The paper was soon curled into crisp blackness that writhed and twisted until its death throes were over. Fire. He would burn the pawnbroker's property until nothing remained.

Where to begin? At the shop on Derby Road where Heilberg lived, at the lock-up on Wigan Road, at the shop in town that was occupied by Heilberg's son? Or . . . what about the houses? If they were wiped out, perhaps the old man would sell the land. After all, he was on good terms with his tenants, would surely be too heartbroken to consider rebuilding. Andrew Worthington agreed with himself, nodded to demonstrate the fact, stopped congratulating himself when another thought struck home. Houses were difficult. Even with three of them empty, there might be people cutting through the lane on their way to Worthington or Spencer Streets. Even in the night, folk arrived home at odd hours after shift work or overtime. A main road might be easier, in fact. A lock-up should be the best bet as a start.

He thought about the names Worthington and Spencer for a second or two. The houses of Worthington and Spencer had been joined together in unholy matrimony and by Paradise Lane. Paradise had seemed such a wonderful title for the bond he had expected to develop between himself and his young wife. But, with the carelessness of youth, he had failed to acquire that land. Andrew had always taken for granted the idea that Paradise was there for the taking. His father, too, had apparently been of the same opinion, because the original mill – Worthington's – had stood on this very site.

Then . . . then, along had come the people's hero, Joseph Heilberg. He was from rich stock, from a family of successful Austrian businessmen. Every penny the man could collect during Hitler's rise had been diverted across the English Channel. And now, that clever little foreigner stood between the mill and the rest of Paradise.

He picked up the phone, gave his home number to the operator. Prudence hated the telephone. It would ring for ages before she plucked up courage enough to—

'Hello,' said Prudence after the third ring.

'Get Simpson,' replied her lord and master.

There was a pause. 'Is that you, Andrew?'

'Who the bloody hell else would it be?' He was feeling uneasy, had heard a new note in his wife's voice.

'Any one of a number of people,' she told him. 'Just wait a moment, please.'

He tapped on his blotter with a pen.

'Andrew?'

'What?' he shouted. 'Where is he?'

'Mr Simpson is weeding the garden,' she informed him. 'There was rain last night, so he is muddy. When he has finished the gardening and cleaned himself, I'll get him to telephone you. Goodbye.'

Andrew Worthington stared into the dumb instrument as if it was some terrifying apparition. What the hell was going on? She was supposed to answer the thing and do as she was told. Furiously, he rattled the phone and barked at the operator, demanded to be reconnected. 'The line is busy, sir,' announced the disembodied woman.

'Busy?' he roared. 'I don't care whether it's busy or not, it's my bloody phone. Connect me at once.'

'Is this an emergency, sir?'

'Is that anything to do with you? It's my phone in my house and—'

'Sorry, sir. Do try later.'

Again, he sat with a dead receiver in his hand. Oh, he would put a stop to Prudence Spencer's behaviour right away. She couldn't do this and get off scot-free. He marched through the main office, snapped orders at those who laboured there, went out into the mill yard and climbed into his car. As he pulled past the open gates, he saw the Blunt woman sweeping the flags in front of her house. She, too, was on his list, though the bigger fish must sizzle first.

He pulled into the semicircular driveway of Worthington House, dragged his ever increasing corpulence out of the car. His wife was in the drawing room chattering away with Gert Simpson. The two women separated quickly, but he had seen them, all right. He marched into the hall, threw open the drawing room door. 'Mrs Simpson? A word.'

Gert followed Worthington into the dining room, stood mutely with a yellow duster in her hand.

'What the bloody hell are you up to?' he asked in a whisper.

Gert shrugged, placed the duster on a side table. 'It's called gaining her trust, sir.'

'To what end?'

'I'm going to take her to town and lose her, sir. Her's not set foot outside this here house for many a year, so I'm persuading her, like, trying to get her to come out with me.'

'Ah.' He didn't trust Gert, yet he had to, must force himself. Bert was another matter, because the man owed a few favours to the master of Worthington House. 'Where's your husband?'

'Back garden, sir. He's covered in nettle stings. I've put some calamine on him, but he's in a right state.'

Without another word, the monarch of all he surveyed walked through the kitchen and awarded Cora Miles a grunt before stepping into the garden. It was a large area with two lawns separated by flower-beds, but it had gone to seed since the jobbing gardener had been slowed by age. Simpson was near the fish-pond, leather gloves on his hands as he tore at weeds.

'Hello, Mr Worthington.' Glad of an excuse, Bert dragged off the gloves and showed the boss the condition of his hands. 'Your missus doesn't half lay the law down,' he commented.

An unease crept through Andrew Worthington's veins, but he shrugged it off. No, she couldn't have changed – the old fears and phobias would still be there. It must be a phase of some sort, and it wouldn't last. No, she wouldn't reign long with her list of orders for these new servants. 'I want you to do a job for me. A very special job. Remember how I spoke up for you when you were charged with disorderly behaviour?'

The man nodded mutely.

'And how I still hold the evidence about the robbery at Foster's shop?'

'Aye,' breathed the reluctant gardener.

'Time for you to scratch my back, Simpson. I want a

favour. Tonight, when your wife is asleep, come round here. Because this will be between just the two of us. You will tell her nothing. Is that understood?'

Bert's eyes narrowed. He was beginning to know this man, understood that none of Worthington's threats were ever empty. 'I get your drift,' he said finally.

'There'll be a hundred pounds in it for you.'

The man's face lit up for a second. But he realized very quickly that such a sum must mean a very special request. 'Right,' he muttered lamely. 'I'll have to get on with shifting these nettles.'

Andrew Worthington nodded curtly, then strode back into the house. Prudence was waiting for him in the hall. There definitely was something different about her. What was it? Ah yes, she was staring straight at him – almost through him – and her hands, which usually fidgeted in his presence, were folded neatly just below her waist. 'Why did you not bring Simpson to the phone?'

The nervousness sat in her chest, as always, but it failed to bubble up into her tone. 'These people are being paid to attend to domestic matters. I should have thought your workload at the mill would be sufficient to keep you occupied.'

He stepped closer to her. 'Don't try to get clever with me, Prudence.'

'I wouldn't dream of it,' she replied.

A thrill of alarm snaked its way the length of his spine, while his heart thudded faster. 'Remember who is master here.'

'I remember.'

God, she had changed, was altering here and now, right in front of his eyes. 'What's happened?' he asked.

'I beg your pardon?'

'Why are you . . . different?'

A shoulder raised itself, the movement all but imperceptible. 'I'm a grown woman, that's all. I can't seem to worry about things any more. There comes a time when one must take a firm hold on one's own destiny.'

'Must one?' he sneered.

She nodded just once. 'Oh, yes. One must.' Prudence turned away and walked into the drawing room, her head held high. Once inside, she leaned against the closed door, a hand pressed to her lips. Sometimes, she thought she might be living with a close relative of Satan. What was he cooking up now with Bert Simpson? Gert wasn't as bad as she had first appeared, but the husband was . . . sly, shifty about the eyes. She moved away from the door, watched the car as it swung into Wigan Road. 'I wish you would go away and never come back,' she mouthed as the vehicle disappeared from view.

Gert entered the room. 'He's gone, madam.'

'Yes.'

'Stick to your guns,' said the brown-haired woman. The crowning glory was still not a convincing shade, as the rinse had been forced to mingle with red dye, but she looked better. 'Whatever Mr Worthington wants out of Bert, I'll get to the bottom of it, don't you worry.'

Prudence smiled. 'Thank you for telling me what was afoot. My husband wants me to leave, and you were in danger of becoming a pawn in his evil game. Are you sure about Mr Simpson? Does he not suspect that you have spoken to me?'

Gert shook her head. 'If Bert wants to go about trying to hurt you, that's his problem. As for me, I want that kiddy, you know. But I'm not like Mr Worthington. I'd not go to all kinds of lengths to get me hands on Sally. But my Bert's under your husband's thumb, madam. And your husband wants Ivy Crumpsall's heart in his hand so he can crush it till the blood flows. On top of that, he wants to kill Joseph Heilberg. Any road, I'm with you, but I have to pretend I'm not.'

Prudence smiled. 'Complicated, isn't it?'

'You've never smiled before,' said Gert. 'You should do it again, because it suits you.'

Prudence was a light sleeper. When she heard the front
door opening, she switched on a bedside lamp, looked at
her watch, doused the light immediately. Twenty-five
minutes past twelve. What on earth was happening? Who
could possibly want to visit Worthington House in the
middle of the night? She rose from the bed, crept to her
door and listened. Was that a murmur of voices? If so,
who could be here at this ungodly hour? She drew back
both bolts, turned the key quietly.

The landing was like a mined beach – it was difficult to
know where to step without setting off squeaks and
creaks. But she managed not to draw attention to herself,
got downstairs and pinned an ear to the dining room
door.

'Nay, that's going too far, is that,' said Bert Simpson. 'I
could finish up in jail.'

'I can put you away tomorrow if you'd rather. I know
who broke into Foster's – remember? I'll help you on your
way to court, Simpson. I'll tell the police of my suspicions
and—'

'She'd leave me.' Bert's tone was frantic. 'Our Gert
wouldn't stand for nothing like that. Stealing's only
stealing, Mr Worthington. This caper's in another league
altogether.'

Prudence pressed a hand against her heart, hoped that
nobody could hear the pounding in her chest. Footsteps
approached and she twisted on the spot, her eyes searching
frantically for somewhere to hide. Just in time, she
concealed herself behind the drawing room door, waited
for whoever had moved to return to the dining room.

She heard a clatter in the kitchen, then heavy footfalls
retracing the route. 'Here's an ashtray,' said Worthington.
'Smoke if you wish.'

Prudence leaned heavily on the wall. It occurred to her
that Gert might be double bluffing. No. There had been
just two voices in the dining room, one she knew and

hated well, the second a high-pitched whine that she was learning to detest. Unless Gert was being extraordinarily quiet, Bert had come alone, must have waited for his wife to be asleep.

It seemed like ages before Bert left. Prudence positioned herself behind closed curtains, watched through a tiny gap while the odious little man walked down the driveway. He was alone. She suddenly felt grateful, almost happy. It seemed that Gert was trustworthy after all. And Simpson's words still echoed in her mind, 'Our Gert wouldn't stand for nothing like that.'

Andrew was on his way to bed. She moved to the doorway, listened as he muttered a few words under his breath, thought she heard the name 'Heilberg' being spat. Should she contact the pawnbroker? And what would she tell him? 'I think my husband is planning to . . .' To what? To have Bert Simpson break into a shop? Oh, what a furore such a warning could cause!

Hard evidence was needed. Hard evidence would not present itself until after whatever had happened. Even then, Prudence's suspicions might well remain no more than hearsay, and it was not usual for a wife to testify against her husband. This required a lot of thought. And would Gert prove useful, would that very ordinary woman have the strength to go on the attack against Bert?

When all was quiet, Prudence Spencer-Worthington made her way back to bed. Along the landing, she could hear his snoring as she closed and locked the door of her room. On her knees, she prayed for the Heilbergs, prayed that her husband's malice would be found out and punished. Most of all, she begged God to keep Gert on the side of righteousness. Then she slept fitfully, woke knowing that the dreams had been bad, though she remembered none of their content.

Maureen Mason was a disappointed woman. She had come back from Ireland to find that Tom Goodfellow had returned only fleetingly from Hampshire. And now, Rosie Blunt was sitting here in the front room of number 3 with the truth tripping lightly from her tongue. 'He's some sort of a lord. Ivy told me in a letter. Great big house, he's got, servants too. His dad died, you see, so Tom's inherited this Goodfellow Hall and a load of farms.'

'Well, it was nice of him to give Sally and Ivy a holiday,' said Maureen, working hard to keep the sadness from her voice.

'Ivy says he's selling up and coming back.'

Maureen's eyebrows stopped short of hitting the ceiling, but only just. 'To Bolton?' Surely any man would choose to live the grand life instead of returning to an industrial town? 'Why isn't he staying where he rightly belongs, Rosie?'

The little old lady shook her head. 'Summat to do with his dad, Ivy thinks. Like a family feud of some sort – you know how they go on, these gentry. If you go and marry trade, or bring any disgrace, you're out on the lug-ole before you can say suit of armour. Any road, I shall have to go back to Ollie, 'cos he's gone all peculiar.'

Maureen, who had always found Ollie a bit strange, didn't know what to say. The man had been going on about green fingers and rotted vegetable matter for years, had always struck most people as odd when he theorized on the subject of gardening.

'He can hardly remember his own name,' said Rosie. 'And he keeps wandering off like a kiddy. I could put him on reins, I suppose. But it's getting hard, Maureen. He's not clean any more. I have to keep changing him and making him sit on the lav. We'd no children, and now he's becoming a child.'

Maureen put her arms around the dear lady. 'If there's anything you want me to do, any help you need, just come and get me. If I'm down at the shop, Mr Heilberg will understand should I close for the odd half-hour.'

Rosie sniffed. 'I'm frightened, Maureen.'

'Will I stay at your house, then? Will I move in till things get sorted?'

The wrinkled face brightened. 'Would you really do that for me, lass?'

'I would and I will.'

The two women clung together for a few moments, then Rosie extracted herself from the embrace and went back to Ollie. Maureen sank into a chair, looked round the room at all her half-mended treasures. Tom would have real treasures, she supposed, ornaments that would make her shepherd and sheepdog look like plaster prizes from the fair.

She was restless, missed the sound of Tom's pigeons, the noises he made when rattling his fire to life. 'I can't just sit here,' she told herself. 'I must pull myself together and find my toothbrush, go up to Rosie's for the night.' But she didn't want to do that, not just yet. She needed a bit of thinking time, yet she wanted to be on the move. Also, she must get her mind off Tom Goodfellow, must force herself to look elsewhere for a husband. There had been one or two possibilities in Ireland, but Tom had been a hard act to follow. Oh, she should occupy herself, find something to do.

The answer came. Yes, that was it. She would go down to the shop and see if Ruth Heilberg had bought anything interesting. The sky was darkening towards night, but she would go all the same. She was always like this after a few weeks in Ireland, restless, raring to get back into the swing.

With her coat over her arm, she walked along Paradise Lane and turned left into Spencer Street, carried on to the bottom until she met Wigan Road. She passed the butcher's and the greengrocery, unlocked the gate, let herself into the shop doorway. The three brass orbs that advertised Heilberg's wanted polishing. Tomorrow, she would root out the metal wadding and a stepladder. With the door locked behind her, Maureen peered into the gloom.

She thought about lighting the mantles, decided against it. The last time she had been down here in the evening several people had knocked at the door. 'You open, love? Only I want to pawn me coat and me husband's best shoes afore he gets back from the Wheatsheaf,' and so on. So she remained in the meagre light of dusk, examined things by carrying them to the window.

Next to the wooden cash box was a chair where Maureen was supposed to sit between customers. It was seldom used, because this active lady preferred to spend her time drifting about among purchases. She never investigated pledges unless they were out of date, but items that had been sold to the shop formed the basis of Maureen's motley collection of 'mended' memorabilia. She found some lead soldiers, wondered about welding, decided it was beyond her. But there was a beautiful china doll in Victorian dress, its face scarred only by a missing nose. The dolls' hospital would have a nose, she felt sure. So she placed the doll in a box with a statue of St Theresa who had lost a hand. Would the dolls' hospital do a saint's hand? she wondered.

There were some old books, too, including a family bible dating back to 1840 and a leather-bound missal. She peered at these, decided to leave them till morning. Then, as she placed these below the counter, a flash of light illuminated the room. For a split second, she saw a face behind the light, then she sank to the floor under a pile of merchandise that was falling from burning shelves.

In the store room, Bert Simpson seemed riveted to the spot. He had entered by a small window, had made the bomb out of a pale ale bottle, some rag and half a pint of paraffin. The last twenty-two hours had been terrifying, and he should have been glad that the ordeal was over. But if this woman burned to death, he would be a murderer. In one short day, he had possibly gone from petty opportunist to arsonist to killer. Worthington had insisted that the shop would be empty. The fire was raging – he could smell burning paint. What could he do?

Galvanized by fear, he fled from the scene, his short, fat legs pumping as he raced to the Parry Rec. Once there, he gathered his breath near the railings, waited until his heart had slowed. Then he forced himself to saunter along Worthington Street towards a public house on Derby Road. Once inside the pub's back yard, he visited the gents', made sure that no sign of his crime showed, rinsed off the smell of paraffin at a tap in a corner.

He went to the bar, grinned half-heartedly at his comrades in drink.

'You were gone a long while,' remarked one.

Bert picked up his glass of flat beer, tried to still his trembling hand. 'Me stomach's playing up,' he said. 'I went for a breath of air.'

'Aye, and you look as if you've used all the toilet paper and all.'

Everyone laughed at the feeble quip, though Bert's smile was at half-mast. All he could see was that woman's face. By now, she could be scorched to a crisp.

EIGHT

'I'm coming with you.' Ivy stood in the middle of a country lane, arms akimbo, black skirt sweeping the floor. 'There's no road I'm letting you go piking back to Bolton on your own.'

Tom breathed in deeply, prayed for patience. 'Sally is settled in the village school. Just let her carry on until the end of term—'

'That's still a month away from now. Joseph and Ruth Heilberg have lost one of their shops, so I want to talk to them. Maureen's my friend and all, you know. If she's in hospital, I'd like to go and see her. And it looks like arson, doesn't it?'

Tom, who had his own opinion in the matter, shook his head, turned on the spot, allowed his eyes to scan the fields. Looking at the land he owned never pleased him. He didn't want these farms, these complications. He wanted to go home . . . yes, home and he wanted to . . .

He swallowed, allowed the thought to return. He wanted to make sure that Maureen was going to improve. Because he loved her and hoped to marry her. As long as she wanted no children, that was. In spite of the summer heat, he shivered at the memory of a brother he had tried to love until another summer many years ago. A Goodfellow child could be a curse, another Jonathan.

Tom dragged himself back to the here and now, knew he would have to say something to Ivy. Oh well, in for a penny, in for a pound. 'I want to go alone,' he insisted, his back turned on Ivy. 'I need to see her.'

'So do I. And Ollie and Rosie. Who's helping Rosie now

with Maureen in hospital? Eh? Go on, your clever lordship, and answer me that one.'

He swivelled on the spot and faced the difficult old woman. 'You are a difficult old woman,' he informed her. 'Look, Ivy, I am going to propose to Maureen.'

She took a step back, waited until her breathing returned to normal. Then a thought struck. 'What if she doesn't look the same? What if she's scarred?'

Tom smiled. 'Then we must try to mend her, just as she has tried to mend so many broken things.' Just as he and others had tried to mend the broken bodies and souls of countless airmen after the Battle of Britain . . .

'She never managed to do it proper.' Ivy smiled sadly. 'There's more glue on her carpet than on her broken ornaments.'

'Well, I shall manage. I am very good with glue.'

Ivy's grin disappeared as quickly as sunlight in a storm. 'And then there's Rosie. Ollie's halfway to Manchester in the brain department, absent without bloody leave, poor soul. Rosie Blunt needs me—'

'Sally needs you.'

Ivy grunted, stepped behind the gate of Rose Cottage, closed it. 'Then you mun fetch Rosie and Ollie here, Tom. If he's going to be confused, he might as well be confused in fresh air.' She left a small pause. 'Is it a deal? After all, yon house is called Rose Cottage.' She jerked a thumb over her shoulder. 'So Rosemary Blunt should be here by rights. Me and our Sal can go in the back bedroom, then the Blunts can have the front.'

'Fine.' He turned as if to leave.

'Hold your horses,' she ordered. 'I want a word with you, lad.'

He crept like a reluctant schoolboy and stood near the gate. 'Yes, miss?'

'Why did you never ask her before? She's been after you for nigh on twelve month, but you said nowt.'

He stared steadily into eyes that were frighteningly

intelligent and alert. 'Because she knows now.'

'Knows what?'

'That I'm landed gentry.'

'And what's that got to do with the price of fish? I mean, we've all had our thoughts about you, Tom Goodfellow. She knew you weren't normal. We all knew as how you weren't blinking normal, come to that. So what's changed?'

He shrugged. 'If she's interested in me now, while I'm a lord, before I've offloaded the title, then that proves something.'

Ivy stared ahead for a few seconds. 'Aye, and if her bonny face is burnt and you still want her, then that'll be true love and all.' She perked up, beamed at him again. 'And then, you can buy me a frock and a hat for the wedding. Lilac, remember. I'll get feisty in lilac, so warn all the old fellows.'

He leaned over the gate and kissed the lovely lady whose face reflected her thoughts and feelings like a barometer. 'I miss Derek,' he muttered, his tone thickened by emotion. 'He was a good man, because you made him so.'

'Stop mauling about,' she laughed, pushing him away. 'Else it's me you'll be dragging up the aisle, not poor Maureen. Eeh, I do hope she's all right.' She wiped a rheumy tear from the corner of an eye, told herself she'd stopped crying for Derek.

'The reports are encouraging,' he said. 'The smoke made her ill, and there are some minor burns to her hands. They said nothing about the rest of her. Did you know she saved a doll and a statue of a saint? She told the ambulance driver to take them to the dolls' hospital. And he did, on his day off.'

'She's fey,' pronounced Ivy. 'Like a lot of Irish, she's got what you might call an imagination, plus a sixth sense. A good lass, is Maureen Mason.'

Tom studied his shoes for a while, then raised his head and looked hard at Ivy. 'Do you think it was Worthington? The fire, I mean.'

Her lip curled. 'I'd put nowt past him. If he'd been around at the time, I'd have blamed him instead of Guy flaming Fawkes and all his merry men. Eeh, I don't know, Tom, and that's a fact. Rosie sent that lad down the hospital – him with the funny hair.'

'Red Trubshaw?'

'Aye, that's the one. Ugly little so-and-so, but good at heart. And Maureen told him the same as she'd told the bobbies – she saw a white face with shocked eyes, then after that she remembered nowt else till she came to proper in the ambulance. Any road, Andrew Worthington wouldn't do his own dirty work. Oh no, he'd have some other daft bugger acting as mop rag.'

Tom stepped aside to allow a cow to pass by. The herdsman came round the corner with the rest of the beasts, tipped his hat at Tom and Ivy. 'Hello, Master Tom, Messus Ivy,' he said, a grin displaying many gaps between teeth.

'That's as near as I can get,' complained Tom when the cattle had moved on. 'They've dropped the "M'lord", but they can't call me by just my Christian name.'

Ivy laughed at him. 'How's it going, then? Are you still selling land off?'

'No.' He straightened, peered at the sky to assess the time. Time hadn't mattered till lately, so he'd lost the habit of wearing a watch. He'd had plenty of time to study and see to his birds in Bolton. 'I must go to Africa.'

He didn't make sense all the time, thought Ivy. That was happen something to do with all the inbreeding that had gone on in the upper classes. 'I thought you were bound for Bolton?'

'I am. I'll go to Africa later on, at the end of the year. My sister must be found, you see. If she has married and borne a child, she may want him to take over here. And she should be given some compensation for having lived with Father. So I'm not disposing of anything more until I've talked to Patricia.'

'It's all yours in the will, isn't it?'

'Legally, yes. Morally – well, we'll see. So I'll bid you good evening, Mrs Crumpsall. When I've separated Sally from Gus and the pigeons, I'll send her home.'

Ivy stood at the gate of the little house that was now the property of her granddaughter. She watched Tom as he walked away, dejection showing in the slope of his shoulders. He was using that brass-headed cane again, she noticed. His heart must be aching all the way down to his mended knee. The poor man didn't want to be here. After twenty-odd years' absence from Goodfellow Hall, he valued his freedom above all else.

She went inside, set the kettle on the fire. There was more than that to it, she thought as she lowered her bones into a chair. It was something to do with his dead brother, something very sad. This place was Tom's birthright, yet he seemed to hate it with a passion he had never shown before. He was mild mannered, sensible and kind. But in this beautiful part of the world, a memory plagued him, made his eyes dark and his soul uneasy.

She dozed off, slept till Sally came home.

'You should stay here for ever, Granny Ivy,' said the child in the grass-stained frock.

'Why? And where've you been to get so mucky?'

'In the fields with a girl from school. You look a lot better than you did at home.'

'Don't change the subject till you've changed your frock and put that one in soak. And Rosie's coming down with Ollie. He's gone funny.'

Sally bit into a red apple, looked at her grandmother with large and innocent eyes. 'He's never made me laugh,' she said.

'Not that sort of funny, Sal.'

'Oh.' Sally chewed, swallowed, considered all she remembered about the folk next door. 'He's always been the other sort of funny, Gran.'

'I know. But he's worse.'

Sally grinned. 'This place will put him right,' she declared happily. 'It's put you right, hasn't it?'

'Get that frock in soak, lady.'

'Right, Gran.'

Tom marched through the corridors of the Bolton Infirmary, a large bunch of summer flowers clutched in a damp hand. He was nervous, easily as scared as he had been before sending 'his' boys on a mission. A bomb was going to be dropped in the next few minutes. Having piloted a fighter, he was less than thoroughly conversant with the positioning of larger missiles.

He stood at the door of a ward, waited with ten or twelve others who were visiting the sick. They were an impatient lot, moaning about the delay, shuffling their feet, fidgeting. But none of them had come to offer a diamond to a woman who wouldn't be able to wear it until burns had mended. He needed this time, needed to stand still and be calm until the sweat on his brow had evaporated . . . 'Mr Goodfellow?'

Tom looked over his shoulder, saw Lottie Crumpsall's dreadful sister. 'Mrs Simpson?'

She nodded, allowing him a better view of hair streaked with many shades of brown. 'I'm going to see my Bert. He's got a terrible stomach. Doctor told him he's digging his grave with his teeth, you know. Ulcers, I think.'

A reply was expected. 'I've come to see Mrs Mason.'

'Aye,' she said, her tone softer. 'Terrible thing, that were. They lost the whole shop, you know. My husband were very upset with it. That's what started his stomach off, when he heard about that Irishwoman getting burnt. I've not seen him in this state since the war finished.'

Tom suddenly saw the woman in a different light. She was ill-dressed, heavily made-up, but she seemed softer, gentler than the female who had come to 'snatch' Sally. 'I do hope your husband will recover, Mrs Simpson.'

'So do I.' She shuffled nearer to Tom, placed her mouth near his ear. 'Is our Sally all right? She'd never let me visit, you know. Our Lottie, I mean. It's not like I weren't interested, only our Lottie never spoke to me for years. Then that letter come out of the blue, like.'

Immediately, Tom was on his mettle. 'I presume she is well enough.'

'And her gran?'

'Again, I have heard nothing to the contrary.'

Gert pulled herself up to full height. 'Just make sure they stay that way,' she whispered. 'Don't forget, I'm that little girl's auntie and I mean her no harm.' Worthington just wanted the Simpsons to get the kiddy away from Ivy, but Gert was convinced that her own motives were more honest. 'And watch out for Worthington,' she added.

Before Tom could stop her, Gert was clattering up the corridor with her bag of apples.

Tom was borne on a tide of humanity into the ward that contained Maureen. He passed several beds, recognized none of the occupants. Well, that was a good sign. Sicker people were stored nearer to the sister's office and nearer to the door in case they needed wheeling out for treatment or for . . . for cold storage.

She was in the last bed on the left, her beautiful black hair uneven and patchy against a mound of pillows. He smiled encouragingly, kept his eyes averted from bandaged hands the size of footballs. 'Hello,' he said. 'I brought you some flowers.'

Maureen looked at him steadily. He had come out of pity, no doubt. No-one could possibly take an interest in a woman with burnt hair. And no member of the gentry would allow himself to love a poor Irish girl who was no longer a girl.

'Shall I leave them here?' He waved the spray of carnations and long-stemmed roses, pointed to her locker.

'Yes.'

He found a chair, drew it near to the bed, wished that he

could hold her close and tell her that she was beautiful.

'Tell everyone my hands are all right, will you? It's just the top layer of skin that got damaged.' She waved the unwieldy wrappings. 'A precautionary measure, they said. To stop infection.' After a pause, she went on, 'My hair is burnt at the back. I'll have to get it cut.' As if this were the final straw, she burst into tears. 'It's vanity, I know that for certain sure. But I've had long hair since I was a child.'

'Short will suit you,' he told her. 'Don't cry, Maureen. Please don't cry. Your hair will curl if you have it shortened.' He didn't know where to start, whether to start. But he had to start in order to finish, and he had to finish because he was taking the Blunts back to Hampshire soon and—

'Why did you come?' she asked, a padded hand mopping up the tears.

'To see you. To visit the Heilbergs and to take Rosie and Ollie back to Hampshire. Ivy ordered me to take them, because I refused to bring her with me, you see.' He paused, licked drying lips. 'It's important that no-one finds out where Sally and Ivy are. Mrs Simpson and her husband wanted Sally and—'

'And they're working for Worthington. I hear they've a cottage near Worthington House.'

Tom sat awhile and allowed the light to dawn fully in his mind. Bert Simpson was in a ward just along the corridor. He had become ill after hearing about Maureen's plight. Bert Simpson worked for Worthington. Worthington, having failed to acquire the recreation ground during the war, would go to any lengths to hurt Joseph Heilberg. The same man wanted to damage Ivy, too. 'My God,' said Tom.

'What? What is it?'

He sat bolt upright. 'The face you saw – could it have belonged to Bert Simpson?'

She pondered. 'It could have been the devil himself,

because it all happened at the speed of lightning. No, no, I'll never be sure. Staring eyes.'

'Bulging? Like Andrew Worthington's?'

'No. I don't know.'

No, it wouldn't have been the mill owner. Tom was convinced that Worthington had paid someone else, a man of poor character who needed money. 'We'll talk about other things,' he told Maureen. He looked over his shoulder, made sure that no-one else was listening. 'I had to see you.' The words sounded clumsy. 'I just had to come.'

'Why?'

He lifted a shoulder. 'I missed you.'

'Oh.' Her heart was pounding like the big bass drum at a brass band concert. 'It was . . . quiet with you and the Crumpsalls gone,' she said. 'And without the noise of the birds.'

'But your washing should be cleaner.'

'Yes.'

She was going to be no help at all. He couldn't go down on one knee, not in a hospital. Apart from anything else, his leg was playing up again. And he couldn't offer her an engagement ring while her hands were mummified. 'You know about my title?'

'Yes.' She scoured her mind for something intelligent to say, came up with nothing.

'I don't want it. I never wanted it, Maureen. Since the Great War, I've seen very little of the ancestral home and its occupants. But my older brother died, you see. There's a sister – she is older, too. Anyway, I am left with the house, the farms, the tenants and the livestock. First, I must find Patricia.'

'Your sister?' At last, she had managed two words.

'In Africa. I shall ignore the title and revert to the old family name – Marchant. Then, if Patricia agrees, Goodfellow Hall will become Marchant House, and that will be used as an orphanage.' His mind took a brief detour, wondered whether Goodfellow Hall might sound more cheerful, welcoming. Perhaps the silly name could serve a purpose after all.

She smiled at him. 'You always were a good man, Tom.'

Tom got up, walked to a window at the side of Maureen's bed, looked down into the hospital grounds. 'Not good enough for my father, I'm afraid. My father was not unlike Andrew Worthington. He saw what he wanted, took what he wanted and made few apologies. Jonathan was the same.'

'Oh.' Maureen was back to monosyllables. She pushed herself to say more. 'Sit down, please. My neck is aching from twisting to look at you.'

He sat, touched a bandaged hand. 'Are you in pain?'

'No. The burns looked worse than they actually were, and my coverings come off later today.' She didn't want to think about that, didn't want to see those scarred fingers ever again. 'It's my own stupid fault,' she added. 'Instead of running out, I think I picked up a doll and a statue and put them on the counter. Then I must have collapsed and been carried outside. I even sent the ambulance man and a fireman back into the shop for those things. Would you ever believe that, now? There were those poor men risking life and limb for a couple of broken items.' She sniffed back another tear. 'My hands got a bit scorched. And my hair is frizzled. However, I'll know the worst this afternoon, though everyone's sure that my hands will heal in time.'

'Then I shall come back this evening.'

Maureen studied him closely. 'The thing you have to speak of is best dealt with now. You're like a cat on a hotplate, so get it done with.'

He thought for a moment, wondered whether either of them was ready for the sombre tale. But he was here, had come here to talk, so he must get the whole thing straight before returning south. 'After the Great War, I went up to Oxford. When I was on leave at the end of one term, I returned home. Often, I stayed with friends or at college, because I could not bear to share space with my father.'

She nodded. 'Isn't that often the case? You grow up with your parents and you love them. But when you become an adult, then you see them in a different light altogether.'

He shook his head slowly. 'I always detested my father, Maureen. My mother died young because of his philandering. It was her money that allowed me to break free. After years of gambling and roaming about, I came to Bolton intending to study, then to publish a thesis and gain my doctorate. Instead, I diverted in to pigeons.'

She laughed out loud. 'Well, you won some prizes.'

'Yes.' It was his turn to search for words now. 'I went home that one time many years before living in Bolton, found that my brother was in the same mould as my father. He . . . Jonathan attacked the daughter of an earl. He had no control over his baser instincts, so I knew that my father had been born all over again. It was the drink that finished Jon. Had he been sober, he would have chosen a different victim.'

'Please don't punish yourself with these memories.'

He looked straight at her. 'I must. You told me to get it off my chest, so I'm doing just that.' He took a deep breath, continued. 'Even in drink, Jonathan knew he had gone too far with Lady Sarah. He threw her into the lake, then overbalanced and fell in after her.' For a moment, he was back there, could see Sarah flailing in the water. 'He could not swim at all. I was and still am a poor swimmer. The decision made itself, really.'

Maureen stared hard at him. 'You saved her and let him drown.'

His head jerked quickly, caused a painful crick to send red-hot fingers of pain leaping into his skull. 'Yes. How did you know?'

'I guessed,' she replied softly.

'My father was furious,' said Tom. 'The news that his

older son had died was not too disturbing. His main concern was the fact that Sarah was still alive. "She will tell the whole bloody county," he screamed at me. "He should have used one of the servants." My father had used servants, you see. So had Jonathan. I knew all about that, tried to forgive myself for leaving a brother to drown. But I could never forgive my father.'

Maureen sighed, blinked as if to clear vision and mind. 'And what happened to Sarah?'

'She killed herself eventually. Her father died soon after the suicide. He left me money.' *Blood money*, said a little voice in Tom's head. *Blood money because you left your own brother to die. That act proves that the bad blood is in you, too, Tom. Bad blood will out . . .*

Tom leaned forward, placed his mouth near Maureen's ear. 'I never married because I didn't want children. The blood is tainted, you see. I could not contemplate the idea of fathering a Goodfellow.'

'That's rubbish,' she answered calmly. 'Children are not made of blood alone. Where they live matters. How they are loved and cared for, how they are educated. Blood is only a part of it.'

He studied her wonderful green eyes, admired the flaw-less complexion, the shock of black hair that made the Irish skin even paler, more translucent. 'Marry me,' he mouthed.

She closed her eyes, remained silent for what seemed like ages. 'I want children. Even if my hands are no good, I want to be a mother. Thirty-five, I am now. There isn't much time for me. Without children, there is no mar-riage.' The eyes flew open, seemed to scour his soul. 'I'm a Catholic. That doesn't mean I need the pomp and Latin, doesn't mean I have to marry in my own church and drag my family screaming up the aisle every week to Holy Communion. But it indicates that the basic principles of the oldest Christianity are part of who I am. The prime reason for marriage is to create children.'

'Maureen, I—'

'No, Tom. Marriage is important to me. But it is a foundation for family life. Two people do not make a family.'

He drew back. 'Then I am sorry for disturbing you at this difficult time, Maureen. We shall forget that this ever happened. It would be a pity to lose a good friendship because of my clumsy behaviour today.'

'I love you,' she said softly. 'I would go to the ends of the earth for you, Lord Goodfellow. To bear your child would be a joy and a privilege.'

He ran a hand through his thick brown hair. 'Think about it,' he begged.

She shook her head, the movement slowed by pillows. 'I have nothing to think about. It's yourself who must go away and consider the problem.'

She was so clever, so astute, obviously well-read, too. All the instincts of womankind were honed to painful perfection within this one female. Maureen knew what she wanted, had the strength and control to deny herself, the honesty not to pretend agreement. Her easiest path would have been to accept the proposal and to create an 'accidental' pregnancy. 'I'm sorry,' he muttered. 'It's impossible. I am the product of a bad lot. I gave no thought to my brother, preferred to rescue a mere acquaintance—'

'A casualty,' she said. 'Just as I was a casualty a few days ago. Would you have chosen to save the man with the fuel and the matches? No. You would have collected me first and—'

'I didn't go back for him. Once Lady Sarah was revived, I stayed with her.'

'You can't swim.'

'I swam to her.'

Maureen shrugged. 'Stalemate.'

'I should never have taught you the rudiments of chess.'

She tried a smile, failed. 'Has it not occurred to you that

your mother has played a part in your existence? Why must you look to the Goodfellows for your character? Perhaps there is more of your mother in you. We noticed this with horses and cows at home. Some were like their sire, others favoured the dam.'

'Maureen—'

'Go home. Go and rescue poor Rosie from the clutches of Ollie's confusion.'

'What will you do?' he asked, his tone crippled by disappointment.

'Back to Ireland, I suppose.'

He rose, picked up his hat. 'Get well,' he whispered.

'I shall.'

Mrs Mason cried for so long after her visitor's exit that the bandages were left alone for a while. Sister gave her a mild sedative, brought a cup of tea with a straw. 'They're not worth it,' announced the large, starched female.

'I beg your pardon?'

'Men. All the same, not one to mend another.'

Maureen sipped the tepid tea. 'Some are different,' she said finally. 'And he is one of them.'

Tom Goodfellow stood in the grounds of the hospital for half an hour. He wanted to run back in, to tell the staff to bugger off with their rules about visiting hours. He wanted to pluck Maureen Mason from her bed and run away to a far country.

But he couldn't. So many people depended on him. There were the Crumpsalls and the Blunts, tenant farmers, servants at Goodfellow Hall. So he walked away from Maureen and towards other responsibilities. Yet his heart remained beside a hospital bed where an Irish widow keened for the rest of the day.

Cora Miles sank into a kitchen chair. 'Why are you telling me this, madam?' It was as if Prudence Worthington needed to find a shoulder to lean on and a listening ear. Mrs Miles was not quite ready for this. She thought a lot of the mistress, had wondered for years how the good woman had tolerated that brute of a husband. But now, the servant was being dragged into waters whose depths were murky and dangerous.

'Because there is no-one else.' Visitors were a rarity. The sad and gloomy house made no caller welcome. 'I have to go out. I have to look at that shop and talk to Mr Heilberg.'

Mrs Miles, who knew very well that the name 'Heilberg' was a red rag to a certain bully in this house, swallowed audibly. 'You've not been out for a while, madam.' She wanted to help the mistress, had decided weeks ago to do all she could for this poor woman, yet the fear of Worthington had renewed itself since . . . since that fire in Heilberg's on Wigan Road.

Prudence inclined her head. 'Gert offered to take me. I like Gert, but she is married to that dreadful little man. I know what I heard, Mrs Miles. They were planning something. I think I know now what that something was.'

'You've no proof.'

'Then I shall make an effort to get it and you will help me . . . Cora.'

The housekeeper twisted a dish towel in her hands. 'I'm scared of him.'

'So am I.'

'But . . .' But Cora could not think of one word to say.

'I'll look after you,' said Prudence.

Could Mrs Worthington look after herself? the servant wondered. 'He'll stop at nowt, missus,' she muttered. 'We both know that. Mr Heilberg knows it, the mill folk know it, the pawnshops' customers, the—'

'He must be stopped.' Prudence's voice was soft, ordinary. 'Only I can stop him. I and a woman called Crumpsall. Gert mentioned her some days ago.'

'Ivy Crumpsall?'

'That's the one.'

194

'She's gone, done a bunk. Mind, she's not flitted, as far as I've heard. Gone for a rest, like. She's took Mr Worthington on lately, yelled at him in the mill yard about her son's funeral. Ivy's feared of no man.'

Ivy would suit Prudence perfectly, then. The lady of the house placed herself in a chair next to her servant. 'Cora, you and I will be leaving here very soon. Of course, I shall have to explain to Victor first. He is my son and he deserves some respect. But I cannot tolerate life here for much longer. You will come with me. I have money, Cora. We shall buy a small house and I shall leave it to you in my will. There are some very pretty places on Crompton Way, not too cramped, pleasant gardens and three bedrooms. But first, I must . . . first, there are things to do.'

Cora Miles almost shook with fear. There was a new set to Prudence's jaw, and a look in her eyes that seemed to shout at anyone who looked closely, 'I've had enough and I am about to ruin him.' There were depths to this pleasant, quiet and frightened woman that had never before been plumbed. An old saying popped its head into Cora's thoughts, something about a worm turning. A worm turning was one thing, but causing earthquakes was another matter altogether. 'Mrs Worthington, I don't want no trouble.'

Prudence studied her nails for a moment. 'I must send to the chemist for some more of that lanolin cream,' she said absently before focusing her attention on the nerve-racked housekeeper. 'Don't worry,' she said, her tone almost cheerful. 'Get my coat, Cora. We shall go out for a walk.'

'But—'

'I need to start right away.' She kept her tone even, worked to disguise the dread she experienced when contemplating the outside world. There had been times when even the garden had been out of bounds. It was as if the world were too big, too full of air and space. Everything would rush into her, filling her lungs, her ears, her mind. No, no, she intended to go carefully, slowly. 'Help me, Cora.'

The woman's heart was awash with pity for her employer. 'Course I will. You know I'll always help you.'

Ten minutes later, Prudence stepped through the front doorway of Worthington House, her breath held against sudden bursts of wind. But the day was still and quiet, so she took a few infant steps down the drive, pointed out the hollyhocks, said how well they were doing.

'Lupins, too,' added Cora Miles. 'And your roses are better this year. Have you never thought of a climber round the door? Honeysuckle's nice.'

'I'll remember that.' The words forced themselves past a barrier formed by gritted teeth. Once she could get away from here, once she was settled in another place, she would buy a sweet-smelling climber and train it round the front door. Round her own front door.

They reached the gate. 'Shall we stop a minute?' asked Cora.

Prudence inhaled through her nose, allowed the air to escape slowly from her mouth. 'Cora, we open this gate as wide as it will go. Then we turn right and walk.'

The housekeeper followed orders, followed her mistress along Wigan Road. 'Tell me when you've had enough,' she said.

'I'm fine,' snapped Prudence. 'Just keep up with me.' A fire had lit itself in the proximity of her chest, a terrifying heat whose base was anger and hatred. There was no space for terror. While the fuel lasted, she would use it and carry on to . . . To where? She slowed her pace while her brain homed in on the 'where'. She was going to hell; she was heading for Paradise.

Cora Miles was of the opinion that a man starved of food and drink should not overindulge when sustenance finally appeared. Similarly, a woman who had stayed inside a house for months on end should not set out to walk the

Great Wall of China on her first outing. But with at least two miles under her belt, Prudence showed no intention of giving up the struggle. 'Happen we should go back now,' Cora said several times. Her own legs were aching, so the pain in Mrs Worthington's muscles was bound to be acute.

But Prudence ploughed ahead until she stood outside the charred remains of Joseph Heilberg's Wigan Road shop. She raked her eyes over the shell, breathed in fumes produced by heat and damp. Pools created by firemen had settled among scattered relics that used to be furniture, clothing, books and jewellery. 'My God,' she mumbled softly. 'Something has to be done.'

'Police won't want to know, madam.'

Prudence nodded just once. 'Some crimes, Cora, are too bad to require evidence. My husband – the man I married – will do all in his power to ruin Joseph Heilberg. He wants that Recreation Ground, you see, wants to extend his little paradise. Mr Heilberg has other shops. His son lives above one, and Mr and Mrs Heilberg have rooms above the Derby Road shop. If all the businesses are destroyed, then Andrew may get his hands on Mr Heilberg's land.'

'Murder?' breathed Cora Miles.

'Exactly that. Come along. We shall walk up Spencer Street to the shop on Derby Road. I cannot sit back and watch while people are killed and maimed. Already, one Irishwoman is in hospital with burns to her hands and hair – it was all over the newspapers. Fortunately, her injuries are minor, but I could not live with myself if I allowed that – and worse – to happen again.'

Grimly, Cora Miles struggled to keep up with the newborn Mrs Worthington. As if her heels were winged, Prudence was skipping along the flags while Cora lagged behind wondering when the agony in her feet was going to stop. The mistress seemed to be on a suicide mission, because nobody in this town had ever 'bested' Andrew Worthington.

'Come along,' chided Prudence. 'Nearly there.' Her lip twisted again when she thought about the naming of this street. Andrew's father had been a hard man, but the whimsical side of his nature had dictated that the joining of the Worthington and Spencer dynasties should be marked for prosperity. So the parallel streets had been joined by a short lane called Paradise. Prudence carried on, pushed the unsavoury reminiscences from her mind. At least the Paradise Lane houses belonged to someone else. By the time Andrew had shifted himself to make a bid, the dwellings had been sold to an immigrant from Austria.

They reached the top of Spencer Street and turned left into Derby Road. Prudence turned to her housekeeper. 'Now, you may go home if you wish. Go to Worthington House or return to your own. There is no need for you to be a witness. As for myself – well – I've come a long way, so I can surely get home on a tram.'

Cora stared straight ahead. She was the wrong side of sixty and she was tired. What had she to lose at this point? There would be no place for her with Mr Worthington once the mistress had left for good. And if she left Mrs W here, would the woman be able to get herself back up to the top of Wigan Road? 'I'll stop with you,' she announced. There was no alternative. Someone needed to supervise these strange goings-on.

'Are you sure?'

'Positive. And it's not just so's you'll leave me a house on Crompton Way, 'cos I'll be dead long before you. Any road, my kin will see to me. I'm staying because . . . well . . . you need somebody. I mean, Master Victor's too busy to help you with all this, and he can't be expected to pick and choose between his parents.' She closed her lips tight against the suspicion that Victor was his dad all over again. Prudence was blinded by motherhood and, anyway, the idea that Victor Worthington might turn out to be another nasty piece of work was best left undiscussed for now.

198

'As long as you are sure.'

Cora nodded, followed Prudence into Heilberg's.

Joseph looked up from a ledger, closed his sagging jaw with a snap. The shock he felt at seeing this reclusive woman must not show. 'Mrs Worthington?' he said. 'Good day to you.'

Prudence nodded curtly. 'Will you close the shop, please?'

Joseph studied the face of the unexpected visitor. 'Ruth will come down and—'

'No. I need both of you.'

The pawnbroker knew that this was not going to be a simple matter of pledging an item for money. With his heart pounding in his ears, he walked round the counter, locked the door, turned the sign so that it displayed CLOSED. 'Follow me,' he said.

Prudence went through the door marked PRIVATE, motioned Cora to follow. Upstairs, they found Ruth Heilberg busy with some needlework. 'Very pretty,' said Prudence. 'Will it be a cushion?'

Ruth, silenced by shock, nodded.

Everyone sat down after Joseph's invitation. The married couple stayed side by side on a sofa beneath the window. Cora placed herself at the dining table, her experienced eye recognizing good polish and plenty of elbow grease in the shine.

'Shall I make tea?' asked Ruth, her gaze fastened to the elegant woman who occupied an armchair.

'Later,' replied Prudence. 'I shall come straight to the point. Mr Heilberg, I have been to see your shop on Wigan Road.'

The man nodded. 'Very sad. But I have insurance and my friend, Mrs Mason, is making a good recovery. For this reason, Ruth and I are counting blessings.'

'Your premiums will increase,' said Prudence. 'And if anything of that nature were to happen again, you would be entered in the register of bad risks.' She inclined her head for a moment, seemed to be studying her hands. 'You must be careful.'

Joseph, wondering whether this might be some form of blackmail, bridled. But no, this good woman would not hurt him – surely? 'A Jew who comes out of Austria does not need to be reminded about taking care, Mrs Worthington,' he replied softly. 'Ruth and I lost many among our families, so we are already warned.'

'I am still warning you.' Prudence's tone was even.

'For this, I thank you.' The man sounded wary.

Prudence Worthington jumped from her chair with a suddenness that startled the other three. She walked to the sofa, towered over the small couple who sat side by side. 'He is just behind you,' she announced clearly. 'His office is yards from where you sit. There is nothing he would not do to see you ruined.'

The ensuing silence was decorated by the elaborate chimes of a German clock. 'Is this your husband of whom you speak?' asked Joseph.

'It is indeed.'

'But why?' asked Ruth, black eyebrows scurrying upward in her startled face. 'If he threatens us, why do you come here?'

Prudence smiled, though her eyes remained clouded. 'Because I hate him, Mrs Heilberg. Because I know his mind, his greed and his cunning. He will not be easy to catch, even for the police. That is the first in his list of commandments – thou shalt not get caught. He has money, ambition and a cruel understanding of people. Worthington will find a weak man, a man who needs money, and he will pay such a man to damage you. The creature he used to fire the Wigan Road shop is in hospital. I know this because the man's wife works in my house. She told me that "her Bert" has been troubled with his stomach since that night.'

'I know who you mean, but he was ill,' interrupted the pawnbroker. 'I, too, have asked questions. All those in the public houses were interviewed, and Bert Simpson had spent a long time . . . he was indisposed, so he used the facilities and—'

'And he burned your shop,' Prudence finished for him. 'While he was supposedly sick, he was, in fact, committing arson.' She walked back to her chair, sat.

'He does have a nervous stomach,' said Cora Miles. 'From the war. His wife told me all about it. It flares up something shocking when he's frightened. And setting light to property won't do his health any good. Aye, I reckon he did it.'

Prudence, pleased with Cora, flashed her a smile. 'Incidentally, Bert Simpson had a win on the horses. That is what he told his wife. Gert Simpson is pleased with the dress she bought with money from her husband. Very appropriately, the dress is flame coloured and the money came not from her husband, not from the horses, but from Andrew Worthington.'

Joseph gripped his wife's hand. 'What can I do?' he asked.

'You can know,' answered Prudence. 'Knowledge is a powerful weapon. Let's have some tea, then we shall discuss tactics. There are many retired dog owners who would gladly give up their nights to watch your shops, Mr Heilberg. A few shillings here and there would almost guarantee your safety.' She patted her hair, leaned back and closed her eyes. 'No sugar for me,' she told the hostess. 'And two heaped spoonfuls for Cora.'

NINE

It was a long walk from the station, but Ivy persevered with the same solid determination that had accompanied her through motherhood, widowhood and the premature demise of her son. As self-appointed matriarch and sage of the Paradise streets, she recognized that her presence in times of crisis was compulsory. Also, she was feeling better, had gained some strength while living in Hampshire. Yes, Hampshire was the real paradise, she told herself as she looked up into a soot-speckled sky. Chimneys belched, trams clanged, trolley buses whined. A ragman's horse was leaving a deposit outside the Wheatsheaf while its master sustained himself in the taproom of the same inn, no doubt. Ivy grinned, remembered that she had no roses to fertilize in Lancashire. She patted the animal, gave him a lump of sugar. Lately, she had taken to carrying treats for the horses in farms surrounding Oakmead.

When she took a short cut through the open market, many stallholders and customers greeted her, told her how well she was looking, asked for the recipe. At the bottom of Wigan Road, she rested for a while, placed her small case on the pavement, tried to count the members of a battalion of mill chimneys whose nostrils pierced the sky. Home. This place was home. No matter how dirty it looked, no matter how foul the smells from furnace and fishmarket, she loved her home town, knew that she could never leave it, not in her heart. But she would go back to Hampshire because Sally was there. 'Them servants had best see to her,' she mumbled under her breath. 'Only she's got to carry on at school. I'll fetch her next time.'

'Talking to yourself, Ivy?' The voice was full of surprise.

'Rosie!' Ivy joined her neighbour, looked her up and down. 'You look like a streak of white paint,' Ivy declared. 'Is he worse?'

Rosie shrugged, tried to smile. 'I don't know.'

Ivy understood. 'Aye, it's hard to make judgement when you see somebody every day, isn't it?'

The little white-haired lady leaned against a wall. 'I've not seen him since yesterday tea,' she said. 'He went missing with a garden spade and no teeth. Police is looking for him now. And I've been combing the streets for him. He'll feel the business end of my temper when he comes home.'

He wouldn't, thought Ivy. This tiny woman was diminished, had lost her will to argue with anything or anybody. 'Eeh, whatever next? There's poor Maureen in hospital, Joseph and Ruth with a shop gone, you traipsing about looking everywhere for Ollie. I can't turn my back for five minutes, can I? Any road, when we find the owld bugger, you can both come back to Hampshire along of me and Tom, have a change.' She wondered fleetingly what Tom would say when he found out that Ivy had travelled hundreds of miles without company. Still, she was old enough to look after herself, she said inwardly. 'You'll like Hampshire,' she advised Rosie. 'There's hills and forests and loads of farms. The air down there's as pure as crystal. And the folk are all right, dead ordinary, no side to them at all.'

Rosie's face was glum. 'We're not coming, Ivy.'

'What? Why not?'

Rosie lifted her shoulders. 'If he doesn't know where he is when he's here, how will he carry on when he's somewhere where he doesn't know where he is in the first place?'

Ivy analysed the question, found a reply. 'If he doesn't

know where he is, why should it matter if he's somewhere else?'

Rosie didn't know. 'I don't know,' she replied. 'But it does matter. Anyway, what are you doing up here? Tom said he'd left you and young Sally down yonder.'

Ivy took her friend's arm. 'There's a few folk I want to see, but first, I need a cuppa and to make sure your Ollie finds his way home. Come on, lass. Me throat's like sandpaper.'

They walked arm in arm up Wigan Road, stopped when they reached Heilberg's. Ivy cast an eye over charred remains. 'Could have been Maureen and all,' she said. 'At least it's nobbut things that were burnt to a crisp. At least she lived through it, eh? Not that yon Worthington would have worried if she had passed on, like. Bad bastard.'

Rosie, who was with Ivy only in body, made no reply.

'There's two people in this town that have stood up to Worthington,' Ivy continued. 'There's me and there's Joseph Heilberg. We're the only two who've not run about like whipped dogs. He wants that land. And he wants to hurt me and our Sal. Oh aye, he'd be tickled pink if yon Gert and Bert took Sally away from me. As for Joseph, I reckon Worthington'd go to the ends of the earth to get at him. So this is just a start.'

Rosie looked puzzled. 'Eh?'

'Never mind, lass. We'll get something organized and find your Ollie. He'll not have gone far, not without his teeth. He won't even answer the door without his gnashers in.'

'He's changed.'

'I know, love—'

'There's no help for him. Sometimes, I wish he were out of his bloody misery.'

Ivy tugged at Rosie's sleeve, dragged her up Spencer Street and into Paradise Lane. 'There,' she exclaimed. 'He's back.'

Ollie was standing in the middle of the cobbles, his arms

204

poised over a pigeon. As soon as he bent to retrieve the bird, it scuttered away, seemed to be enjoying this game. 'Come here, you stupid piece of vermin,' yelled Ollie. 'I've got to find the rest and all. Stand still a minute.'

In different circumstances, the women would have laughed, but neither showed any inclination towards mirth on this occasion. 'Looks as if he's even lost the bloody spade,' said Rosie. 'And his head's full of pigeons. If we could see inside his brain, it'd be all feathers and droppings.'

Between them, Ivy and Rosie managed to steer the old man into his house. 'You'll have to lock the doors and hide the keys,' said Ivy. 'He's not fit to be out on his own.'

Rosie Blunt sank into a rocking chair. 'I can't stand much more of this, Ivy. I mean, he's allers been a bit daft, what with his gardening and all that, but he's like a baby now. It's getting beyond me, is this. And with you gone and Tom and Maureen, I've nobody to turn to, so I—'

'So you come back down yonder with me. Tom's pigeons are all settled – I think he only lost two – but the rest are in a hut near the big house. Ollie can find what he's looking for in Oakmead. You know, it's amazing what a bit of sun and fresh air can do. You should see our Sal – brown as a berry and her hair's thickening up something lovely, like corn in a summer field. It were Tom as said that.'

Rosie continued doubtful. 'I don't know nobody down yon.'

'You know me and our Sal and Tom.'

'Aye, Lord Tom,' muttered Rosie. 'And I bet they all talk funny, don't they?'

Ivy agreed. 'But so do we.'

This was news to Rosie. 'Do we heck as like. Least we can all understand one another. They all talk London down there.'

Ivy laughed. 'No, they don't. They talk soft, like. Gentle and a bit slow. Sometimes, they near put me to sleep in the queue at the post office. And they don't go dashing about. There's no mill hooter, no smoke, no clogs sparking at half past five in a morning. I mean, they start early, but everything's muffled. Even the horses sound as if they've slippers on. Cows wander past our cottage twice a day, big daft eyes, udders swelled up with milk. Sheep and all, they've got. Hens, fresh eggs, loads of cheese. Farm butter, Rosie. You can have all that for nowt. The only trouble with the country is you get to be on nodding terms with Sunday's roast pork. Our Sal won't eat pork from any farms near us, 'cos she says pigs is too nice to eat. So I have to get a joint she's not had words with. It's great, Rosie. So get bloody packed and no messing.'

Rosie made tea, gave Ollie a mug and some bread and butter. 'Where were you all night?' she asked him.

Ivy sipped from her cup, noticed that Rosie no longer addressed her husband in her 'just-you-wait' voice.

'I'm here now, aren't I?' The old man sounded more cantankerous than confused. 'And I don't want no cheek from you, Rosie. It were a hard shift last night. I think I'll have a sleep before me bath.' He dropped the mug, started to snore almost before the last syllable had left his lips.

Rosie stood and watched while the peg rug absorbed tea, milk and sugar. Tears poured silently down her face, making her older and weaker.

Ivy was determined to have no more nonsense. 'I'm going looking for His Lordship,' she said as her cup clattered into its saucer. 'And I'll call in on the Heilbergs, then into the hospital. There's big trouble out there, Rosie. And Worthington's at the back of it.' She got up, walked to her neighbour's side, placed a hand on a trembling shoulder. 'Ollie's happy, love,' she whispered. 'Sometimes, nature is kind to us that's getting on a bit. Yon man's having a second childhood. But you need company, lass. Will you pack up while I'm out?'

'Aye.' The withered cheeks were dried on a corner of

the shawl. 'Aye, we'll come back with you, give Ollie a holiday. I told Tom we weren't going, so you put him right.'

'I will.'

Rosie studied her neighbour quizzically for a few seconds. 'Does Tom know you've come?'

'No.'

'You always were a difficult woman, Ivy Crumpsall.' A faint smile visited the pale lips.

'Just one thing,' said Ivy. 'Leave all your weapons at home, will you? Somehow, I don't think the Hampshire folk would take kindly to your posser.'

Tom opened his door. 'God,' he exclaimed.

Ivy looked over her shoulder. 'Where?' she asked. 'Nay, it's only me, Tom. Far as I know, God's in His heaven but all's not well with the world.'

He held the door wide, allowed Ivy into the lobby, followed her through to the kitchen. 'When did you get here?' he asked. 'And where's Sally?'

'An hour ago and she's with the servants in Goodfellow Hall. Any more questions? Or does that conclude the case for the persecution?'

He pretended to glower at her. 'Did you come as you are?'

'My bag's at Rosie's. Ollie's back. He's still chasing pigeons thinking they're yours. Poor old boy's lost a spade, but Rosie's found his teeth.'

Tom dropped into a chair, ran a hand through his hair. He had visited Joseph and Ruth, had heard about their encounter with Prudence Worthington and her house-keeper, so the plot was thickening. He didn't know who to trust any more. Was Cora Miles a spy from Worthington? Was Lottie Crumpsall's sister Gert a goody or a baddy? Did Bert Simpson set fire to the Heilbergs' shop on Wigan Road? And on top of all that, Maureen was still refusing to marry him.

'What's up with you?' asked Ivy. 'You look like you've swallowed a cockroach.'

'She won't marry me.'

'Oh.' Ivy settled back in an armchair. 'Happen she's seen the state of your physog, lad. That mush of yours would stop Magee's Brewery's horses and curdle the bloody ale. Try straightening your gob. Like this.' She used her fingers to drag her own mouth into a semblance of a smile. 'And ask her again.'

He tapped his hands on the arms of the chair. 'What the hell's going on round here, Ivy? The Heilbergs are in real danger, I'm sure. They're getting watchmen with dogs – a couple of fellows who will stop all night in the shops for a small consideration – but who can guarantee the safety of Ruth and Joseph? Or was the attack on the Wigan Road premises an isolated incident?'

'No,' she said immediately. 'It were deliberate. I'd stake me life on it. That's why I'm here, Tom. There's things I remember, things I've wrote down over the years. Oh aye, we'll put a stop to Worthington and his bullying. But first, you can tell me about Maureen.'

He told her. Not just about the rejected proposal, but about his whole life. 'And that's why I don't want children,' he concluded.

Ivy put her head on one side, studied him for several seconds. A clock on the mantel ticked loudly, each sound definite enough to be a pronouncement in itself. 'You're a big-headed pie-can,' said Ivy, whose metaphors were often confused when she felt strongly. 'Why should any child of Maureen's take after your lot?'

'You've not seen the true colour of Goodfellow blood,' he replied.

Ivy's face and voice did justice to the word caustic. 'She's got a past and all, you know. Maureen comes from generations of hard-working Irish farmers. What makes you think your blood's stronger than hers? She's a good Christian woman. A Catholic, mind, but you can't hold that against her – I don't, never have. That girl would make a good mother, Tom.'

'I had a good mother—'

'Not for long, eh? You were only young when your mam popped her clogs. That there Jon might have been a lot different if your mam had been around. And, while you're talking so clever, how come you never turned out like your dad?'

He stared at her for what seemed an eternity. 'I've had my moments.' His voice was soft, almost a whisper. 'Gambling, chasing women and so forth.'

'But you've never hurt nobody.'

'Not deliberately.'

Ivy leaned forward, craned her neck at him. 'Then get off your backside and take your good blood down to the infirmary. Tell Maureen I'm here. Oh, and while you're there, think on what I said. Her ancestors might not have owned half of Ireland, but they were just as important as your family. Get married and take your chances the same road as the rest of us does. There's never a one of us knows how children will turn out, 'cos marriage is a gamble, and you know all about gambling, eh? There's vicars whose dads were murderers, then there's thieves with nice kiddies. Tom, you keep pretending you're just an ordinary bloke, but when it suits, you start on about being gentry with bad ways. Fact is, you make no more sense than Ollie Blunt, and he talks like he's been twice through the bloody mangle. So get weaving before I thump you. I know Rosie'll lend me her yardbrush if I ask nice. Ever been clocked with a yardbrush, Tom?'

He shook his head absently. Ivy had probably said to him all the things his own mother might have voiced, though the language would have been slightly different and no broom would have entered into the conversation, he thought. The old woman was right. How could he presume that his 'blue' line would be predominant? 'Thank you,' he said gruffly.

'What for?'

He shrugged, tried to lighten the atmosphere. 'For putting me in my place, Mrs Crumpsall.'

Ivy got out of the chair, announced her intention to visit the Heilbergs. 'Come seven o'clock tonight, I want everybody in number one,' she told him.

'Everyone?'

'Aye. That's me, you, Maureen if they let her out, Joseph, Ruth, Rosie and Ollie.'

'Mrs Worthington and her housekeeper are supposedly with us, too.' He told her of the two women visiting the Heilbergs.

Ivy's eyes blazed in near triumph. 'I knew it. I knew that lass would turn on him one day.' The grin was replaced by a frown. 'Chairs,' she said. 'There's not enough in our house.'

'I'll bring mine,' he volunteered.

She shook her head. 'Fetch Maureen's and Rosie's and all.'

'Why so many?'

The old woman tapped the side of her nose. 'Just you wait, son,' she said. 'I've not even started yet.' She turned to leave, changed her mind. 'Get in yon car and up to Worthington's house,' she ordered. 'Tell the missus about the meeting.'

He thought for a moment. 'What if Mrs Miles and Mrs Worthington are part of some evil plan?'

Ivy smiled grimly. 'Nay. Cora Miles is a good lass – I used to push her out in her pram when she were little. As for Mrs W, she must be feeling strongly about summat if she's putting more than the end of her nose past the front door.'

'Agoraphobia?' he asked.

Ivy fixed him with a stare of cast iron. 'Aye, if there's enough chairs, he can come and all.'

He scratched his head.

'Aggery-wotsit.'

'Phobia.'

She smiled properly this time. 'Funny name, but as long as he's on our side, we'll make room for him.' She awarded him one of her vast store of knowing looks. 'All right, leave Mrs Worthington till later. We'll think about it. Happen she's best left out of it, or happen she's best warned. We'll stew on that.'

When the old lady had left, Tom walked to the grate and pulled a little box from behind the clock. Inside, on a bed of satin, lay a sizeable diamond in a ring of rose gold. Would the bandages be off by now? Even if they weren't, Maureen could wear the ring on a chain or a ribbon round her neck. She had a pretty neck, long and elegant.

Tom sat by the grate, stroked the velvet lid of the tiny container. She wanted a child. Like most other humans on the globe, Tom Goodfellow had never completely subdued the urge to procreate and continue his line. His own line, the Marchant line.

Ivy was right. He must take his chances and trust that the 'blue' in his veins would be diluted by Maureen's healthier corpuscles. At forty-odd, he could surely manage fatherhood – no matter what that status brought into his life.

Her hands were so small, made purple and red by the burns. 'I've got to let the air to them,' she told her visitors. 'It's only the surface that's damaged, but my fingers feel tight, you see. I have to go for some kind of therapy to get myself moving properly again. But they're not as bad as I thought they might be.'

'Aye, there's nowt beats oxygen for healing,' said the sage in the brown coat.

Maureen studied Ivy for a while. 'Ah, now I know what's wrong with you,' she exclaimed. 'You're in a coat and no shawl. I only just now realized that I've never seen you without shawl and apron. The coat suits you.'

'And your hair suits you and all.' Ivy stood up so that

she could admire the newly cropped cap of black curls. 'Eeh, you've an Irish head on you, girl. That's one thing about the Irish – they always have good hair and strong teeth.'

'That's two things,' replied Maureen, who was feeling more like her usual self. She hadn't yet spoken to her other visitor except for a brief greeting, but she was pleased with her hairdo, gratified by the doctor's assurance that most scars on her hands would disappear in weeks or months. 'In fact, it's a lot of things, thirty-two teeth and more than a few thousand hairs.'

'Back to bloody normal,' groaned Ivy. 'Clever answers, contrarywise look in her eyes, ready to argue.' She turned to Tom. 'She's all yours, lad. I'll go and muster an army for tonight.'

Maureen watched while the old lady walked down the ward. 'What's she up to?'

'War,' replied Tom.

'Oh.' Maureen looked at him, knew that she could get lost in eyes as blue as his. Did children really matter? She knew folk who hadn't been blessed, yet they seemed happy enough. In fact, it was often the arrival of babies that sounded the death-knell of a marriage by relegating husbands to back seats. 'What kind of war?'

He fingered the box in his pocket. 'An "Ivy" kind of war.'

'I see. There'll be no prisoners taken, then.'

'Very few.'

She wanted him. She had wanted him for ages, had been inventing excuses to drop into his house just to see him, just to stand next to him, to breathe the same air . . . 'Sure, it was nice of you to come, Tom,' she told him. 'If you'll go outside and wait, I'll get one of the nurses to help me dress. The doctor says I can come home as long as somebody takes me and looks after me. I'm sure Rosie and Mrs Heilberg will see to my needs.' She held up the discoloured hands, stared at them. 'It's all on the surface, thank God,' she said. 'The flesh underneath wasn't touched.' She looked at him. 'Go on, then.'

'Right.' He opened his mouth to continue, thought better of it, walked the length of the ward with one hand gripping the jewellery case as if his life depended on its contents.

Eventually, she joined him in the corridor, a nurse by her side. 'Thank you,' said Maureen. 'I promise I'll be right back if I can't manage.'

'Ah, you were lucky,' said the nurse. 'But go easy, won't you?'

'I'll be fine,' Maureen told her. 'There are neighbours who will see to me.'

'Goodbye, Mrs Mason.'

Tom smiled almost nervously at his companion, slowed his pace to match hers as they made for the main door. 'Let's go through the park,' he suggested.

She blinked against the afternoon brightness. 'Lead on,' she said. There was something in the Bible that seemed apt at this point, a woman speaking to her mother-in-law, Maureen thought. Was it the Book of Ruth? 'Whither thou goest I will go, and where thou lodgest I will lodge. And thy people shall be my people, and thy God my God.' She felt like that. If he had suggested sailing to China, she would have gone with him. Though she was glad it was just the park, because she still felt tired.

'Maureen?'

'Oh, I beg pardon. I was miles away.'

'Where?'

'China.'

He smiled, told himself that he might have to get used to the vagaries of this lovely woman's mind. Women in general had a tendency to allow their thoughts to wander unleashed, and this particular lady was possessed of a fine brain and a colourful turn of phrase. Life with Maureen would never be dull. Life with Maureen would be full of broken things and glue. If she would have him, that was.

213

'Look at the children playing.' She nodded towards a group of rascals jumping on and off the 'crown', a roundabout that bore a strong resemblance to a monarch's headgear. 'They'll be all cuts and bruises come bedtime.'

'You like children.' It was not a question.

She sighed heavily. 'I've come this far without a baby, so I suppose I can make the rest of the journey without one.'

'No need,' he told her. 'It was Ivy who put me straight, of course. A child of mine would be a child of yours. The goodness in you would teach him how to behave.'

She stopped dead, swung on a heel and stared at him. 'Is this you proposing again?'

He nodded, his face very solemn.

'You look fit for a requiem,' she said.

Copying Ivy, he used his fingers to stretch his lips into a smile. Her laughter was infectious, so they dropped on to a bench and let the mirth fly. 'Will you wear a ring?' he asked between giggles.

She glanced down at her hands, suddenly found the scars to be extremely amusing. 'When I can bear it,' she replied.

When both were almost composed, he took the diamond from its nest of white satin and allowed the sun to dance along its smooth table. 'Wear it on a chain for now,' he said, a note of satisfaction in his voice. 'When your hands settle down, we can see if the ring's the right size for you.'

Maureen fixed her gaze on the gem. Its facets split the sun's rays into a thousand shards that pricked her eyes. But she wouldn't cry. No, it would be bad luck to weep over an engagement ring. 'Tom,' she managed finally. 'Did this cost a lot of money?'

'Only an arm and a leg.'

'Ah well, sure it's a good thing you have two of each.' She smiled broadly at him. 'I don't have to be a lady, do I?'

He tried to look worried. 'If you are less than a lady, ma'am, I shall be forced to withdraw the proposal.'

She dug him in the ribs. 'You know what I mean.'

'No. You can be plain Mrs Marchant.'

The children in the playground continued their reckless games, shrieking and shouting as knees and elbows were grazed and bruised. To them, there was nothing special about the moment. But had they stopped their play for a time, they would have noticed a man and a woman embracing on a park bench. Of course, that would have been nothing new, as many lovers walked these paths on summer evenings. And who might have guessed that a lord of the realm was about to relinquish title and lands to settle in a mill town with a woman of ordinary stock?

The games went on and so did the kissing.

The last of the shift had disappeared in all directions, backs stained with the sweat that made for discomfort in summer, pneumonia in winter. Some mill owners had managed, at great cost, to ventilate the sheds, but Worthington stuck to his money and to the old law, an eleventh commandment that stated, 'Thou shalt open no windows during thy shift, or a plague of unemployment shall descend upon thee and thy families.'

Ivy had discarded the coat, was back in uniform – white blouse, grey skirt, black shawl, snowy apron. She leaned against a gatepost, remembered how ill and weak she had felt while standing here a few months ago after Derek's death. Her breathing and her mind had been cleared by the fresh country air, and she was ready for him. Oh yes, on this occasion she was more than fit to face the devil.

A man emerged from the carding shed, his face grim. 'Ivy.' He reached out a hand in greeting. 'Come inside, love. I've facts and figures in me book.' He glanced up at the window of the boss's office. 'He can take a bloody running jump up his own back passage after today,' he said. 'Sixty-five, I am, Ivy. Sixty-bloody-five. Except for the first war, I've spent fifty-three year in this hole. And the war weren't what you might call a holiday, neither. Come on, hurry up afore you get clocked. If he sets eyes on you, he'll know there's summat afoot.'

Together, Ivy and the old foreman pored over newspaper advertisements and lists of names. 'There's nigh on thirty spinners applied to Ainsworth's and Deane Top for a kick-off,' said the old man. 'And at least another thirty are asking round and about – Kippax's, Beehive and others. The lads and lasses who've been interviewed have took references from me and other foremen – 'cos bosses with decent workplaces know Worthington won't give nobody a character.' He picked up more papers. 'Monday morning, Worthington'll be seventeen weavers down. And them boys and girls as leave here next week'll be nicely settled in mills with proper union representation and a bit of a thank you along of the wage packet.'

'Nobody's give notice?'

He shook his head. 'Not a man-jack nor a woman-jill. Why the bloody hell should they? He's fought tooth and nail to stop them getting organized proper, so they owe him nowt at all. Fortnight from now, Paradise'll be near gutted, not enough workers to run at half-mast.'

She leaned back in the hard wooden chair and inhaled deeply. 'What response have you had from the other mill owners?'

'Disgusted, they are. I mean, you'd think Worthington'd show a bit of sense what with trained folk being thinner on the ground and the unions spreading like wildfire. We're still a lot of folk short, 'cos some went fighting and never came back. I mean, whether they were weavers or goldsmiths, the bloody Germans still shot them. Yon feller's made no effort to shape this place decent, so all the sensible bosses are opening their doors wide, 'cos they know a Paradise worker's worth having.'

'Aye, you're right there, Sam.'

'And for them who've stopped here because it's near

home, there's mills putting on free transport to fetch folk there and back.' He nodded pensively. 'Next news, there'll be a government inspector coming up. I know that, 'cos I've sent word about this dump. There's very few mills like this one now, thank God. I've visited a fair few these last weeks, and they've air-conditioning, bright electric lights, space between mules. Canteens and all. Walls painted pale yellow. Nice. Cheerful. Expanding too, keeping up with the times and employing more folk.'

Ivy sighed. 'Tom Goodfellow reckons even proper mills'll bottom out, though. They want millions spending on them, you know. New machinery and all that. Nobody can afford what's needed, but I'm glad to hear they're making things better for the poor buggers that's doing the grafting. Aye, well, that'll put one spoke in his wheel.'

Sam Greenhalgh rolled up the evidence, pushed it into a drawer. 'I'm not really retiring,' he said, a wide grin showing many gaps among few teeth. 'This afternoon, I leave here. Monday I start at Heilberg's with our Lassie. She's an alsatian. I'm going in for night-watchman and he's paying fair, too.'

'Joseph's a good man.'

'He is that, lass. Now, you'd best be shifting. Are they all coming to your house, then? Did you manage to persuade them?'

Ivy nodded. 'I wrote to each and every one while I were away, then I sent young Red Trubshaw chasing them all up today. We're going to need every chair in Paradise Lane. Even then, there'll be standing room only for the stragglers.'

Sam shook her hand warmly. 'You'll shut this mill,' he said, a note of satisfaction in his tone.

Ivy laughed. 'Oh no, Sam. This mill won't shut.'

'Eh?' Grey eyebrows shunted upward. 'What do you mean?'

She touched the side of her nose. 'Wait and see, lad. Just you wait and see. Because, my old mate, things is

217

coming to the boil very nicely. As they say in Sherlock Holmes stories, all will be revealed in time.'

Maureen was ignoring her hands. She was so busy showing off her ring that the burns were no longer important. Ivy smiled kindly upon her neighbour, offered her congratulations, hoped that the words hid a fury she had carefully damped down to simmering point. Worthington had scarred Maureen's hands. Ivy admired the ring on its chain of pale gold, but she concentrated on the burns and prayed that her plan would work.

The house was already crammed. Behind the parlour sofa, a row of assorted chairs lined the wall. Maureen had saved two for herself and Tom by placing her bag on one and her cardigan on the other. Ruth and Joseph Heilberg sat next to these reserved seats, then Rosie and Ollie Blunt occupied the displaced kitchen sofa with Ivy. Other chairs were ranked under the window directly facing the Paradise Lane residents and the owner of the houses. The landlord tried not to fret about this being the beginning of the sabbath. For the first time, no candle would be lit in his house when sunset approached. He held his wife's hand, advised her and the Lord of Israel that this was a special occasion. Ivy stared at the empty places beneath the window, crossed her fingers beneath the fringe of her shawl, hoped with all her heart that the people she had invited would turn up.

Tom left Maureen, bent down over Ivy. 'Do you still want me to go up for Mrs Worthington? You know how she hates going out. And he might be home—'

'Not at this time. Not on a Friday. Like Scrooge, he counts his gold religiously every week. And he'll not be alone. There'll be some woman there with him, you can bet your life on that. Let's hope she's willing and getting a few bob for her trouble. Any road, I still think Mrs Worthington'd be better not coming. She shouldn't get involved with what I'm doing here tonight, 'cos he might even bloody kill her. Only you must tell her what's afoot, 'cos she'll cop the flak later on. Just warn her, Tom. You'll not be giving her any news. She knows the names of most of them that's expected.' They must come; they had to come! Ivy sniffed meaningfully. 'Aye, the main thing is to make sure she's warned and ready for the rotten mood he'll be in tonight.'

Tom whispered in Maureen's ear, left the house. Maureen claimed her seat, waited with the rest for whatever was going to happen.

'Has he found them bloody pigeons?' asked Ollie.

'Yes.' His wife's voice held no expression. It was plain that she had answered this question many times.

'Where are they?' he insisted.

'Away.'

'Will they come home? They're homing pigeons.'

'They've moved house,' answered Rosie.

Ivy took Ollie's hand, stroked the liver-spotted skin. 'Be quiet, lad,' she advised. 'We need our wits tonight.'

He smiled at her. In a moment of clarity, he hit the truth. 'You'll get no bloody sense out of me, love.'

'We still want you here,' Ivy told him. 'You're part of what's happening, Ollie.'

He nodded slowly. 'Aye, happen I am.' He gazed round the room.

Ivy was more determined than ever to get Ollie down to Hampshire. That beautiful and fruitful county would surely cheer the old man. He still had some strength, was wiry enough to withstand a night in the cold looking for Tom's departed pigeons. She could picture him in the autumn sitting on a cart while the harvest came home. At last, he would reap something after years of failure in his own back garden.

The front door was opened and a voice floated up the lobby. 'Mrs Crumpsall?'

Ivy's heart lightened immediately. 'Come in unless you

want money.' She kept her tone light. 'Make yourself at home, don't be shy.'

A woman's head poked itself into the room, the hair hidden by a scarf. 'There's a lot of us,' she said. 'Nine, I think. Phyllis Caldwell's only fetched one, 'cos the other's abroad in the army.' She looked shocked when she saw the congregation. 'You look as if you're waiting for the main picture to start.'

Ivy got up, pulled the woman into the room. 'They're all with you, lass. Is it Rita? Rita Eckersley-as-was?'

The visitor nodded. 'Aye, I found a good lad at the finish. He took me and Roy on even though Roy weren't his.' She addressed the whole room. 'It were rape. He got me up in his office and . . . I were only fifteen.'

Ivy put her arms round Rita and comforted her. 'Friends, lass. These are all friends.'

Rita dabbed at her eyes, turned, jerked an arm at those behind her. Roy came in, a fine lad in his mid-twenties. He was followed by Mary Shaw and her two teenage daughters, then Tilly Saxton entered timidly with a girl of about twelve. Phyllis Caldwell brought up the rear with Lizzie. Lizzie's twin brother was the only absentee, as he was tidying up the British mess in India.

Before taking her seat, Mary Shaw burst into tears.

'What's up with you now?' enquired Rita Eckersley-as-was. When she got no answer, she decided to speak up for the distressed woman. 'Mary's upset in case you think she's cheap with having the two kiddies to that bad bugger. But it were blackmail. Worthington knew summat about her dad, threatened to put him in prison. So it's a wonder she didn't have more than the two.' Pleased with her explanation, Rita sat down.

Joseph rose to his feet. 'We are not here to judge. Each man and woman carries a burden, but none must criticize another. Do not weep,' he advised Mary. 'You have beautiful children. For this we must be thankful.'

Mary cheered up. 'They're good girls.'

220

Joseph beamed upon the gathering. 'All in this room have suffered or witnessed the tyranny of one man. He will be stopped. This is not about revenge or retribution. To stop the cancer will be enough.'

Ivy kept her mouth shut for a few minutes. Deep in her heart, she wanted revenge, but Joseph Heilberg was right. Worthington must be brought to heel so that no more people would suffer. When the room was quiet, she composed herself before speaking. 'We have to be quick,' she began. 'Mr Heilberg is going to the mill in a minute. He's going to tell Worthington to come here and talk business. It's time you lot stood up to him.' She pointed to the mothers, then to the offspring who stood in an uneasy row behind their parents' chairs. 'And I'll tell you now – in case you don't already know – that I were nearly in the same boat. I were older than his usual girls, but he had a go and got stopped.'

Joseph picked up his hat and walked to the door. 'Be calm,' he advised. 'We are many and he is but one man.'

Ivy sat down, waited. If any of them wanted to clear off, she had no intention of stopping them. But the fingers under her shawl were crossed again as she watched the troubled faces. He had never admitted paternity, had progressed from one woman to another, had tossed aside each one as soon as his eye had moved along the line to another pretty young thing. Well, these were only some of his children. But there were enough, she thought grimly. If they would all stay, there would be enough.

Prudence ran an eye over Tom Goodfellow. He seemed a fine man, a trustworthy soul. She allowed him inside, placed him in the dining room. 'I shall be back directly,' she advised him before rushing off to consult her house-keeper.

In the kitchen, Cora Miles was washing dishes. She listened as her mistress outlined Tom's message, wrung out the dishcloth, picked up a tea towel. 'I don't think I should be there for the comeuppance,' she said. 'And I don't think you should be here, either. When the master gets in, he'll be mortallious.'

Prudence lowered herself into a chair. 'I must get out of this house, Cora. Tonight. This is more than my nerves can tolerate. I shall go to Victor.'

Mrs Miles, who had her own opinion of the young master, carried on drying dishes.

'What will you do?' asked Prudence.

Cora shrugged. 'If you want to go down Paradise Lane with Tom Goodfellow, I'll come with you. But your husband'll murder you if he knows you're in with the Paradisers. As for what you might call the long-term, there's no future here for me if you're not stopping. I'm all right, I don't want you fretting over me. There's a bob or two put by, and I shall get a few little cleaning jobs up Wigan Road and—'

'You are coming with me.'

The housekeeper opened a cupboard, clattered some pans into place. 'I've got me own place. I shan't need to stop at Master Victor's.'

'Your home is rented. How much is the rent?'

'I'll manage.'

Prudence swallowed her pride and it tasted bitter. 'I need you,' she said softly. 'Victor will marry soon, I'm sure. Miss West is just right for him.'

Cora nodded to herself. If anybody could keep that young rapscallion in his place, Margaret West might prove to be the one. 'Then I'll do whatever you want, Mrs Worthington.' This lady had always been good to Cora. When new bedroom furniture had been delivered, the old stuff had gone to the housekeeper. She understood Mrs Worthington, recognized her weaknesses, knew that this woman could not be left alone. 'Happen we should go to a hotel for a while, madam. We could stop at the Pack Horse till you find a house. As long as the rent's paid, I can leave my belongings round the corner.' She jerked a thumb in the direction of her home. 'But take my advice and leave Ivy Crumpsall to get on with her own doings. He'll be took down tonight, I'm telling you. Ivy never pulls a punch. Stop out of his road.'

Prudence left the kitchen, stood in the hall for a few moments before entering the dining room. Tom was plainly in a hurry, was pacing about the floor. 'I am sorry to have kept you waiting,' she said.

'No matter. Mrs Crumpsall heard about your visit to the Heilbergs, so she wanted you to know what's going on tonight. There's no need for you to come. In fact . . .'

'I'll be safer out of it?'

'Yes.'

She guided him to the front door. 'Please give my regards to Mrs Crumpsall and tell her that I shall not be living here from now on.' She straightened her shoulders, looked him in the eye. 'For a short time, Mrs Miles and I will be staying at the Pack Horse. I shall telephone for transport shortly, so please go about your business.'

He lingered for a few seconds. 'Are you sure that this is the right thing for you?' She was not one for getting out and about, he thought. The shock of so many changes might prove too much for her.

She read his mind. 'Mr Goodfellow, my life in this house has not been easy. The . . . nervousness was born of unhappiness. A fresh start may well be the best thing.'

He shook her hand, walked down the drive to his car. Second thoughts prompted him to return. 'Mrs Worthington—'

'Spencer-Worthington. Shortly to be simply Spencer, I hope.'

He understood that well enough. 'I, too, intend to change my name.' And their reasons were not dissimilar, he mused. 'If you ever need me, go to Joseph Heilberg. While I am abroad – I must go to Africa soon – Mr Heilberg will help you. I hope you find some joy in life soon.'

She smiled at him. 'I shall do my best.'

Tom drove away, slammed his foot to the floor. It would be happening now, and he needed to be there. In his pocket lay a letter from Peregrine Fotheringay. The money was available, the project was attracting interest. Soon, very soon, Andrew Worthington's world would be torn apart. Tom, his fiancée and his neighbours needed to postpone the planned return to Hampshire, because there was much to do.

TEN

There was no way out. Behind him, the little pawnbroker stood with his back wedged against the door. Andrew Worthington was a large man, but an exit made by forcefully removing Heilberg from the doorway would have been undignified and an admission of guilt.

'Business?' roared Worthington. 'What kind of business is this?' He pointed to Ivy. 'And I thought we were rid of you at last.' Swinging round, he faced the man who had brought him here on false pretences. 'Considering selling the houses and the land, are you?' he asked with heavy sarcasm. 'I take what you say in good faith, and what do I find? Ivy Crumpsall and her cronies. Yes, I thought we'd seen the back of her.' He swivelled again, stared at the woman he had hated for a lifetime.

Ivy bared her teeth in a mockery of a smile. 'Eeh, you don't get shut of me that easy, Mr Worthington. I'm one of them things that has to be took down brick by brick, you know.' She glanced round the room. 'Does anybody want to give their seat to this here important man?'

Nobody moved.

'No respect,' pronounced Ivy. 'That's the trouble with folk today. They show no respect for their elders and betters.' She glared at Mary Shaw who was blubbering again into a handkerchief. 'We just want you to meet a few of your kiddies, sir,' continued the hostess. 'That's Roy, then there's Pauline, Pamela, Amy and Lizzie. Oh, Donald couldn't make it all the way from India, but he'll call in to see you as soon as he gets a bit of home leave.'

Worthington's heart pounded in his ears, seemed louder

225

than the big steelworks' hammers. He was in a corner, had been backed into it by more than a dozen enemies. The women were ugly, dried out and worn out, and some of the so-called children were practically adults.

'He's a big lad, my Donald,' announced Phyllis Caldwell, determined to speak for her absent son. 'For years he's wanted to get his hands round your throat. After all that training for the army, he's got muscles like Samson.'

Ivy smiled kindly upon Phyllis, turned the full glare of her attention on Worthington. 'Com-pen-sa-tion.' The syllables were clearly separated, as if she were speaking to a child of three or four. 'Safety in numbers, you see. If they all go to court, you'll need good legs to stand on, Mr Worthington. It doesn't matter whether these folk win or lose, 'cos Roy and Donald will sort you out.' She looked Roy up and down. 'That's a fine lad you've got there, Rita. How old is he?'

'I'm twenty-six and I can talk for meself, ta.' Roy's eyes were fixed on the face of his biological father. 'Mam suffered and so did I,' he snapped. 'So you'd best pay up.'

Ivy judged Roy to be a man of few words and hasty actions. 'Leave him a minute, son,' she advised. 'Let him get used to being a daddy to so many. Happen we can find some of the others, eh? I reckon we might fill the Victoria Hall if we try hard enough. We could get a band in and have pie and peas.'

The youngest girl stepped forward, pushed her way past all the mothers' chairs. She stood in the centre of the room, her face scarlet, bright blue eyes brimming with some indefinable emotion. All her life, Amy Saxton had been without a dad. Tilly had explained over the years that the man who had fathered her was married to someone else, but Amy had now reached the age when she could reason for herself. Every time a child at school had threatened to tell his or her dad about something, Amy had fumed. She had a dad, but she had been ordered by

226

her mother never to approach him, had not been able to beg him to fight the many battles of childhood.

Worthington, dismayed by the girl's penetrating gaze, shifted his feet and turned his head slightly. She looked like him. The bloody girl had his markedly convex eyes, his chin.

'Are you my dad?' she asked, though she needed no reply. If she were to turn now and look in the overmantel mirror, the answer would be there.

'I am not your father,' spat Worthington. 'There is no proof, not for any of you.'

Amy stood her ground. 'You were never there,' she said accusingly. 'When I got beat up, you weren't there. The others had dads at home, but I didn't. It's better now, because some of the dads got killed in the war. I moved to another school and told everybody you'd been shot in France.' She nodded, then put her head on one side as she studied this creature who had ignored and neglected her and her mother. 'I wish you were dead,' she told him. 'Dead is better than not there, 'cos they can't help being killed, can they? But you were here and you never helped my mam.'

A dreadful silence hung over the room. Maureen glanced at the clock, wondered where Tom had got to. She hoped with all her heart that Mrs Worthington would stay away from this terrible scene, yet she was glad that the lady was being informed about events. The mill owner was furious, and his wife needed to be prepared for repercussions. Where was Tom?

Ivy pulled Amy away from her father, told her to go and stand with her mother. Tilly wept softly until her daughter returned and put an arm across her shoulders. 'I'm glad he never came to our house,' pronounced the girl. 'He's not a nice man, Mam. Like Mrs Crumpsall said in her letter, he's not worth knowing except for money.'

The centre of attention glared at Ivy. She'd set him up all right – and she'd probably got Prudence involved, too.

No wonder the atmosphere at home had deteriorated – this old crone had, he felt sure, given Prudence her new-found 'confidence'. Oh yes, Ivy Crumpsall was the one who deserved all the credit for this little scenario. And all because he'd chased her round the yard one evening donkey's years ago. Unconsciously, he touched his cheek, as if remembering the blow delivered by Ivy Crumpsall's neighbour, a smash across the face that had sent him reeling. He heard words he had almost managed to forget, 'Keep your hands off Ivy Crumpsall, you filthy bastard, else I'll set a full shift of my mates on you.' She'd been a startlingly attractive woman, had never looked her age.

'Well?' asked Ivy. 'Cat got your tongue?'

'I've nothing to say.' She looked her age now, all right. Though there was vigour in her stance, strength in her tone . . . He folded his arms and waited. They couldn't keep him here for ever. It was tantamount to kidnapping. If he stood his ground, he would get through it. He gritted his teeth, concentrated on breathing steadily.

'A hundred pounds apiece will do for now,' declared Ivy. 'A hundred for each mother and the same for every one of your children. After that, a fiver a month will do. You can send Donald's to Phyllis and she'll save it for him till he gets leave. Aye, you mun get a Bolton Savings Bank book for your lad,' she advised Phyllis. 'It'll set him up when he leaves the forces.'

Worthington's face was colouring towards magenta. 'You'll not get away with this,' he shouted. 'I'll give not one penny piece. My lawyer will see to that.' He inhaled, searched for words, searched for an exit from a room that was crammed with people and with hatred. 'These slovenly bitches are nothing to do with me,' he shouted. 'I've never touched a woman who wasn't willing.'

A snort escaped Ivy's lips. 'Oh aye? And I'm the Queen of flaming Sheba.'

Worthington glared at Ivy. She knew. Ah yes, she knew

him far too well for comfort. Unable to look any longer into the old woman's unflinching gaze, he turned on the rest of the company. He would stick to his guns, all right. 'Sue me,' he spat. 'Go on – you just try it and see what—' The remainder of his words were amputated as he was shunted further into the room by Joseph Heilberg, who moved quickly away from the opening door.

'Sorry,' said Tom to Joseph. He entered fully, stood between Joseph and Worthington. 'Good evening, sir.' He took a card from his pocket and placed it in the mill owner's hand. 'Were you discussing lawyers? Well, there is my solicitor's card. He liaises with these people.' A second square of printed matter changed hands. 'Those are my northern representatives, though Marsh, Marsh and Fotheringay of Regent Street in London will, if necessary, be willing to take on the case for these good people.' He smiled benignly upon the gathering. 'Good evening to you, also,' he said. 'I am so pleased to meet you all at last.'

Worthington's fury could no longer be contained. 'What the bloody hell is this to do with you?' he demanded of Tom.

Tom remained cool. 'A good question, sir. When I came north, it was my intention to publish a paper about the industrial revolution and its effects on cotton factors. It was for a doctorate, you see.'

Worthington, who had little time for the products of universities, curled his lip into a snarl.

'My father, Lord Goodfellow of Oakmead in Hampshire, was keen on education, you see.' He tried not to laugh as he deliberately dropped the title into the arena. His father hadn't been keen on anything or anybody – unless the 'anybodies' turned out to be women who couldn't run very quickly. 'I studied your mill, sir, found it to be . . . wanting.' Tom stopped for a moment. This awful man reminded him of his own father and of Jonathan, too . . . 'The workers in the Paradise Mill are not being treated fairly. Others in your position have installed certain basic comforts and amenities, but you are lagging behind the times. In fact, the progress made in your factory since the revolution is virtually nil.'

Worthington swallowed audibly into the small silence that followed. A lord. A bloody lord with bloody London lawyers. No, this wasn't kidnap – it was blackmail. Yet he felt himself deflating, was being diminished by Goodfellow's presence. Even without the title, this bloke was not to be taken lightly. He had breeding and brains, was of a different class, a level of society that was feared and even revered by Worthington and his kind.

Tom carried on. 'These other ladies and young people have suffered in a different way. We are here to attempt an equable settlement that might preclude the need for court proceedings.' He smiled benevolently upon his victim. 'I suggest you sleep on this, Mr Worthington.'

'No time for sleep,' snarled the purple-faced man. 'Things to do in the mill, yet. Things none of the idle workforce can do, Your Lordship. As for this lot . . .' He swept a none too steady hand across Ivy Crumpsall's parlour. 'The demands will be met.' These five words emerged quietly, as if he had difficulty in allowing them to find a way out. Completely routed for the first time ever, he turned to leave.

But Tom and Joseph blocked the doorway. 'In writing, please,' said the pawnbroker, a hand emerging from his breast pocket. 'Your signature.'

Tom obliged by offering his back as a suitable surface for the paper.

When the words had been scanned, Worthington added a flourish, then Ivy Crumpsall and Rosemary Blunt stepped forward as signatory witnesses.

Lord Goodfellow, when his shoulders were no longer required, faced the enemy and performed a neat bow. 'Thank you, sir,' he said. 'Your co-operation in these matters is appreciated.'

Worthington pushed the men aside and made for the lobby.

'Oy!' called Ollie.

The big man froze, one foot in the parlour, the other in the narrow passageway. 'Yes?'

'If you see any pigeons, bring them home, lad.'

The assembly waited until heavy footfalls had disappeared from earshot. Ivy, Rosie and Ruth burst into laughter that was completely beyond control. Tom grinned at Maureen, then the whole gathering began to giggle and guffaw, though few knew why they were suddenly amused.

Ollie, without knowing how, had gladdened all hearts by mentioning pigeons. He twisted and turned in his seat, saw all the happy faces, mistook the mothers' hysteria for mirth. 'Hey,' he yelled. 'Were that Worthington?'

'Yes, love.' Rosie mopped at her tears. 'And you've sent him looking for pigeons.'

Ollie thought about that. 'Nay,' he announced solemnly. 'Only place yon man would see a pigeon's under a pie crust.'

While everyone continued to laugh away their tensions, Ivy went into the kitchen to brew tea in a huge pot borrowed from the Spencer Street Chapel. 'Eeh, Ollie,' she muttered to herself. 'It's right what they say – "out of the mouths of babes" – 'cos you're a child all over again.' The tears she dried had nothing to do with merriment.

He drove erratically up Wigan Road, his eyes glued to tram-tracks as if he needed a course to steer him homeward. His heart pounded frighteningly, and sweat coursed into his eyes, causing them to sting as he stared ahead. Ivy Crumpsall. If only he knew somebody who could put a stop to her once and for all. Simpson was useless. He'd started the fire on Wigan Road, had then turned frantic with terror after hearing about the Irishwoman's burns. The man was in hospital now, his stomach affected by nervousness. Too much acid? Acid of the most caustic variety should be thrown into the face of that horrible, unsightly old hag. His flesh crawled when he thought of touching her. But Ivy Crumpsall hadn't always been ugly, hadn't always been old . . .

There was a hollow quality to the sound when he slammed the front door of Worthington House. He paused, listened, heard nothing. Prudence was probably upstairs, would be reading in her locked and bolted bedroom. On Fridays, Mrs Miles left cold meat and salad, so he noticed nothing new when he carried his plate through from the kitchen. His place was not set at the dining table, and he gathered that the ageing housekeeper had suffered a slight loss of memory again. She'd not been on form lately, would probably benefit from a talking-to. After taking silver from the sideboard, he sat to eat his solitary meal, hadn't the heart to flick through the *Bolton Evening News*.

Six. He threw down his fork and took a draught of water. Six of his so-called children, the Crumpsall witch had found. That youngest one – he could not recall her name – was so like him. Any man who wasn't blind would easily see the resemblance. He would have to pay up. The sums did themselves in his mind – he had always been good with numbers. With the mothers included, he'd have to lay out a thousand pounds to start with, then fifty pounds a month for life. Unless or until somebody died. God, he wished he could find some person to do a few unsavoury little jobs. But no. He had signed, had been witnessed. If any of that motley crew popped off, Lord Fauntleroy would be on to his lawyers quicker than sugar sliding off a shovel.

'Damn him, too,' he roared, his left arm sweeping plate, glass, silver and food from the table. He glanced sideways, watched a radish as it rolled beneath the sideboard. Lettuce decorated a skirting board, and slices of egg lay on the parquet, each one looking like a tiny sun peering through white cloud. It was her fault. This was all the doing of that cold bitch upstairs. If she'd been anything like a wife, he wouldn't have needed to look elsewhere for comfort. As ever, he conveniently forgot that many liaisons had taken place before his marriage.

His face lifted itself until he was staring at the ceiling. Prudence bloody Spencer. How pleased Father had been about the alliance. Permission had been granted to name the streets Worthington and Spencer, then Paradise Lane had been born when the factory's chimney had begun to wear the name 'Paradise' instead of 'Worthington's Fine Calico'. Why hadn't Father bought the lane then? Why hadn't he acquired the waste ground in the lower portion of the H?

Over a cigarette, he pondered on something he had heard in his mill some years previously. A winder had been summarily dismissed for saying, 'H is for hell, not for Paradise, and this place is hell.' Oh, how little they knew, those idiots who merely kept the mill ticking over. Hell was here, in the midst of so-called affluence. This big, proud house at the top of Wigan Brow was the real Hades.

She was icy, terrified of sex. Like any young man, he had been adventurous, inquisitive, keen to experiment. Nothing abnormal had been expected of her, he told himself firmly for the hundredth time. Women had to do these things. It was their duty, their role in life. She had been beautiful, rounded, supple. And she had refused to allow him into her bed after Victor's birth. She had done her duty by producing a son. If he had forced himself upon her, she would have returned to her parents with tales of his 'perversions'.

To hell with her. He rose, pushed back his chair so fiercely that it fell over and clattered on to the wooden floor at the edge of the central rug. She wanted telling. He paused, the hand holding a Navy Cut cigarette frozen mid-air. How loud that falling chair had sounded. It was as if every noise echoed right through the house and up into the gables. Were the bedroom doors standing open? he wondered.

He climbed the stairs, stopped on the landing. Her bedroom door hung wide open, as did the door to her dressing room. The single bed with its white cover of broderie anglaise looked unslept in, virginal. An uneasy feeling crept from the base of his spine right up into his skull, an icy finger that seemed to trace a warning along the surface of his body. The dressing table was bare except for a free-standing set of mirrors, three ovals edged in cream and gold. A hanger lay on the floor next to a tan-coloured shoe.

The dressing room led off her bedroom, its outward-opening door hanging free against the cane chair in which she often sat while reading. Two steps covered the area between rooms, and he found himself standing in an oblong of perfect emptiness. Bars from which her clothes had hung were naked, as were the shoe racks. No, there was one thing left. He reached across to a shelf and picked up a band of gold. She had gone. His fingers folded over the wedding ring as if to crush it.

In his own room, he removed studs and collar, threw Prudence's ring into a bin and rinsed his hands at the washbasin. Alone. He had never been alone before. Life had been solitary, but she had always been here, a parallel line whose existence had merely served to mirror his.

A niggling headache caressed his temples, began to weave its sadistic web across his forehead and into his brain. Today, he had lost a wife and found six children. Victor. Would Prudence have gone to him? He lifted the telephone receiver, barked his son's number at the operator.

'Hello?'

'Victor? This is your father. Is your mother there?'

'No.'

The big man fell back on to his bed, decided to be comfortable. 'She's gone,' he said baldly. 'She's taken all her clothes, so I assumed that she would be with you.'

'I haven't seen Mother,' replied Victor. 'But she phoned and said she'd be staying in a hotel.'

'Did she give a reason?'

'No.'

Without bidding goodbye, Andrew Worthington slammed down the receiver, then lay glaring at the instrument for several seconds as if laying the blame at its feet. The pain in his head was less severe, so a walk might do him good. He replaced his collar, fastened the tie, pulled on his jacket. He would go and fetch Mrs Miles. After all, somebody would be needed to clean up. He couldn't leave that mess in the dining room.

With a determinedly carefree stride, he set off along the road, wondered whether any of the neighbours had noticed Prudence's exit. He smiled to himself. She wouldn't go far, wouldn't stay away long. The woman had an irrational fear of everything beyond the bounds of her own home. Though she seemed to have gained some strength of late. A chill visited his spine again, but he shrugged it off. Prudence would not move on, not after all these years . . . would she?

In Kitchener Street, he hammered at the housekeeper's door, watched a few curtains twitching when he got no response. The woman in the next house emerged, teeth removed, woven headscarf failing to conceal a row of steel curlers. 'She's gone,' announced the crone, a hand clawing at the front of her grey shawl.

'Gone?'

'Took things. Bags, like. Went off with your wife in a taxi cab. Nobbut half an hour ago, it were, happen nearer three-quarters.'

He tried to act nonchalant, felt his eyes glazing over with the effort of appearing unshaken. 'I see. I thought they were going tomorrow,' he explained. 'A little holiday, you understand.'

She smiled, bared gums that glistened in the evening

light. 'I heard them talking,' she said. 'Nowt up with my hearing, Mr Worthington. Your missus said as how she hoped you wouldn't find them.'

He swallowed. 'Where?'

'Can't remember.'

He jangled some coins, approached the woman. 'Will this jog your memory?'

'Might.'

He dropped a handful of silver into outstretched talons.

'Pack Horse,' she said gleefully. 'Till they can find a house.'

'Thank you.' He tipped his hat, turned on his heel and walked away. In a gap between houses, he found the bottom of Randall Street. The other woman lived there, the floozie whose stupid husband was in hospital with a ticklish stomach. He marched along, tried to hold up his head.

Gert saw him coming, ran to the door. 'Mr Worthington,' she exclaimed. 'I called round your house after coming back from town, let meself in. Where've they gone?' She had half expected the exit, but not yet. For days, she had watched Mrs Worthington's increasing unease, yet she felt hurt now, because she had received no warning from the mistress or from Cora. Perhaps they didn't trust her, then. 'Do you know where they are?' she asked again.

'That's no concern of yours,' he snapped. 'I need you to come and clean up the dining room – had a bit of an accident, dropped my plate. And, as from tomorrow you will take over the position as housekeeper.'

Gert didn't like this man, didn't trust him. Her loyalty lay with his wife. 'Isn't Cora coming back, then?' she asked.

He looked at her blankly. 'Cora?'

'Your housekeeper.' Even after all these years, he had no idea of his servant's name, thought Gert. She found herself hoping that Mrs Worthington would stay away from this husband of hers. Gert had seen a lot of life and she knew a nasty bloke when she saw one. 'I'm going down to see Bert. They have an extra visiting hour on a Friday evening.'

He nodded. 'Right. If you'll walk to the house, I'll drive you to the hospital and bring you back. Then you can clean the dining room.'

She hesitated. She had never been alone with Andrew Worthington. There had always been his wife or Cora Miles or Bert – sometimes all three. 'I'm tired,' she muttered. 'I've been to visit Bert this afternoon and all. He's very low in his spirits.'

Worthington bit back a flippant remark about a bottle of whisky being the cure. No, he had better take this seriously. If Bert Simpson were to crack and tell the truth . . . The man was too lily-livered for that. Anyway, the main thing was to keep life ticking over as normally as possible, to shrug off the Ivy Crumpsalls and the Prudence Worthingtons of this world. 'I'll take you and bring you back,' he insisted. 'Then we shall discuss the terms of your employment. Of course, your wage will be commensurate with the level of responsibility.'

Gert couldn't manage to care about the wage. Oh, she knew she was a cut below most folk, but this was the way Bert liked her to be, nicely turned out and made-up to look cheerful. Yet for all that, something deep inside her was a cut above this chap. He had a special slyness about him, an arrogance, as if he expected the whole world to do his bidding just for money. 'I'm not sure I want to be a housekeeper, Mr Worthington,' she said carefully. 'I were took on as a general help, like. And Bert's the odd-job man and driver. Them were the jobs we went for.'

He lowered head and tone. 'I pay your rent,' he reminded her.

She heard the threat, remembered the days when she and Bert had been penniless and tramping about the streets with a few possessions. The thought of homelessness was Gert's Achilles heel. She sniffed, took a step back into the house. 'I'll be two minutes.'

Worthington did not wish to be seen in the company of the brash-looking woman, so he set off for home. Let her follow him, he thought. Let her walk behind, as that would illustrate her position in life. And his. He held up his chin and marched back to the hated house.

Joseph and Ruth finally cobbled together their sabbath, though they had never been so late in the past. They begged forgiveness, divided the bread, looked at each other in the candlelight. 'I can't stop thinking about that man,' said Joseph, his eyes raised to the ceiling. 'May I be forgiven again for my anger.'

Ruth sighed, swallowed a lump of bread that threatened to stick in her throat. 'We learn our lessons. We are taught to treat all men as equal children of God, yet I cannot think with charity about Worthington.'

'There is something wrong with that man, Ruth. He feels nothing for other people, worries only about himself. To him, I would never admit this, but those staring eyes terrify me. He is, perhaps, insane.'

'A demon.' Ruth looked into the flickering candles.

'Maureen escaped the madness.' Joseph blinked away some wetness. 'She must have felt that fear, the same fear our people endured in the camps. We must take care of Maureen.'

Ruth smiled. 'His Lordship will do the caring, Joseph. Let us thank God that her pretty face was saved. On hands, she can wear gloves, and they will heal fully in time. But at least she needs no mask to hide her face.'

He nodded. 'The rest of the business begins on Monday.'

'We should not talk business now,' she told him.

'I know. But the men from London will come soon. Worthington's workers are on the move as we speak. He is in for some shocks, because his reign is almost over, Ruth. It would have been better for him if he had allowed the workers to make a union. Now, he stands to lose everything.'

'Yes. For the mill workers we must give thanks.'

They gave thanks, though their hearts were heavy with worry about the days to come.

Ivy stood in the doorway, arms folded across her chest. 'They'd never miss me,' said Arthur 'Red' Trubshaw. 'If you took me to Sally, there'd be one less mouth to feed round our house. And after a bit, I could come back meself on the train. I'm ten, nearly eleven.'

This poor lad missed Sal something terrible, thought Ivy. His little sister had died, and Red had loved Alice with a ferocity that showed again now in his concern for Sally Crumpsall. 'Lad, I can't traipse halfway up and down England with you. And what do you want with our Sal? She's nobbut seven, no company for a boy your age.'

He shrugged. 'I don't know. She 'minds me of Alice, I think. She were good fun, our Alice, not like a girl. Like she stuck up for herself. Sally does and all. And she's got no mam and dad to look after her.' He eyed the old woman up and down. 'You're getting on, Mrs Crumpsall. I could help you.'

'How?'

'Different things. Same as lifting and carrying and cleaning up. And I can paint windows.'

Ivy nodded wisely. 'Aye, I've seen your painting, son. There's more green on the bloody glass than there is on yon frames.'

'I were only nine.' His tone was indignant, hurt. 'I'm older now. A lot older.'

Ivy struggled to hide a grin. This Trubshaw kiddy was a gem, rough round the edges, but worth his weight in gold. Would Tom mind, she wondered, if Red came to Hampshire with them in a week or so? Schools would be closed soon, and the Crumpsalls would be returning to Lancashire in September. They could spend holidays in

Hampshire. Oh, how posh that sounded! She imagined herself saying jokingly, 'My granddaughter has a little place in Hampshire – Oakmead. It's only a cottage, but it makes a wonderful holiday home'. The details needed completing, but Tom was positive that Rose Cottage would be Sally's as soon as the paperwork was completed. 'I'll see,' she told the boy. 'I'm promising nowt.'

The smile almost split the homely face into two distinct halves. 'Ta, missus.' He whooped along the lane, feet flailing in mid-air as he cleared imaginary hurdles.

Ivy went back inside, made yet more tea. 'Do you think we could get six folk in yon Rolls Royce?' she asked Rosie.

'Six?' Rosie kept her voice down because Ollie was sleeping in the chair.

'Me, you and Ollie, Tom and Maureen.'

'That's five.'

'And Arthur Trubshaw.'

Rosie almost dropped a saucer. 'You what? Nay, if you're thinking of taking him, you ought to send a telegram first. Folk should be warned. Do you know what he did last week?'

Ivy raised a shoulder. 'I weren't here last week.'

'Well, I were. He took a pair of Elsie Bickerstaffe's unmentionables off the line and climbed the Paradise chimney. Then he stood there waving Elsie's doo-dahs round his head and shouting, "Take cover, here comes the Zeppelin." She never come out of her house till Friday, and that were only to fetch her husband's best suit from Heilberg's.'

Ivy lifted the teapot from its stand. 'Well,' she managed while squashing her mirth. 'Have you seen the size of Elsie Bickerstaffe's knickers?'

'Aye,' said Rosie. 'And so has everybody else between here and bloody Manchester. Tea-rose in colour, they were. Tea-rose with the elastic missing in one leg. Proper shown up, she were.'

'Farming'll sort him,' declared the matriarch. 'Give him

a pitchfork and he'll soon learn manners.'

Rosie took a sip of tea. 'Give him a pitchfork and he'll be armed and dangerous.'

Ivy fled to the scullery and laughed quietly. There was nothing to laugh at, really. The next few days were going to be very trying. Tom's plan might work, but it might not. It all depended on how desperate Worthington got. All the same, if it came to a battle of wills, she would certainly put her money on Lord Goodfellow.

Lord Goodfellow leaned over the bed and made eye contact with its occupant. 'Nothing will happen to you,' he whispered. 'If you did fire the shop, you were under orders. We have all committed unsavoury acts while under orders from a superior.'

Bert swallowed, tasted bile. 'Nowt to do with me,' he managed. 'And you'd best be off, 'cos Gert'll be here in a minute.'

Tom straightened, sat down, smoothed the creases in his trousers. 'Then I shall have a word with Gert,' he said pleasantly. 'Perhaps she can throw light on the subject, just as you threw an incendiary of some sort into Heilberg's on Wigan Road.' He paused, waited for an answer, received none. 'Were you blackmailed?'

Bert shivered, though the ward was overheated. 'Look here,' he said softly. 'I'm getting cut open tomorrow. Haven't I enough on with doctors poking about me insides? I don't need no more bother than I've already got. Like I said before, that fire were nowt to do with me. I were in the pub. In fact, I might have been in the lav, 'cos I'd started being bad with me ulcers. So just leave me alone. I could be dead tomorrow.'

Tom nodded his agreement. 'So might we all, old chap. In fact, my fiancée is lucky to be alive. Maureen Mason. Do you know her?'

Bert closed his mouth and set it in a tight, thin line.

'She worked in that shop. She's an Irish lady with a very

241

pretty face. Fortunately for Worthington, her beauty is still intact, though her fingers will be painful for a while and her hair had to be cut short.'

Bert's eyes lit up for a split second. 'She's all right, then?'

Tom nodded. 'No further, Bert. You have my word as a gentleman that you will not be prosecuted. I know you did it. You know you did it. And we both know the name of the real perpetrator.'

Bert wasn't very well up on fancy words, but he got the drift, looked over Tom's shoulder and saw the time on the clock, was anxious because Gert would appear at any moment. 'I were under pressure,' he said softly. 'He had one or two things on me, see. I'd . . . I'd took a few things as wasn't strictly mine. He said he'd get the bobbies.'

'So you set fire to a shop.'

The man in the bed nodded. 'Aye, but I didn't know she were there. That shop were a lock-up. It were closed come six o'clock every night. I got a shock when I saw her.' He gulped painfully. 'I caught sight of her just as I let fly with the bottle of paraffin. It were one of the worst moments in my whole life. Any road, she didn't recognize me, else she'd have said.'

'So you thought you'd got away with it, I suppose.' Tom took a deep breath, tried to unclench his fists, but the fingers that had tightened instinctively refused to relax. 'Worthington paid you.' This was not a question.

'Aye.'

'Why?'

Bert licked dry lips, wished with all his heart that the man and the pain would both go away. 'The land. I suppose if the Heilbergs got ruined, they'd sell their bit of Paradise.'

'And Sally? Is Worthington paying you to take Sally away from her grandmother?'

Several moments elapsed before Bert spoke. 'I've told you what you wanted to know. As for owt else, you said you'd be a gentleman. So be a gentleman and get the hell out of this bloody hospital before Gert turns up.'

Tom picked up his hat, found himself crushing that, too. 'I trust that you will get well, Mr Simpson,' he said before leaving the ward.

In the corridor, he saw Gert tottering along in ridiculous shoes with high wedges and strappy uppers out of which stuck hammer-toes with crimson nails. Behind her walked the mill owner. Gert stopped, said hello, stumbled towards Bert with a bag of green grapes clutched to her ample breast.

'Lord Goodfellow.' Worthington bowed with a flourish. 'Been visiting?'

'Yes.'

'Bert Simpson?'

A small silence was laden with so much energy that it seemed to crackle in the air between them, like electricity looking anxiously for an earth. 'Indeed,' replied Tom at last.

Worthington leaned against the wall in an effort to retain his balance. He'd been knocked sideways more than once today. He crossed his feet, tried to make the stance casual. 'Lying bugger, that one,' he muttered. 'Don't know why I took him on.'

'Quite.'

There was something in Goodfellow's eyes, a look that screamed his adversary's infamy. Worthington pulled himself upright, went into the ward. The floozie was hanging over Simpson's bed, was stroking the man's waxy face. Worthington tapped her on the shoulder, inhaled the stink of California Poppy. 'Go and find the sister,' he advised gently. 'Ask about the operation. You need to know exactly what is going to be done to Bert tomorrow.'

Gert clapped a hand to her mouth. 'Ooh, you're right, Mr Worthington. I never thought of that—'

'Hang on,' begged Bert, dreading the thought of being

left alone with the boss. 'They've told me.' He lifted his pyjama top. 'I'll be cut here, then they'll get rid of me ulcers and patch me stomach up after.'

Worthington shook his head. 'Sounds like mending a puncture,' he commented. 'I think Gert should ask all the same.'

'I will.' She rose, swayed till she got her balance, then minced off towards the office.

'Well?' asked Worthington.

'Well what?'

'His Lorship is what. Why did he come?'

Bert shrugged. 'To see if I were all right.'

'Nothing else?'

Bert was fed up to the back teeth. On the following morning, he would be going down to theatre without even a cup of tea and a ciggy for breakfast. If he survived all the messing, he'd be weeks on just drinks and bits of rice pudding and suchlike. And here stood Worthington with a face like a stopped clock, the bulging eyes looking like a pair of cuckoos ready to jump out on wires and scream the time. 'Nowt else.'

'Did he ask about the fire?'

Bert closed his eyes, shook his head slowly. 'He said as how he'd got engaged to that woman in the shop, her as got burnt.' A sudden brainwave overtook the pain. He opened his eyes. 'He'd come for dressings for her hands, he said. Burn cream and stuff, remembered I were still in here. So he dropped by.'

'That had better be the truth, Simpson.'

Simpson suddenly failed to care. He fixed his eyes on his employer and landlord. 'Will you please go away? I'm ill. I'll see you when I get out of here.'

The mill owner turned on his heel and walked out of the ward. He didn't trust Bert, but there was no more he could do.

*　　*　　*

244

She didn't like him, didn't want to be near him. There was a terrible anger simmering just beneath his skin; she could see veins throbbing and swelling in his neck, while his breathing had become fast and shallow, as if he were starved of oxygen after a long run. 'I can come early tomorrow instead, Mr Worthington. Six o'clock, I'll clean up the dining room and—'

'Get it done now.' He swung the nose of the car into the driveway of Worthington House, shivered slightly when he faced the blank, empty eyes of the place he called home. Although he hated himself for it, he knew that he was missing Prudence. He didn't miss who she was, didn't care if he never saw the blasted woman again. But she'd been there, always.

Gert's feelings were similar to her employer's. She didn't want to go inside that place. It was an unattractive house with big, squared bays and a solid door that didn't seem to want visitors. Everything was brown. Brown window frames, brown door, brown curtains. Even the plants in the garden hadn't managed a true green. They were a sort of khaki, she supposed. A browny-green. 'I don't feel well,' she told him.

He got out of the car, strode to the porch, opened the door.

There was no escaping him, she decided. She would have to go in and clean the blinking room so that he might leave her in peace. The idea of homelessness and un-employment held no appeal. With reluctance illustrated in every step, she walked through the hall and into the dining room. He had thrown his meal at the wall. His chair, too, had been tossed aside. Gert righted this item, began to scrape salad off the floor.

Worthington watched her from the doorway. She didn't look so bad now. When she bent to retrieve the radish, he glimpsed a stocking top and the fastener on a suspender. The skin above the nylon was surprisingly supple and inviting. What would it matter? he asked himself. Who would miss another little slice off a cut loaf?

She piled the mess onto his plate, walked towards him, almost dropped the crockery when she saw the bulky man blocking the doorway. 'I'll get a cloth,' she murmured.

He grinned, though there was nothing pleasant in the expression. 'Would you like to earn a little bit extra?' he asked.

Gert swallowed. 'No, I'm satisfied, ta.'

'I'm not. It's a while since I've been satisfied. A cold bitch, my wife. Didn't like anything that wasn't strictly kosher, if you get my drift. No imagination, no style.'

She looked directly into the ugly, dome-shaped eyes, noticed that they were almost black, as if the pupils had swollen and swallowed up surrounding irises. If he touched her, she would die. She hadn't taken after their Lottie. Liking a good time and the odd drink was one thing, but adultery was another matter altogether. Her Bert wasn't much, but he was hers exclusively. 'I'm sure I don't know what you mean,' she said carefully. 'I want to get home. My husband's having a big operation in the morning.'

He reached out and ran a finger along her arm, chuckled when she shivered. 'Just this once,' he whispered. 'And I'll pay you well.'

'I don't want money.'

'I see.' A huge hand enveloped her left breast, crushed the flesh until she almost screamed. 'You'll do as you're told, Gertrude,' he muttered. 'Because I'm on your side.'

As red-hot needles of pain stung the twisted nipple, she brought up the plate and smashed it into his nose. Blood spurted everywhere, splashed on her blouse, on her face. The metallic smell of his life fluid sickened her, almost made her heave.

With a roar of pain, he hit her across the head, causing her to smash into the edge of the open door. As she slithered to the floor, he used his handkerchief to staunch the flow from his nose, employed his foot to keep her still.

Gert lay half-conscious beneath the huge black shoe, decided that she must remain alive. To remain alive, she would need to be compliant. Through a haze, she watched while he mopped his nose, while he knelt beside her, while he tore off her clothes. Alive. She must stay alive. The things he did weren't right, weren't normal. She was turned this way and that while he used her body, while he defiled her. To stay sane, she shepherded together her remaining faculties to chant nursery rhymes in her head. A friend of hers had done that during labour, had said that the little songs had helped to overcome the agony. But Gert couldn't shout the words; she could only think them. When he threw her face down on the dining table and performed more unspeakable acts, she went through the words of Little Bo Peep and wondered whether death might have been the easier option.

At last, he was spent. He dragged himself away from her and blundered out of the room. On the way upstairs, he stumbled, fell down to the hall, began the climb all over again. She didn't matter. She was a woman of no importance and, like all the rest of her kind, she would keep quiet.

Gert slid to the floor, was suddenly alert. A terrible agony racked her lower body and she saw spots of blood on the carpet. Whose blood was this? she wondered. When she attempted to stand, she knew that the blood was hers, heard it dropping softly and steadily onto the Persian rug. He had ripped her open, had pleasured himself in parts of her body that should have remained intact for life. She could taste him, smell him, feel him inside her. There were no tears, because she was beyond such luxuries.

Her cheap, garish garments were torn, but she managed to cover herself. The shoes would be beyond her. Even when she was at her best, these wedges were a bit on the high side. No matter – she would get home barefoot if necessary.

'Here's your money.' He tossed a handful of coins and notes across the room.

She jumped, wondered how such a big man had come downstairs without making a sound, then noticed that he had removed his shoes. 'I don't want it,' she mumbled.

'That's up to you,' he barked. 'Clean up, get washed, then get out of here. One word out of you and I'll deny everything.'

Even now, she looked at him steadily. No wonder Mrs Worthington had taken herself off into another room then off into another place altogether. The man was sick, out of order. 'I won't be back,' she informed him. 'And neither will my Bert.'

'Then you can clear out of that house,' he bellowed. 'And I hope your damn fool of a man can find a job he's capable of doing.'

Gert picked up her bag and shoes. 'One day,' she announced clearly. 'One day, somebody will do you in. And don't think about denying what's gone on here, 'cos a load of folk will have seen you leaving the hospital with me. You're a dead man. As for that mucky little house, you can shove it up somebody else's privates – your own'll do.' He walked towards her, but she neither budged nor flinched. 'Kill me and they'll know it's you. Mark me any more and I'll be a bonny sight for the police.'

All his life, he had dreaded this moment. The young ones were the easiest but, these days, even they were feistier, less afraid. 'I'm sorry,' he mumbled with difficulty. He had seldom apologized, found the words sticking to his tongue so that they came out softly. 'I didn't mean . . .' He swallowed the rest of the lie. She wasn't even young, wasn't even pretty. He didn't know why this had happened, though he remembered wanting to punish somebody, anybody, everybody. 'Sorry,' he repeated lamely.

'Sorry? Does that stop me bleeding where I should never have been touched?'

He took a step back. 'I'm on your side,' he told her. 'I was the one who got Lottie to write to you before she left.

I was the one she sent for when Ivy Crumpsall's cronies robbed her at Trinity Street Station. I got rid of your sister so that you could have a child.' He sniffed. 'Simpson could never give you one.'

Gert found herself counting beats of time before she spoke. 'So you paid her to go?'

'I gave her some money, yes.'

'And to write asking me to fettle for Sally?'

He nodded.

'You'd do anything to hurt Ivy Crumpsall, wouldn't you? And the Heilbergs and all, come to that. Did you burn yon shop?'

He bared his teeth. 'Ask your husband about that.'

She staggered back, leaned against the table on which she had just been made filthy. 'He did that job for you?'

He shrugged. 'He did it. But it was his own idea.' He lit a cigarette and his hands were surer, steadier. 'Go to the police with your little tale and I'll have him arrested the minute he regains consciousness after his operation.'

Gert was sharing a room with the personification of evil. She glanced at his feet, wondered whether the hooves inside the woollen socks were cloven. At school, they'd been told that Satan had strange toes. But there was no fear in her now, because she was looking not at a boss, but at a man in plain black socks. Gert's head and heart were filled with a mixture of anger and despair. Because she had just lost Bert. If Bert had set light to Mr Heilberg's shop, then her marriage was over. 'Do what you like,' she snapped. 'I'll not be staying married to a bloody criminal. I've never minded his bits of thieving, but hurting folk is summat different.'

He drew on the cigarette, smiled through a fug of smoke. 'Oh, I'd still be careful if I were you. After all, who is going to believe that you weren't in it with him? If you leave him now, such an action will be construed by the court as a demonstration of fear brought on by guilt. You can shout all you like about being uninvolved, but no-one will listen. I am a Freemason, you know. I have friends in high places.'

'And in hell,' she replied.

'Gertrude, Gertrude.' He shook his head in a mockery of concern. 'I've tried to get that child for you and look how you repay me.'

'Bugger off,' she screamed. 'I wanted Sally for the proper reasons, to see to her and make sure she were all right. But you're not all right. The things you did to me were nasty, evil. Is the devil your father?'

He fixed his eyes on her, used the glare that worked so well on spinners and weavers. She was nothing, a plain and painted creature of the slums, yet she was standing up to him. It was becoming more and more difficult to train women, to make them understand their proper place in the scheme of things. Women were for housework, bedroom pleasures and for the performing of industrial tasks that were too menial and ill-paid for men. They were not meant to have brains. They were not meant to argue. His nose hurt. Her face was covered in bruises. She must not talk. He had to make sure that she kept her big mouth closed. 'My father was a Worthington. His first name was neither Lucifer nor Beelzebub.'

Gert kicked out at the money, sent it spinning in all directions. 'Right, we'll play it your way, then. I'll try to be fair with you, Mr Worthington. So listen, eh? I might have a short life or a long one, but I'm going to spend it making sure you pay for what's happened. Aye, so you do know a few Freemasons, but I know folk and all, folk who don't need the bloody masons. You're a dead man, sweetheart. Make sure you're never alone in a dark place. There's no lock as'll keep you safe, no guard dog. You're dead, dead, dead. I'm going to make sure you suffer.'

He could feel the blood pounding round his body and into his head. She was so cool and casual that he feared her with every fibre of his being. 'Never be alone,' she had said. 'No lock will save you.' The headache was back, this time loud and angry like a huge drum behind his temples. 'You don't scare me,' he snapped.

Gert smiled knowingly. 'Is that right? Then you're not just a bad bugger. You're a stupid swine and all. Wedge summat under your door handle tonight, Mr Worthington. And keep your windows shut. My friends can get past most barriers.'

His lips curled. She was talking as if she were educated, was using words he hadn't expected to hear from a slut. 'Get out,' he said.

'If you shift out of me road, I will.' Hoping that her trembling did not show, Gert squeezed past him, walked down the hall and through the front door.

He followed her, grabbed her arm, pulled her back into the porch. 'Listen, bitch.' The words rasped as they emerged, as if his throat were sore. 'If anybody has a right to that kid, it's me.' With his other hand, he pounded his chest. 'Remember how your sister had a ten-month pregnancy? Her man had gone abroad, but the stupid bugger believed her when she wrote and said she was having his baby. The child I tried to get for you is a Worthington. Remember that. Tell the old witch whose child that is.'

She spat into his grinning face.

He leered at her, wiped the spittle from his face. 'The letter I handed over to you and Bert was only half the story, Gertrude. Lottie and I both signed another statement the day she left Bolton. That document is locked away in a safe. It states categorically that I am Sally's father.'

Gert shivered. 'I don't give that much for our Lottie and her carryings-on.' She snapped her fingers beneath his slightly swollen and reddened nose. Her heart was hopping about in her chest, seemed to have lost its rhythm, but she fought to keep a cool exterior. 'We didn't get on. I know she's a cheap little tart. Anybody who goes with twisted folk like you has to be a tart.'

251

He tightened his hold on her arm. 'Derek Crumpsall was no more use than your Bert when it came to fathering. He'd nothing in him, no life, no go. But Lottie was a goer.' He nodded quickly. 'Every time I got desperate, she came to the mill. And I gave her the odd quid.' He sniffed, removed the smile from his face. 'By my reckoning, that Sally Crumpsall owes me a tenner. Because that's approximately what I paid her mother in 1939.'

She pulled away from him, backed down the driveway. Clutching bag and shoes, she crossed the road and hid behind some bushes at the edge of the park. Within half an hour, a smile lurked at the corner of her lips. The evening was hot and clammy, yet Worthington had just closed all his windows.

ELEVEN

Ivy opened her door, looked at the crumpled mess that had deposited itself on the flags below the step. 'What have you come for?' she asked, her tone sharp. She'd no time for Gert Simpson, no time for anybody at present. There was a lot going on, including Maureen and Tom's wedding in a matter of days. And she wanted to get back to Oakmead, back to Sal. The departure date had been postponed twice already. Then there was the other business, the business that was going to put Worthington out of business . . . 'What do you want?' The woman had plainly taken a battering. But her husband was still in hospital. Who had belted her, then?

'Just to come in.'

Ivy allowed her gaze to stray past the dishevelled and bruised woman, saw two dilapidated suitcases, a shopping bag and some brown paper parcels. 'What's all that?' she asked.

'Me clothes. And a few bits and pieces. I've nowhere to go, Mrs Crumpsall. Worthington's chucked me out of the house we were renting. I didn't fancy stopping there any road.'

Ivy paused for a second, processed the information. 'Sounds just like him, does that. Come in for a bit, then.'

Gert gathered her belongings and staggered inside beneath the weight of all the baggage.

'Stick that lot in the parlour while I think,' commanded Ivy. She went off to make tea.

The unexpected visitor placed her packages on the floor and looked round the parlour. It was so clean, so tidy.

There wasn't much money here, but the place was homely, especially with that lovely clock ticking gently on the mantelpiece. She perched on the edge of the sofa, took out her powder compact and studied her face. Even under thick cream and powder, the bruises showed.

'What happened?' asked Ivy from the doorway.

'He raped me,' replied Gert immediately, though she hadn't expected to come out with it so baldly. There was something about Ivy Crumpsall that invited – perhaps demanded – the whole truth without any dressing. 'And other things, things I'd never have thought of.' She turned her head so that the older woman might get a better view of the damage. 'I'm not the only one what finished up bleeding, though. I split his nose, but that weren't enough. I want him dead, Mrs Crumpsall. If somebody'll arrange for him to be dead, I'll dig the grave myself – with these.' She stretched out ten nails whose painted surface was chipped.

Ivy lowered herself into the fireside rocker. There was something so vulnerable about Gert's damaged nail varnish. It probably wasn't like her to have such tatty hands. 'We'll go in the kitchen and have a cuppa in a minute.' The tone had lost its raw and angry edge. 'You're not the first, love. And you won't be his last, neither.'

'I know.' Gert gulped back a sob of self-pity. 'I've even give up me job in Woolworths, 'cos me and Bert were working for Worthington – cleaning, odd jobs and all that. But I've lost that place as well – I've no intention of going anywhere near Worthington's house again – and I've nowhere to live.'

'I'm sorry, lass.' And Ivy was sorry, wondered whether she might have misjudged this woman before. Gert's next words convinced Ivy that Lottie and Gert were poles apart.

'It were Worthington as got Lottie to write and ask me to come down here for Sally. I mean, I didn't even know Lottie were going abroad, did I? So when I came and asked for Sally, that were because I thought Lottie wanted me to have her. I came here in good faith, Mrs Crumpsall. But Bert were in on it with Worthington, I think. I've finished with Bert and all. I went on the phone at the corner shop and the hospital says he's all right. I mean, I didn't want him to die or nothing. But he's no husband of mine.'

'What'll you do?'

'I don't know.'

Ivy studied her peg rug for a moment or two. 'So you're not here to find out where our Sal is? You're not here to try and take her off me?'

Gert shook her head so hard that the multi-coloured curls flew all around her face. 'Lottie wrote in that letter as how you weren't fit to mind Sally.' She eyed the old woman. 'And when I came that first time, I have to tell you I agreed with her, 'cos you were pale and sick looking. You seem all right now. Yon kiddy's your grandchild . . .'

'She's not, she's not!' cried a voice in Gert's head. But Gert closed her inner ear and continued stolidly, 'If owt ever happens to you, Mrs Crumpsall, I'll do my bit for Sally. I'm not like our Lottie, I promise you.'

'I know that. Aye, I know now, lass. You'd make ten of yon Lottie Kerrigan.'

The kind tone brought tears spurting from Gert's already crimson-lidded eyes. 'I've nowt,' she cried between sobs. 'Nowt and nobody and nowhere of me own.'

Ivy rose and crossed the room. 'You've me and little Sal and you've here,' she whispered. 'Get yon pile of stuff up the dancers and into our Sal's room. She's still away, but we're keeping this house on. Our lass has been given a cottage by Lord Tom. He said she'd rabbited on for years about a house in the country, so he's gone and given her a lovely place. But we'll not be there a lot. She'll be coming back here, to her own school. So, when me and Sal come home, you'll have to manage on the sofa till I get another bed. Any road, you can keep the place dusted for me, eh? Now, pull yourself together and we'll have a drink.'

'I can't,' sobbed Gert. 'I can't live in your house and act as if nowt's happened—'

'Course you can.'

'He did it!' she shouted. 'My Bert. He did that fire, you know. And Ruth and Joseph Heilberg are your mates and Maureen Wotsername—'

'We know all about it,' announced Ivy firmly. 'Bert's a damn fool of a man, but we all guessed from the kick-off that it were Worthington's plan, that arson attack. He blackmailed Bert, I bet.'

'Aye.' Gert dried her face. 'But that doesn't make no difference, not to me. Nothing's worse than hurting folk. Burns are awful. And Bert can say he didn't know she were there, but that doesn't matter to me, neither. The pawnshop were in a terraced row. Fire spreads. Loads of folk could have died that night.' She blew her nose. 'Any road, Bert can bugger off. I've done me best. Time I had a new life.'

While they drank tea in the kitchen, Ivy kept one eye on Gert and the other on the clock. The disruption of Paradise Mill had started some days ago, but the best was yet to come. Today, at twelve noon, three sheds were going to down tools and walk out. Ivy, who was only human, wanted to see the fun. 'When did he do all that to you?' she asked.

'Thursday.'

This was Monday. 'So you looked a lot worse afore today?'

Gert sniffed. 'I felt ashamed. I couldn't go out looking like the loser in a boxing match, could I? This morning, I thought of you, thought you might just help me.'

Ivy clattered the spoon in her saucer. 'Would you like to see something really exciting?'

'Eh?'

The old woman leaned forward and whispered, as if she

imagined the kitchen to be full of people. 'We're fetching him down, Gert.'

'Eh?' repeated the guest. 'Who?'

'The man who bruised your face, love.' And worse, mused Ivy. Aye, the real damage was hidden, because although the body would heal, a woman was never the same after rape, since it was an invasion of the soul, too.

'Bloody hell,' breathed Gert.

'I agree,' said Ivy. 'With custard.'

Gert excused herself to go down the garden. Before leaving the room, she smiled at Ivy. 'Thanks for . . . for trying to help me. You're the only one I could turn to except for Mrs Worthington – and she's got trouble enough of her own.' The brave expression melted, leaving her face old and wise. 'That poor woman, eh? How's she managed all these years? No wonder there's bolts and locks on her bedroom door.' Gert bit her lip, shook her head, then went out into the back garden.

Ivy Crumpsall closed her eyes and leaned back in her chair. She pictured him suspended from a rope, the ugly eyes bulging even further than usual from their hooded sockets. Her right hand clasped as if it held the lever to a trapdoor. Aye, she'd like to send him from here to eternity, all right. And, if ever given half a chance, she wouldn't even wear the hangman's mask. Her eyes flew open. She wanted him to know, wanted him to see her face today.

Gert came in, lowered herself gingerly into a chair.

'All right?'

'Not as bad as it were, ta.'

Ivy smiled kindly, though her face managed to remain tight. 'He'll be stopped and all, Gert. Nigh on a quarter of his workforce did a disappearing act a couple of days since. He's been running round like a screw-necked chicken trying to get folk to change their minds and come back to Paradise. The whole town's in on it, you know. Mill owners know what's afoot – even the bloody Freemasons want shut of him, 'cos they're decent men at heart. That's why we've stayed on, me and Lord Tom. Well – there's the wedding and all, of course. Them as have left Worthington's have been took on by other mills – better pay, nice conditions, a union to speak up for them. They're not all fools, the mill owners. Today, we've another fifty-odd coming out, only they're planning on a bit of a show. They'll lose nowt, because every man and woman starts a new job tomorrow. Fancy a front seat?'

Gert gulped, didn't like the idea of seeing the monster again. She was genuinely frightened, jumpy and ill at ease. 'Eeh, Mrs Crumpsall, I don't know as I'm rightly up to it. I've been . . . having nightmares. I've got so as I don't want to go to sleep. When I'm awake, I can tell meself I'm all right, only your dreams have a mind of their own, don't they?'

'Call me Ivy and call me daft, but if you stand next to me, he'll know you've told me. Scared to bloody death of me, he is, and not without cause. I'll tell you summat else and all – a few others who got interfered with have come forward. With their children – his children.'

Sally was his child. Gert closed her mouth with a snap, commanded the words to go away. She would never tell this lady that Sally was not a Crumpsall. 'How awful,' she managed.

'He's got to pay. We fixed it so he'll pay.'

Gert rose unsteadily and picked up her handbag. It was no use sitting here waiting for Christmas, she told herself. The man had to be punished – ruined if possible. 'Paradise'll close, then,' she remarked.

'No.' Ivy stood up, threw the shawl around her shoulders, smoothed the spotless apron. 'It'll change hands, lass. Six months from now, yon mill will be working full pelt.'

'But how?'

'Just watch,' Ivy told her. 'Watch and learn that the ordinary people can have power. It's just a matter of grabbing the reins and taking over. Oh, and knowing somebody with a bit of money and clout helps. That bad bugger stands no chance. No chance at all.'

Tom replaced the receiver, sat down in Joseph's favourite chair. The Heilbergs were downstairs running the shop while Tom completed a list of tasks that covered two sheets of paper. He ticked off another item, picked up the phone yet again, asked for a London number. 'Perry!' he exclaimed. 'How are you?'

'Fine. I'll see you tomorrow. Is everything going to plan?'

Tom grinned to himself. 'Listen, are you sure you've got a suit that fits?'

A laugh drifted all the way from Regent Street into Tom's ear. 'Tom, that's below the belt.'

'Yes, and make sure you have belt and braces, old chap. I'd rather you wore something that fits above and below the meridian. Any news about the other business?'

'Done.'

'Nutty?'

'He's delighted, Tom. Doesn't know whether to laugh or cry. Good of you to pay for his mother's funeral. Nutty's never forgotten the day you came and gave him a fiver. A fiver of mine, I believe?'

Tom nodded to himself. 'You'll get it back if the suit fits.' He thought about poor old Nutty with his damaged face and hands. Nutty Clarke would be coming up with his wife and family for the wedding, would be staying on to mind certain interests while Tom and Maureen went to Africa, while Ivy and Sally continued to gain health and strength in Hampshire. 'See you tomorrow, then,' said Tom. 'And no loud ties – none of those kipper things you used to sport. Remember, you're the best man at my wedding.'

'I've always been the best, Tom. At long last, my superiority will be recognized.'

Tom Goodfellow severed the connection, pondered awhile, sat quietly with the Heilbergs' treasures all around him. He ran his eyes over pieces of Austrian crystal and German porcelain, admired a 'school of' Monet and a tablecloth of Spanish lace. It was a calm place, a beautiful room for two beautiful people. This was what he wanted for Sally and Ivy. Peace and prettiness. They would find that in Hampshire, would be able to visit Rose Cottage several times a year.

He smiled, considered all the other people who would be involved in his schemes. Tenant farmers would be owners of a few acres; Goodfellow Hall could become an orphanage, a place of sanctuary for unloved children. Oh, Sally. Little Sally, whose father had died, whose mother had absconded, had no need of a place in the Hall, because she was loved by so many. How many times had she visited him in Paradise Lane? How many times had she described the home of her dreams? 'But I've bigger dreams for you, Sally,' he muttered before leaving the room.

'Cup of tea, Tom?' asked Ruth.

He shook his head. 'No, thank you. I'm going off to watch the pantomime. Are you coming, Joseph?'

The pawnbroker continued to stack boots and shoes in a corner of the shop. 'No. I am no *tricoteuse*. You may cut off his head, but I shall not look at the blood.'

Ruth came to stand by Tom. 'Me, I shall come,' she announced. 'Because we need to be witnesses.' She looked at her husband. 'Will you change your mind, Joseph?'

'No.' He straightened, ran a hand through his hair. 'You go and do what needs to be done. Ruthie, if you go you go. I cannot stop you. But it will not be pleasant.'

'So speaks the chairman of the board,' laughed Ruth. 'Come, Tom. We go now to see the death of an era and—'

'And you come back in time for the meal,' said her husband. 'Or I shall send out a search party.'

Ruth took Tom's arm and walked out of the shop with him.

When the door closed, Joseph sat behind the counter and looked at all the things that would soon be gone. Mrs Armstrong's Easter costume rubbed shoulders with Ernest Wray's Sunday best. A hunter with a cracked face ticked alongside a jackknife that opened bottles, peeled potatoes, took stones from the hooves of a horse. A statue of the infant Jesus in Mary's arms sat under a glass dome next to Bernard Crompton's prize-winning darts.

Joseph had loved this shop. He hadn't enjoyed people's poverty, had tried not to take advantage of their needs, but he had become something of a sage and mentor, a younger, masculine version of Ivy Crumpsall. Each item on the shelves, under the counter, in the safe and in the window had a tale attached to it. He would miss this business.

After a few moments' thought, he took out his keys and locked all the cases, pulled down the window blinds and turned the sign to CLOSED. He was going, he told himself, just to keep an eye on Ruth. When the walkout happened, Worthington might lose his temper and lash out at somebody. A sensible bystander was needed, he decided. And it was a lovely morning for a walk.

Paradise Lane was packed with people. They kept to the side where the houses stood, though, leaving the cobbled area and the pavement outside the mill as the stage for the central characters. These personae arrived in ones and twos, Maureen Mason emerging from number 3 at five minutes to twelve, her right hand gloved, the left and less affected member on display so that all might see the sun reflected in her diamond. Forcing it onto the scorched finger had been a bit painful, but Maureen was proud enough to bear that.

A couple of minutes later, Ruth Heilberg and Tom Goodfellow hove into view from Worthington Street, closely followed by the pawnbroker in his best Homburg. Although there were few clouds, Joseph Heilberg carried a rolled umbrella, looked every inch the affluent southern gentleman waiting for a London train. The two pairs sorted themselves so that Ruth stood with her husband while Tom put an arm across Maureen's shoulders.

From Spencer Street, Rosie Blunt marched along with her husband dragging his feet behind her. 'They'll not be here,' cried the old man. 'Not with all these folk. We'll have to go back to the Rec.'

'The pigeons don't live here any more,' shouted Rosie. 'They've moved house.'

'I'm minding them for Tom!'

Tom left Maureen's side and went to rescue Rosie. 'Ollie,' he said clearly and patiently. 'In a few days, we'll go to the pigeons.'

Ollie stared at Tom, the old eyes full of confusion. 'Why? Have they lost their bloody wings? They should come to us, not the other road round.'

Tom drew in a deep breath, thought Rosie had a hard job here. 'Ollie, take my word. Next week, you will see my pigeons again. In the meantime, go easy on Rosie, will you?'

A memory link stirred itself in Ollie's slowly decaying brain. 'Rosie? Go easy on my Rosie? It's nobbut yesterday she chased me all down the gardens with the coal shovel. Have you felt the end of yon coal shovel?'

Tom nodded gravely. 'Just once.'

'Try a bloody lifetime,' grumbled Ollie quietly.

The Town Hall clock struck the hour. Even Ollie Blunt was silenced, because the air of expectation that hung over the street was almost tangible.

Ivy emerged from her house, a three-deep crowd of women and retired men parting as if by magic or act of God to allow her through. Behind her tottered Gert Kerrigan-as-was, her face bruised, her walk affected not just by the silly shoes, but also by other kinds of pain.

The twelfth tone died away and the assembly fell into total silence, each man and woman contemplating the

262

various reasons for attending these last rites. A few younger matrons sniffed away a tear or two, remembered their days as weavers and doffers, hoped their kiddies were all right for the moment with neighbours or grandparents. The faces of old men hardened as they recalled Worthington Senior, the devil from whom the current Satan had received tuition in the art of subjugating human souls. Had a bird dropped a feather during these moments, it would have hit the floor with a thud.

Ivy stood rigidly still, the edges of her shawl held tightly in one hand. How many of these people had waited for how many years? She felt the support behind her, as if it lifted her, guided and strengthened her. It would be a cold day in hell before Worthington showed his ugly mug in Paradise after this.

A door in one corner of the mill yard opened slowly and a man emerged, some packages clutched to his chest. The contents of a locker built up over the years – old shoes, wrapping paper, a cracked cup, the lid from some long-lost billycan. He was followed by another, then a third. Suddenly, the larger exits were thrown wide, and a tangle of people thrust its way out, separating into individuals as soon as the yard was reached. Like the observers outside the gates, these escapees stopped and stood in deathly silence, most eyes raised towards the boss's window.

Ivy Crumpsall sauntered forward, her walk deliberately slow and casual. He would be working hard up there, she thought. He was probably on the phone trying to cull employees from surrounding towns, because many of his workforce had already left Paradise. Well, she would get him to show his face, would make sure he saw the past laid out before those bulging eyes, his future in rags and tatters that defied any kind of darning. 'Worthington?' she called. 'Come on, show yourself.'

A window shot upward. Worthington poked his head through the gap, stared down at the yard. 'What the bloody hell's going on?' he yelled.

'They're off,' answered Ivy. 'To Ainsworth's and Kippax's and Swan Lane – they're going for an extra bob or two and a canteen dinner and a boss as does a fair imitation of being human.' She could not keep the glee from her final words. 'They're off to where the union'll look after them, to proper mills where owners recognize unions as a step forward.'

'Who rattled the bars of your cage?' roared the man at the window. He paused, did some counting of heads, knew that his mill would close today for lack of labour. 'Get back in here,' he advised them none too quietly. 'And we'll talk about pay.'

'And a canteen?' asked Ivy.

He glared at her. 'None of your business, Mrs Crumpsall.'

Joseph Heilberg spoke quietly to his wife. 'Ruth, go to the end of the lane and see if anyone is coming. What was planned may prove unwise. Also, the timing is important.'

Ruth nodded, went off to keep watch along Spencer Street.

Ivy fixed hard eyes on the man she loathed, then turned away and beckoned Gert. When the two women stood together, Andrew Worthington's face twisted itself into a horrible grimace. He could say nothing, do nothing. They were in it together, these common female creatures who should be allowed no power, no say in the world of industry. He cursed the day when he had first seen Ivy, damned the evening when he had last encountered Gert.

Ivy took Gert's hand, guided her back into the lane. 'That's our bit done, lass. And thanks for being so brave. With the two of us stood there, the bugger knew he'd lost.'

The former employees of the Paradise Calico Company filed through the gates for the last time. They were greeted and congratulated by onlookers before separating to go back to hearth and home. Many were led away by family members who had come to lend encouragement, and not a few walked towards a crate of ale. After all, a free weekday afternoon was going to be a novelty.

Ivy, Gert and Tom lingered while Rosie guided Ollie back into number 2. The little woman stood with her arms folded against the inevitable when Ollie found a bird to chase. Joseph walked towards Spencer Street, and Maureen was swept towards Worthington Street in the company of a gaggle of chattering doffers who wanted details of the wedding and a closer look at the ring.

Worthington glared down at Lord Goodfellow. 'Why?' he cried. 'What have I done to them?'

In that moment, Tom almost understood the man, almost pitied him. But almost was not enough, because a picture of Maureen's scorched hands shot through his mind. No, Tom must feel no guilt, no sorrow. There were the poor illegitimates to think of, and their mothers, too. 'You have despised them,' he replied eventually. 'You've used their women and cast them aside, then you've underpaid everyone, left them to work in archaic and filthy conditions. What do you expect from them – respect? You've been your own undoing, Worthington.'

Now that the free show was all but over, the audience began to melt away like snow on the first day of spring. Ivy, Tom and Gert remained while Rosie finally tracked down her frail husband and propelled him back into their house. 'Do you think she'll come?' asked Ivy.

'Who? Who's coming?' Gert's fear showed in small, frantic movements of her eyes.

'His wife,' replied Ivy.

Gert swallowed. 'Mrs Worthington?'

'Aye.' Ivy folded the shawl about her chest, felt chilled in spite of the summer heat. 'She's a word or two to say to him.'

'He'll bloody kill her,' muttered Gert.

Tom shook his head. 'The lady won't be alone. It seems that when old man Spencer allowed his daughter to marry, he made sure that his investment in the Paradise Mill would be returnable – with interest – in the event of any

marital difficulties. What a wise man he must have been.'
He looked at Ivy, wondered whether he was saying too
much in front of Gert.

Ivy responded to the raised eyebrow with a nod. 'This
one can be trusted,' she told him. 'She's even abandoned
her husband over what's gone on. Aye, Gert's all right.'

Gert smiled nervously at His Lordship, wondered
whether she ought to curtsey. 'I'm not like our Lottie,' she
informed him with a newborn shyness that owed much to
Tom Goodfellow's elevation in status. 'I can be depended
on – honest.'

'Good.' Tom looked left and right, saw Maureen
approaching from Worthington Street. 'Mrs Worthington
may not come,' he said quietly. 'Perhaps she has had
second thoughts.'

But she hadn't. Prudence Worthington came round the
Spencer Street corner in the company of the Heilbergs,
Cora Miles and a dark-suited man who was a stranger.

'That's a lawyer,' predicted Ivy. 'They always have
round shoulders, do lawyers. It's with bending over and
reading stuff.'

Tom wondered what Ivy's reaction to Peregrine Fotheringay might be. There was no roundness to Perry's stance,
because the good man was too carefree to be poring over
old deeds, wills and manuscripts. But for all that, he was a
useful man to know.

The party turned into the mill yard, Joseph pausing for
a split second to raise his black hat in Ivy's direction. The
little pawnbroker quickened his pace and followed his wife
into the future. Within a matter of months, the looms and
mules of Paradise would turn again. There was work to be
done, and little of it was clean . . .

The owner of Paradise Mill glowered over a pair of half-
moon reading glasses. At the other side of his desk stood
Prudence and a man called Sutcliffe. The latter was a
lawyer with a lot of papers, a grim face and a tendency to

stutter. 'What is this man talking about?' The question was directed towards the female with whom Andrew Worthington had shared a house for many years.

'Divorce,' she said calmly.

Worthington removed his spectacles and placed them on a leather-bound blotter. He decided now to address his wife's companion, who was male, at least. The stutter was annoying, but it was no use talking to Prudence. Pru-dish, she should have been christened. Or Frigid, perhaps. 'I've a mill to run,' he barked. 'No time for foolishness. There have been no divorces in our family. You will get precious little help from me,' he informed the lawyer.

Sutcliffe remained motionless, made no comment.

'Adultery,' said Prudence quietly. 'We have the name of one of your consorts, Andrew.' She waved a hand in the direction of her lawyer's papers. 'The woman rents a cottage of ours on Halliwell Road. Well, she pays no rent, I gather. Her instalments are delivered in kind, I understand.'

Mildred, thought Worthington. Mildred would never talk.

Prudence read his thoughts. 'The neighbours will testify with regard to your movements, as will the woman's estranged husband. If this is not enough, I can find others.'

He was finished. He sat in a chair that had been his father's, in a mill office that had been his father's, and he knew that the people of Paradise, together with his own wife, had routed him. Paradise Mill was running at less than half its true capacity. A whole weaving shed and two spinning rooms were completely empty, while none of the other units could boast a full complement of workers.

Prudence narrowed her eyes. 'What did you do to Mrs Simpson?' she enquired, her tone deliberately sweet. 'Mrs Miles – who will be staying with me, incidentally – called to see Gert Simpson, and was informed by a neighbour that Gert had returned from somewhere or other in a very sorry state, incapable of walking properly, her face bruised, her clothes torn. Mrs Simpson is staying with the Crumpsalls, I understand.'

Silence would be best, decided Worthington.

'You raped her.'

Sutcliffe shuffled some documents, placed them in a cardboard folder.

'I can get Gert Simpson to testify against you,' continued Prudence. 'You were seen on the evening in question. The same neighbour noticed you in the street, then saw Gert following you towards Wigan Road.'

'Visiting her husband in hospital,' blustered the seated man.

Prudence tapped the floor with the toe of her shoe, could scarcely believe that she was here and facing up to him, that she was experiencing very little discomfort. 'Did she come to the house later, after the hospital visit?'

He bit his lip. He had been seen at the infirmary, had probably been noticed driving away with his passenger. There was nothing he could say.

'I can get Gert to prosecute you,' repeated Prudence softly. 'She may well decide to do just that without my interference. But unless you give me my freedom, I shall make bloody sure that the case goes to court.'

She had never sworn before. The timbre of her voice was low, almost conversational. The woman was angry, so deeply furious that she dared not let her feelings rise to the surface. 'Rubbish,' he managed.

Sutcliffe decided to earn his money. 'Mrs Simpson was forced to inform her neighbour of the circumstances which led to her injuries, Mr Worthington. The lady next door did the shopping, as Mrs Simpson was too ill to go outside.'

Where's the bloody stammer now? thought the man behind the desk. When the solicitor had introduced himself, he had come out as 'Sut-c-c-cliffe'. The lawyer's deep-set eyes were bright, mobile, seemed to be boring through the mill owner and into the wall behind his head. 'I trust that you will see sense, Mr Worthington,' concluded Sutcliffe. 'Things might become quite messy, you see.'

Andrew Worthington stared at his wife. She would force him into destitution. Even if he fought old Spencer's will, he could not win because Prudence knew too much. 'The place is no use anyway.' He swept a hand across the space between himself and his wife, pointed the index finger in the direction of the sheds. 'No workers, no money. Do your worst.'

She nodded. 'Sell it,' she advised clearly.

'I'll not get much for it, not while it's producing so little.'

Prudence inclined her head again. 'I think it might be best if you cut your losses, Andrew. Of course, my father's wishes must be upheld. Mr Sutcliffe is here to represent me in this matter.'

'I'll be penniless.' The large man considered trying to appeal to her better nature, rejected the concept when he saw the set of her jaw. 'The house is mine.'

'Yes,' she replied. 'But the other properties are joint, as is the business.'

'So you've won,' he snapped.

'This is neither game nor war,' she told him. 'It was supposed to be a marriage. Whatever it was, we must liquidate immediately.'

Sutcliffe touched his client's arm, led her to the door. 'You will hear from me in due course,' he said plainly before stepping outside. 'G-g-good day, sir.'

Andrew Worthington picked up a huge onyx paperweight and hurled it against the door. It bounced off, hit a dark green jardinière, sent a crimson-crowned geranium spinning across the room in the company of shattered earthenware. His heart sounded loudly in his ears and breathing was difficult. It was as if some magnetic force had pulled all the oxygen out of the room. Soil and compost was deposited everywhere. A clock on the wall pronounced the time by giving out a solitary chime. Half past twelve. At half past twelve on a summer Monday, Andrew Worthington had been bankrupted.

He picked up his spectacles, pushed them into a pocket, breathed in and out, in and out, tried to slow his heart. A pain was spreading across his chest and into shoulders and arms. After tearing at his collar stud, he leaned back, waited for the discomfort to pass. It was his father's disease, an ailment that had plagued Worthington Senior for many years. Angina. She was killing him. They were all killing him. A plot had been hatched and all the conspirators were just outside, some in terraced hovels, one with a title and a gobful of plums, one on the arm of a disarmingly astute solicitor with a slight speech impediment. 'I'll burn it first,' he muttered. 'I'll tear it brick from brick before I'll hand it over to Prudence.' But there was no energy in the words. He had not the strength to fight, had not the stamina to defend himself, even. The mill must be sold; there was nothing else for it.

He walked to the window, thought about Victor. Would he be able to help? Would the youngest Worthington find some investors who might pull Paradise Mill out of its nosedive? No. No, Victor was a mummy's boy. 'She spoiled him,' he spat. 'I'll get no co-operation from that quarter.'

At one o'clock, the ex-master of Paradise Mill left his post, walked down the stairs and through the yard, stood for a few seconds with his eyes glued to the massive frontage of the cotton factory. After a while, he swivelled and stared at the houses. Heilberg's houses. The pain in his chest started up again, slim fingers of heat that probed his ribs and left him panting. Soon, he would die. With this certainty in mind, he climbed into his car and drove home. Whatever, he had no intention of going out whimpering. What was that quote? he asked himself idly as he drove up Wigan Road. Something about the world ending not with a bang? He smiled grimly. His own exit would be loud. And some would perish in the aftershock.

The wedding was over. Ivy had been disappointed, because the ceremony – if such it might have been called – had taken place in the town registry office. She'd bought a lilac frock, too, had caused a stir by wearing toning hat and gloves in darker purple. And it had all flashed by in seconds, a civil job with no pastor, no bridesmaids and no confetti. Maureen and Tom had worn their best clothes, but a very tall chap from London had turned up in a strange brown suit with too-short trousers and sleeves.

She stirred her tea, looked at the weird creature who was seated at the other side of her table. 'What sort of a name is that?' she asked. 'I've never heard nowt like it.'

He nodded, wiped his mouth with a hanky that had seen better days. 'Nor have I. My father was probably to blame.'

'Any brothers and sisters?'

'No.'

'Well, there's a bit of luck,' declared Ivy Crumpsall. 'Because there's not a lot of names as would fit with Featheringay.' Only a slight twitch of her lip gave away the fact that she was aware of her mistaken pronunciation. 'Mind, John would have been better. Or Joe or Jim. But Perry-green's a gobful on its own, isn't it?'

He grinned. 'I'm used to it. Now, I want you to sign a couple of papers, Mrs Crumpsall.'

Ivy sipped at the tea, eyed him warily. 'I hope you know what you're doing, lad.' He looked as if he didn't know whether it was Tuesday, Easter Sunday or breakfast time. 'And I'll have you understand here and now that I've never directed nothing before.'

Perry sighed. Of late, life had become extremely busy. Tom Goodfellow and Joseph Heilberg, together with a handful of investors from the south, were preparing to buy

Paradise Mill. Prudence Worthington's share would be easy to acquire, but her husband's portion was going to be a problem.

'Is it legal, what you're doing?' asked Ivy.

Perry shrugged. 'Legal, yes. Mr Goodfellow and Mr Heilberg are investing money in a workers' co-operative. Initially, you and they will form the board, though the employees will, in time, have the opportunity to buy shares in their own company. At that point, they will elect representation, so the board will be expanded.'

Ivy chewed absently on her lower lip. 'I'm getting on,' she said. 'Me old bones are creaking with age.'

Perry grinned cheekily. 'Borrow an oil can from Paradise. Believe me, you still have a lot to offer, in spite of your years – probably because of your age. You are all to be in this together, Mrs Crumpsall. Mr Heilberg, Tom and yourself will supervise the running of the workers' co-operative. Really, apart from a bit of welfare work, your sole responsibility will be to look at the books in the company of an auditor. There will be meetings, of course, but there won't be a lot for you to do. Mr Heilberg will be running the show—'

'And the workers are going to get bonus shares and seats on the committee. Aye, you've told me all this once. But where's the money coming from?'

'That is not your worry.'

Ivy bit into a biscuit. 'I can answer me own question if I think on. A lot of it's Tom's money. He's using what his dad left him. Well, some of it. He's saving most of the land and property till he finds his sister. But I'm putting no money in, Mr Featheringay, 'cos I haven't got none.' She awarded him a hard look. 'You really should do summat about that, Perry-green. I mean, Tom's changed his family name back to Marchant, and he said it were easy. He's plain Mr Marchant now. If he can get rid of Goodfellow, why don't you have a go at shifting your daft name?'

'I like it.'

He was as daft as a cat with fleas, she told herself. Couldn't sit still, always messing about in his pockets, didn't want to have a decent handle. 'You're crackers,' she informed him.

'Eccentric. It's deliberate.'

'Is it?'

He nodded soberly. 'With a name like mine, I've had to be eccentric—'

'Then alter it, get a new one.'

He smiled. 'I'm too eccentric to have an ordinary surname.'

'Like I said afore – bloody daft.'

He leaned back, started rocking in the straight-backed dining chair. 'Back to business, Mrs Crumpsall. You will be consulted. You will be valued for your expertise.'

'Eh?'

'You've lived in these parts for some time. You know the workers, you know cotton. We'll need you to see that things run smoothly.' He heard Tom's voice, remembered every word. 'She's a character, Perry. Even a few weeks ago, none of us would have expected her to stay alive for much longer. Hampshire has enlivened her, but she needs reasons, work, responsibility and respect. Not a great, fat job, but a niche of her own.'

'I'll be useless,' she declared.

Perry noticed a glimmer of hope in the fading eyes. 'You'll be wonderful. You can listen to their troubles, go to their homes and give advice. Without you, we are a bit stuck.'

He talked lovely, she thought. A haircut and a shave would have been nice, but he was all there with his lemon drops. 'You should sack your tailor,' she advised him. 'And give that suit to one of Tom's farmers. It'd look a treat on a scarecrow.'

Peregrine Fotheringay stopped rocking, threw back his head and howled with glee. He wasn't used to such

273

forthrightness. She was a grand old girl, half-granite and half-velvet. 'I must go. The offer will be made in half an hour. I am to meet with Worthington's lawyer.'

Gert Simpson popped her head into the room. 'Ivy?'

'Hello?'

'They're off. Are you coming?'

Ivy jumped up. 'Come on, Featheringay. Let's see Tom and Maureen on their way. Africa,' she mumbled to no-one in particular. 'I bet they come back with malaria and all sorts.'

Paradise emptied itself into the lane and watched while Maureen and Tom set off on their honeymoon. Ivy wiped a tear from her face, clung to Tom's hand for a moment. 'Write, lad,' she said gruffly.

'Are you with us?' he asked.

'Aye, yon daft lawyer of yours has got me in up to me neck. And we're off back to Hampshire tomorrow. That chap of yours is coming up for me and Ollie and Rosie. Aye, Red and all, God help us.' She sniffed. 'Our Sal will be wondering where I am.'

Maureen put her arms round the old lady. 'Give Sally my love.'

Tom eyed Perry, wondered where this particular set of dreadful clothing had come from. The craftsmen of Savile Row probably paid Perry to stay out of the area. 'Get that mill,' he said quietly. 'And make sure that Prudence Worthington's rights are upheld. She's ready to sell her share, but make sure she gets a decent sum for it.'

'I will.'

Tom clapped the trilby onto his head. 'There'll be no other bids from Bolton. The decent mill owners are with us all the way. Watch for interest from out of town. If things get difficult, get Sutcliffe to have a word in the right ears. I'll be back when I've found my sister.' He climbed into the taxi cab with his new wife.

A small figure ran along Paradise Lane. 'Tom!' called Joseph Heilberg. 'A moment, please.' He reached the car and poked his head inside. 'If you see an elephant on his own, do not approach him.'

Ivy stepped back towards her house, remembered what Derek had said to Joseph just a few months ago.

'Are you all right, love?' asked Gert.

'Aye, I'll do.'

Joseph joined the two women. 'Your son was a good man, Ivy.'

'He was.'

'And his daughter will make a good woman, I think. Tom will bring her a photograph of some elephants. I promised Derek that I would bring pictures for Sally if I ever went to Africa.'

Gert Simpson carried her terrible secret into the house. The man birthed by Ivy Crumpsall was not Sally's father. Sally's father was up Wigan Road in a huge and empty house. Gert's hands travelled of their own accord to cover her belly, and she remembered the pain, could almost feel it again.

'You ill, lass?'

Gert turned on the spot. 'No. I'll finish packing your bag.'

Ivy sat by the window and fixed her eyes on Paradise Mill. Soon, a painter would be employed to redecorate the chimney. THE GOODFELLOW CO-OPERATIVE should be in existence soon. She smiled, thanked everyone's lucky stars that Tom had not been burdened with a horrible name. In fact, Goodfellow was cheerful, which was why they'd decided to hang on to it for business purposes. But Fotheringay? It didn't bear thinking about.

TWELVE

Andrew Worthington had done the rounds of Winchester during his brief visit. He had stayed at an inn for the night, had ambled along to a house on College Street inside which a female called Jane Austen had died. She had been some sort of a writer, he thought, though he had never spent a lot of time on novels. Prudence would have read the woman's work, no doubt.

He cast an eye over the College of St Mary, remained unimpressed by a notice declaring this to be the oldest public school in England. There was no real pleasure to be gained from walking; he did it simply because the doctor had advised gentle exercise and a light, alcohol-free diet. Behind a hand, he belched and caught an echo of this morning's breakfast – bacon, eggs, sausages and toast. The exercise was just about manageable, but dieting was proving impossible.

Determined to persevere until his mission had been accomplished, he climbed into his car and placed the trilby on the lid of a small suitcase. Lord Goodfellow. Very soon, Andrew Worthington would arrive at the Goodfellow estate. Sir Peter had died, it seemed, had left all his goods and chattels to a man who had been living in a scruffy, cramped Paradise hovel belonging to a foreigner called Joseph Heilberg.

The pain paid a brief visit, was shooed away by one of those funny little pills. He waited, sat perfectly still until the tightness relaxed. That Jane Austen woman had come here to be near her doctor, but she had died anyway. Amused by the concept, he started the engine and pulled away. With or without medical intervention, he intended to have his moment of triumph.

Finding Goodfellow's hide had not been difficult. In the reference department of Bolton's Central Library, he had pored through a list of gentry, had discovered the tale of the Goodfellows' laughable beginnings. After hunting wild boar at the other end of Hampshire, a Marchant had been knighted by the inebriated Henry VIII. The woman would be there, thought Worthington. Ivy Crumpsall and the brat were no doubt living on the fat of Goodfellow's ancestors' land.

He left Winchester, followed a ribbon of road through fields where harvesters toiled. The anger seethed just beneath the surface, making his skin hot and wet. When the discomfort became intense, he pulled over and braked, climbed out, removed his jacket and waistcoat.

Prudence was buying a little semi-detached on Crompton Way, just a couple of living rooms, a tiny morning room, a kitchen. The Miles woman had given up her house to stay with Prudence, while Gert Simpson was residing at number 1, Paradise Lane. About this house-sitting arrangement he could do nothing, because Heilberg was the landlord. A sigh of relief bubbled past the large man's lips. If that trollop had brought a case against him . . .

Gert had not prosecuted him. Like the rest, she would probably come to terms with what had happened. Because, in line with all the other women he had known, Gert had been asking for trouble by flaunting her assets in front of a full-blooded male. Some damned fool of a Cockney had taken over Goodfellow's cottage, a chap with burns, a thin wife and a couple of babies. The rest . . . the rest did not bear thinking about too closely.

But the story wove itself through his mind, would not leave him in peace. He had sold his portion of the mill to a so-called conglomerate from the south, a group of business-men who were anxious to upgrade the cotton trade. But these invisible purchasers had been non-existent. He ground teeth and gears, managed not to hit a milestone as he steered himself out of a ditch. Fotheringay and a little, grey-suited friend from London had signed on the dotted line, had handed over a sizeable cheque before handing over the mill to Goodfellow, now Marchant, and Joseph Heilberg. Oh, how that had hurt! He had been tricked, swindled, made to look a fool.

Worthington tried to control his breathing, in, out, in, out. The deed had been done and he must simply accept that Heilberg and company had won. They were forming a co-operative, were preparing to labour under the socialist delusion that workers should hold shares in their factories. How easily that Fotheringay chap had twisted the truth. 'We shall get exactly what we need from Mr Heilberg,' the Londoner had said. 'As we speak, plans are waiting for a signature, Mr Worthington. The bottom of the H – the place now known as the Paradise Recreation Ground – will soon become part and parcel of the mill.'

He slowed the car, told himself to be more careful. After all, he had to survive to take his revenge. Those bloody London lawyers had been in on the plot to oust the mill's rightful owner. Oh yes, the recreation ground was going to be developed, but not under the watchful eye of a Worthington, not with the guidance of a family steeped in cotton. For years he had fought to acquire that land, but it had remained beyond his reach. Now, the dream would finally materialize, but Heilberg and Lord Wotsisname would be in charge.

The rightful owner of Paradise drove steadily, shirt sleeves rolled for comfort, his window lowered to stir the placid air of this warm autumn day. They had duped him into handing over his livelihood. No, no, he must not think . . .

Gears ground again as an unexpected hairpin bend was negotiated. The Recreation area would soon sprout a canteen, half a dozen baths, a medical room, some classrooms and a hall for indoor sports and social gatherings. The thieves had taken everything, right down to the office chair in which two generations of Worthingtons had sat.

The Blunts, too, had disappeared, were probably here, in Hampshire, with Ivy Crumpsall and her granddaughter. He covered his mouth to stifle a laugh. That child was no kin to the Crumpsalls. She was just another by-blow, a thing that had been conceived against an office wall or across a desk. Lottie had been a lively lass, too feisty for the numbskull she had married. He sneered again, patted the steering-wheel. Lottie Crumpsall had given him many a good time, and he had given her a daughter.

He passed an inn, decided not to stop just yet. His denial of paternity had been fierce, but the pregnancy had lasted over ten months. Derek had been abroad for forty-two weeks by the time 'his' daughter had put in an appearance. Lottie had been wont to remind Andrew Worthington of his obligations, but he had stuck to his guns until her departure for foreign parts. On Trinity Street, he had pushed money into the hands of a tomato-spattered whore, had admitted paternity in writing and in exchange for a letter penned in the waiting room. The missive had been intended for Lottie's sister – its contents stating that Gertrude Simpson should rear Sally. But Bert and Gert Simpson had failed to wrench the girl from Ivy Crumpsall's arms. Now, Andrew Worthington would grab his pound of flesh.

He entered Oakmead, took his bearings from a signpost at the end of the street. The place was silent, almost asleep. Two large dogs lay in the doorway of a thatched cottage, their ears pricking as if to mark the arrival of a stranger. But they neither moved nor barked as Andrew Worthington stepped from his car and walked along the pavement. A post-office-cum-general-store had the word CLOSED printed on cardboard in its window. Across the way, a row of cottages bore the legend 'ALMSHOUSES' and 'AD 1815', which date was repeated on a wall of the adjoining school. Where was Goodfellow Hall?

He entered the Boar's Head, felt swamped by the gloom inside. Tiny windows allowed very little light to infiltrate the small and stuffy room. Behind a bar counter, a dim shape moved. 'What's your pleasure, sir?' asked the formless creature.

The newcomer blinked, waited for his eyes to adjust. 'A pint of bitter and the directions to Goodfellow Hall, please.' It was a woman of about forty, he realized. She had black hair and was wearing a dark dress, but the bared teeth were shining between parted lips. She poured the beer, placed it on the counter. 'The Hall's a couple of miles that way.' She waved a cloth. 'Big gates and a long drive. The master's not there – he's in Africa with his wife. Got married, he did. Though there were some hereabouts who said he never would, not after the tragedy.'

He decided to act cannily. 'Quite. That was a dreadful business.'

The barmaid leaned against the counter. 'You from the north, then?'

He nodded, took a draught from the glass, gave himself time to think. 'That's where I met Lord Goodfellow.'

'Mr Marchant now. That's what he likes to be called these days.'

'I know.' He licked froth from his upper lip, cursed the doctor who had tried to no avail to separate him from his pint of ale. 'Tom and I have been close for many years,' he informed her.

She picked up a tankard and polished it with a yellow duster. 'He's got other folk from the north around here. Rose Cottage, they're staying in. There's a woman called Ivy and a little girl . . . now, what's her name?'

'Sally,' he said, his tone warm and helpful. 'Sally Crumpsall. And her grandmother is Ivy.'

'That's it. Then the other lady's Rosie something or other—'

'Blunt,' he told her. 'Her husband is Ollie.'

'Daft in the head. Nice man, comes here with servants from the Hall. The farmers are letting him help bring the harvest in, bless him. Then there's a lad they call Red – on account of his hair, I shouldn't wonder. Nice lot of people.'

He drained his glass. 'The same again and one for yourself.'

'That's kind of you, sir.'

While she pulled at the pump handle, he gazed round the bar and saw that he was the sole customer. 'Quiet today.'

'Harvest,' she replied. 'Another ten minutes and they'll all be in with a terrible thirst. Bring their own sandwiches, they do.' Her accent was mellow, as if it had ripened like fruit in the sun-splashed atmosphere of this bucolic setting. Though her sallow skin spoke of many hours in the twilight of Oakmead's sole public house.

He had to be out of here quickly, then. Ollie Blunt might be ageing, but he would surely recognize the boss from Paradise Mill. 'I hope Tom will be happy now,' he said. 'After the other business, he deserves a chance.' She had talked of trouble, and he wanted to know more.

The woman leaned on the counter, gave him the dubious benefit of a full if somewhat wrinkled cleavage. 'That Master Jonathan was never any good. What he did to Lady Sarah was terrible, by all accounts. Course, when she put an end to herself, we all knew why. Even after all these years she wasn't getting over it. That's what they all say, anyway.' She paused, plainly expecting a comment.

'Sad ending,' he managed.

'Killed her dad, too. Lord Collingford took some sort of fit and keeled over in his bedroom a few days after Lady Sarah's death. Had nightmares, did Lady Sarah. So it was like she was raped over and over again.'

The cogs in his brain began to mesh. 'By Master Jonathan.' He shook his head. 'Rape is a disgusting crime.'

'Well . . .' She rolled her eyes, batted the too-fine lashes. 'I mean, what else could Master Tom have done? He was standing there watching when Lady Sarah was tossed into the lake. Then, I suppose he saw his brother falling in. He could only save one of them, being a poor swimmer and all. So Master Jonathan was drowned and Lady Sarah was saved by Master Tom.'

The bloody hero of the piece, thought Worthington. Goodfellow should have been in films as the leader of the sheriff's posse, a white-hatted man on a pale, prancing horse. Damn him. In Africa, was he? So Ivy and the girl would be completely unprotected. He said goodbye, made for the door.

'Your change, sir. Don't you want it?'

'Keep it,' he replied.

Outside, he walked the length of the street, cast an eye over a square church tower that looked old enough to be Norman or Saxon. From a safe distance, he watched the harvesters arriving on flat carts, waited while feedbags were fastened to the horses. Ollie Blunt was among the throng. Even from this distance the man's voice was recognizable as he shouted about green fingers and the potatoes he had grown in Lancashire. The old stranger was borne on a tide of humanity into the inn, then the village settled back to doze once more in the burnished tints of autumn.

Worthington sat in his car and wondered how he might use the information he had gleaned today. Should he tell the holidaying residents of Paradise that their new master had committed a crime akin to fratricide? No. It was a pity, but the tale of Tom Marchant's tragic youth would not be useful. In fact, it could serve only to reinforce the concept of 'Lord Tom' as the champion of women, a white-clad knight of unblemished chivalry and fortitude.

He would go now and find Goodfellow Hall. He wanted to see the true size of Mr Marchant's wealth and power. Then, he would come face to face with his own daughter.

The plans were still vague, but he intended to make Ivy Crumpsall suffer. More than anything, he craved the pleasure that would surely result from her pain.

Being a country girl suited Sally. Within a couple of months of her arrival in Oakmead, she had gained weight and a golden tan that showed off the thickened mass of sun-bleached hair. Ivy often looked at the dimples in her granddaughter's cheeks, sighed to herself when she thought of her dead son. 'Derek,' she would say inside her head while possing her whites. 'If you could only see her now, lad. If you could only see them strong legs and them lovely blue eyes.'

Red Trubshaw, that stalwart young man who always shadowed Sally's every move, had become one huge, walking freckle. The spattering of melanin that had decorated his face seemed to have joined forces, so that the lad appeared brown and healthy. Sturdy limbs had become muscular during bouts of harvesting, and Red had become an altogether quieter boy.

Ivy watched the two of them playing in the garden, grinned when Red helped Sally up after a tumble. No harm would come to the lass, not while Arthur Trubshaw had a breath in his body. 'A good soul,' Ivy told Rosie. 'Just shows you – never judge a book by its cover.'

'It's me own bloody book I'm thinking on,' replied the small, white-haired woman. 'Harvesting? Yon Ollie Blunt's not fit to pour a cup of tea. Imagine what damage he could do with a bloody pitchfork.'

Ivy dried the last cup, swung round to face her friend. 'Look, love. Ollie's lost a few slates off his roof – we all know that. Now, you can either have him sat here in the kitchen like half-set jelly, or you can let him play out.'

Rosie stretched her spine, achieving her full height of four feet and eleven inches. 'It's kiddies as plays out. Not grown men.'

'He's not a grown man no more, Rosie.'

'Have you seen the size of his feet and—?'

'Nowt to do with the size of his feet and hands, and well you know it.' Ivy tapped her skull. 'It's in here. The man's gone into his second childhood, so he needs occupying.'

Rosie flopped into a chair. 'I know all that, Ivy. I didn't land with the last lot of rain. It's a child's mind in a man's body. You don't let childer out in the street with a razor blade, do you? He's worse than an ordinary child, 'cos he's got a man's power. If somebody riles him—'

'Nobody will. They're lovely folk round here, full of fun and patience. They'll see to him. Stop worrying about summat as hasn't happened yet.'

Rosie stared through the kitchen window, looked past the playing children and into the fields and woods beyond the garden. 'It's bonny here, Ivy,' she said thickly.

'Aye.'

'We're lucky to have this little holiday.'

Ivy sat opposite her neighbour and grasped the tiny hands. 'This'll allers be here for us. It's Sally's now. We got a letter from Tom this morning. He's found yon sister of his, and she says he can turn the Hall into an orphanage. Then all these tenant farmers'll get a house and a bit of land. But Rose Cottage is our Sal's. We can come again.'

Rosie bit her lip for a moment. 'We'll come, Ivy. But not my Ollie. It's going to be soon.'

'I know, lass.'

Rosie gulped back a sob. 'What will I do without that big, soft bugger?'

'You'll give your legs a rest and stick with me, Rosie. Aye, you stick with me and we'll get through some road or other.'

The tears flowed. 'Thanks, Ivy.'

Ivy nodded quickly, left Rosie at the table and went to fill the kettle yet again. 'They've gone,' she remarked.

'Who?' Rosie blew her nose.

'Our Sal and Red. They'll be jumping about in that

trout stream again. I wouldn't care, Sal's more feared of the bloody fish than they are of her.'

'Will the kiddies be all right?'

Ivy nodded as she reached for the tea caddy. 'As long as Red's around, no harm'll come to our lass.'

He stopped the car and cast an eye over Goodfellow's mansion. It was a massive pile, the sort of place that screamed 'old money' from every pillar, window and door. The garden, though slightly neglected, was roughly the size of Burnden Park, and Andrew Worthington guessed that the land at the back of the house might well be sufficient to accommodate the Bolton Wanderers plus Blackburn Rovers, Manchester United and all reserves. There was power here, because there was land.

Uneasy in the face of such riches, he leaned against the bonnet of his car and thought about the next move. Goodfellow – Marchant, he reminded himself yet again – was not here. Also, the more he stared at Goodfellow Hall, the more he was encouraged by imperfections caused by neglect. There were slates missing, some lying crookedly against others, some shunted into small piles which had slid along to rest on rainwater troughing. A length of guttering had broken free to hang its metal length down the face of the old house like a black scar over the twin front doors.

He reached into the car's body, brought forth a pair of binoculars and focused them on the Hall. A dome of stained glass sat in the centre of the roof, proclaiming the fact that the entrance chamber rose through three storeys and more. A single spiked finial topped the orb, its dagger-shaped point aiming straight into an azure sky. But Andrew Worthington missed the beauty and homed in on bits of patchwork, pieces of tarpaulin and plain glass that had been used to darn the ageing structure.

He smiled, imagined the inside of the house. A minstrels' gallery, perhaps? Two staircases converging along a landing, the banisters broken, the treads covered in threadbare carpeting? He swung the glasses, settled on a Rolls Royce parked just below the balustrade. A man was polishing the car, his whole body seeming to throw itself into the movement. There was money here even now, he thought uncomfortably. Members of the gentry were often eccentric. And, after the trouble over Lady Wotsername and the death of his older son, the recently defunct Sir Peter might have gone to the dogs for a while.

Worthington sat in his car and pondered for a while. The Crumpsalls would have friends here. They and the Blunts were no doubt in the care of Marchant's minions. If the servants and tenants of the Goodfellow estate were all as meticulous as the chap cleaning the Rolls, then there might be trouble.

He lit a cigarette, leaned back in the uncomfortable seat, wished he could afford a Rolls Royce with good upholstery and a paid driver. Oh, he had some money, all right, the few thousand he'd managed to bleed away from Paradise, then the payment he had received from those who had manipulated Peregrine Fotheringay's strings. Workers' co-operative? Heilberg and the erstwhile Lord Goodfellow had taken away the mill. Daylight robbery, that had been. He must keep going, stay sane and mobile, because the list of grudges was expanding by the day.

Still, at least he had the little nest egg, a well-hidden fund that could not be touched by Prudence's lawyer. As for the group of so-called dependants who had assembled in Ivy Crumpsall's house – let them find him first. So, what else could he lose at this point? Nothing. What he needed most of all was to watch Ivy Crumpsall's face when she learned the true identity of her 'granddaughter's' father. He needed only to produce Lottie's written declaration, then the child would be his.

His. He closed his eyes and wondered what the hell he would do with a seven-year-old daughter. Bloody Victor had been difficult enough, always whining over a cut knee, a bit of a bruise, a new toy he'd seen in town. And if it came to a legal fight, no court or welfare committee on earth would award a failed mill owner custody of the girl. He was older than his years, ill, relatively poor. But what if he . . . what if he kidnapped her and simply took her away from the Crumpsall woman for a while? If arrested, he could say his conscience had pricked him and that he had wanted to give the urchin a treat. As for the reaction of the Bolton folk – he had no ties in the town, no need to return.

A snuffling sound made him sit up sharply, and he found himself face to face with a black-and-white cow whose sole aim in life seemed to be to lick its way through the windscreen. A thick, velvet tongue stroked the transparent sheet, leaving smears and bubbling spittle. 'Shoo,' mumbled the car's inhabitant.

The animal blinked slowly, pressed its soft nose against the glass.

Andrew Worthington fought the pain brought on by panic, fingered the silver-gilt pillbox in a breast pocket. It was too soon for another pill, far too soon. And this big, stupid beast refused to move even when he shook a fist at it. Its lower jaw moved rhythmically from side to side as it ground food against huge, yellowing teeth. Each time he caught sight of these tombstones, Worthington shivered. This was his first encounter with a bovine creature, and the pain in his chest was increasing. What should he do?

A familiar voice called out, 'Get out of the road, Primrose.' The Friesian mooed, backed away, trotted off along the lane.

Ivy Crumpsall stared through the messy windscreen and shuddered. He was here. The biggest nightmare of her whole life was sitting white-faced outside the gate of Goodfellow Hall. She inhaled deeply, waved her walking stick at Primrose, tried to ignore the thoughts that danced around inside her brain. He was here for a reason. He was here because she had been instrumental in removing him from Paradise Mill.

'Mrs Crumpsall?' He closed the car door, attempted to stand upright, though his legs seemed shaky.

Once the cow had sauntered off, Ivy turned slowly and looked into the bulging eyes of the man she had detested for much of her life. 'What are you doing here?' she snapped. 'Long way from home, isn't it?'

'I have no home.' He rested against the car door, fished a tiny tablet from the box and pushed it into his mouth. When relief arrived, he forced himself upright. 'You and the lord of this manor made sure I finished up with nothing.'

'There were others involved,' she replied carefully. 'Like your wife and a couple of hundred workers and—'

'And Gert Simpson.'

She shrugged, tried to make the gesture light. She was alone with a monster on a deserted country road. 'They all had their reasons.'

His mouth twisted in a travesty of a smile that further distorted a face already made ugly by bitterness. 'You'll pay, missus,' he whispered.

'What with? I've no money.'

'You've something of mine,' he spat.

She allowed her eyes to travel the length of his body. 'I've not got time for this,' she said after a moment or two. 'I've two children to find.'

His head shook slowly from side to side. 'And one of them's mine.'

Ivy, suddenly chilled in spite of the sun's kindness, wrapped the shawl tightly about her upper body. She had not expected this, had imagined that he would never admit the truth. For years, she had tried to deny it herself. The little girl's eyes were so like Derek's had been. But no, no, the baby had been delivered not quite full term, tiny, underweight, fingernails barely grown. Had Lottie gone the distance, Sally might even have been born eleven months after Derek's departure for foreign soil.

The old woman inhaled deeply, maintained her position. 'Our Sal?' Her eyebrows raised themselves, deepening the furrows of age on her forehead. 'You're telling me nowt new, Andrew Worthington. Me and our Derek guessed from the kick-off as how Sally weren't a Crumpsall.' They had discussed the matter just once, when the child had been five years old. After that day, Sally had been theirs. Not Lottie's, not Worthington's, but hers and Derek's. And the neighbours', of course. So many people had figured in the rearing of Sally while her feckless mother played her games.

His lower jaw sagged until it all but met his chest.

Ivy folded her arms beneath the knitted wool shawl. 'But it didn't matter, you see. 'Cos my Derek were a good man and he saw it this road.' She took a small step in his direction. 'It weren't no fault of the kiddy's. Her mother's a whore, and you're a rotten bugger, but that doesn't make our Sal a bad lot.' She smiled grimly. 'It were a ten-month pregnancy, Worthington. And Lottie Kerrigan-as-was were very flush with money. We all knew where she'd earned it. We all knew she'd been flitting in and out of your bloody office, even though she did live at the other end of town. Things like that gets noticed, like. That were your doing, all right, 'cos Loose Lottie didn't get her chance to start messing about with the Yanks till they turned up a couple of years later. And you were her man of the moment in 1939. But you're no father.'

He could not believe what he was hearing. 'And you never said a word.'

'There were none of us wanted owt to do with you, so we kept our gobs shut. And Sally needed protecting. Why should we make her go through life knowing she were another one of your mistakes? We took to her, me and Derek. I kept writing to him and telling him what a little love she were. Then, when he got demobbed, he saw for himself as how our Sal were a good 'un. Derek loved his daughter for who she were, not for where she'd come from.' Derek had enjoyed just one short year of health with the child he had thought of as a daughter. 'He were more of a dad than you could ever be,' she said now. 'Even when he were dying, he watched over our Sal. You?' She laughed mirthlessly. 'That Victor of yours could turn out to be another rotten swine. I'm right sorry for that po-faced woman he's walking out with.'

He felt like a punctured balloon, could feel the power draining out of him. His final weapon had been removed from his hands. How many hundreds of miles had he driven to have his moment with this harridan? And she had taken even that away from him. 'I'll be claiming her,' he muttered. 'I've a letter from her mother—'

'Try,' she said softly. 'Try and Bolton will hang you from the minute hand of the Town Hall clock.'

'I'll not set foot in that place again.'

Ivy inclined her head. 'Very wise. In fact, there's a phone in yon Hall, and I can go now and talk to some very big Labour Party folk from our neck of the woods. Cotton workers' union's got a bob or two put by, so they'll think nowt of having you tailed, Worthington. Some big lads up yonder, eh? Steelmen and all, them as sweats in foundries. They don't like you. Even the bosses of other mills can't stand the sight of your mush. Didn't you get chucked out of the Lodge on top of everything else? Eeh, what a shame that were.'

His heart felt as if it were held in a vice. A hammer seemed to pound in his chest, a large weapon that echoed sounds from the steel factories she had just mentioned. 'You bitch,' he murmured.

Ivy suddenly realized that this man was very ill and that she didn't care how ill he was. 'Bitches and cows make you feared, don't they? Just bugger off away from Mr Marchant's lands, Worthington. There's a dozen men in them fields who'll kill you as soon as look at your horrible face.' She swivelled on her heel and marched away. Not long ago, she had been weak, might have been too frail to manage these encounters with Worthington. She inhaled the clean air, said a silent prayer of thanks to Hampshire. Now, she must do what she had intended in the first place, which was to find Sally and Red. At a four-way junction of country lanes, she paused, then turned towards the brook.

Worthington slumped to the ground and sat in an undignified heap while he fought for oxygen. Death was near, so near that he could almost smell the stench of decay. Reason seemed to be deserting him completely. Even as the anger roared in his skull, a level of consciousness told him that he was losing control. But he didn't care any more. There was nothing left for him, no work, no home, no future. All he wanted now was the chance to kick back at those who had conspired against him.

He lifted his head and stared across the field just as a pair of children danced into his line of vision. The blonde girl was probably Sally Crumpsall, and the red-headed lad seemed familiar. In a few minutes, once his lungs had settled, he would walk slowly across the fallow land and take the child. She was the only weapon left to him.

Sally watched the silver trout as they cavorted in the stream. There were so many fish that there seemed insufficient water to accommodate them. 'Do they drown?' she asked her companion. 'If there's not enough water, do they choke?'

Red nodded. 'Aye, same as we do if there's no air.'

'They need more water, then,' she said.

'Oh, they'll be all right. Once they get round yon bend, they'll be in a wider part of the river. That's why they're all rushing about.' He dropped to the ground and breathed in the smell of damp grass. Red Trubshaw was not a fanciful boy, yet he was beginning to think that smells had colours attached to them. Grass and peas straight from the pod had a green smell, while not-quite-ripe tomatoes definitely carried a burnt yellowish aroma. He wondered for a moment whether, because of his nickname, he ponged of red like strawberries did . . . Sally's colour was yellow, he mused.

'We're going home soon,' Sally moaned. There were things and people that she missed; there were others best not thought about. The headmaster belonged to the latter category. 'Back to Craddock Street Juniors and old Basher Bates.'

Red had little time for their headmaster. 'Don't worry. Once he's seen you with me, he'll leave you alone. I put jumping jacks through his letterbox last bonfire night 'cos he'd thumped me and our Charlie. He never said nowt, old Basher, only when he looked at me, I knew he knew it were me as had done it. And he knew I knew he knew.'

Sally, who had got lost after the second 'knew', poked her companion in the ribs. 'There's a car stopped over yonder,' she told him. 'And a man coming across to us.'

Red yawned. The countryside was great, but it seemed to make him excessively hungry and in need of sleep. The idea of going home to share a bed with three brothers did not appeal. Also, the smell of his house in Paradise matched no colour at all. Brown, perhaps. Dirty, smelly brown full of germs and mildew and cockroaches and—

'Hello, Mr Worthington,' said Sally, surprise showing in her tone. 'What are you doing here?'

Red, instantly alert, shot upright and glared at the shadow between him and the sun.

'I've come to see you,' announced the intruder. 'I thought you might like a ride in my car.'

Red poked a hand through his hair so that it stood to attention above raised eyebrows. 'We've to go home in a minute,' he told the man.

'Home? Isn't your home in Bolton, lad?'

Sally answered for both of them. 'We've got a house here and all, Mr Worthington. Rose Cottage. It's mine, because Uncle Tom gave it me. When I'm twenty-one, I get the doings.'

'She means the deeds,' explained Red. He didn't like this man, didn't trust him. 'Get moving, Sal. Your gran'll be wondering where we've got to.'

Worthington placed a heavy hand on Sally's shoulder. 'Come on,' he wheedled, his voice rising in pitch as if he were coaxing a pet cat. 'I've things to tell you, Sally. Things about me and the man you called Dad, things about your mother and—'

Sensing danger, Red threw himself at the unwelcome guest. 'Bugger off,' he said clearly. 'We want nowt off you. Me and her's got all we want. I don't know why you've come all this way. Is it 'cos they've took the mill off you?' He thrust a balled fist into the man's soft gut.

Worthington let out a formless roar and grabbed the boy by the throat. 'Don't you dare speak to me like that. I'll have your hide. This girl is mine – do you hear? She is mine, I tell you.' Although Red was a big lad, Andrew Worthington's temper allowed him to shake the substantial child as if he were a doll. 'I've lost enough, boy, and it's time Ivy Crumpsall shared the pain. This is my daughter and—'

Red's boot made sharp contact with the large man's groin. 'Shut your mouth,' roared the furious boy. 'You shouldn't be here.' He stood back and watched with interest while Worthington folded himself into a ball on the ground. 'I know where to kick folk,' shouted Red. 'And so does she and all.' He jerked a thumb at Sally. 'She's like me sister, is Sal—'

'If you say "Sally, Sally, Sally" very fast, it sounds like Alice,' said Sally. 'Red had an Alice, only she died, so he's got me instead.' Why was she talking about foolish things while this man was pretending to be her dad? Because she didn't want him for a dad, she told herself. Her dad was dead and in heaven with Jesus and God and a load of angels with harps and wings. Talking and thinking daft seemed to take her mind off the confusion.

Red, who had always been a good eavesdropper, had

heard tales at home, when his own mam had chatted with neighbours over a couple of jugs from the outdoor licence. There were a lot of boys and girls on a list of what Mam called Worthington's cast-offs. Surely Sally was in no way connected with this great heap of humanity that writhed about in the grass? He grabbed Sally's hand. 'Come on,' he urged. 'Let's get away from him.'

But Sally shook her head. 'I'm stopping here till he tells me I'm not his girl,' she said. 'I'm not his daughter, I'm not, not, not.'

Red stared at Sally. Her cheeks were fiery and there was a set to her jaw, a stubbornness in her eyes. This was how she had looked that day in the playground when Red and his friends had taunted her about the new clothes. 'Come on, Sal,' he begged. 'Yon feller's only trying to make trouble for you.' He pulled at her, tried to drag her away from the scene.

'He's got to tell the truth!' Sally screamed at the top of her voice. 'Make him tell the truth, Red.'

Worthington waited for the pain to subside, hoped that the discomfort in his chest would not increase. Everything around him was bathed in a dark red light, as if his temper had spilled out to stain the air, the clouds, the faces of these children. He was a doomed man. Within weeks – perhaps days – his heart would give up the fight. The woman he was seeking to punish had been ill, yet she seemed to have been given a reprieve. There had been strength in Ivy Crumpsall's voice today, energy in her demeanour.

Red pulled hard on Sally's closed fist. 'Come on, let's run.' A half-crown landed by his boot, and he studied it for a moment. 'I don't want your mucky money,' he said eventually. He hadn't owned a coin of such value in his whole life. The nearest he ever came to more than a shilling was while doing Mam's shopping on a Saturday morning. Even then, the change had been counted like gold dust.

Worthington rose to his feet. 'Pick it up,' he ordered.

'No.'

'Why not?'

'Don't want it. Don't want nothing off you.'

'There's a lot more,' whispered the sweating man. 'A fiver if you'll take it.'

Red swallowed a hollow lump of surprise. Five quid? He could go to Blackpool for a fortnight, get new shoes, eat all the chips he could carry. Or he could buy a fancy stone for his dead sister's grave. He glanced at Sally. Sally was real, because she was here and now. For little Alice, there was no hope – and a piece of cold, white marble with writing on would not warm his sister back to life. 'Not interested,' he breathed.

Worthington's lip curled. 'How much do you want for her, then?'

Sally glanced sideways at the boy who had always supported her. 'I'm not in Mr Heilberg's shop window,' she said quietly. 'And I am not your girl. You can't make me be your girl. You can't buy me, Mr Worthington.'

'You heard her,' snapped Red. 'Her's not been pledged like somebody's Sunday suit. Sally's not for sale.'

'Ten pounds, then. That's my last offer.'

Sally exploded. 'Shut up, you!' she yelled. 'You're not my dad, because my dad died with being in the pit and the war and you're a horrible man with ugly eyes and Gran hates you.' She pulled herself out of Red's grip. 'Go away. This is a nice place with nice people, fields and everything.' She knew what she meant, but the words did not arrive easily. He didn't belong here, looked out of context in such a beautiful setting. 'Mills is smelly and horrible just like you, so go back. You've no house here.' She stretched her spine. 'I have a house here, my own house. Go back to yours.'

The man lunged forward and scooped the girl into his arms. She rained blows on his face, but he seemed not to notice.

Red, temporarily frozen by shock, simply stood and watched while people began to arrive from two or three directions, men who wielded the tools of harvest time. 'What's going on here?' asked a farm-hand. 'Put her down,' he told the stranger.

Worthington backed away from the field workers. 'Touch me with those forks and you'll hit the girl,' he said. 'She's my daughter. Ivy Crumpsall kidnapped her and brought her here. There's proof in my pocket, a letter from the child's mother. It states that this child should be reared by an aunt.' And a second sheet, the page he had never given to Gert, named Andrew Worthington as the child's father. 'I advise you all to keep perfectly still.' He allowed his eyes to travel round the semicircle of men.

Red bit down on his lower lip until he tasted the tang of blood. They must all stay as they were and say nothing, because Worthington didn't have eyes in the back of his head. Ollie Blunt was creeping softly through the field, the pitchfork held out before him like Britannia's trident with a prong missing. He didn't look daft any more. Ollie's face was set in lines of concentration as he came up behind the hated intruder.

Ivy appeared and stood panting next to a ramshackle stile. She could not believe what she was seeing. Half a dozen workers had placed their implements on the ground, but Ollie continued to stalk his prey. She opened her mouth to scream, but she was too late. As the red-faced Worthington stumbled over a clump of weeds, he dropped Sally and fell back onto Ollie's pitchfork.

The cruel points entered Worthington's body, while Sally, screaming with shock and relief, was dragged away by Red. With a strength born of terror, Worthington rolled sideways, heaved himself onto his knees, his mouth set in a perfect O that seemed to illustrate amazement rather than pain.

Ollie stood very still and watched while his victim crumpled slowly. Somebody was screaming. 'It's all right,

Sally,' Ollie said. 'He can't hurt you no more now.'

One of the harvesters stepped forward and placed his hands on the wooden steel. 'Leave it,' shouted Ivy. 'He'll bleed less if you don't pull it out.' She jerked her head in response to movement from the lane, saw Rosie making haste towards her husband. 'Don't touch that fork,' yelled Ivy to her neighbour. Poor Rosie. A pang of guilt shot through Ivy's heart, its shards as wicked as the prongs of any hay fork. If Rosie and Ollie had stayed in Paradise, this would never have happened . . .

Worthington sank face down in the grass, lifted his head, saw Ivy Crumpsall standing over him. His mouth widened in a sneer. 'She knows now, Mrs Crumpsall. That's no granddaughter of yours – I've told her . . .' Flecks of blood splashed from his mouth and onto the grass. 'Mine,' he moaned. 'Just another one of . . .' A red-hot pain shot through his chest and into his left arm. Compared to this agony, the buried pitchfork was a minor nuisance. There seemed to be no air, no sun. A darkness encircled him, dragging him down and down until his only comfort was the cool pasture that touched his face. Behind Ivy Crumpsall stood a cow, probably the same animal that had terrified him earlier. Now, he was too tired to experience fear.

'The man's at death's door,' whispered a bystander whose cheeks had whitened beneath the warm glister of summer. The labourer raised his head and shouted, 'Quick, get a cart – send for the ambulance.'

'He's still with us,' said Ivy. His head was turned sideways, so that just one hideous eyeball stared up into her face. She bent, touched his neck, felt the feeble flicker of a wavering pulse. 'Repent,' she beseeched. 'Do it now, Mr Worthington. If you pray now, the gates will open for you.'

The agony abated slightly when she touched his hand, as if she had the ability to remove even the pain of death. 'You . . . pray,' he mumbled.

Ivy Crumpsall clasped his stiffening fingers between her palms and said the Lord's Prayer. The harvesters joined in with the amen, then stood in an uncertain group while this woman from the north ministered to the felled man.

A flat cart arrived, the shire in its shafts nodding patiently while Worthington was placed face down on a bed of stooks. Two men in working garb climbed aboard and steadied the pitchfork to prevent it doing further damage to Worthington's innards. The driver clicked his tongue before setting off with the wounded man, the labourers, and Ivy Crumpsall. Ivy glanced down from the cart, hoping with all her heart that Red would settle Sally. Beneath the tan, the poor girl was grey with shock, was plainly reeling from twin blows. She had found an unwanted father, she had seen him felled.

When the vehicle had disappeared, Ollie wandered about, his gaze fastened to the sky. 'Them's homing birds up yon,' he announced to no-one in particular. 'They'll be from number four. He's gone off, has Tom. I'm in charge of things while he's away.' He swivelled slowly, saw his wife in tears. 'Don't cry, Rosie,' he muttered. 'Birds'll come back, you'll see.'

'What do we do now, missus?' This question was directed at Rosie by a weather-beaten man in a dusty smock. 'I mean, that man looked just about done for, didn't he? There be trouble coming, I don't doubt.'

Rosie faced them. They were good folk, the salt of an earth that was not too far removed from the land from which she had hailed. The only difference was that this lot worked outside. But they toiled like any spinner for wages that depended on the generosity of a master. These were the lucky ones, because Tom Marchant was a fair man, though they and their families had suffered at the hands of his forefathers. 'I think he had a heart attack,' she said softly, one eye on Sally.

'Pitchfork didn't help, though,' drawled the spokesman. 'Questions will be asked. Got a couple of holes right through his back, he has. Ask me, the police are going to take an interest.' He chewed on his lip for a moment. 'Mind, when all's said and done with, this was an accident. And that stranger was trying to take young Sally off to God knows where. We saw what happened, didn't we?' he asked the surrounding farm-hands.

A chorus of ayes and yeses answered the question.

Rosie waved a hand towards Ollie. 'Look at him. He's forgot already. This weren't his fault, 'cos he hardly knows what he's doing. And, like you said, Worthington were going to kidnap little Sal.' She sighed heavily. The truth might have to come out now, because Ollie needed protecting. The world must be told of the dead man's past so that Ollie might be kept safe. 'You all saw what were going on here. Speak up for my Ollie when the time comes.' Rosie squared her shoulders against the suspicion that Ollie might be arrested today. She cleared her thickening throat and thought about all the anguish that would surely follow today's happenings. 'There's nowt we can mend here,' she concluded. 'I suppose we'll just have to do our best.'

Sally whimpered, turned her head and buried it in Red's chest. There had been a still, white body in the grass and she was glad it had gone away. And her head was all mixed up, because Dad wasn't Dad any more and both her fathers were dead.

Rosie stepped to Sally's side, placed a hand on the child's head. 'You'll understand in time, love. Derek were your dad. It's the one that brings you up that's important, Sal. In time, lass. In time . . .'

Worthington survived. Against all the odds and in spite of medical opinion to the contrary, the man was hanging on in defiance of a bad heart and two stab wounds that had miraculously avoided most major organs.

Ollie Blunt, having been cleared by all the witnesses, had been released without spending even one night in the cells. He used up his days looking for pigeons, getting in the way of farm labourers, or snoozing in front of the kitchen fire in Rose Cottage.

Ivy's main worry was Sally. Each time the subject of parents was raised, the child flew either into a temper or out of the house. There was no reasoning with her. 'There's no talking to her,' said Ivy to Rosie Blunt.

Rosie raised her eyebrows. 'What are you expecting? A bloody encore like what they have at the Grand after a good turn? There's no good turn been done for that lass, I can tell you. Her's disturbed, Ivy. Her's had the breath knocked out of her body and her little world turned upside down.'

Ivy flopped into a chair and pushed a string of hair away from her eyes. 'How can I explain summat as a child can't understand in the first place? Where do I find an answer when she's not even old enough for the flipping question?'

Rosie dropped the sock she had been darning and stared hard at her best friend. In spite of all the worries, Ivy still looked well. In fact, she seemed to have started counting her years backwards. 'I'd not rate you as seventy-seven, Ivy. But even if you do look younger than your age, stop taking too much on yourself. Let me do it.'

'Eh?' Ivy sat bolt upright. 'You? How would you go about fettling for a young kiddy?'

'Same as I do for Ollie. With short words, a hug and a smile.'

'Get away. There's more than that to be done here. I mean, she doesn't even know where babies come from, does she? As far as our Sal knows, they could be left on your step with the milk jug or fetched in with the coal. So how do I tell her about her mother messing about in Paradise Mill with a bloke who weren't fit to wipe the muck off our Derek's clogs?'

'You don't need to say none of that, Ivy.'

Ivy blew another strand of hair from her face. 'It's been all over the papers, too. There'll be trouble when she gets back to Craddock Street School, everybody pointing at her and saying she's one of Worthington's accidents.'

Rosie cast a glance in the direction of the 'criminal' who was snoring peacefully with his slippered feet propped on a stool. 'He very near killed him, Ivy. My poor old feller were trying to do the world a favour, and he doesn't even understand that. He's got no memory of that day, or of the day in court. Even when he spoke to them doctors, he talked about pigeons and green spuds. I gave him the *Daily Herald* so he could read about the scandal, and he never even looked at it.'

Ivy nodded sagely. 'Bloody hornets' nest we stirred up there, Rosie. They all got listed – Rita Eckersley, Mary Shaw, Tilly Saxton, Phyllis Caldwell. Every last one of them spoke to the papers about Worthington's carryings-on. Their kids'll be branded and all. But we had to tell the truth, didn't we? Worthington had that letter from Lottie in his pocket. He thought he were dying, so he made sure the letter got to the *Daily Herald*. There were nowt else for it, so we had to fight back and damn a sick man.' Ivy forgave herself for wishing he had died. Had Worthington not survived, many of her troubles would have been six feet under. 'Mind, damage were already done to our Sal,' she said quietly.

'Aye.' Rosie stood up and looked through the window. 'I think I'll go and look for Sally and Red. Keep an eye on yon hero, will you? Don't let him start wandering off. Remember – we must make sure he doesn't go messing about with pitchforks and suchlike. An accident's all right, but he'd better not make a habit of it. Any road, I'll try and have a word with Sally, see what I can do.'

'All right. But don't go upsetting her. I don't want no more of her tantrums.'

Rosie, who understood perfectly why a hitherto 'good' child was suddenly difficult, stepped outside and enjoyed a few moments of solitude. It was a bonny place, she thought. Rose Cottage was about halfway between

Oakmead and the Hall. It was a story-book house, painted white and with a thatched roof that hung over the upper windows.

She walked along the lane, nodded at a couple of drovers. The folk round these parts were friendly and hard-working, only too pleased to lend a hand to four strange migrants from the north. They had pleaded for Ollie, had worn best suits and shiny boots to give evidence on his behalf. Ollie would never hurt a fly, not deliberately, the Hampshire farm-hands had insisted. As mild as a lamb and as biddable as any sheepdog, they had told the court. In their opinion, the incident had been an unfortunate mishap rather than an act of aggression on Ollie's part. Worthington had slipped and Ollie had not moved away quickly enough.

Rosie peered through a hedge, watched the cows walking homeward. Red and Sally could be near the herd, she thought, because both had a fondness for animals. Then Red hove into view, his hair on end above a pink and sweaty face. 'She ran off, Mrs Blunt.'

Rosie placed her hands on Red's shoulders, waited until his breathing eased. 'You shouldn't go dashing about, not with your colouring. You look like a beetroot.'

'She's come over hot and all, went a right funny colour, she did. And she started talking daft. I were trying to catch her.'

'I know, but don't be getting overheated.'

Red turned this way and that, his eyes scanning fields and hedgerows as they searched for his adopted sister. 'She asked me. So I told her.'

'Ah.' Rosie sat on a milestone and waited for him to continue.

'Well, we saw this bull and this cow, see. And I told her what they were doing. "They're practising for making next year's calves," I said to her. Then she asked me if her mam had been practising with Mr Worthington, so I said I wouldn't believe anything Worthington told me. But her eyes went funny and she ran off. She can get through some small gaps, can Sally. So I lost her.'

'Oh, heck.'

Red sat on the ground near Rosie's feet. 'It wouldn't make no difference if it were me this had happened to, 'cos me dad's nowt to be proud of. But Sally loved her dad, Mrs Blunt. And now, she thinks this other dad of hers is a bad 'un.'

'He is and all.'

'Aye, I know.'

He sounded like an old man, mused Rosie. 'Come on, son.' She got up, smoothed her skirt, took his hand. 'We've got to show her that we love her, Red. See, she doesn't know who she is no more. A couple of weeks back, she were Derek's lass. She's still Derek's. But she'll not take that in till we make her know we love her.'

'I love her.' He gripped the old lady's hand tightly and stared at his feet, his face brightened even further by embarrassment. 'I want to look after Sally. For always.'

'You will, lad. When we can blinking well find her.'

The sun had begun its descent by the time they found Sally. At first, the child seemed to be sleeping, her legs drawn up to her chest, a hand embracing the dry bole of a felled tree. But when Red walked round the stump and saw Sally's face, he could not keep the panic from his tone. 'Like Alice,' he gasped. 'All white round the edges and pink in the middle.'

Rosie leaned against a sycamore whose leaves were beginning to curl towards autumn. 'What?' She was tired, thirsty and seventy-five years old. It was as if she had walked for a whole day, because every bone in her body was screaming for mercy.

'Fever,' cried Red. 'You stop here. I'll go to the Hall and get somebody.'

'Eh?' The old woman watched while her companion ran away, then summoned her will to step in where energy had failed. The boy was right. Sally's breathing was shallow and fast, and the little white cheeks glowed along their fine bones. She was not asleep, but ill, very ill. Rosie tore off her shawl and wrapped it round the child. 'Sweet Jesus, have mercy,' prayed the old woman.

Sally moved, opened her eyes. 'Go away,' she croaked. 'You're just a nasty man. My dad were good.'

'That's right, love,' whispered Rosie.

'You can't be my dad. You're really ugly and me gran says you're a nasty bugger.'

Rosie sucked in her lower lip, ordered the tears to stay off her face and out of her words. 'Derek Crumpsall were your father, pet. It takes more nor a bull and a cow to make a calf, Sal. God's in it and all, you know. God makes life. He's the one what breathes it into everything. Sometimes, He creates a special soul, summat as needs a bit of looking after. God looked at you and decided to give you to Derek. Derek didn't live long, and he were at the war for most of your little life, but Derek made you into a good girl. Him and your Granny Ivy between them were your mam and dad, lass.'

Sally stared right through her companion. A beautiful smile appeared on the child's face as she gazed past the haze of fever and into a face she had known and loved. 'Dad,' she said before entering a deep sleep.

Rosie shivered, told herself firmly that she was missing her shawl. Yet deep inside herself, Rosie Blunt knew that the child had been looking in to another dimension, another place. And Sally Crumpsall should not be ready to step forth into the next life. 'Hurry up, Red,' breathed the old woman. 'Get a move on while there's still signs of life.'

Help came eventually. Ivy bustled along through the bushes, dragged two labourers to Sally's side. They lifted her gently, avoided the flailing arms of Arthur 'Red' Trubshaw. 'Don't hurt her,' screamed the agitated boy. 'Watch her head . . . hold her legs . . . keep that shawl on her.'

'Come on,' urged Rosie. 'There's nowt'll come of you fretting, lad.'

But the boy was beyond reason. He climbed into the cart with Ivy and Rosie, kept his eyes fixed on Sally's face. From now on, he would be good. He would be obedient and willing, would get washed twice a day . . . Well, if she lived, that was. 'She'll not die, will she?' he asked Ivy.

'No,' replied Ivy. Sal mustn't die. Sal was one of the few worthwhile creatures on the earth. 'Our Sal's going to come through with flying colours,' she told the troubled lad. 'She's got more than enough to live for.'

THIRTEEN

'Will you please stop making such a nuisance of yourself, boy?' The woman's quiet tone belied the harshness of her words. She bent and pretended to tug Red's earlobe. 'Out,' she whispered. 'Go and play in the garden. Sally's going to be fine, I assure you.'

Red stuck out his chest, pushed his shoulders back. What were these folk doing here, anyway? It was none of their business. But, following the furore about the terrible accident, some newspapers, after investigating fully the history of the injured man, had turned Sally's illness into everyone's concern. And Prudence Worthington was here with somebody called Mrs Miles from Bolton. Red's eyebrows knitted themselves into a long, auburn frown. 'Are you going to visit Mr Worthington in hospital?'

Prudence awarded the boy a tight smile. 'No.' Oh, she might well go, but not yet, not for a while. That all depended on the man's level of recovery . . .

'Why?' He leaned against the window sill. 'He's your husband, isn't he?'

'Yes.'

'And he's been hurt and he's got a bad heart.' As ever, Red felt not the slightest twinge of conscience. In fact, the kick he had delivered to Worthington's groin had been deliberately wiped from his thoughts. Of course, should the memory ever become useful, then details of that fateful day would rekindle themselves in glowing colour.

'That is correct. Now, will you go outside while I make Sally comfortable? Or must I get Mrs Crumpsall to deal with you? That poor lady needs a rest.'

Arthur 'Red' Trubshaw, for all his tenacity, was not in the market for another load of earache from Sally's gran. Mrs Worthington seemed to know what she was doing, he thought grudgingly. Sally had been too ill to be taken to the hospital, had deteriorated considerably while being carried from the woods and into Rose Cottage. So Red, Ivy and Rosie had watched over the child during something called a crisis. And now, this important woman had turned up to tell everybody what to do. Still, she and Mrs Miles would return to their hotel soon. 'What's a crisis?' Red asked Andrew Worthington's wife.

She wiped Sally's face with a flannel. 'In pneumonia, it's the height of fever. Sometimes, people die during a crisis. But Sally's fever broke and she's still with us.'

'So are you,' the boy muttered softly. 'Why did you come?'

The woman shrugged. 'Because I was needed.'

'What about Mr Worthington?'

Prudence shook a finger at this frightful but lovable boy. 'It's all far too complicated for a child of your tender years.'

Nothing was too complicated for Red. He seemed to have been born old and knowing, had been dragged up in a crowded household where feelings ran amok, where the behaviour patterns of maladjusted adults were on display for all to see. Still, at least Mr and Mrs Trubshaw still communicated, even if half of their conversations were accompanied by flying fists, plates and swearwords. 'Stopped talking to him, haven't you?' he asked, wisdom etched prematurely into every plane of his homely face. 'You don't care about him no more.' He sniffed. 'Me mam says he's horrible, and Sally's nan calls him a monster.'

Prudence studied this dreadful creature. The grey socks had slid into wrinkles above battered clogs, his hair stood on end like a forest of flame, while all points in between were untidy, as if he had thrown himself into the clothing from a great distance or while blindfolded. 'You need to tidy yourself,' she said.

Red glanced at Sally. 'I will when she wakes up.'

'She may not wake until tomorrow.'

He shrugged. 'Right, I'll get meself straight tomorrow, then.' Red was no coward. He was cock of the school, had survived Basher Bates's cane, Ivy Crumpsall's earachings, his dad's iron-bottomed clogs. But something in this woman's face suddenly made him squirm. She was quiet, but very, very strong – as if she had lived through much worse things than the business ends of Basher's cane and Mrs Blunt's posser. Almost unawares, he tucked the shirt-tail into his trousers, rubbed the toe of a clog against a rolled-down sock.

Prudence found herself grinning. The lad had spirit enough for two men with plenty to spare, she thought. 'Arthur, she is—'

'Red,' he told her as firmly as possible. It was difficult to be firm with someone so . . . so nice, so reasonable.

'Red, then. Sally is in a very deep sleep. Sleep is the cure now. Please go outside quietly. Mrs Crumpsall and Mrs Blunt are exhausted. You might, perhaps, take charge of Mr Blunt for a while, take him for a walk or—'

'He's nobbut tenpence in the bob. What if he starts looking for pigeons again? Or pitchforks?'

'Take him out, Red.'

He smiled. 'If he had a collar and lead, I might.'

'Red!'

'I'm going, I'm going,' he cried.

'Don't go,' said a tiny voice.

Woman and boy turned in perfect harmony, strode to the bed. 'You're awake,' pronounced Red.

'Yes.' She was so, so tired. She wanted to look at the lady and at Red, but her eyelids wouldn't stay up, not without props. 'I've seen me dad,' she said softly.

'He weren't your dad,' advised the boy. 'He were just a troublemaker – this here woman's his wife – and I reckon he's had no visitors at the hospital. Even Mrs Worthington can't be bothered going to see him. He's nobody's dad, Sal.'

With a great effort of will, Sally forced her laden eyelids to raise themselves. 'Not him,' she whispered. 'Me dad. He spoke to me. Told me to come back to Granny Ivy.'

Prudence Worthington felt the girl's forehead, found it to be cool. 'You saw Mr Crumpsall?' she asked, her tone normal, as if she were asking the time of the next tram.

Red thought all this was bloody daft, though he kept the sentiment and expletive away from his tongue.

'He were covered in coal dust,' Sally said quietly. 'He's got a new job.'

'Really?' Prudence patted the sick child's hand. 'What does he do, Sally?'

'Fetches the miners up. After explosions and collapses. Fetches them up to heaven. Says he doesn't mind, like.' Sally yawned. 'Says he's me proper dad no matter what. Says Mr Worthington's nowt a pound. He's not ready to die yet, Mr Worthington. Years, he's got. Years and years. Dad told me to watch out . . . Not frightened no more. Not frightened . . .' She closed her eyes and slept.

Prudence shuddered. It was all nonsense, of course. The child was ill, had suffered appallingly high temperatures, had fought for every breath. Sick people were prone to fancies, she told herself firmly. Mother had 'spoken' to Father many times before going off to join him. For a split second, Prudence was standing at her own mother's bedside, was listening while her female parent went into details about the hereafter. 'Your father is not singing,' Mrs Spencer had said. 'God is good, but even He could not tolerate George's total tone-deafness.' In a perfect heaven, would not Father's voice have been mended? And in a perfect world, would not Andrew Worthington perish before he got the opportunity to inflict more damage on innocents?

Red thought it was time to speak up. 'Mrs Worthington, I—'

'Spencer,' she said automatically. She dragged herself back to the here and now. 'Go and tell Ivy that her granddaughter is improving. Then take Mr Blunt for a walk.'

'Aye aye, sir. I mean madam.'

Prudence fixed the wayward lad with a glare that was not quite severe. 'How do your parents cope?' she asked.

'They don't,' he replied in a low voice. 'They just ignore us.' He left the room and went in search of Ollie.

Prudence Spencer, recently Spencer-Worthington, patted her hair absently. 'I shall take that boy in hand,' she murmured before tending her patient. 'It's time somebody did.'

Everything was pale green or white. At first, he hadn't noticed much, but the place was beginning to get on his nerves. Hospitals. He'd never liked them much, hadn't enjoyed calling in on the sick. Not that he'd been a regular visitor . . . He remembered the last time he had entered a torture chamber – Bert Simpson had been in one of these high and far from comfortable beds. A stomach job, that had been. How had Simpson fared? Worthington wondered idly. Had it hurt like this? Had it hurt like hell?

'Time for your medicine, Mr Worthington.'

He rolled his eyes, allowed them to rest on the uncomely creature that stood by his bed. 'Bugger off,' he mumbled.

'I see. We're naughty today, are we?'

The ugly bitch always spoke in the plural, as if attempting to copy the late and great Victoria, that one and only woman who had been as good as any man. 'I'll not take it.'

The sister's apron crackled with starch as she lowered her bulk into the bedside chair. 'Then what colour shall we use to line our coffin?' she asked.

'You can please your bloody self about that,' he replied. Still tired, he had not the energy to remind her that she would not find a place on any man's list of chosen bedfellows – even in death.

'You're a lucky person,' she reminded him for the umpteenth time.

Lucky? Of course he was lucky. After all, few people of his acquaintance had suffered heart disease and both prongs of a pitchfork thrust between their ribs. He bared his teeth at her, made sure that she would not interpret this gesture as a smile.

'No need for faces,' she went on, her voice monotonous. 'We are extremely fortunate, believe me. That poor man who accidentally stabbed you did a great service, Mr Worthington. So now, we must take our medicine like—'

'A service?' he managed.

She nodded vigorously, though not one carefully ironed hair changed position, and the rigid cap remained in situ on top of the grey coiffure. 'It gave our surgeon the opportunity to do some minor repairs. Had you not required an operation to clean the stab wounds, your life might have been very short. As things are, your mended heart will carry on beating for some years. With the medicine, of course. If we do not take the medicine, then we are ruining the work of our wonderful surgeon.'

Surgeon should have a capital S, decided the man in the bed. When she spoke of the mechanic whose tools were used on humanity, she bowed her head as if she were in church. He opened his mouth, accepted the spoonful of vile liquid.

'We'll get used to it,' she said.

'You might,' he grumbled. 'It tastes like cat doings.'

She patted his hand. 'Now, how can we be sure of that?'

Worthington fixed his eyes on her. 'We can be sure because four fifths of taste is really smell. Did we not learn that in order to become a nurse?'

The sister removed her hand, placed the spoon on a locker, closed the bottle. 'This afternoon, you will sit in a chair. It is time for you to begin healing, Mr Worthington.

After all, we shall want to return to our families.' There was a barbed edge to the words, as she, like everyone else with functioning eyes, had read about Worthington's many misdeeds. 'And to our businesses,' she added belatedly.

She knew. In that moment, Worthington realized that the whole affair had gone public. 'Newspapers?' he asked. 'Has there been any . . . publicity?' He should never have handed over that bloody document! And whoever had taken it should have waited before sending it on to some flaming newspaper. 'I wasn't in my right mind when I gave the letter to somebody's visitor.' He had expected death, not recovery. And before death, he had made sure that the whole country would know about Sally Crumpsall's real father. Now, he had to live with all that.

The nurse jerked her head just once. 'Well, your letter started the publicity. Without that, you would have been just another statistic. People who work the land are killed and maimed in accidents every day.' She sniffed. 'It's been on the wireless, too, I believe. Home Service.'

It would hardly have provided material for the Light Programme, he thought. So. It was out in the open now. Would the authorities search him out; would they try to enforce the agreement he had signed at what amounted to knife-point? Would they lay a dozen or more paternity orders at his feet? He had some money, enough to provide for himself. How on earth could he be expected to maintain all his so-called offspring?

She read his mind. 'They'll not bother you while you're in here. But afterwards . . .' She raised both shoulders.

Afterwards, he would make himself scarce. 'Thank you,' he snapped.

'You're welcome.' The large woman rose and walked into her office. After a pause of about ten seconds, she lifted the telephone receiver and asked for a number. 'Mrs Spencer-Worthington?'

'Yes,' replied the distant voice.

'You asked me to keep you informed of your . . . of Mr Worthington's progress. He will live. In fact, he is probably in better health than he was before the accident. I think he'll be out of hospital in about three weeks.'

'Oh. Thank you so much for keeping me informed.'

'Hello? Are you still there, Mrs Spencer-Worthington? Hello?' Sister Gladys Merton rattled the telephone, realized eventually that Worthington's wife had cut herself off. And for that, decided the nurse, the woman could not be blamed.

'Joseph, you are like a man on fire. Sit, or shall I bring a bucket of water to put out the flames?' Ruth forced her husband into a chair, kept her hands on his shoulders, tutted quietly. 'You will be ill. There is no man on earth who can be here and there at the same time. You are dealing with this, that, these and those all at once. Soon, you will meet your own shadow as you walk up and down Paradise.'

'I hope my shadow has a good brain,' replied Joseph. 'He can help me to study these plans.' He gestured towards the table where blueprints lay in place of a cloth. 'While I sit here doing nothing, the architect is trying to squeeze a quart into a pint pot. Should we have four baths or six? Will the medical room be on the ground floor, what size must the apprentices' classroom be, when will Tom come home?'

'This is too much for you,' sighed Ruth.

Joseph shook his head, wagged a finger under his wife's nose. 'No, I am truly alive. This project is awesome and brilliant. I do not understand why no-one thought of it before. So simple, it is.'

Ruth walked to the other side of the table, poured tea into cups on the trolley. 'Soon, I shall get my table back,' she pretended to grumble. Joseph was carrying so much responsiblity. Tom and Maureen were away, as were Ivy, Sally and the Blunts. Fotheringay had flitted up and down

313

the country a few times, had brought people from London stores and factories. Simple? Here they sat, two displaced Austrian Jews who used to deal in antiquities, and they were situated at the helm of a ship that intended to dock across the road from Harrods. She swallowed a sip of tea, toyed with a small piece of strudel. 'Harrods,' she whispered reverently. 'So near to Harrods.' It was a daunting prospect. The new company intended to treat and spin cotton, to weave it, send some for dyeing, then turn it into finished products intended for sale in many major cities, including London.

Joseph laughed. 'This is a free country, Ruth. If a man can pay his way, he can set up shop where he will. Tom has vision. This enterprise reeks already of success. We buy the raw and sell the completely finished. Except for dyeing, we keep the business in the family from start to retail. Many middle men will be cut out, so our prices will be low.'

'Eat,' she commanded. 'Or you will become a pale shadow.' Tom had made it sound so easy. Labour in the north was cheap, purses in the south were fatter. But even the rich had been rendered careful by the war, so products should be tailored to fit the average expendable income. There were charts in a drawer somewhere, figures that meant little to Ruth. Accountants and bankers had worked out interest rates, projected capital expenditure, percentages, expected inflation levels. The result was that Joseph Heilberg was toiling eighteen hours a day and his wife was worried.

He read her mind. 'It will work.'

Ruth shrugged, pushed away the plate. 'The people of Paradise have never made such things. How do we know how to—?'

'A weaver is a weaver. He follows a pattern, my dear. Did you look at the Lancashire quilts? For those, the cotton was dyed then woven into beautiful designs. So what is different now? The fact that some of our plain

314

cotton will go away to have a pattern stamped onto it? The fact that we will manufacture the end products? There is nothing terrifying about furniture and household linens. Our materials will be the best, as will the workforce. In ten years, you will laugh at your fear. Also, we have good carpenters and other craftsmen here in Bolton. All they need is a chance, Ruth. Just as we needed a chance twelve years ago.'

Ruth washed the dishes, wondered when she would laugh again. The streets had buzzed with the news of Worthington's misfortune, had hummed with gossip when the names of all those sad women had appeared in the press. Sally. Poor little Sally was just another product of that vile man and Lottie Crumpsall. The world was such an uncertain place. Worthington's children were known now, and they could easily become targets for people with small minds. 'She should not come back to Paradise,' Ruth said aloud.

Joseph stood in the kitchen doorway. 'Ivy and Sally must not be forced from their proper home,' he said softly.

Ruth turned, looked at him, remembered a young man who had travelled from Vienna to meet her. 'Do you have regrets, Joseph?' she asked.

'No.'

'We lost our country. We lost so much, so many loved ones,' she murmured.

Joseph kept his regrets where they belonged. If others had listened, if they had heeded him and come to England or America, they would have remained untouched by the devil's servants. If, if. How many times could a man say and think that tiny word . . . ? 'I am glad I came to your father's farm, Ruth. For myself, I am happy.' He looked back through the years, saw the crystal-cut facets of the Alps, heard cows lowing as they made their way home. The matchmaker had been right in this case, because he and Ruth were still suited.

'I, too, am glad,' she told him.

Clouds that had touched the ice-capped peaks had been white, like small bundles of cotton set haphazardly against an azure backcloth. There had been no warning of the storm to come, not in those early days. But in Vienna, the whispers had begun. And Joseph had listened. 'We slid down on our toboggan and this is where we landed,' he said.

'You steered me away from danger, Joseph.'

He laughed, recalled the mess he had made of his first ride on that home-made sleigh. 'So wet, we were.' The snowdrift had been cold enough to burn his fingers. Ruth's dark hair had looked so pretty against the whiteness. 'Now, we are safe. And we must make others safe, too. This is the right way.'

While Ruth performed kitchen tasks, Joseph Heilberg looked again at the paper dream. The middle classes were about to establish themselves, Tom had said. The middle classes wanted furnishings that would be better than Utility, cheaper by far than Chippendale. In a place called Paradise, several hundred people were about to embark on a scheme to provide complete suites of furniture, bales of fabric, plans for whole rooms, whole houses. The Paradise Look would swamp the country within twelve months. Advertising costs were going to be astronomical, as was the rent in the centre of London. London mattered, Tom had said. Although most cities should be targeted, the capital must provide the hub of the web.

'Joseph?'

He swung round, looked at her. She was older, rounder than the child he had chased through crisp, green fields. Beneath her eyes, slight shadows reminded him of soft bruising on the down of a peach. Together, he and Ruth had brought home the cattle, had milked and churned, had sung with her family in a firelit kitchen. Together, they had abandoned their families, had escaped to England. 'Yes?' he asked, noting the sparkle in her eyes.

'How shall I address you when you take the throne?'

316

He tapped his brow, pretended to think. 'Sir should do,' he replied finally. 'Yes, as Managing Director, I shall be a sir.'

Prudence Spencer's steps did not falter as she made her way through a maze of corridors. Cora Miles followed her mistress and new-found friend, hoped that Prudence's nerves would not let her down. After all, this good woman had come a long distance in more ways than one. Within a matter of weeks, the recluse had taken on a divorce lawyer, a house move and the journey from Lancashire to Hampshire. Not to mention a proposed active part in the running of Paradise. Cora crossed her fingers.

'I shall be perfectly all right,' announced Prudence in a voice loud enough to bounce itself off walls and along careworn brown lino. 'Stop worrying, Cora.'

The housekeeper's mouth twitched, though she could find little to smile about. Prudence was a new woman. She had lost weight, thereby allowing near-perfect bone structure to enhance a face that had always been comely. Her body, too, had fined down, was almost elegant in the dove-grey costume. A stiff frill of cream lace hid a slight crêping at the throat, while a cameo brooch in Wedgwood blue echoed the misleading gentleness of those soft eyes. 'Where shall I wait?' asked Cora.

Prudence glanced at a gold wrist-watch. 'Outside the ward, I suppose. Ten minutes should suffice here. The shops will still be open. We must get games and books for Sally, some small toys to occupy her time. The period of recovery is always difficult for an energetic child.'

Mrs Worthington, now Spencer, was treating this expedition as just another errand. Cora Miles, who had been wondering for some time about the strange rebirth of her mistress, was nearing the conclusion that oppressed folk must develop a core of inner strength, a power created by deep anger. 'If you want me, just come and—'

'I shan't need you,' interrupted Prudence. 'This is

something I must face alone.' She left Cora at the door, marched into the ward. Several visitors had already arrived, were placing gifts of fruit and flowers on lockers. Empty handed, Prudence walked steadily towards a man who might have looked thoroughly familiar had he not shrunk.

'Prudence,' he mumbled, his features stiffening with shock. Bloodshot eyes glowed like pools of hot steel in twin crucibles of dark stone. 'How nice of you to take the trouble,' he said, the voice more certain.

She turned from the bed, found a wooden chair, sat in it and stared at the creature on the pillows. He had aged. Fat had melted from his face, leaving the jowls hanging vacantly above striped winceyette. 'You are smaller,' she remarked, her tone light.

'So are you.'

'Ah.' She removed the grey gloves, folded ring-free hands in her lap. 'Business will suit me, I think.'

'What?'

She awarded him a tight smile. 'The Paradise Look.'

Andrew Worthington hung on to his temper by swallowing words he dared not say. This person wasn't just different, wasn't just slim and elegant. No, she was . . . she was . . .

'The mill,' she advised him. 'We are going to make furniture, curtains, bed linens, cushions – even wardrobes and so on. Diversification will be necessary if the cotton industry is to survive. I shall work as a buyer of yarns. After all, I've learned over the years what to look for in the purchasing of cotton. Goodness only knows how you rambled on about the batches. It used to bore me so, but I am finding your teachings useful at last. Of course, there'll be linen, then mixtures, perhaps a bit of wool in time. I go to Yorkshire next month to negotiate with a wool merchant. The help and advice of the wool factors will be invaluable.' She drew breath, hoped that the soliloquy had been born of self-confidence rather than nervousness.

'Whatever, the venture will be brave and exciting.'

She was jumping all over him. It felt as if she had picked up the pitchfork, driven it home, twisted it in a wound that was already raw. 'You are enjoying this, aren't you?'

Prudence arched her brows. 'Not really. I abhor violence and hate to see its victims. I trust that your injuries are healing.'

'I'll sue that Blunt fellow,' he spat.

'Waste of time, Andrew.' She smoothed the grey gloves, folded them, placed them in her bag. 'He has the mental age of a two-year-old and very little money. Also, it was decided that the accident was your fault.' She sighed. 'Of course, you may yet be charged with attempted kidnap—'

'Nonsense,' he spat. The Crumpsall woman would not put her so-called granddaughter through such an ordeal. 'You've thought of everything, haven't you?'

The eyes still protruded slightly, she thought as she prepared an answer. But the sockets that contained them had darkened considerably. 'I have had years of thinking time, Andrew. And I am not alone in this new venture.'

'Heilberg?' The two syllables were forced between clenched incisors.

'Managing Director.'

'That Jew?'

She inclined her head. 'That businessman, yes. Tom and Maureen Marchant will be on the board, as will Ivy Crumpsall and I. Ivy is ageing, but her wisdom is valuable.'

His lip curled. 'I'm sure.'

Prudence allowed her gaze to travel round the cheerless room. Even the splashes of colour provided by flowers failed to hide the inherent misery. ' A coat of paint would not go amiss,' she ventured. 'And a few quilts in pastels.' She looked directly into his eyes. 'You will not return to Bolton, I suppose?'

'Why should I?'

'I can think of several reasons why you should not. After

all, many of those reasons would be seeking paternity payments.'

'Most of the so-called children are grown up,' he snarled.

She smiled grimly. 'At least you are admitting to their existence. However, I should perhaps make my intentions plain, Andrew. This is not a social call.'

Andrew Worthington swallowed, realized that his throat was abnormally dry. She made him uneasy, unsure. For years, he had lived with Prudence Spencer, had kept her in her place. But now, she was the strong one. Oh yes, she was the one with a full pack of cards. 'I did not think you had visited me out of kindness. Duty, perhaps, but—'

'I have no sense of duty towards you.' There was little malice in the words. Actually, the more she looked at him, the more she saw him for what he really was – a coward and a bully. She no longer hated him. Had she ever really hated this man? 'In fact, I am prepared to honour on your behalf the agreement you made with certain women in Bolton. I shall pay your price, Andrew.'

He raised his head, studied the ceiling, saw several patches where various fluids had seeped through from the ward above. 'Why?' he asked at last.

'To keep you away from the town, of course. If I ever see you again, the payments will stop and your many offspring will sue you. Of course, I shall gladly meet the cost of any action they might be forced to bring against you.'

He smiled, lowered his head. 'Thought it all through, haven't you?'

Prudence did not flinch as she looked into his mad eyes. 'Parts of Hampshire, too, will be out of bounds, I'm afraid. Sally and Ivy Crumpsall have property here, so you must keep your distance.'

He nodded just once, raked his eyes over her face.

'You will have little money,' she said. 'However, when you sell the house on Wigan Road, you should have enough to buy a small place somewhere—'

'But not in Bolton.'

'No.'

'And not in Hampshire.'

'Exactly.'

He pushed his hands against the mattress, urged his body to sit straighter in the bed. Pain from the pitchfork wounds had eased greatly, though he still felt some discomfort from the surgeon's probings inside his chest.

'Your heart condition is improved, then?' asked the visitor.

He shrugged. 'The chap mended a puncture, I think. It seems I might live for years.' The last word was drawn out and allowed to linger in a sneer.

Prudence shuddered, hoped that her sudden disquiet did not show. Sally had 'seen' Derek Crumpsall, had foretold that the man in this hospital bed would live for a long time yet. 'You must stay away from that child.'

He sat perfectly still, kept his eyes on her, said nothing.

'I will protect them all, Andrew. No-one in Paradise would be pleased to see you again. The workers will soon have representation at board level, shares in their own company, a reason to labour and make the firm a success. They will also be encouraged to unionize.'

'Balderdash,' he spat.

Suddenly and for no clear reason, she needed to question him. 'Why have you always been so . . . so horrible?'

Twin dark eyebrows journeyed quickly up the high forehead. 'Marriage to you hasn't been easy,' he replied eventually. 'You're a cold fish.'

'Really?' She said no more, simply sat with her hands folded in her lap. She would not twitch, would not avoid his eyes.

'Of course you are. It was like sleeping with a piece of frozen cod.'

'Oh. Do go on, Andrew. Your philosophy is so interesting. Leaving me aside, do you hate all Jews, or is

321

your malice reserved just for Joseph Heilberg? Have you a habit of setting fire to people's properties? Are all women natural victims? Did you never stop to wonder about the pain of those you attacked? Is the world here so that you might use it as you will?' Even as she spoke, she knew that there would be no answers.

His jaw dropped. 'Get out,' he finally managed.

Prudence shook her head softly. 'I believe, Andrew, that you are incapable of putting yourself in another person's shoes. You are the only one who suffers pain, the only one who deserves protection. A man who cannot sympathize or hypothesize is a cripple. You are unable to mourn for another's loss. You cannot share grief, joy, excitement.' She paused, allowed her gaze to search his face. 'It is such a shame that you bear no mark. Some poor soul with an injured spine sits in a chair, is wheeled about with his disability on show. Unfortunately, there is no sling for a damaged mind, no outward mark from which the rest of us might take warning.'

'Go,' he whispered harshly.

Prudence showed no sign of preparing to leave. 'You know, I think I have finally become an adult,' she told him. 'For too long, I was a bewildered child, afraid of my own shadow. That must have made your life of debauchery so much easier.' She dropped her head for a second, stared vacantly at the floor. 'I suppose some of it was my fault, then, so it is right that I should pay your debts.'

'I am telling you now, if you don't get out of here—'

'What?' Her chin raised itself. 'You'll what? Hit me, burn down my shop, take away my dignity? There is nothing you can do to me, Andrew Worthington. As I have already been in close contact with your disease, my system has raised an army of immunity against you.' She thought for a moment, put her head on one side. 'Disease,' she repeated slowly. 'Like the lepers in the Bible, you should carry a bell to warn others of your progress towards them.'

In thirty-odd years of marriage, he had never known her to make a speech. In thirty-odd years of marriage, she had never defied him. In fact he could not remember when she had last expressed an opinion. 'It won't succeed,' he said quietly.

'I beg your pardon?'

'This workers' co-operative, this furniture game. I shall await developments.'

She pursed her lips for a moment. 'Yes, I suppose we might allow you to do that. As long as you await developments from a safe distance, that is.'

He looked hard at her face, found that her eyes were cold, that the jaw had set itself. 'Clever all of a sudden, aren't you?'

Prudence rose from the chair, removed the gloves from her handbag. 'No single man can win against the masses,' she informed him, the tone matter-of-fact. 'We are simply too many and too much for you, Andrew. Goodbye.'

His heart pounded loudly as he followed her progress through the ward. Through narrowed eyes, he saw the woman who had been his wife going through the double doors without a single backward glance. Another face appeared briefly, its homely contours framed in an upper panel of glass. Mrs Miles. They were all in it together, then.

Women. Andrew Worthington picked at the fringe of a bottle-green bed cover, hoped that his heart would calm down before bursting all the surgeon's needlework. Ivy Crumpsall, Prudence Spencer, Rosie Blunt, the Miles woman – they were all joined in the plot to destroy him, had even made allies of the loose females who had given themselves to him over the years.

Sister arrived at the bedside. 'A visitor, then?'

He glared at the nurse, was convinced that she, too, was a part of the plot. 'Go to hell,' he spat.

The craggy features smiled down upon him. 'We are out of sorts today, aren't we?'

Andrew Worthington mustered his resources. 'Speak for yourself. But with a face like yours, I'm not surprised if you feel a bit depressed.' He closed his eyes, willed her to go away.

Sister Gladys Merton bit back the reply, told herself that it would be unprofessional behaviour if she were to tell him how ugly he was.

He lay as still as stone, listened to her heavy footfalls as she walked into her office. Women. He would need to stay out of the picture for a few years, would need to regain his strength.

But he wasn't finished. Oh no, he wasn't going to take this lying down. In time, he told himself. In time . . .

'So that's where we're going to live.' Ivy plonked the snapshot on the table right in front of Sally. 'Next door to Mrs Worthington and Mrs Miles. We'll pay rent to Mrs Worthington, 'cos she owns the house.'

'She doesn't,' replied Sally, an impish smile decorating her face. 'Mrs Spencer owns it.'

'Less of your cheek, Clever Clogs.' Ivy transferred her attention to Arthur 'Red' Trubshaw. Red, whose appetites for life and for food were becoming legendary in Hampshire, was pushing porridge round his bowl. 'What's up with you? That porridge'll curdle if you don't straighten your mush.'

Red shrugged. He didn't want to go home, didn't want to end up in a bed containing eight or ten limbs and at least two adenoidal snorers. 'I'm all right,' he answered quietly.

'All right? You look like a week of wet Mondays,' pronounced the matriarch. 'I think I'd better give you some working medicine.'

The threat of working medicine was something that hung like a black cloud over any day when one of Ivy's charges felt unwell. Liquid laxative was prescribed by the good woman for any ailment from headaches to sore feet, and the children usually enjoyed a total and apparently miraculous recovery when offered a spoonful of California Syrup of Figs. But Red shrugged, made no move towards escape.

'What's up with you?' asked Ivy. 'Have I to get that bottle out and dose you up?'

'I'm not bothered.'

Sally studied her stalwart friend with interest. Normally, he would have been halfway to Oakmead or Goodfellow Hall when threatened with an inner cleansing. 'Are you poorly?' she asked him.

He raised a shoulder. 'No.'

'Are you fed up?'

He fixed his gaze on Sally. 'Course I'm fed up. I'll be back to our house and Basher Bates inside a week. You're having a new house and a new school.' He did not resent Sally's good fortune, he told himself inwardly. It was just that Hampshire had been so nice, no bugs in the bedroom walls, no cockroaches, no brothers pinching his catapults and glass marbles. The conker season would start soon, too. A lad living round here could be a millionaire when it came to conkers.

Ivy winked at Sally. 'Shall I tell him?'

'If you want.'

'Tell me what?' He looked at their smiling faces, knew that they had a secret. 'Go on, then,' he shouted.

Rosie peered in from the kitchen. 'Shut up, Red,' she advised him. 'Else I'll come out there and give you a clout. Yon husband of mine's just spilled his tea when you yelled out.'

'Sorry.' He was sorry, too, very sorry for poor Mr Blunt whose mind was wandering, very sorry for Mrs Blunt who did all the cleaning up of the old man's various accidents.

Ivy took Red's hands, noticed the dirt under fingernails. 'You'll have to be clean,' she told him. 'Mrs Spencer won't put up with no dirt. As for Cora, she'll likely shove your head under the cold tap and do your ears with carbolic and steel wool.'

325

'Eh?' He looked from one to the other, snatched back his hand.

'Your mam says you can come along of us to Crompton Way,' said Ivy. 'Mr Heilberg called round at your house and asked, then he wrote to us. You'll be sleeping next door, mind, in Mrs Spencer's house, but you'll still be our Red. And your mam and dad's Red, too. They're only letting you go on account of overcrowding. You've got to visit them every weekend.'

Red let out a sigh of relief that was short-lived. His mam was letting him go. It didn't feel right. Surely Mam wasn't going to get rid of him as if he were ready for the rag cart? He glanced at little Sally, realized how awful she must have felt when her mother upped and offed without a by-your-leave or a ta-ra. 'Did . . . did me mam not say owt about me going, like?'

Ivy nodded. 'Aye, lad. Joseph Heilberg said as how your mother come over all faint, had to be brought round with Mrs Heilberg's sally-volley-tiles. Them's smelling salts, you know. Any road, Mrs Trubshaw said she wanted you to have a chance for a better life. Oh, and if you don't visit home every Saturday, she'll sell your hide to Walker's Tannery.'

Red could not believe his luck. He was ugly, big and clumsy. His mother loved him enough to hang on to him, enough to let him go. He was ugly and stupid, but Ivy and Sally liked him anyway. He was going to live in a house with a garden and . . . A thought struck. 'Can I change schools and all?' he asked.

'Aye, if you must.' Ivy's face wore a thin mask of severity. 'Any trouble and you'll go straight back to Basher Bates.'

Sally was going to miss her own teacher. She remembered all the little kindnesses, the many occasions when Irene Lever had passed food to the malnourished child whose mother was Lottie Crumpsall. 'I wish Miss Lever were going to be at our new school,' she said sadly.

Ivy coughed. 'She won't be at no school at all, won't Miss Lever.'

'Why?' chorused the two children.

The old woman patted the steel-grey bun at the nape of her neck. 'Her's been in a lot of bother,' she told them.

Sally glanced at Red. 'But she were all right, Miss Lever,' she protested. 'She never hit nobody, never sent us to Basher for a caning, never hit us with a ruler, never—'

'She sorted yon feller out,' Ivy informed her small audience.

Red's jaw dropped. 'Eh?'

Ivy was plainly savouring the moment. 'Walked in his office when he were giving a lad six of the best. Seems she lost her rag, like.'

'No,' gasped Red.

'Yes,' insisted Ivy. 'Grabbed the cane off him and broke it in two, she did. Then she put both pieces in the bin and said as how it were a pity she couldn't stick him in the rubbish and all. Then, just to top it all, she told him what he could do with his job.'

Sally's loud gulp broke the small silence that followed.

'Everybody knows about it,' continued the old woman. 'The lad as were being punished put it around, told the whole school. Miss Lever walked out and never came back.'

'Her mam's ill,' whispered Sally. 'She looks after her mam. They live over a shop in town. They need money.'

Ivy nodded. 'Aye. That's where Joseph Heilberg found her. Above a shop in town.' To spin out the drama, she spent a second or two clattering dishes on the parlour table. She straightened, winked at Red. 'And that's where he offered her the job. Irene Lever's coming to work at the mill. She'll be helping the apprentices to learn about their trades. And she's good at adding up, so she can keep the books.' Ivy sniffed. 'We've dispensed with Victor Worthington's services. Mrs Worthington – I mean Spencer –

wanted to keep his firm on as accountants, but we've persuaded her to have a complete break for all our sakes.'

Sally didn't care about Victor Worthington. All she could feel was relief because Miss Lever and her old mother would be safe from financial worry. 'Can I play out, Granny Ivy?' she asked sweetly.

Ivy considered. 'What if you start coming over all lacksy-daisy behind a tree again? What if you start traipsing through holes as aren't big enough for Red?' And what about when Worthington gets out of hospital? wondered Ivy, though she kept the thought to herself.

'I won't,' promised Sally.

'She won't,' vowed Red.

Prudence-Spencer-as-was should have sorted Worthington out by this time. Once the man realized there were thousands of folk after him, he would surely learn to behave. 'Go on, then. No climbing and no leaving gates open. If that bloody Primrose gets in our garden again, I'll turn you and her into best steak.'

Sally ran to her grandmother, held her close. 'Gran, you're all talk,' she said.

'And you'll be fifty next birthday,' forecast Ivy. 'Go on, hop it, the pair of you. Get from under me feet.'

Sally and Red hopped it. 'I'll be next door to you,' grinned the flame-haired urchin.

'With Mrs Spencer. She's posh, you know.'

They both stopped in their tracks and considered the awesomeness of poshdom.

After a couple of minutes, Red came up with an answer. 'I think I'll manage,' he declared.

'How? It'll be all clean boots and matching cups and saucers.'

Red nodded. 'Aye, I know. But it won't take me long.'

'Long to do what?'

'Train them,' he pronounced. 'I'll soon have them to rights, Sal. Come on, let's go and find Primrose.'

*   *   *

Joseph Heilberg, in black coat and hat, a rolled umbrella in his hand, strode down Spencer Street and paused at Paradise Lane. Gert Simpson was standing in the middle of the cobbles with a wooden tray in her hands. 'Keeping the workers fed, Mrs Simpson?' shouted Joseph. 'Very commendable. But we should go now and join Ruth, because the ceremony must begin.'

Gert placed her burden on the ground, removed a scarf from a quieter head of hair. 'Shame they're not here,' she told Mr Heilberg. 'Maureen and Tom should have seen this. And Ivy and our Sally. Still. We can't be expecting folk to rush back from Africa just to watch the first sod being turned, eh? Then Sally needs her rest after that pneumonia do.'

Joseph, who had discovered in his heart a great fondness for Lottie Crumpsall's sister, took her arm. 'We shall represent them, my dear.'

Gert fluffed up her hair, folded her lips so that the applied colour might be evenly spread. All around her, great areas of pavement were missing, so she was forced to depend on her companion as she struggled along in the most sensible shoes she had found among her collection. 'Even low heels gets stuck,' she complained. 'And I wouldn't be caught dead in owt flatter than these.' She gave the workmen a brilliant smile. 'They'll be nice, these houses, when they've been decorated. Electric, too. Eeh, we are going up in the world, Mr Heilberg.'

Joseph nodded. The four Paradise Lane houses were for mill management and for Nutty Clarke, the young Londoner who was to be caretaker of the factory buildings. 'Where will you live?' Joseph asked his companion.

Gert shrugged. 'I don't know yet. Nay, don't be worrying about me, 'cos I always fall on me feet. Mind, with these shoes, I might be better falling on me head.'

'I will find you a home,' he promised.

Gert shook the brownish curls. 'I've told you – stop

mithering. It's Ivy and Sally as counts, then that young London man with the burns. I mean, you've got to see to the Blunts and all. He's a few slates short, is old Ollie and—'

'They will live with Ivy and Sally. Mrs Miles and Mrs Spencer will be next door, so the Blunts will be cared for. You, dear lady, must come into the business. There will be many suitable jobs.'

Gert smiled, her teeth dazzling against a frame of scarlet lipstick. 'Too busy looking after everybody, you are.'

Joseph laughed. 'This has been my mission in life. My wife, also, tells me off for being too busy. But I am happy.'

They stopped at the recreation ground, watched while the mayor wielded a shining spade to begin the excavations. Many in the crowd had worked for Worthington, had come to see the day when a new beginning promised to wipe out the poison.

Joseph made his way through the gathering, thanked the officials and mentioned absent friends.

Gert Simpson remained with the throng while Joseph Heilberg did the honours. Mrs Heilberg would be in the Methodist Hall preparing tea and snacks for the visiting dignitaries. Along with the rest, Gert applauded when the speeches were finished, then turned to make her way back to the little house that had become her temporary home.

'Gert?'

She froze in her tracks, could not move. 'Go away,' she managed. There was no need to turn her head, because the voice was a very familiar one.

'I've nowhere to sleep, Gert. Me stomach's still bad and I can't get work.'

Suddenly galvanized, Gert stumbled across the lane to the door of number 1.

'Please,' he begged breathlessly.

She swivelled, looked at him, saw that he was ragged and unshaven. 'There's nowt I can do for you, Bert.'

'But Gert—'

'Sorry,' she said softly.

'It were him, not me! It were him as made me do it.'

She swept her eyes the length of his body. 'Did he hold a gun to your head?'

'No, but he threatened me.'

Gert nodded. 'You should have seen what he did to me. Sorry, Bert. You and me is finished. Fact is, it were you as burned that shop down. I can't help you no more, so off with you.'

He reached out, touched her hand. 'Just a cup of tea, girl. I'll not stop, I promise.'

'No,' she said firmly before closing the door in his face.

Inside, Gert Simpson brewed tea for herself, boiled an egg, made toast at the range. It occurred to her that she had just brought down the shutters on the first half of her life. What would the rest of her time bring? she wondered.

Gert was not a fanciful type, yet it seemed to her that the wielding of that silver spade had been significant for everyone, herself included. A new beginning. Ivy knew that Sally wasn't Derek's, knew that Gert would make no move to claim the child. Everything was out in the open – clean, clear and visible.

She settled by the fire, raised her skirt so that the flames might caress her cool limbs. It would all be down to goodwill from now on, she told herself. No bickering, no fighting, just everyone pulling his or her weight to make life bearable.

Gert dozed, saw a horrible face leering down. 'Clean up that salad,' he shouted.

'Don't touch me,' she moaned. 'Leave me alone, don't—' Her eyes flew open. He was alive, recovering. She glanced at the clock, realized that she had slept for just a few seconds. 'God help us,' she muttered.

Unable to sit still, Gert Simpson pulled on her coat and went to watch the builders laying pipes in the street. Things were going to be all right, she told herself firmly. Then she saw her husband lingering on the corner, his eyes narrowed against a thin stream of smoke from his cigarette. Would Bert help Worthington again? Should she allow Bert back into her life so that she could keep an eye on him?

No. Gert turned her back, fastened her coat and walked towards Spencer Street. She would go to the Methodist Hall and drink tea with the mayor and Ruth and Joseph. She would not falter, would not look over her shoulder. With a firm stride, Gert marched towards the future.

FOURTEEN

On 24 July, 1954, life was continuing apace for the residents of Bromley Cross. The village of quaint stone houses dozed peacefully through the summer Saturday, obviously unperturbed by the government's threat to pay Members of Parliament the princely allowance of two pounds per day, plainly unmoved by Maureen Connolly's third successive Wimbledon title.

A raw-boned man, whose loosened facial skin announced that he had once been larger, shambled along to Darwen Road, stopped outside the newsagent's shop, appeared to study headlines. A handwritten poster declared that the Chinese were apologetic about yesterday's small error of judgement, which tiny mistake had resulted in the shooting down of a British airliner. A bulletin board bore Westminster's promise to furnish the populace with written plans for civil defence in the event of an H-bomb attack. Even this perplexing concept seemed to have failed to stir local residents. The road continued its siesta without a flicker of a lace curtain at the windows of the old weavers' cottages.

The man yawned, straightened, rattled coins in a pocket. He was Alan Westford now, had hung on to his initials in some small attempt to preserve his diminishing identity. Would anyone recognize him after all these years? he wondered. Who could possibly tell that this slim, weather-touched man was once Andrew Worthington, owner of the Paradise Calico Company and a bad heart?

He entered the shop, asked the woman to put him on

333

the list for delivery. '*The Times* and the *Bolton Evening News*,' he said.

She pulled herself up from the stool and out of a reverie, licked the tip of an indelible pencil. 'Name?'

'Westford. Alan Westford.' His heart pounded, threatened, slowed when he breathed deeply. For the sake of his health, Alan Westford had given up beer, tobacco and large meals. To survive, he had taken on a job that had necessitated a certain amount of exercise. To stay alive, he had relinquished most pleasures. At the age of sixty-eight, he was now ready to down tools and pick up the cudgels for his final assault on life. The Crumpsall woman remained alive. For a pound a week, Bert Simpson had been happy to send regular bulletins to London. For another ten bob, the same man had kept Worthington's new identity to himself.

Westford supplied the shopkeeper with his address.

'Nice cottage, that end one,' she said in an effort to start a conversation. After all, the gaining of a new patron was not an everyday event. 'It were only on the market three weeks. Kept it ever so nice, did old Mrs Cummings. All on her own for years, poor soul. Aye, she were a proper little worker, Ada Cummings. Lovely garden isn't it?'

'Yes.' He glanced round the shop, suddenly found the Lancashire tongue to be unfamiliar, slow and almost annoying. 'Have you today's *Evening News*?'

'Sorry. There's the *Green Final*—'

'No.' He shook his head. His interest in sport had never been strong, and the *Final* contained no news unless such reports had been written during or after a match.

'So you'll not be wanting the *Green Final* delivered?'

'No.' He looked over her shoulder, almost salivated when his eye rested on a carton of twenty Capstan Full Strength. Even after a total of seven years' abstinence, his urge to smoke was strong. 'Just the papers I mentioned, thank you.'

The newsagent snapped the daily orders book into the

closed position. 'Anything else? Magazines, periodicals, *Radio Times?*'

'Not just now.'

Disappointed in her failure to draw out her new customer, the woman watched him as he walked through the door and down the road. 'One of them as keeps to himself,' she mumbled regretfully under her breath.

Outside, Alan Westford let out a sigh of relief. Bromley Cross was some miles outside Bolton but, even here, he had feared recognition. After resting for about two years in Bournemouth, he had moved to London, had saved most of the equity from the Wigan Road house, had even managed to put away some of the pittance he had earned on Billingsgate Market. A remembered smell entered his nostrils, as if he had conjured up once more the stench of cod, haddock, tainted plaice. For what had seemed a lifetime, he had risen at dawn to await the arrival of stock from the ports. He had scrubbed, weighed, distributed the stuff to retailers. Fish. He coughed, shuddered. If he never saw another piece of cold-blooded marine flesh, he would not be disappointed.

As he made his way homeward, he lifted his head, inhaled air that was clean and fresh, told himself that he must act normal. If he went about doubled over and trying to avoid being noticed, such attempts at invisibility might even make him all the more remarkable.

He closed his gate, stood for a while in the front garden, saw many flowers whose names he did not know. Another stretch down the side of the end-of-terrace cottage was laid as lawn with patches here and there that contained roses. Alan Westford knew about roses. They looked pleasant, but they had a tendency to bite back. Like women, he supposed. Because of women, he had lost the mill, had been forced to work like a common man. Because of women and Joseph Heilberg, he had lost everything.

Behind the row of houses, moors rolled away towards the horizon, their many greens enhanced by a dipping midsummer sun. But he did not notice the beauty, failed to see the gentle slopes that advertised the advent of the Pennine Chain. He was a man with a purpose, a man with a memory. Just a few miles down the road, Ivy Crumpsall was living with his daughter and next door to his wife. When would the Crumpsall hag die? She had to be at least eighty-four by now. But no, she must remain alive so that the plan would fell her. This time, he could not fail. This time, he intended to furnish himself with a well-qualified accomplice.

He turned his face to the sun, knew that the orange orb would soon slip away to the west, knew that his west was about to become someone else's east. Across an ocean, ships bearing cargo and passengers docked almost daily in British ports. Within weeks or even days, his ship would come in. It had taken time and money, but sweet vengeance was on its way.

Alan Westford entered the cottage, closed a front door that was his own. The Paradise Look. He could see that damned shop now, its bold as brass face staring defiantly at the best West End stores. He had spent many Saturday afternoons staring at Heilberg's and Goodfellow's triumph, had watched customers milling in and out of a store whose fame was spreading. By now, Prudence and her cronies should be millionaires.

In, out, he ordered his lungs. The art of total relaxation was relatively new to him, but he had been a good pupil, had never missed a session with his Soho-based therapist. Chinese medicine had its good points, he thought now as he took complete control of his own mechanism. To finish the exercise, he wrapped his right hand around his left wrist, allowed his fingers to encircle the snake bracelet. Ho Lin had told him that though the bracelet had no powers, it was there to serve as a reminder. 'Hold on to the snake and hold on to your calm,' the Chinese man had said. At the grand age of 103, Ho Lin knew a lot about survival.

In London's East End, Alan Westford had rented a tiny

room with a cooker and a sink hidden in a corner behind a filthy curtain. Apart from a bed and a table, there had been no comforts. Christmases had passed unmarked, because even his son had not been informed of the new name and address. His only contacts had been fish-mongers and a little Chinese person who had seemed older than time itself.

He sank into a deep chair, glanced at all the ornaments and pictures, slid his eyes over side tables, bookshelves, brasses and fire-irons. The whole lot had been sold with the house, so he had stepped into a ready-made home. The previous owner had died, and her relatives had left every-thing, right down to salt cellar and cutlery. At last, he was comfortable. At last, he was in a position to win.

Sally was doing her homework. Latin wasn't so bad, but she was always at odds with French, could not quite settle to it. Where did the verb come? She threw down her pen, counted on her fingers, chanted, 'Nous and vous before le, la, les, before . . .' Exasperated, she began again.

'They do everything backwards road about, that lot,' said Ivy. 'They don't have a white cow, they have a cow white and—'

'How do you know?' asked Sally.

Ivy tapped the side of her nose. 'I just do. Even folk what never got to Bolton School know a bit about this and that. Shift while I put me cloth on.'

Sally picked up her books, held them high until the tablecloth was settled.

'Why don't you do your homework upstairs?' asked the old lady. 'You've a desk and a lamp and bookshelves.'

'Because I like being down here,' replied Sally. She couldn't quite explain – even to herself – why she needed to be with Ivy as often as possible. Granny Ivy was . . . safety. At fourteen, Sally knew a little about human nature, but she was still not mature enough to work out the reasons for her dependency on Ivy. Gran had always

337

been there, had always been strong, had always been on Sally's side.

'What are you staring at, Sal?'

'You.'

'Why? Have I got dirt on me face?'

'No.'

Ivy walked into the hall, closed the door and made for the kitchen. She filled the kettle, set it on the gas stove, gazed at the blue-and-white wallpaper. With her eighty-fifth birthday looming on the near horizon, Ivy was fully aware of her own mortality. Rosie, who had been widowed for almost three years, was confined to the back bedroom. While tending the little woman, Ivy had come face to face with her own destiny. Fortunately, Gert Simpson had left her prefab to move in with Sally and Ivy. When it came to caring for the elderly, Gert Simpson was a princess . . .

Ivy tutted at herself for allowing her mind to wander again. Sal. She should be thinking about Sal. 'Oh, I hope Pru and Cora and Gert will see to my lass,' she mouthed at the teapot. 'She's always watching me, is our Sal, always looking to see if I'm all right.' She couldn't be all right for ever, that was certain sure. There'd been a few near dos, a couple of brushes with bronchial pneumonia, flu, shingles. Sometimes, she was out of breath before she'd even got up off a chair. Thinking about moving could be tiring enough. And her health had been uncertain for many years, so she must have eaten well into her borrowed time.

'Sit down, Gran. I'll brew up and see to everything.'

Ivy turned, looked at the pretty picture who was the dearest person in the whole world. 'Sal?'

'Yes?'

Ivy swallowed. 'There's none of us goes on for ever, love.'

The girl bit her lip, nodded. 'I know that.' Death was upstairs. His ugly face was not visible, yet his presence seeped beneath the door behind which Rosie Blunt's frail body continued to breathe. Sometimes, Death reached the landing. There was a coldness in the house, an icy draught that defied the warmth of summer. Sally shook herself inwardly, told herself to stop being what Gran would surely call 'all fanciful'.

'I'm halfway through me eighties now.' Oh God. This poor girl had lost her mam and dad, one to America and the other to the Lord. 'There's not just me for you.'

'I know that, too, Gran.'

'Mrs Spencer and Cora and Gert – they'll fettle for you. Tom and Maureen, too. I mean, I'm not shuffling off this minute. It's just – well – these things has to be faced up to sooner or later.'

Sally shivered again, hoped that this involuntary movement did not show. After all, she was a big girl now, a supposedly clever girl who had won a scholarship to Bolton School. If she could just conquer a modern language, she would be sure of a university place. Oxford. Even now, after seven years, she still rememberd that first visit, was still in touch with the childish excitement that had seemed to pierce the very core of her existence. If Granny Ivy died . . .

'Sal?'

If Granny Ivy died, nothing would be worth anything. And if Granny Ivy lived, Sally would have to stay here, on Crompton Way, to watch over the woman who had reared her, loved her and kept her away from harm.

'Sal?'

Granny Ivy wasn't even her real grandmother. 'Yes, Gran?'

'Stop thinking, love. Just for a minute, give your brain a rest.'

At first, when they had returned from Hampshire in 1947, things had been hard. Sally had been recognized, jeered at occasionally, had been whispered about in playgrounds and parks. But like most gossip, the topic had died and gone to rest. Sally and Red had both won places at grammar school, and the subject of parenthood seldom troubled either of them. Red Trubshaw spent half his time with Prudence Spencer, the other half with his family in Paradise. Sally lived with Ivy, who was, she supposed, her adopted grandmother, and with Gert Simpson, her real auntie.

'You'll set that frown,' warned Ivy. 'Come 1960, you'll have two deep lines between your eyes.'

'I don't care.'

Ivy perched on a stool while the young one clattered cups, brewed tea, dashed upstairs with a tray for Gert. She was easy on the eye, was Sal. Tall and slender, she was, with big blue eyes and blond hair that was too healthy for obedience. Long strands were always escaping from their prison of plaits to dangle down Sal's face until pushed impatiently behind the ears.

'You'll not cut it, will you?' asked Ivy. Apart from a quarterly trim, Sal's hair had never been shortened.

'I don't know. I don't think so.'

'You've bonny hair.'

Sally buttered a scone. 'So you keep saying. But you're not the one who has to let it dangle in your dinner.'

Gert put her head round the door. She had altered beyond recognition, had become a confident woman who wore little make-up and quiet, sensible clothes. 'I'm fetching the doctor,' she announced.

'Is she bad?' One of Ivy's hands pressed itself against the lean bosom.

Gert nodded. 'Aye, she's took a bit of a downward turn. I'll ask Mrs Spencer to drop in.' Gert had never managed to call her ex-employer by her Christian name.

Sally was out of the kitchen in a flash. She bounded upstairs and let herself into the back bedroom. Rosie Blunt, who was no bigger than the average ten-year-old, lay sleeping against a mound of pillows whose height was supposed to ease congestion in her lungs. There was no medicine for her now. Rosie was drifting peacefully towards her end on a vehicle called double pneumonia.

Gran had named this particular malady the old person's friend, because it was usually peaceful and easy. The young girl smiled fondly as she recalled Rosie's anger and her need to carry weaponry. At four feet and eleven inches, Rosie Blunt had needed armaments to reinforce her bossy nature.

Sally thought back to her own illness, remembered that pneumonia had brought her peace. Andrew Worthington was the man who had started her life, but Derek Crumpsall would always be her dad. Dead or alive, Derek was her father. Yes, pneumonia had been quiet, she thought. Was Rosie having a visitor at this moment? Was Mr Blunt reaching out a hand to guide his wife into the next world? In spite of the sadness, Sally smiled again. Mr Blunt would be pleased to see his wife, because she would probably arrive in heaven unarmed.

Derek had not helped Sally to cross over. No, he had pushed her back to Granny Ivy, to Red, to the Blunts and Maureen and Tom, had made her return to Rose Cottage. Andrew Worthington had disappeared from sight, had never been heard of since his stay in hospital. Sally shook off the feeling of unease. He would not come back. Even if he did, she was a big girl, almost old enough to deal with him.

'All right, lass?' Ivy, breathless after climbing the stairs, sat on the edge of Gert's bed. 'Is she with us?'

'Yes.'

Ivy put her head on one side, looked at the face of her old friend. 'She looks peaceful. I'd say her time's nearly up.'

Sally swallowed, then allowed the truth to spill from her tongue and into a room that was suddenly hollow, as if all the furniture had been moved out. 'I don't want you to die, Gran.'

'Well, I'm not that keen on it meself, you know. But the flesh is weak, love. I'm living in a worn-out shell. Any road, death's a natural part of life, isn't it?'

'I just can't imagine . . . well, I can't.'

Ivy sighed and studied her hands. The fingers were gnarled and twisted like the wind-whipped branches of a winter tree. Aye, the sun was shining outside, the air was warm and the sky remained as blue as Sally's eyes. But this was the winter of life, all right. She wouldn't cry. No, no, she wasn't going to kick off howling and skriking in front of Sal. Skriking? Yes, that had been one of Ivy's mother's words . . .

'Gran?'

'What, love?'

'She's stopped breathing.'

Ivy gulped back a lump of pain. 'Aye, well. Happen it's best for her.' Ivy stayed where she was. Wearied by the sheer length of her life, she was beyond kicking up a fuss. Anyway, Rosie would be better out of it, because she'd said nothing for days, was plainly ready to be on her way. 'Remember Ollie's spuds?' Ivy asked her granddaughter.

'Yes.'

'Green, they were. Green enough to put an army in hospital. Bad for you, green potatoes.' She shook her head again. 'He struggled day in and day out with that garden. Couldn't even grow weeds proper. Always made a big do out of it, he did. Always moaned at Rosie.'

Sally blinked away her tears, touched Mrs Blunt's cooling face. 'It's not fair, you know. People work so hard and have no money. Then they die.'

'Like Jesus,' Ivy reminded her. 'He worked hard and never had nowt, but He still had to go back to heaven.' She sniffed back a threatening moisture. 'Any road, there's no such thing as death. Little Rosie's gone to another place, that's all. Jesus showed us as how death weren't real.'

Sally crossed the room, placed her hands on Granny Ivy's shoulders. There was no substance to the bone any more, no vigour in the flesh. Mrs Blunt lay dead at the other side of the room, while Ivy Crumpsall simply waited for the reaper's call. 'Oh, Gran,' sobbed the girl.

'Stop it.' Ivy looked into Sally's eyes. 'No matter what happens, I want you to get an education. Do you know what education means, our Sal?'

The girl nodded mutely.

'Looked it up in the library, I did,' continued the old woman. 'It's from some daft foreign language – might have been Latin. You do Latin, don't you?'

Again, the girl simply inclined her head.

'It means leading out, Sal. It means being brought out of the dark and into the light. It means coming away from mills and factories and going into a better world.' She paused, inhaled, tried to strangle at birth the sobs created by Rosie Blunt's passing. 'Education means chances and choices, lass. I don't want you stood here weeping when I go. There's no need to look back. Just lead yourself out of here and read all them books you've always wanted.'

'Gran, I . . .' The rest of the sentence was drowned by tears.

'Don't let me down,' whispered Ivy. 'There's me shares in Paradise and there's the cottage. Sell the lot and get down to Oxford. Have a bike and a black cloak, go on one of them stupid boats with a long pole. Start your own life.'

'Not . . . without you.'

Ivy struggled to her feet and allowed her grief to spill over. She would have been taller than Sally but for the hump, she thought irrelevantly. Five foot seven, she used to be. 'They called me beanpole at school,' she mumbled. 'And Thin Lizzie. Till I clouted them.' She waved a hand towards Rosie. 'She had a little policy for this, Sal. Same as her Ollie. They even tidied up for themselves after they were dead. Good folk.' The real sobbing began.

Sally mopped at Gran's tears with a handkerchief.

'Sal?'

'Yes?'

Ivy pulled what remained of herself together and gripped her granddaughter's arm. 'Let me go, love.

343

Promise me you'll let me go when it's my turn. I don't want to go hovering about with no harp because you're keeping me earthbound. Me and Rosie are time-served, you know. We're both due for wings, 'cos . . .' The old lady coughed, heaved for breath. ''Cos we went to chapel when we could.'

For what seemed to be the first time, Sally saw Granny Ivy's vulnerability. Like everyone else, this lady had her weaknesses. The end of life had to be faced, because no-one could possibly continue for ever in earthly form. The young girl straightened, looked into intelligent eyes whose irises were no longer clearly defined. 'When . . . when God takes you, Gran, I'll cry. But I'll let go.'

Ivy nodded, felt a drop of moisture as it leapt from her face and onto the surface of a starch-crisped blouse. 'Growing up is letting go, lass. You let go of the child you used to be, then you let go of them as minded you. When I start to fail proper, like, don't give up owt for me. 'Cos one day, you'll be a mother. That'll be your turn at doing the minding. Remember, I'm not your kiddy.'

'Right, Gran.'

Ivy sniffed. 'I'm not really your grandma, either. Only we've never talked much about that, have we? You got chosen, pet. Me and your dad chose to have you. And as I stand here this very minute with me best friend just gone, I can tell you I regret nowt. You were the most wonderful thing as ever happened to me – apart from my Derek.'

Gert arrived and tripped lightly into the room, saw the grief in the faces of two people who were dear to her, knew that the third precious soul had gone. 'Eeh, Ivy,' she breathed. 'Mrs Spencer and Cora's gone out – so has the doctor.' She crossed the floor, looked down on Rosie's calm face. 'God bless you, old lass,' she said softly. 'Even though you near clocked me with yon posser, I did love you.' She dashed away a tear, turned to look at Sally and Ivy. 'Go down,' she whispered. 'I'll see to her.'

But Ivy remained where she was, her hand clasped around Sally's. 'Gert?'

'What?'

'If . . . when it's my turn, will you see to me?'

Gert nodded. 'Don't start talking daft, Ivy. Don't—'

'I want Sally to have a good life. I want her to go to that there Oxford place and get one of them university degrees and a funny hat. Then, if she wants to come back and work in Paradise, she can. And if she wants to be a teacher or some such fancy thing, she can do that and all.'

Gert tried to lighten the situation. After all, Rosie wouldn't have wanted everybody to be morbid and grisling. 'Talk to Irene Lever about teachers first, Sally. Remember what she did? Aye, her got the sack for breaking Basher Bates's cane. Glad of the job in Paradise, she were. There's worse than Paradise, Ivy. But I know what you mean.'

'Good.' Ivy kept her gimlet eye pinned to Lottie-Kerrigan-as-was's sister's face. 'You'd make ten of yon sister of yours, girl.'

Gert pretended to bridle. 'Fifty, more like. Look, if that one ever shows her face round here, I'll have a thing or two to say to her. I will, you know.'

Ivy bit her lip. 'And Worthington?' She felt Sally stiffen. 'What about him?'

'Same,' snapped Gert. 'The very same.' She watched while the young one guided Ivy out of the bedroom, listened to the aged woman's faltering steps as she was led downstairs. Then Gert Simpson got on with the job. She talked to Rosie all the time, said things which had been held inside for too long. 'I did love him, you know. Bert, I mean. He weren't much, but he were mine and we were suited. Only he killed the love when he near killed Maureen Marchant.'

She washed and dried Rosie's still-warm body, arranged the hair, dressed Rosie in the best pink winceyette nightie with a bit of white lace round its collar. 'No kiddies for me, love. And none for Maureen, either. In her forties now, same as me. All that love and she still got no babies.'

Rosie would have made a good mam, too, Gert thought. Aye, this lovely woman would have reared some bonny kiddies if only God had been more willing.

For a few moments, Gert lingered near the window and remembered Bert. She'd seen him from time to time, had bumped into him in town, had turned him away from the door of her prefab. It had been nice, that prefab. Two bedrooms, a nice living room, a kitchen with a fridge built in. And she'd given it up to come and mind Rosie.

Poor Rosie. Gert returned to the bed and smiled down at the relaxed face. 'Won't be the same without your snoring, lass. But I'll stop on here and see to Ivy. She gets fed up on her own all day while Sally's at school.' Worthington would have done anything to get his hands on Sally. Oh, he hadn't wanted the child, but he'd longed to break Ivy's heart. 'Where is he, Rosie?' she mouthed. Even now, she could feel him, could smell his filth, was often awake in the night after one of those terrible dreams. The man was still alive. Gert could sense his existence, felt certain that his death would have brought her peace. 'I'll know when you're dead, all right,' she said. 'I won't need no notice in the papers, 'cos I'll rest after you've gone.' She jerked her head upward, stared at the ceiling. 'World'll be cleaner when yon man's out of it,' she advised the Almighty. 'And You'd be saving me from murder and all, 'cos I'll swing for that rotten swine if needs be.'

Gert sat with Rosie and waited patiently for the doctor to arrive. She lingered with her thoughts, recalled who and how she used to be, wondered how her life might have turned out had she not been raped. Ever since that evening, Gert had kept herself to herself. If she couldn't have Bert, she wouldn't have anybody. And she couldn't have Bert because Bert was weak and stupid.

Ivy next, no doubt. Poor old love was bone weary and ready for off. What then? Gert straightened her spine, sat bolt upright in the rocker that had occupied Rosie's kitchen for a lifetime. 'I'll stop here,' she whispered into the room. 'I'll stop near Mrs Spencer and Cora and I'll be Sally's auntie. And God help any bugger who stands in my way.'

A crowd had gathered outside number 2 Paradise Lane, which now belonged to a foreman. Nutty Clarke, caretaker of Paradise, lived in number 4, while the other cottages were occupied by various members of staff. These men and their wives stood at the gateway to Paradise, their heads bowed, their bodies draped in black clothing.

When the horse-drawn hearse finally pulled up, there was not a dry eye in the street. The flagpole in Paradise's yard bore a Union Jack at half-mast, and not a single sound emerged from the factory. As a mark of honour, business had closed because of the death of a founder member.

Tom Marchant took the handkerchief from his wife, dabbed at his own moist cheeks, returned the square of white cloth. 'Bear up,' he said to Maureen.

Maureen smiled at him, looked past him, 'saw' Rosie chasing Ollie out of number 2. 'Don't talk to me about gardening, you bloody pie-can. It were your dad had the green fingers. If you want to grow summat, grow a brain.' The posser or the shovel or the yardbrush would be raised above that little head. Maureen could see it as clearly as she saw the horse and the coffin covered in flowers. 'I'll give thee a damn good hiding when I catch thee, Ollie Blunt! Daft? That's not the word for thee.' When seriously angry, Rosie had often used 'thee' instead of 'you'.

Little Rosie had finished up as an advisor in the weaving sheds. Little Rosie had owned shares in a very successful company. Would Rosie have left her shares to Sally? Maureen wondered. Yes. Maureen glanced sideways at her husband. A proportion of the Marchant interest in Paradise would go to Sally, too. Aside from a bequest to the orphanage at Goodfellow Hall, all the Marchant money was willed to Sally Crumpsall. Still, what was money?

Maureen tugged at Tom's sleeve. 'What have they done with it?' she asked.

'I beg your pardon, dear?'

'Rosie's dolly-posser.'

'I don't know. It's probably at Crompton Way.'

Maureen nodded. If possible, she would get that weapon and put it in the garden, train a climber round it. She had a lovely garden, a beautiful house, a wonderful husband. And no children. The tears flowed anew, but they were not just for Rosie. Maureen wept for the tiny boy child who had torn his way out into the light only to die after a few moments. She had called him David.

'Stop it, Maureen,' whispered Tom. He knew her every thought, her every mood. She was still mourning a child who would have been five years old by now.

'Sorry,' she muttered.

He sighed heavily, said nothing. No matter what, Maureen would never recover, not completely. She would go through the motions, would continue to enjoy much of life. But at least once a day, she would grieve. At funerals, her pain was compounded. He squeezed her hand, tried to lend her some strength.

Ivy, who had been forced by Gert to use a bathchair, sat right behind the hearse. They'd had some good times, she and Rosie. Rosie and the rest of Paradise Lane had minded Sally, too, while Lottie-Kerrigan-as-was got on with her evil doings. She sniffed, fixed her eyes on the glass case that held a good woman. They'd talked, she and Rosie. They'd had real discussions and arguments. There'd been no reserve between them, no embarrassment.

'All right, Ivy?' asked Gert.

'I'd be a sight better on me feet.'

'You can't—'

'Don't start, Gert. If I want to get meself out of this pram, then I will. The only road you'll keep me in here is if you tie me down with two clothes lines and a pair of handcuffs.'

Gert swallowed her sadness, thanked God that she'd had the sense to start wearing low heels. Paradise was on a bit of a slope, so pushing the chair was hard enough without worrying about cobbles and high heels and—

'Gert?' Bert had forced his way through, was standing right next to his wife. 'I'm sorry,' he managed. 'About Mrs Blunt.' He twisted a cap in his hands, kept his head down. Behind Gert stood Tom and Maureen Marchant. Bert could not bear to look at that woman's hands. The slightest sign of a scar would have borne testament to what Bert had perpetrated in the past. This time, he told himself, he was working properly for Andrew Worthington. This time, he was being paid to keep pace with developments so that Worthington could set up in legitimate opposition. So why did he feel so . . . so uneasy?

'Go away,' Gert advised him. 'This is a funeral.'

Bert raised just his eyes, saw Gert's set mouth. It didn't matter whether or not Worthington's intentions were genuine. He shouldn't allow himself to be employed by the man, even on a casual basis. If Gert knew . . . If she knew that Bert was spying for Alan Westford by getting Paradisers to loosen their tongues in pubs . . . 'I wish you'd have me back, love.' If she would only take him back, he would give up Worthington's cash, would even get a proper job. He gulped nervously. 'Job' was not a favourite word.

'No. And this isn't the right time for you to be plaguing me.'

Ivy swivelled, stared at Bert. 'There's no right time for you to be mithering,' she announced. 'Gert doesn't want you. She's set for life where she is, 'cos Mrs Spencer'll let her keep the house after I've gone. And Gert's got a grand job, too, when she wants it back. Turned out to be a good little weaver, didn't she, Ro—?'

Ivy bit off the second syllable. There was no Rosie, not any more. She fixed her eyes on the coffin and waited to be wheeled towards the inevitable.

Sally arrived, breathless and still dressed in her uniform. 'Gran?'

'How many marks for that French homework?' Ivy needed something to concentrate on, a subject that might take her mind off Rosie being dead and Bert Simpson being at the funeral, bold as brass and ugly as sin itself.

'Nine out of ten.'

Ivy nodded. 'Why not ten?'

'Got the verb wrong.'

Ivy pointed at the hearse. 'Good job Rosie's not here, Sal. She'd have give you a good talking-to.'

Sally placed a hand on her aunt's arm. 'I'll help you to push, Gert.'

'I'll manage,' replied Gert. 'Only I'll fettle better when he's gone away.' She waved a hand towards the 'he', waited until Bert had shuffled his way back into the crowd. 'You've missed nowt there,' she advised her niece. 'He were never an uncle to you. He were never on the side of the angels.'

'You still love him,' pronounced the seated Ivy.

Gert raised her eyes to heaven. 'Aye, and you always loved Richard Tauber, Ivy. But that didn't mean you were going to chase after him.'

Without turning, Ivy bridled. They could tell she was bridling from the set of her shoulders. 'At least he could sing,' she said in defence of the tenor. 'Yon man can't do owt except lift a glass to his gob.'

Gert bowed her head. They hadn't lived together for years, but she still hurt when anyone criticized Bert. Anyway, they remained wed, because no divorce papers had been served by either party, so happen she should feel something for a man she was tied to. Perhaps, inside herself, in a place too deep to be obvious, she wanted him back. No, she said inwardly. Not after Maureen's hands.

She looked over her shoulder and smiled at Maureen and Tom. Now, that was a gradely couple.

Ruth and Joseph Heilberg joined the line. They bowed their heads and waited for the procession to move, each praying to the God of Israel for the soul of the departed Rosie. Joseph cast his mind back over recent years, remembered the beginning of it all when Rosie and Ivy had worked day in and day out to bring about the triumph that was now called The Paradise Look.

'Joseph?'

'Yes, Ruth?'

'We will go afterwards to the hall. The food will not be kosher, but God must forgive us.'

Joseph smiled at his lovely wife. 'It is the same God for us and for Christians.' He raised both shoulders, lifted his hands. 'So who are we to say that they are wrong? Perhaps kosher is wrong.'

Ruth smiled sadly. 'So, who was Jesus?'

'Messiah or prophet, Jesus was a good man, Ruth. So even if they are mistaken, these Methodists follow a saint.' Would that members of all religions could accept each other as easily, he thought. How many wars had been fought in the name of Jesus, in the names of other spiritual leaders?

'Joseph?' Tom shook the hand of Paradise's Managing Director. 'Will you come to the Methodist Hall afterwards?'

Ruth answered. 'Of course we will.' She reached out a hand to welcome the newly arrived Prudence Spencer and Cora Miles. Behind them, the polished face of Arthur 'Red' Trubshaw was grim beneath a black cap. Below the neb, a few spikes of red hair had escaped from their prison of hair dressing. Red nodded at Sally, then took his place next to Mrs Spencer.

Sally looked round at Paradise, saw the house in which she had lived, first with Mam and Dad, then with Granny Ivy. She remembered Red Trubshaw with his scabby knees and holey socks, remembered how he had cared for her. He was different now. Red had changed and so had she. One day, she would go to Oxford and take a degree in English or history. She glanced at the back of Gran's hat, recalled the lecture. Yes, she would go to university, no matter what. As for Red – well – he had turned out to be some kind of scientific genius. The Municipal Grammar School was full of itself, because it had found a 'natural' scholar from the slums surrounding Paradise.

Sally's eyes edged along brickwork until they rested on the door that had belonged to the Blunts. The houses were improved, had become almost pretty with their new windows and doors. They were all electric, too, with bathrooms and inside toilets. Poor Mrs Blunt. It was right that the cortège should leave from here, from the place where Rosie Blunt had spent at least a quarter of her eighty-odd years. The young girl crossed her fingers and allowed her eyelids to close. Not Gran, she said inwardly. Not Gran, not yet.

'Sal?'

'Yes?' Startled blue eyes were wide open again.

'I've told you,' said Ivy softly. 'Stop thinking, or your face'll set.'

Sally stopped thinking, then walked with the others along the slow hundred yards to Spencer Street.

'Well?' Westford stroked his newly grown beard. 'Is the place empty?' He glanced around, though no-one ever came into this narrow alley at the rear of the Kippax Mill.

Bert Simpson nodded. 'Aye. Everybody's gone round to the Spencer Street chapel. Even the Paradise caretaker's left his post.' He steeled himself. 'Rosie Blunt had a lot to do with the opening of the workers' co-operative. She were very highly thought of. Some of Kippax's have gone to pay their respects and all.' He gestured towards the mill in whose shadow they were standing.

Westford simmered, hung on to his temper, was

352

determined not to allow his emotions to boil over on the doorstep of an empire that was rightfully his. 'Let's go, then.'

Bert sagged against the wall. Nobody would ever recognize Worthington, not now. Of that much, Bert was certain. But he didn't want to be involved, didn't want to put himself in a position where he could be asked to do . . . anything at all. Working for the absentee Worthington/Westford had been one thing, but having the man here was another matter altogether.

'Well?'

Bert shrugged, pushed his hands deep into trouser pockets. 'I don't want to be involved no more, Mr . . . Westford. It were bad enough last time when I set fire to yon shop. Nay, you're taking on a whole town here. Paradise is the only mill where workers gets shares and a say in their own right. No, I'm going no further.'

Westford counted to eight, because ten would have taken too long. 'I know a lot of things about you, Bert, and—'

'And I know a lot about you, Mr Worthington. I've got your new name and address. If I say one word to Tom Marchant, he'll have you tarred and feathered.'

The Town Hall clock sounded a knell, intoned the eleven o'clock chime that marked Rosie Blunt's final visit to her chapel. There would be at least another two hours, thought Westford. Oh yes, that factory could well remain unoccupied till mid-afternoon. This was the one chance, probably the sole opportunity he would get to investigate the size of his enemies' might. And now, at the actual eleventh hour, Simpson was panicking.

'You've no hold over me no more,' said the shorter man. 'Things I did all them years ago is nothing towards what you did. Attempted kidnapping's serious, like. It's not the same as pinching a bit of stuff from the back of a shop—'

'Or setting fire to a pawnbroker's?' Sarcasm decorated Westford's words.

353

Bert eased himself into an erect position. 'Say what you want. I'll tell the police you did it. After all this time, who's to know the bloody difference?'

Westford smirked. 'Your wife, for a start.'

'Eh?'

In for a penny, thought the ex-owner of Paradise. 'Free with her favours like her sister, is Gert. Yes, I spent time with both the Kerrigan girls, and one gave me a daughter.'

'Aye, we know all about Sally,' replied Bert. But this man was lying, surely? Gert would never have gone with Worthington, not willingly.

Westford nodded. 'Yes, I had Lottie Crumpsall many a time. She's a lively woman, you know. And her sister's pretty feisty, too. Bert, your wife and I had an interesting time while you were in hospital.'

Bert was glad of the wall, suddenly needed its rough support. 'No,' he managed. 'Not my Gert.'

'Yes. Your Gert is anybody's Gert. There's no point in your trying to turn a new leaf. Nothing will get you back into Gert's good books, I'm afraid. It's over. You'll just have to face up to it. Nothing will induce Gert to take you back, because she'll never be satisfied with any one man. She needs her own stud farm.'

Bert's face was white. He removed his hands from their pockets and placed them palms down against the wall. 'She's changed,' he managed. 'Even the road she dresses.' He shook his head quickly. 'No, no. My Gert were never like that.'

'Sheep's clothing is what she wears now. Where there are wolves, there are she-wolves.'

Bert grappled with all the confusing concepts that were rooting in his brain. Gert was respectable, had always been a good girl. Even though she'd dressed up a bit on the colourful side, she'd acted decent. There was something very wrong here. No way would Ivy Crumpsall have a loose woman living in her house with the young girl she

354

had raised as a granddaughter. Even when Gert had lived in the little prefab house, she had been up and down to the Crumpsalls' house, had worked full-time in Paradise as a weaver.

'Well?' Westford glanced at his watch.

'I'm thinking.'

'And just how long will that process take?'

Bert Simpson looked directly into the eyes of Andrew Worthington. He was still Andrew Worthington, no matter what. This bad bugger had never even been prosecuted for grabbing Sally, because everything had been glossed over when Ollie Blunt had accidentally impaled the lunatic on a pitchfork. Andrew Worthington had been a doomed man whose life had been saved by Ollie Blunt. Without the surgery that followed, Worthington could have died within weeks.

'Still thinking?'

'No.'

'Then what are you going to do about our plan?'

'Your plan, not mine.' They definitely wouldn't recognize Worthington, thought Bert. He had shrunk like a wool garment in hot water, had emerged wrinkled and worn-out. Even the eyes, which had protruded so markedly in his ugly face, were now partially shrouded beneath veils of collapsing flesh. 'You're on your own,' he said softly. 'Do what you want and say what you want, but I'm out of it.' He turned and took a step away.

Westford clapped a hand on the shoulder of his cohort. 'There's money in it for you. If you come with me now, I'll pay you fifty pounds. Think what you could do with fifty pounds.'

'Nowt is what I could do,' snapped Bert as he swung round to face his tormentor. 'The sleep I've lost over Maureen Mason's hands . . . well . . . you'd not be interested in that, would you? Fifty quid's no good to me without Gert. Fifty thousand's no good, come to that. And from what you've said, there's no way she'll come back.

355

Not while she's having such a good time, like.'

Westford cursed himself inwardly. He should never have taken that tack, should not have tried to discredit Gert. He had wanted Bert to forget all about his wife, to forsake any misguided loyalty towards the woman. But in damning Gert, he had removed Simpson's reason for staying alive. 'Look, I was wrong. I made all that up so that you would stay away from your wife. After all, you know some of my little secrets, don't you? And if you were to return to Gert, you might just tell her my new name and address.' He paused, rooted round for further comment. 'And Gert's loyal to Ivy Crumpsall. She might have ruined any chance I might have of . . . of . . .'

'Of destroying Paradise?' Bert nodded slowly, pensively. 'Aye, Gert's a loyal woman. Salt of the earth, she is, the sort who'd stick with anybody who treated her right. And summat else and all, Mr Worthington—'

'Westford—'

'Please your bloody self about that, 'cos I know who you are and what you are.' Bert suddenly felt very cold – chilled to the bone, but stronger, almost brave. 'My Gert's on the right side. Yon Crumpsall woman worked hard well past retirement age, 'cos she believed in Paradise. Ivy Crumpsall'd make ten of you, me and half a dozen others. So bugger off, I'm done with you.'

A dart of pure fear shot through Westford's body, seeming to hit the spot where Ollie Blunt had impaled him years earlier. Simpson was walking away, would put the word about that Worthington was back and looking for revenge. He groped for his wallet, hailed Bert. 'Take your wages. At least let me pay you for what you've done so far.'

Bert Simpson stopped dead in his tracks, frozen not by the promise of money, but by something far more important. Slowly, he pivoted and walked back along the tiny passageway. 'You . . . you forced her, didn't you?'

Westford took a small step back.

This slight movement and a certain look in Westford's eyes was enough for Bert. 'You bloody bastard. You raped my girl, didn't you? I know it, I can tell by that smirk on your rotten face.' Bert paused, inhaled, took another pace. 'That's it, then. I'm going through Kippax's yard and I'm going to tell every bugger I meet that you're back and looking for trouble. Tom Marchant'll have your card marked before teatime, I'm telling you. It's over, Worthington. And you can tell your mate Westford that he's finished and all—' The sentence died suddenly when pain flooded Bert's chest. Was he the one having the heart attack? Shouldn't it have been the other fellow?

'Go to hell,' snarled the man who called himself Westford.

It was then that Bert understood what was happening to him. Too late, he realized that Worthington was upon him, that a knife was slipping into his chest for the second time. Or was it the third?

'Die, you whining coward,' spat the assailant.

Bert fell against the wall, saw that the sky had darkened. Rain? he wondered. No, no, it was his eyes. He was slipping down the wall and into the next life. 'You'll not get away . . .' The words bubbled wetly on his tongue before spilling colour down his chin. 'You . . . finished . . . Worthing . . . ton.' He slumped, tried to breathe, gave up the unequal fight.

Westford straightened, wiped the all-purpose army knife on a handkerchief, spat on his hands and cleaned them. There was not much blood, he thought. There was less blood here than had come out of his own nose the night he had conquered Gert Simpson. He looked over his shoulder, saw no-one, knew that he was relatively safe.

When his pulse slowed, Westford dragged the body across the dirt track and covered it in rubbish. When what remained of Bert Simpson was hidden, the murderer turned his face towards Wigan Road and the place known as Paradise.

FIFTEEN

For several minutes, Alan Westford remained in the alley. He positioned himself about halfway between Bert Simpson's body and the passageway's junction with Wigan Road. He had done it. He had killed a man, so nothing mattered from now on. Whatever happened, no single occurrence could possibly result in anything as marrow chilling as those moments of terror while Bert Simpson had hung between life and death.

The Town Hall clock struck the quarter. Fifteen minutes. Fifteen minutes ago, Simpson had been alive, speaking, moaning, threatening. The way was clear now, because Westford was finally alone and completely responsible for his own destiny. Bert had been an obstacle, he told himself by way of reassurance. The man had been besotted with the cheap slut he had married, might easily have told her everything. Now, Simpson would talk no more.

He checked his hands and clothing for blood spots, combed his hair, straightened the new tie. For some inexplicable reason, he found himself to be calm and steady. With his confidence swollen by this morning's uneventful walk through the centre of Bolton, he stepped firmly out of the ginnel and onto Wigan Road. Nobody would know him. When he had looked in a mirror of late, he had scarcely recognized himself. Also, he simply couldn't seem to worry any more. It was as if any barrier in his path could be moved or destroyed. After this morning's event, he was unable to fret about something as insignificant as being recognized. From now, his time was borrowed; from now, he would always be a murderer. Yet this knowledge did not trouble him unduly.

In the bottom of the H, where the Recreation Ground had once sat doing nothing apart from incubating weeds, a new building showed off its smug facia of red Accrington brick. Westford looked right and left, saw no movement on Paradise Lane, knew that everyone was at Rosie Blunt's funeral. He stepped through a gateway, noticed that the word PARADISE would have been formed had the wrought iron gates stood closed.

He strolled up a path to the main doorway, rattled a knob, was not surprised to learn that the place was locked. As he wandered around the structure, he found his mouth gaping when the size of Marchant's gamble finally hit home. There was a huge hall with chairs stacked to one side and gymnastic equipment stored along walls. Doors at one side of the large room were labelled BATHS, MEDICAL, LIBRARY. Library? What did this lot round here want with books? At the rear of the building, another locked entrance plainly led to a staircase. A notice read, THIS WAY TO CLASSROOMS AND APPRENTICES' TUTORIALS. An arrow pointing upward verified the functions of the upper storey.

Westford's need for a cigarette was great. Had he been carrying tobacco and the means to light a smoke, he could have tossed the match into the workers' co-operative's dream world. No. It was too big for him. There was city money here too, so any damage would be closely investigated then righted by insurers. And, of course, he might get caught. So what? he asked himself. Wasn't he already in trouble? With surprise, he realized that he had not given a thought to Bert Simpson for several minutes.

'Can I help you?'

Westford swung round, his heart beating loudly in his ears. 'Just looking,' he replied. The man wore a flat cap and gloves, had scars on his face.

'You shut'n be here.'

Westford heard the now familiar Cockney accent. Grateful for his ability to mimic, he smiled tentatively. 'You from the East End?'

'Yes.'

'Wotcher doing up here, then?' The job at Billingsgate was paying off. After years as a listener, Westford had picked up the accent. 'I'm just visiting, meself. Gotta sister on Wigan Road, but she ain't in. Left me bags in her yard and came to the mill, thought she might work here.'

'What's her name?'

Westford covered the pause with a cough. 'Too much bleeding smoke round here. Gets to me chest. Hilda. Hilda Dobson. Married a weaver.'

Nutty Clarke nodded. 'They've all gone to a funeral. I been meself to the service. One of the founders died. Nice old girl, she was.' Nutty ran his eyes over the intruder. 'Dobson, you say?'

'That's right.'

The caretaker, who had left the funeral service to check on security, took a key from his pocket. 'Follow me, sir. The workers are all listed in the office.'

Westford followed Nutty Clarke across Paradise Lane and into the mill yard. As he entered what he still considered to be his own domain, Westford was suddenly Worthington again. This was his family's business. It had been built and run on Worthington sweat and blood, had been handed down from father to son, only to be snatched by a jumped-up ex-lord from Hampshire. He simmered, tried not to think about Heilberg. Marchant annoyed him, but Heilberg was the leading light here now, was probably using the Worthington office, the Worthington desk and chair.

'You all right?' asked Nutty.

'Yes.' He cleared his throat. 'Just hoping we find me sister, that's all.' Dobson, he told himself firmly. He must remember that his non-existent sister's name was Hilda Dobson.

Inside the building, Worthington stopped abruptly, all the breath seeming to leave his body in one long sigh. The mill had been rearranged; he and the caretaker were standing in a room, a proper drawing room with furniture, curtains, a carpet. 'What's this?' he asked before giving himself time to think.

'This is where buyers sit,' replied Nutty. 'It gives them an idea of what The Paradise Look can do for their customers. We put these arrangements in department stores all over the country. It's one of the services we provide.'

The 'we' did not pass unnoticed. Paradise belonged to everyone, from the management right down to the fellow who swept the floors. Shares, of course, would be an optional extra, a perk to be picked up in lieu of bonus. Worthington knew the folk round here very well. They were a canny lot, so they probably carried the forty-nine per cent between them for a rainy day. 'Lovely,' he managed. 'I remember seeing a shop down in the West End – The Paradise Look, it was called. So the stuff made here goes off down to London?'

Nutty shrugged. 'London, Birmingham – anywhere and everywhere. We make three-piece suites, odd sofas and armchairs, curtains, bed linens, tablecloths, cushions—'

'Where's the employees' list?' snapped Worthington. He was suddenly furious. The anger was usually deep inside, in a part of him that stayed cold and dark no matter what the weather, no matter what his mood. But now, it bubbled like lava under a too-thin crust of mock-indifference. 'I need to find me sister.'

Nutty scrutinized the stranger. 'You're a funny bugger,' he commented casually. 'Half and half, eh? Bit of London, bit of Lancashire—'

'I was born up here,' said Worthington hastily. 'Then we moved, came back, moved again. My sister married and stayed in Bolton.'

'Come upstairs,' said Nutty. 'Mr Heilberg must have taken the lists and left them in his desk.'

They entered the office. On the desk that had belonged to Worthington Senior, a photograph of Ruth Heilberg sat in a silver frame. The chair was still there. The chair from which Worthington had ruled the roost was here for the use of . . . Joseph Heilberg.

'You ill or something?'

'No, no. I'm just tired from all the travelling.'

Nutty pored through the pages. 'Well, she's not a spinner or a weaver. And the only women in the carpentry department are cleaners . . . no, she's not a cleaner . . . not an upholsterer . . . and I can't find her name among the sewing machinists. Sorry.'

'Never mind. She must be in some other mill.'

The caretaker put away the book, went to the door. 'You coming?'

He didn't want to go. He wanted to stay, wanted to shout for the lad from the general office. Except that the general office was now a sort of fairyland of tastefully draped fabrics where customers could, no doubt, browse at leisure while drinking tea and choosing their lines for next spring. 'Yes, I'm coming.'

They strolled across the yard together. 'Is it a happy ship, then?' Worthington kept his tone light.

Nutty guffawed. 'You could say that, mate. Anything would be an improvement on the bastard who used to own this place. No love lost there, from what I've heard.'

'Really?'

Nutty laughed again. 'I think he ran himself out of town, you know. Turned up in Hampshire, tried to grab one of his kids, a girl called Sally Crumpsall. Seems he had children left, right and centre, thought nothing of troubling a young woman. But Sally's very highly thought of in these parts. She'll come into this pile one day – mark my words. I mean, Mr Heilberg's got money in it, and so have some others, but Tom Marchant's is the lion's share. He's no children of his own, so his share'll fall to Sally. He's got an orphanage now, you know. Used to be a lord, but he gave the house away. Brought his sister back from abroad, told her she could run the orphanage and be a missionary in her own country.' He locked a door, pocketed the bunch of keys. 'Still, Sally Crumpsall's the light of Mr Marchant's life, so she'll be the boss here one day, I reckon. A woman in charge, eh?'

Sally again. Lottie's brat was going to end up running the Paradise Mill. 'Thanks,' said Worthington tersely. 'I'll go and wait at my sister's house.'

Back in Paradise Lane, Worthington watched the caretaker dashing off to pay his last respects to an old woman who hadn't mattered. She'd assaulted Worthington once, had driven a posser into his belly. And her husband had stuck a pitchfork in his back.

Revenge. He ambled down Worthington Street towards Wigan Road, realized that he was virtually helpless. For a start, he was on his own. Bert Simpson hadn't been up to much, but he had been there. And this whole thing was just too big to cope with. He'd no money to speak of, no means of punishing the Jew or Tom Marchant. But Ivy Crumpsall . . .

He stood on Wigan Road at the bottom of Spencer Street, watched the funeral procession as it came to order outside the chapel. Prudence. There she stood in new clothes, her figure trim, her housekeeper by her side. The Crumpsall woman was in a wheelchair. The wheelchair was being pushed into line by Gert Simpson. Another widow, he thought. Still, that was no great loss, because Bert Simpson had been a stranger to work, had shown a marked distaste for anything involving physical movement.

A woman left the crowd, ran down the street towards Wigan Road. Worthington stepped back, but not before she had looked straight into his eyes. After a small beat of time marked by a straining heart, he returned to normal.

363

She hadn't recognized him, because he hadn't known her. And he had changed so radically that no-one could possibly identify him through old newspaper photographs.

Irene Lever slipped into the chemist shop and bought a packet of Fisherman's Friends. A ticklish cough had troubled her right through the service, and she didn't want to stand hacking over Mrs Blunt's grave.

'Here you are,' said the shopkeeper. 'Miss Lever?'

'Oh.' She pulled out of her reverie, paid for the pastilles and left the shop. Only once had she met a man with eyes as markedly cold and cruel as those in the face of that stranger. The unknown newcomer had backed away, too, had looked uneasy, almost guilty. No, she told herself firmly. That had been no more than a common courtesy or a mark of respect at the sight of the cortège.

She crossed the road, saw no sign of the man. Slowly, she walked up Spencer Street and joined the others. As they set off towards the cemetery, Irene Lever remembered. Basher Bates's eyes had been wicked, especially on that fateful day when she had snapped his cane and left teaching for ever. The eyes of the man on Wigan Road had been similar to Basher Bates's . . .

But there was a funeral to attend, so she put away her ridiculous thoughts and concentrated on saying a final farewell to Rosie Blunt.

Victor had turned out to be decent after all. Cora Miles was glad that she'd kept her opinion of him to herself over the years. She watched him now with his wife and son, noticed how he looked after Margaret West-as-was, how he handed round sandwiches and made sure that everyone's cup or glass was full. 'He's a credit to you, Prudence.' After many years, her employer's Christian name had begun to slip out easily. 'That's a good lad.'

Prudence smiled, nodded her agreement. 'And Margaret's pleasant once you get used to her.' She pondered for a moment. 'I used to worry in case . . .

in case Victor turned out like his father.'

Cora shivered. The thought of a second Andrew Worthington was not one that sat happily in her imagination, though she had, for a long time, expected to see such a creature evolving in Victor. But he was, at last, a good lad.

Prudence sat with her hands in her lap. She was remembering. All those years when she had stayed in Worthington House, her lips tightly sealed, her bedroom door tightly bolted. Then the day when the chrysalis had finally split . . . Her mouth twitched as she recalled bursting in on the Heilbergs – 'He is so near,' she had insisted. 'So near and so dangerous.' Suddenly, she shivered, as if a draught had entered the hall. But no, the place was warm, made hotter by the existence of a couple of hundred occupants who talked, ate, drank, moved about to form different groups. In fact, the room was quite stuffy.

She shuddered once more. That coldness had come from inside herself. The pores on her arms had opened to make all the downy hairs stand proud. But she dismissed the mood, told herself not to be silly. After all, sixty-one was not an age at which one should act fanciful. Nevertheless, Prudence Spencer looked over her shoulder before stepping forward to talk to her friends.

After several evenings spent in public houses, Alan Westford was absolutely certain that he would never be recognized. He had even been in the company of people he had employed or traded with, had kept the groans inside himself when the subject of the Goodfellow Workers' Co-operative came up. It was plain that the scheme was successful and highly thought of. The buildings were still called Paradise, and the merchandise bore tickets marked THE PARADISE LOOK, but the business was registered as the GWC.

He drained his glass, decided to hang for a sheep.

Having returned to one bad habit, he might as well indulge another. That first bite of Virginia hit his throat like a bullet and sent his head reeling towards the upper atmosphere, but he was soon smoking along with the rest. Bad ways died hard, he told himself. There had been no mention of Bert Simpson. Clearly, the body had not been found, because so few people walked through that badly-pitted passageway.

Worthington glanced at a calendar on the wall, took note of the date. How much longer? he asked himself. He had sent the money, was beginning to think it had been squandered. It had to happen quickly. The Crumpsall crone was already in a wheelchair and he wanted her to remain alive so that the final dart could be fired into her decrepit body.

'Having another?' asked a man at his elbow.

'No, thanks.' He was suddenly wary. After glancing sideways a couple of times, Worthington realized that he was in the company of a carder from Paradise. 'I'll have to be off,' he mumbled.

The man followed Worthington to the door. 'Don't I know you?'

'No.' He was shaking. After spending so many days without a flicker of recognition in a single face, his confidence was crumbling as easily as Lancashire cheese. 'No, we have never met,' he said somewhat firmly.

The carder pushed past Worthington and stood outside the Wheatsheaf. 'Oh, I'm sorry,' he said. 'I thowt I'd seen a bloody ghost. Spitting image of me Uncle Ted, you are. If he'd not been dead these two years, I'd have been asking you about Auntie Kitty.'

Worthington shook his head. 'I'm just visiting a sister,' he said. 'Then I'm going back to London.'

The man frowned. 'Eeh, you do look like owld Ted,' he insisted. 'Well, him and somebody else. Only I can't remember who the other feller is.'

'We all have doubles.'

'Aye.' The carder scratched his head and went back into the public bar.

Worthington waited until the big bass drum in his chest had settled down a bit. He had just been forced to come to terms with two things. The first was that he was in danger of being spotted too early; the second fact was that the beer and the cigarettes were stirring up the old trouble. Oh, he wanted the Bolton folk to know about his return. But not yet.

He trudged to the bus stop on Bradshawgate, waited for the transport that would take him back to Bromley Cross. Until the time was right, he had better stay close to his new home. Eventually, Alan Westford could be laid to rest and Andrew Worthington would take centre stage once more.

On the bus, he sat and pondered, wished that he could play a part in what he considered to be the main plot. No. He had no chance of retrieving Paradise, no chance of acting out a main part. But once he was cued to step into his own small role, he might well disturb the founder members of the workers' co-operative.

The unsteadying of a vital corner of Paradise would have to be enough. That, and the final destruction of Ivy Crumpsall's dream.

He bought a small van, an inconspicuous piece of merchandise that had seen better days. Driving round in this heap of rust was safer than lingering in a bus queue.

For weeks on end, he waited for a letter or a telegram, spent the rest of his time driving round Bolton. He saw Tom Marchant and his wife motoring up the driveway of a sizeable house on Chorley New Road, a double-fronted detached with large gardens. He watched Joseph and Ruth Heilberg enjoying the fruits of their labour – another sizeable property at the edge of a farm in Harwood. And, of course, he kept a weather eye on Crompton Way, where a pair of semi-detached houses contained Ivy Crumpsall, the child and Gert Simpson, then Prudence, Cora Miles and, occasionally, that argumentative boy with the bright orange hair.

Twice, he caught sight of his son, his daughter-in-law and a lad who was probably a grandson. Victor still looked like a mother's boy, a big soft thing who held Margaret Wotsername's arm and clung to the hand of the child. Each Sunday, Victor and his family visited Prudence. From various vantage points, Worthington watched Victor kissing Prudence and smiling kindly upon Cora Miles before climbing into his car. No chance there of any support, thought the watcher. Oh, when was it going to happen? When would that final opportunity arise?

It arrived when least expected, in the early part of December. He was sitting next to a blazing coal fire, a copy of *The Times* spread out, his feet resting on a brass fender that wanted polish. The house had got itself into a bit of a mess, with dirty dishes piled here and there, papers on the floor, a pile of washing on a chair. He had been surprised to discover that housework was rather complicated, that the organization of a tidy life required thought and effort. In London, the room had already been squalid, and the woman in the next room had done his washing for a couple of bob a week. Peace and solitude had its price, apparently.

He had loaded the copper and heaped coal on the fire, was preparing to tackle a dozen shirts and what seemed like a million items of underwear. While the water heated, he dozed in the warmth, his copy of the daily paper slipping down his chest, the top sheet flickering in time with his snores.

The alley was full of people in the dream. Something horrible was clawing its way out of a pile of wet cardboard and rotted food matter, its fleshless fingers clicking like a lobster's bony pincers. Everyone smiled and talked about the weather while the thing climbed into an erect position. It had no eyes, just circles of bone surrounded by tatters of yellowing skin.

Worthington jumped to wakefulness before the people in the alley could accuse him. He had scoured the *Bolton Evening News* each night, had pored over column after column, had searched headlines for news of his victim. Nothing. No-one had missed Simpson because he lived alone and had no permanent place of work. Even after all these weeks, the body had not been found. Surely, someone would miss him eventually? Surely his landlord would notify police that a tenant had gone missing?

He sat up, poked the fire, listened while the copper sang its intention to boil. There was a packet of Acdo in the scullery with some Lux flakes and a bar of plain green soap for his collars. Although he had no idea of how to go about the task, he leaned forward and gathered up his soiled clothing. Whites first. He knew that much, at least. Boil the whites, then soak the coloureds. As for Dolly-Blue and starch – well – he wouldn't bother, not on this trial run. At least he was making an effort. For months, his clothes had flapped greyly in the back garden after a quick swill in tepid water. It was time to pull himself together on the outside, at least.

When he remembered the dream, he froze. At first, he hadn't been bothered about anything, hadn't cared. After all, Simpson had been a ne'er do well with a drink problem and a marked aversion to work. For quite a long time, Worthington had been untroubled about being caught, philosophical about staying free. But the longer the corpse lay in that ginnel, the more obsessed he became. He should move it. He should stick it in a bag with a pile of bricks and tip it into the river.

A knock at the door wiped washing and crime out of his mind. Had they come for him? Apart from the milkman and the paper lad, no-one had visited the cottage. He walked towards the window, peeped through the lace curtain, saw a bike. It was a telegram boy.

He grabbed the envelope, pushed a florin into the boy's hand, slammed the door. It was happening. His eyes flew

over the words. ON MY WAY UP STOP ARRIVING TRINITY
STREET 6PM THURSDAY STOP MEET THE TRAIN STOP LOTTIE
STOP.

'Yes!' He jumped into the room, gathered up his shirts
and shoved them into the dresser. Another day would do.
This afternoon, he would drive to town and buy himself
some new clothes. After all, it wasn't every day a man
prepared for his wedding . . .

Lottie Crumpsall closed the window and plucked a mirror
from her handbag. The soot from the engine had done
little to enhance her appearance, so she used a great deal of
spit to rub the specks from her face. It was important to
return looking triumphant, she felt. There was no sense in
arriving with a face like a sweep's.

The man sitting opposite tried to ignore Lottie's far
from hygienic attempt at cleanliness. The woman was a
tart. From the bottoms of her high-heeled shoes to the top
of her ridiculous hat, this female looked every inch the
whore. He coughed, retreated behind his *Daily Herald*.

Lottie, unmoved by her companion's obvious disapproval, stood up and straightened her seams. The
lime-green skirt was cut short to show off her legs, and she
twisted this way and that to achieve a better picture of
what she considered to be her greatest assets. Had she
been able to do the impossible by walking behind herself,
she would surely have seen that the muscles, pushed out
of position by her teetering posture, bulged like the
biceps of a prize fighter beneath their veil of thirty-denier
nylon.

She righted the hat, made sure that it clung, just about,
to the left side of her head. Blond hair suited her, she
thought. The curls had gone a bit crisp with the perm on
top of bleach, but they would settle in time. When her face
was powdered and rouged, she applied bright red lipstick
in the middle of her lips, pouted at the Cupid's bow effect
she had created.

The man, fascinated in spite of himself, folded his newspaper and glanced again at the vision before him. In his opinion, however uneducated he might have been when it came to fashion, scarlet and lime-green did not make for a perfect partnership. And this strange person had used powder so pale that she looked as if she had quarrelled with a flour bin and lost the argument. Twin spots of rouge made a clown of her, while the low-cut blouse failed completely to achieve the effect she so clearly sought.

'What are you staring at?' Her voice was strange, high-pitched, with an accent that sat about halfway between mid-Lancashire and Jean Harlow.

'I'm sorry,' he managed. 'Are you American?'

She grinned, stuffed a stick of gum in her mouth and chewed noisily. 'Half and half,' she giggled. 'Want a piece?'

He wanted no piece of gum and no piece of her. 'No, thanks.'

'I'm coming home,' she advised him. 'To get married.'

'Really?' Perhaps her fiancé was blind. Or perhaps this had been a courtship carried out by post. God help the poor devil when he set eyes on this lot! 'Wonderful,' he added lamely.

'Known each other for years, of course. But I've been working in New York.' The 'new' came out as 'noo', while the second word, in accordance with Lancashire speech, emerged as 'Yoerk'. What a mess she was.

'Bought this costoom special,' she said. 'It was on sale in Macey's. I had to fight for it, but I always get what I want.'

The man pulled out his watch and wished time would fly.

'You married?' she asked, one finger and thumb stretching a length of gum from bared teeth.

He had never seen a grown woman playing with chewing gum. 'Yes, I'm married with three children.'

'I have a daughter,' drawled Lottie. 'Fourteen now. My intended's got a nice cottage up Bromley Cross. We're gonna live there after the wedding.'

He nodded, because he had run out of trite comments.

'So I've a lot to look forward to.' She pulled a manicure set from her bag and began sawing at her nails. He was a boring man, so she gave up on him. Another few minutes and she would be home. Home? She stopped the laugh from bubbling over into the carriage. For years, she'd had nowhere to call home. Morton Amerson had turned out to be a nasty piece of work. The bar position had never materialized, though she had certainly been placed in many other positions during her seven years abroad.

When her manicure was finished, she stared at her reflection in the dark mirror created by evening blackness behind the window. From day one, she had worked the clubs. Not as a barmaid or a waitress, but as a companion. As a companion-hostess, she had made the men pay for drinks, then for favours. Morton, her pimp, had allowed her twenty-five per cent of all she had earned. The wages were low so that the 'girls' could not escape.

Her Englishness had almost guaranteed that she would be busy. Enlivened by the idea of something different, men had queued to lie down with her. She twiddled the gum. The lying down hadn't been too bad, but she could have done without some of the sessions in back alleys and doorways. Well, she was away from all that now. Mr Worthington – Mr Westford – had sent her the money and she had escaped at last. Soon, she would be a decent married woman with a nice stone cottage and a daughter.

Thinking about Sally always made Lottie uneasy. Over the years, she had managed to forget the kid for most of the time, had been too busy staying alive and fit for work. But occasionally, in the dark hours of the few nights she had spent alone, she would wonder about Sally. She would never have another live kid. After all the proddings and probings by various 'doctors', her inner workings were useless. Anyway, who wanted to be pregnant at forty? She didn't look forty, she told herself by way of reassurance. She just looked tired. Anybody would have looked a bit worn out after half a dozen abortions and countless men with strange tastes.

Worthington, now Westford, was another oddity. Still, she reckoned she could cope with one pervert. With just the one, she would know where she stood. Or lay. She giggled, covered her mouth and pretended to cough, told the bloke that she'd swallowed some of her gum.

He rolled up his paper as the train slowed down. 'Bolton,' he advised her.

'I know.' For some reason, she was all excited. Was she looking forward to meeting Worthington again? No. She picked up her bag, gave the man a nice smile when he lifted down her suitcase. 'Ta,' she said.

He suddenly felt sorry for her. She was a grown-up infant with no idea of how to dress, how to behave. 'I hope you'll be happy,' he said before disappearing from her life.

Lottie sat on the edge of her seat. Happiness was not something she understood. She understood a full stomach, a not-too-cruel client, a laugh with the other girls who had shared the brownstone at the bottom end of 42nd Street. What was happiness?

As Lottie Crumpsall stumbled off the Manchester train onto Trinity Street's platform 1, she thought she had an answer. Someone of her own. Somebody who belonged to her and only to her. That kind of closeness came only from a child. She had a child, her own child, a daughter who had grown in her belly. Ivy Crumpsall had no rights at all when it came to Sally.

She saw the people on the platform, looked for Worthington, could not pick him out. An old man came forward and picked up her suitcase. 'Lottie,' he said quietly.

'Is that you?' she asked stupidly.

'No,' he replied, attempting some levity. 'It's my twin brother.'

She saw the shock in his face, knew that her own features wore a similar expression. This man was as old as Father Time.

'You've changed,' he remarked, a note of disapproval entering the words.

Lottie straightened her spine, decided that she would just get on with it. If she had to live with an old man, at least that was better than working the streets. 'You'll get used to me,' she advised him. 'And I suppose I'll get used to you.' It was only a matter of time, she told herself firmly. She needed Worthington. Through him, she might get a chance to reclaim the one person who might give her a taste of happiness.

'You look a bloody sight worse than you did before,' he said. 'What the hell happened?'

Lottie stood in front of the mirror and looked at herself. 'It's not so bad if the sun don't shine,' she told him. 'It only looks green in bright light.'

Westford sank into his chair. She was supposed to be cleaning up, but the place still looked like a rag yard. He had refused to marry a bottle blonde, so Lottie had been to a salon for a brown dye. She had come out khaki and she still looked like a tramp. 'We're supposed to be getting our daughter back,' he told her. 'Can't you find something decent to wear?'

Lottie looked down at her frock. It was the longest dress she had, and it reached halfway down her calves. Its only saving grace lay in the fact that it was a lovely colour called burnt tangerine. 'This is decent,' she snapped. 'I ain't wearing navy blue just to keep you happy, feller.'

'You'll do as you're told,' he advised her.

Lottie Crumpsall, whose travels had taken her thousands of miles into all kinds of trouble, was not afraid of this man. Next to Morton Amerson and his bully-boys, Andrew Worthington, now Alan Westford, was going to be a pussy cat. 'Don't tell me what I can't do and what I can do. Any more of your lip and I'll go after Sally without your help.'

He paused, thought for a second or two. 'What can you offer her? You've no place, no money, no chance of—'

'Aw, pipe down,' she shouted. 'Do you think I'm a crazy woman? I saved.' She had kept a tin under a loose floorboard, had stashed away the odd few dollars every week. Even when Morton had battered her, she had continued to lie, had insisted that she was not creaming off some of the profit. 'I got money,' she said now. 'Not a lot, but enough to set me up in a rented place till I find work.'

He stared at her. Who the hell would employ this woman? She was so unattractive, so coarse and shabby. 'We must do this together, Lottie. You won't get her back without me. We have to prove that there's a decent home for her, enough money to carry on her education and see to her needs.'

Lottie wet her fingers and smoothed her eyebrows before turning to look at him. 'I don't need you at all. She's my kid – that's not hard to prove. But who's to know that you're her real father? Anyway, I can't see the authorities being impressed by a bloke who lost a fortune, left his wife and tried to kidnap a child.'

He hung on to his temper, just about. It was vital that he kept peace with Lottie. Even if they didn't go through with the marriage, even if they didn't manage to get Sally away from Ivy, he wanted the old woman to know that he and Lottie would be here after her death. The realization that Lottie had returned for Sally would be sufficient to finish the old woman. If she knew that Sally's real father was waiting, too, she would surely perish in misery.

'I can wear a hat,' said Lottie.   •

'Yes, that would be an improvement.' He stood up, joined her at the mirror. 'Look, I'll take you to Manchester tomorrow and buy you a new outfit. I'm not completely poor, you know. I, too, have worked and saved.'

Lottie turned once more and viewed their reflection. 'What happened to you?' she asked. 'You've shrunk like a prune.'

Again, he sat on his anger. 'We're none of us the same as we were, Lottie. Now. Are you going to clean up a bit?' He waved an arm across the untidy room.

Lottie shrugged. 'I ain't used to it,' she advised him. 'We had servants.' The 'servants' had been young girls serving a sort of apprenticeship. These unfortunates had swept and polished until they reached the age when they, too, could earn money in a horizontal position. 'Cleaning is one thing I can't do.'

He took a deep breath. 'Let's do it together, then. I'll sweep while you dust.' Andrew Worthington listened to Alan Westford, found him pathetic. No way would the owner of Paradise have taken up a sweeping brush. But he wanted everything to be right, wanted to make sure that he and Lottie were organized in case the Welfare stepped into the arena. As he moved a stack of dishes, he wondered again what the outcome would be. Sally had been safe all these years, but she had been living with a grandmother who was no blood relative. Maureen and Tom Marchant might bring in some big guns to oppose Lottie's claim, but neither were they related by blood to Sally Crumpsall.

He pushed some cold potato into the bin, clanged the lid, scowled at the woman next door who was hanging out her sheets. The Heilbergs would come in on the act, no doubt. As long as they knew that he and Lottie were in the vicinity, they would be upset and anxious about the girl's future. As long as they all knew that the girl's mother and father would be visiting with gifts and treats . . . He would have to marry Lottie, there was nothing else for it. The thought of Joseph Heilberg's face when his old enemy claimed Sally as his own daughter . . . Westford went inside and slammed the door, a smile lingering at the corners of his mouth.

In the sitting room, Alan Westford took charge. 'Our

surname will be Westford,' he informed Lottie. 'I've changed my name by deed poll. You'll be Mrs Westford.'

Mrs Westford-to-be put down the nail-file and took up a yellow duster. She wasn't sure. 'I've not made my mind up yet,' she told him airily. 'I might not be the marrying type.'

Westford stifled a growl. 'Nice jewellers in Manchester,' he said. 'A new outfit and an engagement ring?'

Lottie flicked a bit of dust around the dresser. 'I'll think about it,' she said.

They were all in Ivy's house having the usual Friday treat – cod, chips and peas from the fat ladies' chip shop on Tonge Moor Road. Of course, the place wasn't called the Fat Ladies', but the pair of women who ran it were huge and friendly, always gave a waiting child a couple of hot chips wrapped in a little paper holder to keep fingers safe.

'Eeh, that were good,' sighed Ivy. She had rallied yet again, was up and about, though she still had to be pushed in the chair from time to time.

Prudence, who thoroughly enjoyed not being a lady, screwed up the paper that had contained her supper, then licked vinegar from her fingers.

'The state of you,' chided Ivy, who always had a plate. 'Anybody'd think you were dragged up at the bottom end of Deane Road with jam jars for cups and nits in your hair.'

Prudence shrugged, tossed the ball of newsprint into the grate.

Sally retrieved it, threw it to Red. Red feinted to the right, bowled to the left, grinned when Cora Miles caught the missile. 'You can't fool me,' said Cora, who had grown used to the young imp.

Ivy watched the impromptu game, smiled to herself. They were both doing so well. Sal was near the top of her class in everything except French, while Red Trubshaw, that mucky urchin from the slums, had long since left his science teacher at the starting post. 'Give over,' she told the assembly. 'You know I get a stitch when I laugh.'

Sally yawned, caught the bundle of paper and fed it to the fire. 'Where's Gert?' she asked.

Ivy shrugged. 'She's all mithered because she's not seen yon daft husband of hers for a few weeks. I think she's gone piking up Bromwich Street to see if he's moved. If he has moved, it'll be the first time he's showed any signs of life. If he were burning, he'd be too lazy to run away from the fire.' She stopped abruptly, remembered that Bert had been closely acquainted with the flames that had temporarily damaged the hands of a good friend. 'Gert won't be long,' she told her granddaughter. 'All she has to do is find the pub nearest to his lodgings.'

As if summoned by the conversation, Gert burst into the room, her face flushed. 'He's gone,' she announced. 'There were a black pudding in the meat safe crawling with maggots. Bread and milk's gone green, and I chucked out a pound of stinking manifold. Nobody's seen him for ages and the landlord says he's going to let the room if Bert doesn't come back soon.'

Prudence closed her eyes. For weeks, she had forced herself to carry on as normal in spite of a . . . a what? A feeling, a silly premonition that had plagued her since Rosie Blunt's funeral? It was as if she were being watched or followed. Cora was worried, too. Even through closed eyelids, Prudence could feel Cora's gaze. 'You must tell the police,' she said.

'Don't worry, I have,' replied Gert. 'They talk as if he's left of his own accord, like. They kept telling me about some bloke who went out for a box of matches in 1936 and never came back. But I know Bert. He wouldn't have gone without eating his tripe. He wouldn't have gone without his money. There were fifteen and thre'pence in one of his old boots. Landlord had been through the place looking for rent, like, but he never found that bit of savings.' She opened her fingers and let the money trickle out into the other hand. 'He's dead,' she pronounced.

Sally walked across the room and put her arms round the woman she had never called Aunt. Gert was more like a friend, a chosen person who was a valued part of Sally's life. 'They'll find him,' she said softly. 'They will. Have they tried the hospitals? If he had to go in suddenly, he might have been forced to leave all his things.'

Gert nodded jerkily. 'They're doing that now, love, going round all the hospitals. That's me only hope, isn't it? All I can pray for is that he's had an accident or a funny stomach again.' She swallowed. 'But unless it were TB or summat, they'd not keep him this long. With TB, he'd have got warning. He'd have been able to tell me about it.' Her head dropped. 'No, he's not in no sanatorium, Sal. He'd have wrote to me so's I'd visit him.'

Sally understood Gert's terrible dilemma. Without knowing all the details, she realized that Gert loved a man who was not good enough for her. Love had nothing to do with reason, Sally thought now. You could love somebody without liking them. Sally had loved her own mother, had even missed her for a while, but there seemed to be nothing likeable about Lottie Crumpsall.

Red joined Sally and Gert. 'I'd best get searching,' he said. 'I'll fetch the Spencer Street gang out. There'll have to be an armistice between Spencers and Worthingtons while this search gets going.' Realizing what he had said, he smiled apologetically at Prudence. 'They fight one another, them two streets,' he said.

Prudence nodded. 'Yes.' There was enmity between the two who had named the streets, and confirmation of this further trouble served only to make her more uneasy. Spencers and Worthingtons should never have met. She gulped down some air. No-one knew the whereabouts of her ex-husband, either. She and Gert were in the same situation, though Gert did retain some affection for her man. Oh, surely Bert's disappearance had nothing to do with this . . . this feeling? It wasn't even a feeling, she informed herself. It was just a lump in her chest, a heavy mass that sometimes made swallowing difficult. 'Do what you can, Red. Will you go home or come home?'

'Go,' he answered. 'I'll stop with Mam for a couple of nights.' With no sign of embarrassment, he kissed his adoptive mother and Cora Miles. 'See you soon,' he said before disappearing into the night.

Ivy's rheumy eyes fixed themselves on Prudence Spencer's face. 'What's up with you?' she asked. 'You've had a face like the dog's dinner for months.'

Prudence shrugged. 'A bit of indigestion,' she replied lamely.

'Then you'd best get a spoonful of bicarb and go to the doctor's on Monday.' That was not stomach trouble, thought Ivy as her good friend left the room. 'Is she fretting?' she asked Cora.

Cora shrugged, didn't want to upset the frail old lady. 'It comes and goes,' she answered. With her hands joined in her lap, she prayed for God to take away Prudence Spencer's troubles.

SIXTEEN

Lottie was worried. As Mrs Alan Westford, she had the status of a married woman, a house that promised to be pretty once she got round to cleaning it, and a husband whose sexual appetite had dwindled to nothing. At the age of forty, Lottie remained young in her mind, had never considered herself to be ageing. But being stuck with a man of sixty-eight was not her idea of fun. The thing that bothered her most was the terrible coldness in his expression. Sometimes, when the two of them talked about getting Sally back, the ice would melt a little, and he would liven up considerably. Lottie knew that it was anger that melted the frost, and she was not comfortable living day to day with the man's terrifying pent-up rage.

She placed some whites in the dolly, picked up the posser and stamped it against the washing. He was inside messing with a second-hand Hoover cleaner, a terrible thing that coughed and spat dust all over the place. In the lean-to scullery, Lottie lit a cigarette and warmed her hands by cupping them round the match.

She felt that nothing would ever warm her soul again, though. Her attitude was a puzzle, because she ought to be grateful, really. She had entertained so many men in the past that a rest should have been welcome. Yet she missed being held, kissed, stroked, talked to. If she thought about it, the final act had been an also-ran, a thing to be endured. She dragged at the Woodbine, spat a bit of loose tobacco into the suds. Sometimes, she had enjoyed being with a man, had achieved her share of pleasurable moments. But that had happened when her partner had been kind, gentle and talkative.

Lottie dragged out a shirt, pushed it through the mangle and into the sink for rinsing. He wanted his shirts white, he had insisted. She toyed with a packet of Dolly-Blue, couldn't be bothered with the instructions, threw it in with the rinse water.

'What are you doing?'

She turned on her heel, looked him up and down. 'Flying an aeroplane,' she replied.

'I've fixed the Hoover.'

'Good.' She dipped the Woodbine in the water, threw it into a bucket. 'I'll be done soon.'

He stared at her for a few seconds. 'Where did you go yesterday afternoon?'

Lottie shrugged. 'Here and there. Shopping.'

'For what?'

Again, she raised her shoulders. 'Nowt. I found nowt worth buying.'

Westford frowned. 'The word is "nothing" Charlotte. You must learn to improve your speech.'

With the washing pincers held aloft, she approached him. 'My name is Lottie. I can't be doing with the full handle, and I ain't taking no elocution lessons from you, neither. Who do you think you are, eh? A mill owner?' She laughed mirthlessly. 'If you'd still owned Paradise, you'd never have looked at me. I'm here because I'm useful. I'm here because you want to get Sally away from Ivy and that po-faced first wife of yours. But if you think I vomited my way across the Atlantic in that rotten boat just to do your bloody washing, you'd better go and get your head tested for woodworm.' She slammed down the pincers and pushed past him.

He followed, watched as she dragged on her coat. 'Where are you going?'

Lottie grinned. 'That's for me to know and for you to worry about.' She measured his temper by the quick movements of his now sunken eyes. 'Go on. Hit me.'

He closed his fists tightly, slammed a hand against each side of his body. His anger must continue hidden, he told himself. If he alienated Lottie, his chances of having his day with the Crumpsalls, the Marchants and the Heilbergs would be greatly reduced. 'I'll see you later,' he managed at last.

'Don't hold your breath,' advised Lottie. 'I'll come back when I'm good and ready.' She turned towards the front door, stopped, looked over her shoulder. 'Oh, by the way – you'd best see to them shirts before the water gets cold. If you want 'em white, you have to wash 'em hot.'

Westford glared at the closed door for at least a minute after his wife had left. What the hell had he done? She was ugly, she couldn't cook, wash or sew. Sighing deeply, he walked to the scullery to rescue a shirt soaked in enough Dolly-Blue to turn it navy. The one piece of sanity he clung to was the knowledge that Lottie was Sally's mother. Surely no-one could keep a child from its natural parents? He turned on the tap and rinsed the shirt. It would all come out in the wash. Wouldn't it?

The school was on Chorley New Road. Lottie had stood here at letting-out time for three days on the trot, and she had at last plucked up enough courage to ask about her daughter. On the previous day, a girl had pointed out Sally, but Sally had been getting on a bus with some other girls. Lottie sighed, pulled up the collar of her coat. School would probably close today for Christmas.

She didn't really know why she was here. Yesterday, when she had finally seen her little girl, she had been terrified. Sally wasn't a little girl. She was as tall as Lottie, with a healthy body and the sort of hair that should belong to a film star. Unconsciously, Lottie fingered the mass of greenish-brown frizz that peeped out beneath the front fold of her headscarf. Sally was above her and beyond her.

She didn't deserve such a daughter, not after the way she'd carried on.

The school doors opened and the girls came out. They didn't push and shove and scream like normal children, because this was Bolton School. At Bolton School, the pupils did Greek, Latin, the sciences. Lottie, who considered herself to be as thick as a double-brick wall, tried to melt behind a tree. She was a sight. Even in this fur coat he'd bought her she looked a freak. Even if she took off her gloves and flashed the three diamonds on a twist, she would still be out of place.

Her heart seemed to turn upside down when she realized that the group crossing the road towards her included Sally. She grabbed her dorothy bag, opened it, pretended to search for something.

'Sally already has a boyfriend,' laughed one of the girls. 'She lives next door to the famous Arthur Trubshaw.'

'Be quiet, Chloe.' Lottie had just heard her daughter's voice for the first time in over seven years. 'He is not my boyfriend. Red's more of a brother.'

Another girl spoke. 'He'll walk into Oxbridge without even trying. I'm sure he's ready now, before the Higher Certificate. Supposed to be a genius.'

Sally giggled. 'Whereas I will have to master French first.'

'Oh, you're fine now, Sally. Sixty per cent isn't bad.'

'Not where my grandmother's concerned,' answered Sally. 'She accepts nothing less than a ninety, and even then she wants to know what happened to the other ten. Come on, girls, there's the bus.'

Lottie sagged with relief and shock. Her daughter talked like a woman, an educated woman. Sally's mother lingered near the tree long after the bus had moved off with its cargo of chattering young people. 'You don't belong here,' she told herself in a whisper. 'That girl has no need of you.' And no need of the monster that showed sometimes in the eyes of Alan Westford.

After realizing how cold she had become, Lottie began the long walk to . . . to where? She wandered on in a more or less straight line, turned left at the fire station, continued until she found herself at the junction of Bradshawgate, Churchgate, Deansgate and Bank Street. Should she go left or right? Should she carry on or double back to a bus stop? Before taking time to think, she strode down the slope of Bank Street, her head down, her feet slipping against a thin film of ice. It took her a long time to reach Crompton Way, and she was glad that she had found Ivy's address among papers at the cottage. Crompton Way was a ring road, but Westford's notes had been with a map he had drawn, so Lottie was able to place the house between Thicketford Road and Bury Road.

She stood on the opposite side, looked across the road and saw her daughter again. Sally, who seemed to be alone in the front parlour, was pinning a bunch of holly above the fireplace. Festoons of crêpe paper hung from the ceiling, and a wreath of fir and ribbon was fastened to the front door. Christmas. When had she, Lottie Westford, previously Crumpsall, née Kerrigan had a Christmas? Mam had always been drunk, too drunk for cooking and filling stockings. Lottie should have learned from her mother, should have made sure that her little daughter had enjoyed a few decent Christmases. Derek had bought little gifts, had trimmed a tree once or twice.

Tears trickled down her face, threatened to freeze in the merciless cold. Her exhalations hung in the air like miniature clouds, and her hands were numb even though encased in thick gloves. How she wanted to walk to that door and raise the knocker above the yule-tide decoration. How she wanted to sit with Sally by a roaring fire. They could drink tea and have a mince pie and talk about Sally's dreams for the future.

Reluctantly, Lottie left the scene and cut through to Tonge Moor Road. Here, she could catch a bus for Bromley Cross and home. But home was a man with a stony heart and no love. Perhaps Sally would change all that. Next year, the three of them might sit down to eat a Christmas dinner with all the trimmings, candles, silver thre'pences in the pudding, an iced cake.

When her long journey was over, she trudged up the path to the cottage, braced herself, threw open the door.

'Where've you been?' he asked.

She pulled off her gloves, held out blue fingers to the fire. 'Looking at me daughter,' she replied. 'We leave her till after Christmas.'

Westford, who had been looking forward with glee to the chance of ruining Ivy Crumpsall's seasonal festivities, said nothing. There was an edge to Lottie, a coating she had acquired overseas. She was manageable, but only just. He speared a piece of bread and held it to the fire. 'Toast?' he asked.

Lottie made no reply.

They'd had a terrific Christmas. Red, who had matured considerably, was now sufficiently genteel to use his stink bombs outdoors. The recipe he had perfected over recent months produced a remarkable stench that went far beyond any smell created by a shop-bought bomb. When he had released three on Crompton Way on Christmas morning, dogs had howled, cats had fled the neighbourhood and four housewives had spent an hour or so fretting because they thought the smell was their meat going off.

Sally and Red sat on the wall. 'I think I'll try for Imperial in London,' he said. 'Oxford and Cambridge would be too hoity-toity for me.'

'No, they wouldn't. Education's for everybody these days, and you're cleverer than most. Oxford's so beautiful. You'd love it.' She poked him in the ribs. 'Are you going to get a degree in stink bombs?'

He awarded her a glance that was meant to be withering. 'Physics,' he told her. 'I want to get into something new. Like nuclear energy.'

It was all a mystery to Sally. She enjoyed the classics, was not particularly inspired by pipettes, Bunsen burners and the digestive system of a worm. 'Mrs Spencer's gone strange again.' She jerked a thumb towards the house that was a twin to hers. 'Depressed, Gran says.'

Red stuck out his tongue, said he could taste snow on the way. 'She'll be all right,' he said. 'Living with Worthington all those years didn't do her any good.'

Sally sighed, tried to think about something else. Derek was her dad. Ever since pneumonia, she had managed to keep that knowledge wedged safely inside her head. But Worthington had performed the mechanical act which had started her existence. 'Does she think he's come back, then?'

Red shrugged. 'She's not said. But she sits still a lot, as if she's waiting for something.' He looked over his shoulder and waved at Ivy. 'Is your gran in there on her own?'

Sally nodded. 'Gert's still out somewhere looking for Bert. She's strange, you know. First she tells me that he's no good, that I've missed nothing because he wouldn't have been any use as an uncle. Then she starts running about wringing her hands looking for him.'

The boy nodded sagely. 'That's love,' he informed her. 'It doesn't make sense because it doesn't have to. Take my old man. If you do take him, you're welcome, but wear a suit of armour. He's a right bastard, always clouting my mother and screaming at the kids. But Mam loves him. She's always saving him the best bits of meat and ironing his clothes just the way he likes them.' He shook his head slowly. 'No sense at all. She should have thrown him out years ago, but she can't. It's like that with Gert and Bert.'

Sally jumped down. 'Coming? I don't like leaving her alone for too long.'

'Right.' He got down from the wall and walked towards one of the people who had saved him all those years ago. He was well-fed, well-educated; he had stopped being an urchin. All the same, he thought as he entered Ivy's house, the people at number 200 deserved a stink bomb. They

387

were always peeping through the curtains, always trying to keep one step in front of everyone else.

He paused on the doorstep, watched while the woman at 200 backed away from the window. Yes. He would plant a nice big one in her garden tomorrow, one with a delayed action that would not give off its odour until it rained or snowed. That should get her back up. She'd probably have her husband and son scrubbing for days while she sat on the sofa with the vapours. He laughed at the pun and closed the door, was glad that he had not abandoned his roots completely.

'Go on,' he urged. 'There's no point in sitting here. At this rate, next Christmas could come round before you've made your move.'

Lottie edged away from her husband. She hated to be near him, couldn't stand the sound or the smell of him. They slept in separate bedrooms because of his snoring. She looked down at her wedding band and engagement ring, wondered briefly about grounds for annulment. He snored, all right, but not enough to merit such total isolation. The man had never kissed her, not even in the registry office. He had merely forced the ring onto her finger, scowled at the registrar, then steered his new wife out of the building. 'Why did you marry me?' she asked.

He thumped the steering-wheel with the heel of a leather-gloved hand. 'What sort of a question is that? And what sort of a time is this to be asking?'

'I want an answer.'

He turned his head and looked at her. 'Because it was the right thing. Because Sally's our daughter and she's living with a very old woman who might not last till Easter.'

Lottie opened her bag and took out a small mirror. 'Why didn't you marry one of the others, then? You've a dozen or more kids you could feel sorry for.'

'Sally's bright. She deserves a chance.'

She closed the bag with a loud snap. 'She's getting her chance. She's at a damned good school and she's living in a lovely house. My sister's living with her, so we know she'll be all right. Our Gert might be a bit of a daft bugger, but she won't turn her back on Sally once Ivy's dead. Why can't we leave her where she is?'

Westford ground his teeth, held back an oath. 'Look, I want to do one decent thing before I die. I want to make sure that our child has the best.'

Lottie stifled a groan, opened the van door, stepped outside. With her heart fluttering like a cabbage-white butterfly, she walked towards the house. She didn't know what she wanted any more. It would be nice to have a daughter. It would be nice to get the opportunity to make things right with Sally. But time and geography had distanced mother and child, and Sally might not be willing to allow her mother a second chance. She walked up the path and knocked.

'Who is it? Come in unless you want money.'

Lottie closed her eyes and was transported back seven years and two miles. They closed in on her, tore her clothes, took her money and spattered her with rotten tomatoes. The voice she had just heard belonged to the woman behind that horrible farewell.

'Come in, I said.'

Lottie entered the hall, saw a runner of red carpet with polished parquet round its edges. A grandmother clock ticked. Pegs on a light oak coat stand bore scarves, jackets, a black blazer with a Bolton School crest on its pocket. She touched it, breathed it in, tried to discover the scent of her daughter.

'Who is it?'

'It's me, Ivy,' she answered.

The clock struck the hour. Lottie lifted her head and saw a photograph on the wall. It was Sally. Perhaps she should just take this and run, because she was so afraid of the woman behind the door.

'Get in here, Lottie,' said the disembodied voice. 'I knew you'd be back. Bad pennies always turn up at the finish.'

Shaking in her shoes, Lottie Westford entered the living room. A very old, thin woman sat next to the fire, her hair sparse and white, her hands pale and folded on a bony lap. 'Hello, Ivy,' Lottie managed at last.

Ivy inclined her head very slightly. 'Sit down. Sorry I can't make a brew, only this is one of me bad days.'

The visitor perched uncomfortably on the edge of an armchair. It was a lovely room, clean as a new pin, furnished well and with carpet of a warm, welcoming red. 'Arthritis?' she asked.

'Aye. Me bones are crumbling away to nowt.'

'That's a shame.'

Ivy cleared her throat, took a sip of water from a glass at her elbow. 'You sound like a Yank.'

'I was over there a long time.'

'Yes. Yes, you were gone a fair while.' Ivy replaced the tumbler on a little side table. 'What brings you back?'

Lottie shrugged, remembered her husband's instructions. 'I'm married. We live on Darwen Road up Bromley Cross.'

'Oh.'

'He's called Westford. Alan Westford.' She had been forbidden to disclose her husband's true identity at this early stage. 'I'd like to see Sally.'

The old woman's eyes were hard as she fixed them on her daughter-in-law. 'Why? You never wrote to her, never sent a card on her birthday or at Christmas. Sally's likely forgot all about you.'

Lottie inhaled deeply. 'She's my daughter, Ivy. I know there's no love lost between you and me, but you have to admit that I'm Sally's mother. I've got rights, you know.'

Ivy's facial expression did not change. 'So has she. She had a right to a mother when she were a little lass, only she never had no mother. She had a right to a hot dinner every day, but it were the neighbours as kept her fed. She has a right to good schooling and a loving home, and she's got them things now. It's not all down to me, you know. Loads of folk love our Sal. There's Tom Goodfellow – only his real name's Marchant – and his wife. Then there's the Heilbergs and Sally's Auntie Gert. Just you leave that lass be, Lottie. Sally's already a woman of property – she has a country house in Hampshire. She's got a good future to look forward to. We've all looked after her between us. You can't come and uproot her just to suit yourself.' Exhausted by the monologue, Ivy leaned back against the cushions.

'I've changed,' mumbled Lottie.

'Have you? What have you changed into?'

Lottie licked her dry lips. 'I'm married. I've got a house with a garden and countryside near it. She should live with me now. What happens when you're not here?'

Ivy raised her head once more. 'It's all been seen to.'

'How? You can't go making arrangements behind my back.'

The invalid's mouth curled into a snarl. 'What were we supposed to do, then? We never knew where you were. It were you as turned your back, Lottie Kerrigan—'

'Westford.'

'A rose by any other name, Lottie. Now, I want you to get out of my house and do what you did all them years ago. Just walk away. Just set off and keep going till you reach the other side of the world. You're not needed. Sally doesn't need a mother like you. That might be a fur coat, but it does nowt for you. Can you imagine how that poor girl would feel if you turned up at prize-giving? You're a tramp, Lottie Kerrigan. No amount of money and good clothes would make a silk purse out of you.' Ivy licked parched lips. 'Now, bugger off out of it.'

Lottie rose to her feet, stumbled over the edge of the hearthrug. She knew how she looked. She knew that no matter how hard she tried, she always came out cheap.

'It's inside I've changed, Ivy,' she said softly. 'In a place where it doesn't show.'

Ivy made no reply.

'You have to make space for folk to improve themselves, you know. I'm older and I've got more sense than I had. I'm older and I've a right to see my only child.' She fastened the buttons on her best coat. 'If you want to be difficult, just carry on. My husband will see a solicitor about all this.' With her head held high, she stalked out of the room.

'Keep away,' called Ivy. 'I'll not fight fair, Lottie.'

'No,' replied the unwelcome guest. 'You never did. That carry-on on Trinity Street weren't fair, half a dozen against one woman. Well, just you wait, that's all I can say.' She slammed her way out of the house.

Ivy waited. She waited until Lottie had been gone for five minutes, then she struggled to her feet, picked up the poker and clattered it against the party wall. Prudence would know what to do. Prudence could telephone Tom and Maureen. Between them and the Heilbergs, they could surely save Sal.

Finding the address hadn't been too difficult. Ivy had made a mental note of the name Westford, had remembered Darwen Road in Bromley Cross. Tom had simply walked into the nearest newsagent and asked for help in tracing his 'brother'.

Tom Marchant stood on Darwen Road, his eyes glued to an end cottage across the way. A man sat by a fire, the evening paper making a barrier in front of his upper body. Every time a page was turned, Tom got a fleeting view of the man's face. He seemed to be seventyish, very wrinkled and grey-complexioned. So this was Lottie Crumpsall's new husband. The word 'new' seemed inappropriate, because the shrivelled man looked as if he had lived twice over in the same skin.

With a hand that trembled in the freezing cold, Tom

undid the catch on a leather case, pulled out a pair of binoculars and pushed the strap of the case further up his shoulder. He stared through the glasses for at least a minute, his breath seeming to hold itself while he studied the seated man.

Back in the car, Tom sat completely motionless, his hands resting on the wheel. It couldn't be. No, no, that wasn't Andrew Worthington. After a moment or two, he made a decision. There was one person in this town who would have an answer. His flesh crawled when he remembered Prudence's tortured face. Of late, she had been quiet, almost depressed, as if waiting for the sky to fall on her head. Tom was a great believer in the sixth sense. As a country boy, he had often noticed how animals 'knew' when danger was near. People were just overdeveloped animals. Many had retained the ability to sniff out misfortune or threat.

He started the car, drove down what locals called the 'brew', made for Crompton Way. He needed to be careful and discreet. No-one else knew about the return of Sally's mother. For the time being, he and Ivy were keeping the news to themselves.

Fortunately, Prudence was alone. Red had gone to visit his family, while Cora Miles had accompanied Gert from next door on another mission to the central police station, because Bert was still missing. 'What is it, Tom?' asked Prudence.

He told her. While he skirted the main cause of his concern, she watched him closely, her face remaining calm, as if what she heard came as no surprise. 'You think it's Andrew, don't you?'

Tom nodded, could find no words.

'I'll get my coat.'

He followed her into the hallway. 'The curtains may be closed by now,' he said.

She fastened her coat, tied a silk scarf around her throat, picked up a pair of fur gloves. 'Curtains will be no

393

hindrance for me, Tom. I already know he's there, you see. If necessary, I shall knock at the door and ask after his health.'

Tom placed a hand on her shoulder, felt the stiffness in her muscles. 'Prudence, my dear, do you think you should—?'

'Oh, but I do. Indeed, I do.' The clear, china-blue eyes searched his face. 'Tom, I need the relief of knowing properly. I need to be sure that I'm not going insane.'

He bowed to the inevitable. This good lady had been making excuses for weeks, had been no further than next door during Christmas and New Year. Soon, the full-blown agoraphobia could return unless someone jolted her out of the doldrums.

As he turned the key and whipped the engine to life, he wished with all his heart that the reason for Prudence's journey could be less traumatic. But they had to go, had to find out.

'What's his name?' she asked as they turned into Tonge Moor Road.

'Westford. Alan Westford.'

A long sigh escaped her lips. 'Just as I thought. He would never completely relinquish his name. A megalomaniac would always hang on to his initials. Whatever we need to do, we must make sure that Sally is kept away from him.'

'You're sure he's Worthington?'

Prudence nodded. 'I'm absolutely certain.'

They argued for ten minutes. 'You should not go in there alone,' Tom insisted.

Prudence, strangely calm, wanted no company. 'It's my nightmare. If I'm not out within a reasonable time, you may come in. If his wife's with him, I should be safe enough.' She got out of the car. 'Stay,' she told him, smiling when she saw him panting like an obedient dog. 'Sorry. I didn't mean to be abrupt.'

'Be careful,' he muttered to himself as he watched her walking up the path. Light showed through closed curtains, but he would have no way of seeing inside the room. He folded his arms, tried to warm cold fingers.

Prudence stood for a moment on the step, her hand raised to the lion's head door-knocker. She could sense Andrew's nearness. It wasn't a smell, wasn't anything she saw or heard, but she simply knew that the man she had married was behind this door. She knocked.

After a few seconds, she knocked again. The door opened to reveal a wedge of light and the left side of a woman's face. 'Hello?' said the apparition. 'Who is it?'

Prudence cleared her throat. 'Prudence Spencer. I used to be Worthington.'

'Oh.' The head bobbed up and down, then a hand came forward and touched the frizzy hair. 'What do you want?'

'To see Worthington.'

'Oh.' Lottie wavered, didn't know what to say or do. Had she said anything out of place to Ivy Crumpsall? She bit her lip. No, no, she had definitely told the old woman that her husband's name was Alan Westford. 'There's no Worthingtons here, sorry.' The door began to close, but Prudence moved quickly, copied the age-old trick of tradesfolk by wedging her foot in the gap.

Lottie glanced down at the lambskin boot. She was unable to close the door. She was unable to tell the woman to bugger off, because Prudence Worthington – or Spencer – was as near to gentry as Lottie had ever encountered.

A man's voice called, 'Shut that bloody door, Lottie.'

Prudence froze. She was already cold on the outside, but hearing him and knowing that her instincts had been right almost undid her altogether. A lump of frost descended to her stomach. 'Let me in,' she said softly. 'Let me in immediately.'

Lottie turned and fled up the stairs, leaving Prudence with one foot in the house and the other on the doorstep.

After a second or two, the visitor stepped into the house, careful to leave the door slightly ajar. She needed an escape route. Just in case she couldn't cope, she wanted an easy way out of what promised to be a terrifying situation. The panic touched her mind, caressed it, swallowed it, sent darts right through her body. The need to run was almost overwhelming, yet she had to persevere for Sally's sake.

'Who the hell is it?' He walked into the tiny hallway, stopped in his tracks when he answered his own question. 'Prudence.'

'I . . . I'm not alone,' she stammered. 'There's someone waiting for me outside.'

He stepped away, backed into the living room. 'Lottie?' he screamed.

'It's not her fault,' said Prudence. 'I guessed. I've known for weeks that you were back.'

He walked to the fireplace, stood with his back to the flames.

Prudence remembered that posture. Whenever she had 'done wrong', he had assumed this stance while delivering a lecture. She stared at him for what seemed an endless time, knew that she would have recognized him even in the dark. He seemed shorter, less square about the shoulders. The eyes, which had always been convex, looked as if they had been pushed into his head, because the once-firm flesh around them had collapsed into unhealthy, grey folds. 'What are you doing here?' she asked eventually.

He lifted his shoulders. 'Free country, isn't it?'

'There are people here who would dance on your grave,' she advised him unnecessarily. 'Women, particularly.'

The eyes screwed themselves tightly as he lit a cigarette from the end of another. 'Since you cleaned me out, you've kindly paid my so-called debts in that sphere. So I've nothing to worry about.'

'Except Sally.' Prudence heard the change in his

breathing, watched a vein as it swelled on his left temple.
'You have come for Sally. You have married that poor,
stupid woman just so that you might take away Ivy's
granddaughter.' She lifted a hand, waited until he had
closed his mouth against the words he wanted to say.
'Hear me out, Andrew—'

'Alan,' he snapped.

She chose to ignore the interruption. 'Listen for once in
your life. Lottie was gone for seven years. There was no
word from her, no message. As is the case when a spouse
goes missing, Lottie was declared dead by the authorities.
Ivy and Tom had papers drawn up in view of Sally's status
as an orphan. Sally is already adopted, Andrew. Her
guardians are Maureen and Tom Marchant. Sally has
continued to live with the grandmother who—'

'She's no grandmother to that child—'

'With the grandmother who has cared for her since
Lottie's disappearance. Lottie abandoned a defenceless
seven-year-old whose father lay dying. No welfare
committee on this earth would send Sally back to her
mother. No court in Britain is going to allow that young
girl to live with you and Lottie.'

Strangely, he was not surprised to hear any of this. Just
as he had not thought about Bert Simpson, he had ignored
reason when thinking about Sally. His only wish had
been to frighten Ivy Crumpsall literally to death. Lottie's
visit to Crompton Way had not been enough, but his own
planned appearance as Sally's rightful father might have
done the trick. And the woman standing here had
removed his chance of pleasure. 'Get out,' he growled.

'I'm not afraid of you any more.' This was the truth. At
last, he was becoming a creature of little import. 'I know
your game, you see. You're fully aware that you and Lottie
won't get Sally. You've never expected to become a father
to her. But your physical presence in the Bolton area is
supposedly sufficient to upset the apple-cart, as is your
alliance with Sally's mother. Checkmate, Andrew. We've

been one step ahead of you for many years.'

He took a stride towards her, stopped abruptly when Lottie appeared in the doorway. 'What are you up to now?' he asked.

Lottie placed a large bag on the floor. 'I'm off,' she told him. She touched Prudence's shoulder. 'Will you give me a lift to town, please?'

'Of course.'

Westford looked at his two wives. Prudence had aged well, was smart and stylish in the dark brown coat. Lottie looked like a magnified version of a cheap prize from Bolton's visiting fair, a badly made doll that had fallen off a shelf to be trampled underfoot by thoughtless pleasure-seekers. And that, he supposed, was exactly what had happened to her in real life. That was what she had deserved, too. 'Bugger off, the pair of you,' he shouted.

Lottie came to stand beside her husband's first wife. 'Listen to me and all,' she said quietly. 'If you go within a mile of my daughter, I'll bloody swing for you.'

Prudence nodded. 'They will need a double gibbet. I, too, am prepared to swing in order to save Sally. I imagine that the Marchants and the Heilbergs have a similar opinion. Sally belongs to all of us, you see. We are all taking care of her. We are all making sure that she gets the best of everything. You are not on the list, Andrew.' She took Lottie's arm. 'Shall we go?'

'Aye.' Without a backward glance, Lottie left her husband and showed no emotion until she was seated in the car.

'Don't cry,' said Prudence.

'I'm not crying,' replied Lottie. 'It's just the relief leaking out of me.'

SEVENTEEN

Sally Crumpsall entered the Pack Horse Inn through the side entrance on Nelson Square. People were going in and out of the education offices or scurrying about with shopping bags, while a man on the corner was pointing out a hat in the window of a gentleman's outfitter's. An assistant stood beside him, the white tape measure around his neck betraying his status. Sally looked at the everyday scene, smiled when a furious attendant chased a lad out of the public toilets. 'Yer not supposed fer t'play marbles in yon,' roared the man as he waved his long-handled mop at the miscreant. 'Them is conveniences, not playgrounds.' A few years ago, Red Trubshaw might have been up to that sort of trick.

She pushed the inner door, went inside. A man at the reception desk looked up. 'Yes, miss?'

Sally undid her coat, smoothed her hair, straightened the collar of her blouse. 'I'm here to see Mrs Crumpsall,' she informed him. 'Only she might be Mrs Worthington. I mean . . . I mean Mrs Westford.' Her cheeks glowed with embarrassment. Had she mentioned Kerrigan, her mother would have had four names to choose from. Determinedly, she stood her ground without biting her nails. She had given up biting her nails, even when standing in a strange place without knowing her own mother's name.

Unaffected by Sally's disquiet, the seasoned clerk pored over the guest register, pinpointed a room. He was used to this sort of thing. The old saying 'there's nowt as queer as folk' was verified daily in the hotel trade.

Sally thanked him, followed his directions up the

thickly carpeted stairs. Outside in the square, normal things were still happening. Men were buying hats, people were carrying home their groceries, the buses were running along nearby Bradshawgate. But meeting a mother after seven years was not commonplace. She was scared and a little bit uneasy in her stomach.

Outside the room, she paused, her heart beating wildly. It occurred to her that she would have preferred to meet a total stranger. At her interview for Bolton School, she had been confronted by all kinds of people, some of whom had been terrifyingly clever. She had been faced by a head-mistress, a bursar and the head of first year in the space of half an hour. Even the caretaker had been well-spoken and smart with his navy-blue overalls and slicked-back hair.

Sally recoiled from the door behind which her mother waited, then leaned against the opposite wall. She remembered. She remembered hunger, dirt, the sound of her father's laboured breathing. A basket had hung outside on a rope, and the neighbours had left bits of food for her. Many times, she had been spanked by her mother. At school she had been ignored because of filthy clothes and nits in her hair. Miss Lever had been kind. She worked in Paradise now, that lovely teacher.

What could she say to the woman at the other side of this door? Granny Ivy had made Sally come here alone. 'You're fourteen now, nearly a young woman. Lottie's your mam, love. Just go and see her. Just go and talk to her. You don't need nobody to hold your hand, not any more.'

She did, though. Standing here trying not to bite her thumbnail, she was suddenly about five years old. Tears and laughter were both only just beneath the surface of her open-pored skin, because her emotions were tangled and raw. Mam. She was going to see her mam who had run off with an American, her mam who had come back and married . . . him.

A maid clattered along the corridor, mops and buckets

rattling in a deep-sided cart. 'You all reet, lass?'

'Er . . . yes.'

'Are you lost?'

'No.'

The cleaner put her turbaned head on one side. 'Nowt's as bad as you think it's going fer t' be. Mind, nowt's as good as you think, neither. Get it over with, flower. Whatever's mithering you, get it finished and done with, then you can put a laugh back in yon bonny eyes.'

Sally tapped at the door, smiled weakly in response to the maid's wink.

Lottie, who had been standing only inches away, was relieved when she could open the door. For what had seemed like ages, the girl had hung back in the corridor. In spite of thick carpets, Lottie had heard every word, every rustle, every sigh. 'Come in. You've no need to be frightened of me.'

Sally entered, stood perfectly still until Lottie came up behind her. When a hand touched her shoulder, Sally flinched automatically.

'Sit down,' said Lottie.

Sally obeyed, watched while her mother turned up the gas fire.

'Cold,' remarked Lottie.

'Yes.'

'Mind, New York were worse. They had to dig their way out of their houses some days. Shall I send for some tea and scones?'

'Not for me. I've to go soon.'

'Oh.' Lottie sank into the chair opposite her daughter's. For this occasion, Lottie had spent quite a bit of her savings on a 'quiet' frock, some good shoes and a hairdo that made her look human. 'You're a very pretty girl,' she said.

Sally blushed. 'Thank you.'

'Clever, too, from what I've heard. What are you going to be?'

'I don't know yet.'

The older woman leaned back, tried to achieve some comfort by placing a cushion in the small of her spine. 'I've left the queer feller. He only wanted me to get you back so's your grandma would suffer. I've never had much time for Ivy, but I weren't going to let him use me. He's used folk all his life, has Worthington. Any road, he can do his own dirty work.'

Sally finally managed to look into her mother's eyes. 'Why did you come back?'

Lottie shrugged. 'Because things didn't work out for me. The chap I followed over there were another rum bugger. When the private detective found me and told me how Worthington wanted to send me the fare home, I jumped at it. And here I am. I've a few bob, not much, like, only Mrs Spencer's paying the hotel bill. I suppose I'd better start looking for a job and somewhere to live.'

Sally straightened, plucked at her meagre store of courage. 'You left my dad to die, Mother. And you left me, too. Why?'

A few beats of time passed while several emotions surfaced to wage war on Lottie's unpretty face. 'Because I'm selfish, Sally. Because I've always grabbed at chances.'

'You didn't love me.'

Lottie studied her hands for a moment. 'No, I didn't.'

The ensuing silence was punctuated by the sound of a bus rattling along Bradshawgate.

Sally chewed her lip, kept her hands away from her mouth. 'Why didn't you love me?' So many whys, she thought. Enough whys to stretch across the Atlantic . . .

Lottie sniffed. 'I don't know. And that is the God's honest truth. You were puny and you moaned a lot as a baby. Then you wanted things, needed things. I weren't ready for none of that, see. And I'd no road of knowing how to go about being a mam.' She paused, scratched her head, then remembered the posh hairdo. 'Me and me sisters used to beg down at Bolton Market. Folk gave us pennies and bits of fruit. We'd no shoes. You could have soled and heeled our feet and we'd have felt nowt, 'cos the skin went hard with all that barefoot traipsing. She were never in. She were always going here and there.'

'Your mother?'

Lottie inclined her head. 'Aye, she were a case, me mam. She'd more blokes than you've had hot dinners.'

Sally's hot dinners had started to arrive with regularity only after this woman had departed for foreign soil. 'I don't remember being fed regularly,' she said quietly. 'Until after you were gone. Uncle Tom bought my uniform. I went to school in lovely new clothes and had a meal with Granny Ivy when I got home. Dad died a couple of days later. Then Gran brought me up with the help of Uncle Tom, Maureen and the Heilbergs. I was lucky to have so many friends.'

Lottie swallowed, found her throat to be as dry as sandpaper. 'I'm sorry, Sally. There's no way I can put right what were done wrong all them years ago. But I sent for you to tell you that I mean no harm. That bad bugger up yon had some scheme for frightening Ivy to death, I think. Oh, we'd not have got you away from your gran, but he'd have made enough noise if I'd stuck by him. Ivy's safe now.'

'Thank you.'

Lottie frowned. 'I'm a bad woman, Sally.'

'Oh.' It was impossible to achieve any reply.

'I've been with men . . . for money. I went with that bastard Worthington because he paid me. Then . . . well . . . you're too young for talking about this kind of caper.'

Sally bit her thumbnail. 'I know about all that stuff, Mother. Worthington might have been the one who started me off, but my dad was a wonderful man. You were too busy going out to notice what a nice man my dad was. He was kind and gentle and . . .' The words dried up when Sally saw her mother's shoulders shaking. She hadn't realized that the woman could cry. 'I'm sorry.'

Lottie jumped up, dragged a handkerchief from her

sleeve and spun around to face the window. 'I can't look at you no more, I can't! You don't have to tell me what sort of a man Derek Crumpsall used to be. I treated him as if he were soft, but he weren't. It were me. I'm bad inside, rotten right through to me bones. Go away, girl. Get the hell out of this place before you catch whatever bloody disease I were born with.'

Sally decided that this mother of hers had an odd voice, because she spoke 'Lanky' and American at the same time. But the tears crossed all language barriers. 'I don't want to leave you crying.'

'Why not? I left you and him bloody skriking, didn't I? I've got what I deserve now, 'cos I've got nowt at all. No daughter, no job, no home and no money. You've to go, do you hear? I don't want you. I never wanted you in the first place. I drank enough gin to stock a pub, and I lived at the slipper baths in near-boiling water for a fortnight trying to get shut of you. Go on, bugger off out of it!'

Sally got up, walked to the door, opened it, closed it loudly. With her back pressed hard against the jamb, she watched while her mother sank to the carpet in a heap of despair.

Lottie sobbed hysterically, made no attempts to raise herself from the floor. 'Jesus . . . that kid . . . deserved . . . What kind of a woman . . . am I?'

Sally's thumbnail was suddenly very short. Having pretended to leave, she lingered now and bore witness to something she was never meant to see. This was like spying, like looking through someone's curtains at night. A knowledge was rooting itself in her mind, a seed whose capillaries responded quickly to the water from Lottie's eyes. Whatever Sally's mother was, whatever she had been, there was a bond, a link that kept them tied.

'Oh God,' moaned the woman. 'I'll not see her . . . no more.'

Sally crossed the room and dropped down next to Lottie.

The tears slowed. 'What the bloody hell do you want now?'

'Nothing.' That was what being related meant, thought Sally. You didn't want anything except just to say . . . hello, how are you?

'I'm no good, Sally. I'm warning you now—'

Sally placed a hand over Lottie's mouth. 'You're not bad, Mother. Most people aren't bad, you know. You just took a long time to grow up, that's all.'

Gert and Lottie dragged Bert's bits and pieces down the driveway. Mucky Singleton, a rag-and-bone collector, had been hired to cart the stuff, and his disgraceful appearance did little to enhance a situation that was already awkward.

In the doorway of the Bromwich Street house, a fat man with a low-hanging beer belly counted notes and coins. 'I should think so and all,' he called after the two women. 'I'd have charged interest if I'd known he were going to do a midnight flit.'

Lottie, who had had more than enough of the landlord, dumped a box in front of Mucky's bedraggled horse. 'Get down off that wagon, you lazy swine,' she told Mucky Singleton. 'You're supposed to be helping.'

Mucky pulled the clay pipe from between yellowed teeth. 'Yer said nowt about carrying. All yer said were as you wanted me and Montgomery.' He pointed to the horse.

Lottie threw a handful of coins onto the cart. 'Here you are, Judas.' Then she went up the path to tackle the landlord. 'Listen, fairy cake,' she said sweetly. 'My sister's had enough harassment without you chucking in your ten penn'orth. Bert's gone missing. He has not done a flit. Any more lip from you and I'll stick a pin in you, see if you pop.'

Gert lifted her husband's things from the pavement, passed them to Mucky. Because of the nature of his work, Mucky came into contact with a lot of women, so he knew

405

when they meant business. The one who talked a bit Yankee was in a mood. He would sooner meet his Maker than contend with a woman of such sharp humour. 'Loaded up, missus,' he told Lottie. 'Where now?'

'Vernon Street,' snapped the 'Yankee' one. 'I'll keep his things at my place,' she told Gert. 'Save you messing Ivy's house up.'

Gert, who wasn't feeling or saying much, nodded her agreement.

'Well?' said Mucky. 'Are you climbing on, or what?'

Lottie bridled. 'I'd not ride on your rotten wagon behind that flea-bitten nag for all the cotton in Lancashire. Just get gone and we'll meet you in Vernon Street.'

Gert pulled at her sister's arm, was suddenly glad that Lottie was with her. They'd never got on, had disliked each other even as children. But now, Lottie was . . . she was all right. 'Thanks, Lottie,' she said softly. 'I don't know what I would have done without you.'

Lottie, who had cheered up considerably since getting her own room and landing a cleaning job in an office building, squeezed Gert's hand. 'He'll turn up, love. They always do, same as tin pennies. There's not one man to mend another, is there? Always piking off and saying nowt, always getting home drunk and disasterly, no bones in their legs and no bloody front door key. See. You come to my little room in Vernon Street. We'll make some toast and have a cuppa, see what we can sort out. He'll not be far away. They don't shift without money for a pint and a ciggy.'

'He's dead,' mumbled Gert.

Lottie, who agreed with her sister, dragged her along Bromwich Street. 'Don't be saying that. He might have won a fortune at the dogs, might have gone off to spend it in Monte Carlo.'

Gert sniffed, said no more. Her Bert was a goner. She knew it in her head and felt it in her heart. Why hadn't they found him, though? Why did the police keep giving her these lectures about Bert being forty-nine and old enough to fettle? 'He's not a creature of regular habits,' the desk sergeant had said. 'With no employer for us to interview, where do we start?' She shivered, wondered when the bobbies would come to their senses and start dragging the waterways.

In spite of bewilderment and grief, Gert followed her sister across the centre of town to Chorley Old Road. After all, there was nothing else she could do, was there?

Alan Westford walked down the narrow hallway and picked up the evening paper. He read a few lines about the nationalization of the railways, poured himself a pint of bottle brown ale, lit a Senior Service. He was glad she'd gone. If she'd stayed, she would have been no use, the state of her. Who on earth would have granted custody of a fourteen-year-old girl to a woman like Lottie? If only she'd returned looking half-decent, the Westfords might have pleaded that Lottie had been abroad to make money and had returned to give the child a good life. But, tramp that she was, no-one could have taken Lottie seriously. Even so, her continued presence in his house might have been sufficient to frighten the Crumpsall hag out of her skin. Still, it was all spilt milk now.

He dragged hungrily at the tobacco, swallowed the beer in one draught, opened another bottle. There was some whisky in the sideboard, blended, but not a bad scotch. In about half an hour, he would make himself a plate of eggs and bacon, and there was some fresh bread and a nice pat of butter.

But when he unfolded the paper properly, all thoughts of food left his brain. They had found him. At last, the police had discovered the remains of a man in that little-used passageway behind the Kippax Mill. By now, there would be sparse physical evidence left, he reassured himself. He need not worry, because no-one would connect the incident with him. All the same, his appetite remained poor, so he dined on whisky and Senior Service.

'In the opinion of the examining doctor the body had been in the alley for several weeks. In spite of the cold weather, there has been some deterioration. In view of this, the cause of death has not yet been established, though foul play is suspected due to chest wounds.'

Foul play. He drank two fingers of scotch, poured another dose. Bloody foul play, eh? Oh, he could tell a few tales on that subject. What about a chap who had worked his fingers to the bone only to finish up in a weaver's cottage with no company except scotch and brown ale? What about a chap whose wife had taken all his money to set up a business with an Austrian Jew, a lord of the realm and a load of idiots from the slums?

Perhaps the dreams would stop now. Perhaps he could enjoy the sleep of a just man, because Bert Simpson was no longer hidden under piles of paper and cotton waste. Westford was all right until he went to bed, seldom gave a conscious thought to the disloyal creature whose life he had ended. But he could have done without all those nightmares full of clicking bones and empty eye sockets. Bert Simpson hadn't been worth all this bother. In his present condition, the stupid man certainly did not merit the trouble and expense of coroner's court, police wages, murder investigation.

He scrutinized the report again, made sure he hadn't missed anything. No, no, he was in the clear thus far. The clothes he had worn on that day had been reduced to ashes in a garden bonfire; he had even destroyed a pair of good shoes. There were those people who knew about the return of the renamed Andrew Worthington, but nothing could be proved, because he had no connection with Bert. Did he?

Through a fog created by best Virginia and drunkenness, Westford remembered the letters. 'Destroy this', he had written at the end of each missive. Had those papers been burnt? Had they? Bromwich Street. Yes, Simpson had taken a room in a house there after separating from his wife. The clock ticked loudly, but Westford's heartbeat drowned the noise. If one single letter from London remained, he would be connected to Bert Simpson.

Westford jumped up, staggered into the kitchen. What could he do? Bromwich Street. That was in the Haulgh area, down Bridgeman Place and along the Bury Road. The police would be there, of course. The police would be sifting through every bus ticket, every scrap of refuse, every letter, because Bert's disappearance had been reported by his slut of a wife, no doubt.

He was suddenly tired. In fact, the adjective did not serve adequately, because tiredness would have been easy compared to the weakness that seemed to pervade his body. Bed. He must get himself upstairs for a nap.

When the door-knocker clattered, he pressed a hand to his heart, half-expecting the final attack that would remove all need to worry about Bert bloody Simpson. But no, his heart had been mended after the pitchfork business, though he had been warned against alcohol and tobacco . . . Whoever stood on the path had no patience. There were lights burning, so he could not pretend to be out. He made a small attempt to straighten his tie, wished he'd had that shave, shambled off to the front door.

Relief flooded his veins, mingled with the ale and whisky, made him attempt a smile. 'Oh,' he said to his only legitimate son. 'Come in.'

Gert was beyond consolation. She fled from the over-populated room, ran upstairs, locked herself in the bathroom. His hands. She had recognized those small hands, though the rest hadn't looked much like Bert. That lady policeman had tried to be nice, but Gert had still screamed like a cornered animal. And the pills the doctor had supplied weren't much use. 'Go away,' she yelled when someone tapped on the door.

Downstairs, Ivy sat near the window, her eyes fixed on

the near-blackness outside. Poor little Gert. There was no harm in the woman, though Ivy had feared her all those years ago when she had first come for Sal. Someone touched Ivy's shoulder. 'She's shut herself in the bathroom, Ivy.' It was Ruth Heilberg's voice. 'Leave her,' said Ivy. 'There's times when folk just has to be by theirselves.'

Tom and Joseph stood in front of the fireplace, the former towering over the latter by at least nine inches. 'For this man, Gert always had love,' said Joseph.

Tom glanced across at Maureen, noticed that she was plucking vacantly at the sleeve of her jumper. 'He was murdered, Joseph.'

'Yes, this much we know.'

'Do you think . . . ?' Tom could not bring himself to verbalize the thoughts.

'I should not be surprised.' Joseph placed his Homburg on the side table where Ivy's store of medicines sat. The wonderful woman was now confined to the house, spent most of her time in this very room. Gert was the one who cared for Ivy. Gert cooked for her, washed her, took her to the bathroom. 'Where is Sally?'

'Next door with Prudence and Cora. Red's there, too, so she'll be all right.' Tom spoke to Ruth. 'Go back upstairs, if you don't mind. You will be able to listen. I don't suppose Gert will do anything silly, but we must be sure of her safety.'

'What can we do, Tom?' Joseph touched the taller man's arm. 'Come, we shall talk in the kitchen.'

The two men went into the hall, but their progress was halted by a frantic banging on the front door. Tom opened it, found Lottie white-faced and shivering on the step. 'You're not wearing a coat. You must be freez—'

'Gert!' screamed Lottie.

Tom drew the newcomer to one side. 'She's in the bathroom. Bert has been found murdered, you see, and—'

'I know that! I bloody know!' Lottie was no more than a

410

hair's breadth from hysteria. 'Get my sister. Get my sister now, this minute.'

Gert appeared on the landing with Ruth hovering in her wake. 'Lottie?' shouted Gert. 'Is that you? I knew his hands straight away, Lottie. He had these little hands. So cold, he looked, stretched out on that tin table. They gave me pills, but I can't stop seeing his hands, Lottie. He never gave over loving me, you know. He never stopped wanting me back, but there was that fire and Maureen's hands. Now his hands. His poor little hands all blue, all dead. Maureen's went red and purple, you know. I never forgave him. Do you think God'll let him in, Lottie?'

Tears poured down Lottie's ashen cheeks. For some inexplicable reason, she had been emotional lately. Had Lottie been able to steal some thinking time, she might have worked out that her sensitivities had come to light after that meeting with her daughter. Lottie saw the state of her older sister, screwed up the paper in her skirt pocket. No, she couldn't do it, not just now, not right away. With a level of determination that showed in the set of her jaw, Lottie reined herself in, then turned and spoke to the two men. 'I realized. When I saw the *Evening News*, I just knew it were Bert. So I've come to take our Gert to the morgue, only it sounds like she's already been.' Thoughts dashed about in her mind, this way, that way, into and out of corners, each idea colliding with the next. She must protect Sally, Gert, herself. She must . . . Must what? Tell these men what she knew, show them the scrap of information she had found among Bert's paltry effects?

'A hot drink, Lottie?' asked Tom.

'Yes. And stick a bit of brandy in it. I'm perishing.' She met her sister halfway up the stairs, drew her down into the warmth.

Ivy turned from the window when the Kerrigan girls came in. 'You all right, Lottie?'

'Aye.'

Gert slumped on to the sofa, her eyes beginning to close

as the sedatives finally hit the spot. Ruth, motherly as ever, lifted Gert's legs and stretched her out, made her comfortable with a cushion. 'Yes, you will sleep now,' she whispered. 'And we are here for you, all of us.'

Lottie walked over to her old enemy. 'She's a good girl at heart, our Gert. As for Bertie Simpson, he were a damned fool, only he didn't deserve killing.'

Ivy stared at the latest visitor. 'Spit it out, Lottie.'

'Eh?' Warmer now, Lottie was calming down, though a solution still eluded her. 'What are you on about?'

'You. You're what I'm on about, girl. What's up with you? No coat, no scarf, no bloody sense. You know summat. You've found what they call evidence, haven't you?'

Lottie inhaled deeply. 'The paper. I read the paper and thought it must be Bert. So I panicked and ran all the way across town.'

'And I'm the Queen of Sheba. You know summat, girl. I'd stake a fortune on that.'

Lottie took a cup from Tom, sipped the scalding tea.

'Will you all go in the other room?' asked Ivy. 'Leave me and Lottie here in case Gert wakes up. Any road, you'd be best going home, I think. There's nowt to be mended here, and nowt as'll worsen overnight.'

When they were alone, Ivy gave Lottie time to finish her tea before tackling her again. While she waited, the old woman's mind flitted about over the years, settled here and there, moved on through some good days and some bad. Sally and her little house in Hampshire, Ollie and Rosie, the day of the pitchfork. Maureen wearing her engagement ring on a chain until her burns healed, Gert leaving her husband after the arson attack.

Ivy closed her eyes, remembered the rebirth of Paradise. Folk from London coming up with drawings, Joseph dashing about with swatches of material. They'd taken on carpenters, cabinet makers, a sales team, the best weavers. Then the shops had opened in cities and towns, people flocking in to buy middle-priced furnishings. As the company had grown, interior designers had been hired to reshape the lives of ordinary folk in nice semi-detached houses. The Paradise Look. 'What do you know, Lottie?'

'Summat and nowt.'

He would have done anything to ruin Paradise. Worthington was a bitter man with few principles and precious little self-control. He was determined, evil and clever enough to reach across the Atlantic to grab Lottie. 'Even if you'd got her, she wouldn't have stayed with you. She's fourteen, too old to be kept where she doesn't want to be.'

'I know.'

Ivy turned her head slowly until her eyes were fixed on the face of her daughter-in-law. 'What do you know?' she asked again.

'Enough.'

Ivy inclined her head. 'What'll you do?'

Lottie placed her cup on the small table next to Ivy's bottles of pills and potions. 'The right thing for once, Ivy.'

'Have you thought on it, then?'

Lottie nodded.

'In that case, go careful. And make sure there's somebody with you.'

'I will.'

Ivy gazed at the prostrate figure on the sofa. 'Think about her. And think about Sally, too. Gert needs an answer, or she will when she's got used to Bert's death. But there's other folk who'd be better going through life with some truths hidden.' Ivy blinked, thought about her lovely granddaughter. Sally's real dad had committed murder. And Sally's mam was here, in the house, with the proof hidden in that pocket of hers, the pocket into which she kept thrusting a nervous hand. 'She's always called Derek Dad, but she knows what's what, Lottie. A murderer? Does she have to be told she were started by a bloody murderer?' Ivy nodded pensively. 'Well, I suppose it'll all have to come out now, one road or another. Eeh, I wish we could save her from that, Lottie.'

Lottie reached out and touched the old lady's shoulder. Never before in her life had she shown affection for Ivy Crumpsall. But Lottie was learning very quickly that there was a lot more to Ivy than she had ever realized. 'I'll stop tonight, if that's all right. I'll help you get settled upstairs, then I'll sit in here with Gert.' She paused. 'Where's our Sal?'

Ivy smiled faintly. 'Your daughter's next door with your husband's first wife. It's a bugger, isn't it?'

When the house had settled into an uneasy rest, Lottie dragged Ivy's chair across the room and sat next to Gert. This was a right pickle and no mistake. Ivy knew everything, but then she always had known everything. Putting the old girl to bed had made Lottie realize how frail Ivy was – huge salt-cellars at the base of her neck, stringy arms, every rib showing through a thin covering of age-slackened skin. But Ivy's mind remained razor-sharp in spite of the passage of time. As for the physical deterioration – well – even strong folk finished up like that, diminished and dependent.

Behind the weight of all her worries, Lottie teetered on the brink of some happiness, because Sally had greeted her like an old friend. 'I'm so glad you've got a job,' Sally had told her mother tonight. 'Isn't this dreadful? Gert will never get over it.' Lottie looked up at the ceiling, decided that she would always remember the date, the month and the year, because she was spending this night under the roof that sheltered Sally, too.

Gert's wide eyes had attached themselves to her sister's face. 'Lottie?'

'When did you wake up?'

'Just now. What were you smiling for?'

Lottie shrugged. 'Just thinking, that's all. Seven years since I saw her, Gert. She's a right little smasher, isn't she?'

414

'Aye.' Gert struggled into a sitting position. 'Were I screaming and carrying on before, like?'

'Not much. I think you did well, love, considering what's gone on.'

Gert stood up, swayed a bit, announced her intention to brew up. In the kitchen, she surprised her companion by saying, 'Funny, but I feel all right now. See, I've known all along as how Bert were dead. It were just seeing him that upset me. Only there's just one thing, Lottie. I want to know who did for him.'

Lottie brought milk to the table, found the sugar bowl.

'I bet it were Worthington.' Gert cleared her throat. 'I mean, why did he change his name, eh? What's he doing calling himself Westford? And Bert always had a bit of money, you know. When he used to visit me at the prefab, he'd bring me a few flowers or some daft ornament. Somebody were giving him that money, Lottie. Bert never worked except for odd jobs, and the oddest job he ever had were setting fire to Mr Heilberg's shop down Wigan Road.'

Lottie stirred the tea, said nothing.

'Lottie?'

'What?'

'You've said nowt.'

'I'd have needed a crowbar to squeeze a word in edgeways.' She picked up the cups and carried them through to the front room, sat down and waited for her sister. 'I found something, Gert. It were in that box full of old betting slips and newspapers. Part of a letter. From London.' She pulled the scrap of paper from her pocket and handed it over. 'Worthington's kept in touch with Bert all along. It says there about money being enclosed.'

'"Destroy this",' read Gert. 'Bert's been spying for that bloody rotten Worthington.' She glanced at Lottie. 'You've no feelings for Worthington, have you?'

Lottie shrugged, stirred her tea. 'He got me home, love. That were all he did for me. Then when he said about getting married, I thought I'd give it a go, 'cos he had a house and all that. Only he never come near me, never touched me, didn't want anything to do with me.'

'You were lucky, then.' Gert screwed up the piece of paper, placed it on the table. 'He did some terrible things to me, Lottie. Before he piked off down south, like. He weren't normal.'

Lottie gritted her teeth, kept her counsel. She had grown used to 'not normal', had serviced men from all walks of the gutter. This sister she had never taken time to know seemed straight, the type who should have had kids, the sort who would have kept to one man.

'Well, I suppose we'll never know,' concluded Gert.

Lottie reached for her handbag, pulled out a sealed envelope. 'I found this and all.'

'What is it?'

'I don't know, do I? I've not opened it, 'cos it's addressed to you. I'm not one for opening other folks' letters. It were in the same box with all sorts of rubbish.'

Gert stared at the envelope. 'Open it,' she said. 'Read it to me.'

Lottie, suddenly all fingers and thumbs, tore at the flap, pulled out a single sheet of lined paper. 'Jesus,' she breathed.

'What? What?'

Lottie swallowed, fingered her throat. '"Dear Gert",' she read. '"I'm writing this in case anything happens to me. Worthington's off his rocker. I can tell just by looking at him that he's gone crackers. There's things he might be asking me to do, like burning Paradise and killing Ivy Crumpsall, happen grabbing little Sally and all. Well, the time is coming when I'll have to tell him to sod off, Gert.

I've done things in the past, like the pawnshop and writing to him and telling him what's going on down Paradise way. Only I can't take no more. I'm worried that he's going to do something to me. This might sound a bit daft, but he could kill me. Any road, you'll only read this if he does, so happen it won't seem daft to you.

I always loved you, Gert. From your loving husband, Bert Simpson."'

Gert's cup clattered in its saucer. 'Well,' she breathed after several seconds had elapsed. 'He's gone and murdered my Bert.'

Lottie threw the letter into her bag as if it had burnt her hands. 'Ivy knows,' she muttered.

'How?'

'Well, she's always been the same, has Ivy. I mean, when I lived in Paradise Lane, she even seemed to know what I were thinking, where I'd been, all that kind of stuff. She as good as told me tonight that Worthington had killed your Bert. And I think the others have a good idea, too. Only . . .'

'Only what? Come on, Lottie. Half a tale's worse than no news at all.'

'Well . . . Sally,' said Lottie hesitantly. 'Sally knows he's her father. She talks about Derek as her dad, like, but she knows about me and the queer feller. She'd be best not finding out as her real dad were a murderer.'

Gert sat perfectly still for at least a minute. 'She's got to know sooner or later,' she pronounced at last. 'Let's find him and face him, Lottie. Let's make damned sure we're right. We can tell him about yon letter and stop him doing any more damage. I mean, it looks as if our Sally'll have to be told. But if we can stop him now, then he'll know we're on to him and he might just bugger off back to London.'

Lottie gulped back her anger. 'He wants punishing, Gert.'

Very slowly, Gert turned her head and faced her sister fully. 'God'll see to that, love. God and the devil can do more than the courts. For what he's done, Worthington won't get the noose or life imprisonment.' She shook her head. 'He'll get eternity. That should be long enough, just about.'

*   *   *

417

Prudence Spencer knocked on the window, placed a finger to her lips when Lottie Crumpsall pulled back the curtain. She hopped from foot to foot impatiently until the door was opened. 'Lottie?' she whispered as she stepped into the house.

'Aye?' It was only just gone seven in the morning. Gert was stretched out fast asleep on the sofa, while Lottie was stiff after spending the night on the floor. She closed the front door and led Prudence into the hall. 'What do you want at this time, Mrs Spencer?'

Prudence crept into the kitchen, closed the door as soon as Lottie had joined her. 'If what I suspect is true, he's nothing to lose now.'

'Eh?'

'Andrew. If he killed Bert, he's already in trouble. And if he killed Bert, he'll be forced to plan the rest of his own dirty work. I've a bad feeling in here.' She clapped a hand to her chest. 'If he can't get Paradise back, he'll destroy it. If he can't hurt Ivy by stealing Sally away from her, he'll find some other way of punishing all of us. We must go for the police.'

Lottie was a great believer in hunches. Many a time, she had refused a client, only to hear later that the same man had injured another working girl. This woman had hunches. This woman didn't need any bits of paper to prove that her husband had killed Bert. 'We can't fetch the bobbies. In fact, our Gert's half hoping as how Worthington won't be found out. He is Sally's dad, you know.' She felt the heat in her face, realized that she was blushing for the first time in twenty-odd years.

Prudence jerked her head upward, as if preparing for the fray. 'My son came to see me last night. He had just visited Andrew. Victor is not a fanciful man, Lottie. In truth, he's very much an accountant – all figures and percentages, no imagination. Victor found his father very drunk and raving about Ivy, the mill, Joseph Heilberg. Andrew was vowing vengeance and shouting about Bert

418

Simpson having come to a suitably sticky end. My son had to put Andrew to bed. He is convinced that his father is completely out of control.'

Lottie put the kettle on, found two cups, fiddled about with the tea caddy. 'We've to put Sally first,' she said.

'But he can't get away with murder and—'

'Sally has to be kept in the dark for as long as possible,' insisted Lottie. 'Happen our so-called husband'll go back south when he knows we're on to him.'

In Ivy's kitchen, Prudence sank into a straight-backed chair, toyed with the cruet set. 'What's the answer, Lottie?' She had to admit that this seemingly ne'er-do-well woman was worldly-wise and fit for any of life's hurdles.

Lottie scalded the pot, counted out three spoons of tea, made the brew. 'Well, you and me and our Gert'll tackle him. Leave the men out of it – they're not devious enough, most men. They can't see round corners like women can. I'm telling you now, Mrs S, that my husband and yours is at death's door. He's smoking like a chimney and drinking enough to launch a battleship. There's no way he's got the strength to be a real threat.'

'Can we be sure?'

Lottie heaped sugar into her cup. 'We can make bloody sure, Mrs Spencer.'

'Use my Christian name, please.'

'Right, I will. Sugar, Prudence?'

'No, thank you. We must hurry and put a stop to him.'

Lottie blew on her tea. 'Leave it to me, Prudence. If nowt else comes to mind, I'll kill the bastard myself.'

'Are you sure you know how to go about this, Prudence?' asked Lottie.

'Of course I do. I drove into town only last week – I have had lessons, you know. Pru's better, by the way.'

'Eh?'

'Better than Prudence.'

'Oh.' Lottie smiled encouragingly at her sister. 'You all right, our Gert?'

'Aye. Are you?'

For a woman bent on murder, Lottie was fine and she said so.

All three stared wordlessly up Crompton Way, then the would-be driver riffled through an instruction book that had arrived with the Ford. 'Open throttle. Ease in choke to halfway. No, no, I think it's the other way round. Oh, why don't they write these things in English? Depress clutch, engage first gear while removing handbrake,' she quoted.

'Is there any danger of us getting there this week?' asked Lottie. It was eight o'clock on a Saturday morning in January 1955. A maniac was on the loose, while the heroines of the piece sat and waited for a car to start. 'We'll still be here come Ash Wednesday,' complained Lottie.

'Shut up,' advised Pru. Unused to ordering people about in such a brusque fashion, she blushed and returned to the instructions. Of the trio, she was the most terrified when the pride and joy that was her new car bounded forward like a drunken kangaroo. 'I shall get to grips with this momentarily,' announced Pru uncertainly. 'Really, there is nothing to it.'

Shaken and bruised, they arrived on Darwen Road at ten minutes past eight. The several death-defying miles that lay behind them were fading to a blessed blur by the time Lottie inserted her key in the door of the cottage. 'I'll do this on me own,' she advised the other two.

Pru was firm. 'No. We are all Andrew's victims.' She took Gert's hand and gripped it tightly. 'We are in this together.'

'The Three Musketeers,'· quipped Lottie weakly. She was scared, but she didn't want it to show. 'Let's go and find the Scarlet rotten Pimple. More like a bloody boil, he is.'

420

They walked round the ground floor of the cottage in a huddle, each one clinging to her sister-in-crime as if life itself depended on human contact. 'He's not down here,' said Gert.

Lottie broke free, ran back to the kitchen and peered through the window overlooking the side of the house. 'Van's gone,' she shouted. 'He always leaves it up the side. We've missed him.'

Gert and Pru were in the front living room, their eyes fastened to pages torn from the *Bolton Evening News*. 'Look,' said Pru. 'An admission of guilt, I'd say. He has removed the article about Bert's death.'

'I married a bloody murderer,' commented Lottie.

'So did I,' Pru reminded her. 'But while I was with him, he stuck to killing people's souls. Now.' She sank into a chair. 'Where do we go from here?'

'Back to Crompton Way,' said Gert, her mouth set in an angry line. 'If his van's there, we make sure we get him away from Ivy. If it's not at Ivy's, we go and look at Joseph's house, then—'

'He'll be in Paradise,' said Pru, her tone even, almost cold. 'He'll destroy that first.'

'Are you sure?' asked Gert.

Pru nodded quickly. 'Oh yes. Property before people, that was his motto. All the same, we'll go via Crompton Way, just to make sure that Ivy is safe. Then, if Andrew isn't at the factory, we'll telephone from there and tell Joseph and Ivy to be watchful. Come along, now, there's no time to waste.'

They bundled themselves back into the vehicle, lurched down the moor and into the road where Prudence and Ivy's houses sat. No van was parked, so they rattled on through the centre of Bolton, up Wigan Road, turning left up Spencer Street, then right into Paradise Lane. His empty van was near the lane's junction with Worthington Street.

'I feel sick,' whispered Gert.

'Stop here, then,' advised Lottie. 'Me and Pru'll see to him.'

Gert shook her head. 'No. It were my husband he killed, Lottie. I want to look in that bugger's horrible eyes and tell him I know all about what's happened.' Her head drooped for a second. She didn't really want to look at him, didn't really want to remember how Worthington had used her. In a way, he had murdered her, too, because she'd never been near a man since that night. Even Bert had stood no chance of touching her. 'Let's get him,' she said softly.

Pru heard something in Gert's voice. 'Don't descend to his level,' she advised Gert. To Lottie, she said, 'As for what you said about killing him – I hope you weren't serious. Sally must be kept secure. If she had a mother and an aunt in prison, she really would be a troubled girl.'

The two sisters looked at one another. 'For Sal,' breathed Lottie. 'For her, we keep our tempers.'

'I'll do me best,' agreed Gert.

As they alighted from the car, a man ran across the yard. 'A bloke's just gone in,' he said breathlessly. 'He didn't see me. I think he's carrying something – it looked like a gun. Then in his other hand, there was a can.'

'Paraffin.' Pru studied Nutty Clarke's scarred face. 'Wait,' she told him gently.

'What?' Nutty's head turned this way and that. 'I'm going into my office to call the coppers and—'

'No.' Although Pru's tone was low, it carried meaning. 'The police must be kept out of this if at all possible. It is, in effect, a family matter.'

'Oh.' Nutty knew Mrs Spencer well, had seen her at many a meeting. 'Well, if you're sure.'

'I am,' Pru told him. 'For the moment, at least.' She turned away from him, almost lost her composure when she saw Gert and Lottie disappearing through one of the entrances and into the dormant factory called Paradise. Had this been a weekday, the coward she had divorced

422

would not have set foot in what he still considered to be his realm. She could not shout after them, could not warn them. Surely they had heard Nutty talking about the possibility of a gun? She made a swift, irrevocable decision, whispered an instruction to Nutty, watched him walk away.

Inside, Gert and Lottie had a whispered conference, then separated, each woman starting to climb one of the twin stairways that flanked the main, central flight. When they reached the first floor, they stopped, peered into the showroom, saw him sitting on a Paradise Look sofa in front of a Paradise Look curtain that was draped over a sham window frame. Lottie shook her head at Gert, withdrew to the landing. Gert also stepped back onto her set of stairs. He had not seen them, she thought.

Westford took a swig from his silver hip flask and rolled whisky over his tongue before allowing its warmth to descend to his stomach. When had he last eaten? he wondered. In a minute or so, he would set fire to this bloody place. He would do a proper job. That rat Simpson couldn't have lit a fire in hell, because he'd been stupid, too scared of shadows. He gazed at the Paradise empire, saw moulded pillars supporting elegant arches where a dark corridor had once existed. They had opened the place up, but had kept the three separate stairways. Here, opposite the middle door, he could cover all possibilities.

At the base of the third, central stairway, Prudence Spencer waited and listened. When Nutty Clarke appeared at her side, she placed a finger to her lips, then beckoned. Stealthily, they climbed the steps. Nutty had done as ordered. 'Police are on their way,' he whispered.

Prudence bit down on her lip. There had been no alternative, really. Poor Sally would have to be told about Andrew's wickedness, because the girl's mother and aunt were in a building where a madman lurked with a gun, paraffin and a temper fit to cause spontaneous human combustion. With Nutty just behind her, Prudence ascended stealthily, her mind occupied by something she had read about people bursting into flames for no apparent reason.

Flames. Prudence paused, glanced over her shoulder into a face whose contours had already been remoulded by fire. 'Wait in the yard if you wish,' she mumbled.

'I'll be all right,' he told her.

How had it felt to be locked in a burning cockpit? Prudence wondered. Perhaps she would find out soon enough; perhaps they would all become closely acquainted with fire within the next few moments.

On the landing, they stopped and listened. Prudence held a restraining hand against her companion before pulling at the door handle. When she peered inside, she found herself looking into the face of Andrew Worthington and into the barrel of a pistol.

'Bitch,' spat the seated man. He waved the gun. 'Come in and close the door, Prudence.' He grinned, stretching sagging and drink-reddened flesh into a smile that was hideous.

She swallowed, heard the clumsy gulp that accompanied this involuntary reaction. 'The police are coming,' she told him, her voice made husky by a fear-dried throat.

'For me?' he asked. 'Are they coming for me, dear wife?'

'Yes.'

He laughed loudly, almost uncontrollably. 'Then I do hope they bring an ambulance, Prudence. Somebody will have to tidy away your remains.'

Nutty stepped into the room. 'Put the gun down, sir,' he advised calmly. 'Just leave it on the floor.' He positioned himself in front of Prudence. 'Lay it down,' he repeated.

Worthington rose to his feet. Yes, he was Worthington. This was his factory, had been his father's factory. The mill chimney no longer bore his name, yet Paradise was still his property. 'What happened to your face?' he asked.

424

'Burnt,' snapped Nutty. 'In a plane. What happened to yours?' He nodded quickly. 'I recognize you. A dial like yours isn't easily forgotten. You were hanging round looking for your sister – or so you said. I've seen you a few times, lurking about like a criminal.'

Worthington watched while the caretaker continued to shield Prudence. There were six bullets in the gun, enough ammunition to blow away this scarred airman and several Prudences. Then a movement caught his eye. He glanced sideways, saw Lottie standing in a corner. 'Ah. Wife the second,' he announced. 'Come in, Charlotte and enjoy the party.'

'Kill me first,' cried a voice from the other end of the showroom. 'You did for Bert, so you might as well finish me and all.'

Worthington stepped back to give himself enough space to cover everyone in the room. If he fired the gun, he might get one or two, but not all of them, because they would surely run for cover. And the police would be here shortly. Which one should he choose, then? Lottie? Lottie who had returned from America to reclaim her daughter? Lottie who had failed him so miserably, so completely?

He moved his head slowly and looked at Gert. Gert and Bert Simpson – what marvellous names for a music hall act. Gert had turned out to be a wet weekend, hadn't she? Tormenting him with her frivolous clothes then screaming rape – a bloody madwoman, she was.

But no. Again, he fixed his attention on Prudence. Prudence, a woman who had given him years of hell, was now struggling physically with a mere caretaker. The shy and agoraphobic woman was suddenly strong, powerful, capable of helping to build a business whose name was displayed in every city store. The Paradise Look? There would be nothing heavenly about her face once he had shot the life out of it.

Prudence pushed Nutty Clarke. 'This is not your fight,' she told him breathlessly. Nutty was not a big man, but she couldn't manage to move him. 'Go down to the yard and meet the police,' she ordered, the words still starved of oxygen. 'This is my business, Mr Clarke.'

'And mine,' replied Nutty. 'I've shares in it.'

'I didn't mean—'

'Keep bloody still!' roared Worthington. His peripheral vision marked the progress of Lottie and Gert as they crept closer to him and further away from the safety of the stairwells. 'And you two,' he shouted. 'Stay where you are.' He waved the gun about until the sisters were still.

With one last tremendous effort, Prudence Spencer drove an elbow into the caretaker's gut. When he collapsed, she bent over to apologize, stopped herself when she saw the look of triumph on her ex-husband's face. Slowly, she straightened, her eyes riveted to his. He was, she thought, Satan incarnate.

'Yes, you'll be the first.' He raised the gun, saw that Nutty Clarke was struggling to raise himself. 'You first, Prudence, then the other two mares,' spat Worthington. 'If I'm to hang for Simpson, I'll take the rest of you with me.'

Prudence froze. She felt Nutty's hands as he gripped her waist, knew that the caretaker was almost upright. The removal of a safety catch caused a loud click that echoed round the showroom. She continued to stare at Worthington, almost felt the bullet as it whizzed past her head.

Worthington steadied himself, cursed the whisky, aimed again. His vision was becoming blurred, while a weakness in his limbs made the pistol heavier. Breathing needed thinking about, was no longer an automatic process. When his knees buckled, he went down, pulled at the trigger, noticed that Nutty Clarke was upright again.

Gert ran and hid behind a bale of cloth, but Lottie simply walked in a straight, slow line towards the man who had tried to hurt her daughter. As she moved, it occurred to Lottie that she actually loved Sally, and that

426

knowledge seemed to strengthen her resolve. If necessary, she would die to save Pru, because Pru had minded Sal, had sheltered the child, Gert and Ivy.

Andrew Worthington was not a strong believer, but he imagined that some divine hand had entered the arena. The trigger would not budge, though every ounce of Worthington's energy was focused on the effort. His arms throbbed and ached. A fist was closing itself around his heart, filling his inner core with a pain that defied description. 'He's having a heart attack,' someone said. Someone? Prudence. Yes, Prudence had delivered that particular verdict.

The gun dropped to the floor with a thud, its arrival on polished wood preceding its owner's head by a mere split second.

'His temper killed him at last,' somebody said. Prudence again. Yes, yes, he knew that voice. The taking in of air was now impossible. Although no longer breathing, he still heard, still knew where he was. He was in Paradise. Though his body had ceased to work, a fury coursed through him and rattled his heart until it fluttered into silence. For a few sweet moments, the agony left him, then he drifted away into a final, painless sleep.

A lone figure made its way along Crompton Way, head lowered in contemplation, black-gloved hands joined together beneath the waist of a princess-line coat of dark grey.

'She's coming,' said the old woman at the window. 'Stick that kettle on, Gert. She'll be fair clemmed after what she's been through, poor lass.'

Lottie jumped up from the sofa and joined her mother-in-law. 'She shouldn't have gone, Ivy. We shouldn't have let her go, not on her own.'

Ivy's head nodded with an ague brought on by advancing years. 'Have you ever tried stopping her when her mind's made up?'

The younger woman managed a rueful grin. 'She's took after you,' she declared without malice. 'Stubborn as a mule. Still, I should have gone with her.'

Outside, Sally Crumpsall lifted her gaze, saw her mother and grandmother looking for her. They hadn't wanted her to go, of course. But going had been important. At the funeral, there had been just a handful of people – a lawyer, Victor Worthington, the undertaker's men. Even the dead man's daughter-in-law had stayed away. Sally waved at Gran, opened the gate, turned into the garden and walked up the path. Next week, Sally would be in Hampshire with her mother. The two of them would need to get to know one another all over again.

The door opened. 'Are you all right?'

'Yes, Mother.'

Lottie sniffed. 'Funny, being called Mother. Funny in a nice way,' she added hastily.

Sally removed the gloves, stuffed them into pockets, took off her coat and hung it on the stand. 'It was like the end of a book,' she told Lottie. 'I had to read all the way through. Anyway, it's over now.' There had been no proper service, because Andrew Worthington had demonstrated few good points on which the vicar might have eulogized.

'Were the papers there?' asked Lottie anxiously.

Sally nodded.

'Did they take your photo?'

'I suppose so.'

Lottie sighed deeply. 'Will there ever be an end to it?'

'Of course,' replied her daughter. 'You see, we all know who we are now. We all know where we belong.'

Lottie wondered anew about Sally's calmness. 'He weren't your dad, love. He didn't count, 'cos it were my fault and—'

'Stop it,' said Sally quietly. 'None of that matters any more, not really. We've got one another and Auntie Gert and Granny Ivy. I went to the funeral because it was part of the story. But for him, it was the last chapter. We have a new page now.' They walked into the sitting room and sat on the sofa.

'Cold day for it,' remarked Ivy by way of greeting. 'Went off all right, did it?'

Sally nodded.

Ivy Crumpsall turned her head and looked out into a leaden sky. She had outlived him. A smile lingered at the corner of her lips, and she ironed it out quickly. Whatever the circumstances, nobody should feel glad about another person's death. 'You growing that tea, Gert?' she shouted.

'I'm cutting parkin,' came the response from the kitchen.

Ivy lifted her head into a steadier position and looked at the daughter-in-law she had once hated. Lottie had been so brave, had quietly laid her life on the line to save Prudence Spencer. By the time Worthington had finally dropped, Lottie had been well within his sights. 'Sally got some of her guts from you and all,' the old woman said. 'Go and help Gert with that cake, Sal. Me stomach thinks me throat's cut.'

Alone, the two women sat in silence for a while, then Ivy cleared her throat. 'Funny, isn't it?'

'What?' asked Lottie.

'The way he died. Where he died.'

Lottie shrugged. 'I suppose so.'

'Think about it,' said Ivy softly. 'Straight from Paradise to hell.'

Lottie opened her mouth to make comment, found nothing to say.

'Whereas my Derek went the other road – from hell to paradise.'

Sally came in with the tray, Gert hot on her heels with a plate of Ivy's favourite cake. 'Here you are, Gran.' The young girl handed a cup to Ivy, watched while the old woman's hands trembled. She'd been so certain, had Granny Ivy. Like a rock, she had always been there. 'I've stirred it,' said Sally.

'I can still fettle, you know,' snapped Ivy. Then, in a gentler tone she asked, 'Will I still do as your granny, love?'

Sally bent and kissed a withered cheek. 'You're my dad's mum, aren't you? So I'm stuck with you whatever I think.'

Ivy wiped away a rheumy tear before sinking her teeth into a piece of cake. 'That's a fair parkin, Gert Simpson,' she announced through a mouthful. 'Given time, you might even get it right.'

While the elders continued their banter, Sally went into the kitchen, looked through the window and saw the sharp winter sun piercing a cloud. She smiled at the ray of light. 'Thanks,' she said to Derek Crumpsall. 'Thanks for being my dad.'